I0524292

Philip K. Dick

The Amazing Sci-Fi Tales of Philip K. Dick - 34 Titles in One Edition

OK Publishing 2021

Philip K. Dick

The Amazing Sci-Fi Tales of Philip K. Dick - 34 Titles in One Edition

Published by

MUSAICUM

Books

- Advanced Digital Solutions & High-Quality book Formatting -

musaicumbooks@okpublishing.info

2021 OK Publishing

ISBN 978-80-272-7794-0

Contents

.

Second Variety

The claws were bad enough in the first place-nasty, crawling little death-robots. But when they began to imitate their creators, it was time for the human race to make peace-if it could!

The Russian soldier made his way nervously up the ragged side of the hill, holding his gun ready. He glanced around him, licking his dry lips, his face set. From time to time he reached up a gloved hand and wiped perspiration from his neck, pushing down his coat collar.

Eric turned to Corporal Leone. "Want him? Or can I have him?" He adjusted the view sight so the Russian's features squarely filled the glass, the lines cutting across his hard, somber features.

Leone considered. The Russian was close, moving rapidly, almost running. "Don't fire. Wait." Leone tensed. "I don't think we're needed."

The Russian increased his pace, kicking ash and piles of debris out of his way. He reached the top of the hill and stopped, panting, staring around him. The sky was overcast, drifting clouds of gray particles. Bare trunks of trees jutted up occasionally; the ground was level and bare, rubble-strewn, with the ruins of buildings standing out here and there like yellowing skulls.

The Russian was uneasy. He knew something was wrong. He started down the hill. Now he was only a few paces from the bunker. Eric was getting fidgety. He played with his pistol, glancing at Leone.

"Don't worry," Leone said. "He won't get here. They'll take care of him."

"Are you sure? He's got damn far."

"They hang around close to the bunker. He's getting into the bad part. Get set!"

The Russian began to hurry, sliding down the hill, his boots sinking into the heaps of gray ash, trying to keep his gun up. He stopped for a moment, lifting his fieldglasses to his face.

"He's looking right at us," Eric said.

* * * * *

The Russian came on. They could see his eyes, like two blue stones. His mouth was open a little. He needed a shave; his chin was stubbled. On one bony cheek was a square of tape, showing blue at the edge. A fungoid spot. His coat was muddy and torn. One glove was missing. As he ran his belt counter bounced up and down against him.

Leone touched Eric's arm. "Here one comes."

Across the ground something small and metallic came, flashing in the dull sunlight of midday. A metal sphere. It raced up the hill after the Russian, its treads flying. It was small, one of the baby ones. Its claws were out, two razor projections spinning in a blur of white steel. The Russian heard it. He turned instantly, firing. The sphere dissolved into particles. But already a second had emerged and was following the first. The Russian fired again.

A third sphere leaped up the Russian's leg, clicking and whirring. It jumped to the shoulder. The spinning blades disappeared into the Russian's throat.

Eric relaxed. "Well, that's that. God, those damn things give me the creeps. Sometimes I think we were better off before."

"If we hadn't invented them, they would have." Leone lit a cigarette shakily. "I wonder why a Russian would come all this way alone. I didn't see anyone covering him."

Lt. Scott came slipping up the tunnel, into the bunker. "What happened? Something entered the screen."

"An Ivan."

"Just one?"

Eric brought the view screen around. Scott peered into it. Now there were numerous metal spheres crawling over the prostrate body, dull metal globes clicking and whirring, sawing up the Russian into small parts to be carried away.

"What a lot of claws," Scott murmured.

"They come like flies. Not much game for them any more."

Scott pushed the sight away, disgusted. "Like flies. I wonder why he was out there. They know we have claws all around."

A larger robot had joined the smaller spheres. It was directing operations, a long blunt tube with projecting eyepieces. There was not much left of the soldier. What remained was being brought down the hillside by the host of claws.

"Sir," Leone said. "If it's all right, I'd like to go out there and take a look at him."

"Why?"

"Maybe he came with something."

Scott considered. He shrugged. "All right. But be careful."

"I have my tab." Leone patted the metal band at his wrist. "I'll be out of bounds."

* * * * *

He picked up his rifle and stepped carefully up to the mouth of the bunker, making his way between blocks of concrete and steel prongs, twisted and bent. The air was cold at the top. He crossed over the ground toward the remains of the soldier, striding across the soft ash. A wind blew around him, swirling gray particles up in his face. He squinted and pushed on.

The claws retreated as he came close, some of them stiffening into immobility. He touched his tab. The Ivan would have given something for that! Short hard radiation emitted from the tab neutralized the claws, put them out of commission. Even the big robot with its two waving eyestalks retreated respectfully as he approached.

He bent down over the remains of the soldier. The gloved hand was closed tightly. There was something in it. Leone pried the fingers apart. A sealed container, aluminum. Still shiny.

He put it in his pocket and made his way back to the bunker. Behind him the claws came back to life, moving into operation again. The procession resumed, metal spheres moving through the gray ash with their loads. He could hear their treads scrabbling against the ground. He shuddered.

Scott watched intently as he brought the shiny tube out of his pocket. "He had that?"

"In his hand." Leone unscrewed the top. "Maybe you should look at it, sir."

Scott took it. He emptied the contents out in the palm of his hand. A small piece of silk paper, carefully folded. He sat down by the light and unfolded it.

"What's it say, sir?" Eric said. Several officers came up the tunnel. Major Hendricks appeared.

"Major," Scott said. "Look at this."

Hendricks read the slip. "This just come?"

"A single runner. Just now."

"Where is he?" Hendricks asked sharply.

"The claws got him."

Major Hendricks grunted. "Here." He passed it to his companions. "I think this is what we've been waiting for. They certainly took their time about it."

"So they want to talk terms," Scott said. "Are we going along with them?"

"That's not for us to decide." Hendricks sat down. "Where's the communications officer? I want the Moon Base."

Leone pondered as the communications officer raised the outside antenna cautiously, scanning the sky above the bunker for any sign of a watching Russian ship.

"Sir," Scott said to Hendricks. "It's sure strange they suddenly came around. We've been using the claws for almost a year. Now all of a sudden they start to fold."

"Maybe claws have been getting down in their bunkers."

"One of the big ones, the kind with stalks, got into an Ivan bunker last week," Eric said. "It got a whole platoon of them before they got their lid shut."

"How do you know?"

"A buddy told me. The thing came back with-with remains."

"Moon Base, sir," the communications officer said.

On the screen the face of the lunar monitor appeared. His crisp uniform contrasted to the uniforms in the bunker. And he was clean shaven. "Moon Base."

"This is forward command L-Whistle. On Terra. Let me have General Thompson."

The monitor faded. Presently General Thompson's heavy features came into focus. "What is it, Major?"

"Our claws got a single Russian runner with a message. We don't know whether to act on it-there have been tricks like this in the past."

"What's the message?"

"The Russians want us to send a single officer on policy level over to their lines. For a conference. They don't state the nature of the conference. They say that matters of —" He consulted the slip. " —Matters of grave urgency make it advisable that discussion be opened between a representative of the UN forces and themselves."

He held the message up to the screen for the general to scan. Thompson's eyes moved.

"What should we do?" Hendricks said.

"Send a man out."

"You don't think it's a trap?"

"It might be. But the location they give for their forward command is correct. It's worth a try, at any rate."

"I'll send an officer out. And report the results to you as soon as he returns."

"All right, Major." Thompson broke the connection. The screen died. Up above, the antenna came slowly down.

Hendricks rolled up the paper, deep in thought.

"I'll go," Leone said.

"They want somebody at policy level." Hendricks rubbed his jaw. "Policy level. I haven't been outside in months. Maybe I could use a little air."

"Don't you think it's risky?"

Hendricks lifted the view sight and gazed into it. The remains of the Russian were gone. Only a single claw was in sight. It was folding itself back, disappearing into the ash, like a crab. Like some hideous metal crab....

"That's the only thing that bothers me." Hendricks rubbed his wrist. "I know I'm safe as long as I have this on me. But there's something about them. I hate the damn things. I wish we'd never invented them. There's something wrong with them. Relentless little —"

"If we hadn't invented them, the Ivans would have."

Hendricks pushed the sight back. "Anyhow, it seems to be winning the war. I guess that's good."

"Sounds like you're getting the same jitters as the Ivans." Hendricks examined his wrist watch. "I guess I had better get started, if I want to be there before dark."

* * * * *

He took a deep breath and then stepped out onto the gray, rubbled ground. After a minute he lit a cigarette and stood gazing around him. The landscape was dead. Nothing stirred. He could see for miles, endless ash and slag, ruins of buildings. A few trees without leaves or branches, only the trunks. Above him the eternal rolling clouds of gray, drifting between Terra and the sun.

Major Hendricks went on. Off to the right something scuttled, something round and metallic. A claw, going lickety-split after something. Probably after a small animal, a rat. They got rats, too. As a sort of sideline.

He came to the top of the little hill and lifted his fieldglasses. The Russian lines were a few miles ahead of him. They had a forward command post there. The runner had come from it.

A squat robot with undulating arms passed by him, its arms weaving inquiringly. The robot went on its way, disappearing under some debris. Hendricks watched it go. He had never seen that type before. There were getting to be more and more types he had never seen, new varieties and sizes coming up from the underground factories.

Hendricks put out his cigarette and hurried on. It was interesting, the use of artificial forms in warfare. How had they got started? Necessity. The Soviet Union had gained great initial success, usual with the side that got the war going. Most of North America had been blasted off the map. Retaliation was quick in coming, of course. The sky was full of circling disc-bombers long before the war began; they had been up there for years. The discs began sailing down all over Russia within hours after Washington got it.

* * * * *

But that hadn't helped Washington.

The American bloc governments moved to the Moon Base the first year. There was not much else to do. Europe was gone; a slag heap with dark weeds growing from the ashes and bones. Most of North America was useless; nothing could be planted, no one could live. A few million people kept going up in Canada and down in South America. But during the second year Soviet parachutists began to drop, a few at first, then more and more. They wore the first really effective anti-radiation equipment; what was left of American production moved to the moon along with the governments.

All but the troops. The remaining troops stayed behind as best they could, a few thousand here, a platoon there. No one knew exactly where they were; they stayed where they could, moving around at night, hiding in ruins, in sewers, cellars, with the rats and snakes. It looked as if the Soviet Union had the war almost won. Except for a handful of projectiles fired off from the moon daily, there was almost no weapon in use against them. They came and went as they pleased. The war, for all practical purposes, was over. Nothing effective opposed them.

* * * * *

And then the first claws appeared. And overnight the complexion of the war changed.

The claws were awkward, at first. Slow. The Ivans knocked them off almost as fast as they crawled out of their underground tunnels. But then they got better, faster and more cunning. Factories, all on Terra, turned them out. Factories a long way under ground, behind the Soviet lines, factories that had once made atomic projectiles, now almost forgotten.

The claws got faster, and they got bigger. New types appeared, some with feelers, some that flew. There were a few jumping kinds.

The best technicians on the moon were working on designs, making them more and more intricate, more flexible. They became uncanny; the Ivans were having a lot of trouble with them. Some of the little claws were learning to hide themselves, burrowing down into the ash, lying in wait.

And then they started getting into the Russian bunkers, slipping down when the lids were raised for air and a look around. One claw inside a bunker, a churning sphere of blades and metal-that was enough. And when one got in others followed. With a weapon like that the war couldn't go on much longer.

Maybe it was already over.

Maybe he was going to hear the news. Maybe the Politburo had decided to throw in the sponge. Too bad it had taken so long. Six years. A long time for war like that, the way they had waged it. The automatic retaliation discs, spinning down all over Russia, hundreds of thousands of them. Bacteria crystals. The Soviet guided missiles, whistling through the air. The chain bombs. And now this, the robots, the claws —

The claws weren't like other weapons. They were *alive*, from any practical standpoint, whether the Governments wanted to admit it or not. They were not machines. They were living things, spinning, creeping, shaking themselves up suddenly from the gray ash and darting toward a man, climbing up him, rushing for his throat. And that was what they had been designed to do. Their job.

They did their job well. Especially lately, with the new designs coming up. Now they repaired themselves. They were on their own. Radiation tabs protected the UN troops, but if a man lost his tab he was fair game for the claws, no matter what his uniform. Down below the surface automatic machinery stamped them out. Human beings stayed a long way off. It was too risky; nobody wanted to be around them. They were left to themselves. And they seemed to be doing all right. The new designs were faster, more complex. More efficient.

Apparently they had won the war.

* * * * *

Major Hendricks lit a second cigarette. The landscape depressed him. Nothing but ash and ruins. He seemed to be alone, the only living thing in the whole world. To the right the ruins of a town rose up, a few walls and heaps of debris. He tossed the dead match away, increasing his pace. Suddenly he stopped, jerking up his gun, his body tense. For a minute it looked like —

From behind the shell of a ruined building a figure came, walking slowly toward him, walking hesitantly.

Hendricks blinked. "Stop!"

The boy stopped. Hendricks lowered his gun. The boy stood silently, looking at him. He was small, not very old. Perhaps eight. But it was hard to tell. Most of the kids who remained were stunted. He wore a faded blue sweater, ragged with dirt, and short pants. His hair was long and matted. Brown hair. It hung over his face and around his ears. He held something in his arms.

"What's that you have?" Hendricks said sharply.

The boy held it out. It was a toy, a bear. A teddy bear. The boy's eyes were large, but without expression.

Hendricks relaxed. "I don't want it. Keep it."

The boy hugged the bear again.

"Where do you live?" Hendricks said.

"In there."

"The ruins?"

"Yes."

"Underground?"

"Yes."

"How many are there?"

"How-how many?"

"How many of you. How big's your settlement?"

The boy did not answer.

Hendricks frowned. "You're not all by yourself, are you?"

The boy nodded.

"How do you stay alive?"

"There's food."

"What kind of food?"

"Different."

Hendricks studied him. "How old are you?"

"Thirteen."

It wasn't possible. Or was it? The boy was thin, stunted. And probably sterile. Radiation exposure, years straight. No wonder he was so small. His arms and legs were like pipecleaners, knobby, and thin. Hendricks touched the boy's arm. His skin was dry and rough; radiation skin. He bent down, looking into the boy's face. There was no expression. Big eyes, big and dark.

"Are you blind?" Hendricks said.

"No. I can see some."

"How do you get away from the claws?"

"The claws?"

"The round things. That run and burrow."

"I don't understand."

Maybe there weren't any claws around. A lot of areas were free. They collected mostly around bunkers, where there were people. The claws had been designed to sense warmth, warmth of living things.

"You're lucky." Hendricks straightened up. "Well? Which way are you going? Back-back there?"

"Can I come with you?"

"With *me*?" Hendricks folded his arms. "I'm going a long way. Miles. I have to hurry." He looked at his watch. "I have to get there by nightfall."

"I want to come."

Hendricks fumbled in his pack. "It isn't worth it. Here." He tossed down the food cans he had with him. "You take these and go back. Okay?"

The boy said nothing.

"I'll be coming back this way. In a day or so. If you're around here when I come back you can come along with me. All right?"

"I want to go with you now."

"It's a long walk."

"I can walk."

Hendricks shifted uneasily. It made too good a target, two people walking along. And the boy would slow him down. But he might not come back this way. And if the boy were really all alone —

"Okay. Come along."

The boy fell in beside him. Hendricks strode along. The boy walked silently, clutching his teddy bear.

"What's your name?" Hendricks said, after a time.

"David Edward Derring."

"David? What-what happened to your mother and father?"

"They died."

"How?"

"In the blast."

"How long ago?"

"Six years."

Hendricks slowed down. "You've been alone six years?"

"No. There were other people for awhile. They went away."

"And you've been alone since?"

"Yes."

Hendricks glanced down. The boy was strange, saying very little. Withdrawn. But that was the way they were, the children who had survived. Quiet. Stoic. A strange kind of fatalism gripped them. Nothing came as a surprise. They accepted anything that came along. There was no longer any *normal*, any natural course of things, moral or physical, for them to expect. Custom, habit, all the determining forces of learning were gone; only brute experience remained.

"Am I walking too fast?" Hendricks said.

"No."

"How did you happen to see me?"

"I was waiting."

"Waiting?" Hendricks was puzzled. "What were you waiting for?"

"To catch things."

"What kind of things?"

"Things to eat."

"Oh." Hendricks set his lips grimly. A thirteen year old boy, living on rats and gophers and half-rotten canned food. Down in a hole under the ruins of a town. With radiation pools and claws, and Russian dive-mines up above, coasting around in the sky.

"Where are we going?" David asked.

"To the Russian lines."

"Russian?"

"The enemy. The people who started the war. They dropped the first radiation bombs. They began all this."

The boy nodded. His face showed no expression.

"I'm an American," Hendricks said.

There was no comment. On they went, the two of them, Hendricks walking a little ahead, David trailing behind him, hugging his dirty teddy bear against his chest.

* * * * *

About four in the afternoon they stopped to eat. Hendricks built a fire in a hollow between some slabs of concrete. He cleared the weeds away and heaped up bits of wood. The Russians' lines were not very far ahead. Around him was what had once been a long valley, acres of fruit trees and grapes. Nothing remained now but a few bleak stumps and the mountains that stretched across the horizon at the far end. And the clouds of rolling ash that blew and drifted with the wind, settling over the weeds and remains of buildings, walls here and there, once in awhile what had been a road.

Hendricks made coffee and heated up some boiled mutton and bread. "Here." He handed bread and mutton to David. David squatted by the edge of the fire, his knees knobby and white. He examined the food and then passed it back, shaking his head.

"No."

"No? Don't you want any?"

"No."

Hendricks shrugged. Maybe the boy was a mutant, used to special food. It didn't matter. When he was hungry he would find something to eat. The boy was strange. But there were many strange changes coming over the world. Life was not the same, anymore. It would never be the same again. The human race was going to have to realize that.

"Suit yourself," Hendricks said. He ate the bread and mutton by himself, washing it down with coffee. He ate slowly, finding the food hard to digest. When he was done he got to his feet and stamped the fire out.

David rose slowly, watching him with his young-old eyes.

"We're going," Hendricks said.

"All right."

Hendricks walked along, his gun in his arms. They were close; he was tense, ready for anything. The Russians should be expecting a runner, an answer to their own runner, but they were tricky. There was always the possibility of a slipup. He scanned the landscape around him.

Nothing but slag and ash, a few hills, charred trees. Concrete walls. But someplace ahead was the first bunker of the Russian lines, the forward command. Underground, buried deep, with only a periscope showing, a few gun muzzles. Maybe an antenna.

"Will we be there soon?" David asked.

"Yes. Getting tired?"

"No."

"Why, then?"

David did not answer. He plodded carefully along behind, picking his way over the ash. His legs and shoes were gray with dust. His pinched face was streaked, lines of gray ash in riverlets down the pale white of his skin. There was no color to his face. Typical of the new children, growing up in cellars and sewers and underground shelters.

* * * * *

Hendricks slowed down. He lifted his fieldglasses and studied the ground ahead of him. Were they there, someplace, waiting for him? Watching him, the way his men had watched the Russian runner? A chill went up his back. Maybe they were getting their guns ready, preparing to fire, the way his men had prepared, made ready to kill.

Hendricks stopped, wiping perspiration from his face. "Damn." It made him uneasy. But he should be expected. The situation was different.

He strode over the ash, holding his gun tightly with both hands. Behind him came David. Hendricks peered around, tight-lipped. Any second it might happen. A burst of white light, a blast, carefully aimed from inside a deep concrete bunker.

He raised his arm and waved it around in a circle.

Nothing moved. To the right a long ridge ran, topped with dead tree trunks. A few wild vines had grown up around the trees, remains of arbors. And the eternal dark weeds. Hendricks studied the ridge. Was anything up there? Perfect place for a lookout. He approached the ridge warily, David coming silently behind. If it were his command he'd have a sentry up there, watching for troops trying to infiltrate into the command area. Of course, if it were his command there would be the claws around the area for full protection.

He stopped, feet apart, hands on his hips.

"Are we there?" David said.

"Almost."

"Why have we stopped?"

"I don't want to take any chances." Hendricks advanced slowly. Now the ridge lay directly beside him, along his right. Overlooking him. His uneasy feeling increased. If an Ivan were up there he wouldn't have a chance. He waved his arm again. They should be expecting someone in the UN uniform, in response to the note capsule. Unless the whole thing was a trap.

"Keep up with me." He turned toward David. "Don't drop behind."

"With you?"

"Up beside me! We're close. We can't take any chances. Come on."

"I'll be all right." David remained behind him, in the rear, a few paces away, still clutching his teddy bear.

"Have it your way." Hendricks raised his glasses again, suddenly tense. For a moment-had something moved? He scanned the ridge carefully. Everything was silent. Dead. No life up there, only tree trunks and ash. Maybe a few rats. The big black rats that had survived the claws. Mutants-built their own shelters out of saliva and ash. Some kind of plaster. Adaptation. He started forward again.

* * * * *

A tall figure came out on the ridge above him, cloak flapping. Gray-green. A Russian. Behind him a second soldier appeared, another Russian. Both lifted their guns, aiming.

Hendricks froze. He opened his mouth. The soldiers were kneeling, sighting down the side of the slope. A third figure had joined them on the ridge top, a smaller figure in gray-green. A woman. She stood behind the other two.

Hendricks found his voice. "Stop!" He waved up at them frantically. "I'm —"

The two Russians fired. Behind Hendricks there was a faint *pop*. Waves of heat lapped against him, throwing him to the ground. Ash tore at his face, grinding into his eyes and nose. Choking, he pulled himself to his knees. It was all a trap. He was finished. He had come to be killed, like a steer. The soldiers and the woman were coming down the side of the ridge toward him, sliding down through the soft ash. Hendricks was numb. His head throbbed. Awkwardly, he got his rifle up and took aim. It weighed a thousand tons; he could hardly hold it. His nose and cheeks stung. The air was full of the blast smell, a bitter acrid stench.

"Don't fire," the first Russian said, in heavily accented English.

The three of them came up to him, surrounding him. "Put down your rifle, Yank," the other said.

Hendricks was dazed. Everything had happened so fast. He had been caught. And they had blasted the boy. He turned his head. David was gone. What remained of him was strewn across the ground.

The three Russians studied him curiously. Hendricks sat, wiping blood from his nose, picking out bits of ash. He shook his head, trying to clear it. "Why did you do it?" he murmured thickly. "The boy."

"Why?" One of the soldiers helped him roughly to his feet. He turned Hendricks around. "Look."

Hendricks closed his eyes.

"Look!" The two Russians pulled him forward. "See. Hurry up. There isn't much time to spare, Yank!"

Hendricks looked. And gasped.

"See now? Now do you understand?"

* * * * *

From the remains of David a metal wheel rolled. Relays, glinting metal. Parts, wiring. One of the Russians kicked at the heap of remains. Parts popped out, rolling away, wheels and springs and rods. A plastic section fell in, half charred. Hendricks bent shakily down. The front of the head had come off. He could make out the intricate brain, wires and relays, tiny tubes and switches, thousands of minute studs —

"A robot," the soldier holding his arm said. "We watched it tagging you."

"Tagging me?"

"That's their way. They tag along with you. Into the bunker. That's how they get in."

Hendricks blinked, dazed. "But —"

"Come on." They led him toward the ridge. "We can't stay here. It isn't safe. There must be hundreds of them all around here."

The three of them pulled him up the side of the ridge, sliding and slipping on the ash. The woman reached the top and stood waiting for them.

"The forward command," Hendricks muttered. "I came to negotiate with the Soviet —"

"There is no more forward command. *They* got in. We'll explain." They reached the top of the ridge. "We're all that's left. The three of us. The rest were down in the bunker."

"This way. Down this way." The woman unscrewed a lid, a gray manhole cover set in the ground. "Get in."

Hendricks lowered himself. The two soldiers and the woman came behind him, following him down the ladder. The woman closed the lid after them, bolting it tightly into place.

"Good thing we saw you," one of the two soldiers grunted. "It had tagged you about as far as it was going to."

* * * * *

"Give me one of your cigarettes," the woman said. "I haven't had an American cigarette for weeks."

Hendricks pushed the pack to her. She took a cigarette and passed the pack to the two soldiers. In the corner of the small room the lamp gleamed fitfully. The room was low-ceilinged, cramped. The four of them sat around a small wood table. A few dirty dishes were stacked to one side. Behind a ragged curtain a second room was partly visible. Hendricks saw the corner of a cot, some blankets, clothes hung on a hook.

"We were here," the soldier beside him said. He took off his helmet, pushing his blond hair back. "I'm Corporal Rudi Maxer. Polish. Impressed in the Soviet Army two years ago." He held out his hand.

Hendricks hesitated and then shook. "Major Joseph Hendricks."

"Klaus Epstein." The other soldier shook with him, a small dark man with thinning hair. Epstein plucked nervously at his ear. "Austrian. Impressed God knows when. I don't remember. The three of us were here, Rudi and I, with Tasso." He indicated the woman. "That's how we escaped. All the rest were down in the bunker."

"And-and *they* got in?"

Epstein lit a cigarette. "First just one of them. The kind that tagged you. Then it let others in."

Hendricks became alert. "The *kind*? Are there more than one kind?"

"The little boy. David. David holding his teddy bear. That's Variety Three. The most effective."

"What are the other types?"

Epstein reached into his coat. "Here." He tossed a packet of photographs onto the table, tied with a string. "Look for yourself."

Hendricks untied the string.

"You see," Rudi Maxer said, "that was why we wanted to talk terms. The Russians, I mean. We found out about a week ago. Found out that your claws were beginning to make up new designs on their own. New types of their own. Better types. Down in your underground factories behind our lines. You let them stamp themselves, repair themselves. Made them more and more intricate. It's your fault this happened."

* * * * *

Hendricks examined the photos. They had been snapped hurriedly; they were blurred and indistinct. The first few showed-David. David walking along a road, by himself. David and another David. Three Davids. All exactly alike. Each with a ragged teddy bear.

All pathetic.

"Look at the others," Tasso said.

The next pictures, taken at a great distance, showed a towering wounded soldier sitting by the side of a path, his arm in a sling, the stump of one leg extended, a crude crutch on his lap. Then two wounded soldiers, both the same, standing side by side.

"That's Variety One. The Wounded Soldier." Klaus reached out and took the pictures. "You see, the claws were designed to get to human beings. To find them. Each kind was better than the last. They got farther, closer, past most of our defenses, into our lines. But as long as they were merely *machines*, metal spheres with claws and horns, feelers, they could be picked off like any other object. They could be detected as lethal robots as soon as they were seen. Once we caught sight of them —"

"Variety One subverted our whole north wing," Rudi said. "It was a long time before anyone caught on. Then it was too late. They came in, wounded soldiers, knocking and begging to be let in. So we let them in. And as soon as they were in they took over. We were watching out for machines...."

"At that time it was thought there was only the one type," Klaus Epstein said. "No one suspected there were other types. The pictures were flashed to us. When the runner was sent to you, we knew of just one type. Variety One. The big Wounded Soldier. We thought that was all."

"Your line fell to —"

"To Variety Three. David and his bear. That worked even better." Klaus smiled bitterly. "Soldiers are suckers for children. We brought them in and tried to feed them. We found out the hard way what they were after. At least, those who were in the bunker."

"The three of us were lucky," Rudi said. "Klaus and I were-were visiting Tasso when it happened. This is her place." He waved a big hand around. "This little cellar. We finished and climbed the ladder to start back. From the ridge we saw. There they were, all around the bunker. Fighting was still going on. David and his bear. Hundreds of them. Klaus took the pictures."

Klaus tied up the photographs again.

* * * * *

"And it's going on all along your line?" Hendricks said.

"Yes."

"How about *our* lines?" Without thinking, he touched the tab on his arm. "Can they —"

"They're not bothered by your radiation tabs. It makes no difference to them, Russian, American, Pole, German. It's all the same. They're doing what they were designed to do. Carrying out the original idea. They track down life, wherever they find it."

"They go by warmth," Klaus said. "That was the way you constructed them from the very start. Of course, those you designed were kept back by the radiation tabs you wear. Now they've got around that. These new varieties are lead-lined."

"What's the other variety?" Hendricks asked. "The David type, the Wounded Soldier-what's the other?"

"We don't know." Klaus pointed up at the wall. On the wall were two metal plates, ragged at the edges. Hendricks got up and studied them. They were bent and dented.

"The one on the left came off a Wounded Soldier," Rudi said. "We got one of them. It was going along toward our old bunker. We got it from the ridge, the same way we got the David tagging you."

The plate was stamped: I-V. Hendricks touched the other plate. "And this came from the David type?"

"Yes." The plate was stamped: III-V.

Klaus took a look at them, leaning over Hendricks' broad shoulder. "You can see what we're up against. There's another type. Maybe it was abandoned. Maybe it didn't work. But there must be a Second Variety. There's One and Three."

"You were lucky," Rudi said. "The David tagged you all the way here and never touched you. Probably thought you'd get it into a bunker, somewhere."

"One gets in and it's all over," Klaus said. "They move fast. One lets all the rest inside. They're inflexible. Machines with one purpose. They were built for only one thing." He rubbed sweat from his lip. "We saw."

They were silent.

"Let me have another cigarette, Yank," Tasso said. "They are good. I almost forgot how they were."

* * * * *

It was night. The sky was black. No stars were visible through the rolling clouds of ash. Klaus lifted the lid cautiously so that Hendricks could look out.

Rudi pointed into the darkness. "Over that way are the bunkers. Where we used to be. Not over half a mile from us. It was just chance Klaus and I were not there when it happened. Weakness. Saved by our lusts."

"All the rest must be dead," Klaus said in a low voice. "It came quickly. This morning the Politburo reached their decision. They notified us-forward command. Our runner was sent out at once. We saw him start toward the direction of your lines. We covered him until he was out of sight."

"Alex Radrivsky. We both knew him. He disappeared about six o'clock. The sun had just come up. About noon Klaus and I had an hour relief. We crept off, away from the bunkers. No one was watching. We came here. There used to be a town here, a few houses, a street. This cellar was part of a big farmhouse. We knew Tasso would be here, hiding down in her little place. We had come here before. Others from the bunkers came here. Today happened to be our turn."

"So we were saved," Klaus said. "Chance. It might have been others. We-we finished, and then we came up to the surface and started back along the ridge. That was when we saw them, the Davids. We understood right away. We had seen the photos of the First Variety, the Wounded Soldier. Our Commissar distributed them to us with an explanation. If we had gone another step they would have seen us. As it was we had to blast two Davids before we got back. There were hundreds of them, all around. Like ants. We took pictures and slipped back here, bolting the lid tight."

"They're not so much when you catch them alone. We moved faster than they did. But they're inexorable. Not like living things. They came right at us. And we blasted them."

Major Hendricks rested against the edge of the lid, adjusting his eyes to the darkness. "Is it safe to have the lid up at all?"

"If we're careful. How else can you operate your transmitter?"

Hendricks lifted the small belt transmitter slowly. He pressed it against his ear. The metal was cold and damp. He blew against the mike, raising up the short antenna. A faint hum sounded in his ear. "That's true, I suppose."

But he still hesitated.

"We'll pull you under if anything happens," Klaus said.

"Thanks." Hendricks waited a moment, resting the transmitter against his shoulder. "Interesting, isn't it?"

"What?"

"This, the new types. The new varieties of claws. We're completely at their mercy, aren't we? By now they've probably gotten into the UN lines, too. It makes me wonder if we're not seeing the beginning of a new species. *The* new species. Evolution. The race to come after man."

* * * * *

Rudi grunted. "There is no race after man."

"No? Why not? Maybe we're seeing it now, the end of human beings, the beginning of the new society."

"They're not a race. They're mechanical killers. You made them to destroy. That's all they can do. They're machines with a job."

"So it seems now. But how about later on? After the war is over. Maybe, when there aren't any humans to destroy, their real potentialities will begin to show."

"You talk as if they were alive!"

"Aren't they?"

24

There was silence. "They're machines," Rudi said. "They look like people, but they're machines."

"Use your transmitter, Major," Klaus said. "We can't stay up here forever."

Holding the transmitter tightly Hendricks called the code of the command bunker. He waited, listening. No response. Only silence. He checked the leads carefully. Everything was in place.

"Scott!" he said into the mike. "Can you hear me?"

Silence. He raised the gain up full and tried again. Only static.

"I don't get anything. They may hear me but they may not want to answer."

"Tell them it's an emergency."

"They'll think I'm being forced to call. Under your direction." He tried again, outlining briefly what he had learned. But still the phone was silent, except for the faint static.

"Radiation pools kill most transmission," Klaus said, after awhile. "Maybe that's it."

Hendricks shut the transmitter up. "No use. No answer. Radiation pools? Maybe. Or they hear me, but won't answer. Frankly, that's what I would do, if a runner tried to call from the Soviet lines. They have no reason to believe such a story. They may hear everything I say —"

"Or maybe it's too late."

Hendricks nodded.

"We better get the lid down," Rudi said nervously. "We don't want to take unnecessary chances."

* * * * *

They climbed slowly back down the tunnel. Klaus bolted the lid carefully into place. They descended into the kitchen. The air was heavy and close around them.

"Could they work that fast?" Hendricks said. "I left the bunker this noon. Ten hours ago. How could they move so quickly?"

"It doesn't take them long. Not after the first one gets in. It goes wild. You know what the little claws can do. Even *one* of these is beyond belief. Razors, each finger. Maniacal."

"All right." Hendricks moved away impatiently. He stood with his back to them.

"What's the matter?" Rudi said.

"The Moon Base. God, if they've gotten there —"

"The Moon Base?"

Hendricks turned around. "They couldn't have got to the Moon Base. How would they get there? It isn't possible. I can't believe it."

"What is this Moon Base? We've heard rumors, but nothing definite. What is the actual situation? You seem concerned."

"We're supplied from the moon. The governments are there, under the lunar surface. All our people and industries. That's what keeps us going. If they should find some way of getting off Terra, onto the moon —"

"It only takes one of them. Once the first one gets in it admits the others. Hundreds of them, all alike. You should have seen them. Identical. Like ants."

"Perfect socialism," Tasso said. "The ideal of the communist state. All citizens interchangeable."

Klaus grunted angrily. "That's enough. Well? What next?"

Hendricks paced back and forth, around the small room. The air was full of smells of food and perspiration. The others watched him. Presently Tasso pushed through the curtain, into the other room. "I'm going to take a nap."

The curtain closed behind her. Rudi and Klaus sat down at the table, still watching Hendricks.

"It's up to you," Klaus said. "We don't know your situation."

Hendricks nodded.

"It's a problem." Rudi drank some coffee, filling his cup from a rusty pot. "We're safe here for awhile, but we can't stay here forever. Not enough food or supplies."

"But if we go outside —"

"If we go outside they'll get us. Or probably they'll get us. We couldn't go very far. How far is your command bunker, Major?"

"Three or four miles."

"We might make it. The four of us. Four of us could watch all sides. They couldn't slip up behind us and start tagging us. We have three rifles, three blast rifles. Tasso can have my pistol." Rudi tapped his belt. "In the Soviet army we didn't have shoes always, but we had guns. With all four of us armed one of us might get to your command bunker. Preferably you, Major."

"What if they're already there?" Klaus said.

Rudi shrugged. "Well, then we come back here."

* * * * *

Hendricks stopped pacing. "What do you think the chances are they're already in the American lines?"

"Hard to say. Fairly good. They're organized. They know exactly what they're doing. Once they start they go like a horde of locusts. They have to keep moving, and fast. It's secrecy and speed they depend on. Surprise. They push their way in before anyone has any idea."

"I see," Hendricks murmured.

From the other room Tasso stirred. "Major?"

Hendricks pushed the curtain back. "What?"

Tasso looked up at him lazily original location of illo2 from the cot. "Have you any more American cigarettes left?"

Hendricks went into the room and sat down across from her, on a wood stool. He felt in his pockets. "No. All gone."

"Too bad."

"What nationality are you?" Hendricks asked after awhile.

"Russian."

"How did you get here?"

"Here?"

"This used to be France. This was part of Normandy. Did you come with the Soviet army?"

"Why?"

"Just curious." He studied her. She had taken off her coat, tossing it over the end of the cot. She was young, about twenty. Slim. Her long hair stretched out over the pillow. She was staring at him silently, her eyes dark and large.

"What's on your mind?" Tasso said.

"Nothing. How old are you?"

"Eighteen." She continued to watch him, unblinking, her arms behind her head. She had on Russian army pants and shirt. Gray-green. Thick leather belt with counter and cartridges. Medicine kit.

"You're in the Soviet army?"

"No."

"Where did you get the uniform?"

She shrugged. "It was given to me," she told him.

"How-how old were you when you came here?"

"Sixteen."

"That young?"

Her eyes narrowed. "What do you mean?"

* * * * *

26

Hendricks rubbed his jaw. "Your life would have been a lot different if there had been no war. Sixteen. You came here at sixteen. To live this way."

"I had to survive."

"I'm not moralizing."

"Your life would have been different, too," Tasso murmured. She reached down and unfastened one of her boots. She kicked the boot off, onto the floor. "Major, do you want to go in the other room? I'm sleepy."

"It's going to be a problem, the four of us here. It's going to be hard to live in these quarters. Are there just the two rooms?"

"Yes."

"How big was the cellar originally? Was it larger than this? Are there other rooms filled up with debris? We might be able to open one of them."

"Perhaps. I really don't know." Tasso loosened her belt. She made herself comfortable on the cot, unbuttoning her shirt. "You're sure you have no more cigarettes?"

"I had only the one pack."

"Too bad. Maybe if we get back to your bunker we can find some." The other boot fell. Tasso reached up for the light cord. "Good night."

"You're going to sleep?"

"That's right."

The room plunged into darkness. Hendricks got up and made his way past the curtain, into the kitchen.

And stopped, rigid.

Rudi stood against the wall, his face white and gleaming. His mouth opened and closed but no sounds came. Klaus stood in front of him, the muzzle of his pistol in Rudi's stomach. Neither of them moved. Klaus, his hand tight around his gun, his features set. Rudi, pale and silent, spread-eagled against the wall.

"What —" Hendricks muttered, but Klaus cut him off.

"Be quiet, Major. Come over here. Your gun. Get out your gun."

Hendricks drew his pistol. "What is it?"

"Cover him." Klaus motioned him forward. "Beside me. Hurry!"

Rudi moved a little, lowering his arms. He turned to Hendricks, licking his lips. The whites of his eyes shone wildly. Sweat dripped from his forehead, down his cheeks. He fixed his gaze on Hendricks. "Major, he's gone insane. Stop him." Rudi's voice was thin and hoarse, almost inaudible.

"What's going on?" Hendricks demanded.

Without lowering his pistol Klaus answered. "Major, remember our discussion? The Three Varieties? We knew about One and Three. But we didn't know about Two. At least, we didn't know before." Klaus' fingers tightened around the gun butt. "We didn't know before, but we know now."

He pressed the trigger. A burst of white heat rolled out of the gun, licking around Rudi.

"Major, this is the Second Variety."

* * * * *

Tasso swept the curtain aside. "Klaus! What did you do?"

Klaus turned from the charred form, gradually sinking down the wall onto the floor. "The Second Variety, Tasso. Now we know. We have all three types identified. The danger is less. I —"

Tasso stared past him at the remains of Rudi, at the blackened, smouldering fragments and bits of cloth. "You killed him."

"Him? *It*, you mean. I was watching. I had a feeling, but I wasn't sure. At least, I wasn't sure before. But this evening I was certain." Klaus rubbed his pistol butt nervously. "We're lucky. Don't you understand? Another hour and it might —"

"You were *certain*?" Tasso pushed past him and bent down, over the steaming remains on the floor. Her face became hard. "Major, see for yourself. Bones. Flesh."

Hendricks bent down beside her. The remains were human remains. Seared flesh, charred bone fragments, part of a skull. Ligaments, viscera, blood. Blood forming a pool against the wall.

"No wheels," Tasso said calmly. She straightened up. "No wheels, no parts, no relays. Not a claw. Not the Second Variety." She folded her arms. "You're going to have to be able to explain this."

Klaus sat down at the table, all the color drained suddenly from his face. He put his head in his hands and rocked back and forth.

"Snap out of it." Tasso's fingers closed over his shoulder. "Why did you do it? Why did you kill him?"

"He was frightened," Hendricks said. "All this, the whole thing, building up around us."

"Maybe."

"What, then? What do you think?"

"I think he may have had a reason for killing Rudi. A good reason."

"What reason?"

"Maybe Rudi learned something."

Hendricks studied her bleak face. "About what?" he asked.

"About him. About Klaus."

* * * * *

Klaus looked up quickly. "You can see what she's trying to say. She thinks I'm the Second Variety. Don't you see, Major? Now she wants you to believe I killed him on purpose. That I'm —"

"Why did you kill him, then?" Tasso said.

"I told you." Klaus shook his head wearily. "I thought he was a claw. I thought I knew."

"Why?"

"I had been watching him. I was suspicious."

"Why?"

"I thought I had seen something. Heard something. I thought I —" He stopped.

"Go on."

"We were sitting at the table. Playing cards. You two were in the other room. It was silent. I thought I heard him —*whirr*."

There was silence.

"Do you believe that?" Tasso said to Hendricks.

"Yes. I believe what he says."

"I don't. I think he killed Rudi for a good purpose." Tasso touched the rifle, resting in the corner of the room. "Major —"

"No." Hendricks shook his head. "Let's stop it right now. One is enough. We're afraid, the way he was. If we kill him we'll be doing what he did to Rudi."

Klaus looked gratefully up at him. "Thanks. I was afraid. You understand, don't you? Now she's afraid, the way I was. She wants to kill me."

"No more killing." Hendricks moved toward the end of the ladder. "I'm going above and try the transmitter once more. If I can't get them we're moving back toward my lines tomorrow morning."

Klaus rose quickly. "I'll come up with you and give you a hand."

* * * * *

The night air was cold. The earth was cooling off. Klaus took a deep breath, filling his lungs. He and Hendricks stepped onto the ground, out of the tunnel. Klaus planted his feet wide apart, the rifle up, watching and listening. Hendricks crouched by the tunnel mouth, tuning the small transmitter.

"Any luck?" Klaus asked presently.

"Not yet."

"Keep trying. Tell them what happened."

Hendricks kept trying. Without success. Finally he lowered the antenna. "It's useless. They can't hear me. Or they hear me and won't answer. Or —"

"Or they don't exist."

"I'll try once more." Hendricks raised the antenna. "Scott, can you hear me? Come in!"

He listened. There was only static. Then, still very faintly —

"This is Scott."

His fingers tightened. "Scott! Is it you?"

"This is Scott."

Klaus squatted down. "Is it your command?"

"Scott, listen. Do you understand? About them, the claws. Did you get my message? Did you hear me?"

"Yes." Faintly. Almost inaudible. He could hardly make out the word.

"You got my message? Is everything all right at the bunker? None of them have got in?"

"Everything is all right."

"Have they tried to get in?"

The voice was weaker.

"No."

Hendricks turned to Klaus. "They're all right."

"Have they been attacked?"

"No." Hendricks pressed the phone tighter to his ear. "Scott, I can hardly hear you. Have you notified the Moon Base? Do they know? Are they alerted?"

No answer.

"Scott! Can you hear me?"

Silence.

Hendricks relaxed, sagging. "Faded out. Must be radiation pools."

* * * * *

Hendricks and Klaus looked at each other. Neither of them said anything. After a time Klaus said, "Did it sound like any of your men? Could you identify the voice?"

"It was too faint."

"You couldn't be certain?"

"No."

"Then it could have been —"

"I don't know. Now I'm not sure. Let's go back down and get the lid closed."

They climbed back down the ladder slowly, into the warm cellar. Klaus bolted the lid behind them. Tasso waited for them, her face expressionless.

"Any luck?" she asked.

Neither of them answered. "Well?" Klaus said at last. "What do you think, Major? Was it your officer, or was it one of *them*?"

"I don't know."

"Then we're just where we were before."

Hendricks stared down at the floor, his jaw set. "We'll have to go. To be sure."

"Anyhow, we have food here for only a few weeks. We'd have to go up after that, in any case."

"Apparently so."

"What's wrong?" Tasso demanded. "Did you get across to your bunker? What's the matter?"

"It may have been one of my men," Hendricks said slowly. "Or it may have been one of *them*. But we'll never know standing here." He examined his watch. "Let's turn in and get some sleep. We want to be up early tomorrow."

"Early?"

"Our best chance to get through the claws should be early in the morning," Hendricks said.

* * * * *

The morning was crisp and clear. Major Hendricks studied the countryside through his field-glasses.

"See anything?" Klaus said.

"No."

"Can you make out our bunkers?"

"Which way?"

"Here." Klaus took the glasses and adjusted them. "I know where to look." He looked a long time, silently.

Tasso came to the top of the tunnel and stepped up onto the ground. "Anything?"

"No." Klaus passed the glasses back to Hendricks. "They're out of sight. Come on. Let's not stay here."

The three of them made their way down the side of the ridge, sliding in the soft ash. Across a flat rock a lizard scuttled. They stopped instantly, rigid.

"What was it?" Klaus muttered.

"A lizard."

The lizard ran on, hurrying through the ash. It was exactly the same color as the ash.

"Perfect adaptation," Klaus said. "Proves we were right. Lysenko, I mean."

They reached the bottom of the ridge and stopped, standing close together, looking around them.

"Let's go." Hendricks started off. "It's a good long trip, on foot."

Klaus fell in beside him. Tasso walked behind, her pistol held alertly. "Major, I've been meaning to ask you something," Klaus said. "How did you run across the David? The one that was tagging you."

"I met it along the way. In some ruins."

"What did it say?"

"Not much. It said it was alone. By itself."

"You couldn't tell it was a machine? It talked like a living person? You never suspected?"

"It didn't say much. I noticed nothing unusual."

"It's strange, machines so much like people that you can be fooled. Almost alive. I wonder where it'll end."

"They're doing what you Yanks designed them to do," Tasso said. "You designed them to hunt out life and destroy. Human life. Wherever they find it."

* * * * *

Hendricks was watching Klaus intently. "Why did you ask me? What's on your mind?"

"Nothing," Klaus answered.

"Klaus thinks you're the Second Variety," Tasso said calmly, from behind them. "Now he's got his eye on you."

Klaus flushed. "Why not? We sent a runner to the Yank lines and he comes back. Maybe he thought he'd find some good game here."

Hendricks laughed harshly "I came from the UN bunkers. There were human beings all around me."

"Maybe you saw an opportunity to get into the Soviet lines. Maybe you saw your chance. Maybe you —"

"The Soviet lines had already been taken over. Your lines had been invaded before I left my command bunker. Don't forget that."

Tasso came up beside him. "That proves nothing at all, Major."

"Why not?"

"There appears to be little communication between the varieties. Each is made in a different factory. They don't seem to work together. You might have started for the Soviet lines without knowing anything about the work of the other varieties. Or even what the other varieties were like."

"How do you know so much about the claws?" Hendricks said.

"I've seen them. I've observed them. I observed them take over the Soviet bunkers."

"You know quite a lot," Klaus said. "Actually, you saw very little. Strange that you should have been such an acute observer."

Tasso laughed. "Do you suspect me, now?"

"Forget it," Hendricks said. They walked on in silence.

"Are we going the whole way on foot?" Tasso said, after awhile. "I'm not used to walking." She gazed around at the plain of ash, stretching out on all sides of them, as far as they could see. "How dreary."

"It's like this all the way," Klaus said.

"In a way I wish you had been in your bunker when the attack came."

"Somebody else would have been with you, if not me," Klaus muttered.

Tasso laughed, putting her hands in her pockets. "I suppose so."

They walked on, keeping their eyes on the vast plain of silent ash around them.

* * * * *

The sun was setting. Hendricks made his way forward slowly, waving Tasso and Klaus back. Klaus squatted down, resting his gun butt against the ground.

Tasso found a concrete slab and sat down with a sigh. "It's good to rest."

"Be quiet," Klaus said sharply.

Hendricks pushed up to the top of the rise ahead of them. The same rise the Russian runner had come up, the day before. Hendricks dropped down, stretching himself out, peering through his glasses at what lay beyond.

Nothing was visible. Only ash and occasional trees. But there, not more than fifty yards ahead, was the entrance of the forward command bunker. The bunker from which he had come. Hendricks watched silently. No motion. No sign of life. Nothing stirred.

Klaus slithered up beside him. "Where is it?"

"Down there." Hendricks passed him the glasses. Clouds of ash rolled across the evening sky. The world was darkening. They had a couple of hours of light left, at the most. Probably not that much.

"I don't see anything," Klaus said.

"That tree there. The stump. By the pile of bricks. The entrance is to the right of the bricks."

"I'll have to take your word for it."

"You and Tasso cover me from here. You'll be able to sight all the way to the bunker entrance."

"You're going down alone?"

"With my wrist tab I'll be safe. The ground around the bunker is a living field of claws. They collect down in the ash. Like crabs. Without tabs you wouldn't have a chance."

"Maybe you're right."

"I'll walk slowly all the way. As soon as I know for certain —"

"If they're down inside the bunker you won't be able to get back up here. They go fast. You don't realize."

"What do you suggest?"

Klaus considered. "I don't know. Get them to come up to the surface. So you can see."

Hendricks brought his transmitter from his belt, raising the antenna. "Let's get started."

* * * * *

Klaus signalled to Tasso. She crawled expertly up the side of the rise to where they were sitting.

"He's going down alone," Klaus said. "We'll cover him from here. As soon as you see him start back, fire past him at once. They come quick."

"You're not very optimistic," Tasso said.

"No, I'm not."

Hendricks opened the breech of his gun, checking it carefully. "Maybe things are all right."

"You didn't see them. Hundreds of them. All the same. Pouring out like ants."

"I should be able to find out without going down all the way." Hendricks locked his gun, gripping it in one hand, the transmitter in the other. "Well, wish me luck."

Klaus put out his hand. "Don't go down until you're sure. Talk to them from up here. Make them show themselves."

* * * * *

Hendricks stood up. He stepped down the side of the rise.

A moment later he was walking slowly toward the pile of bricks and debris beside the dead tree stump. Toward the entrance of the forward command bunker.

Nothing stirred. He raised the transmitter, clicking it on. "Scott? Can you hear me?"

Silence.

"Scott! This is Hendricks. Can you hear me? I'm standing outside the bunker. You should be able to see me in the view sight."

He listened, the transmitter gripped tightly. No sound. Only static. He walked forward. A claw burrowed out of the ash and raced toward him. It halted a few feet away and then slunk off. A second claw appeared, one of the big ones with feelers. It moved toward him, studied him intently, and then fell in behind him, dogging respectfully after him, a few paces away. A moment later a second big claw joined it. Silently, the claws trailed him, as he walked slowly toward the bunker.

Hendricks stopped, and behind him, the claws came to a halt. He was close, now. Almost to the bunker steps.

"Scott! Can you hear me? I'm standing right above you. Outside. On the surface. Are you picking me up?"

* * * * *

He waited, holding his gun against his side, the transmitter tightly to his ear. Time passed. He strained to hear, but there was only silence. Silence, and faint static.

Then, distantly, metallically —

"This is Scott."

The voice was neutral. Cold. He could not identify it. But the earphone was minute.

"Scott! Listen. I'm standing right above you. I'm on the surface, looking down into the bunker entrance."

"Yes."

"Can you see me?"

"Yes."

"Through the view sight? You have the sight trained on me?"

"Yes."

32

Hendricks pondered. A circle of claws waited quietly around him, gray-metal bodies on all sides of him. "Is everything all right in the bunker? Nothing unusual has happened?"

"Everything is all right."

"Will you come up to the surface? I want to see you for a moment." Hendricks took a deep breath. "Come up here with me. I want to talk to you."

"Come down."

"I'm giving you an order."

Silence.

"Are you coming?" Hendricks listened. There was no response. "I order you to come to the surface."

"Come down."

Hendricks set his jaw. "Let me talk to Leone."

There was a long pause. He listened to the static. Then a voice came, hard, thin, metallic. The same as the other. "This is Leone."

"Hendricks. I'm on the surface. At the bunker entrance. I want one of you to come up here."

"Come down."

"Why come down? I'm giving you an order!"

Silence. Hendricks lowered the transmitter. He looked carefully around him. The entrance was just ahead. Almost at his feet. He lowered the antenna and fastened the transmitter to his belt. Carefully, he gripped his gun with both hands. He moved forward, a step at a time. If they could see him they knew he was starting toward the entrance. He closed his eyes a moment.

Then he put his foot on the first step that led downward.

Two Davids came up at him, their faces identical and expressionless. He blasted them into particles. More came rushing silently up, a whole pack of them. All exactly the same.

Hendricks turned and raced back, away from the bunker, back toward the rise.

At the top of the rise Tasso and Klaus were firing down. The small claws were already streaking up toward them, shining metal spheres going fast, racing frantically through the ash. But he had no time to think about that. He knelt down, aiming at the bunker entrance, gun against his cheek. The Davids were coming out in groups, clutching their teddy bears, their thin knobby legs pumping as they ran up the steps to the surface. Hendricks fired into the main body of them. They burst apart, wheels and springs flying in all directions. He fired again through the mist of particles.

A giant lumbering figure rose up in the bunker entrance, tall and swaying. Hendricks paused, amazed. A man, a soldier. With one leg, supporting himself with a crutch.

"Major!" Tasso's voice came. More firing. The huge figure moved forward, Davids swarming around it. Hendricks broke out of his freeze. The First Variety. The Wounded Soldier.

He aimed and fired. The soldier burst into bits, parts and relays flying. Now many Davids were out on the flat ground, away from the bunker. He fired again and again, moving slowly back, half-crouching and aiming.

From the rise, Klaus fired down. The side of the rise was alive with claws making their way up. Hendricks retreated toward the rise, running and crouching. Tasso had left Klaus and was circling slowly to the right, moving away from the rise.

A David slipped up toward him, its small white face expressionless, brown hair hanging down in its eyes. It bent over suddenly, opening its arms. Its teddy bear hurtled down and leaped across the ground, bounding toward him. Hendricks fired. The bear and the David both dissolved. He grinned, blinking. It was like a dream.

"Up here!" Tasso's voice. Hendricks made his way toward her. She was over by some columns of concrete, walls of a ruined building. She was firing past him, with the hand pistol Klaus had given her.

"Thanks." He joined her, grasping for breath. She pulled him back, behind the concrete, fumbling at her belt.

"Close your eyes!" She unfastened a globe from her waist. Rapidly, she unscrewed the cap, locking it into place. "Close your eyes and get down."

* * * * *

She threw the bomb. It sailed in an arc, an expert, rolling and bouncing to the entrance of the bunker. Two Wounded Soldiers stood uncertainly by the brick pile. More Davids poured from behind them, out onto the plain. One of the Wounded Soldiers moved toward the bomb, stooping awkwardly down to pick it up.

The bomb went off. The concussion whirled Hendricks around, throwing him on his face. A hot wind rolled over him. Dimly he saw Tasso standing behind the columns, firing slowly and methodically at the Davids coming out of the raging clouds of white fire.

Back along the rise Klaus struggled with a ring of claws circling around him. He retreated, blasting at them and moving back, trying to break through the ring.

Hendricks struggled to his feet. His head ached. He could hardly see. Everything was licking at him, raging and whirling. His right arm would not move.

Tasso pulled back toward him. "Come on. Let's go."

"Klaus-He's still up there."

"Come on!" Tasso dragged Hendricks back, away from the columns. Hendricks shook his head, trying to clear it. Tasso led him rapidly away, her eyes intense and bright, watching for claws that had escaped the blast.

One David came out of the rolling clouds of flame. Tasso blasted it. No more appeared.

"But Klaus. What about him?" Hendricks stopped, standing unsteadily. "He —"

"Come on!"

* * * * *

They retreated, moving farther and farther away from the bunker. A few small claws followed them for a little while and then gave up, turning back and going off.

At last Tasso stopped. "We can stop here and get our breaths."

Hendricks sat down on some heaps of debris. He wiped his neck, gasping. "We left Klaus back there."

Tasso said nothing. She opened her gun, sliding a fresh round of blast cartridges into place.

Hendricks stared at her, dazed. "You left him back there on purpose."

Tasso snapped the gun together. She studied the heaps of rubble around them, her face expressionless. As if she were watching for something.

"What is it?" Hendricks demanded. "What are you looking for? Is something coming?" He shook his head, trying to understand. What was she doing? What was she waiting for? He could see nothing. Ash lay all around them, ash and ruins. Occasional stark tree trunks, without leaves or branches. "What —"

Tasso cut him off. "Be still." Her eyes narrowed. Suddenly her gun came up. Hendricks turned, following her gaze.

* * * * *

Back the way they had come a figure appeared. The figure walked unsteadily toward them. Its clothes were torn. It limped as it made its way along, going very slowly and carefully. Stopping now and then, resting and getting its strength. Once it almost fell. It stood for a moment, trying to steady itself. Then it came on.

Klaus.

Hendricks stood up. "Klaus!" He started toward him. "How the hell did you —"

Tasso fired. Hendricks swung back. She fired again, the blast passing him, a searing line of heat. The beam caught Klaus in the chest. He exploded, gears and wheels flying. For a moment he continued to walk. Then he swayed back and forth. He crashed to the ground, his arms flung out. A few more wheels rolled away.

Silence.

Tasso turned to Hendricks. "Now you understand why he killed Rudi."

Hendricks sat down again slowly. He shook his head. He was numb. He could not think.

"Do you see?" Tasso said. "Do you understand?"

Hendricks said nothing. Everything was slipping away from him, faster and faster. Darkness, rolling and plucking at him.

He closed his eyes.

* * * * *

Hendricks opened his eyes slowly. His body ached all over. He tried to sit up but needles of pain shot through his arm and shoulder. He gasped.

"Don't try to get up," Tasso said. She bent down, putting her cold hand against his forehead.

It was night. A few stars glinted above, shining through the drifting clouds of ash. Hendricks lay back, his teeth locked. Tasso watched him impassively. She had built a fire with some wood and weeds. The fire licked feebly, hissing at a metal cup suspended over it. Everything was silent. Unmoving darkness, beyond the fire.

"So he was the Second Variety," Hendricks murmured.

"I had always thought so."

"Why didn't you destroy him sooner?" he wanted to know.

"You held me back." Tasso crossed to the fire to look into the metal cup. "Coffee. It'll be ready to drink in awhile."

She came back and sat down beside him. Presently she opened her pistol and began to disassemble the firing mechanism, studying it intently.

"This is a beautiful gun," Tasso said, half-aloud. "The construction is superb."

"What about them? The claws."

"The concussion from the bomb put most of them out of action. They're delicate. Highly organized, I suppose."

"The Davids, too?"

"Yes."

"How did you happen to have a bomb like that?"

Tasso shrugged. "We designed it. You shouldn't underestimate our technology, Major. Without such a bomb you and I would no longer exist."

"Very useful."

Tasso stretched out her legs, warming her feet in the heat of the fire. "It surprised me that you did not seem to understand, after he killed Rudi. Why did you think he —"

"I told you. I thought he was afraid."

"Really? You know, Major, for a little while I suspected you. Because you wouldn't let me kill him. I thought you might be protecting him." She laughed.

"Are we safe here?" Hendricks asked presently.

"For awhile. Until they get reinforcements from some other area." Tasso began to clean the interior of the gun with a bit of rag. She finished and pushed the mechanism back into place. She closed the gun, running her finger along the barrel.

"We were lucky," Hendricks murmured.

"Yes. Very lucky."

"Thanks for pulling me away."

* * * * *

Tasso did not answer. She glanced up at him, her eyes bright in the fire light. Hendricks examined his arm. He could not move his fingers. His whole side seemed numb. Down inside him was a dull steady ache.

"How do you feel?" Tasso asked.

"My arm is damaged."

"Anything else?"

"Internal injuries."

"You didn't get down when the bomb went off."

Hendricks said nothing. He watched Tasso pour the coffee from the cup into a flat metal pan. She brought it over to him.

"Thanks." He struggled up enough to drink. It was hard to swallow. His insides turned over and he pushed the pan away. "That's all I can drink now."

Tasso drank the rest. Time passed. The clouds of ash moved across the dark sky above them. Hendricks rested, his mind blank. After awhile he became aware that Tasso was standing over him, gazing down at him.

"What is it?" he murmured.

"Do you feel any better?"

"Some."

"You know, Major, if I hadn't dragged you away they would have got you. You would be dead. Like Rudi."

"I know."

"Do you want to know why I brought you out? I could have left you. I could have left you there."

"Why did you bring me out?"

"Because we have to get away from here." Tasso stirred the fire with a stick, peering calmly down into it. "No human being can live here. When their reinforcements come we won't have a chance. I've pondered about it while you were unconscious. We have perhaps three hours before they come."

"And you expect me to get us away?"

"That's right. I expect you to get us out of here."

"Why me?"

"Because I don't know any way." Her eyes shone at him in the half-light, bright and steady. "If you can't get us out of here they'll kill us within three hours. I see nothing else ahead. Well, Major? What are you going to do? I've been waiting all night. While you were unconscious I sat here, waiting and listening. It's almost dawn. The night is almost over."

* * * * *

Hendricks considered. "It's curious," he said at last.

"Curious?"

"That you should think I can get us out of here. I wonder what you think I can do."

"Can you get us to the Moon Base?"

"The Moon Base? How?"

"There must be some way."

Hendricks shook his head. "No. There's no way that I know of."

Tasso said nothing. For a moment her steady gaze wavered. She ducked her head, turning abruptly away. She scrambled to her feet. "More coffee?"

"No."

"Suit yourself." Tasso drank silently. He could not see her face. He lay back against the ground, deep in thought, trying to concentrate. It was hard to think. His head still hurt. And the numbing daze still hung over him.

"There might be one way," he said suddenly.

"Oh?"

"How soon is dawn?"

"Two hours. The sun will be coming up shortly."

"There's supposed to be a ship near here. I've never seen it. But I know it exists."

"What kind of a ship?" Her voice was sharp.

"A rocket cruiser."

"Will it take us off? To the Moon Base?"

"It's supposed to. In case of emergency." He rubbed his forehead.

"What's wrong?"

"My head. It's hard to think. I can hardly-hardly concentrate. The bomb."

"Is the ship near here?" Tasso slid over beside him, settling down on her haunches. "How far is it? Where is it?"

"I'm trying to think."

Her fingers dug into his arm. "Nearby?" Her voice was like iron. "Where would it be? Would they store it underground? Hidden underground?"

"Yes. In a storage locker."

"How do we find it? Is it marked? Is there a code marker to identify it?"

Hendricks concentrated. "No. No markings. No code symbol."

"What, then?"

"A sign."

"What sort of sign?"

* * * * *

Hendricks did not answer. In the flickering light his eyes were glazed, two sightless orbs. Tasso's fingers dug into his arm.

"What sort of sign? What is it?"

"I —I can't think. Let me rest."

"All right." She let go and stood up. Hendricks lay back against the ground, his eyes closed. Tasso walked away from him, her hands in her pockets. She kicked a rock out of her way and stood staring up at the sky. The night blackness was already beginning to fade into gray. Morning was coming.

Tasso gripped her pistol and walked around the fire in a circle, back and forth. On the ground Major Hendricks lay, his eyes closed, unmoving. The grayness rose in the sky, higher and higher. The landscape became visible, fields of ash stretching out in all directions. Ash and ruins of buildings, a wall here and there, heaps of concrete, the naked trunk of a tree.

The air was cold and sharp. Somewhere a long way off a bird made a few bleak sounds.

Hendricks stirred. He opened his eyes. "Is it dawn? Already?"

"Yes."

Hendricks sat up a little. "You wanted to know something. You were asking me."

"Do you remember now?"

"Yes."

"What is it?" She tensed. "What?" she repeated sharply.

"A well. A ruined well. It's in a storage locker under a well."

"A well." Tasso relaxed. "Then we'll find a well." She looked at her watch. "We have about an hour, Major. Do you think we can find it in an hour?"

* * * * *

"Give me a hand up," Hendricks said.

Tasso put her pistol away and helped him to his feet. "This is going to be difficult."

"Yes it is." Hendricks set his lips tightly. "I don't think we're going to go very far."

They began to walk. The early sun cast a little warmth down on them. The land was flat and barren, stretching out gray and lifeless as far as they could see. A few birds sailed silently, far above them, circling slowly.

"See anything?" Hendricks said. "Any claws?"

"No. Not yet."

They passed through some ruins, upright concrete and bricks. A cement foundation. Rats scuttled away. Tasso jumped back warily.

"This used to be a town," Hendricks said. "A village. Provincial village. This was all grape country, once. Where we are now."

They came onto a ruined street, weeds and cracks criss-crossing it. Over to the right a stone chimney stuck up.

"Be careful," he warned her.

A pit yawned, an open basement. Ragged ends of pipes jutted up, twisted and bent. They passed part of a house, a bathtub turned on its side. A broken chair. A few spoons and bits of china dishes. In the center of the street the ground had sunk away. The depression was filled with weeds and debris and bones.

"Over here," Hendricks murmured.

"This way?"

"To the right."

They passed the remains of a heavy duty tank. Hendricks' belt counter clicked ominously. The tank had been radiation blasted. A few feet from the tank a mummified body lay sprawled out, mouth open. Beyond the road was a flat field. Stones and weeds, and bits of broken glass.

"There," Hendricks said.

* * * * *

A stone well jutted up, sagging and broken. A few boards lay across it. Most of the well had sunk into rubble. Hendricks walked unsteadily toward it, Tasso beside him.

"Are you certain about this?" Tasso said. "This doesn't look like anything."

"I'm sure." Hendricks sat down at the edge of the well, his teeth locked. His breath came quickly. He wiped perspiration from his face. "This was arranged so the senior command officer could get away. If anything happened. If the bunker fell."

"That was you?"

"Yes."

"Where is the ship? Is it here?"

"We're standing on it." Hendricks ran his hands over the surface of the well stones. "The eye-lock responds to me, not to anybody else. It's my ship. Or it was supposed to be."

There was a sharp click. Presently they heard a low grating sound from below them.

"Step back," Hendricks said. He and Tasso moved away from the well.

A section of the ground slid back. A metal frame pushed slowly up through the ash, shoving bricks and weeds out of the way. The action ceased, as the ship nosed into view.

"There it is," Hendricks said.

The ship was small. It rested quietly, suspended in its mesh frame, like a blunt needle. A rain of ash sifted down into the dark cavity from which the ship had been raised. Hendricks made his way over to it. He mounted the mesh and unscrewed the hatch, pulling it back. Inside the ship the control banks and the pressure seat were visible.

* * * * *

Tasso came and stood beside him, gazing into the ship. "I'm not accustomed to rocket piloting," she said, after awhile.

Hendricks glanced at her. "I'll do the piloting."

"Will you? There's only one seat, Major. I can see it's built to carry only a single person."

Hendricks' breathing changed. He studied the interior of the ship intently. Tasso was right. There was only one seat. The ship was built to carry only one person. "I see," he said slowly. "And the one person is you."

She nodded.

"Of course."

"Why?"

"*You* can't go. You might not live through the trip. You're injured. You probably wouldn't get there."

"An interesting point. But you see, I know where the Moon Base is. And you don't. You might fly around for months and not find it. It's well hidden. Without knowing what to look for —"

"I'll have to take my chances. Maybe I won't find it. Not by myself. But I think you'll give me all the information I need. Your life depends on it."

"How?"

"If I find the Moon Base in time, perhaps I can get them to send a ship back to pick you up. *If* I find the Base in time. If not, then you haven't a chance. I imagine there are supplies on the ship. They will last me long enough —"

Hendricks moved quickly. But his injured arm betrayed him. Tasso ducked, sliding lithely aside. Her hand came up, lightning fast. Hendricks saw the gun butt coming. He tried to ward off the blow, but she was too fast. The metal butt struck against the side of his head, just above his ear. Numbing pain rushed through him. Pain and rolling clouds of blackness. He sank down, sliding to the ground.

* * * * *

Dimly, he was aware that Tasso was standing over him, kicking him with her toe.

"Major! Wake up."

He opened his eyes, groaning.

"Listen to me." She bent down, the gun pointed at his face. "I have to hurry. There isn't much time left. The ship is ready to go, but you must tell me the information I need before I leave."

Hendricks shook his head, trying to clear it.

"Hurry up! Where is the Moon Base? How do I find it? What do I look for?"

Hendricks said nothing.

"Answer me!"

"Sorry."

"Major, the ship is loaded with provisions. I can coast for weeks. I'll find the Base eventually. And in a half hour you'll be dead. Your only chance of survival —" She broke off.

Along the slope, by some crumbling ruins, something moved. Something in the ash. Tasso turned quickly, aiming. She fired. A puff of flame leaped. Something scuttled away, rolling across the ash. She fired again. The claw burst apart, wheels flying.

"See?" Tasso said. "A scout. It won't be long."

"You'll bring them back here to get me?"

"Yes. As soon as possible."

Hendricks looked up at her. He studied her intently. "You're telling the truth?" A strange expression had come over his face, an avid hunger. "You will come back for me? You'll get me to the Moon Base?"

"I'll get you to the Moon Base. But tell me where it is! There's only a little time left."

"All right." Hendricks picked up a piece of rock, pulling himself to a sitting position. "Watch."

Hendricks began to scratch in the ash. Tasso stood by him, watching the motion of the rock. Hendricks was sketching a crude lunar map.

* * * * *

"This is the Appenine range. Here is the Crater of Archimedes. The Moon Base is beyond the end of the Appenine, about two hundred miles. I don't know exactly where. No one on Terra knows. But when you're over the Appenine, signal with one red flare and a green flare, followed by two red flares in quick succession. The Base monitor will record your signal. The Base is under the surface, of course. They'll guide you down with magnetic grapples."

"And the controls? Can I operate them?"

"The controls are virtually automatic. All you have to do is give the right signal at the right time."

"I will."

"The seat absorbs most of the take-off shock. Air and temperature are automatically controlled. The ship will leave Terra and pass out into free space. It'll line itself up with the moon, falling into an orbit around it, about a hundred miles above the surface. The orbit will carry you over the Base. When you're in the region of the Appenine, release the signal rockets."

Tasso slid into the ship and lowered herself into the pressure seat. The arm locks folded automatically around her. She fingered the controls. "Too bad you're not going, Major. All this put here for you, and you can't make the trip."

"Leave me the pistol."

Tasso pulled the pistol from her belt. She held it in her hand, weighing it thoughtfully. "Don't go too far from this location. It'll be hard to find you, as it is."

"No. I'll stay here by the well."

Tasso gripped the take-off switch, running her fingers over the smooth metal. "A beautiful ship, Major. Well built. I admire your workmanship. You people have always done good work. You build fine things. Your work, your creations, are your greatest achievement."

"Give me the pistol," Hendricks said impatiently, holding out his hand. He struggled to his feet.

"Good-bye, Major." Tasso tossed the pistol past Hendricks. The pistol clattered against the ground, bouncing and rolling away. Hendricks hurried after it. He bent down, snatching it up.

The hatch of the ship clanged shut. The bolts fell into place. Hendricks made his way back. The inner door was being sealed. He raised the pistol unsteadily.

* * * * *

There was a shattering roar. The ship burst up from its metal cage, fusing the mesh behind it. Hendricks cringed, pulling back. The ship shot up into the rolling clouds of ash, disappearing into the sky.

Hendricks stood watching a long time, until even the streamer had dissipated. Nothing stirred. The morning air was chill and silent. He began to walk aimlessly back the way they had come. Better to keep moving around. It would be a long time before help came-if it came at all.

He searched his pockets until he found a package of cigarettes. He lit one grimly. They had all wanted cigarettes from him. But cigarettes were scarce.

A lizard slithered by him, through the ash. He halted, rigid. The lizard disappeared. Above, the sun rose higher in the sky. Some flies landed on a flat rock to one side of him. Hendricks kicked at them with his foot.

It was getting hot. Sweat trickled down his face, into his collar. His mouth was dry.

Presently he stopped walking and sat down on some debris. He unfastened his medicine kit and swallowed a few narcotic capsules. He looked around him. Where was he?

Something lay ahead. Stretched out on the ground. Silent and unmoving.

Hendricks drew his gun quickly. It looked like a man. Then he remembered. It was the remains of Klaus. The Second Variety. Where Tasso had blasted him. He could see wheels and relays and metal parts, strewn around on the ash. Glittering and sparkling in the sunlight.

Hendricks got to his feet and walked over. He nudged the inert form with his foot, turning it over a little. He could see the metal hull, the aluminum ribs and struts. More wiring fell out. Like viscera. Heaps of wiring, switches and relays. Endless motors and rods.

He bent down. The brain cage had been smashed by the fall. The artificial brain was visible. He gazed at it. A maze of circuits. Miniature tubes. Wires as fine as hair. He touched the brain cage. It swung aside. The type plate was visible. Hendricks studied the plate.

And blanched.

IV-IV.

For a long time he stared at the plate. Fourth Variety. Not the Second. They had been wrong. There were more types. Not just three. Many more, perhaps. At least four. And Klaus wasn't the Second Variety.

But if Klaus wasn't the Second Variety —

Suddenly he tensed. Something was coming, walking through the ash beyond the hill. What was it? He strained to see. Figures. Figures coming slowly along, making their way through the ash.

Coming toward him.

Hendricks crouched quickly, raising his gun. Sweat dripped down into his eyes. He fought down rising panic, as the figures neared.

The first was a David. The David saw him and increased its pace. The others hurried behind it. A second David. A third. Three Davids, all alike, coming toward him silently, without expression, their thin legs rising and falling. Clutching their teddy bears.

He aimed and fired. The first two Davids dissolved into particles. The third came on. And the figure behind it. Climbing silently toward him across the gray ash. A Wounded Soldier, towering over the David. And —

* * * * *

And behind the Wounded Soldier came two Tassos, walking side by side. Heavy belt, Russian army pants, shirt, long hair. The familiar figure, as he had seen her only a little while before. Sitting in the pressure seat of the ship. Two slim, silent figures, both identical.

They were very near. The David bent down suddenly, dropping its teddy bear. The bear raced across the ground. Automatically, Hendricks' fingers tightened around the trigger. The bear was gone, dissolved into mist. The two Tasso Types moved on, expressionless, walking side by side, through the gray ash.

When they were almost to him, Hendricks raised the pistol waist high and fired.

The two Tassos dissolved. But already a new group was starting up the rise, five or six Tassos, all identical, a line of them coming rapidly toward him.

And he had given her the ship and the signal code. Because of him she was on her way to the moon, to the Moon Base. He had made it possible.

He had been right about the bomb, after all. It had been designed with knowledge of the other types, the David Type and the Wounded Soldier Type. And the Klaus Type. Not designed by human beings. It had been designed by one of the underground factories, apart from all human contact.

The line of Tassos came up to him. Hendricks braced himself, watching them calmly. The familiar face, the belt, the heavy shirt, the bomb carefully in place.

The bomb —

As the Tassos reached for him, a last ironic thought drifted through Hendricks' mind. He felt a little better, thinking about it. The bomb. Made by the Second Variety to destroy the other varieties. Made for that end alone.

They were already beginning to design weapons to use against each other.

The Variable Man

I

Security Commissioner Reinhart rapidly climbed the front steps and entered the Council building. Council guards stepped quickly aside and he entered the familiar place of great whirring machines. His thin face rapt, eyes alight with emotion, Reinhart gazed intently up at the central SRB computer, studying its reading.

"Straight gain for the last quarter," observed Kaplan, the lab organizer. He grinned proudly, as if personally responsible. "Not bad, Commissioner."

"We're catching up to them," Reinhart retorted. "But too damn slowly. We must finally go over-and soon."

Kaplan was in a talkative mood. "We design new offensive weapons, they counter with improved defenses. And nothing is actually made! Continual improvement, but neither we nor Centaurus can stop designing long enough to stabilize for production."

"It will end," Reinhart stated coldly, "as soon as Terra turns out a weapon for which Centaurus can build no defense."

"Every weapon has a defense. Design and discord. Immediate obsolescence. Nothing lasts long enough to —"

"What we count on is the *lag*," Reinhart broke in, annoyed. His hard gray eyes bored into the lab organizer and Kaplan slunk back. "The time lag between our offensive design and their counter development. The lag varies." He waved impatiently toward the massed banks of SRB machines. "As you well know."

At this moment, 9:30 AM, May 7, 2136, the statistical ratio on the SRB machines stood at 21-17 on the Centauran side of the ledger. All facts considered, the odds favored a successful repulsion by Proxima Centaurus of a Terran military attack. The ratio was based on the total information known to the SRB machines, on a gestalt of the vast flow of data that poured in endlessly from all sectors of the Sol and Centaurus systems.

21-17 on the Centauran side. But a month ago it had been 24-18 in the enemy's favor. Things were improving, slowly but steadily. Centaurus, older and less virile than Terra, was unable to match Terra's rate of technocratic advance. Terra was pulling ahead.

"If we went to war now," Reinhart said thoughtfully, "we would lose. We're not far enough along to risk an overt attack." A harsh, ruthless glow twisted across his handsome features, distorting them into a stern mask. "But the odds are moving in our favor. Our offensive designs are gradually gaining on their defenses."

"Let's hope the war comes soon," Kaplan agreed. "We're all on edge. This damn waiting...."

The war would come soon. Reinhart knew it intuitively. The air was full of tension, the *elan*. He left the SRB rooms and hurried down the corridor to his own elaborately guarded office in the Security wing. It wouldn't be long. He could practically feel the hot breath of destiny on his neck-for him a pleasant feeling. His thin lips set in a humorless smile, showing an even line of white teeth against his tanned skin. It made him feel good, all right. He'd been working at it a long time.

First contact, a hundred years earlier, had ignited instant conflict between Proxima Centauran outposts and exploring Terran raiders. Flash fights, sudden eruptions of fire and energy beams.

And then the long, dreary years of inaction between enemies where contact required years of travel, even at nearly the speed of light. The two systems were evenly matched. Screen against screen. Warship against power station. The Centauran Empire surrounded Terra, an iron ring that couldn't be broken, rusty and corroded as it was. Radical new weapons had to be conceived, if Terra was to break out.

Through the windows of his office, Reinhart could see endless buildings and streets, Terrans hurrying back and forth. Bright specks that were commute ships, little eggs that carried businessmen and white-collar workers around. The huge transport tubes that shot masses of workmen to factories and labor camps from their housing units. All these people, waiting to break out. Waiting for the day.

Reinhart snapped on his vidscreen, the confidential channel. "Give me Military Designs," he ordered sharply.

* * * * *

He sat tense, his wiry body taut, as the vidscreen warmed into life. Abruptly he was facing the hulking image of Peter Sherikov, director of the vast network of labs under the Ural Mountains.

Sherikov's great bearded features hardened as he recognized Reinhart. His bushy black eyebrows pulled up in a sullen line. "What do you want? You know I'm busy. We have too much work to do, as it is. Without being bothered by-politicians."

"I'm dropping over your way," Reinhart answered lazily. He adjusted the cuff of his immaculate gray cloak. "I want a full description of your work and whatever progress you've made."

"You'll find a regular departmental report plate filed in the usual way, around your office someplace. If you'll refer to that you'll know exactly what we —"

"I'm not interested in that. I want to *see* what you're doing. And I expect you to be prepared to describe your work fully. I'll be there shortly. Half an hour."

* * * * *

Reinhart cut the circuit. Sherikov's heavy features dwindled and faded. Reinhart relaxed, letting his breath out. Too bad he had to work with Sherikov. He had never liked the man. The big Polish scientist was an individualist, refusing to integrate himself with society. Independent, atomistic in outlook. He held concepts of the individual as an end, diametrically contrary to the accepted organic state Weltansicht.

But Sherikov was the leading research scientist, in charge of the Military Designs Department. And on Designs the whole future of Terra depended. Victory over Centaurus-or more waiting, bottled up in the Sol System, surrounded by a rotting, hostile Empire, now sinking into ruin and decay, yet still strong.

Reinhart got quickly to his feet and left the office. He hurried down the hall and out of the Council building.

A few minutes later he was heading across the mid-morning sky in his highspeed cruiser, toward the Asiatic land-mass, the vast Ural mountain range. Toward the Military Designs labs.

Sherikov met him at the entrance. "Look here, Reinhart. Don't think you're going to order me around. I'm not going to —"

"Take it easy." Reinhart fell into step beside the bigger man. They passed through the check and into the auxiliary labs. "No immediate coercion will be exerted over you or your staff. You're free to continue your work as you see fit-for the present. Let's get this straight. My concern is to integrate your work with our total social needs. As long as your work is sufficiently productive —"

Reinhart stopped in his tracks.

"Pretty, isn't he?" Sherikov said ironically.

"What the hell is it?

"Icarus, we call him. Remember the Greek myth? The legend of Icarus. Icarus flew.... This Icarus is going to fly, one of these days." Sherikov shrugged. "You can examine him, if you want. I suppose this is what you came here to see."

Reinhart advanced slowly. "This is the weapon you've been working on?"

"How does he look?"

Rising up in the center of the chamber was a squat metal cylinder, a great ugly cone of dark gray. Technicians circled around it, wiring up the exposed relay banks. Reinhart caught a glimpse of endless tubes and filaments, a maze of wires and terminals and parts criss-crossing each other, layer on layer.

"What is it?" Reinhart perched on the edge of a workbench, leaning his big shoulders against the wall. "An idea of Jamison Hedge-the same man who developed our instantaneous interstellar vidcasts forty years ago. He was trying to find a method of faster than light travel when he was killed, destroyed along with most of his work. After that ftl research was abandoned. It looked as if there were no future in it."

"Wasn't it shown that nothing could travel faster than light?"

"The interstellar vidcasts do! No, Hedge developed a valid ftl drive. He managed to propel an object at fifty times the speed of light. But as the object gained speed, its length began to diminish and its mass increased. This was in line with familiar twentieth-century concepts of mass-energy transformation. We conjectured that as Hedge's object gained velocity it would continue to lose length and gain mass until its length became nil and its mass infinite. Nobody can imagine such an object."

"Go on."

"But what actually occurred is this. Hedge's object continued to lose length and gain mass until it reached the theoretical limit of velocity, the speed of light. At that point the object, still gaining speed, simply ceased to exist. Having no length, it ceased to occupy space. It disappeared. However, the object had not been *destroyed*. It continued on its way, gaining momentum each moment, moving in an arc across the galaxy, away from the Sol system. Hedge's object entered some other realm of being, beyond our powers of conception. The next phase of Hedge's experiment consisted in a search for some way to slow the ftl object down, back to a sub-ftl speed, hence back into our universe. This counterprinciple was eventually worked out."

"With what result?"

"The death of Hedge and destruction of most of his equipment. His experimental object, in re-entering the space-time universe, came into being in space already occupied by matter. Possessing an incredible mass, just below infinity level, Hedge's object exploded in a titanic cataclysm. It was obvious that no space travel was possible with such a drive. Virtually all space contains *some* matter. To re-enter space would bring automatic destruction. Hedge had found his ftl drive and his counterprinciple, but no one before this has been able to put them to any use."

Reinhart walked over toward the great metal cylinder. Sherikov jumped down and followed him. "I don't get it," Reinhart said. "You said the principle is no good for space travel."

"That's right."

"What's this for, then? If the ship explodes as soon as it returns to our universe —"

"This is not a ship." Sherikov grinned slyly. "Icarus is the first practical application of Hedge's principles. Icarus is a bomb."

"So this is our weapon," Reinhart said. "A bomb. An immense bomb."

"A bomb, moving at a velocity greater than light. A bomb which will not exist in our universe. The Centaurans won't be able to detect or stop it. How could they? As soon as it passes the speed of light it will cease to exist-beyond all detection."

"But —"

"Icarus will be launched outside the lab, on the surface. He will align himself with Proxima Centaurus, gaining speed rapidly. By the time he reaches his destination he will be traveling at ftl-100. Icarus will be brought back to this universe within Centaurus itself. The explosion should destroy the star and wash away most of its planets-including their central hub-planet, Armun. There is no way they can halt Icarus, once he has been launched. No defense is possible. Nothing can stop him. It is a real fact."

"When will he be ready?"

Sherikov's eyes flickered. "Soon."

"Exactly how soon?"

The big Pole hesitated. "As a matter of fact, there's only one thing holding us back."

Sherikov led Reinhart around to the other side of the lab. He pushed a lab guard out of the way.

"See this?" He tapped a round globe, open at one end, the size of a grapefruit. "This is holding us up."

"What is it?"

"The central control turret. This thing brings Icarus back to sub-ftl flight at the correct moment. It must be absolutely accurate. Icarus will be within the star only a matter of a microsecond. If the turret does not function exactly, Icarus will pass out the other side and shoot beyond the Centauran system."

"How near completed is this turret?"

Sherikov hedged uncertainly, spreading out his big hands. "Who can say? It must be wired with infinitely minute equipment-microscope grapples and wires invisible to the naked eye."

"Can you name any completion date?"

Sherikov reached into his coat and brought out a manila folder. "I've drawn up the data for the SRB machines, giving a date of completion. You can go ahead and feed it. I entered ten days as the maximum period. The machines can work from that."

Reinhart accepted the folder cautiously. "You're sure about the date? I'm not convinced I can trust you, Sherikov."

Sherikov's features darkened. "You'll have to take a chance, Commissioner. I don't trust you any more than you trust me. I know how much you'd like an excuse to get me out of here and one of your puppets in."

Reinhart studied the huge scientist thoughtfully. Sherikov was going to be a hard nut to crack. Designs was responsible to Security, not the Council. Sherikov was losing ground-but he was still a potential danger. Stubborn, individualistic, refusing to subordinate his welfare to the general good.

"All right." Reinhart put the folder slowly away in his coat. "I'll feed it. But you better be able to come through. There can't be any slip-ups. Too much hangs on the next few days."

"If the odds change in our favor are you going to give the mobilization order?"

"Yes," Reinhart stated. "I'll give the order the moment I see the odds change."

* * * * *

Standing in front of the machines, Reinhart waited nervously for the results. It was two o'clock in the afternoon. The day was warm, a pleasant May afternoon. Outside the building the daily life of the planet went on as usual.

As usual? Not exactly. The feeling was in the air, an expanding excitement growing every day. Terra had waited a long time. The attack on Proxima Centaurus had to come-and the sooner the better. The ancient Centauran Empire hemmed in Terra, bottled the human race up in its one system. A vast, suffocating net draped across the heavens, cutting Terra off from the bright diamonds beyond.... And it had to end.

The SRB machines whirred, the visible combination disappearing. For a time no ratio showed. Reinhart tensed, his body rigid. He waited.

The new ratio appeared.

Reinhart gasped. 7-6. Toward Terra!

Within five minutes the emergency mobilization alert had been flashed to all Government departments. The Council and President Duffe had been called to immediate session. Everything was happening fast.

But there was no doubt. 7-6. In Terra's favor. Reinhart hurried frantically to get his papers in order, in time for the Council session.

At histo-research the message plate was quickly pulled from the confidential slot and rushed across the central lab to the chief official.

"Look at this!" Fredman dropped the plate on his superior's desk. "Look at it!"

Harper picked up the plate, scanning it rapidly. "Sounds like the real thing. I didn't think we'd live to see it."

Fredman left the room, hurrying down the hall. He entered the time bubble office. "Where's the bubble?" he demanded, looking around.

One of the technicians looked slowly up. "Back about two hundred years. We're coming up with interesting data on the War of 1914. According to material the bubble has already brought up —"

"Cut it. We're through with routine work. Get the bubble back to the present. From now on all equipment has to be free for Military work."

"But-the bubble is regulated automatically."

"You can bring it back manually."

"It's risky." The technician hedged. "If the emergency requires it, I suppose we could take a chance and cut the automatic."

"The emergency requires *everything*," Fredman said feelingly.

"But the odds might change back," Margaret Duffe, President of the Council, said nervously. "Any minute they can revert."

"This is our chance!" Reinhart snapped, his temper rising. "What the hell's the matter with you? We've waited years for this."

The Council buzzed with excitement. Margaret Duffe hesitated uncertainly, her blue eyes clouded with worry. "I realize the opportunity is here. At least, statistically. But the new odds have just appeared. How do we know they'll last? They stand on the basis of a single weapon."

"You're wrong. You don't grasp the situation." Reinhart held himself in check with great effort. "Sherikov's weapon tipped the ratio in our favor. But the odds have been moving in our direction for months. It was only a question of time. The new balance was inevitable, sooner or later. It's not just Sherikov. He's only one factor in this. It's all nine planets of the Sol System-not a single man."

One of the Councilmen stood up. "The President must be aware the entire planet is eager to end this waiting. All our activities for the past eighty years have been directed toward —"

Reinhart moved close to the slender President of the Council. "If you don't approve the war, there probably will be mass rioting. Public reaction will be strong. Damn strong. And you know it."

Margaret Duffe shot him a cold glance. "You sent out the emergency order to force my hand. You were fully aware of what you were doing. You knew once the order was out there'd be no stopping things."

A murmur rushed through the Council, gaining volume. "We have to approve the war!... We're committed!... It's too late to turn back!"

Shouts, angry voices, insistent waves of sound lapped around Margaret Duffe. "I'm as much for the war as anybody," she said sharply. "I'm only urging moderation. An inter-system war is a big thing. We're going to war because a machine says we have a statistical chance of winning."

"There's no use starting the war unless we can win it," Reinhart said. "The SRB machines tell us whether we can win."

"They tell us our *chance* of winning. They don't guarantee anything."

"What more can we ask, beside a good chance of winning?"

Margaret Duffe clamped her jaw together tightly. "All right. I hear all the clamor. I won't stand in the way of Council approval. The vote can go ahead." Her cold, alert eyes appraised Reinhart. "Especially since the emergency order has already been sent out to all Government departments."

"Good." Reinhart stepped away with relief. "Then it's settled. We can finally go ahead with full mobilization."

Mobilization proceeded rapidly. The next forty-eight hours were alive with activity.

Reinhart attended a policy-level Military briefing in the Council rooms, conducted by Fleet Commander Carleton.

"You can see our strategy," Carleton said. He traced a diagram on the blackboard with a wave of his hand. "Sherikov states it'll take eight more days to complete the ftl bomb. During that time the fleet we have near the Centauran system will take up positions. As the bomb goes off the fleet will begin operations against the remaining Centauran ships. Many will no doubt survive the blast, but with Armun gone we should be able to handle them."

Reinhart took Commander Carleton's place. "I can report on the economic situation. Every factory on Terra is converted to arms production. With Armun out of the way we should be able to promote mass insurrection among the Centauran colonies. An inter-system Empire is hard to maintain, even with ships that approach light speed. Local war-lords should pop up all over the place. We want to have weapons available for them and ships starting *now* to reach them in time. Eventually we hope to provide a unifying principle around which the colonies can all collect. Our interest is more economic than political. They can have any kind of government they want, as long as they act as supply areas for us. As our eight system planets act now."

Carleton resumed his report. "Once the Centauran fleet has been scattered we can begin the crucial stage of the war. The landing of men and supplies from the ships we have waiting in all key areas throughout the Centauran system. In this stage —"

Reinhart moved away. It was hard to believe only two days had passed since the mobilization order had been sent out. The whole system was alive, functioning with feverish activity. Countless problems were being solved-but much remained.

He entered the lift and ascended to the SRB room, curious to see if there had been any change in the machines' reading. He found it the same. So far so good. Did the Centaurans know about Icarus? No doubt; but there wasn't anything they could do about it. At least, not in eight days.

Kaplan came over to Reinhart, sorting a new batch of data that had come in. The lab organizer searched through his data. "An amusing item came in. It might interest you." He handed a message plate to Reinhart.

It was from histo-research:

May 9, 2136

This is to report that in bringing the research time bubble up to the present the manual return was used for the first time. Therefore a clean break was not made, and a quantity of material from the past was brought forward. This material included an individual from the early twentieth century who escaped from the lab immediately. He has not yet been taken into protective custody. Histo-research regrets this incident, but attributes it to the emergency.

E. Fredman

Reinhart handed the plate back to Kaplan. "Interesting. A man from the past-hauled into the middle of the biggest war the universe has seen."

"Strange things happen. I wonder what the machines will think."

"Hard to say. Probably nothing." Reinhart left the room and hurried along the corridor to his own office.

As soon as he was inside he called Sherikov on the vidscreen, using the confidential line. The Pole's heavy features appeared. "Good day, Commissioner. How's the war effort?"

"Fine. How's the turret wiring proceeding?"

A faint frown flickered across Sherikov's face. "As a matter of fact, Commissioner —"

"What's the matter?" Reinhart said sharply.

Sherikov floundered. "You know how these things are. I've taken my crew off it and tried robot workers. They have greater dexterity, but they can't make decisions. This calls for more than mere dexterity. This calls for —" He searched for the word. "—for an *artist*."

Reinhart's face hardened. "Listen, Sherikov. You have eight days left to complete the bomb. The data given to the SRB machines contained that information. The 7-6 ratio is based on that estimate. If you don't come through —"

Sherikov twisted in embarrassment. "Don't get excited, Commissioner. We'll complete it."

"I hope so. Call me as soon as it's done." Reinhart snapped off the connection. If Sherikov let them down he'd have him taken out and shot. The whole war depended on the ftl bomb.

The vidscreen glowed again. Reinhart snapped it on. Kaplan's face formed on it. The lab organizer's face was pale and frozen. "Commissioner, you better come up to the SRB office. Something's happened."

"What is it?"

"I'll show you."

Alarmed, Reinhart hurried out of his office and down the corridor. He found Kaplan standing in front of the SRB machines. "What's the story?" Reinhart demanded. He glanced down at the reading. It was unchanged.

Kaplan held up a message plate nervously. "A moment ago I fed this into the machines. After I saw the results I quickly removed it. It's that item I showed you. From histo-research. About the man from the past."

"What happened when you fed it?"

Kaplan swallowed unhappily. "I'll show you. I'll do it again. Exactly as before." He fed the plate into a moving intake belt. "Watch the visible figures," Kaplan muttered.

Reinhart watched, tense and rigid. For a moment nothing happened. 7-6 continued to show. Then —

The figures disappeared. The machines faltered. New figures showed briefly. 4-24 for Centaurus. Reinhart gasped, suddenly sick with apprehension. But the figures vanished. New figures appeared. 16-38 for Centaurus. Then 48-86. 79-15 in Terra's favor. Then nothing. The machines whirred, but nothing happened.

Nothing at all. No figures. Only a blank.

"What's it mean?" Reinhart muttered, dazed.

"It's fantastic. We didn't think this could —"

"What's happened?"

"The machines aren't able to handle the item. No reading can come. It's data they can't integrate. They can't use it for prediction material, and it throws off all their other figures."

"Why?"

"It's —it's a variable." Kaplan was shaking, white-lipped and pale. "Something from which no inference can be made. The man from the past. The machines can't deal with him. The variable man!"

II

Thomas Cole was sharpening a knife with his whetstone when the tornado hit.

The knife belonged to the lady in the big green house. Every time Cole came by with his Fixit cart the lady had something to be sharpened. Once in awhile she gave him a cup of coffee, hot black coffee from an old bent pot. He liked that fine; he enjoyed good coffee.

The day was drizzly and overcast. Business had been bad. An automobile had scared his two horses. On bad days less people were outside and he had to get down from the cart and go to ring doorbells.

But the man in the yellow house had given him a dollar for fixing his electric refrigerator. Nobody else had been able to fix it, not even the factory man. The dollar would go a long way. A dollar was a lot.

He knew it was a tornado even before it hit him. Everything was silent. He was bent over his whetstone, the reins between his knees, absorbed in his work.

He had done a good job on the knife; he was almost finished. He spat on the blade and was holding it up to see-and then the tornado came.

All at once it was there, completely around him. Nothing but grayness. He and the cart and horses seemed to be in a calm spot in the center of the tornado. They were moving in a great silence, gray mist everywhere.

And while he was wondering what to do, and how to get the lady's knife back to her, all at once there was a bump and the tornado tipped him over, sprawled out on the ground. The horses screamed in fear, struggling to pick themselves up. Cole got quickly to his feet.

Where was he?

The grayness was gone. White walls stuck up on all sides. A deep light gleamed down, not daylight but something like it. The team was pulling the cart on its side, dragging it along, tools and equipment falling out. Cole righted the cart, leaping up onto the seat.

And for the first time saw the people.

Men, with astonished white faces, in some sort of uniforms. Shouts, noise and confusion. And a feeling of danger!

Cole headed the team toward the door. Hoofs thundered steel against steel as they pounded through the doorway, scattering the astonished men in all directions. He was out in a wide hall. A building, like a hospital.

The hall divided. More men were coming, spilling from all sides.

Shouting and milling in excitement, like white ants. Something cut past him, a beam of dark violet. It seared off a corner of the cart, leaving the wood smoking.

Cole felt fear. He kicked at the terrified horses. They reached a big door, crashing wildly against it. The door gave-and they were outside, bright sunlight blinking down on them. For a sickening second the cart tilted, almost turning over. Then the horses gained speed, racing across an open field, toward a distant line of green, Cole holding tightly to the reins.

Behind him the little white-faced men had come out and were standing in a group, gesturing frantically. He could hear their faint shrill shouts.

But he had got away. He was safe. He slowed the horses down and began to breathe again.

The woods were artificial. Some kind of park. But the park was wild and overgrown. A dense jungle of twisted plants. Everything growing in confusion.

The park was empty. No one was there. By the position of the sun he could tell it was either early morning or late afternoon. The smell of the flowers and grass, the dampness of the leaves, indicated morning. It had been late afternoon when the tornado had picked him up. And the sky had been overcast and cloudy.

Cole considered. Clearly, he had been carried a long way. The hospital, the men with white faces, the odd lighting, the accented words he had caught-everything indicated he was no longer in Nebraska-maybe not even in the United States.

Some of his tools had fallen out and gotten lost along the way. Cole collected everything that remained, sorting them, running his fingers over each tool with affection. Some of the little chisels and wood gouges were gone. The bit box had opened, and most of the smaller bits had been lost. He gathered up those that remained and replaced them tenderly in the box. He took a key-hole saw down, and with an oil rag wiped it carefully and replaced it.

Above the cart the sun rose slowly in the sky. Cole peered up, his horny hand over his eyes. A big man, stoop-shouldered, his chin gray and stubbled. His clothes wrinkled and dirty. But his eyes were clear, a pale blue, and his hands were finely made.

He could not stay in the park. They had seen him ride that way; they would be looking for him.

Far above something shot rapidly across the sky. A tiny black dot moving with incredible haste. A second dot followed. The two dots were gone almost before he saw them. They were utterly silent.

Cole frowned, perturbed. The dots made him uneasy. He would have to keep moving–and looking for food. His stomach was already beginning to rumble and groan.

Work. There was plenty he could do: gardening, sharpening, grinding, repair work on machines and clocks, fixing all kinds of household things. Even painting and odd jobs and carpentry and chores.

He could do anything. Anything people wanted done. For a meal and pocket money.

Thomas Cole urged the team into life, moving forward. He sat hunched over in the seat, watching intently, as the Fixit cart rolled slowly across the tangled grass, through the jungle of trees and flowers.

* * * * *

Reinhart hurried, racing his cruiser at top speed, followed by a second ship, a military escort. The ground sped by below him, a blur of gray and green.

The remains of New York lay spread out, a twisted, blunted ruin overgrown with weeds and grass. The great atomic wars of the twentieth century had turned virtually the whole seaboard area into an endless waste of slag.

Slag and weeds below him. And then the sudden tangle that had been Central Park.

Histo-research came into sight. Reinhart swooped down, bringing his cruiser to rest at the small supply field behind the main buildings.

Harper, the chief official of the department, came quickly over as soon as Reinhart's ship landed.

"Frankly, we don't understand why you consider this matter important," Harper said uneasily.

Reinhart shot him a cold glance. "I'll be the judge of what's important. Are you the one who gave the order to bring the bubble back manually?"

"Fredman gave the actual order. In line with your directive to have all facilities ready for —"

Reinhart headed toward the entrance of the research building. "Where is Fredman?"

"Inside."

"I want to see him. Let's go."

Fredman met them inside. He greeted Reinhart calmly, showing no emotion. "Sorry to cause you trouble, Commissioner. We were trying to get the station in order for the war. We wanted the bubble back as quickly as possible." He eyed Reinhart curiously. "No doubt the man and his cart will soon be picked up by your police."

"I want to know everything that happened, in exact detail."

Fredman shifted uncomfortably. "There's not much to tell. I gave the order to have the automatic setting canceled and the bubble brought back manually. At the moment the signal reached it, the bubble was passing through the spring of 1913. As it broke loose, it tore off a piece of ground on which this person and his cart were located. The person naturally was brought up to the present, inside the bubble."

"Didn't any of your instruments tell you the bubble was loaded?"

"We were too excited to take any readings. Half an hour after the manual control was thrown, the bubble materialized in the observation room. It was de-energized before anyone noticed what was inside. We tried to stop him but he drove the cart out into the hall, bowling us out of the way. The horses were in a panic."

"What kind of cart was it?"

"There was some kind of sign on it. Painted in black letters on both sides. No one saw what it was."

"Go ahead. What happened then?"

"Somebody fired a Slem-ray after him, but it missed. The horses carried him out of the building and onto the grounds. By the time we reached the exit the cart was half way to the park."

Reinhart reflected. "If he's still in the park we should have him shortly. But we must be careful." He was already starting back toward his ship, leaving Fredman behind. Harper fell in beside him.

Reinhart halted by his ship. He beckoned some Government guards over. "Put the executive staff of this department under arrest. I'll have them tried on a treason count, later on." He smiled ironically as Harper's face blanched sickly pale. "There's a war going on. You'll be lucky if you get off alive."

Reinhart entered his ship and left the surface, rising rapidly into the sky. A second ship followed after him, a military escort. Reinhart flew high above the sea of gray slag, the unrecovered waste area. He passed over a sudden square of green set in the ocean of gray. Reinhart gazed back at it until it was gone.

Central Park. He could see police ships racing through the sky, ships and transports loaded with troops, heading toward the square of green. On the ground some heavy guns and surface cars rumbled along, lines of black approaching the park from all sides.

They would have the man soon. But meanwhile, the SRB machines were blank. And on the SRB machines' readings the whole war depended.

About noon the cart reached the edge of the park. Cole rested for a moment, allowing the horses time to crop at the thick grass. The silent expanse of slag amazed him. What had happened? Nothing stirred. No buildings, no sign of life. Grass and weeds poked up occasionally through it, breaking the flat surface here and there, but even so, the sight gave him an uneasy chill.

Cole drove the cart slowly out onto the slag, studying the sky above him. There was nothing to hide him, now that he was out of the park. The slag was bare and uniform, like the ocean. If he were spotted —

A horde of tiny black dots raced across the sky, coming rapidly closer. Presently they veered to the right and disappeared. More planes, wingless metal planes. He watched them go, driving slowly on.

Half an hour later something appeared ahead. Cole slowed the cart down, peering to see. The slag came to an end. He had reached its limits. Ground appeared, dark soil and grass. Weeds grew everywhere. Ahead of him, beyond the end of the slag, was a line of buildings, houses of some sort. Or sheds.

Houses, probably. But not like any he had ever seen.

The houses were uniform, all exactly the same. Like little green shells, rows of them, several hundred. There was a little lawn in front of each. Lawn, a path, a front porch, bushes in a meager row around each house. But the houses were all alike and very small.

Little green shells in precise, even rows. He urged the cart cautiously forward, toward the houses.

No one seemed to be around. He entered a street between two rows of houses, the hoofs of his two horses sounding loudly in the silence. He was in some kind of town. But there were no dogs or children. Everything was neat and silent. Like a model. An exhibit. It made him uncomfortable.

A young man walking along the pavement gaped at him in wonder. An oddly-dressed youth, in a toga-like cloak that hung down to his knees. A single piece of fabric. And sandals.

Or what looked like sandals. Both the cloak and the sandals were of some strange half-luminous material. It glowed faintly in the sunlight. Metallic, rather than cloth.

A woman was watering flowers at the edge of a lawn. She straightened up as his team of horses came near. Her eyes widened in astonishment-and then fear. Her mouth fell open in a soundless O and her sprinkling can slipped from her fingers and rolled silently onto the lawn.

Cole blushed and turned his head quickly away. The woman was scarcely dressed! He flicked the reins and urged the horses to hurry.

Behind him, the woman still stood. He stole a brief, hasty look back-and then shouted hoarsely to his team, ears scarlet. He had seen right. She wore only a pair of translucent shorts. Nothing else. A mere fragment of the same half-luminous material that glowed and sparkled. The rest of her small body was utterly naked.

He slowed the team down. She had been pretty. Brown hair and eyes, deep red lips. Quite a good figure. Slender waist, downy legs, bare and supple, full breasts —. He clamped the thought furiously off. He had to get to work. Business.

Cole halted the Fixit cart and leaped down onto the pavement. He selected a house at random and approached it cautiously. The house was attractive. It had a certain simple beauty. But it looked frail-and exactly like the others.

He stepped up on the porch. There was no bell. He searched for it, running his hand uneasily over the surface of the door. All at once there was a click, a sharp snap on a level with his eyes. Cole glanced up, startled. A lens was vanishing as the door section slid over it. He had been photographed.

While he was wondering what it meant, the door swung suddenly open. A man filled up the entrance, a big man in a tan uniform, blocking the way ominously.

"What do you want?" the man demanded.

"I'm looking for work," Cole murmured. "Any kind of work. I can do anything, fix any kind of thing. I repair broken objects. Things that need mending." His voice trailed off uncertainly. "Anything at all."

"Apply to the Placement Department of the Federal Activities Control Board," the man said crisply. "You know all occupational therapy is handled through them." He eyed Cole curiously. "Why have you got on those ancient clothes?"

"Ancient? Why, I —"

The man gazed past him at the Fixit cart and the two dozing horses. "What's that? What are those two animals? *Horses?*" The man rubbed his jaw, studying Cole intently. "That's strange," he said.

"Strange?" Cole murmured uneasily. "Why?"

"There haven't been any horses for over a century. All the horses were wiped out during the Fifth Atomic War. That's why it's strange."

Cole tensed, suddenly alert. There was something in the man's eyes, a hardness, a piercing look. Cole moved back off the porch, onto the path. He had to be careful. Something was wrong.

"I'll be going," he murmured.

"There haven't been any horses for over a hundred years." The man came toward Cole. "Who are you? Why are you dressed up like that? Where did you get that vehicle and pair of horses?"

"I'll be going," Cole repeated, moving away.

The man whipped something from his belt, a thin metal tube. He stuck it toward Cole.

It was a rolled-up paper, a thin sheet of metal in the form of a tube. Words, some kind of script. He could not make any of them out. The man's picture, rows of numbers, figures —

"I'm Director Winslow," the man said. "Federal Stockpile Conservation. You better talk fast, or there'll be a Security car here in five minutes."

Cole moved-fast. He raced, head down, back along the path to the cart, toward the street.

Something hit him. A wall of force, throwing him down on his face. He sprawled in a heap, numb and dazed. His body ached, vibrating wildly, out of control. Waves of shock rolled over him, gradually diminishing.

He got shakily to his feet. His head spun. He was weak, shattered, trembling violently. The man was coming down the walk after him. Cole pulled himself onto the cart, gasping and retching. The horses jumped into life. Cole rolled over against the seat, sick with the motion of the swaying cart.

He caught hold of the reins and managed to drag himself up in a sitting position. The cart gained speed, turning a corner. Houses flew past. Cole urged the team weakly, drawing great shuddering breaths. Houses and streets, a blur of motion, as the cart flew faster and faster along.

Then he was leaving the town, leaving the neat little houses behind. He was on some sort of highway. Big buildings, factories, on both sides of the highway. Figures, men watching in astonishment.

After awhile the factories fell behind. Cole slowed the team down. What had the man meant? Fifth Atomic War. Horses destroyed. It didn't make sense. And they had things he knew nothing about. Force fields. Planes without wings-soundless.

Cole reached around in his pockets. He found the identification tube the man had handed him. In the excitement he had carried it off. He unrolled the tube slowly and began to study it. The writing was strange to him.

For a long time he studied the tube. Then, gradually, he became aware of something. Something in the top right-hand corner.

A date. October 6, 2128.

Cole's vision blurred. Everything spun and wavered around him. October, 2128. Could it be?

But he held the paper in his hand. Thin, metal paper. Like foil. And it had to be. It said so, right in the corner, printed on the paper itself.

Cole rolled the tube up slowly, numbed with shock. Two hundred years. It didn't seem possible. But things were beginning to make sense. He was in the future, two hundred years in the future.

While he was mulling this over, the swift black Security ship appeared overhead, diving rapidly toward the horse-drawn cart, as it moved slowly along the road.

Reinhart's vidscreen buzzed. He snapped it quickly on. "Yes?"

"Report from Security."

"Put it through." Reinhart waited tensely as the lines locked in place. The screen re-lit.

"This is Dixon. Western Regional Command." The officer cleared his throat, shuffling his message plates. "The man from the past has been reported, moving away from the New York area."

"Which side of your net?"

"Outside. He evaded the net around Central Park by entering one of the small towns at the rim of the slag area."

"*Evaded?*"

"We assumed he would avoid the towns. Naturally the net failed to encompass any of the towns."

Reinhart's jaw stiffened. "Go on."

"He entered the town of Petersville a few minutes before the net closed around the park. We burned the park level, but naturally found nothing. He had already gone. An hour later we received a report from a resident in Petersville, an official of the Stockpile Conservation Department. The man from the past had come to his door, looking for work. Winslow, the official, engaged him in conversation, trying to hold onto him, but he escaped, driving his cart off. Winslow called Security right away, but by then it was too late."

"Report to me as soon as anything more comes in. We must have him-and damn soon." Reinhart snapped the screen off. It died quickly.

He sat back in his chair, waiting.

Cole saw the shadow of the Security ship. He reacted at once. A second after the shadow passed over him, Cole was out of the cart, running and falling. He rolled, twisting and turning, pulling his body as far away from the cart as possible.

There was a blinding roar and flash of white light. A hot wind rolled over Cole, picking him up and tossing him like a leaf. He shut his eyes, letting his body relax. He bounced, falling and striking the ground. Gravel and stones tore into his face, his knees, the palms of his hands.

Cole cried out, shrieking in pain. His body was on fire. He was being consumed, incinerated by the blinding white orb of fire. The orb expanded, growing in size, swelling like some monstrous sun, twisted and bloated. The end had come. There was no hope. He gritted his teeth —

The greedy orb faded, dying down. It sputtered and winked out, blackening into ash. The air reeked, a bitter acrid smell. His clothes were burning and smoking. The ground under him was hot, baked dry, seared by the blast. But he was alive. At least, for awhile.

Cole opened his eyes slowly. The cart was gone. A great hole gaped where it had been, a shattered sore in the center of the highway. An ugly cloud hung above the hole, black and ominous. Far above, the wingless plane circled, watching for any signs of life.

Cole lay, breathing shallowly, slowly. Time passed. The sun moved across the sky with agonizing slowness. It was perhaps four in the afternoon. Cole calculated mentally. In three hours it would be dark. If he could stay alive until then —

Had the plane seen him leap from the cart?

He lay without moving. The late afternoon sun beat down on him. He felt sick, nauseated and feverish. His mouth was dry.

Some ants ran over his outstretched hand. Gradually, the immense black cloud was beginning to drift away, dispersing into a formless blob.

The cart was gone. The thought lashed against him, pounding at his brain, mixing with his labored pulse-beat. *Gone.* Destroyed. Nothing but ashes and debris remained. The realization dazed him.

Finally the plane finished its circling, winging its way toward the horizon. At last it vanished. The sky was clear.

Cole got unsteadily to his feet. He wiped his face shakily. His body ached and trembled. He spat a couple times, trying to clear his mouth. The plane would probably send in a report. People would be coming to look for him. Where could he go?

To his right a line of hills rose up, a distant green mass. Maybe he could reach them. He began to walk slowly. He had to be very careful. They were looking for him-and they had weapons. Incredible weapons.

He would be lucky to still be alive when the sun set. His team and Fixit cart were gone-and all his tools. Cole reached into his pockets, searching through them hopefully. He brought out some small screwdrivers, a little pair of cutting pliers, some wire, some solder, the whetstone, and finally the lady's knife.

Only a few small tools remained. He had lost everything else. But without the cart he was safer, harder to spot. They would have more trouble finding him, on foot.

Cole hurried along, crossing the level fields toward the distant range of hills.

The call came through to Reinhart almost at once. Dixon's features formed on the vidscreen. "I have a further report, Commissioner." Dixon scanned the plate. "Good news. The man from the past was sighted moving away from Petersville, along highway 13, at about ten miles an hour, on his horse-drawn cart. Our ship bombed him immediately."

"Did-did you get him?"

"The pilot reports no sign of life after the blast."

Reinhart's pulse almost stopped. He sank back in his chair. "Then he's dead!"

"Actually, we won't know for certain until we can examine the debris. A surface car is speeding toward the spot. We should have the complete report in a short time. We'll notify you as soon as the information comes in."

Reinhart reached out and cut the screen. It faded into darkness. Had they got the man from the past? Or had he escaped again? Weren't they ever going to get him? Couldn't he be captured? And meanwhile, the SRB machines were silent, showing nothing at all.

Reinhart sat brooding, waiting impatiently for the report of the surface car to come in.

* * * * *

It was evening.

"Come on!" Steven shouted, running frantically after his brother. "Come on back!"

"Catch me." Earl ran and ran, down the side of the hill, over behind a military storage depot, along a neotex fence, jumping finally down into Mrs. Norris' back yard.

Steven hurried after his brother, sobbing for breath, shouting and gasping as he ran. "Come back! You come back with that!"

"What's he got?" Sally Tate demanded, stepping out suddenly to block Steven's way.

Steven halted, his chest rising and falling. "He's got my intersystem vidsender." His small face twisted with rage and misery. "He better give it back!"

Earl came circling around from the right. In the warm gloom of evening he was almost invisible. "Here I am," he announced. "What you going to do?"

Steven glared at him hotly. His eyes made out the square box in Earl's hands. "You give that back! Or-or I'll tell Dad."

Earl laughed. "Make me."

"Dad'll make you."

"You better give it to him," Sally said.

"Catch me." Earl started off. Steven pushed Sally out of the way, lashing wildly at his brother. He collided with him, throwing him sprawling. The box fell from Earl's hands. It skidded to the pavement, crashing into the side of a guide-light post.

Earl and Steven picked themselves up slowly. They gazed down at the broken box.

"See?" Steven shrilled, tears filling his eyes. "See what you did?"

"You did it. You pushed into me."

"You did it!" Steven bent down and picked up the box. He carried it over to the guide-light, sitting down on the curb to examine it.

Earl came slowly over. "If you hadn't pushed me it wouldn't have got broken."

Night was descending rapidly. The line of hills rising above the town were already lost in darkness. A few lights had come on here and there. The evening was warm. A surface car slammed its doors, some place off in the distance. In the sky ships droned back and forth, weary commuters coming home from work in the big underground factory units.

Thomas Cole came slowly toward the three children grouped around the guide-light. He moved with difficulty, his body sore and bent with fatigue. Night had come, but he was not safe yet.

He was tired, exhausted and hungry. He had walked a long way. And he had to have something to eat-soon.

A few feet from the children Cole stopped. They were all intent and absorbed by the box on Steven's knees. Suddenly a hush fell over the children. Earl looked up slowly.

In the dim light the big stooped figure of Thomas Cole seemed extra menacing. His long arms hung down loosely at his sides. His face was lost in shadow. His body was shapeless, indistinct. A big unformed statue, standing silently a few feet away, unmoving in the half-darkness.

"Who are you?" Earl demanded, his voice low.

"What do you want?" Sally said. The children edged away nervously. "Get away."

Cole came toward them. He bent down a little. The beam from the guide-light crossed his features. Lean, prominent nose, beak-like, faded blue eyes —

Steven scrambled to his feet, clutching the vidsender box. "You get out of here!"

"Wait." Cole smiled crookedly at them. His voice was dry and raspy. "What do you have there?" He pointed with his long, slender fingers. "The box you're holding."

The children were silent. Finally Steven stirred. "It's my inter-system vidsender."

"Only it doesn't work," Sally said.

"Earl broke it." Steven glared at his brother bitterly. "Earl threw it down and broke it."

Cole smiled a little. He sank down wearily on the edge of the curb, sighing with relief. He had been walking too long. His body ached with fatigue. He was hungry, and tired. For a long time he sat, wiping perspiration from his neck and face, too exhausted to speak.

"Who are you?" Sally demanded, at last. "Why do you have on those funny clothes? Where did you come from?"

"Where?" Cole looked around at the children. "From a long way off. A long way." He shook his head slowly from side to side, trying to clear it.

"What's your therapy?" Earl said.

"My therapy?"

"What do you do? Where do you work?"

Cole took a deep breath and let it out again slowly. "I fix things. All kinds of things. Any kind."

Earl sneered. "Nobody fixes things. When they break you throw them away."

Cole didn't hear him. Sudden need had roused him, getting him suddenly to his feet. "You know any work I can find?" he demanded. "Things I could do? I can fix anything. Clocks, type-writers, refrigerators, pots and pans. Leaks in the roof. I can fix anything there is."

Steven held out his inter-system vidsender. "Fix this."

There was silence. Slowly, Cole's eyes focussed on the box. "That?"

"My sender. Earl broke it."

Cole took the box slowly. He turned it over, holding it up to the light. He frowned, concentrating on it. His long, slender fingers moved carefully over the surface, exploring it.

"He'll steal it!" Earl said suddenly.

"No." Cole shook his head vaguely. "I'm reliable." His sensitive fingers found the studs that held the box together. He depressed the studs, pushing them expertly in. The box opened, revealing its complex interior.

"He got it open," Sally whispered.

"Give it back!" Steven demanded, a little frightened. He held out his hand. "I want it back."

The three children watched Cole apprehensively. Cole fumbled in his pocket. Slowly he brought out his tiny screwdrivers and pliers. He laid them in a row beside him. He made no move to return the box.

"I want it back," Steven said feebly.

Cole looked up. His faded blue eyes took in the sight of the three children standing before him in the gloom. "I'll fix it for you. You said you wanted it fixed."

"I want it back." Steven stood on one foot, then the other, torn by doubt and indecision. "Can you really fix it? Can you make it work again?"

"Yes."

"All right. Fix it for me, then."

A sly smile flickered across Cole's tired face. "Now, wait a minute. If I fix it, will you bring me something to eat? I'm not fixing it for nothing."

"Something to eat?"

"Food. I need hot food. Maybe some coffee."

Steven nodded. "Yes. I'll get it for you."

Cole relaxed. "Fine. That's fine." He turned his attention back to the box resting between his knees. "Then I'll fix it for you. I'll fix it for you good."

His fingers flew, working and twisting, tracing down wires and relays, exploring and examining. Finding out about the inter-system vidsender. Discovering how it worked.

Steven slipped into the house through the emergency door. He made his way to the kitchen with great care, walking on tip-toe. He punched the kitchen controls at random, his heart beating excitedly. The stove began to whirr, purring into life. Meter readings came on, crossing toward the completion marks.

Presently the stove opened, sliding out a tray of steaming dishes. The mechanism clicked off, dying into silence. Steven grabbed up the contents of the tray, filling his arms. He carried everything down the hall, out the emergency door and into the yard. The yard was dark. Steven felt his way carefully along.

He managed to reach the guide-light without dropping anything at all.

Thomas Cole got slowly to his feet as Steven came into view. "Here," Steven said. He dumped the food onto the curb, gasping for breath. "Here's the food. Is it finished?"

Cole held out the inter-system vidsender. "It's finished. It was pretty badly smashed."

Earl and Sally gazed up, wide-eyed. "Does it work?" Sally asked.

"Of course not," Earl stated. "How could it work? He couldn't —"

"Turn it on!" Sally nudged Steven eagerly. "See if it works."

Steven was holding the box under the light, examining the switches. He clicked the main switch on. The indicator light gleamed. "It lights up," Steven said.

"Say something into it."

Steven spoke into the box. "Hello! Hello! This is operator 6-Z75 calling. Can you hear me? This is operator 6-Z75. Can you hear me?"

In the darkness, away from the beam of the guide-light, Thomas Cole sat crouched over the food. He ate gratefully, silently. It was good food, well cooked and seasoned. He drank a container of orange juice and then a sweet drink he didn't recognize. Most of the food was strange to him, but he didn't care. He had walked a long way and he was plenty hungry. And he still had a long way to go, before morning. He had to be deep in the hills before the sun came up. Instinct told him that he would be safe among the trees and tangled growth-at least, as safe as he could hope for.

He ate rapidly, intent on the food. He did not look up until he was finished. Then he got slowly to his feet, wiping his mouth with the back of his hand.

The three children were standing around in a circle, operating the inter-system vidsender. He watched them for a few minutes. None of them looked up from the small box. They were intent, absorbed in what they were doing.

"Well?" Cole said, at last. "Does it work all right?"

After a moment Steven looked up at him. There was a strange expression on his face. He nodded slowly. "Yes. Yes, it works. It works fine."

Cole grunted. "All right." He turned and moved away from the light. "That's fine."

The children watched silently until the figure of Thomas Cole had completely disappeared. Slowly, they turned and looked at each other. Then down at the box in Steven's hands. They gazed at the box in growing awe. Awe mixed with dawning fear.

Steven turned and edged toward his house. "I've got to show it to my Dad," he murmured, dazed. "He's got to know. *Somebody's* got to know!"

III

Eric Reinhart examined the vidsender box carefully, turning it around and around.

"Then he did escape from the blast," Dixon admitted reluctantly. "He must have leaped from the cart just before the concussion."

Reinhart nodded. "He escaped. He got away from you-twice." He pushed the vidsender box away and leaned abruptly toward the man standing uneasily in front of his desk. "What's your name again?"

"Elliot. Richard Elliot."

"And your son's name?"

"Steven."

"It was last night this happened?"

"About eight o'clock."

"Go on."

"Steven came into the house. He acted queerly. He was carrying his inter-system vidsender." Elliot pointed at the box on Reinhart's desk. "That. He was nervous and excited. I asked what was wrong. For awhile he couldn't tell me. He was quite upset. Then he showed me the vidsender." Elliot took a deep, shaky breath. "I could see right away it was different. You see I'm an electrical engineer. I had opened it once before, to put in a new battery. I had a fairly good idea how it should look." Elliot hesitated. "Commissioner, it had been *changed*. A lot of the wiring was different. Moved around. Relays connected differently. Some parts were missing. New parts had been jury rigged out of old. Then I discovered the thing that made me call Security. The vidsender-it really *worked*."

"Worked?"

"You see, it never was anything more than a toy. With a range of a few city blocks. So the kids could call back and forth from their rooms. Like a sort of portable vidscreen. Commissioner, I tried out the vidsender, pushing the call button and speaking into the microphone. I —I got a ship of the line. A battleship, operating beyond Proxima Centaurus-over eight light years away. As far out as the actual vidsenders operate. Then I called Security. Right away."

For a time Reinhart was silent. Finally he tapped the box lying on the desk. "You got a ship of the line-with *this?*"

"That's right."

"How big are the regular vidsenders?"

Dixon supplied the information. "As big as a twenty-ton safe."

"That's what I thought." Reinhart waved his hand impatiently. "All right, Elliot. Thanks for turning the information over to us. That's all."

Security police led Elliot outside the office.

Reinhart and Dixon looked at each other. "This is bad," Reinhart said harshly. "He has some ability, some kind of mechanical ability. Genius, perhaps, to do a thing like this. Look at the period he came from, Dixon. The early part of the twentieth century. Before the wars began. That was a unique period. There was a certain vitality, a certain ability. It was a period of incredible growth and discovery. Edison. Pasteur. Burbank. The Wright brothers. Inventions and machines. People had an uncanny ability with machines. A kind of intuition about machines-which we don't have."

"You mean —"

"I mean a person like this coming into our own time is bad in itself, war or no war. He's too different. He's oriented along different lines. He has abilities we lack. This fixing skill of his. It throws us off, out of kilter. And with the war...."

"Now I'm beginning to understand why the SRB machines couldn't factor him. It's impossible for us to understand this kind of person. Winslow says he asked for work, any kind of work. The man said he could do anything, fix anything. Do you understand what that means?"

"No," Dixon said. "What does it mean?"

"Can any of us fix anything? No. None of us can do that. We're specialized. Each of us has his own line, his own work. I understand my work, you understand yours. The tendency in evolution is toward greater and greater specialization. Man's society is an ecology that forces adaptation to it. Continual complexity makes it impossible for any of us to know anything outside our own personal field —I can't follow the work of the man sitting at the next desk over from me. Too much knowledge has piled up in each field. And there's too many fields."

"This man is different. He can fix anything, do anything. He doesn't work with knowledge, with science-the classified accumulation of facts. He *knows* nothing. It's not in his head, a form of learning. He works by intuition-his power is in his hands, not his head. Jack-of-all-trades. His hands! Like a painter, an artist. In his hands-and he cuts across our lives like a knife-blade."

"And the other problem?"

"The other problem is that this man, this variable man, has escaped into the Albertine Mountain range. Now we'll have one hell of a time finding him. He's clever-in a strange kind of way. Like some sort of animal. He's going to be hard to catch."

Reinhart sent Dixon out. After a moment he gathered up the handful of reports on his desk and carried them up to the SRB room. The SRB room was closed up, sealed off by a ring of armed Security police. Standing angrily before the ring of police was Peter Sherikov, his beard waggling angrily, his immense hands on his hips.

"What's going on?" Sherikov demanded. "Why can't I go in and peep at the odds?"

"Sorry." Reinhart cleared the police aside. "Come inside with me. I'll explain." The doors opened for them and they entered. Behind them the doors shut and the ring of police formed outside. "What brings you away from your lab?" Reinhart asked.

Sherikov shrugged. "Several things. I wanted to see you. I called you on the vidphone and they said you weren't available. I thought maybe something had happened. What's up?"

"I'll tell you in a few minutes." Reinhart called Kaplan over. "Here are some new items. Feed them in right away. I want to see if the machines can total them."

"Certainly, Commissioner." Kaplan took the message plates and placed them on an intake belt. The machines hummed into life.

"We'll know soon," Reinhart said, half aloud.

Sherikov shot him a keen glance. "We'll know what? Let me in on it. What's taking place?"

"We're in trouble. For twenty-four hours the machines haven't given any reading at all. Nothing but a blank. A total blank."

Sherikov's features registered disbelief. "But that isn't possible. *Some* odds exist at all times."

"The odds exist, but the machines aren't able to calculate them."

"Why not?"

"Because a variable factor has been introduced. A factor which the machines can't handle. They can't make any predictions from it."

"Can't they reject it?" Sherikov said slyly. "Can't they just-just *ignore* it?"

"No. It exists, as real data. Therefore it affects the balance of the material, the sum total of all other available data. To reject it would be to give a false reading. The machines can't reject any data that's known to be true."

Sherikov pulled moodily at his black beard. "I would be interested in knowing what sort of factor the machines can't handle. I thought they could take in all data pertaining to contemporary reality."

"They can. This factor has nothing to do with contemporary reality. That's the trouble. Histo-research in bringing its time bubble back from the past got overzealous and cut the circuit too quickly. The bubble came back loaded-with a man from the twentieth century. A man from the past."

"I see. A man from two centuries ago." The big Pole frowned. "And with a radically different Weltanschauung. No connection with our present society. Not integrated along our lines at all. Therefore the SRB machines are perplexed."

Reinhart grinned. "Perplexed? I suppose so. In any case, they can't do anything with the data about this man. The variable man. No statistics at all have been thrown up-no predictions have been made. And it knocks everything else out of phase. We're dependent on the constant showing of these odds. The whole war effort is geared around them."

"The horse-shoe nail. Remember the old poem? 'For want of a nail the shoe was lost. For want of the shoe the horse was lost. For want of the horse the rider was lost. For want —'"

"Exactly. A single factor coming along like this, one single individual, can throw everything off. It doesn't seem possible that one person could knock an entire society out of balance-but apparently it is."

"What are you doing about this man?"

"The Security police are organized in a mass search for him."

"Results?"

"He escaped into the Albertine Mountain Range last night. It'll be hard to find him. We must expect him to be loose for another forty-eight hours. It'll take that long for us to arrange the annihilation of the range area. Perhaps a trifle longer. And meanwhile —"

"Ready, Commissioner," Kaplan interrupted. "The new totals."

The SRB machines had finished factoring the new data. Reinhart and Sherikov hurried to take their places before the view windows.

For a moment nothing happened. Then odds were put up, locking in place.

Sherikov gasped. 99-2. In favor of Terra. "That's wonderful! Now we —"

The odds vanished. New odds took their places. 97-4. In favor of Centaurus. Sherikov groaned in astonished dismay. "Wait," Reinhart said to him. "I don't think they'll last."

The odds vanished. A rapid series of odds shot across the screen, a violent stream of numbers, changing almost instantly. At last the machines became silent.

Nothing showed. No odds. No totals at all. The view windows were blank.

"You see?" Reinhart murmured. "The same damn thing!"

Sherikov pondered. "Reinhart, you're too Anglo-Saxon, too impulsive. Be more Slavic. This man will be captured and destroyed within two days. You said so yourself. Meanwhile, we're all working night and day on the war effort. The warfleet is waiting near Proxima, taking up positions for the attack on the Centaurans. All our war plants are going full blast. By the time the attack date comes we'll have a full-sized invasion army ready to take off for the long trip to the Centauran colonies. The whole Terran population has been mobilized. The eight supply planets are pouring in material. All this is going on day and night, even without odds showing. Long before the attack comes this man will certainly be dead, and the machines will be able to show odds again."

Reinhart considered. "But it worries me, a man like that out in the open. Loose. A man who can't be predicted. It goes against science. We've been making statistical reports on society for two centuries. We have immense files of data. The machines are able to predict what each person and group will do at a given time, in a given situation. But this man is beyond all prediction. He's a variable. It's contrary to science."

"The indeterminate particle."

"What's that?"

"The particle that moves in such a way that we can't predict what position it will occupy at a given second. Random. The random particle."

"Exactly. It's —it's *unnatural.*"

Sherikov laughed sarcastically. "Don't worry about it, Commissioner. The man will be captured and things will return to their natural state. You'll be able to predict people again, like laboratory rats in a maze. By the way-why is this room guarded?"

"I don't want anyone to know the machines show no totals. It's dangerous to the war effort."

"Margaret Duffe, for example?"

Reinhart nodded reluctantly. "They're too timid, these parliamentarians. If they discover we have no SRB odds they'll want to shut down the war planning and go back to waiting."

"Too slow for you, Commissioner? Laws, debates, council meetings, discussions.... Saves a lot of time if one man has all the power. One man to tell people what to do, think for them, lead them around."

Reinhart eyed the big Pole critically. "That reminds me. How is Icarus coming? Have you continued to make progress on the control turret?"

A scowl crossed Sherikov's broad features. "The control turret?" He waved his big hand vaguely. "I would say it's coming along all right. We'll catch up in time."

Instantly Reinhart became alert. "Catch up? You mean you're still behind?"

"Somewhat. A little. But we'll catch up." Sherikov retreated toward the door. "Let's go down to the cafeteria and have a cup of coffee. You worry too much, Commissioner. Take things more in your stride."

"I suppose you're right." The two men walked out into the hall. "I'm on edge. This variable man. I can't get him out of my mind."

"Has he done anything yet?"

"Nothing important. Rewired a child's toy. A toy vidsender."

"Oh?" Sherikov showed interest. "What do you mean? What did he do?"

"I'll show you." Reinhart led Sherikov down the hall to his office. They entered and Reinhart locked the door. He handed Sherikov the toy and roughed in what Cole had done. A strange look crossed Sherikov's face. He found the studs on the box and depressed them. The box opened. The big Pole sat down at the desk and began to study the interior of the box. "You're sure it was the man from the past who rewired this?"

"Of course. On the spot. The boy damaged it playing. The variable man came along and the boy asked him to fix it. He fixed it, all right."

"Incredible." Sherikov's eyes were only an inch from the wiring. "Such tiny relays. How could he —"

"What?"

"Nothing." Sherikov got abruptly to his feet, closing the box carefully. "Can I take this along? To my lab? I'd like to analyze it more fully."

"Of course. But why?"

"No special reason. Let's go get our coffee." Sherikov headed toward the door. "You say you expect to capture this man in a day or so?"

"*Kill* him, not capture him. We've got to eliminate him as a piece of data. We're assembling the attack formations right now. No slip-ups, this time. We're in the process of setting up a cross-bombing pattern to level the entire Albertine range. He must be destroyed, within the next forty-eight hours."

Sherikov nodded absently. "Of course," he murmured. A preoccupied expression still remained on his broad features. "I understand perfectly."

* * * * *

Thomas Cole crouched over the fire he had built, warming his hands. It was almost morning. The sky was turning violet gray. The mountain air was crisp and chill. Cole shivered and pulled himself closer to the fire.

The heat felt good against his hands. *His hands.* He gazed down at them, glowing yellow-red in the firelight. The nails were black and chipped. Warts and endless calluses on each finger, and the palms. But they were good hands; the fingers were long and tapered. He respected them, although in some ways he didn't understand them.

Cole was deep in thought, meditating over his situation. He had been in the mountains two nights and a day. The first night had been the worst. Stumbling and falling, making his way uncertainly up the steep slopes, through the tangled brush and undergrowth —

But when the sun came up he was safe, deep in the mountains, between two great peaks. And by the time the sun had set again he had fixed himself up a shelter and a means of making a fire. Now he had a neat little box trap, operated by a plaited grass rope and pit, a notched stake. One rabbit already hung by his hind legs and the trap was waiting for another.

The sky turned from violet gray to a deep cold gray, a metallic color. The mountains were silent and empty. Far off some place a bird sang, its voice echoing across the vast slopes and ravines. Other birds began to sing. Off to his right something crashed through the brush, an animal pushing its way along.

Day was coming. His second day. Cole got to his feet and began to unfasten the rabbit. Time to eat. And then? After that he had no plans. He knew instinctively that he could keep himself alive indefinitely with the tools he had retained, and the genius of his hands. He could kill game and skin it. Eventually he could build himself a permanent shelter, even make clothes but of hides. In winter —

But he was not thinking that far ahead. Cole stood by the fire, staring up at the sky, his hands on his hips. He squinted, suddenly tense. Something was moving. Something in the sky, drifting slowly through the grayness. A black dot.

He stamped out the fire quickly. What was it? He strained, trying to see. A bird?

A second dot joined the first. Two dots. Then three. Four. Five. A fleet of them, moving rapidly across the early morning sky. Toward the mountains.

Toward him.

Cole hurried away from the fire. He snatched up the rabbit and carried it along with him, into the tangled shelter he had built. He was invisible, inside the shelter. No one could find him. But if they had seen the fire —

He crouched in the shelter, watching the dots grow larger. They were planes, all right. Black wingless planes, coming closer each moment. Now he could hear them, a faint dull buzz, increasing until the ground shook under him.

The first plane dived. It dropped like a stone, swelling into a great black shape. Cole gasped, sinking down. The plane roared in an arc, swooping low over the ground. Suddenly bundles tumbled out, white bundles falling and scattering like seeds.

The bundles drifted rapidly to the ground. They landed. They were men. Men in uniform.

Now the second plane was diving. It roared overhead, releasing its load. More bundles tumbled out, filling the sky. The third plane dived, then the fourth. The air was thick with drifting bundles of white, a blanket of descending weed spores, settling to earth.

On the ground the soldiers were forming into groups. Their shouts carried to Cole, crouched in his shelter. Fear leaped through him. They were landing on all sides of him. He was cut off. The last two planes had dropped men behind him.

He got to his feet, pushing out of the shelter. Some of the soldiers had found the fire, the ashes and coals. One dropped down, feeling the coals with his hand. He waved to the others. They were circling all around, shouting and gesturing. One of them began to set up some kind of gun. Others were unrolling coils of tubing, locking a collection of strange pipes and machinery in place.

Cole ran. He rolled down a slope, sliding and falling. At the bottom he leaped to his feet and plunged into the brush. Vines and leaves tore at his face, slashing and cutting him. He fell again, tangled in a mass of twisted shrubbery. He fought desperately, trying to free himself. If he could reach the knife in his pocket —

Voices. Footsteps. Men were behind him, running down the slope. Cole struggled frantically, gasping and twisting, trying to pull loose. He strained, breaking the vines, clawing at them with his hands.

A soldier dropped to his knee, leveling his gun. More soldiers arrived, bringing up their rifles and aiming.

Cole cried out. He closed his eyes, his body suddenly limp. He waited, his teeth locked together, sweat dripping down his neck, into his shirt, sagging against the mesh of vines and branches coiled around him.

Silence.

Cole opened his eyes slowly. The soldiers had regrouped. A huge man was striding down the slope toward them, barking orders as he came.

Two soldiers stepped into the brush. One of them grabbed Cole by the shoulder.

"Don't let go of him." The huge man came over, his black beard jutting out. "Hold on."

Cole gasped for breath. He was caught. There was nothing he could do. More soldiers were pouring down into the gulley, surrounding him on all sides. They studied him curiously, murmuring together. Cole shook his head wearily and said nothing.

The huge man with the beard stood directly in front of him, his hands on his hips, looking him up and down. "Don't try to get away," the man said. "You can't get away. Do you understand?"

Cole nodded.

"All right. Good." The man waved. Soldiers clamped metal bands around Cole's arms and wrists. The metal dug into his flesh, making him gasp with pain. More clamps locked around his legs. "Those stay there until we're out of here. A long way out."

"Where-where are you taking me?"

Peter Sherikov studied the variable man for a moment before he answered. "Where? I'm taking you to my labs. Under the Urals." He glanced suddenly up at the sky. "We better hurry. The Security police will be starting their demolition attack in a few hours. We want to be a long way from here when that begins."

* * * * *

Sherikov settled down in his comfortable reinforced chair with a sigh. "It's good to be back." He signalled to one of his guards. "All right. You can unfasten him."

The metal clamps were removed from Cole's arms and legs. He sagged, sinking down in a heap. Sherikov watched him silently.

Cole sat on the floor, rubbing his wrists and legs, saying nothing.

"What do you want?" Sherikov demanded. "Food? Are you hungry?"

"No."

"Medicine? Are you sick? Injured?"

"No."

Sherikov wrinkled his nose. "A bath wouldn't hurt you any. We'll arrange that later." He lit a cigar, blowing a cloud of gray smoke around him. At the door of the room two lab guards stood with guns ready. No one else was in the room beside Sherikov and Cole.

Thomas Cole sat huddled in a heap on the floor, his head sunk down against his chest. He did not stir. His bent body seemed more elongated and stooped than ever, his hair tousled and unkempt, his chin and jowls a rough stubbled gray. His clothes were dirty and torn from crawling through the brush. His skin was cut and scratched; open sores dotted his neck and cheeks and forehead. He said nothing. His chest rose and fell. His faded blue eyes were almost closed. He looked quite old, a withered, dried-up old man.

Sherikov waved one of the guards over. "Have a doctor brought up here. I want this man checked over. He may need intravenous injections. He may not have had anything to eat for awhile."

The guard departed.

"I don't want anything to happen to you," Sherikov said. "Before we go on I'll have you checked over. And deloused at the same time."

Cole said nothing.

Sherikov laughed. "Buck up! You have no reason to feel bad." He leaned toward Cole, jabbing an immense finger at him. "Another two hours and you'd have been dead, out there in the mountains. You know that?"

Cole nodded.

"You don't believe me. Look." Sherikov leaned over and snapped on the vidscreen mounted in the wall. "Watch, this. The operation should still be going on."

The screen lit up. A scene gained form.

"This is a confidential Security channel. I had it tapped several years ago-for my own protection. What we're seeing now is being piped in to Eric Reinhart." Sherikov grinned. "Reinhart arranged what you're seeing on the screen. Pay close attention. You were there, two hours ago."

Cole turned toward the screen. At first he could not make out what was happening. The screen showed a vast foaming cloud, a vortex of motion. From the speaker came a low rumble, a deep-throated roar. After a time the screen shifted, showing a slightly different view. Suddenly Cole stiffened.

He was seeing the destruction of a whole mountain range.

The picture was coming from a ship, flying above what had once been the Albertine Mountain Range. Now there was nothing but swirling clouds of gray and columns of particles and debris, a surging tide of restless material gradually sweeping off and dissipating in all directions.

The Albertine Mountains had been disintegrated. Nothing remained but these vast clouds of debris. Below, on the ground, a ragged plain stretched out, swept by fire and ruin. Gaping wounds yawned, immense holes without bottom, craters side by side as far as the eye could see. Craters and debris. Like the blasted, pitted surface of the moon. Two hours ago it had been rolling peaks and gulleys, brush and green bushes and trees.

Cole turned away.

"You see?" Sherikov snapped the screen off. "You were down there, not so long ago. All that noise and smoke-all for you. All for you, Mr. Variable Man from the past. Reinhart arranged that, to finish you off. I want you to understand that. It's very important that you realize that."

Cole said nothing.

Sherikov reached into a drawer of the table before him. He carefully brought out a small square box and held it out to Cole. "You wired this, didn't you?"

Cole took the box in his hands and held it. For a time his tired mind failed to focus. What did he have? He concentrated on it. The box was the children's toy. The inter-system vidsender, they had called it.

"Yes. I fixed this." He passed it back to Sherikov. "I repaired that. It was broken."

Sherikov gazed down at him intently, his large eyes bright. He nodded, his black beard and cigar rising and falling. "Good. That's all I wanted to know." He got suddenly to his feet, pushing his chair back. "I see the doctor's here. He'll fix you up. Everything you need. Later on I'll talk to you again."

Unprotesting, Cole got to his feet, allowing the doctor to take hold of his arm and help him up.

After Cole had been released by the medical department, Sherikov joined him in his private dining room, a floor above the actual laboratory.

The Pole gulped down a hasty meal, talking as he ate. Cole sat silently across from him, not eating or speaking. His old clothing had been taken away and new clothing given him. He was shaved and rubbed down. His sores and cuts were healed, his body and hair washed. He looked much healthier and younger, now. But he was still stooped and tired, his blue eyes worn and faded. He listened to Sherikov's account of the world of 2136 AD without comment.

"You can see," Sherikov said finally, waving a chicken leg, "that your appearance here has been very upsetting to our program. Now that you know more about us you can see why Commissioner Reinhart was so interested in destroying you."

Cole nodded.

"Reinhart, you realize, believes that the failure of the SRB machines is the chief danger to the war effort. But that is nothing!" Sherikov pushed his plate away noisily, draining his coffee mug. "After all, wars *can* be fought without statistical forecasts. The SRB machines only describe. They're nothing more than mechanical onlookers. In themselves, they don't affect the course of the war. *We* make the war. They only analyze."

Cole nodded.

"More coffee?" Sherikov asked. He pushed the plastic container toward Cole. "Have some."

Cole accepted another cupful. "Thank you."

"You can see that our real problem is another thing entirely. The machines only do figuring for us in a few minutes that eventually we could do for our own selves. They're our servants, tools. Not some sort of gods in a temple which we go and pray to. Not oracles who can see into the future for us. They don't see into the future. They only make statistical predictions-not prophecies. There's a big difference there, but Reinhart doesn't understand it. Reinhart and his kind have made such things as the SRB machines into gods. But I have no gods. At least, not any I can see."

Cole nodded, sipping his coffee.

"I'm telling you all these things because you must understand what we're up against. Terra is hemmed in on all sides by the ancient Centauran Empire. It's been out there for centuries, thousands of years. No one knows how long. It's old-crumbling and rotting. Corrupt and venal. But it holds most of the galaxy around us, and we can't break out of the Sol system. I told you about Icarus, and Hedge's work in ftl flight. We must win the war against Centaurus. We've waited and worked a long time for this, the moment when we can break out and get room among the stars for ourselves. Icarus is the deciding weapon. The data on Icarus tipped the SRB odds in our favor-for the first time in history. Success in the war against Centaurus will depend on Icarus, not on the SRB machines. You see?"

Cole nodded.

"However, there is a problem. The data on Icarus which I turned over to the machines specified that Icarus would be completed in ten days. More than half that time has already passed. Yet, we are no closer to wiring up the control turret than we were then. The turret baffles us." Sherikov grinned ironically. "Even *I* have tried my hand at the wiring, but with no success. It's intricate-and small. Too many technical bugs not worked out. We are building only one, you understand. If we had many experimental models worked out before —"

"But this is the experimental model," Cole said.

"And built from the designs of a man dead four years-who isn't here to correct us. We've made Icarus with our own hands, down here in the labs. And he's giving us plenty of trouble." All at once Sherikov got to his feet. "Let's go down to the lab and look at him."

They descended to the floor below, Sherikov leading the way. Cole stopped short at the lab door.

"Quite a sight," Sherikov agreed. "We keep him down here at the bottom for safety's sake. He's well protected. Come in. We have work to do."

In the center of the lab Icarus rose up, the gray squat cylinder that someday would flash through space at a speed of thousands of times that of light, toward the heart of Proxima Centaurus, over four light years away. Around the cylinder groups of men in uniform were laboring feverishly to finish the remaining work.

"Over here. The turret." Sherikov led Cole over to one side of the room. "It's guarded. Centauran spies are swarming everywhere on Terra. They see into everything. But so do we. That's how we get information for the SRB machines. Spies in both systems."

The translucent globe that was the control turret reposed in the center of a metal stand, an armed guard standing at each side. They lowered their guns as Sherikov approached.

"We don't want anything to happen to this," Sherikov said. "Everything depends on it." He put out his hand for the globe. Half way to it his hand stopped, striking against an invisible presence in the air.

Sherikov laughed. "The wall. Shut it off. It's still on."

One of the guards pressed a stud at his wrist. Around the globe the air shimmered and faded.

"Now." Sherikov's hand closed over the globe. He lifted it carefully from its mount and brought it out for Cole to see. "This is the control turret for our enormous friend here. This is what will slow him down when he's inside Centaurus. He slows down and re-enters this universe. Right in the heart of the star. Then-no more Centaurus." Sherikov beamed. "And no more Armun."

But Cole was not listening. He had taken the globe from Sherikov and was turning it over and over, running his hands over it, his face close to its surface. He peered down into its interior, his face rapt and intent.

"You can't see the wiring. Not without lenses." Sherikov signalled for a pair of micro-lenses to be brought. He fitted them on Cole's nose, hooking them behind his ears. "Now try it. You can control the magnification. It's set for 1000X right now. You can increase or decrease it."

Cole gasped, swaying back and forth. Sherikov caught hold of him. Cole gazed down into the globe, moving his head slightly, focussing the glasses.

"It takes practice. But you can do a lot with them. Permits you to do microscopic wiring. There are tools to go along, you understand." Sherikov paused, licking his lip. "We can't get it done correctly. Only a few men can wire circuits using the micro-lenses and the little tools. We've tried robots, but there are too many decisions to be made. Robots can't make decisions. They just react."

Cole said nothing. He continued to gaze into the interior of the globe, his lips tight, his body taut and rigid. It made Sherikov feel strangely uneasy.

"You look like one of those old fortune tellers," Sherikov said jokingly, but a cold shiver crawled up his spine. "Better hand it back to me." He held out his hand.

Slowly, Cole returned the globe. After a time he removed the micro-lenses, still deep in thought.

"Well?" Sherikov demanded. "You know what I want. I want you to wire this damn thing up." Sherikov came close to Cole, his big face hard. "You can do it, I think. I could tell by the way you held it-and the job you did on the children's toy, of course. You could wire it up right, and in five days. Nobody else can. And if it's not wired up Centaurus will keep on running the galaxy and Terra will have to sweat it out here in the Sol system. One tiny mediocre sun, one dust mote out of a whole galaxy."

Cole did not answer.

Sherikov became impatient. "Well? What do you say?"

"What happens if I don't wire this control for you? I mean, what happens to *me?*"

"Then I turn you over to Reinhart. Reinhart will kill you instantly. He thinks you're dead, killed when the Albertine Range was annihilated. If he had any idea I had saved you —"

"I see."

"I brought you down here for one thing. If you wire it up I'll have you sent back to your own time continuum. If you don't —"

Cole considered, his face dark and brooding.

"What do you have to lose? You'd already be dead, if we hadn't pulled you out of those hills."

"Can you really return me to my own time?"

"Of course!"

"Reinhart won't interfere?"

Sherikov laughed. "What can he do? How can he stop me? I have my own men. You saw them. They landed all around you. You'll be returned."

"Yes. I saw your men."

"Then you agree?"

"I agree," Thomas Cole said. "I'll wire it for you. I'll complete the control turret-within the next five days."

IV

Three days later Joseph Dixon slid a closed-circuit message plate across the desk to his boss.

"Here. You might be interested in this."

Reinhart picked the plate up slowly. "What is it? You came all the way here to show me this?"

"That's right."

"Why didn't you vidscreen it?"

Dixon smiled grimly. "You'll understand when you decode it. It's from Proxima Centaurus."

"Centaurus!"

"Our counter-intelligence service. They sent it direct to me. Here, I'll decode it for you. Save you the trouble."

Dixon came around behind Reinhart's desk. He leaned over the Commissioner's shoulder, taking hold of the plate and breaking the seal with his thumb nail.

"Hang on," Dixon said. "This is going to hit you hard. According to our agents on Armun, the Centauran High Council has called an emergency session to deal with the problem of Terra's impending attack. Centauran relay couriers have reported to the High Council that the Terran bomb Icarus is virtually complete. Work on the bomb has been rushed through final stages in the underground laboratories under the Ural Range, directed by the Terran physicist Peter Sherikov."

"So I understand from Sherikov himself. Are you surprised the Centaurans know about the bomb? They have spies swarming over Terra. That's no news."

"There's more." Dixon traced the message plate grimly, with an unsteady finger. "The Centauran relay couriers reported that Peter Sherikov brought an expert mechanic out of a previous time continuum to complete the wiring of the turret!"

Reinhart staggered, holding on tight to the desk. He closed his eyes, gasping.

"The variable man is still alive," Dixon murmured. "I don't know how. Or why. There's nothing left of the Albertines. And how the hell did the man get half way around the world?"

Reinhart opened his eyes slowly, his face twisting. "Sherikov! He must have removed him before the attack. I told Sherikov the attack was forthcoming. I gave him the exact hour. He had to get help—from the variable man. He couldn't meet his promise otherwise."

Reinhart leaped up and began to pace back and forth. "I've already informed the SRB machines that the variable man has been destroyed. The machines now show the original 7-6 ratio in our favor. But the ratio is based on false information."

"Then you'll have to withdraw the false data and restore the original situation."

"No." Reinhart shook his head. "I can't do that. The machines must be kept functioning. We can't allow them to jam again. It's too dangerous. If Duffe should become aware that —"

"What are you going to do, then?" Dixon picked up the message plate. "You can't leave the machines with false data. That's treason."

"The data can't be withdrawn! Not unless equivalent data exists to take its place." Reinhart paced angrily back and forth. "Damn it, I was *certain* the man was dead. This is an incredible situation. He must be eliminated-at any cost."

Suddenly Reinhart stopped pacing. "The turret. It's probably finished by this time. Correct?"

Dixon nodded slowly in agreement. "With the variable man helping, Sherikov has undoubtedly completed work well ahead of schedule."

Reinhart's gray eyes flickered. "Then he's no longer of any use-even to Sherikov. We could take a chance.... Even if there were active opposition...."

"What's this?" Dixon demanded. "What are you thinking about?"

"How many units are ready for immediate action? How large a force can we raise without notice?"

"Because of the war we're mobilized on a twenty-four hour basis. There are seventy air units and about two hundred surface units. The balance of the Security forces have been transferred to the line, under military control."

"Men?"

"We have about five thousand men ready to go, still on Terra. Most of them in the process of being transferred to military transports. I can hold it up at any time."

"Missiles?"

"Fortunately, the launching tubes have not yet been disassembled. They're still here on Terra. In another few days they'll be moving out for the Colonial fracas."

"Then they're available for immediate use?"

"Yes."

"Good." Reinhart locked his hands, knotting his fingers harshly together in sudden decision. "That will do exactly. Unless I am completely wrong, Sherikov has only a half-dozen air units and no surface cars. And only about two hundred men. Some defense shields, of course —"

"What are you planning?"

Reinhart's face was gray and hard, like stone. "Send out orders for all available Security units to be unified under your immediate command. Have them ready to move by four o'clock this afternoon. We're going to pay a visit," Reinhart stated grimly. "A surprise visit. On Peter Sherikov."

* * * * *

"Stop here," Reinhart ordered.

The surface car slowed to a halt. Reinhart peered cautiously out, studying the horizon ahead.

On all sides a desert of scrub grass and sand stretched out. Nothing moved or stirred. To the right the grass and sand rose up to form immense peaks, a range of mountains without end, disappearing finally into the distance. The Urals.

"Over there," Reinhart said to Dixon, pointing. "See?"

"No."

"Look hard. It's difficult to spot unless you know what to look for. Vertical pipes. Some kind of vent. Or periscopes."

Dixon saw them finally. "I would have driven past without noticing."

"It's well concealed. The main labs are a mile down. Under the range itself. It's virtually impregnable. Sherikov had it built years ago, to withstand any attack. From the air, by surface cars, bombs, missiles —"

"He must feel safe down there."

"No doubt." Reinhart gazed up at the sky. A few faint black dots could be seen, moving lazily about, in broad circles. "Those aren't ours, are they? I gave orders —"

"No. They're not ours. All our units are out of sight. Those belong to Sherikov. His patrol."

Reinhart relaxed. "Good." He reached over and flicked on the vidscreen over the board of the car. "This screen is shielded? It can't be traced?"

"There's no way they can spot it back to us. It's non-directional."

The screen glowed into life. Reinhart punched the combination keys and sat back to wait.

After a time an image formed on the screen. A heavy face, bushy black beard and large eyes.

Peter Sherikov gazed at Reinhart with surprised curiosity. "Commissioner! Where are you calling from? What —"

"How's the work progressing?" Reinhart broke in coldly. "Is Icarus almost complete?"

Sherikov beamed with expansive pride. "He's done, Commissioner. Two days ahead of time. Icarus is ready to be launched into space. I tried to call your office, but they told me —"

"I'm not at my office." Reinhart leaned toward the screen. "Open your entrance tunnel at the surface. You're about to receive visitors."

Sherikov blinked. "Visitors?"

"I'm coming down to see you. About Icarus. Have the tunnel opened for me at once."

"Exactly where are you, Commissioner?"

"On the surface."

Sherikov's eyes flickered. "Oh? But —"

"Open up!" Reinhart snapped. He glanced at his wristwatch. "I'll be at the entrance in five minutes. I expect to find it ready for me."

"Of course." Sherikov nodded in bewilderment. "I'm always glad to see you, Commissioner. But I —"

"Five minutes, then." Reinhart cut the circuit. The screen died. He turned quickly to Dixon. "You stay up here, as we arranged. I'll go down with one company of police. You understand the necessity of exact timing on this?"

"We won't slip up. Everything's ready. All units are in their places."

"Good." Reinhart pushed the door open for him. "You join your directional staff. I'll proceed toward the tunnel entrance."

"Good luck." Dixon leaped out of the car, onto the sandy ground. A gust of dry air swirled into the car around Reinhart. "I'll see you later."

Reinhart slammed the door. He turned to the group of police crouched in the rear of the car, their guns held tightly. "Here we go," Reinhart murmured. "Hold on."

The car raced across the sandy ground, toward the tunnel entrance to Sherikov's underground fortress.

Sherikov met Reinhart at the bottom end of the tunnel, where the tunnel opened up onto the main floor of the lab.

The big Pole approached, his hand out, beaming with pride and satisfaction. "It's a pleasure to see you, Commissioner. This is an historic moment."

Reinhart got out of the car, with his group of armed Security police. "Calls for a celebration, doesn't it?" he said.

"That's a good idea! We're two days ahead, Commissioner. The SRB machines will be interested. The odds should change abruptly at the news."

"Let's go down to the lab. I want to see the control turret myself."

A shadow crossed Sherikov's face. "I'd rather not bother the workmen right now, Commissioner. They've been under a great load, trying to complete the turret in time. I believe they're putting a few last finishes on it at this moment."

"We can view them by vidscreen. I'm curious to see them at work. It must be difficult to wire such minute relays."

Sherikov shook his head. "Sorry, Commissioner. No vidscreen on them. I won't allow it. This is too important. Our whole future depends on it."

Reinhart snapped a signal to his company of police. "Put this man under arrest."

Sherikov blanched. His mouth fell open. The police moved quickly around him, their gun tubes up, jabbing into him. He was searched rapidly, efficiently. His gun belt and concealed energy screen were yanked off.

"What's going on?" Sherikov demanded, some color returning to his face. "What are you doing?"

"You're under arrest for the duration of the war. You're relieved of all authority. From now on one of my men will operate Designs. When the war is over you'll be tried before the Council and President Duffe."

Sherikov shook his head, dazed. "I don't understand. What's this all about? Explain it to me, Commissioner. What's happened?"

Reinhart signalled to his police. "Get ready. We're going into the lab. We may have to shoot our way in. The variable man should be in the area of the bomb, working on the control turret."

Instantly Sherikov's face hardened. His black eyes glittered, alert and hostile.

Reinhart laughed harshly. "We received a counter-intelligence report from Centaurus. I'm surprised at you, Sherikov. You know the Centaurans are everywhere with their relay couriers. You should have known —"

Sherikov moved. Fast. All at once he broke away from the police, throwing his massive body against them. They fell, scattering. Sherikov ran-directly at the wall. The police fired wildly. Reinhart fumbled frantically for his gun tube, pulling it up.

Sherikov reached the wall, running head down, energy beams flashing around him. He struck against the wall-and vanished.

"Down!" Reinhart shouted. He dropped to his hands and knees. All around him his police dived for the floor. Reinhart cursed wildly, dragging himself quickly toward the door. They had to get out, and right away. Sherikov had escaped. A false wall, an energy barrier set to respond to his pressure. He had dashed through it to safety. He —

From all sides an inferno burst, a flaming roar of death surging over them, around them, on every side. The room was alive with blazing masses of destruction, bouncing from wall to wall. They were caught between four banks of power, all of them open to full discharge. A trap —a death trap.

* * * * *

Reinhart reached the hall gasping for breath. He leaped to his feet. A few Security police followed him. Behind them, in the flaming room, the rest of the company screamed and struggled, blasted out of existence by the leaping bursts of power.

Reinhart assembled his remaining men. Already, Sherikov's guards were forming. At one end of the corridor a snub-barreled robot gun was maneuvering into position. A siren wailed. Guards were running on all sides, hurrying to battle stations.

The robot gun opened fire. Part of the corridor exploded, bursting into fragments. Clouds of choking debris and particles swept around them. Reinhart and his police retreated, moving back along the corridor.

They reached a junction. A second robot gun was rumbling toward them, hurrying to get within range. Reinhart fired carefully, aiming at its delicate control. Abruptly the gun spun convulsively. It lashed against the wall, smashing itself into the unyielding metal. Then it collapsed in a heap, gears still whining and spinning.

"Come on." Reinhart moved away, crouching and running. He glanced at his watch. *Almost time*. A few more minutes. A group of lab guards appeared ahead of them. Reinhart fired. Behind him his police fired past him, violet shafts of energy catching the group of guards as they entered the corridor. The guards spilled apart, falling and twisting. Part of them settled into dust, drifting down the corridor. Reinhart made his way toward the lab, crouching and leaping, pushing past heaps of debris and remains, followed by his men. "Come on! Don't stop!"

* * * * *

Suddenly from around them the booming, enlarged voice of Sherikov thundered, magnified by rows of wall speakers along the corridor. Reinhart halted, glancing around.

"Reinhart! You haven't got a chance. You'll never get back to the surface. Throw down your guns and give up. You're surrounded on all sides. You're a mile, under the surface."

Reinhart threw himself into motion, pushing into billowing clouds of particles drifting along the corridor. "Are you sure, Sherikov?" he grunted.

Sherikov laughed, his harsh, metallic peals rolling in waves against Reinhart's eardrums. "I don't want to have to kill you, Commissioner. You're vital to the war: I'm sorry you found out about the variable man. I admit we overlooked the Centauran espionage as a factor in this. But now that you know about him —"

Suddenly Sherikov's voice broke off. A deep rumble had shaken the floor, a lapping vibration that shuddered through the corridor.

Reinhart sagged with relief. He peered through the clouds of debris, making out the figures on his watch. Right on time. Not a second late.

The first of the hydrogen missiles, launched from the Council buildings on the other side of the world, were beginning to arrive. The attack had begun.

At exactly six o'clock Joseph Dixon, standing on the surface four miles from the entrance tunnel, gave the sign to the waiting units.

The first job was to break down Sherikov's defense screens. The missiles had to penetrate without interference. At Dixon's signal a fleet of thirty Security ships dived from a height of ten miles, swooping above the mountains, directly over the underground laboratories. Within five minutes the defense screens had been smashed, and all the tower projectors leveled flat. Now the mountains were virtually unprotected.

"So far so good," Dixon murmured, as he watched from his secure position. The fleet of Security ships roared back, their work done. Across the face of the desert the police surface cars were crawling rapidly toward the entrance tunnel, snaking from side to side.

Meanwhile, Sherikov's counter-attack had begun to go into operation.

Guns mounted among the hills opened fire. Vast columns of flame burst up in the path of the advancing cars. The cars hesitated and retreated, as the plain was churned up by a howling vortex, a thundering chaos of explosions. Here and there a car vanished in a cloud of particles. A group of cars moving away suddenly scattered, caught up by a giant wind that lashed across them and swept them up into the air.

Dixon gave orders to have the cannon silenced. The police air arm again swept overhead, a sullen roar of jets that shook the ground below. The police ships divided expertly and hurtled down on the cannon protecting the hills.

The cannon forgot the surface cars and lifted their snouts to meet the attack. Again and again the airships came, rocking the mountains with titanic blasts.

The guns became silent. Their echoing boom diminished, died away reluctantly, as bombs took critical toll of them.

Dixon watched with satisfaction as the bombing came to an end. The airships rose in a thick swarm, black gnats shooting up in triumph from a dead carcass. They hurried back as emergency anti-aircraft robot guns swung into position and saturated the sky with blazing puffs of energy.

Dixon checked his wristwatch. The missiles were already on the way from North America. Only a few minutes remained.

The surface cars, freed by the successful bombing, began to regroup for a new frontal attack. Again they crawled forward, across the burning plain, bearing down cautiously on the battered wall of mountains, heading toward the twisted wrecks that had been the ring of defense guns. Toward the entrance tunnel.

An occasional cannon fired feebly at them. The cars came grimly on. Now, in the hollows of the hills, Sherikov's troops were hurrying to the surface to meet the attack. The first car reached the shadow of the mountains....

A deafening hail of fire burst loose. Small robot guns appeared everywhere, needle barrels emerging from behind hidden screens, trees and shrubs, rocks, stones. The police cars were caught in a withering cross-fire, trapped at the base of the hills.

Down the slopes Sherikov's guards raced, toward the stalled cars. Clouds of heat rose up and boiled across the plain as the cars fired up at the running men. A robot gun dropped like a slug onto the plain and screamed toward the cars, firing as it came.

Dixon twisted nervously. Only a few minutes. Any time, now. He shaded his eyes and peered up at the sky. No sign of them yet. He wondered about Reinhart. No signal had come up from below. Clearly, Reinhart had run into trouble. No doubt there was desperate fighting going on in the maze of underground tunnels, the intricate web of passages that honeycombed the earth below the mountains.

In the air, Sherikov's few defense ships were taking on the police raiders. Outnumbered, the defense ships darted rapidly, wildly, putting up a futile fight.

Sherikov's guards streamed out onto the plain. Crouching and running, they advanced toward the stalled cars. The police airships screeched down at them, guns thundering.

Dixon held his breath. When the missiles arrived —

The first missile struck. A section of the mountain vanished, turned to smoke and foaming gasses. The wave of heat slapped Dixon across the face, spinning him around. Quickly he re-entered his ship and took off, shooting rapidly away from the scene. He glanced back. A second and third missile had arrived. Great gaping pits yawned among the mountains, vast sections missing like broken teeth. Now the missiles could penetrate to the underground laboratories below.

On the ground, the surface cars halted beyond the danger area, waiting for the missile attack to finish. When the eighth missile had struck, the cars again moved forward. No more missiles fell.

Dixon swung his ship around, heading back toward the scene. The laboratory was exposed. The top sections of it had been ripped open. The laboratory lay like a tin can, torn apart by mighty explosions, its first floors visible from the air. Men and cars were pouring down into it, fighting with the guards swarming to the surface.

* * * * *

Dixon watched intently. Sherikov's men were bringing up heavy guns, big robot artillery. But the police ships were diving again. Sherikov's defensive patrols had been cleaned from the sky. The police ships whined down, arcing over the exposed laboratory. Small bombs fell, whistling down, pin-pointing the artillery rising to the surface on the remaining lift stages.

Abruptly Dixon's vidscreen clicked. Dixon turned toward it.

Reinhart's features formed. "Call off the attack." His uniform was torn. A deep bloody gash crossed his cheek. He grinned sourly at Dixon, pushing his tangled hair back out of his face. "Quite a fight."

"Sherikov —"

"He's called off his guards. We've agreed to a truce. It's all over. No more needed." Reinhart gasped for breath, wiping grime and sweat from his neck. "Land your ship and come down here at once."

"The variable man?"

"That comes next," Reinhart said grimly. He adjusted his gun tube. "I want you down here, for that part. I want you to be in on the kill."

Reinhart turned away from the vidscreen. In the corner of the room Sherikov stood silently, saying nothing. "Well?" Reinhart barked. "Where is he? Where will I find him?"

Sherikov licked his lips nervously, glancing up at Reinhart. "Commissioner, are you sure —"

"The attack has been called off. Your labs are safe. So is your life. Now it's your turn to come through." Reinhart gripped his gun, moving toward Sherikov. "*Where is he?*"

For a moment Sherikov hesitated. Then slowly his huge body sagged, defeated. He shook his head wearily. "All right. I'll show you where he is." His voice was hardly audible, a dry whisper. "Down this way. Come on."

Reinhart followed Sherikov out of the room, into the corridor. Police and guards were working rapidly, clearing the debris and ruins away, putting out the hydrogen fires that burned everywhere. "No tricks, Sherikov."

"No tricks." Sherikov nodded resignedly. "Thomas Cole is by himself. In a wing lab off the main rooms."

"Cole?"

"The variable man. That's his name." The Pole turned his massive head a little. "He has a name."

Reinhart waved his gun. "Hurry up. I don't want anything to go wrong. This is the part I came for."

"You must remember something, Commissioner."

"What is it?"

Sherikov stopped walking. "Commissioner, nothing must happen to the globe. The control turret. Everything depends on it, the war, our whole —"

"I know. Nothing will happen to the damn thing. Let's go."

"If it should get damaged —"

"I'm not after the globe. I'm interested only in-in Thomas Cole."

They came to the end of the corridor and stopped before a metal door. Sherikov nodded at the door. "In there."

Reinhart moved back. "Open the door."

"Open it yourself. I don't want to have anything to do with it."

Reinhart shrugged. He stepped up to the door. Holding his gun level he raised his hand, passing it in front of the eye circuit. Nothing happened.

Reinhart frowned. He pushed the door with his hand. The door slid open. Reinhart was looking into a small laboratory. He glimpsed a workbench, tools, heaps of equipment, measuring devices, and in the center of the bench the transparent globe, the control turret.

"Cole?" Reinhart advanced quickly into the room. He glanced around him, suddenly alarmed. "Where —"

The room was empty. Thomas Cole was gone.

When the first missile struck, Cole stopped work and sat listening.

Far off, a distant rumble rolled through the earth, shaking the floor under him. On the bench, tools and equipment danced up and down. A pair of pliers fell crashing to the floor. A box of screws tipped over, spilling its minute contents out.

Cole listened for a time. Presently he lifted the transparent globe from the bench. With carefully controlled hands he held the globe up, running his fingers gently over the surface, his faded blue eyes thoughtful. Then, after a time, he placed the globe back on the bench, in its mount.

The globe was finished. A faint glow of pride moved through the variable man. The globe was the finest job he had ever done.

The deep rumblings ceased. Cole became instantly alert. He jumped down from his stool, hurrying across the room to the door. For a moment he stood by the door listening intently. He could hear noise on the other side, shouts, guards rushing past, dragging heavy equipment, working frantically.

A rolling crash echoed down the corridor and lapped against his door. The concussion spun him around. Again a tide of energy shook the walls and floor and sent him down on his knees.

The lights flickered and winked out.

Cole fumbled in the dark until he found a flashlight. Power failure. He could hear crackling flames. Abruptly the lights came on again, an ugly yellow, then faded back out. Cole bent down and examined the door with his flashlight. A magnetic lock. Dependent on an externally induced electric flux. He grabbed a screwdriver and pried at the door. For a moment it held. Then it fell open.

Cole stepped warily out into the corridor. Everything was in shambles. Guards wandered everywhere, burned and half-blinded. Two lay groaning under a pile of wrecked equipment. Fused guns, reeking metal. The air was heavy with the smell of burning wiring and plastic. A thick cloud that choked him and made him bend double as he advanced.

"Halt," a guard gasped feebly, struggling to rise. Cole pushed past him and down the corridor. Two small robot guns, still functioning, glided past him hurriedly toward the drumming chaos of battle. He followed.

At a major intersection the fight was in full swing. Sherikov's guards fought Security police, crouched behind pillars and barricades, firing wildly, desperately. Again the whole structure shuddered as a great booming blast ignited some place above. Bombs? Shells?

Cole threw himself down as a violet beam cut past his ear and disintegrated the wall behind him. A Security policeman, wild-eyed, firing erratically. One of Sherikov's guards winged him and his gun skidded to the floor.

A robot cannon turned toward him as he made his way past the intersection. He began to run. The cannon rolled along behind him, aiming itself uncertainly. Cole hunched over as he shambled rapidly along, gasping for breath. In the flickering yellow light he saw a handful of Security police advancing, firing expertly, intent on a line of defense Sherikov's guards had hastily set up.

The robot cannon altered its course to take them on, and Cole escaped around a corner.

He was in the main lab, the big chamber where Icarus himself rose, the vast squat column.

Icarus! A solid wall of guards surrounded him, grim-faced, hugging guns and protection shields. But the Security police were leaving Icarus alone. Nobody wanted to damage him. Cole evaded a lone guard tracking him and reached the far side of the lab.

It took him only a few seconds to find the force field generator. There was no switch. For a moment that puzzled him-and then he remembered. The guard had controlled it from his wrist.

Too late to worry about that. With his screwdriver he unfastened the plate over the generator and ripped out the wiring in handfuls. The generator came loose and he dragged it away from the wall. The screen was off, thank God. He managed to carry the generator into a side corridor.

Crouched in a heap, Cole bent over the generator, deft fingers flying. He pulled the wiring to him and laid it out on the floor, tracing the circuits with feverish haste.

The adaptation was easier than he had expected. The screen flowed at right angles to the wiring, for a distance of six feet. Each lead was shielded on one side; the field radiated outward, leaving a hollow cone in the center. He ran the wiring through his belt, down his trouser legs, under his shirt, all the way to his wrists and ankles.

He was just snatching up the heavy generator when two Security police appeared. They raised their blasters and fired point-blank.

Cole clicked on the screen. A vibration leaped through him that snapped his jaw and danced up his body. He staggered away, half-stupefied by the surging force that radiated out from him. The violet rays struck the field and deflected harmlessly.

He was safe.

He hurried on down the corridor, past a ruined gun and sprawled bodies still clutching blasters. Great drifting clouds of radioactive particles billowed around him. He edged by one cloud nervously. Guards lay everywhere, dying and dead, partly destroyed, eaten and corroded by the hot metallic salts in the air. He had to get out-and fast.

At the end of the corridor a whole section of the fortress was in ruins. Towering flames leaped on all sides. One of the missiles had penetrated below ground level.

Cole found a lift that still functioned. A load of wounded guards was being raised to the surface. None of them paid any attention to him. Flames surged around the lift, licking at the wounded. Workmen were desperately trying to get the lift into action. Cole leaped onto the lift. A moment later it began to rise, leaving the shouts and the flames behind.

The lift emerged on the surface and Cole jumped off. A guard spotted him and gave chase. Crouching, Cole dodged into a tangled mass of twisted metal, still white-hot and smoking. He ran for a distance, leaping from the side of a ruined defense-screen tower, onto the fused ground and down the side of a hill. The ground was hot underfoot. He hurried as fast as he could, gasping for breath. He came to a long slope and scrambled up the side.

The guard who had followed was gone, lost behind in the rolling clouds of ash that drifted from the ruins of Sherikov's underground fortress.

Cole reached the top of the hill. For a brief moment he halted to get his breath and figure where he was. It was almost evening. The sun was beginning to set. In the darkening sky a few dots still twisted and rolled, black specks that abruptly burst into flame and fused out again.

Cole stood up cautiously, peering around him. Ruins stretched out below, on all sides, the furnace from which he had escaped. A chaos of incandescent metal and debris, gutted and wrecked beyond repair. Miles of tangled rubbish and half-vaporized equipment.

He considered. Everyone was busy putting out the fires and pulling the wounded to safety. It would be awhile before he was missed. But as soon as they realized he was gone they'd be after him. Most of the laboratory had been destroyed. Nothing lay back that way.

Beyond the ruins lay the great Ural peaks, the endless mountains, stretching out as far as the eye could see.

Mountains and green forests. A wilderness. They'd never find him there.

Cole started along the side of the hill, walking slowly and carefully, his screen generator under his arm. Probably in the confusion he could find enough food and equipment to last him indefinitely. He could wait until early morning, then circle back toward the ruins and load up. With a few tools and his own innate skill he would get along fine. A screwdriver, hammer, nails, odds and ends —

A great hum sounded in his ears. It swelled to a deafening roar. Startled, Cole whirled around. A vast shape filled the sky behind him, growing each moment. Cole stood frozen, utterly transfixed. The shape thundered over him, above his head, as he stood stupidly, rooted to the spot.

Then, awkwardly, uncertainly, he began to run. He stumbled and fell and rolled a short distance down the side of the hill. Desperately, he struggled to hold onto the ground. His hands dug wildly, futilely, into the soft soil, trying to keep the generator under his arm at the same time.

A flash, and a blinding spark of light around him.

The spark picked him up and tossed him like a dry leaf. He grunted in agony as searing fire crackled about him, a blazing inferno that gnawed and ate hungrily through his screen. He spun dizzily and fell through the cloud of fire, down into a pit of darkness, a vast gulf between two hills. His wiring ripped off. The generator tore out of his grip and was lost behind. Abruptly, his force field ceased.

Cole lay in the darkness at the bottom of the hill. His whole body shrieked in agony as the unholy fire played over him. He was a blazing cinder, a half-consumed ash flaming in a universe of darkness. The pain made him twist and crawl like an insect, trying to burrow into the ground. He screamed and shrieked and struggled to escape, to get away from the hideous fire. To reach the curtain of darkness beyond, where it was cool and silent, where the flames couldn't crackle and eat at him.

He reached imploringly out, into the darkness, groping feebly toward it, trying to pull himself into it. Gradually, the glowing orb that was his own body faded. The impenetrable chaos of night descended. He allowed the tide to sweep over him, to extinguish the searing fire.

Dixon landed his ship expertly, bringing it to a halt in front of an overturned defense tower. He leaped out and hurried across the smoking ground.

From a lift Reinhart appeared, surrounded by his Security police. "He got away from us! He escaped!"

"He didn't escape," Dixon answered. "I got him myself."

Reinhart quivered violently. "What do you mean?"

"Come along with me. Over in this direction." He and Reinhart climbed the side of a demolished hill, both of them panting for breath. "I was landing. I saw a figure emerge from a lift and run toward the mountains, like some sort of animal. When he came out in the open I dived on him and released a phosphorus bomb."

"Then he's —*dead?*"

"I don't see how anyone could have lived through a phosphorus bomb." They reached the top of the hill. Dixon halted, then pointed excitedly down into the pit beyond the hill. "There!"

They descended cautiously. The ground was singed and burned clean. Clouds of smoke hung heavily in the air. Occasional fires still flickered here and there. Reinhart coughed and bent over to see. Dixon flashed on a pocket flare and set it beside the body.

The body was charred, half destroyed by the burning phosphorus. It lay motionless, one arm over its face, mouth open, legs sprawled grotesquely. Like some abandoned rag doll, tossed in an incinerator and consumed almost beyond recognition.

"He's alive!" Dixon muttered. He felt around curiously. "Must have had some kind of protection screen. Amazing that a man could —"

"It's him? It's really him?"

"Fits the description." Dixon tore away a handful of burned clothing. "This is the variable man. What's left of him, at least."

Reinhart sagged with relief. "Then we've finally got him. The data is accurate. He's no longer a factor."

Dixon got out his blaster and released the safety catch thoughtfully. "If you want, I can finish the job right now."

At that moment Sherikov appeared, accompanied by two armed Security police. He strode grimly down the hillside, black eyes snapping. "Did Cole —" He broke off. "Good God."

"Dixon got him with a phosphorus bomb," Reinhart said noncommittally. "He had reached the surface and was trying to get into the mountains."

Sherikov turned wearily away. "He was an amazing person. During the attack he managed to force the lock on his door and escape. The guards fired at him, but nothing happened. He had rigged up some kind of force field around him. Something he adapted."

"Anyhow, it's over with," Reinhart answered. "Did you have SRB plates made up on him?"

Sherikov reached slowly into his coat. He drew out a manila envelope. "Here's all the information I collected about him, while he was with me."

"Is it complete? Everything previous has been merely fragmentary."

"As near complete as I could make it. It includes photographs and diagrams of the interior of the globe. The turret wiring he did for me. I haven't had a chance even to look at them." Sherikov fingered the envelope. "What are you going to do with Cole?"

"Have him loaded up, taken back to the city-and officially put to sleep by the Euthanasia Ministry."

"Legal murder?" Sherikov's lips twisted. "Why don't you simply do it right here and get it over with?"

Reinhart grabbed the envelope and stuck it in his pocket. "I'll turn this right over to the machines." He motioned to Dixon. "Let's go. Now we can notify the fleet to prepare for the attack on Centaurus." He turned briefly back to Sherikov. "When can Icarus be launched?"

"In an hour or so, I suppose. They're locking the control turret in place. Assuming it functions correctly, that's all that's needed."

"Good. I'll notify Duffe to send out the signal to the warfleet." Reinhart nodded to the police to take Sherikov to the waiting Security ship. Sherikov moved off dully, his face gray and haggard. Cole's inert body was picked up and tossed onto a freight cart. The cart rumbled into the hold of the Security ship and the lock slid shut after it.

"It'll be interesting to see how the machines respond to the additional data," Dixon said.

"It should make quite an improvement in the odds," Reinhart agreed. He patted the envelope, bulging in his inside pocket. "We're two days ahead of time."

* * * * *

Margaret Duffe got up slowly from her desk. She pushed her chair automatically back. "Let me get all this straight. You mean the bomb is finished? Ready to go?"

Reinhart nodded impatiently. "That's what I said. The Technicians are checking the turret locks to make sure it's properly attached. The launching will take place in half an hour."

"Thirty minutes! Then —"

"Then the attack can begin at once. I assume the fleet is ready for action."

"Of course. It's been ready for several days. But I can't believe the bomb is ready so soon." Margaret Duffe moved numbly toward the door of her office. "This is a great day, Commissioner. An old era lies behind us. This time tomorrow Centaurus will be gone. And eventually the colonies will be ours."

"It's been a long climb," Reinhart murmured.

"One thing. Your charge against Sherikov. It seems incredible that a person of his caliber could ever —"

"We'll discuss that later," Reinhart interrupted coldly. He pulled the manila envelope from his coat. "I haven't had an opportunity to feed the additional data to the SRB machines. If you'll excuse me, I'll do that now."

* * * * *

For a moment Margaret Duffe stood at the door. The two of them faced each other silently, neither speaking, a faint smile on Reinhart's thin lips, hostility in the woman's blue eyes.

"Reinhart, sometimes I think perhaps you'll go too far. And sometimes I think you've *already* gone too far...."

"I'll inform you of any change in the odds showing." Reinhart strode past her, out of the office and down the hall. He headed toward the SRB room, an intense thalamic excitement rising up inside him.

A few moments later he entered the SRB room. He made his way to the machines. The odds 7-6 showed in the view windows. Reinhart smiled a little. 7-6. False odds, based on incorrect information. Now they could be removed.

Kaplan hurried over. Reinhart handed him the envelope, and moved over to the window, gazing down at the scene below. Men and cars scurried frantically everywhere. Officials coming and going like ants, hurrying in all directions.

The war was on. The signal had been sent out to the warfleet that had waited so long near Proxima Centaurus. A feeling of triumph raced through Reinhart. He had won. He had destroyed the man from the past and broken Peter Sherikov. The war had begun as planned. Terra was breaking out. Reinhart smiled thinly. He had been completely successful.

"Commissioner."

Reinhart turned slowly. "All right."

Kaplan was standing in front of the machines, gazing down at the reading. "Commissioner —"

Sudden alarm plucked at Reinhart. There was something in Kaplan's voice. He hurried quickly over. "What is it?"

Kaplan looked up at him, his face white, his eyes wide with terror. His mouth opened and closed, but no sound came.

"*What is it?*" Reinhart demanded, chilled. He bent toward the machines, studying the reading.

And sickened with horror.

100-1. *Against* Terra!

He could not tear his gaze away from the figures. He was numb, shocked with disbelief. 100-1. *What had happened?* What had gone wrong? The turret was finished, Icarus was ready, the fleet had been notified —

There was a sudden deep buzz from outside the building. Shouts drifted up from below. Reinhart turned his head slowly toward the window, his heart frozen with fear.

Across the evening sky a trail moved, rising each moment. A thin line of white. Something climbed, gaining speed each moment. On the ground, all eyes were turned toward it, awed faces peering up.

The object gained speed. Faster and faster. Then it vanished. Icarus was on his way. The attack had begun; it was too late to stop, now.

And on the machines the odds read a hundred to one-for failure.

At eight o'clock in the evening of May 15, 2136, Icarus was launched toward the star Centaurus. A day later, while all Terra waited, Icarus entered the star, traveling at thousands of times the speed of light.

Nothing happened. Icarus disappeared into the star. There was no explosion. The bomb failed to go off.

At the same time the Terran warfleet engaged the Centauran outer fleet, sweeping down in a concentrated attack. Twenty major ships were seized. A good part of the Centauran fleet was destroyed. Many of the captive systems began to revolt, in the hope of throwing off the Imperial bonds.

Two hours later the massed Centauran warfleet from Armun abruptly appeared and joined battle. The great struggle illuminated half the Centauran system. Ship after ship flashed briefly and then faded to ash. For a whole day the two fleets fought, strung out over millions of miles of space. Innumerable fighting men died-on both sides.

At last the remains of the battered Terran fleet turned and limped toward Armun-defeated. Little of the once impressive armada remained. A few blackened hulks, making their way uncertainly toward captivity.

Icarus had not functioned. Centaurus had not exploded. The attack was a failure.

The war was over.

"We've lost the war," Margaret Duffe said in a small voice, wondering and awed. "It's over. Finished."

The Council members sat in their places around the conference table, gray-haired elderly men, none of them speaking or moving. All gazed up mutely at the great stellar maps that covered two walls of the chamber.

"I have already empowered negotiators to arrange a truce," Margaret Duffe murmured. "Orders have been sent out to Vice-Commander Jessup to give up the battle. There's no hope. Fleet Commander Carleton destroyed himself and his flagship a few minutes ago. The Centauran High Council has agreed to end the fighting. Their whole Empire is rotten to the core. Ready to topple of its own weight."

Reinhart was slumped over at the table, his head in his hands. "I don't understand.... *Why?* Why didn't the bomb explode?" He mopped his forehead shakily. All his poise was gone. He was trembling and broken. "*What went wrong?*"

Gray-faced, Dixon mumbled an answer. "The variable man must have sabotaged the turret. The SRB machines knew.... They analyzed the data. *They knew!* But it was too late."

Reinhart's eyes were bleak with despair as he raised his head a little. "I knew he'd destroy us. We're finished. A century of work and planning." His body knotted in a spasm of furious agony. "All because of Sherikov!"

* * * * *

Margaret Duffe eyed Reinhart coldly. "Why because of Sherikov?"

"He kept Cole alive! I wanted him killed from the start." Suddenly Reinhart jumped from his chair. His hand clutched convulsively at his gun. "And he's *still* alive! Even if we've lost I'm going to have the pleasure of putting a blast beam through Cole's chest!"

"Sit down!" Margaret Duffe ordered.

Reinhart was half way to the door. "He's still at the Euthanasia Ministry, waiting for the official —"

"No, he's not," Margaret Duffe said.

Reinhart froze. He turned slowly, as if unable to believe his senses. "*What?*"

"Cole isn't at the Ministry. I ordered him transferred and your instructions cancelled."

"Where-where is he?"

There was unusual hardness in Margaret Duffe's voice as she answered. "With Peter Sherikov. In the Urals. I had Sherikov's full authority restored. I then had Cole transferred there, put in Sherikov's safe keeping. I want to make sure Cole recovers, so we can keep our promise to him-our promise to return him to his own time."

Reinhart's mouth opened and closed. All the color had drained from his face. His cheek muscles twitched spasmodically. At last he managed to speak. "You've gone insane! The traitor responsible for Earth's greatest defeat —"

"We have lost the war," Margaret Duffe stated quietly. "But this is not a day of defeat. It is a day of victory. The most incredible victory Terra has ever had."

Reinhart and Dixon were dumbfounded. "What —" Reinhart gasped. "What do you —" The whole room was in an uproar. All the Council members were on their feet. Reinhart's words were drowned out.

"Sherikov will explain when he gets here," Margaret Duffe's calm voice came. "He's the one who discovered it." She looked around the chamber at the incredulous Council members. "Everyone stay in his seat. You are all to remain here until Sherikov arrives. It's vital you hear what he has to say. His news transforms this whole situation."

* * * * *

Peter Sherikov accepted the briefcase of papers from his armed technician. "Thanks." He pushed his chair back and glanced thoughtfully around the Council chamber. "Is everybody ready to hear what I have to say?"

"We're ready," Margaret Duffe answered. The Council members sat alertly around the table. At the far end, Reinhart and Dixon watched uneasily as the big Pole removed papers from his briefcase and carefully examined them.

"To begin, I recall to you the original work behind the ftl bomb. Jamison Hedge was the first human to propel an object at a speed greater than light. As you know, that object diminished in length and gained in mass as it moved toward light speed. When it reached that speed it vanished. It ceased to exist in our terms. Having no length it could not occupy space. It rose to a different order of existence.

"When Hedge tried to bring the object back, an explosion occurred. Hedge was killed, and all his equipment was destroyed. The force of the blast was beyond calculation. Hedge had placed his observation ship many millions of miles away. It was not far enough, however. Originally, he had hoped his drive might be used for space travel. But after his death the principle was abandoned.

"That is-until Icarus. I saw the possibilities of a bomb, an incredibly powerful bomb to destroy Centaurus and all the Empire's forces. The reappearance of Icarus would mean the annihilation of their System. As Hedge had shown, the object would re-enter space already occupied by matter, and the cataclysm would be beyond belief."

"But Icarus never came back," Reinhart cried. "Cole altered the wiring so the bomb kept on going. It's probably still going."

"Wrong," Sherikov boomed. "The bomb *did* reappear. But it didn't explode."

Reinhart reacted violently. "You mean —"

"The bomb came back, dropping below the ftl speed as soon as it entered the star Proxima. But it did not explode. There was no cataclysm. It reappeared and was absorbed by the sun, turned into gas at once."

"Why didn't it explode?" Dixon demanded.

"Because Thomas Cole solved Hedge's problem. He found a way to bring the ftl object back into this universe without collision. Without an explosion. The variable man found what Hedge was after...."

The whole Council was on its feet. A growing murmur filled the chamber, a rising pandemonium breaking out on all sides.

"I don't believe it!" Reinhart gasped. "It isn't possible. If Cole solved Hedge's problem that would mean —" He broke off, staggered.

"Faster than light drive can now be used for space travel," Sherikov continued, waving the noise down. "As Hedge intended. My men have studied the photographs of the control turret. They don't know *how* or *why*, yet. But we have complete records of the turret. We can duplicate the wiring, as soon as the laboratories have been repaired."

Comprehension was gradually beginning to settle over the room. "Then it'll be possible to build ftl ships," Margaret Duffe murmured, dazed. "And if we can do that —"

"When I showed him the control turret, Cole understood its purpose. Not *my* purpose, but the original purpose Hedge had been working toward. Cole realized Icarus was actually an incomplete spaceship, not a bomb at all. He saw what Hedge had seen, an ftl space drive. He set out to make Icarus work."

"We can go *beyond* Centaurus," Dixon muttered. His lips twisted. "Then the war was trivial. We can leave the Empire completely behind. We can go beyond the galaxy."

"The whole universe is open to us," Sherikov agreed. "Instead of taking over an antiquated Empire, we have the entire cosmos to map and explore, God's total creation."

Margaret Duffe got to her feet and moved slowly toward the great stellar maps that towered above them at the far end of the chamber. She stood for a long time, gazing up at the myriad suns, the legions of systems, awed by what she saw.

"Do you suppose he realized all this?" she asked suddenly. "What we can see, here on these maps?"

"Thomas Cole is a strange person," Sherikov said, half to himself. "Apparently he has a kind of intuition about machines, the way things are supposed to work. An intuition more in his hands than in his head. A kind of genius, such as a painter or a pianist has. Not a scientist. He has no verbal knowledge about things, no semantic references. He deals with the things themselves. Directly.

"I doubt very much if Thomas Cole understood what would come about. He looked into the globe, the control turret. He saw unfinished wiring and relays. He saw a job half done. An incomplete machine."

"Something to be fixed," Margaret Duffe put in.

"Something to be fixed. Like an artist, he saw his work ahead of him. He was interested in only one thing: turning out the best job he could, with the skill he possessed. For us, that skill has opened up a whole universe, endless galaxies and systems to explore. Worlds without end. Unlimited, *untouched* worlds."

Reinhart got unsteadily to his feet. "We better get to work. Start organizing construction teams. Exploration crews. We'll have to reconvert from war production to ship designing. Begin the manufacture of mining and scientific instruments for survey work."

"That's right," Margaret Duffe said. She looked reflectively up at him. "But you're not going to have anything to do with it."

Reinhart saw the expression on her face. His hand flew to his gun and he backed quickly toward the door. Dixon leaped up and joined him. "Get back!" Reinhart shouted.

Margaret Duffe signalled and a phalanx of Government troops closed in around the two men. Grim-faced, efficient soldiers with magnetic grapples ready.

Reinhart's blaster wavered-toward the Council members sitting shocked in their seats, and toward Margaret Duffe, straight at her blue eyes. Reinhart's features were distorted with insane fear. "Get back! Don't anybody come near me or she'll be the first to get it!"

Peter Sherikov slid from the table and with one great stride swept his immense bulk in front of Reinhart. His huge black-furred fist rose in a smashing arc. Reinhart sailed against the wall, struck with ringing force and then slid slowly to the floor.

The Government troops threw their grapples quickly around him and jerked him to his feet. His body was frozen rigid. Blood dripped from his mouth. He spat bits of tooth, his eyes glazed over. Dixon stood dazed, mouth open, uncomprehending, as the grapples closed around his arms and legs.

Reinhart's gun skidded to the floor as he was yanked toward the door. One of the elderly Council members picked the gun up and examined it curiously. He laid it carefully on the table. "Fully loaded," he murmured. "Ready to fire."

Reinhart's battered face was dark with hate. "I should have killed all of you. *All* of you!" An ugly sneer twisted across his shredded lips. "If I could get my hands loose —"

"You won't," Margaret Duffe said. "You might as well not even bother to think about it." She signalled to the troops and they pulled Reinhart and Dixon roughly out of the room, two dazed figures, snarling and resentful.

For a moment the room was silent. Then the Council members shuffled nervously in their seats, beginning to breathe again.

Sherikov came over and put his big paw on Margaret Duffe's shoulder. "Are you all right, Margaret?"

She smiled faintly. "I'm fine. Thanks...."

Sherikov touched her soft hair briefly. Then he broke away and began to pack up his briefcase busily. "I have to go. I'll get in touch with you later."

"Where are you going?" she asked hesitantly. "Can't you stay and —"

"I have to get back to the Urals." Sherikov grinned at her over his bushy black beard as he headed out of the room. "Some very important business to attend to."

* * * * *

Thomas Cole was sitting up in bed when Sherikov came to the door. Most of his awkward, hunched-over body was sealed in a thin envelope of transparent airproof plastic. Two robot attendants whirred ceaselessly at his side, their leads contacting his pulse, blood-pressure, respiration, body temperature.

Cole turned a little as the huge Pole tossed down his briefcase and seated himself on the window ledge.

"How are you feeling?" Sherikov asked him.

"Better."

"You see we've quite advanced therapy. Your burns should be healed in a few months."

"How is the war coming?"

"The war is over."

Cole's lips moved. "Icarus —"

"Icarus went as expected. As *you* expected." Sherikov leaned toward the bed. "Cole, I promised you something. I mean to keep my promise-as soon as you're well enough."

"To return me to my own time?"

"That's right. It's a relatively simple matter, now that Reinhart has been removed from power. You'll be back home again, back in your own time, your own world. We can supply you with some discs of platinum or something of the kind to finance your business. You'll need a new Fixit truck. Tools. And clothes. A few thousand dollars ought to do it."

Cole was silent.

"I've already contacted histo-research," Sherikov continued. "The time bubble is ready as soon as you are. We're somewhat beholden to you, as you probably realize. You've made it possible for us to actualize our greatest dream. The whole planet is seething with excitement. We're changing our economy over from war to —"

"They don't resent what happened? The dud must have made an awful lot of people feel downright bad."

"At first. But they got over it-as soon as they understood what was ahead. Too bad you won't be here to see it, Cole. A whole world breaking loose. Bursting out into the universe. They want me to have an ftl ship ready by the end of the week! Thousands of applications are already on file, men and women wanting to get in on the initial flight."

Cole smiled a little, "There won't be any band, there. No parade or welcoming committee waiting for them."

"Maybe not. Maybe the first ship will wind up on some dead world, nothing but sand and dried salt. But everybody wants to go. It's almost like a holiday. People running around and shouting and throwing things in the streets.

"Afraid I must get back to the labs. Lots of reconstruction work being started." Sherikov dug into his bulging briefcase. "By the way.... One little thing. While you're recovering here, you might like to look at these." He tossed a handful of schematics on the bed.

Cole picked them up slowly. "What's this?"

"Just a little thing I designed." Sherikov arose and lumbered toward the door. "We're realigning our political structure to eliminate any recurrence of the Reinhart affair. This will block any more one-man power grabs." He jabbed a thick finger at the schematics. "It'll turn power over to all of us, not to just a limited number one person could dominate-the way Reinhart dominated the Council.

"This gimmick makes it possible for citizens to raise and decide issues directly. They won't have to wait for the Council to verbalize a measure. Any citizen can transmit his will with one of these, make his needs register on a central control that automatically responds. When a large enough segment of the population wants a certain thing done, these little gadgets set up an active field that touches all the others. An issue won't have to go through a formal Council. The citizens can express their will long before any bunch of gray-haired old men could get around to it."

* * * * *

Sherikov broke off, frowning.

"Of course," he continued slowly, "there's one little detail...."

"What's that?"

"I haven't been able to get a model to function. A few bugs.... Such intricate work never was in my line." He paused at the door. "Well, I hope I'll see you again before you go. Maybe if you feel well enough later on we could get together for one last talk. Maybe have dinner together sometime. Eh?"

But Thomas Cole wasn't listening. He was bent over the schematics, an intense frown on his weathered face. His long fingers moved restlessly over the schematics, tracing wiring and terminals. His lips moved as he calculated.

Sherikov waited a moment. Then he stepped out into the hall and softly closed the door after him.

He whistled merrily as he strode off down the corridor.

Adjustment Team

SOMETHING WENT WRONG…AND ED FLETCHER GOT MIXED UP IN THE BIGGEST THING IN HIS LIFE.

It was bright morning. The sun shone down on the damp lawns and sidewalks, reflecting off the sparkling parked cars. The Clerk came walking hurriedly, leafing through his instructions, flipping pages and frowning. He stopped in front of the small green stucco house for a moment, and then turned up the walk, entering the back yard.

The dog was asleep inside his shed, his back turned to the world. Only his thick tail showed.

"For Heaven's sake," the Clerk exclaimed, hands on his hips. He tapped his mechanical pencil noisily against his clipboard. "Wake up, you in there."

The dog stirred. He came slowly out of his shed, head first, blinking and yawning in the morning sunlight. "Oh, it's you. Already?" He yawned again.

"Big doings." The Clerk ran his expert finger down the traffic-control sheet. "They're adjusting Sector T137 this morning. Starting at exactly nine o'clock." He glanced at his pocket watch. "Three hour alteration. Will finish by noon."

"T137? That's not far from here."

The Clerk's lips twisted in contempt. "Indeed. You're showing astonishing perspicacity, my black-haired friend. Maybe you can divine why I'm here."

"We overlap with T137."

"Exactly. Elements from this sector are involved. We must make sure they're properly placed when adjustment begins." The Clerk glanced toward the small green stucco house. "Your particular task concerns the man in there. He is employed by a business establishment lying within Sector T137. It's essential he be there before nine o'clock.

The dog studied the house. The shades had been let up. The kitchen light was on. Beyond the lace curtains dim shapes could be seen, stirring around the table. A man and woman. They were drinking coffee.

"There they are," the dog murmured. "The man, you say? He's not going to be harmed, is he?"

"Of course not. But he must be at his office early. Usually he doesn't leave until after nine. Today he must leave at eight-thirty. He must be within Sector T137 before the process begins, or he won't be altered to coincide with the new adjustment."

The dog sighed. "That means I have to summon."

"Correct." The Clerk checked his instruction sheet. "You're to summon at precisely eight-fifteen. You've got that? Eight-fifteen. No later."

"What will an eight-fifteen summons bring?"

The Clerk flipped open his instruction book, examining the code columns. "It will bring A Friend with a Car. To drive him to work early." He closed the book and folded his arms, preparing to wait. "That way he'll get to his office almost an hour ahead of time. Which is vital."

"Vital," the dog murmured. He lay down, half inside his shed. His eyes closed. "Vital."

"Wake up! This must be done exactly on time. If you summon too soon or too late —"

The dog nodded sleepily. "I know. I'll do it right. I *always* do it right."

Ed Fletcher poured more cream in his coffee. He sighed, leaning back in his chair. Behind him the oven hissed softly, filling the kitchen with warm fumes. The yellow overhead light beamed down.

"Another roll?" Ruth asked.

"I'm full." Ed sipped his coffee. "You can have it."

"Have to go." Ruth got to her feet, unfastening her robe. "Time to go to work."

"Already?"

"Sure. You lucky bum! Wish I could sit around." Ruth moved toward the bathroom, running her fingers through her long black hair. "When you work for the Government you start early."

"But you get off early," Ed pointed out. He unfolded the *Chronicle*, examining the sporting green. "Well, have a good time today. Don't type any wrong words, any double-entendres."

The bathroom door closed, as Ruth shed her robe and began dressing.

Ed yawned and glanced up at the clock over the sink. Plenty of time. Not even eight. He sipped more coffee and then rubbed his stubbled chin. He would have to shave. He shrugged lazily. Ten minutes, maybe.

Ruth came bustling out in her nylon slip, hurrying into the bedroom. "I'm late." She rushed rapidly around, getting into her blouse and skirt, her stockings, her little white shoes. Finally she bent over and kissed him. "Goodbye, honey. I'll do the shopping tonight."

"Goodbye." Ed lowered his newspaper and put his arm around his wife's trim waist, hugging her affectionately. "You smell nice. Don't flirt with the boss."

Ruth ran out the front door, clattering down the steps. He heard the click of her heels diminish down the sidewalk.

She was gone. The house was silent. He was alone.

Ed got to his feet, pushing his chair back. He wandered lazily into the bathroom and got his razor down. Eight-ten. He washed his face, rubbing it down with shaving cream, and began to shave. He shaved leisurely. He had plenty of time.

The Clerk bent over his round pocket watch, licking his lips nervously. Sweat stood out on his forehead. The second hand ticked on. Eight-fourteen. Almost time.

"Get ready!" the Clerk snapped. He tensed, his small body rigid. "Ten seconds to go!"

"Time!" the Clerk cried.

Nothing happened.

The Clerk turned, eyes wide with horror. From the little shed a thick black tail showed. The dog had gone back to sleep.

"TIME!" the Clerk shrieked. He kicked wildly at the furry rump. "In the name of God —"

The dog stirred. He thumped around hastily, backing out of the shed. "My goodness." Embarrassed, he made his way quickly to the fence. Standing up on his hind paws, he opened his mouth wide. "Woof!" he summoned. He glanced apologetically at the Clerk. "I beg your pardon. I can't understand how —"

The Clerk gazed fixedly down at his watch. Cold terror knotted his stomach. The hands showed eight-sixteen. "You failed," he grated. "You failed! You miserable flea-bitten rag-bag of a wornout old mutt! You failed!"

The dog dropped and came anxiously back. "I failed, you say? You mean the summons time was —?"

"You summoned too late." The Clerk put his watch away slowly, a glazed expression on his face. "You summoned too late. We won't get A Friend with a Car. There's no telling what will come instead. I'm afraid to see what eight-sixteen brings."

"I hope he'll be in Sector T137 in time."

"He won't," the Clerk wailed. "He won't be there. We've made a mistake. We've made things go wrong!"

Ed was rinsing the shaving cream from his face when the muffled sound of the dog's bark echoed through the silent house.

"Damn," Ed muttered. "Wake up the whole block." He dried his face, listening. Was somebody coming?

A vibration. Then —

The doorbell rang.

Ed came out of the bathroom. Who could it be? Had Ruth forgotten something? He tossed on a white shirt and opened the front door.

A bright young man, face bland and eager, beamed happily at him. "Good morning, sir." He tipped his hat. "I'm sorry to bother you so early —"

"What do you want?"

"I'm from the Federal Life Insurance Company. I'm here to see you about —"

Ed pushed the door closed. "Don't want any. I'm in a rush. Have to get to work."

"Your wife said this was the only time I could catch you." The young man picked up his briefcase, easing the door open again. "She especially asked me to come this early. We don't usually begin our work at this time, but since she asked me, I made a special note about it"

"Okay." Sighing wearily, Ed admitted the young man. "You can explain your policy while I get dressed."

The young man opened his briefcase on the couch, laying out heaps of pamphlets and illustrated folders. "I'd like to show you some of these figures, if I may. It's of great importance to you and your family to —"

Ed found himself sitting down, going over the pamphlets. He purchased a ten-thousand-dollar policy on his own life and then eased the young man out. He looked at the clock. Practically nine-thirty!

"Damn." He'd be late to work. He finished fastening his tie, grabbed his coat, turned off the oven and the lights, dumped the dishes in the sink, and ran out on the porch.

As he hurried toward the bus stop he was cursing inwardly. Life insurance salesmen. Why did the jerk have to come just as he was getting ready to leave?

Ed groaned. No telling what the consequences would be, getting to the office late. He wouldn't get there until almost ten. He set himself in anticipation. A sixth sense told him he was in for it. Something bad. It was the wrong day to be late.

If only the salesman hadn't come.

Ed hopped off the bus a block from his office. He began walking rapidly. The huge clock in front of Stein's Jewelry Store told him it was almost ten.

His heart sank. Old Douglas would give him hell for sure. He could see it now. Douglas puffing and blowing, red-faced, waving his thick finger at him; Miss Evans, smiling behind her typewriter; Jackie, the office boy, grinning and snickering; Earl Hendricks; Joe and Tom; Mary, dark-eyed, full bosom and long lashes. All of them, kidding him the whole rest of the day.

He came to the corner and stopped for the light. On the other side of the street rose the big white concrete building, the towering column of steel and cement, girders and glass windows-the office building. Ed flinched. Maybe he could say the elevator got stuck. Somewhere between the second and third floor.

The street light changed. Nobody else was crossing. Ed crossed alone. He hopped up on the curb on the far side —

And stopped, rigid.

The sun had winked off. One moment it was beaming down. Then it was gone. Ed looked sharply up. Gray clouds swirled above him. Huge, formless clouds. Nothing more. An ominous, thick haze that made everything waver and dim. Uneasy chills plucked at him. *What was it?*

He advanced cautiously, feeling his way through the mist. Everything was silent. No sounds-not even the traffic sounds. Ed peered frantically around, trying to see through the rolling haze. No people. No cars. No sun. Nothing.

The office building loomed up ahead, ghostly. It was an indistinct gray. He put out his hand uncertainly —

A section of the building fell away. It rained down, a torrent of particles. Like sand. Ed gaped foolishly. A cascade of gray debris, spilling around his feet. And where he had touched the building, a jagged cavity yawned-an ugly pit marring the concrete.

Dazed, he made his way to the front steps. He mounted them. The steps gave way underfoot. His feet sank down. He was wading through shifting sand, weak, rotted stuff that broke under his weight.

He got into the lobby. The lobby was dim and obscure. The overhead lights flickered feebly in the gloom. An unearthly pall hung over everything.

He spied the cigar stand. The seller leaned silently, resting on the counter, toothpick between his teeth, his face vacant. *And gray.* He was gray all over.

"Hey," Ed croaked. "What's going on?"

The seller did not answer. Ed reached out toward him. His hand touched the seller's gray arm-and passed right through.

"Good God," Ed said.

The seller's arm came loose. It fell to the lobby floor, disintegrating into fragments. Bits of gray fiber. Like dust. Ed's senses reeled.

"Help!" he shouted, finding his voice.

No answer. He peered around. A few shapes stood here and there: a man reading a newspaper, two women waiting at the elevator.

Ed made his way over to the man. He reached out and touched him.

The man slowly collapsed. He settled into a heap, a loose pile of gray ash. Dust. Particles. The two women dissolved when he touched them. Silently. They made no sound as they broke apart.

Ed found the stairs. He grabbed hold of the bannister and climbed. The stairs collapsed under him. He hurried faster. Behind him lay a broken path-his footprints clearly visible in the concrete. Clouds of ash blew around him as he reached the second floor.

He gazed down the silent corridor. He saw more clouds of ash. He heard no sound. There was just darkness-rolling darkness.

He climbed unsteadily to the third floor. Once, his shoe broke completely through the stair. For a sickening second he hung, poised over a yawning hole that looked down into a bottomless nothing.

Then he climbed on, and emerged in front of his own office: DOUGLAS AND BLAKE, REAL ESTATE.

The hall was dim, gloomy with clouds of ash. The overhead lights flickered fitfully. He reached for the door handle. The handle came off in his hand. He dropped it and dug his fingernails into the door. The plate glass crashed past him, breaking into bits. He tore the door open and stepped over it, into the office.

Miss Evans sat at her typewriter, fingers resting quietly on the keys. She did not move. She was gray, her hair, her skin, her clothing. She was without color. Ed touched her. His fingers went through her shoulder, into dry flakiness.

He drew back, sickened. Miss Evans did not stir.

He moved on. He pushed against a desk. The desk collapsed into rotting dust. Earl Hendricks stood by the water cooler, a cup in his hand. He was a gray statue, unmoving. Nothing stirred. No sound. No life. The whole office was gray dust-without life or motion.

Ed found himself out in the corridor again. He shook his head, dazed. What did it mean? Was he going out of his mind? Was he —?

A sound.

Ed turned, peering into the gray mist. A creature was coming, hurrying rapidly. A man —a man in a white robe. Behind him others came. Men in white, with equipment. They were lugging complex machinery.

"Hey —" Ed gasped weakly.

The men stopped. Their mouths opened. Their eyes popped.

"Look!"

"Something's gone wrong!"

"One still charged."

"Get the de-energizer."

"We can't proceed until —"

The men came toward Ed, moving around him. One lugged a long hose with some sort of nozzle. A portable cart came wheeling up. Instructions were rapidly shouted.

Ed broke out of his paralysis. Fear swept over him. Panic. Something hideous was happening. He had to get out. Warn people. Get away.

He turned and ran, back down the stairs. The stairs collapsed under him. He fell half a flight, rolling in heaps of dry ash. He got to his feet and hurried on, down to the ground floor.

The lobby was lost in the clouds of gray ash. He pushed blindly through, toward the door. Behind him, the white-clad men were coming, dragging their equipment and shouting to each other, hurrying quickly after him.

He reached the sidewalk. Behind him the office building wavered and sagged, sinking to one side, torrents of ash raining down in heaps. He raced toward the corner, the men just behind him. Gray clouds swirled around him. He groped his way across the street, hands outstretched. He gained the opposite curb —

The sun winked on. Warm yellow sunlight streamed down on him. Cars honked. Traffic lights changed. On all sides men and women in bright spring clothes hurried and pushed: shoppers, a blue-clad cop, salesmen with briefcases. Stores, windows, signs ... noisy cars moving up and down the street...

And overhead was the bright sun and familiar blue sky.

Ed halted, gasping for breath. He turned and looked back the way he had come. Across the street was the office building-as it had always been. Firm and distinct. Concrete and glass and steel.

He stepped back a pace and collided with a hurrying citizen. "Hey," the man grunted. "Watch it."

"Sorry." Ed shook his head, trying to clear it. From where he stood, the office building looked like always, big and solemn and substantial, rising up imposingly on the other side of the street.

But a minute ago —

Maybe he was out of his mind. He had seen the building crumbling into dust. Building-and people. They had fallen into gray clouds of dust. And the men in white-they had chased him. Men in white robes, shouting orders, wheeling complex equipment.

He was out of his mind. There was no other explanation. Weakly, Ed turned and stumbled along the sidewalk, his mind reeling. He moved blindly, without purpose, lost in a haze of confusion and terror.

The Clerk was brought into the top-level Administrative chambers and told to wait.

He paced back and forth nervously, clasping and wringing his hands in an agony of apprehension. He took off his glasses and wiped them shakily.

Lord. All the trouble and grief. And it wasn't his fault. But he would have to take the rap. It was his responsibility to get the Summoners routed out and their instructions followed. The miserable flea-infested Summoner had gone back to sleep-and *he* would have to answer for it.

The doors opened. "All right," a voice murmured, preoccupied. It was a tired, care-worn voice. The Clerk trembled and entered slowly, sweat dripping down his neck into his celluloid collar.

The Old Man glanced up, laying aside his book. He studied the Clerk calmly, his faded blue eyes mild —a deep, ancient mildness that made the Clerk tremble even more. He took out his handkerchief and mopped his brow.

"I understand there was a mistake," the Old Man murmured. "In connection with Sector T137. Something to do with an element from an adjoining area."

"That's right." The Clerk's voice was faint and husky. "Very unfortunate."

"What exactly occurred?"

"I started out this morning with my instruction sheets. The material relating to T137 had top priority, of course. I served notice on the Summoner in my area that an eight-fifteen summons was required."

"Did the Summoner understand the urgency?"

"Yes, sir." The Clerk hesitated. "But —"

"But what?"

The Clerk twisted miserably. "While my back was turned the Summoner crawled back in his shed and went to sleep. I was occupied, checking the exact time with my watch. I called the moment-but there was no response."

"You called at eight-fifteen exactly?"

"Yes, sir! Exactly eight-fifteen. But the Summoner was asleep. By the time I managed to arouse him it was eight-*sixteen*. He summoned, but instead of A Friend with a Car we got a —A Life Insurance Salesman." The Clerk's face screwed up with disgust. "The Salesman kept the element there until almost nine-thirty. Therefore he was late to work instead of early."

For a moment the Old Man was silent. "Then the element was not within T137 when the adjustment began."

"No. He arrived about ten o'clock."

"During the middle of the adjustment." The Old Man got to his feet and paced slowly back and forth, face grim, hands behind his back. His long robe flowed out behind him. "A serious matter. During a Sector Adjustment all related elements from other Sectors must be included. Otherwise, their orientations remain out of phase. When this element entered T137 the adjustment had been in progress fifty minutes. The element encountered the Sector at its most de-energized stage. He wandered about until one of the adjustment teams met him."

"Did they catch him?"

"Unfortunately no. He fled, out of the Sector. Into a nearby fully energized area."

"What-what then?"

The Old Man stopped pacing, his lined face grim. He ran a heavy hand through his long white hair. "We do not know. We lost contact with him. We will reestablish contact soon, of course. But for the moment he is out of control."

"What are you going to do?"

"He must be contacted and contained. He must be brought up here. There's no other solution."

"Up *here!*"

"It is too late to de-energize him. By the time he is regained he will have told others. To wipe his mind clean would only complicate matters. Usual methods will not suffice. I must deal with this problem myself."

"I hope he's located quickly," the Clerk said.

"He will be. Every Watcher is alerted. Every Watcher and every Summoner." The Old Man's eyes twinkled. "Even the Clerks, although we hesitate to count on them."

The Clerk flushed. "I'll be glad when this thing is over," he muttered.

Ruth came tripping down the stairs and out of the building, into the hot noonday sun. She lit a cigarette and hurried along the walk, her small bosom rising and falling as she breathed in the spring air.

"Ruth." Ed stepped up behind her.

"Ed!" She spun, gasping in astonishment. "What are you doing away from —?"

"Come on." Ed grabbed her arm, pulling her along. "Let's keep moving."

"But what —?"

"I'll tell you later." Ed's face was pale and grim. "Let's go where we can talk. In private."

"I was going down to have lunch at Louie's. We can talk there." Ruth hurried along breathlessly. "What is it? What's happened? You look so strange. And why aren't you at work? Did you-did you get fired?"

They crossed the street and entered a small restaurant. Men and women milled around, getting their lunch. Ed found a table in the back, secluded in a corner. "Here." He sat down abruptly. "This will do." She slid into the other chair.

Ed ordered a cup of coffee. Ruth had salad and creamed tuna on toast, coffee and peach pie. Silently, Ed watched her as she ate, his face dark and moody.

"Please tell me," Ruth begged.

"You really want to know?"

"Of course I want to know!" Ruth put her small hand anxiously on his. "I'm your wife."

"Something happened today. This morning. I was late to work. A damn insurance man came by and held me up. I was half an hour late."

Ruth caught her breath. "Douglas fired you."

"No." Ed ripped a paper napkin slowly into bits. He stuffed the bits in the half-empty water glass. "I was worried as hell. I got off the bus and hurried down the street. I noticed it when I stepped up on the curb in front of the office."

"Noticed what?"

Ed told her. The whole works. Everything.

When he had finished, Ruth sat back, her face white, hands trembling. "I see," she murmured. "No wonder you're upset." She drank a little cold coffee, the cup rattling against the saucer. "What a terrible thing."

Ed leaned intently toward his wife. "Ruth. Do you think I'm going crazy?"

Ruth's red lips twisted. "I don't know what to say. It's so strange..."

"Yeah. Strange is hardly the word for it. I poked my hands right through them. Like they were clay. Old dry clay. Dust. Dust figures." Ed lit a cigarette from Ruth's pack. "When I got out I looked back and there it was. The office building. Like always."

"You were afraid Mr. Douglas would bawl you out, weren't you?"

"Sure. I was afraid-and guilty." Ed's eyes flickered. "I know what you're thinking. I was late and I couldn't face him. So I had some sort of protective psychotic fit. Retreat from reality." He stubbed the cigarette out savagely. "Ruth, I've been wandering around town since. Two and a half hours. Sure, I'm afraid. I'm afraid like hell to go back."

"Of Douglas?"

"No! The men in white." Ed shuddered. "God. Chasing me. With their damn hoses and-and equipment."

Ruth was silent. Finally she looked up at her husband, her dark eyes bright. "You have to go back, Ed."

"Back? Why?"

"To prove something."

"Prove what?"

"Prove it's all right." Ruth's hand pressed against his. "You have to, Ed. You have to go back and face it. To show yourself there's nothing to be afraid of."

"The hell with it! After what I saw? Listen, Ruth. I saw the fabric of reality split open. I saw —*behind*. Underneath. I saw what was really there. And I don't want to go back. I don't want to see dust people again. Ever."

Ruth's eyes were fixed intently on him. "I'll go back with you," she said.

"For God's sake."

"For *your* sake. For your sanity. So you'll know." Ruth got abruptly to her feet, pulling her coat around her. "Come on, Ed. I'll go with you. We'll go up there together. To the office of Douglas and Blake, Real Estate. I'll even go in with you to see Mr. Douglas."

Ed got up slowly, staring hard at his wife. "You think I blacked out. Cold feet. Couldn't face the boss." His voice was low and strained. "Don't you?"

Ruth was already threading her way toward the cashier. "Come on. You'll see. It'll all be there. Just like it always was."

"Okay," Ed said. He followed her slowly. "We'll go back there-and see which of us is right."

They crossed the street together, Ruth holding on tight to Ed's arm. Ahead of them was the building, the towering structure of concrete and metal and glass.

"There it is," Ruth said. "See?"

There it was, all right. The big building rose up, firm and solid, glittering in the early afternoon sun, its windows sparkling brightly.

Ed and Ruth stepped up onto the curb. Ed tensed himself, his body rigid. He winced as his foot touched the pavement —

But nothing happened: the street noises continued; cars, people hurrying past; a kid selling papers. There were sounds, smells, the noises of the city in the middle of the day. And overhead was the sun and the bright blue sky.

"See?" Ruth said. "I was right."

They walked up the front steps, into the lobby. Behind the cigar stand the seller stood, arms folded, listening to the ball game. "Hi, Mr. Fletcher," he called to Ed. His face lit up good-naturedly. "Who's the dame? Your wife know about this?"

Ed laughed unsteadily. They passed on toward the elevator. Four or five businessmen stood waiting. They were middle-aged men, well dressed, waiting impatiently in a bunch. "Hey, Fletcher," one said. "Where you been all day? Douglas is yelling his head off."

"Hello, Earl," Ed muttered. He gripped Ruth's arm. "Been a little sick."

The elevator came. They got in. The elevator rose. "Hi, Ed," the elevator operator said. "Who's the good-looking gal? Why don't you introduce her around?"

Ed grinned mechanically. "My wife."

The elevator let them off at the third floor. Ed and Ruth got out, heading toward the glass door of Douglas and Blake, Real Estate.

Ed halted, breathing shallowly. "Wait." He licked his lips. "I —"

Ruth waited calmly as Ed wiped his forehead and neck with his handkerchief. "All right now?"

"Yeah." Ed moved forward. He pulled open the glass door.

Miss Evans glanced up, ceasing her typing. "Ed Fletcher! Where on earth have you been?"

"I've been sick. Hello, Tom."

Tom glanced up from his work. "Hi, Ed. Say, Douglas is yelling for your scalp. Where have you been?"

"I know." Ed turned wearily to Ruth. "I guess I better go in and face the music."

Ruth squeezed his arm. "You'll be all right. I know." She smiled, a relieved flash of white teeth and red lips. "Okay? Call me if you need me."

"Sure." Ed kissed her briefly on the mouth. "Thanks, honey. Thanks a lot. I don't know what the hell went wrong with me. I guess it's over."

"Forget it. So long." Ruth skipped back out of the office, the door closing after her. Ed listened to her race down the hall to the elevator.

"Nice little gal," Jackie said appreciatively.

"Yeah." Ed nodded, straightening his necktie. He moved unhappily toward the inner office, steeling himself. Well, he had to face it. Ruth was right. But he was going to have a hell of a time explaining it to the boss. He could see Douglas now, thick red wattles, big bull roar, face distorted with rage —

Ed stopped abruptly at the entrance to the inner office. He froze rigid. The inner office-it was *changed*.

The hackles of his neck rose. Cold fear gripped him, clutching at his windpipe. The inner office was different. He turned his head slowly, taking in the sight: the desks, chairs, fixtures, file cabinets, pictures.

. Changes. Little changes. Subtle. Ed closed his eyes and opened them slowly. He was alert, breathing rapidly, his pulse racing. It was changed, all right. No doubt about it.

"What's the matter, Ed?" Tom asked. The staff watched him curiously, pausing in their work.

Ed said nothing. He advanced slowly into the inner office. The office had been *gone over*. He could tell. Things had been altered. Rearranged. Nothing obvious-nothing he could put his finger on. But he could tell.

Joe Kent greeted him uneasily. "What's the matter, Ed? You look like a wild dog. Is something —?"

Ed studied Joe. He was different. Not the same. What was it?

Joe's face. It was a little fuller. His shirt was blue-striped. Joe never wore blue stripes. Ed examined Joe's desk. He saw papers and accounts. The desk-it was too far to the right. And it was bigger. It wasn't the same desk.

The picture on the wall. It wasn't the same. It was a different picture entirely. And the things on top of the file cabinet-some were new, others were gone.

He looked back through the door. Now that he thought about it, Miss Evans' hair was different, done a different way. And it was lighter.

In here, Mary, filing her nails, over by the window-she was taller, fuller. Her purse, lying on the desk in front of her —a red purse, red knit.

"You always...have that purse?" Ed demanded.

Mary glanced up. "What?"

"That purse. You always have that?"

Mary laughed. She smoothed her skirt coyly around her shapely thighs, her long lashes blinking modestly. "Why, Mr. Fletcher. What do you mean?"

Ed turned away. *He knew.* Even if she didn't. She had been redone-changed: her purse, her clothes, her figure, everything about her. None of them knew-but him. His mind spun dizzily. They were all changed. All of them were different. They had all been remolded, recast. Subtly-but it was there.

The wastebasket. It was smaller, not the same. The window shades-white, not ivory. The wall paper was not the same pattern. The lighting fixtures...

Endless, subtle changes.

Ed made his way back to the inner office. He lifted his hand and knocked on Douglas' door.

"Come in."

Ed pushed the door open. Nathan Douglas looked up impatiently. "Mr. Douglas —" Ed began. He came into the room unsteadily-and stopped.

Douglas was not the same. Not at all. His whole office was changed: the rugs, the drapes. The desk was oak, not mahogany. And Douglas himself...

Douglas was younger, thinner. His hair, brown. His skin not so red. His face smoother. No wrinkles. Chin reshaped. Eyes green, not black. He was a different man. But still Douglas —a different Douglas. A different version!

"What is it?" Douglas demanded impatiently. "Oh, it's you, Fletcher. Where were you this morning?"

Ed backed out. Fast.

He slammed the door and hurried back through the inner office. Tom and Miss Evans glanced up, startled. Ed passed by them, grabbing the hall door open.

"Hey!" Tom called. "What —?"

Ed hurried down the hall. Terror leaped through him. He had to hurry. He had *seen.* There wasn't much time. He came to the elevator and stabbed the button.

No time.

He ran to the stairs and started down. He reached the second floor. His terror grew. It was a matter of seconds.

Seconds!

The public phone. Ed ran into the phone booth. He dragged the door shut after him. Wildly, he dropped a dime in the slot and dialed. He had to call the police. He held the receiver to his ear, his heart pounding.

Warn them. Changes. Somebody tampering with reality. Altering it. He had been right. The white-clad men...their equipment...going through the building.

"Hello!" Ed shouted hoarsely. There was no answer. No hum. Nothing.

Ed peered frantically out the door.

And he sagged, defeated. Slowly, he hung up the telephone receiver.

He was no longer on the second floor. The phone booth was rising, leaving the second floor behind, carrying him up, faster and faster. It rose floor by floor, moving silently, swiftly.

The phone booth passed through the ceiling of the building and out into the bright sunlight. It gained speed. The ground fell away below. Buildings and streets were getting smaller each moment. Tiny specks hurried along, far below, cars and people, dwindling rapidly.

Clouds drifted between him and the earth. Ed shut his eyes, dizzy with fright. He held on desperately to the door handles of the phone booth.

Faster and faster the phone booth climbed. The earth was rapidly being left behind, far below. Ed peered up wildly. *Where?* Where was he going? Where was it taking him?

He stood gripping the door handles, waiting.

The Clerk nodded curtly. "That's him, all right. The element in question."

Ed Fletcher looked around him. He was in a huge chamber. The edges fell away into indistinct shadows. In front of him stood a man with notes and ledgers under his arm, peering at him through steel-rimmed glasses. He was a nervous little man, sharp-eyed, with celluloid collar, blue-serge suit, vest, watch chain. He wore black shiny shoes.

And beyond him —

An old man sat quietly, in an immense modern chair. He watched Fletcher calmly, his blue eyes mild and tired. A strange thrill shot through Fletcher. It was not fear. Rather it was a vibration, rattling his bones —a deep sense of awe, tinged with fascination.

"Where-what is this place?" he asked faintly. He was still dazed from his quick ascent.

"Don't ask questions!" the nervous little man snapped angrily, tapping his pencil against his ledgers. "You're here to answer, not ask."

The Old Man moved a little. He raised his hand. "I will speak to the element alone," he murmured. His voice was low. It vibrated and rumbled through the chamber. Again the wave of fascinated awe swept Ed.

"Alone?" The little fellow backed away, gathering his books and papers in his arms. "Of course." He glanced hostilely at Ed Fletcher. "I'm glad he's finally in custody. All the work and trouble just for —"

He disappeared through a door. The door closed softly behind him. Ed and the Old Man were alone.

"Please sit down," the Old Man said.

Ed found a seat. He sat down awkwardly, nervously. He got out his cigarettes and then put them away again.

"What's wrong?" the Old Man asked.

"I'm just beginning to understand."

"Understand what?"

"That I'm dead."

The Old Man smiled briefly. "Dead? No, you're not dead. You're...visiting. An unusual event, but necessitated by circumstances." He leaned toward Ed. "Mr. Fletcher, you have got yourself involved in something."

"Yeah," Ed agreed. "I wish I knew what it was. Or how it happened."

"It was not your fault. You're the victim of a clerical error. A mistake was made-not by you. But involving you."

"What mistake?" Ed rubbed his forehead wearily. "I —I got in on something. I saw *through.* I saw something I wasn't supposed to see."

The Old Man nodded. "That's right. You saw something you were not supposed to see-something few elements have been aware of, let alone witnessed."

"Elements?"

"An official term. Let it pass. A mistake was made, but we hope to rectify it. It is my hope that —"

"Those people," Ed interrupted. "Heaps of dry ash. And gray. Like they were dead. Only it was everything: the stairs and walls and floor. No color or life."

"That Sector had been temporarily de-energized. So the adjustment team could enter and effect changes."

"Changes." Ed nodded. "That's right. When I went back later, everything was alive again. But not the same. It was all different."

"The adjustment was complete by noon. The team finished its work and re-energized the Sector."

"I see," Ed muttered.

"You were supposed to have been in the Sector when the adjustment began. Because of an error you were not. You came into the Sector late-during the adjustment itself. You fled, and when you returned it was over. You saw, and you should not have seen. Instead of a witness you should have been part of the adjustment. Like the others, you should have undergone changes."

Sweat came out on Ed Fletcher's head. He wiped it away. His stomach turned over. Weakly, he cleared his throat. "I get the picture." His voice was almost inaudible. A chilling premonition moved through him. "I was supposed to be changed like the others. But I guess something went wrong."

"Something went wrong. An error occurred. And now a serious problem exists. You have seen these things. You know a great deal. And you are not coordinated with the new configuration."

"Gosh," Ed muttered. "Well, I won't tell anybody." Cold sweat poured off him. "You can count on that. I'm as good as changed."

"You have already told someone," the Old Man said coldly.

"Me?" Ed blinked. "Who?"

"Your wife."

Ed trembled. The color drained from his face, leaving it sickly white. "That's right. I did."

"Your wife knows." The Old Man's face twisted angrily. "A woman. Of all the things to tell —"

"I didn't know." Ed retreated, panic leaping through him. "But I know *now*. You can count on me. Consider me changed."

The ancient blue eyes bored keenly into him, peering far into his depths. "And you were going to call the police. You wanted to inform the authorities."

"But I didn't know *who* was doing the changing."

"Now you know. The natural process must be supplemented-adjusted here and there. Corrections must be made. We are fully licensed to make such corrections. Our adjustment teams perform vital work."

Ed plucked up a measure of courage. "This particular adjustment. Douglas. The office. What was it for? I'm sure it was some worthwhile purpose."

The Old Man waved his hand. Behind him in the shadows an immense map glowed into existence. Ed caught his breath. The edges of the map faded off in obscurity. He saw an infinite web of detailed sections, a network of squares and ruled lines. Each square was marked. Some glowed with a blue light. The lights altered constantly.

"The Sector Board," the Old Man said. He sighed wearily. "A staggering job. Sometimes we wonder how we can go on another period. But it must be done. For the good of all. For *your* good."

"The change. In our-our Sector."

"Your office deals in real estate. The old Douglas was a shrewd man, but rapidly becoming infirm. His physical health was waning. In a few days Douglas will be offered a chance to purchase a large unimproved forest area in western Canada. It will require most of his assets. The older, less virile Douglas would have hesitated. It is imperative he not hesitate. He must purchase the area and clear the land at once. Only a younger man —a younger Douglas-would undertake this.

"When the land is cleared, certain anthropological remains will be discovered. They have already been placed there. Douglas will lease his land to the Canadian Government for scientific study. The remains found there will cause international excitement in learned circles.

"A chain of events will be set in motion. Men from numerous countries will come to Canada to examine the remains. Soviet, Polish, and Czech scientists will make the journey.

"The chain of events will draw these scientists together for the first time in years. National research will be temporarily forgotten in the excitement of these non-national discoveries. One of the leading Soviet scientists will make friends with a Belgian scientist. Before they depart they will agree to correspond-without the knowledge of their governments, of course.

"The circle will widen. Other scientists on both sides will be drawn in. A society will be founded. More and more educated men will transfer an increasing amount of time to this international society. Purely national research will suffer a slight but extremely critical eclipse. The war tension will somewhat wane.

"This alteration is vital. And it is dependent on the purchase and clearing of the section of wilderness in Canada. The old Douglas would not have dared take the risk. But the altered Douglas, and his altered, more youthful staff, will pursue this work with wholehearted enthusiasm. And from this, the vital chain of widening events will come about. The beneficiaries will be *you*. Our methods may seem strange and indirect. Even incomprehensible. But I assure you we know what we're doing."

"I know that now," Ed said.

"So you do. You know a great deal. Much too much. No element should possess such knowledge. I should perhaps call an adjustment team in here..."

A picture formed in Ed's mind: swirling gray clouds, gray men and women. He shuddered. "Look," he croaked. "I'll do anything. Anything at all. Only don't de-energize me." Sweat ran down his face. "Okay?"

The Old Man pondered. "Perhaps some alternative could be found. There is another possibility..."

"What?" Ed asked eagerly. "What is it?"

The Old Man spoke slowly, thoughtfully. "If I allow you to return, you will swear never to speak of the matter? Will you swear not to reveal to anyone the things you saw? The things you know?"

"Sure!" Ed gasped eagerly, blinding relief flooding over him. "I swear!"

"Your wife. She must know nothing more. She must think it was only a passing psychological fit-retreat from reality."

"She thinks that already."

"She must continue to."

Ed set his jaw firmly. "I'll see that she continues to think it was a mental aberration. She'll never know what really happened."

"You are certain you can keep the truth from her?"

"Sure," Ed said confidently. "I know I can."

"All right." The Old Man nodded slowly. "I will send you back. But you must tell no one." He swelled visibly. "Remember: you will eventually come back to me-everyone does, in the end-and your fate will not be enviable."

"I won't tell her," Ed said, sweating. "I promise. You have my word on that. I can handle Ruth. Don't give it a second thought."

Ed arrived home at sunset.

He blinked, dazed from the rapid descent. For a moment he stood on the pavement, regaining his balance and catching his breath. Then he walked quickly up the path.

He pushed the door open and entered the little green stucco house.

"Ed!" Ruth came flying, face distorted with tears. She threw her arms around him, hugging him tight. "Where the hell have you been?"

"Been?" Ed murmured. "At the office, of course."

Ruth pulled back abruptly. "No, you haven't."

Vague tendrils of alarm plucked at Ed. "Of course I have. Where else —?"

"I called Douglas about three. He said you left. You walked out, practically as soon as I turned my back. Eddie —"

Ed patted her nervously. "Take it easy, honey." He began unbuttoning his coat. "Everything's okay. Understand? Things are perfectly all right."

Ruth sat down on the arm of the couch. She blew her nose, dabbing at her eyes. "If you knew how much I've worried." She put her handkerchief away and folded her arms. "I want to know where you were."

Uneasily, Ed hung his coat in the closet. He came over and kissed her. Her lips were ice cold. "I'll tell you all about it. But what do you say we have something to eat? I'm starved."

Ruth studied him intently. She got down from the arm of the couch. "I'll change and fix dinner."

She hurried into the bedroom and slipped off her shoes and nylons. Ed followed her. "I didn't mean to worry you," he said carefully. "After you left me today I realized you were right."

"Oh?" Ruth unfastened her blouse and skirt, arranging them over a hanger. "Right about what?"

"About me." He manufactured a grin and made it glow across his face. "About...what happened."

Ruth hung her slip over the hanger. She studied her husband intently as she struggled into her tight-fitting jeans. "Go on."

The moment had come. It was now or never. Ed Fletcher braced himself and chose his words carefully. "I realized," he stated, "that the whole darn thing was in my mind. You were right, Ruth. Completely right. And I even realize what caused it."

Ruth rolled her cotton T-shirt down and tucked it in her jeans. "What was the cause?"

"Overwork."

"Overwork?"

"I need a vacation. I haven't had a vacation in years. My mind isn't on my job. I've been daydreaming." He said it firmly, but his heart was in his mouth. "I need to get away. To the mountains. Bass fishing. Or —" He searched his mind frantically. "Or —"

Ruth came toward him ominously. "Ed!" she said sharply. "Look at me!"

"What's the matter?" Panic shot through him. "Why are you looking at me like that?"

"*Where were you this afternoon?*"

Ed's grin faded. "I told you. I went for a walk. Didn't I tell you? A walk. To think things over."

"Don't lie to me, Eddie Fletcher! I can tell when you're lying!" Fresh tears welled up in Ruth's eyes. Her breasts rose and fell excitedly under her cotton shirt. "Admit it! You didn't go for a walk!"

Ed stammered weakly. Sweat poured off him. He sagged helplessly against the door. "What do you mean?"

Ruth's black eyes flashed with anger. "Come on! I want to know where you were! Tell me! I have a right to know. What really happened?"

Ed retreated in terror, his resolve melting like wax. It was going all wrong. "Honest. I went out for a —"

"Tell me!" Ruth's sharp fingernails dug into his arm. "I want to know where you were-and who you were with!"

Ed opened his mouth. He tried to grin, but his face failed to respond. "I don't know what you mean."

"You know what I mean. Who were you with? Where did you go? Tell me! I'll find out, sooner or later."

There was no way out. He was licked-and he knew it. He couldn't keep it from her. Desperately he stalled, praying for time. If he could only distract her, get her mind on something else. If she would only let up, even for a second. He could invent something —a better story. Time-he needed more time. "Ruth, you've got to —"

Suddenly there was a sound: the bark of a dog, echoing through the dark house.

Ruth let go, cocking her head alertly. "That was Dobbie. I think somebody's coming."

The doorbell rang.

"You stay here. I'll be right back." Ruth ran out of the room, to the front door. "Darn it." She pulled the front door open.

"Good evening!" The young man stepped quickly inside, loaded down with objects, grinning broadly at Ruth. "I'm from the Sweep-Rite Vacuum Cleaner Company."

Ruth scowled impatiently. "Really, we're about to sit down at the table."

"Oh, this will only take a moment." The young man set down the vacuum cleaner and its attachments with a metallic crash. Rapidly, he unrolled a long illustrated banner, showing the vacuum cleaner in action. "Now, if you'll just hold this while I plug in the cleaner —"

He bustled happily about, unplugging the TV set, plugging in the cleaner, pushing the chairs out of his way.

"I'll show you the drape scraper first." He attached a hose and nozzle to the big gleaming tank. "Now, if you'll just sit down I'll demonstrate each of these easy-to-use attachments." His happy voice rose over the roar of the cleaner. "You'll notice —"

Ed Fletcher sat down on the bed. He groped in his pocket until he found his cigarettes. Shakily he lit one and leaned back against the wall, weak with relief.

He gazed up, a look of gratitude on his face. "Thanks," he said softly. "I think we'll make it-after all. Thanks a lot."

The Hanging Stranger

Five o'clock Ed Loyce washed up, tossed on his hat and coat, got his car out and headed across town toward his TV sales store. He was tired. His back and shoulders ached from digging dirt out of the basement and wheeling it into the back yard. But for a forty-year-old man he had done okay. Janet could get a new vase with the money he had saved; and he liked the idea of repairing the foundations himself.

It was getting dark. The setting sun cast long rays over the scurrying commuters, tired and grim-faced, women loaded down with bundles and packages, students swarming home from the university, mixing with clerks and businessmen and drab secretaries. He stopped his Packard for a red light and then started it up again. The store had been open without him; he'd arrive just in time to spell the help for dinner, go over the records of the day, maybe even close a couple of sales himself. He drove slowly past the small square of green in the center of the street, the town park. There were no parking places in front of LOYCE TV SALES AND SERVICE. He cursed under his breath and swung the car in a U-turn. Again he passed the little square of green with its lonely drinking fountain and bench and single lamppost.

From the lamppost something was hanging. A shapeless dark bundle, swinging a little with the wind. Like a dummy of some sort. Loyce rolled down his window and peered out. What the hell was it? A display of some kind? Sometimes the Chamber of Commerce put up displays in the square.

Again he made a U-turn and brought his car around. He passed the park and concentrated on the dark bundle. It wasn't a dummy. And if it was a display it was a strange kind. The hackles on his neck rose and he swallowed uneasily. Sweat slid out on his face and hands.

It was a body. A human body.

*****

"Look at it!" Loyce snapped. "Come on out here!"

Don Fergusson came slowly out of the store, buttoning his pin-stripe coat with dignity. "This is a big deal, Ed. I can't just leave the guy standing there."

"See it?" Ed pointed into the gathering gloom. The lamppost jutted up against the sky-the post and the bundle swinging from it. "There it is. How the hell long has it been there?" His voice rose excitedly. "What's wrong with everybody? They just walk on past!"

Don Fergusson lit a cigarette slowly. "Take it easy, old man. There must be a good reason, or it wouldn't be there."

"A reason! What kind of a reason?"

Fergusson shrugged. "Like the time the Traffic Safety Council put that wrecked Buick there. Some sort of civic thing. How would I know?"

Jack Potter from the shoe shop joined them. "What's up, boys?"

"There's a body hanging from the lamppost," Loyce said. "I'm going to call the cops."

"They must know about it," Potter said. "Or otherwise it wouldn't be there."

"I got to get back in." Fergusson headed back into the store. "Business before pleasure."

Loyce began to get hysterical. "You see it? You see it hanging there? A man's body! A dead man!"

"Sure, Ed. I saw it this afternoon when I went out for coffee."

"You mean it's been there all afternoon?"

"Sure. What's the matter?" Potter glanced at his watch. "Have to run. See you later, Ed."

Potter hurried off, joining the flow of people moving along the sidewalk. Men and women, passing by the park. A few glanced up curiously at the dark bundle-and then went on. Nobody stopped. Nobody paid any attention.

"I'm going nuts," Loyce whispered. He made his way to the curb and crossed out into traffic, among the cars. Horns honked angrily at him. He gained the curb and stepped up onto the little square of green.

The man had been middle-aged. His clothing was ripped and torn, a gray suit, splashed and caked with dried mud. A stranger. Loyce had never seen him before. Not a local man. His face was partly turned, away, and in the evening wind he spun a little, turning gently, silently. His skin was gouged and cut. Red gashes, deep scratches of congealed blood. A pair of steel-rimmed glasses hung from one ear, dangling foolishly. His eyes bulged. His mouth was open, tongue thick and ugly blue.

"For Heaven's sake," Loyce muttered, sickened. He pushed down his nausea and made his way back to the sidewalk. He was shaking all over, with revulsion-and fear.

Why? Who was the man? Why was he hanging there? What did it mean?

And-why didn't anybody notice?

He bumped into a small man hurrying along the sidewalk. "Watch it!" the man grated, "Oh, it's you, Ed."

Ed nodded dazedly. "Hello, Jenkins."

"What's the matter?" The stationery clerk caught Ed's arm. "You look sick."

"The body. There in the park."

"Sure, Ed." Jenkins led him into the alcove of LOYCE TV SALES AND SERVICE. "Take it easy."

Margaret Henderson from the jewelry store joined them. "Something wrong?"

"Ed's not feeling well."

Loyce yanked himself free. "How can you stand here? Don't you see it? For God's sake —"

"What's he talking about?" Margaret asked nervously.

"The body!" Ed shouted. "The body hanging there!"

More people collected. "Is he sick? It's Ed Loyce. You okay, Ed?"

"The body!" Loyce screamed, struggling to get past them. Hands caught at him. He tore loose. "Let me go! The police! Get the police!"

"Ed —"

"Better get a doctor!"

"He must be sick."

"Or drunk."

Loyce fought his way through the people. He stumbled and half fell. Through a blur he saw rows of faces, curious, concerned, anxious. Men and women halting to see what the disturbance was. He fought past them toward his store. He could see Fergusson inside talking to a man, showing him an Emerson TV set. Pete Foley in the back at the service counter, setting up a new Philco. Loyce shouted at them frantically. His voice was lost in the roar of traffic and the murmur around him.

"Do something!" he screamed. "Don't stand there! Do something! Something's wrong! Something's happened! Things are going on!"

The crowd melted respectfully for the two heavy-set cops moving efficiently toward Loyce.

*****

"Name?" the cop with the notebook murmured.

"Loyce." He mopped his forehead wearily. "Edward C. Loyce. Listen to me. Back there —"

"Address?" the cop demanded. The police car moved swiftly through traffic, shooting among the cars and buses. Loyce sagged against the seat, exhausted and confused. He took a deep shuddering breath.

"1368 Hurst Road."

"That's here in Pikeville?"

"That's right." Loyce pulled himself up with a violent effort. "Listen to me. Back there. In the square. Hanging from the lamppost —"

"Where were you today?" the cop behind the wheel demanded.

"Where?" Loyce echoed.

"You weren't in your shop, were you?"

"No." He shook his head. "No, I was home. Down in the basement."

"In the *basement*?"

"Digging. A new foundation. Getting out the dirt to pour a cement frame. Why? What has that to do with —"

"Was anybody else down there with you?"

"No. My wife was downtown. My kids were at school." Loyce looked from one heavy-set cop to the other. Hope flicked across his face, wild hope. "You mean because I was down there I missed-the explanation? I didn't get in on it? Like everybody else?"

After a pause the cop with the notebook said: "That's right. You missed the explanation."

"Then it's official? The body-it's *supposed* to be hanging there?"

"It's supposed to be hanging there. For everybody to see."

Ed Loyce grinned weakly. "Good Lord. I guess I sort of went off the deep end. I thought maybe something had happened. You know, something like the Ku Klux Klan. Some kind of violence. Communists or Fascists taking over." He wiped his face with his breast-pocket handkerchief, his hands shaking. "I'm glad to know it's on the level."

"It's on the level." The police car was getting near the Hall of Justice. The sun had set. The streets were gloomy and dark. The lights had not yet come on.

"I feel better," Loyce said. "I was pretty excited there, for a minute. I guess I got all stirred up. Now that I understand, there's no need to take me in, is there?"

The two cops said nothing.

"I should be back at my store. The boys haven't had dinner. I'm all right, now. No more trouble. Is there any need of —"

"This won't take long," the cop behind the wheel interrupted. "A short process. Only a few minutes."

"I hope it's short," Loyce muttered. The car slowed down for a stoplight. "I guess I sort of disturbed the peace. Funny, getting excited like that and —"

Loyce yanked the door open. He sprawled out into the street and rolled to his feet. Cars were moving all around him, gaining speed as the light changed. Loyce leaped onto the curb and raced among the people, burrowing into the swarming crowds. Behind him he heard sounds, shouts, people running.

They weren't cops. He had realized that right away. He knew every cop in Pikeville. A man couldn't own a store, operate a business in a small town for twenty-five years without getting to know all the cops.

They weren't cops-and there hadn't been any explanation. Potter, Fergusson, Jenkins, none of them knew why it was there. They didn't know-and they didn't care. *That* was the strange part.

Loyce ducked into a hardware store. He raced toward the back, past the startled clerks and customers, into the shipping room and through the back door. He tripped over a garbage can and ran up a flight of concrete steps. He climbed over a fence and jumped down on the other side, gasping and panting.

There was no sound behind him. He had got away.

He was at the entrance of an alley, dark and strewn with boards and ruined boxes and tires. He could see the street at the far end. A street light wavered and came on. Men and women. Stores. Neon signs. Cars.

And to his right-the police station.

He was close, terribly close. Past the loading platform of a grocery store rose the white concrete side of the Hall of Justice. Barred windows. The police antenna. A great concrete wall rising up in the darkness. A bad place for him to be near. He was too close. He had to keep moving, get farther away from them.

Them?

Loyce moved cautiously down the alley. Beyond the police station was the City Hall, the old-fashioned yellow structure of wood and gilded brass and broad cement steps. He could see the endless rows of offices, dark windows, the cedars and beds of flowers on each side of the entrance.

And-something else.

Above the City Hall was a patch of darkness, a cone of gloom denser than the surrounding night. A prism of black that spread out and was lost into the sky.

He listened. Good God, he could hear something. Something that made him struggle frantically to close his ears, his mind, to shut out the sound. A buzzing. A distant, muted hum like a great swarm of bees.

Loyce gazed up, rigid with horror. The splotch of darkness, hanging over the City Hall. Darkness so thick it seemed almost solid. *In the vortex something moved.* Flickering shapes. Things, descending from the sky, pausing momentarily above the City Hall, fluttering over it in a dense swarm and then dropping silently onto the roof.

Shapes. Fluttering shapes from the sky. From the crack of darkness that hung above him. He was seeing-them.

*****

For a long time Loyce watched, crouched behind a sagging fence in a pool of scummy water.

They were landing. Coming down in groups, landing on the roof of the City Hall and disappearing inside. They had wings. Like giant insects of some kind. They flew and fluttered and came to rest-and then crawled crab-fashion, sideways, across the roof and into the building.

He was sickened. And fascinated. Cold night wind blew around him and he shuddered. He was tired, dazed with shock. On the front steps of the City Hall were men, standing here and there. Groups of men coming out of the building and halting for a moment before going on.

Were there more of them?

It didn't seem possible. What he saw descending from the black chasm weren't men. They were alien-from some other world, some other dimension. Sliding through this slit, this break in the shell of the universe. Entering through this gap, winged insects from another realm of being.

On the steps of the City Hall a group of men broke up. A few moved toward a waiting car. One of the remaining shapes started to re-enter the City Hall. It changed its mind and turned to follow the others.

Loyce closed his eyes in horror. His senses reeled. He hung on tight, clutching at the sagging fence. The shape, the man-shape, had abruptly fluttered up and flapped after the others. It flew to the sidewalk and came to rest among them.

Pseudo-men. Imitation men. Insects with ability to disguise themselves as men. Like other insects familiar to Earth. Protective coloration. Mimicry.

Loyce pulled himself away. He got slowly to his feet. It was night. The alley was totally dark. But maybe they could see in the dark. Maybe darkness made no difference to them.

He left the alley cautiously and moved out onto the street. Men and women flowed past, but not so many, now. At the bus-stops stood waiting groups. A huge bus lumbered along the street, its lights flashing in the evening gloom.

Loyce moved forward. He pushed his way among those waiting and when the bus halted he boarded it and took a seat in the rear, by the door. A moment later the bus moved into life and rumbled down the street.

*****

Loyce relaxed a little. He studied the people around him. Dulled, tired faces. People going home from work. Quite ordinary faces. None of them paid any attention to him. All sat quietly, sunk down in their seats, jiggling with the motion of the bus.

The man sitting next to him unfolded a newspaper. He began to read the sports section, his lips moving. An ordinary man. Blue suit. Tie. A businessman, or a salesman. On his way home to his wife and family.

Across the aisle a young woman, perhaps twenty. Dark eyes and hair, a package on her lap. Nylons and heels. Red coat and white angora sweater. Gazing absently ahead of her.

A high school boy in jeans and black jacket.

A great triple-chinned woman with an immense shopping bag loaded with packages and parcels. Her thick face dim with weariness.

Ordinary people. The kind that rode the bus every evening. Going home to their families. To dinner.

Going home-with their minds dead. Controlled, filmed over with the mask of an alien being that had appeared and taken possession of them, their town, their lives. Himself, too. Except that he happened to be deep in his cellar instead of in the store. Somehow, he had been overlooked. They had missed him. Their control wasn't perfect, foolproof.

Maybe there were others.

Hope flickered in Loyce. They weren't omnipotent. They had made a mistake, not got control of him. Their net, their field of control, had passed over him. He had emerged from his cellar as he had gone down. Apparently their power-zone was limited.

A few seats down the aisle a man was watching him. Loyce broke off his chain of thought. A slender man, with dark hair and a small mustache. Well-dressed, brown suit and shiny shoes. A book between his small hands. He was watching Loyce, studying him intently. He turned quickly away.

Loyce tensed. One of *them*? Or-another they had missed?

The man was watching him again. Small dark eyes, alive and clever. Shrewd. A man too shrewd for them-or one of the things itself, an alien insect from beyond.

The bus halted. An elderly man got on slowly and dropped his token into the box. He moved down the aisle and took a seat opposite Loyce.

The elderly man caught the sharp-eyed man's gaze. For a split second something passed between them.

A look rich with meaning.

Loyce got to his feet. The bus was moving. He ran to the door. One step down into the well. He yanked the emergency door release. The rubber door swung open.

"Hey!" the driver shouted, jamming on the brakes. "What the hell —"

Loyce squirmed through. The bus was slowing down. Houses on all sides. A residential district, lawns and tall apartment buildings. Behind him, the bright-eyed man had leaped up. The elderly man was also on his feet. They were coming after him.

Loyce leaped. He hit the pavement with terrific force and rolled against the curb. Pain lapped over him. Pain and a vast tide of blackness. Desperately, he fought it off. He struggled to his knees and then slid down again. The bus had stopped. People were getting off.

Loyce groped around. His fingers closed over something. A rock, lying in the gutter. He crawled to his feet, grunting with pain. A shape loomed before him. A man, the bright-eyed man with the book.

Loyce kicked. The man gasped and fell. Loyce brought the rock down. The man screamed and tried to roll away. *"Stop!* For God's sake listen —"

He struck again. A hideous crunching sound. The man's voice cut off and dissolved in a bubbling wail. Loyce scrambled up and back. The others were there, now. All around him. He ran, awkwardly, down the sidewalk, up a driveway. None of them followed him. They had stopped and were bending over the inert body of the man with the book, the bright-eyed man who had come after him.

Had he made a mistake?

But it was too late to worry about that. He had to get out-away from them. Out of Pikeville, beyond the crack of darkness, the rent between their world and his.

*****

"Ed!" Janet Loyce backed away nervously. "What is it? What —"

Ed Loyce slammed the door behind him and came into the living room. "Pull down the shades. Quick."

Janet moved toward the window. "But —"

"Do as I say. Who else is here besides you?"

"Nobody. Just the twins. They're upstairs in their room. What's happened? You look so strange. Why are you home?"

Ed locked the front door. He prowled around the house, into the kitchen. From the drawer under the sink he slid out the big butcher knife and ran his finger along it. Sharp. Plenty sharp. He returned to the living room.

"Listen to me," he said. "I don't have much time. They know I escaped and they'll be looking for me."

"Escaped?" Janet's face twisted with bewilderment and fear. "Who?"

"The town has been taken over. They're in control. I've got it pretty well figured out. They started at the top, at the City Hall and police department. What they did with the *real* humans they —"

"What are you talking about?"

"We've been invaded. From some other universe, some other dimension. They're insects. Mimicry. And more. Power to control minds. Your mind."

"My mind?"

"Their entrance is *here*, in Pikeville. They've taken over all of you. The whole town-except me. We're up against an incredibly powerful enemy, but they have their limitations. That's our hope. They're limited! They can make mistakes!"

Janet shook her head. "I don't understand, Ed. You must be insane."

"Insane? No. Just lucky. If I hadn't been down in the basement I'd be like all the rest of you." Loyce peered out the window. "But I can't stand here talking. Get your coat."

"My coat?"

"We're getting out of here. Out of Pikeville. We've got to get help. Fight this thing. They *can* be beaten. They're not infallible. It's going to be close-but we may make it if we hurry. Come on!" He grabbed her arm roughly. "Get your coat and call the twins. We're all leaving. Don't stop to pack. There's no time for that."

White-faced, his wife moved toward the closet and got down her coat. "Where are we going?"

Ed pulled open the desk drawer and spilled the contents out onto the floor. He grabbed up a road map and spread it open. "They'll have the highway covered, of course. But there's a back road. To Oak Grove. I got onto it once. It's practically abandoned. Maybe they'll forget about it."

"The old Ranch Road? Good Lord-it's completely closed. Nobody's supposed to drive over it."

"I know." Ed thrust the map grimly into his coat. "That's our best chance. Now call down the twins and let's get going. Your car is full of gas, isn't it?"

Janet was dazed.

"The Chevy? I had it filled up yesterday afternoon." Janet moved toward the stairs. "Ed, I —"

"Call the twins!" Ed unlocked the front door and peered out. Nothing stirred. No sign of life. All right so far.

"Come on downstairs," Janet called in a wavering voice. "We're-going out for awhile."

"Now?" Tommy's voice came.

"Hurry up," Ed barked. "Get down here, both of you."

Tommy appeared at the top of the stairs. "I was doing my home work. We're starting fractions. Miss Parker says if we don't get this done —"

"You can forget about fractions." Ed grabbed his son as he came down the stairs and propelled him toward the door. "Where's Jim?"

"He's coming."

Jim started slowly down the stairs. "What's up, Dad?"

"We're going for a ride."

"A ride? Where?"

Ed turned to Janet. "We'll leave the lights on. And the TV set. Go turn it on." He pushed her toward the set. "So they'll think we're still —"

He heard the buzz. And dropped instantly, the long butcher knife out. Sickened, he saw it coming down the stairs at him, wings a blur of motion as it aimed itself. It still bore a vague resemblance to Jimmy. It was small, a baby one. A brief glimpse-the thing hurtling at him, cold, multi-lensed inhuman eyes. Wings, body still clothed in yellow T-shirt and jeans, the mimic outline still stamped on it. A strange half-turn of its body as it reached him. What was it doing?

A stinger.

Loyce stabbed wildly at it. It retreated, buzzing frantically. Loyce rolled and crawled toward the door. Tommy and Janet stood still as statues, faces blank. Watching without expression. Loyce stabbed again. This time the knife connected. The thing shrieked and faltered. It bounced against the wall and fluttered down.

Something lapped through his mind. A wall of force, energy, an alien mind probing into him. He was suddenly paralyzed. The mind entered his own, touched against him briefly, shockingly. An utterly alien presence, settling over him-and then it flickered out as the thing collapsed in a broken heap on the rug.

It was dead. He turned it over with his foot. It was an insect, a fly of some kind. Yellow T-shirt, jeans. His son Jimmy....He closed his mind tight. It was too late to think about that. Savagely he scooped up his knife and headed toward the door. Janet and Tommy stood stone-still, neither of them moving.

The car was out. He'd never get through. They'd be waiting for him. It was ten miles on foot. Ten long miles over rough ground, gulleys and open fields and hills of uncut forest. He'd have to go alone.

Loyce opened the door. For a brief second he looked back at his wife and son. Then he slammed the door behind him and raced down the porch steps.

A moment later he was on his way, hurrying swiftly through the darkness toward the edge of town.

*****

The early morning sunlight was blinding. Loyce halted, gasping for breath, swaying back and forth. Sweat ran down in his eyes. His clothing was torn, shredded by the brush and thorns through which he had crawled. Ten miles-on his hands and knees. Crawling, creeping through the night. His shoes were mud-caked. He was scratched and limping, utterly exhausted.

But ahead of him lay Oak Grove.

He took a deep breath and started down the hill. Twice he stumbled and fell, picking himself up and trudging on. His ears rang. Everything receded and wavered. But he was there. He had got out, away from Pikeville.

A farmer in a field gaped at him. From a house a young woman watched in wonder. Loyce reached the road and turned onto it. Ahead of him was a gasoline station and a drive-in. A couple of trucks, some chickens pecking in the dirt, a dog tied with a string.

The white-clad attendant watched suspiciously as he dragged himself up to the station. "Thank God." He caught hold of the wall. "I didn't think I was going to make it. They followed me most of the way. I could hear them buzzing. Buzzing and flitting around behind me."

"What happened?" the attendant demanded. "You in a wreck? A hold-up?"

Loyce shook his head wearily. "They have the whole town. The City Hall and the police station. They hung a man from the lamppost. That was the first thing I saw. They've got all the roads blocked. I saw them hovering over the cars coming in. About four this morning I got beyond them. I knew it right away. I could feel them leave. And then the sun came up."

The attendant licked his lip nervously. "You're out of your head. I better get a doctor."

"Get me into Oak Grove," Loyce gasped. He sank down on the gravel. "We've got to get started-cleaning them out. Got to get started right away."

*****

They kept a tape recorder going all the time he talked. When he had finished the Commissioner snapped off the recorder and got to his feet. He stood for a moment, deep in thought. Finally he got out his cigarettes and lit up slowly, a frown on his beefy face.

"You don't believe me," Loyce said.

The Commissioner offered him a cigarette. Loyce pushed it impatiently away. "Suit yourself." The Commissioner moved over to the window and stood for a time looking out at the town of Oak Grove. "I believe you," he said abruptly.

Loyce sagged. "Thank God."

"So you got away." The Commissioner shook his head. "You were down in your cellar instead of at work. A freak chance. One in a million."

Loyce sipped some of the black coffee they had brought him. "I have a theory," he murmured.

"What is it?"

"About them. Who they are. They take over one area at a time. Starting at the top-the highest level of authority. Working down from there in a widening circle. When they're firmly in control they go on to the next town. They spread, slowly, very gradually. I think it's been going on for a long time."

"A long time?"

"Thousands of years. I don't think it's new."

"Why do you say that?"

"When I was a kid....A picture they showed us in Bible League. A religious picture-an old print. The enemy gods, defeated by Jehovah. Moloch, Beelzebub, Moab, Baalin, Ashtaroth —"

"So?"

"They were all represented by figures." Loyce looked up at the Commissioner. "Beelzebub was represented as —a giant fly."

The Commissioner grunted. "An old struggle."

"They've been defeated. The Bible is an account of their defeats. They make gains-but finally they're defeated."

"Why defeated?"

"They can't get everyone. They didn't get me. And they never got the Hebrews. The Hebrews carried the message to the whole world. The realization of the danger. The two men on the bus. I think they understood. Had escaped, like I did." He clenched his fists. "I killed one of them. I made a mistake. I was afraid to take a chance."

The Commissioner nodded. "Yes, they undoubtedly had escaped, as you did. Freak accidents. But the rest of the town was firmly in control." He turned from the window. "Well, Mr. Loyce. You seem to have figured everything out."

"Not everything. The hanging man. The dead man hanging from the lamppost. I don't understand that. Why? Why did they deliberately hang him there?"

"That would seem simple." The Commissioner smiled faintly. *"Bait."*

Loyce stiffened. His heart stopped beating. "Bait? What do you mean?"

"To draw you out. Make you declare yourself. So they'd know who was under control-and who had escaped."

Loyce recoiled with horror. "Then they *expected* failures! They anticipated —" He broke off. "They were ready with a trap."

"And you showed yourself. You reacted. You made yourself known." The Commissioner abruptly moved toward the door. "Come along, Loyce. There's a lot to do. We must get moving. There's no time to waste."

Loyce started slowly to his feet, numbed. "And the man. *Who was the man?* I never saw him before. He wasn't a local man. He was a stranger. All muddy and dirty, his face cut, slashed —"

There was a strange look on the Commissioner's face as he answered. "Maybe," he said softly, "you'll understand that, too. Come along with me, Mr. Loyce." He held the door open, his eyes gleaming. Loyce caught a glimpse of the street in front of the police station. Policemen, a platform of some sort. A telephone pole-and a rope! "Right this way," the Commissioner said, smiling coldly.

*****

As the sun set, the vice-president of the Oak Grove Merchants' Bank came up out of the vault, threw the heavy time locks, put on his hat and coat, and hurried outside onto the sidewalk. Only a few people were there, hurrying home to dinner.

"Good night," the guard said, locking the door after him.

"Good night," Clarence Mason murmured. He started along the street toward his car. He was tired. He had been working all day down in the vault, examining the lay-out of the safety deposit boxes to see if there was room for another tier. He was glad to be finished.

At the corner he halted. The street lights had not yet come on. The street was dim. Everything was vague. He looked around-and froze.

From the telephone pole in front of the police station, something large and shapeless hung. It moved a little with the wind.

What the hell was it?

Mason approached it warily. He wanted to get home. He was tired and hungry. He thought of his wife, his kids, a hot meal on the dinner table. But there was something about the dark bundle, something ominous and ugly. The light was bad; he couldn't tell what it was. Yet it drew him on, made him move for a better look. The shapeless thing made him uneasy. He was frightened by it. Frightened-and fascinated.

And the strange part was that nobody else seemed to notice it.

The Eyes Have It

It was quite by accident I discovered this incredible invasion of Earth by lifeforms from another planet. As yet, I haven't done anything about it; I can't think of anything to do. I wrote to the Government, and they sent back a pamphlet on the repair and maintenance of frame houses. Anyhow, the whole thing is known; I'm not the first to discover it. Maybe it's even under control.

I was sitting in my easy-chair, idly turning the pages of a paperbacked book someone had left on the bus, when I came across the reference that first put me on the trail. For a moment I didn't respond. It took some time for the full import to sink in. After I'd comprehended, it seemed odd I hadn't noticed it right away.

The reference was clearly to a nonhuman species of incredible properties, not indigenous to Earth. A species, I hasten to point out, customarily masquerading as ordinary human beings. Their disguise, however, became transparent in the face of the following observations by the author. It was at once obvious the author knew everything. Knew everything — and was taking it in his stride. The line (and I tremble remembering it even now) read:

> ... his eyes slowly roved about the room.

Vague chills assailed me. I tried to picture the eyes. Did they roll like dimes? The passage indicated not; they seemed to move through the air, not over the surface. Rather rapidly, apparently. No one in the story was surprised. That's what tipped me off. No sign of amazement at such an outrageous thing. Later the matter was amplified.

> ... his eyes moved from person to person.

There it was in a nutshell. The eyes had clearly come apart from the rest of him and were on their own. My heart pounded and my breath choked in my windpipe. I had stumbled on an accidental mention of a totally unfamiliar race. Obviously non-Terrestrial. Yet, to the characters in the book, it was perfectly natural — which suggested they belonged to the same species.

And the author? A slow suspicion burned in my mind. The author was taking it rather *too easily* in his stride. Evidently, he felt this was quite a usual thing. He made absolutely no attempt to conceal this knowledge. The story continued:

> ... presently his eyes fastened on Julia.

Julia, being a lady, had at least the breeding to feel indignant. She is described as blushing and knitting her brows angrily. At this, I sighed with relief. They weren't *all* non-Terrestrials. The narrative continues:

> ... slowly, calmly, his eyes examined every inch of her.

Great Scott! But here the girl turned and stomped off and the matter ended. I lay back in my chair gasping with horror. My wife and family regarded me in wonder.

"What's wrong, dear?" my wife asked.

I couldn't tell her. Knowledge like this was too much for the ordinary run-of-the-mill person. I had to keep it to myself. "Nothing," I gasped. I leaped up, snatched the book, and hurried out of the room.

* * * * *

In the garage, I continued reading. There was more. Trembling, I read the next revealing passage:

...he put his arm around Julia. Presently she asked him if he would remove his arm. He immediately did so, with a smile.

It's not said what was done with the arm after the fellow had removed it. Maybe it was left standing upright in the corner. Maybe it was thrown away. I don't care. In any case, the full meaning was there, staring me right in the face.

Here was a race of creatures capable of removing portions of their anatomy at will. Eyes, arms —and maybe more. Without batting an eyelash. My knowledge of biology came in handy, at this point. Obviously they were simple beings, uni-cellular, some sort of primitive single-celled things. Beings no more developed than starfish. Starfish can do the same thing, you know.

I read on. And came to this incredible revelation, tossed off coolly by the author without the faintest tremor:

...outside the movie theater we split up. Part of us went inside, part over to the cafe for dinner.

Binary fission, obviously. Splitting in half and forming two entities. Probably each lower half went to the cafe, it being farther, and the upper halves to the movies. I read on, hands shaking. I had really stumbled onto something here. My mind reeled as I made out this passage:

...I'm afraid there's no doubt about it. Poor Bibney has lost his head again.

Which was followed by:

...and Bob says he has utterly no guts.

Yet Bibney got around as well as the next person. The next person, however, was just as strange. He was soon described as:

...totally lacking in brains.

* * * * *

There was no doubt of the thing in the next passage. Julia, whom I had thought to be the one normal person, reveals herself as also being an alien life form, similar to the rest:

...quite deliberately, Julia had given her heart to the young man.

It didn't relate what the final disposition of the organ was, but I didn't really care. It was evident Julia had gone right on living in her usual manner, like all the others in the book. Without heart, arms, eyes, brains, viscera, dividing up in two when the occasion demanded. Without a qualm.

...thereupon she gave him her hand.

I sickened. The rascal now had her hand, as well as her heart. I shudder to think what he's done with them, by this time.

...he took her arm.

Not content to wait, he had to start dismantling her on his own. Flushing crimson, I slammed the book shut and leaped to my feet. But not in time to escape one last reference to those carefree bits of anatomy whose travels had originally thrown me on the track:

...her eyes followed him all the way down the road and across the meadow.

I rushed from the garage and back inside the warm house, as if the accursed things were following me. My wife and children were playing Monopoly in the kitchen. I joined them and played with frantic fervor, brow feverish, teeth chattering.

I had had enough of the thing. I want to hear no more about it. Let them come on. Let them invade Earth. I don't want to get mixed up in it.

I have absolutely no stomach for it.

The Skull

"What is this opportunity?" Conger asked. "Go on. I'm interested."

The room was silent; all faces were fixed on Conger-still in the drab prison uniform. The Speaker leaned forward slowly.

"Before you went to prison your trading business was paying well-all illegal-all very profitable. Now you have nothing, except the prospect of another six years in a cell."

Conger scowled.

"There is a certain situation, very important to this Council, that requires your peculiar abilities. Also, it is a situation you might find interesting. You were a hunter, were you not? You've done a great deal of trapping, hiding in the bushes, waiting at night for the game? I imagine hunting must be a source of satisfaction to you, the chase, the stalking —"

Conger sighed. His lips twisted. "All right," he said. "Leave that out. Get to the point. Who do you want me to kill?"

The Speaker smiled. "All in proper sequence," he said softly.

* * * * *

The car slid to a stop. It was night; there was no light anywhere along the street. Conger looked out. "Where are we? What is this place?"

The hand of the guard pressed into his arm. "Come. Through that door."

Conger stepped down, onto the damp sidewalk. The guard came swiftly after him, and then the Speaker. Conger took a deep breath of the cold air. He studied the dim outline of the building rising up before them.

"I know this place. I've seen it before." He squinted, his eyes growing accustomed to the dark. Suddenly he became alert. "This is —"

"Yes. The First Church." The Speaker walked toward the steps. "We're expected."

"Expected? *Here?*"

"Yes." The Speaker mounted the stairs. "You know we're not allowed in their Churches, especially with guns!" He stopped. Two armed soldiers loomed up ahead, one on each side.

"All right?" The Speaker looked up at them. They nodded. The door of the Church was open. Conger could see other soldiers inside, standing about, young soldiers with large eyes, gazing at the ikons and holy images.

"I see," he said.

"It was necessary," the Speaker said. "As you know, we have been singularly unfortunate in the past in our relations with the First Church."

"This won't help."

"But it's worth it. You will see."

* * * * *

They passed through the hall and into the main chamber where the altar piece was, and the kneeling places. The Speaker scarcely glanced at the altar as they passed by. He pushed open a small side door and beckoned Conger through.

"In here. We have to hurry. The faithful will be flocking in soon."

Conger entered, blinking. They were in a small chamber, low-ceilinged, with dark panels of old wood. There was a smell of ashes and smoldering spices in the room. He sniffed. "What's that? The smell."

"Cups on the wall. I don't know." The Speaker crossed impatiently to the far side. "According to our information, it is hidden here by this —"

Conger looked around the room. He saw books and papers, holy signs and images. A strange low shiver went through him.

"Does my job involve anyone of the Church? If it does —"

The Speaker turned, astonished. "Can it be that you believe in the Founder? Is it possible, a hunter, a killer —"

"No. Of course not. All their business about resignation to death, non-violence —"

"What is it, then?"

Conger shrugged. "I've been taught not to mix with such as these. They have strange abilities. And you can't reason with them."

The Speaker studied Conger thoughtfully. "You have the wrong idea. It is no one here that we have in mind. We've found that killing them only tends to increase their numbers."

"Then why come here? Let's leave."

"No. We came for something important. Something you will need to identify your man. Without it you won't be able to find him." A trace of a smile crossed the Speaker's face. "We don't want you to kill the wrong person. It's too important."

"I don't make mistakes." Conger's chest rose. "Listen, Speaker —"

"This is an unusual situation," the Speaker said. "You see, the person you are after-the person that we are sending you to find-is known only by certain objects here. They are the only traces, the only means of identification. Without them —"

"What are they?"

He came toward the Speaker. The Speaker moved to one side. "Look," he said. He drew a sliding wall away, showing a dark square hole. "In there."

Conger squatted down, staring in. He frowned. "A skull! A skeleton!"

"The man you are after has been dead for two centuries," the Speaker said. "This is all that remains of him. And this is all you have with which to find him."

For a long time Conger said nothing. He stared down at the bones, dimly visible in the recess of the wall. How could a man dead centuries be killed? How could he be stalked, brought down?

Conger was a hunter, a man who had lived as he pleased, where he pleased. He had kept himself alive by trading, bringing furs and pelts in from the Provinces on his own ship, riding at high speed, slipping through the customs line around Earth.

He had hunted in the great mountains of the moon. He had stalked through empty Martian cities. He had explored —

The Speaker said, "Soldier, take these objects and have them carried to the car. Don't lose any part of them."

The soldier went into the cupboard, reaching gingerly, squatting on his heels.

"It is my hope," the Speaker continued softly, to Conger, "that you will demonstrate your loyalty to us, now. There are always ways for citizens to restore themselves, to show their devotion to their society. For you I think this would be a very good chance. I seriously doubt that a better one will come. And for your efforts there will be quite a restitution, of course."

The two men looked at each other; Conger, thin, unkempt, the Speaker immaculate in his uniform.

"I understand you," Conger said. "I mean, I understand this part, about the chance. But how can a man who has been dead two centuries be —"

"I'll explain later," the Speaker said. "Right now we have to hurry!" The soldier had gone out with the bones, wrapped in a blanket held carefully in his arms. The Speaker walked to the door. "Come. They've already discovered that we've broken in here, and they'll be coming at any moment."

They hurried down the damp steps to the waiting car. A second later the driver lifted the car up into the air, above the house-tops.

* * * * *

The Speaker settled back in the seat.

"The First Church has an interesting past," he said. "I suppose you are familiar with it, but I'd like to speak of a few points that are of relevancy to us.

"It was in the twentieth century that the Movement began-during one of the periodic wars. The Movement developed rapidly, feeding on the general sense of futility, the realization that each war was breeding greater war, with no end in sight. The Movement posed a simple answer to the problem: Without military preparations-weapons-there could be no war. And without machinery and complex scientific technocracy there could be no weapons.

"The Movement preached that you couldn't stop war by planning for it. They preached that man was losing to his machinery and science, that it was getting away from him, pushing him into greater and greater wars. Down with society, they shouted. Down with factories and science! A few more wars and there wouldn't be much left of the world.

"The Founder was an obscure person from a small town in the American Middle West. We don't even know his name. All we know is that one day he appeared, preaching a doctrine of non-violence, non-resistance; no fighting, no paying taxes for guns, no research except for medicine. Live out your life quietly, tending your garden, staying out of public affairs; mind your own business. Be obscure, unknown, poor. Give away most of your possessions, leave the city. At least that was what developed from what he told the people."

The car dropped down and landed on a roof.

"The Founder preached this doctrine, or the germ of it; there's no telling how much the faithful have added themselves. The local authorities picked him up at once, of course. Apparently they were convinced that he meant it; he was never released. He was put to death, and his body buried secretly. It seemed that the cult was finished."

The Speaker smiled. "Unfortunately, some of his disciples reported seeing him after the date of his death. The rumor spread; he had conquered death, he was divine. It took hold, grew. And here we are today, with a First Church, obstructing all social progress, destroying society, sowing the seeds of anarchy —"

"But the wars," Conger said. "About them?"

"The wars? Well, there were no more wars. It must be acknowledged that the elimination of war was the direct result of non-violence practiced on a general scale. But we can take a more objective view of war today. What was so terrible about it? War had a profound selective value, perfectly in accord with the teachings of Darwin and Mendel and others. Without war the mass of useless, incompetent mankind, without training or intelligence, is permitted to grow and expand unchecked. War acted to reduce their numbers; like storms and earthquakes and droughts, it was nature's way of eliminating the unfit.

"Without war the lower elements of mankind have increased all out of proportion. They threaten the educated few, those with scientific knowledge and training, the ones equipped to direct society. They have no regard for science or a scientific society, based on reason. And this Movement seeks to aid and abet them. Only when scientists are in full control can the —"

* * * * *

He looked at his watch and then kicked the car door open. "I'll tell you the rest as we walk."

They crossed the dark roof. "Doubtless you now know whom those bones belonged to, who it is that we are after. He has been dead just two centuries, now, this ignorant man from the Middle West, this Founder. The tragedy is that the authorities of the time acted too slowly. They allowed him to speak, to get his message across. He was allowed to preach, to start his cult. And once such a thing is under way, there's no stopping it.

"But what if he had died before he preached? What if none of his doctrines had ever been spoken? It took only a moment for him to utter them, that we know. They say he spoke just once, just one time. *Then* the authorities came, taking him away. He offered no resistance; the incident was small."

The Speaker turned to Conger.

"Small, but we're reaping the consequences of it today."

They went inside the building. Inside, the soldiers had already laid out the skeleton on a table. The soldiers stood around it, their young faces intense.

Conger went over to the table, pushing past them. He bent down, staring at the bones. "So these are his remains," he murmured. "The Founder. The Church has hidden them for two centuries."

"Quite so," the Speaker said. "But now we have them. Come along down the hall."

They went across the room to a door. The Speaker pushed it open. Technicians looked up. Conger saw machinery, whirring and turning; benches and retorts. In the center of the room was a gleaming crystal cage.

The Speaker handed a Slem-gun to Conger. "The important thing to remember is that the skull must be saved and brought back-for comparison and proof. Aim low-at the chest."

Conger weighed the gun in his hands. "It feels good," he said. "I know this gun-that is, I've seen them before, but I never used one."

The Speaker nodded. "You will be instructed on the use of the gun and the operation of the cage. You will be given all data we have on the time and location. The exact spot was a place called Hudson's field. About 1960 in a small community outside Denver, Colorado. And don't forget-the only means of identification you will have will be the skull. There are visible characteristics of the front teeth, especially the left incisor —"

Conger listened absently. He was watching two men in white carefully wrapping the skull in a plastic bag. They tied it and carried it into the crystal cage. "And if I should make a mistake?"

"Pick the wrong man? Then find the right one. Don't come back until you succeed in reaching this Founder. And you can't wait for him to start speaking; that's what we must avoid! You must act in advance. Take chances; shoot as soon as you think you've found him. He'll be someone unusual, probably a stranger in the area. Apparently he wasn't known."

Conger listened dimly.

"Do you think you have it all now?" the Speaker asked.

"Yes. I think so." Conger entered the crystal cage and sat down, placing his hands on the wheel.

"Good luck," the Speaker said.

"We'll be awaiting the outcome. There's some philosophical doubt as to whether one can alter the past. This should answer the question once and for all."

Conger fingered the controls of the cage.

"By the way," the Speaker said. "Don't try to use this cage for purposes not anticipated in your job. We have a constant trace on it. If we want it back, we can get it back. Good luck."

Conger said nothing. The cage was sealed. He raised his finger and touched the wheel control. He turned the wheel carefully.

He was still staring at the plastic bag when the room outside vanished.

For a long time there was nothing at all. Nothing beyond the crystal mesh of the cage. Thoughts rushed through Conger's mind, helter-skelter. How would he know the man? How could he be certain, in advance? What had he looked like? What was his name? How had he acted, before he spoke? Would he be an ordinary person, or some strange outlandish crank?

Conger picked up the Slem-gun and held it against his cheek. The metal of the gun was cool and smooth. He practiced moving the sight. It was a beautiful gun, the kind of gun he could fall in love with. If he had owned such a gun in the Martian desert-on the long nights when he had lain, cramped and numbed with cold, waiting for things that moved through the darkness —

He put the gun down and adjusted the meter readings of the cage. The spiraling mist was beginning to condense and settle. All at once forms wavered and fluttered around him.

Colors, sounds, movements filtered through the crystal wire. He clamped the controls off and stood up.

* * * * *

He was on a ridge overlooking a small town. It was high noon. The air was crisp and bright. A few automobiles moved along a road. Off in the distance were some level fields. Conger went to the door and stepped outside. He sniffed the air. Then he went back into the cage.

He stood before the mirror over the shelf, examining his features. He had trimmed his beard-they had not got him to cut it off-and his hair was neat. He was dressed in the clothing of the middle-twentieth century, the odd collar and coat, the shoes of animal hide. In his pocket was money of the times. That was important. Nothing more was needed.

Nothing, except his ability, his special cunning. But he had never used it in such a way before. He walked down the road toward the town.

The first things he noticed were the newspapers on the stands. April 5, 1961. He was not too far off. He looked around him. There was a filling station, a garage, some taverns, and a ten-cent store. Down the street was a grocery store and some public buildings.

A few minutes later he mounted the stairs of the little public library and passed through the doors into the warm interior.

The librarian looked up, smiling.

"Good afternoon," she said.

He smiled, not speaking because his words would not be correct; accented and strange, probably. He went over to a table and sat down by a heap of magazines. For a moment he glanced through them. Then he was on his feet again. He crossed the room to a wide rack against the wall. His heart began to beat heavily.

Newspapers-weeks on end. He took a roll of them over to the table and began to scan them quickly. The print was odd, the letters strange. Some of the words were unfamiliar.

He set the papers aside and searched farther. At last he found what he wanted. He carried the *Cherrywood Gazette* to the table and opened it to the first page. He found what he wanted:

PRISONER HANGS SELF

An unidentified man, held by the county sheriff's office for suspicion of criminal syndicalism, was found dead this morning, by —

He finished the item. It was vague, uninforming. He needed more. He carried the *Gazette* back to the racks and then, after a moment's hesitation, approached the librarian.

"More?" he asked. "More papers. Old ones?"

She frowned. "How old? Which papers?"

"Months old. And-before."

"Of the *Gazette*? This is all we have. What did you want? What are you looking for? Maybe I can help you."

He was silent.

"You might find older issues at the *Gazette* office," the woman said, taking off her glasses. "Why don't you try there? But if you'd tell me, maybe I could help you —"

He went out.

The *Gazette* office was down a side street; the sidewalk was broken and cracked. He went inside. A heater glowed in the corner of the small office. A heavy-set man stood up and came slowly over to the counter.

"What did you want, mister?" he said.

"Old papers. A month. Or more."

"To buy? You want to buy them?"

"Yes." He held out some of the money he had. The man stared.

"Sure," he said. "Sure. Wait a minute." He went quickly out of the room. When he came back he was staggering under the weight of his armload, his face red. "Here are some," he grunted. "Took what I could find. Covers the whole year. And if you want more —"

Conger carried the papers outside. He sat down by the road and began to go through them.

What he wanted was four months back, in December. It was a tiny item, so small that he almost missed it. His hands trembled as he scanned it, using the small dictionary for some of the archaic terms.

MAN ARRESTED FOR UNLICENSED DEMONSTRATION

An unidentified man who refused to give his name was picked up in Cooper Creek by special agents of the sheriff's office, according to Sheriff Duff. It was said the man was recently noticed in this area and had been watched continually. It was —

Cooper Creek. December, 1960. His heart pounded. That was all he needed to know. He stood up, shaking himself, stamping his feet on the cold ground. The sun had moved across the sky to the very edge of the hills. He smiled. Already he had discovered the exact time and place. Now he needed only to go back, perhaps to November, to Cooper Creek —

He walked back through the main section of town, past the library, past the grocery store. It would not be hard; the hard part was over. He would go there; rent a room, prepare to wait until the man appeared.

He turned the corner. A woman was coming out of a doorway, loaded down with packages. Conger stepped aside to let her pass. The woman glanced at him. Suddenly her face turned white. She stared, her mouth open.

Conger hurried on. He looked back. What was wrong with her? The woman was still staring; she had dropped the packages to the ground. He increased his speed. He turned a second corner and went up a side street. When he looked back again the woman had come to the entrance of the street and was starting after him. A man joined her, and the two of them began to run toward him.

He lost them and left the town, striding quickly, easily, up into the hills at the edge of town. When he reached the cage he stopped. What had happened? Was it something about his clothing? His dress?

He pondered. Then, as the sun set, he stepped into the cage.

Conger sat before the wheel. For a moment he waited, his hands resting lightly on the control. Then he turned the wheel, just a little, following the control readings carefully.

The grayness settled down around him.

But not for very long.

*   *   *   *   *

The man looked him over critically. "You better come inside," he said. "Out of the cold."

"Thanks." Conger went gratefully through the open door, into the living-room. It was warm and close from the heat of the little kerosene heater in the corner. A woman, large and shapeless in her flowered dress, came from the kitchen. She and the man studied him critically.

"It's a good room," the woman said. "I'm Mrs. Appleton. It's got heat. You need that this time of year."

"Yes." He nodded, looking around.

"You want to eat with us?"

"What?"

"You want to eat with us?" The man's brows knitted. "You're not a foreigner, are you, mister?"

"No." He smiled. "I was born in this country. Quite far west, though."

"California?"

"No." He hesitated. "In Oregon."

"What's it like up there?" Mrs. Appleton asked. "I hear there's a lot of trees and green. It's so barren here. I come from Chicago, myself."

"That's the Middle West," the man said to her. "You ain't no foreigner."

"Oregon isn't foreign, either," Conger said. "It's part of the United States."

The man nodded absently. He was staring at Conger's clothing.

"That's a funny suit you got on, mister," he said. "Where'd you get that?"

Conger was lost. He shifted uneasily. "It's a good suit," he said. "Maybe I better go some other place, if you don't want me here."

They both raised their hands protestingly. The woman smiled at him. "We just have to look out for those Reds. You know, the government is always warning us about them."

"The Reds?" He was puzzled.

"The government says they're all around. We're supposed to report anything strange or unusual, anybody doesn't act normal."

"Like me?"

They looked embarrassed. "Well, you don't look like a Red to me," the man said. "But we have to be careful. The *Tribune* says —"

Conger half listened. It was going to be easier than he had thought. Clearly, he would know as soon as the Founder appeared. These people, so suspicious of anything different, would be buzzing and gossiping and spreading the story. All he had to do was lie low and listen, down at the general store, perhaps. Or even here, in Mrs. Appleton's boarding house.

"Can I see the room?" he said.

"Certainly." Mrs. Appleton went to the stairs. "I'll be glad to show it to you."

They went upstairs. It was colder upstairs, but not nearly as cold as outside. Nor as cold as nights on the Martian deserts. For that he was grateful.

* * * * *

He was walking slowly around the store, looking at the cans of vegetables, the frozen packages of fish and meats shining and clean in the open refrigerator counters.

Ed Davies came toward him. "Can I help you?" he said. The man was a little oddly dressed, and with a beard! Ed couldn't help smiling.

"Nothing," the man said in a funny voice. "Just looking."

"Sure," Ed said. He walked back behind the counter. Mrs. Hacket was wheeling her cart up.

"Who's he?" she whispered, her sharp face turned, her nose moving, as if it were sniffing. "I never seen him before."

"I don't know."

"Looks funny to me. Why does he wear a beard? No one else wears a beard. Must be something the matter with him."

"Maybe he likes to wear a beard. I had an uncle who —"

"Wait." Mrs. Hacket stiffened. "Didn't that-what was his name? The Red-that old one. Didn't he have a beard? Marx. He had a beard."

Ed laughed. "This ain't Karl Marx. I saw a photograph of him once."

Mrs. Hacket was staring at him. "You did?"

"Sure." He flushed a little. "What's the matter with that?"

"I'd sure like to know more about him," Mrs. Hacket said. "I think we ought to know more, for our own good."

* * * * *

"Hey, mister! Want a ride?"

Conger turned quickly, dropping his hand to his belt. He relaxed. Two young kids in a car, a girl and a boy. He smiled at them. "A ride? Sure."

Conger got into the car and closed the door. Bill Willet pushed the gas and the car roared down the highway.

"I appreciate a ride," Conger said carefully. "I was taking a walk between towns, but it was farther than I thought."

"Where are you from?" Lora Hunt asked. She was pretty, small and dark, in her yellow sweater and blue skirt.

"From Cooper Creek."

"Cooper Creek?" Bill said. He frowned. "That's funny. I don't remember seeing you before."

"Why, do you come from there?"

"I was born there. I know everybody there."

"I just moved in. From Oregon."

"From Oregon? I didn't know Oregon people had accents."

"Do I have an accent?"

"You use words funny."

"How?"

"I don't know. Doesn't he, Lora?"

"You slur them," Lora said, smiling. "Talk some more. I'm interested in dialects." She glanced at him, white-teethed. Conger felt his heart constrict.

"I have a speech impediment."

"Oh." Her eyes widened. "I'm sorry."

They looked at him curiously as the car purred along. Conger for his part was struggling to find some way of asking them questions without seeming curious. "I guess people from out of town don't come here much," he said. "Strangers."

"No." Bill shook his head. "Not very much."

"I'll bet I'm the first outsider for a long time."

"I guess so."

Conger hesitated. "A friend of mine-someone I know, might be coming through here. Where do you suppose I might —" He stopped. "Would there be anyone certain to see him? Someone I could ask, make sure I don't miss him if he comes?"

They were puzzled. "Just keep your eyes open. Cooper Creek isn't very big."

"No. That's right."

They drove in silence. Conger studied the outline of the girl. Probably she was the boy's mistress. Perhaps she was his trial wife. Or had they developed trial marriage back so far? He could not remember. But surely such an attractive girl would be someone's mistress by this time; she would be sixteen or so, by her looks. He might ask her sometime, if they ever met again.

* * * * *

The next day Conger went walking along the one main street of Cooper Creek. He passed the general store, the two filling stations, and then the post office. At the corner was the soda fountain.

He stopped. Lora was sitting inside, talking to the clerk. She was laughing, rocking back and forth.

Conger pushed the door open. Warm air rushed around him. Lora was drinking hot chocolate, with whipped cream. She looked up in surprise as he slid into the seat beside her.

"I beg your pardon," he said. "Am I intruding?"

"No." She shook her head. Her eyes were large and dark. "Not at all."

The clerk came over. "What do you want?"

Conger looked at the chocolate. "Same as she has."

Lora was watching Conger, her arms folded, elbows on the counter. She smiled at him. "By the way. You don't know my name. Lora Hunt."

She was holding out her hand. He took it awkwardly, not knowing what to do with it. "Conger is my name," he murmured.

"Conger? Is that your last or first name?"

"Last or first?" He hesitated. "Last. Omar Conger."

"Omar?" She laughed. "That's like the poet, Omar Khayyam."

"I don't know of him. I know very little of poets. We restored very few works of art. Usually only the Church has been interested enough —" He broke off. She was staring. He flushed. "Where I come from," he finished.

"The Church? Which church do you mean?"

"The Church." He was confused. The chocolate came and he began to sip it gratefully. Lora was still watching him.

"You're an unusual person," she said. "Bill didn't like you, but he never likes anything different. He's so-so prosaic. Don't you think that when a person gets older he should become-broadened in his outlook?"

Conger nodded.

"He says foreign people ought to stay where they belong, not come here. But you're not so foreign. He means orientals; you know."

Conger nodded.

The screen door opened behind them. Bill came into the room. He stared at them. "Well," he said.

Conger turned. "Hello."

"Well." Bill sat down. "Hello, Lora." He was looking at Conger. "I didn't expect to see you here."

Conger tensed. He could feel the hostility of the boy. "Something wrong with that?"

"No. Nothing wrong with it."

There was silence. Suddenly Bill turned to Lora. "Come on. Let's go."

"Go?" She was astonished. "Why?"

"Just go!" He grabbed her hand. "Come on! The car's outside."

"Why, Bill Willet," Lora said. "You're jealous!"

"Who is this guy?" Bill said. "Do you know anything about him? Look at him, his beard —"

She flared. "So what? Just because he doesn't drive a Packard and go to Cooper High!"

Conger sized the boy up. He was big-big and strong. Probably he was part of some civil control organization.

"Sorry," Conger said. "I'll go."

"What's your business in town?" Bill asked. "What are you doing here? Why are you hanging around Lora?"

Conger looked at the girl. He shrugged. "No reason. I'll see you later."

He turned away. And froze. Bill had moved. Conger's fingers went to his belt. *Half pressure,* he whispered to himself. *No more. Half pressure.*

He squeezed. The room leaped around him. He himself was protected by the lining of his clothing, the plastic sheathing inside.

"My God —" Lora put her hands up. Conger cursed. He hadn't meant any of it for her. But it would wear off. There was only a half-amp to it. It would tingle.

Tingle, and paralyze.

He walked out the door without looking back. He was almost to the corner when Bill came slowly out, holding onto the wall like a drunken man. Conger went on.

* * * * *

As Conger walked, restless, in the night, a form loomed in front of him. He stopped, holding his breath.

"Who is it?" a man's voice came. Conger waited, tense.

"Who is it?" the man said again. He clicked something in his hand. A light flashed. Conger moved.

"It's me," he said.

"Who is 'me'?"

"Conger is my name. I'm staying at the Appleton's place. Who are you?"

The man came slowly up to him. He was wearing a leather jacket. There was a gun at his waist.

"I'm Sheriff Duff. I think you're the person I want to talk to. You were in Bloom's today, about three o'clock?"

"Bloom's?"

"The fountain. Where the kids hang out." Duff came up beside him, shining his light into Conger's face. Conger blinked.

"Turn that thing away," he said.

A pause. "All right." The light flickered to the ground. "You were there. Some trouble broke out between you and the Willet boy. Is that right? You had a beef over his girl —"

"We had a discussion," Conger said carefully.

"Then what happened?"

"Why?"

"I'm just curious. They say you did something."

"Did something? Did what?"

"I don't know. That's what I'm wondering. They saw a flash, and something seemed to happen. They all blacked out. Couldn't move."

"How are they now?"

"All right."

There was silence.

"Well?" Duff said. "What was it? A bomb?"

"A bomb?" Conger laughed. "No. My cigarette lighter caught fire. There was a leak, and the fluid ignited."

"Why did they all pass out?"

"Fumes."

Silence. Conger shifted, waiting. His fingers moved slowly toward his belt. The Sheriff glanced down. He grunted.

"If you say so," he said. "Anyhow, there wasn't any real harm done." He stepped back from Conger. "And that Willet is a trouble-maker."

"Good night, then," Conger said. He started past the Sheriff.

"One more thing, Mr. Conger. Before you go. You don't mind if I look at your identification, do you?"

"No. Not at all." Conger reached into his pocket. He held his wallet out. The Sheriff took it and shined his flashlight on it. Conger watched, breathing shallowly. They had worked hard on the wallet, studying historic documents, relics of the times, all the papers they felt would be relevant.

Duff handed it back. "Okay. Sorry to bother you." The light winked off.

When Conger reached the house he found the Appletons sitting around the television set. They did not look up as he came in. He lingered at the door.

"Can I ask you something?" he said. Mrs. Appleton turned slowly. "Can I ask you-what's the date?"

"The date?" She studied him. "The first of December."

"December first! Why, it was just November!"

They were all looking at him. Suddenly he remembered. In the twentieth century they still used the old twelve-month system. November fed directly into December; there was no Quartember between.

He gasped. Then it was tomorrow! The second of December! Tomorrow!

"Thanks," he said. "Thanks."

122

He went up the stairs. What a fool he was, forgetting. The Founder had been taken into captivity on the second of December, according to the newspaper records. Tomorrow, only twelve hours hence, the Founder would appear to speak to the people and then be dragged away.

* * * * *

The day was warm and bright. Conger's shoes crunched the melting crust of snow. On he went, through the trees heavy with white. He climbed a hill and strode down the other side, sliding as he went.

He stopped to look around. Everything was silent. There was no one in sight. He brought a thin rod from his waist and turned the handle of it. For a moment nothing happened. Then there was a shimmering in the air.

The crystal cage appeared and settled slowly down. Conger sighed. It was good to see it again. After all, it was his only way back.

He walked up on the ridge. He looked around with some satisfaction, his hands on his hips. Hudson's field was spread out, all the way to the beginning of town. It was bare and flat, covered with a thin layer of snow.

Here, the Founder would come. Here, he would speak to them. And here the authorities would take him.

Only he would be dead before they came. He would be dead before he even spoke.

Conger returned to the crystal globe. He pushed through the door and stepped inside. He took the Slem-gun from the shelf and screwed the bolt into place. It was ready to go, ready to fire. For a moment he considered. Should he have it with him?

No. It might be hours before the Founder came, and suppose someone approached him in the meantime? When he saw the Founder coming toward the field, then he could go and get the gun.

Conger looked toward the shelf. There was the neat plastic package. He took it down and unwrapped it.

He held the skull in his hands, turning it over. In spite of himself, a cold feeling rushed through him. This was the man's skull, the skull of the Founder, who was still alive, who would come here, this day, who would stand on the field not fifty yards away.

What if *he* could see this, his own skull, yellow and eroded? Two centuries old. Would he still speak? Would he speak, if he could see it, the grinning, aged skull? What would there be for him to say, to tell the people? What message could he bring?

What action would not be futile, when a man could look upon his own aged, yellowed skull? Better they should enjoy their temporary lives, while they still had them to enjoy.

A man who could hold his own skull in his hands would believe in few causes, few movements. Rather, he would preach the opposite —

A sound. Conger dropped the skull back on the shelf and took up the gun. Outside something was moving. He went quickly to the door, his heart beating. Was it *he*? Was it the Founder, wandering by himself in the cold, looking for a place to speak? Was he meditating over his words, choosing his sentences?

What if he could see what Conger had held!

He pushed the door open, the gun raised.

Lora!

He stared at her. She was dressed in a wool jacket and boots, her hands in her pockets. A cloud of steam came from her mouth and nostrils. Her breast was rising and falling.

Silently, they looked at each other. At last Conger lowered the gun.

"What is it?" he said. "What are you doing here?"

She pointed. She did not seem able to speak. He frowned; what was wrong with her?

"What is it?" he said. "What do you want?" He looked in the direction she had pointed. "I don't see anything."

"They're coming."

"They? Who? Who are coming?"

"They are. The police. During the night the Sheriff had the state police send cars. All around, everywhere. Blocking the roads. There's about sixty of them coming. Some from town, some around behind." She stopped, gasping. "They said-they said —"

"What?"

"They said you were some kind of a Communist. They said —"

* * * * *

Conger went into the cage. He put the gun down on the shelf and came back out. He leaped down and went to the girl.

"Thanks. You came here to tell me? You don't believe it?"

"I don't know."

"Did you come alone?"

"No. Joe brought me in his truck. From town."

"Joe? Who's he?"

"Joe French. The plumber. He's a friend of Dad's."

"Let's go." They crossed the snow, up the ridge and onto the field. The little panel truck was parked half way across the field. A heavy short man was sitting behind the wheel, smoking his pipe. He sat up as he saw the two of them coming toward him.

"Are you the one?" he said to Conger.

"Yes. Thanks for warning me."

The plumber shrugged. "I don't know anything about this. Lora says you're all right." He turned around. "It might interest you to know some more of them are coming. Not to warn you-just curious."

"More of them?" Conger looked toward the town. Black shapes were picking their way across the snow.

"People from the town. You can't keep this sort of thing quiet, not in a small town. We all listen to the police radio; they heard the same way Lora did. Someone tuned in, spread it around —"

The shapes were getting closer. Conger could, make out a couple of them. Bill Willet was there, with some boys from the high school. The Appletons were along, hanging back in the rear.

"Even Ed Davies," Conger murmured.

The storekeeper was toiling onto the field, with three or four other men from the town.

"All curious as hell," French said. "Well, I guess I'm going back to town. I don't want my truck shot full of holes. Come on, Lora."

She was looking up at Conger, wide-eyed.

"Come on," French said again. "Let's go. You sure as hell can't stay here, you know."

"Why?"

"There may be shooting. That's what they all came to see. You know that don't you, Conger?"

"Yes."

"You have a gun? Or don't you care?" French smiled a little. "They've picked up a lot of people in their time, you know. You won't be lonely."

He cared, all right! He had to stay here, on the field. He couldn't afford to let them take him away. Any minute the Founder would appear, would step onto the field. Would he be one of the townsmen, standing silently at the foot of the field, waiting, watching?

Or maybe he was Joe French. Or maybe one of the cops. Anyone of them might find himself moved to speak. And the few words spoken this day were going to be important for a long time.

And Conger had to be there, ready when the first word was uttered!

"I care," he said. "You go on back to town. Take the girl with you."

Lora got stiffly in beside Joe French. The plumber started up the motor. "Look at them, standing there," he said. "Like vultures. Waiting to see someone get killed."

* * * * *

The truck drove away, Lora sitting stiff and silent, frightened now. Conger watched for a moment. Then he dashed back into the woods, between the trees, toward the ridge.

He could get away, of course. Anytime he wanted to he could get away. All he had to do was to leap into the crystal cage and turn the handles. But he had a job, an important job. He had to be here, here at this place, at this time.

He reached the cage and opened the door. He went inside and picked up the gun from the shelf. The Slem-gun would take care of them. He notched it up to full count. The chain reaction from it would flatten them all, the police, the curious, sadistic people —

They wouldn't take him! Before they got him, all of them would be dead. *He* would get away. He would escape. By the end of the day they would all be dead, if that was what they wanted, and he —

He saw the skull.

Suddenly he put the gun down. He picked up the skull. He turned the skull over. He looked at the teeth. Then he went to the mirror.

He held the skull up, looking in the mirror. He pressed the skull against his cheek. Beside his own face the grinning skull leered back at him, beside *his* skull, against his living flesh.

He bared his teeth. And he knew.

It was his own skull that he held. He was the one who would die. He was the Founder.

After a time he put the skull down. For a few minutes he stood at the controls, playing with them idly. He could hear the sound of motors outside, the muffled noise of men. Should he go back to the present, where the Speaker waited? He could escape, of course —

Escape?

He turned toward the skull. There it was, his skull, yellow with age. Escape? Escape, when he had held it in his own hands?

What did it matter if he put it off a month, a year, ten years, even fifty? Time was nothing. He had sipped chocolate with a girl born a hundred and fifty years before his time. Escape? For a little while, perhaps.

But he could not *really* escape, no more so than anyone else had ever escaped, or ever would. Only, he had held it in his hands, his own bones, his own death's-head.

They had not.

He went out the door and across the field, empty handed. There were a lot of them standing around, gathered together, waiting. They expected a good fight; they knew he had something. They had heard about the incident at the fountain.

And there were plenty of police-police with guns and tear gas, creeping across the hills and ridges, between the trees, closer and closer. It was an old story, in this century.

One of the men tossed something at him. It fell in the snow by his feet, and he looked down. It was a rock. He smiled.

"Come on!" one of them called. "Don't you have any bombs?"

"Throw a bomb! You with the beard! Throw a bomb!"

"Let 'em have it!"

"Toss a few A Bombs!"

* * * * *

They began to laugh. He smiled. He put his hands to his hips. They suddenly turned silent, seeing that he was going to speak.

"I'm sorry," he said simply. "I don't have any bombs. You're mistaken."

There was a flurry of murmuring.

"I have a gun," he went on. "A very good one. Made by science even more advanced than your own. But I'm not going to use that, either."

They were puzzled.

"Why not?" someone called. At the edge of the group an older woman was watching. He felt a sudden shock. He had seen her before. Where?

He remembered. The day at the library. As he had turned the corner he had seen her. She had noticed him and been astounded. At the time, he did not understand why.

Conger grinned. So he *would* escape death, the man who right now was voluntarily accepting it. They were laughing, laughing at a man who had a gun but didn't use it. But by a strange twist of science he would appear again, a few months later, after his bones had been buried under the floor of a jail.

And so, in a fashion, he would escape death. He would die, but then, after a period of months, he would live again, briefly, for an afternoon.

An afternoon. Yet long enough for them to see him, to understand that he was still alive. To know that somehow he had returned to life.

And then, finally, he would appear once more, after two hundred years had passed. Two centuries later.

He would be born again, born, as a matter of fact, in a small trading village on Mars. He would grow up, learning to hunt and trade —

A police car came on the edge of the field and stopped. The people retreated a little. Conger raised his hands.

"I have an odd paradox for you," he said. "Those who take lives will lose their own. Those who kill, will die. But he who gives his own life away will live again!"

They laughed, faintly, nervously. The police were coming out, walking toward him. He smiled. He had said everything he intended to say. It was a good little paradox he had coined. They would puzzle over it, remember it.

Smiling, Conger awaited a death foreordained.

Mr. Spaceship

Kramerleaned back. "You can see the situation. How can we deal with a factor like this? The perfect variable."

"Perfect? Prediction should still be possible. A living thing still acts from necessity, the same as inanimate material. But the cause-effect chain is more subtle; there are more factors to be considered. The difference is quantitative, I think. The reaction of the living organism parallels natural causation, but with greater complexity."

Gross and Kramer looked up at the board plates, suspended on the wall, still dripping, the images hardening into place. Kramer traced a line with his pencil.

"See that? It's a pseudopodium. They're alive, and so far, a weapon we can't beat. No mechanical system can compete with that, simple or intricate. We'll have to scrap the Johnson Control and find something else."

"Meanwhile the war continues as it is. Stalemate. Checkmate. They can't get to us, and we can't get through their living minefield."

Kramer nodded. "It's a perfect defense, for them. But there still might be one answer."

"What's that?"

"Wait a minute." Kramer turned to his rocket expert, sitting with the charts and files. "The heavy cruiser that returned this week. It didn't actually touch, did it? It came close but there was no contact."

"Correct." The expert nodded. "The mine was twenty miles off. The cruiser was in space-drive, moving directly toward Proxima, line-straight, using the Johnson Control, of course. It had deflected a quarter of an hour earlier for reasons unknown. Later it resumed its course. That was when they got it."

"It shifted," Kramer said. "But not enough. The mine was coming along after it, trailing it. It's the same old story, but I wonder about the contact."

"Here's our theory," the expert said. "We keep looking for contact, a trigger in the pseudopodium. But more likely we're witnessing a psychological phenomena, a decision without any physical correlative. We're watching for something that isn't there. The mine *decides* to blow up. It sees our ship, approaches, and then decides."

"Thanks." Kramer turned to Gross. "Well, that confirms what I'm saying. How can a ship guided by automatic relays escape a mine that decides to explode? The whole theory of mine penetration is that you must avoid tripping the trigger. But here the trigger is a state of mind in a complicated, developed life-form."

"The belt is fifty thousand miles deep," Gross added. "It solves another problem for them, repair and maintenance. The damn things reproduce, fill up the spaces by spawning into them. I wonder what they feed on?"

"Probably the remains of our first-line. The big cruisers must be a delicacy. It's a game of wits, between a living creature and a ship piloted by automatic relays. The ship always loses." Kramer opened a folder. "I'll tell you what I suggest."

"Go on," Gross said. "I've already heard ten solutions today. What's yours?"

"Mine is very simple. These creatures are superior to any mechanical system, but only because they're alive. Almost any other life-form could compete with them, any higher life-form. If the yuks can put out living mines to protect their planets, we ought to be able to harness some of our own life-forms in a similar way. Let's make use of the same weapon ourselves."

"Which life-form do you propose to use?"

"I think the human brain is the most agile of known living forms. Do you know of any better?"

"But no human being can withstand outspace travel. A human pilot would be dead of heart failure long before the ship got anywhere near Proxima."

"But we don't need the whole body," Kramer said. "We need only the brain."

"What?"

"The problem is to find a person of high intelligence who would contribute, in the same manner that eyes and arms are volunteered."

"But a brain...."

"Technically, it could be done. Brains have been transferred several times, when body destruction made it necessary. Of course, to a spaceship, to a heavy outspace cruiser, instead of an artificial body, that's new."

The room was silent.

"It's quite an idea," Gross said slowly. His heavy square face twisted. "But even supposing it might work, the big question is *whose* brain?"

* * * * *

It was all very confusing, the reasons for the war, the nature of the enemy. The Yucconae had been contacted on one of the outlying planets of Proxima Centauri. At the approach of the Terran ship, a host of dark slim pencils had lifted abruptly and shot off into the distance. The first real encounter came between three of the yuk pencils and a single exploration ship from Terra. No Terrans survived. After that it was all out war, with no holds barred.

Both sides feverishly constructed defense rings around their systems. Of the two, the Yucconae belt was the better. The ring around Proxima was a living ring, superior to anything Terra could throw against it. The standard equipment by which Terran ships were guided in outspace, the Johnson Control, was not adequate. Something more was needed. Automatic relays were not good enough.

—Not good at all, Kramer thought to himself, as he stood looking down the hillside at the work going on below him. A warm wind blew along the hill, rustling the weeds and grass. At the bottom, in the valley, the mechanics had almost finished; the last elements of the reflex system had been removed from the ship and crated up.

All that was needed now was the new core, the new central key that would take the place of the mechanical system. A human brain, the brain of an intelligent, wary human being. But would the human being part with it? That was the problem.

Kramer turned. Two people were approaching him along the road, a man and a woman. The man was Gross, expressionless, heavy-set, walking with dignity. The woman was-He stared in surprise and growing annoyance. It was Dolores, his wife. Since they'd separated he had seen little of her....

"Kramer," Gross said. "Look who I ran into. Come back down with us. We're going into town."

"Hello, Phil," Dolores said. "Well, aren't you glad to see me?"

He nodded. "How have you been? You're looking fine." She was still pretty and slender in her uniform, the blue-grey of Internal Security, Gross' organization.

"Thanks." She smiled. "You seem to be doing all right, too. Commander Gross tells me that you're responsible for this project, Operation Head, as they call it. Whose head have you decided on?"

"That's the problem." Kramer lit a cigarette. "This ship is to be equipped with a human brain instead of the Johnson system. We've constructed special draining baths for the brain, electronic relays to catch the impulses and magnify them, a continual feeding duct that supplies the living cells with everything they need. But —"

"But we still haven't got the brain itself," Gross finished. They began to walk back toward the car. "If we can get that we'll be ready for the tests."

"Will the brain remain alive?" Dolores asked. "Is it actually going to live as part of the ship?"

"It will be alive, but not conscious. Very little life is actually conscious. Animals, trees, insects are quick in their responses, but they aren't conscious. In this process of ours the individual personality, the ego, will cease. We only need the response ability, nothing more."

Dolores shuddered. "How terrible!"

"In time of war everything must be tried," Kramer said absently. "If one life sacrificed will end the war it's worth it. This ship might get through. A couple more like it and there wouldn't be any more war."

* * * * *

They got into the car. As they drove down the road, Gross said, "Have you thought of anyone yet?"

Kramer shook his head. "That's out of my line."

"What do you mean?"

"I'm an engineer. It's not in my department."

"But all this was your idea."

"My work ends there."

Gross was staring at him oddly. Kramer shifted uneasily.

"Then who is supposed to do it?" Gross said. "I can have my organization prepare examinations of various kinds, to determine fitness, that kind of thing —"

"Listen, Phil," Dolores said suddenly.

"What?"

She turned toward him. "I have an idea. Do you remember that professor we had in college. Michael Thomas?"

Kramer nodded.

"I wonder if he's still alive." Dolores frowned. "If he is he must be awfully old."

"Why, Dolores?" Gross asked.

"Perhaps an old person who didn't have much time left, but whose mind was still clear and sharp —"

"Professor Thomas." Kramer rubbed his jaw. "He certainly was a wise old duck. But could he still be alive? He must have been seventy, then."

"We could find that out," Gross said. "I could make a routine check."

"What do you think?" Dolores said. "If any human mind could outwit those creatures —"

"I don't like the idea," Kramer said. In his mind an image had appeared, the image of an old man sitting behind a desk, his bright gentle eyes moving about the classroom. The old man leaning forward, a thin hand raised —

"Keep him out of this," Kramer said.

"What's wrong?" Gross looked at him curiously.

"It's because *I* suggested it," Dolores said.

"No." Kramer shook his head. "It's not that. I didn't expect anything like this, somebody I knew, a man I studied under. I remember him very clearly. He was a very distinct personality."

"Good," Gross said. "He sounds fine."

"We can't do it. We're asking his death!"

"This is war," Gross said, "and war doesn't wait on the needs of the individual. You said that yourself. Surely he'll volunteer; we can keep it on that basis."

"He may already be dead," Dolores murmured.

"We'll find that out," Gross said speeding up the car. They drove the rest of the way in silence.

* * * * *

For a long time the two of them stood studying the small wood house, overgrown with ivy, set back on the lot behind an enormous oak. The little town was silent and sleepy; once in awhile a car moved slowly along the distant highway, but that was all.

"This is the place," Gross said to Kramer. He folded his arms. "Quite a quaint little house."

Kramer said nothing. The two Security Agents behind them were expressionless.

Gross started toward the gate. "Let's go. According to the check he's still alive, but very sick. His mind is agile, however. That seems to be certain. It's said he doesn't leave the house. A woman takes care of his needs. He's very frail."

They went down the stone walk and up onto the porch. Gross rang the bell. They waited. After a time they heard slow footsteps. The door opened. An elderly woman in a shapeless wrapper studied them impassively.

"Security," Gross said, showing his card. "We wish to see Professor Thomas."

"Why?"

"Government business." He glanced at Kramer.

Kramer stepped forward. "I was a pupil of the Professor's," he said. "I'm sure he won't mind seeing us."

The woman hesitated uncertainly. Gross stepped into the doorway. "All right, mother. This is war time. We can't stand out here."

The two Security agents followed him, and Kramer came reluctantly behind, closing the door. Gross stalked down the hall until he came to an open door. He stopped, looking in. Kramer could see the white corner of a bed, a wooden post and the edge of a dresser.

He joined Gross.

In the dark room a withered old man lay, propped up on endless pillows. At first it seemed as if he were asleep; there was no motion or sign of life. But after a time Kramer saw with a faint shock that the old man was watching them intently, his eyes fixed on them, unmoving, unwinking.

"Professor Thomas?" Gross said. "I'm Commander Gross of Security. This man with me is perhaps known to you —"

The faded eyes fixed on Kramer.

"I know him. Philip Kramer.... You've grown heavier, boy." The voice was feeble, the rustle of dry ashes. "Is it true you're married now?"

"Yes. I married Dolores French. You remember her." Kramer came toward the bed. "But we're separated. It didn't work out very well. Our careers —"

"What we came here about, Professor," Gross began, but Kramer cut him off with an impatient wave.

"Let me talk. Can't you and your men get out of here long enough to let me talk to him?"

Gross swallowed. "All right, Kramer." He nodded to the two men. The three of them left the room, going out into the hall and closing the door after them.

The old man in the bed watched Kramer silently. "I don't think much of him," he said at last. "I've seen his type before. What's he want?"

"Nothing. He just came along. Can I sit down?" Kramer found a stiff upright chair beside the bed. "If I'm bothering you —"

"No. I'm glad to see you again, Philip. After so long. I'm sorry your marriage didn't work out."

"How have you been?"

"I've been very ill. I'm afraid that my moment on the world's stage has almost ended." The ancient eyes studied the younger man reflectively. "You look as if you have been doing well. Like everyone else I thought highly of. You've gone to the top in this society."

Kramer smiled. Then he became serious. "Professor, there's a project we're working on that I want to talk to you about. It's the first ray of hope we've had in this whole war. If it works, we may be able to crack the yuk defenses, get some ships into their system. If we can do that the war might be brought to an end."

"Go on. Tell me about it, if you wish."

"It's a long shot, this project. It may not work at all, but we have to give it a try."

"It's obvious that you came here because of it," Professor Thomas murmured. "I'm becoming curious. Go on."

* * * * *

After Kramer finished the old man lay back in the bed without speaking. At last he sighed.

"I understand. A human mind, taken out of a human body." He sat up a little, looking at Kramer. "I suppose you're thinking of me."

Kramer said nothing.

"Before I make my decision I want to see the papers on this, the theory and outline of construction. I'm not sure I like it. —For reasons of my own, I mean. But I want to look at the material. If you'll do that —"

"Certainly." Kramer stood up and went to the door. Gross and the two Security Agents were standing outside, waiting tensely. "Gross, come inside."

They filed into the room.

"Give the Professor the papers," Kramer said. "He wants to study them before deciding."

Gross brought the file out of his coat pocket, a manila envelope. He handed it to the old man on the bed. "Here it is, Professor. You're welcome to examine it. Will you give us your answer as soon as possible? We're very anxious to begin, of course."

"I'll give you my answer when I've decided." He took the envelope with a thin, trembling hand. "My decision depends on what I find out from these papers. If I don't like what I find, then I will not become involved with this work in any shape or form." He opened the envelope with shaking hands. "I'm looking for one thing."

"What is it?" Gross said.

"That's my affair. Leave me a number by which I can reach you when I've decided."

Silently, Gross put his card down on the dresser. As they went out Professor Thomas was already reading the first of the papers, the outline of the theory.

* * * * *

Kramer sat across from Dale Winter, his second in line. "What then?" Winter said.

"He's going to contact us." Kramer scratched with a drawing pen on some paper. "I don't know what to think."

"What do you mean?" Winter's good-natured face was puzzled.

"Look." Kramer stood up, pacing back and forth, his hands in his uniform pockets. "He was my teacher in college. I respected him as a man, as well as a teacher. He was more than a voice, a talking book. He was a person, a calm, kindly person I could look up to. I always wanted to be like him, someday. Now look at me."

"So?"

"Look at what I'm asking. I'm asking for his life, as if he were some kind of laboratory animal kept around in a cage, not a man, a teacher at all."

"Do you think he'll do it?"

"I don't know." Kramer went to the window. He stood looking out. "In a way, I hope not."

"But if he doesn't —"

"Then we'll have to find somebody else. I know. There would be somebody else. Why did Dolores have to —"

The vidphone rang. Kramer pressed the button.

"This is Gross." The heavy features formed. "The old man called me. Professor Thomas."

"What did he say?" He knew; he could tell already, by the sound of Gross' voice.

"He said he'd do it. I was a little surprised myself, but apparently he means it. We've already made arrangements for his admission to the hospital. His lawyer is drawing up the statement of liability."

Kramer only half heard. He nodded wearily. "All right. I'm glad. I suppose we can go ahead, then."

"You don't sound very glad."

"I wonder why he decided to go ahead with it."

"He was very certain about it." Gross sounded pleased. "He called me quite early. I was still in bed. You know, this calls for a celebration."

"Sure," Kramer said. "It sure does."

* * * * *

Toward the middle of August the project neared completion. They stood outside in the hot autumn heat, looking up at the sleek metal sides of the ship.

Gross thumped the metal with his hand. "Well, it won't be long. We can begin the test any time."

"Tell us more about this," an officer in gold braid said. "It's such an unusual concept."

"Is there really a human brain inside the ship?" a dignitary asked, a small man in a rumpled suit. "And the brain is actually alive?"

"Gentlemen, this ship is guided by a living brain instead of the usual Johnson relay-control system. But the brain is not conscious. It will function by reflex only. The practical difference between it and the Johnson system is this: a human brain is far more intricate than any man-made structure, and its ability to adapt itself to a situation, to respond to danger, is far beyond anything that could be artificially built."

Gross paused, cocking his ear. The turbines of the ship were beginning to rumble, shaking the ground under them with a deep vibration. Kramer was standing a short distance away from the others, his arms folded, watching silently. At the sound of the turbines he walked quickly around the ship to the other side. A few workmen were clearing away the last of the waste, the scraps of wiring and scaffolding. They glanced up at him and went on hurriedly with their work. Kramer mounted the ramp and entered the control cabin of the ship. Winter was sitting at the controls with a Pilot from Space-transport.

"How's it look?" Kramer asked.

"All right." Winter got up. "He tells me that it would be best to take off manually. The robot controls —" Winter hesitated. "I mean, the built-in controls, can take over later on in space."

"That's right," the Pilot said. "It's customary with the Johnson system, and so in this case we should —"

"Can you tell anything yet?" Kramer asked.

"No," the Pilot said slowly. "I don't think so. I've been going over everything. It seems to be in good order. There's only one thing I wanted to ask you about." He put his hand on the control board. "There are some changes here I don't understand."

"Changes?"

"Alterations from the original design. I wonder what the purpose is."

Kramer took a set of the plans from his coat. "Let me look." He turned the pages over. The Pilot watched carefully over his shoulder.

"The changes aren't indicated on your copy," the Pilot said. "I wonder —" He stopped. Commander Gross had entered the control cabin.

"Gross, who authorized alterations?" Kramer said. "Some of the wiring has been changed."

"Why, your old friend." Gross signaled to the field tower through the window.

"My old friend?"

"The Professor. He took quite an active interest." Gross turned to the Pilot. "Let's get going. We have to take this out past gravity for the test they tell me. Well, perhaps it's for the best. Are you ready?"

"Sure." The Pilot sat down and moved some of the controls around. "Anytime."

"Go ahead, then," Gross said.

"The Professor —" Kramer began, but at that moment there was a tremendous roar and the ship leaped under him. He grasped one of the wall holds and hung on as best he could. The cabin was filling with a steady throbbing, the raging of the jet turbines underneath them.

The ship leaped. Kramer closed his eyes and held his breath. They were moving out into space, gaining speed each moment.

* * * * *

"Well, what do you think?" Winter said nervously. "Is it time yet?"

"A little longer," Kramer said. He was sitting on the floor of the cabin, down by the control wiring. He had removed the metal covering-plate, exposing the complicated maze of relay wiring. He was studying it, comparing it to the wiring diagrams.

"What's the matter?" Gross said.

"These changes. I can't figure out what they're for. The only pattern I can make out is that for some reason —"

"Let me look," the Pilot said. He squatted down beside Kramer. "You were saying?"

"See this lead here? Originally it was switch controlled. It closed and opened automatically, according to temperature change. Now it's wired so that the central control system operates it. The same with the others. A lot of this was still mechanical, worked by pressure, temperature, stress. Now it's under the central master."

"The brain?" Gross said. "You mean it's been altered so that the brain manipulates it?"

Kramer nodded. "Maybe Professor Thomas felt that no mechanical relays could be trusted. Maybe he thought that things would be happening too fast. But some of these could close in a split second. The brake rockets could go on as quickly as —"

"Hey," Winter said from the control seat. "We're getting near the moon stations. What'll I do?"

They looked out the port. The corroded surface of the moon gleamed up at them, a corrupt and sickening sight. They were moving swiftly toward it.

"I'll take it," the Pilot said. He eased Winter out of the way and strapped himself in place. The ship began to move away from the moon as he manipulated the controls. Down below them they could see the observation stations dotting the surface, and the tiny squares that were the openings of the underground factories and hangars. A red blinker winked up at them and the Pilot's fingers moved on the board in answer.

"We're past the moon," the Pilot said, after a time. The moon had fallen behind them; the ship was heading into outer space. "Well, we can go ahead with it."

Kramer did not answer.

"Mr. Kramer, we can go ahead any time."

Kramer started. "Sorry. I was thinking. All right, thanks." He frowned, deep in thought.

"What is it?" Gross asked.

"The wiring changes. Did you understand the reason for them when you gave the okay to the workmen?"

Gross flushed. "You know I know nothing about technical material. I'm in Security."

"Then you should have consulted me."

"What does it matter?" Gross grinned wryly. "We're going to have to start putting our faith in the old man sooner or later."

The Pilot stepped back from the board. His face was pale and set. "Well, it's done," he said. "That's it."

"What's done?" Kramer said.

"We're on automatic. The brain. I turned the board over to it-to him, I mean. The Old Man." The Pilot lit a cigarette and puffed nervously. "Let's keep our fingers crossed."

* * * * *

The ship was coasting evenly, in the hands of its invisible pilot. Far down inside the ship, carefully armoured and protected, a soft human brain lay in a tank of liquid, a thousand minute electric charges playing over its surface. As the charges rose they were picked up and amplified, fed into relay systems, advanced, carried on through the entire ship —

Gross wiped his forehead nervously. "So *he* is running it, now. I hope he knows what he's doing."

Kramer nodded enigmatically. "I think he does."

"What do you mean?"

"Nothing." Kramer walked to the port. "I see we're still moving in a straight line." He picked up the microphone. "We can instruct the brain orally, through this." He blew against the microphone experimentally.

"Go on," Winter said.

"Bring the ship around half-right," Kramer said. "Decrease speed."

They waited. Time passed. Gross looked at Kramer. "No change. Nothing."

"Wait."

Slowly, the ship was beginning to turn. The turbines missed, reducing their steady beat. The ship was taking up its new course, adjusting itself. Nearby some space debris rushed past, incinerating in the blasts of the turbine jets.

"So far so good," Gross said.

They began to breathe more easily. The invisible pilot had taken control smoothly, calmly. The ship was in good hands. Kramer spoke a few more words into the microphone, and they swung again. Now they were moving back the way they had come, toward the moon.

"Let's see what he does when we enter the moon's pull," Kramer said. "He was a good mathematician, the old man. He could handle any kind of problem."

The ship veered, turning away from the moon. The great eaten-away globe fell behind them. Gross breathed a sigh of relief. "That's that."

"One more thing." Kramer picked up the microphone. "Return to the moon and land the ship at the first space field," he said into it.

"Good Lord," Winter murmured. "Why are you —"

"Be quiet." Kramer stood, listening. The turbines gasped and roared as the ship swung full around, gaining speed. They were moving back, back toward the moon again. The ship dipped down, heading toward the great globe below.

"We're going a little fast," the Pilot said. "I don't see how he can put down at this velocity."

* * * * *

The port filled up, as the globe swelled rapidly. The Pilot hurried toward the board, reaching for the controls. All at once the ship jerked. The nose lifted and the ship shot out into space, away from the moon, turning at an oblique angle. The men were thrown to the floor by the sudden change in course. They got to their feet again, speechless, staring at each other.

The Pilot gazed down at the board. "It wasn't me! I didn't touch a thing. I didn't even get to it."

The ship was gaining speed each moment. Kramer hesitated. "Maybe you better switch it back to manual."

The Pilot closed the switch. He took hold of the steering controls and moved them experimentally. "Nothing." He turned around. "Nothing. It doesn't respond."

134

No one spoke.

"You can see what has happened," Kramer said calmly. "The old man won't let go of it, now that he has it. I was afraid of this when I saw the wiring changes. Everything in this ship is centrally controlled, even the cooling system, the hatches, the garbage release. We're helpless."

"Nonsense." Gross strode to the board. He took hold of the wheel and turned it. The ship continued on its course, moving away from the moon, leaving it behind.

"Release!" Kramer said into the microphone. "Let go of the controls! We'll take it back. Release."

"No good," the Pilot said. "Nothing." He spun the useless wheel. "It's dead, completely dead."

"And we're still heading out," Winter said, grinning foolishly. "We'll be going through the first-line defense belt in a few minutes. If they don't shoot us down —"

"We better radio back." The Pilot clicked the radio to *send*. "I'll contact the main bases, one of the observation stations."

"Better get the defense belt, at the speed we're going. We'll be into it in a minute."

"And after that," Kramer said, "we'll be in outer space. He's moving us toward outspace velocity. Is this ship equipped with baths?"

"Baths?" Gross said.

"The sleep tanks. For space-drive. We may need them if we go much faster."

"But good God, where are we going?" Gross said. "Where-where's he taking us?"

* * * * *

The Pilot obtained contact. "This is Dwight, on ship," he said. "We're entering the defense zone at high velocity. Don't fire on us."

"Turn back," the impersonal voice came through the speaker. "You're not allowed in the defense zone."

"We can't. We've lost control."

"Lost control?"

"This is an experimental ship."

Gross took the radio. "This is Commander Gross, Security. We're being carried into outer space. There's nothing we can do. Is there any way that we can be removed from this ship?"

A hesitation. "We have some fast pursuit ships that could pick you up if you wanted to jump. The chances are good they'd find you. Do you have space flares?"

"We do," the Pilot said. "Let's try it."

"Abandon ship?" Kramer said. "If we leave now we'll never see it again."

"What else can we do? We're gaining speed all the time. Do you propose that we stay here?"

"No." Kramer shook his head. "Damn it, there ought to be a better solution."

"Could you contact *him*?" Winter asked. "The Old Man? Try to reason with him?"

"It's worth a chance," Gross said. "Try it."

"All right." Kramer took the microphone. He paused a moment. "Listen! Can you hear me? This is Phil Kramer. Can you hear me, Professor. Can you hear me? I want you to release the controls."

There was silence.

"This is Kramer, Professor. Can you hear me? Do you remember who I am? Do you understand who this is?"

Above the control panel the wall speaker made a sound, a sputtering static. They looked up.

"Can you hear me, Professor. This is Philip Kramer. I want you to give the ship back to us. If you can hear me, release the controls! Let go, Professor. Let go!"

Static. A rushing sound, like the wind. They gazed at each other. There was silence for a moment.

"It's a waste of time," Gross said.

"No-listen!"

The sputter came again. Then, mixed with the sputter, almost lost in it, a voice came, toneless, without inflection, a mechanical, lifeless voice from the metal speaker in the wall, above their heads.

"...Is it you, Philip? I can't make you out. Darkness.... Who's there? With you...."

"It's me, Kramer." His fingers tightened against the microphone handle. "You must release the controls, Professor. We have to get back to Terra. You must."

Silence. Then the faint, faltering voice came again, a little stronger than before. "Kramer. Everything so strange. I was right, though. Consciousness result of thinking. Necessary result. Cognito ergo sum. Retain conceptual ability. Can you hear me?"

"Yes, Professor —"

"I altered the wiring. Control. I was fairly certain.... I wonder if I can do it. Try...."

Suddenly the air-conditioning snapped into operation. It snapped abruptly off again. Down the corridor a door slammed. Something thudded. The men stood listening. Sounds came from all sides of them, switches shutting, opening. The lights blinked off; they were in darkness. The lights came back on, and at the same time the heating coils dimmed and faded.

"Good God!" Winter said.

Water poured down on them, the emergency fire-fighting system. There was a screaming rush of air. One of the escape hatches had slid back, and the air was roaring frantically out into space.

The hatch banged closed. The ship subsided into silence. The heating coils glowed into life. As suddenly as it had begun the weird exhibition ceased.

"I can do-everything," the dry, toneless voice came from the wall speaker. "It is all controlled. Kramer, I wish to talk to you. I've been-been thinking. I haven't seen you in many years. A lot to discuss. You've changed, boy. We have much to discuss. Your wife —"

The Pilot grabbed Kramer's arm. "There's a ship standing off our bow. Look."

* * * * *

They ran to the port. A slender pale craft was moving along with them, keeping pace with them. It was signal-blinking.

"A Terran pursuit ship," the Pilot said. "Let's jump. They'll pick us up. Suits —"

He ran to a supply cupboard and turned the handle. The door opened and he pulled the suits out onto the floor.

"Hurry," Gross said. A panic seized them. They dressed frantically, pulling the heavy garments over them. Winter staggered to the escape hatch and stood by it, waiting for the others. They joined him, one by one.

"Let's go!" Gross said. "Open the hatch."

Winter tugged at the hatch. "Help me."

They grabbed hold, tugging together. Nothing happened. The hatch refused to budge.

"Get a crowbar," the Pilot said.

"Hasn't anyone got a blaster?" Gross looked frantically around. "Damn it, blast it open!"

"Pull," Kramer grated. "Pull together."

"Are you at the hatch?" the toneless voice came, drifting and eddying through the corridors of the ship. They looked up, staring around them. "I sense something nearby, outside. A ship? You are leaving, all of you? Kramer, you are leaving, too? Very unfortunate. I had hoped we could talk. Perhaps at some other time you might be induced to remain."

"Open the hatch!" Kramer said, staring up at the impersonal walls of the ship. "For God's sake, open it!"

There was silence, an endless pause. Then, very slowly, the hatch slid back. The air screamed out, rushing past them into space.

One by one they leaped, one after the other, propelled away by the repulsive material of the suits. A few minutes later they were being hauled aboard the pursuit ship. As the last one of them was lifted through the port, their own ship pointed itself suddenly upward and shot off at tremendous speed. It disappeared.

Kramer removed his helmet, gasping. Two sailors held onto him and began to wrap him in blankets. Gross sipped a mug of coffee, shivering.

"It's gone," Kramer murmured.

"I'll have an alarm sent out," Gross said.

"What's happened to your ship?" a sailor asked curiously. "It sure took off in a hurry. Who's on it?"

"We'll have to have it destroyed," Gross went on, his face grim. "It's got to be destroyed. There's no telling what it-what *he* has in mind." Gross sat down weakly on a metal bench. "What a close call for us. We were so damn trusting."

"What could he be planning," Kramer said, half to himself. "It doesn't make sense. I don't get it."

* * * * *

As the ship sped back toward the moon base they sat around the table in the dining room, sipping hot coffee and thinking, not saying very much.

"Look here," Gross said at last. "What kind of man was Professor Thomas? What do you remember about him?"

Kramer put his coffee mug down. "It was ten years ago. I don't remember much. It's vague."

He let his mind run back over the years. He and Dolores had been at Hunt College together, in physics and the life sciences. The College was small and set back away from the momentum of modern life. He had gone there because it was his home town, and his father had gone there before him.

Professor Thomas had been at the College a long time, as long as anyone could remember. He was a strange old man, keeping to himself most of the time. There were many things that he disapproved of, but he seldom said what they were.

"Do you recall anything that might help us?" Gross asked. "Anything that would give us a clue as to what he might have in mind?"

Kramer nodded slowly. "I remember one thing...."

One day he and the Professor had been sitting together in the school chapel, talking leisurely.

"Well, you'll be out of school, soon," the Professor had said. "What are you going to do?"

"Do? Work at one of the Government Research Projects, I suppose."

"And eventually? What's your ultimate goal?"

Kramer had smiled. "The question is unscientific. It presupposes such things as ultimate ends."

"Suppose instead along these lines, then: What if there were no war and no Government Research Projects? What would you do, then?"

"I don't know. But how can I imagine a hypothetical situation like that? There's been war as long as I can remember. We're geared for war. I don't know what I'd do. I suppose I'd adjust, get used to it."

The Professor had stared at him. "Oh, you do think you'd get accustomed to it, eh? Well, I'm glad of that. And you think you could find something to do?"

Gross listened intently. "What do you infer from this, Kramer?"

"Not much. Except that he was against war."

"We're all against war," Gross pointed out.

"True. But he was withdrawn, set apart. He lived very simply, cooking his own meals. His wife died many years ago. He was born in Europe, in Italy. He changed his name when he came to the United States. He used to read Dante and Milton. He even had a Bible."

"Very anachronistic, don't you think?"

"Yes, he lived quite a lot in the past. He found an old phonograph and records, and he listened to the old music. You saw his house, how old-fashioned it was."

"Did he have a file?" Winter asked Gross.

"With Security? No, none at all. As far as we could tell he never engaged in political work, never joined anything or even seemed to have strong political convictions."

"No," Kramer, agreed. "About all he ever did was walk through the hills. He liked nature."

"Nature can be of great use to a scientist," Gross said. "There wouldn't be any science without it."

"Kramer, what do you think his plan is, taking control of the ship and disappearing?" Winter said.

"Maybe the transfer made him insane," the Pilot said. "Maybe there's no plan, nothing rational at all."

"But he had the ship rewired, and he had made sure that he would retain consciousness and memory before he even agreed to the operation. He must have had something planned from the start. But what?"

"Perhaps he just wanted to stay alive longer," Kramer said. "He was old and about to die. Or —"

"Or what?"

"Nothing." Kramer stood up. "I think as soon as we get to the moon base I'll make a vidcall to earth. I want to talk to somebody about this."

"Who's that?" Gross asked.

"Dolores. Maybe she remembers something."

"That's a good idea," Gross said.

* * * * *

"Where are you calling from?" Dolores asked, when he succeeded in reaching her.

"From the moon base."

"All kinds of rumors are running around. Why didn't the ship come back? What happened?"

"I'm afraid he ran off with it."

"He?"

"The Old Man. Professor Thomas." Kramer explained what had happened.

Dolores listened intently. "How strange. And you think he planned it all in advance, from the start?"

"I'm certain. He asked for the plans of construction and the theoretical diagrams at once."

"But why? What for?"

"I don't know. Look, Dolores. What do you remember about him? Is there anything that might give a clue to all this?"

"Like what?"

"I don't know. That's the trouble."

On the vidscreen Dolores knitted her brow. "I remember he raised chickens in his back yard, and once he had a goat." She smiled. "Do you remember the day the goat got loose and wandered down the main street of town? Nobody could figure out where it came from."

"Anything else?"

"No." He watched her struggling, trying to remember. "He wanted to have a farm, sometime, I know."

"All right. Thanks." Kramer touched the switch. "When I get back to Terra maybe I'll stop and see you."

"Let me know how it works out."

He cut the line and the picture dimmed and faded. He walked slowly back to where Gross and some officers of the Military were sitting at a chart table, talking.

"Any luck?" Gross said, looking up.

"No. All she remembers is that he kept a goat."

"Come over and look at this detail chart." Gross motioned him around to his side. "Watch!"

Kramer saw the record tabs moving furiously, the little white dots racing back and forth.

"What's happening?" he asked.

"A squadron outside the defense zone has finally managed to contact the ship. They're maneuvering now, for position. Watch."

The white counters were forming a barrel formation around a black dot that was moving steadily across the board, away from the central position. As they watched, the white dots constricted around it.

"They're ready to open fire," a technician at the board said. "Commander, what shall we tell them to do?"

Gross hesitated. "I hate to be the one who makes the decision. When it comes right down to it —"

"It's not just a ship," Kramer said. "It's a man, a living person. A human being is up there, moving through space. I wish we knew what —"

"But the order has to be given. We can't take any chances. Suppose he went over to them, to the yuks."

Kramer's jaw dropped. "My God, he wouldn't do that."

"Are you sure? Do you know what he'll do?"

"He wouldn't do that."

Gross turned to the technician. "Tell them to go ahead."

"I'm sorry, sir, but now the ship has gotten away. Look down at the board."

* * * * *

Gross stared down, Kramer over his shoulder. The black dot had slipped through the white dots and had moved off at an abrupt angle. The white dots were broken up, dispersing in confusion.

"He's an unusual strategist," one of the officers said. He traced the line. "It's an ancient maneuver, an old Prussian device, but it worked."

The white dots were turning back. "Too many yuk ships out that far," Gross said. "Well, that's what you get when you don't act quickly." He looked up coldly at Kramer. "We should have done it when we had him. Look at him go!" He jabbed a finger at the rapidly moving black dot. The dot came to the edge of the board and stopped. It had reached the limit of the chartered area. "See?"

—Now what? Kramer thought, watching. So the Old Man had escaped the cruisers and gotten away. He was alert, all right; there was nothing wrong with his mind. Or with his ability to control his new body.

Body-The ship was a new body for him. He had traded in the old dying body, withered and frail, for this hulking frame of metal and plastic, turbines and rocket jets. He was strong, now. Strong and big. The new body was more powerful than a thousand human bodies. But how long would it last him? The average life of a cruiser was only ten years. With careful handling he might get twenty out of it, before some essential part failed and there was no way to replace it.

And then, what then? What would he do, when something failed and there was no one to fix it for him? That would be the end. Someplace, far out in the cold darkness of space, the ship would slow down, silent and lifeless, to exhaust its last heat into the eternal timelessness of outer space. Or perhaps it would crash on some barren asteroid, burst into a million fragments.

It was only a question of time.

"Your wife didn't remember anything?" Gross said.

"I told you. Only that he kept a goat, once."

"A hell of a lot of help that is."

Kramer shrugged. "It's not my fault."

"I wonder if we'll ever see him again." Gross stared down at the indicator dot, still hanging at the edge of the board. "I wonder if he'll ever move back this way."

"I wonder, too," Kramer said.

* * * * *

That night Kramer lay in bed, tossing from side to side, unable to sleep. The moon gravity, even artificially increased, was unfamiliar to him and it made him uncomfortable. A thousand thoughts wandered loose in his head as he lay, fully awake.

What did it all mean? What was the Professor's plan? Maybe they would never know. Maybe the ship was gone for good; the Old Man had left forever, shooting into outer space. They might never find out why he had done it, what purpose-if any-had been in his mind.

Kramer sat up in bed. He turned on the light and lit a cigarette. His quarters were small, a metal-lined bunk room, part of the moon station base.

The Old Man had wanted to talk to him. He had wanted to discuss things, hold a conversation, but in the hysteria and confusion all they had been able to think of was getting away. The ship was rushing off with them, carrying them into outer space. Kramer set his jaw. Could they be blamed for jumping? They had no idea where they were being taken, or why. They were helpless, caught in their own ship, and the pursuit ship standing by waiting to pick them up was their only chance. Another half hour and it would have been too late.

But what had the Old Man wanted to say? What had he intended to tell him, in those first confusing moments when the ship around them had come alive, each metal strut and wire suddenly animate, the body of a living creature, a vast metal organism?

It was weird, unnerving. He could not forget it, even now. He looked around the small room uneasily. What did it signify, the coming to life of metal and plastic? All at once they had found themselves inside a *living* creature, in its stomach, like Jonah inside the whale.

It had been alive, and it had talked to them, talked calmly and rationally, as it rushed them off, faster and faster into outer space. The wall speaker and circuit had become the vocal cords and mouth, the wiring the spinal cord and nerves, the hatches and relays and circuit breakers the muscles.

They had been helpless, completely helpless. The ship had, in a brief second, stolen their power away from them and left them defenseless, practically at its mercy. It was not right; it made him uneasy. All his life he had controlled machines, bent nature and the forces of nature to man and man's needs. The human race had slowly evolved until it was in a position to operate things, run them as it saw fit. Now all at once it had been plunged back down the ladder again, prostrate before a Power against which they were children.

Kramer got out of bed. He put on his bathrobe and began to search for a cigarette. While he was searching, the vidphone rang.

He snapped the vidphone on.

"Yes?"

The face of the immediate monitor appeared. "A call from Terra, Mr. Kramer. An emergency call."

"Emergency call? For me? Put it through." Kramer came awake, brushing his hair back out of his eyes. Alarm plucked at him.

From the speaker a strange voice came. "Philip Kramer? Is this Kramer?"

"Yes. Go on."

"This is General Hospital, New York City, Terra. Mr. Kramer, your wife is here. She has been critically injured in an accident. Your name was given to us to call. Is it possible for you to —"

"How badly?" Kramer gripped the vidphone stand. "Is it serious?"

"Yes, it's serious, Mr Kramer. Are you able to come here? The quicker you can come the better."

"Yes." Kramer nodded. "I'll come. Thanks."

* * * * *

The screen died as the connection was broken. Kramer waited a moment. Then he tapped the button. The screen relit again. "Yes, sir," the monitor said.

"Can I get a ship to Terra at once? It's an emergency. My wife —"

"There's no ship leaving the moon for eight hours. You'll have to wait until the next period."

"Isn't there anything I can do?"

"We can broadcast a general request to all ships passing through this area. Sometimes cruisers pass by here returning to Terra for repairs."

"Will you broadcast that for me? I'll come down to the field."

"Yes sir. But there may be no ship in the area for awhile. It's a gamble." The screen died.

Kramer dressed quickly. He put on his coat and hurried to the lift. A moment later he was running across the general receiving lobby, past the rows of vacant desks and conference tables. At the door the sentries stepped aside and he went outside, onto the great concrete steps.

The face of the moon was in shadow. Below him the field stretched out in total darkness, a black void, endless, without form. He made his way carefully down the steps and along the ramp along the side of the field, to the control tower. A faint row of red lights showed him the way.

Two soldiers challenged him at the foot of the tower, standing in the shadows, their guns ready.

"Kramer?"

"Yes." A light was flashed in his face.

"Your call has been sent out already."

"Any luck?" Kramer asked.

"There's a cruiser nearby that has made contact with us. It has an injured jet and is moving slowly back toward Terra, away from the line."

"Good." Kramer nodded, a flood of relief rushing through him. He lit a cigarette and gave one to each of the soldiers. The soldiers lit up.

"Sir," one of them asked, "is it true about the experimental ship?"

"What do you mean?"

"It came to life and ran off?"

"No, not exactly," Kramer said. "It had a new type of control system instead of the Johnson units. It wasn't properly tested."

"But sir, one of the cruisers that was there got up close to it, and a buddy of mine says this ship acted funny. He never saw anything like it. It was like when he was fishing once on Terra, in Washington State, fishing for bass. The fish were smart, going this way and that —"

"Here's your cruiser," the other soldier said. "Look!"

An enormous vague shape was setting slowly down onto the field. They could make nothing out but its row of tiny green blinkers. Kramer stared at the shape.

"Better hurry, sir," the soldiers said. "They don't stick around here very long."

"Thanks." Kramer loped across the field, toward the black shape that rose up above him, extended across the width of the field. The ramp was down from the side of the cruiser and he caught hold of it. The ramp rose, and a moment later Kramer was inside the hold of the ship. The hatch slid shut behind him.

As he made his way up the stairs to the main deck the turbines roared up from the moon, out into space.

Kramer opened the door to the main deck. He stopped suddenly, staring around him in surprise. There was nobody in sight. The ship was deserted.

"Good God," he said. Realization swept over him, numbing him. He sat down on a bench, his head swimming. "Good God."

The ship roared out into space leaving the moon and Terra farther behind each moment.

And there was nothing he could do.

* * * * *

"So it was you who put the call through," he said at last. "It was you who called me on the vidphone, not any hospital on Terra. It was all part of the plan." He looked up and around him. "And Dolores is really—"

"Your wife is fine," the wall speaker above him said tonelessly. "It was a fraud. I am sorry to trick you that way, Philip, but it was all I could think of. Another day and you would have been back on Terra. I don't want to remain in this area any longer than necessary. They have been so certain of finding me out in deep space that I have been able to stay here without too much danger. But even the purloined letter was found eventually."

Kramer smoked his cigarette nervously. "What are you going to do? Where are we going?"

"First, I want to talk to you. I have many things to discuss. I was very disappointed when you left me, along with the others. I had hoped that you would remain." The dry voice chuckled. "Remember how we used to talk in the old days, you and I? That was a long time ago."

The ship was gaining speed. It plunged through space at tremendous speed, rushing through the last of the defense zone and out beyond. A rush of nausea made Kramer bend over for a moment.

When he straightened up the voice from the wall went on, "I'm sorry to step it up so quickly, but we are still in danger. Another few moments and we'll be free."

"How about yuk ships? Aren't they out here?"

"I've already slipped away from several of them. They're quite curious about me."

"Curious?"

"They sense that I'm different, more like their own organic mines. They don't like it. I believe they will begin to withdraw from this area, soon. Apparently they don't want to get involved with me. They're an odd race, Philip. I would have liked to study them closely, try to learn something about them. I'm of the opinion that they use no inert material. All their equipment and instruments are alive, in some form or other. They don't construct or build at all. The idea of *making* is foreign to them. They utilize existing forms. Even their ships —"

"Where are we going?" Kramer said. "I want to know where you are taking me."

"Frankly, I'm not certain."

"You're not certain?"

"I haven't worked some details out. There are a few vague spots in my program, still. But I think that in a short while I'll have them ironed out."

"What is your program?" Kramer said.

"It's really very simple. But don't you want to come into the control room and sit? The seats are much more comfortable than that metal bench."

Kramer went into the control room and sat down at the control board. Looking at the useless apparatus made him feel strange.

"What's the matter?" the speaker above the board rasped.

* * * * *

Kramer gestured helplessly. "I'm —powerless. I can't do anything. And I don't like it. Do you blame me?"

"No. No, I don't blame you. But you'll get your control back, soon. Don't worry. This is only a temporary expedient, taking you off this way. It was something I didn't contemplate. I forgot that orders would be given out to shoot me on sight."

"It was Gross' idea."

"I don't doubt that. My conception, my plan, came to me as soon as you began to describe your project, that day at my house. I saw at once that you were wrong; you people have no understanding of the mind at all. I realized that the transfer of a human brain from an organic body to a complex artificial space ship would not involve the loss of the intellectualization faculty of the mind. When a man thinks, he *is*.

"When I realized that, I saw the possibility of an age-old dream becoming real. I was quite elderly when I first met you, Philip. Even then my life-span had come pretty much to its end. I could look ahead to nothing but death, and with it the extinction of all my ideas. I had made no mark on the world, none at all. My students, one by one, passed from me into the world, to take up jobs in the great Research Project, the search for better and bigger weapons of war.

"The world has been fighting for a long time, first with itself, then with the Martians, then with these beings from Proxima Centauri, whom we know nothing about. The human society has evolved war as a cultural institution, like the science of astronomy, or mathematics. War is a part of our lives, a career, a respected vocation. Bright, alert young men and women move into it, putting their shoulders to the wheel as they did in the time of Nebuchadnezzar. It has always been so.

"But is it innate in mankind? I don't think so. No social custom is innate. There were many human groups that did not go to war; the Eskimos never grasped the idea at all, and the American Indians never took to it well.

"But these dissenters were wiped out, and a cultural pattern was established that became the standard for the whole planet. Now it has become ingrained in us.

"But if someplace along the line some other way of settling problems had arisen and taken hold, something different than the massing of men and material to —"

"What's your plan?" Kramer said. "I know the theory. It was part of one of your lectures."

"Yes, buried in a lecture on plant selection, as I recall. When you came to me with this proposition I realized that perhaps my conception could be brought to life, after all. If my theory were right that war is only a habit, not an instinct, a society built up apart from Terra with a minimum of cultural roots might develop differently. If it failed to absorb our outlook, if it could start out on another foot, it might not arrive at the same point to which we have come: a dead end, with nothing but greater and greater wars in sight, until nothing is left but ruin and destruction everywhere.

"Of course, there would have to be a Watcher to guide the experiment, at first. A crisis would undoubtedly come very quickly, probably in the second generation. Cain would arise almost at once.

"You see, Kramer, I estimate that if I remain at rest most of the time, on some small planet or moon, I may be able to keep functioning for almost a hundred years. That would be time enough, sufficient to see the direction of the new colony. After that-Well, after that it would be up to the colony itself.

"Which is just as well, of course. Man must take control eventually, on his own. One hundred years, and after that they will have control of their own destiny. Perhaps I am wrong, perhaps war is more than a habit. Perhaps it is a law of the universe, that things can only survive as groups by group violence.

"But I'm going ahead and taking the chance that it is only a habit, that I'm right, that war is something we're so accustomed to that we don't realize it is a very unnatural thing. Now as to the place! I'm still a little vague about that. We must find the place, still.

"That's what we're doing now. You and I are going to inspect a few systems off the beaten path, planets where the trading prospects are low enough to keep Terran ships away. I know of one planet that might be a good place. It was reported by the Fairchild Expedition in their original manual. We may look into that, for a start."

The ship was silent.

* * * * *

Kramer sat for a time, staring down at the metal floor under him. The floor throbbed dully with the motion of the turbines. At last he looked up.

"You might be right. Maybe our outlook is only a habit." Kramer got to his feet. "But I wonder if something has occurred to you?"

"What is that?"

"If it's such a deeply ingrained habit, going back thousands of years, how are you going to get your colonists to make the break, leave Terra and Terran customs? How about *this* generation, the first ones, the people who found the colony? I think you're right that the next generation would be free of all this, if there were an —" He grinned. " —An Old Man Above to teach them something else instead."

Kramer looked up at the wall speaker. "How are you going to get the people to leave Terra and come with you, if by your own theory, this generation can't be saved, it all has to start with the next?"

The wall speaker was silent. Then it made a sound, the faint dry chuckle.

"I'm surprised at you, Philip. Settlers can be found. We won't need many, just a few." The speaker chuckled again. "I'll acquaint you with my solution."

At the far end of the corridor a door slid open. There was sound, a hesitant sound. Kramer turned.

"Dolores!"

Dolores Kramer stood uncertainly, looking into the control room. She blinked in amazement. "Phil! What are you doing here? What's going on?"

They stared at each other.

"What's happening?" Dolores said. "I received a vidcall that you had been hurt in a lunar explosion —"

The wall speaker rasped into life. "You see, Philip, that problem is already solved. We don't really need so many people; even a single couple might do."

Kramer nodded slowly. "I see," he murmured thickly. "Just one couple. One man and woman."

"They might make it all right, if there were someone to watch and see that things went as they should. There will be quite a few things I can help you with, Philip. Quite a few. We'll get along very well, I think."

Kramer grinned wryly. "You could even help us name the animals," he said. "I understand that's the first step."

"I'll be glad to," the toneless, impersonal voice said. "As I recall, my part will be to bring them to you, one by one. Then you can do the actual naming."

"I don't understand," Dolores faltered. "What does he mean, Phil? Naming animals. What kind of animals? Where are we going?"

Kramer walked slowly over to the port and stood staring silently out, his arms folded. Beyond the ship a myriad fragments of light gleamed, countless coals glowing in the dark void. Stars, suns, systems. Endless, without number. A universe of worlds. An infinity of planets, waiting for them, gleaming and winking from the darkness.

He turned back, away from the port. "Where are we going?" He smiled at his wife, standing nervous and frightened, her large eyes full of alarm. "I don't know where we are going," he said. "But somehow that doesn't seem too important right now.... I'm beginning to see the Professor's point, it's the result that counts."

And for the first time in many months he put his arm around Dolores. At first she stiffened, the fright and nervousness still in her eyes. But then suddenly she relaxed against him and there were tears wetting her cheeks.

"Phil...do you really think we can start over again-you and I?"

He kissed her tenderly, then passionately.

And the spaceship shot swiftly through the endless, trackless eternity of the void....

Beyond The Door

That night at the dinner table he brought it out and set it down beside her plate. Doris stared at it, her hand to her mouth. "My God, what is it?" She looked up at him, bright-eyed.

"Well, open it."

Doris tore the ribbon and paper from the square package with her sharp nails, her bosom rising and falling. Larry stood watching her as she lifted the lid. He lit a cigarette and leaned against the wall.

"A cuckoo clock!" Doris cried. "A real old cuckoo clock like my mother had." She turned the clock over and over. "Just like my mother had, when Pete was still alive." Her eyes sparkled with tears.

"It's made in Germany," Larry said. After a moment he added, "Carl got it for me wholesale. He knows some guy in the clock business. Otherwise I wouldn't have —" He stopped.

Doris made a funny little sound.

"I mean, otherwise I wouldn't have been able to afford it." He scowled. "What's the matter with you? You've got your clock, haven't you? Isn't that what you want?"

Doris sat holding onto the clock, her fingers pressed against the brown wood.

"Well," Larry said, "what's the matter?"

He watched in amazement as she leaped up and ran from the room, still clutching the clock. He shook his head. "Never satisfied. They're all that way. Never get enough."

He sat down at the table and finished his meal.

The cuckoo clock was not very large. It was hand-made, however, and there were countless frets on it, little indentations and ornaments scored in the soft wood. Doris sat on the bed drying her eyes and winding the clock. She set the hands by her wristwatch. Presently she carefully moved the hands to two minutes of ten. She carried the clock over to the dresser and propped it up.

Then she sat waiting, her hands twisted together in her lap-waiting for the cuckoo to come out, for the hour to strike.

As she sat she thought about Larry and what he had said. And what she had said, too, for that matter-not that she could be blamed for any of it. After all, she couldn't keep listening to him forever without defending herself; you had to blow your own trumpet in the world.

She touched her handkerchief to her eyes suddenly. Why did he have to say that, about getting it wholesale? Why did he have to spoil it all? If he felt that way he needn't have got it in the first place. She clenched her fists. He was so mean, so damn mean.

But she was glad of the little clock sitting there ticking to itself, with its funny grilled edges and the door. Inside the door was the cuckoo, waiting to come out. Was he listening, his head cocked on one side, listening to hear the clock strike so that he would know to come out?

Did he sleep between hours? Well, she would soon see him: she could ask him. And she would show the clock to Bob. He would love it; Bob loved old things, even old stamps and buttons. He liked to go with her to the stores. Of course, it was a little *awkward*, but Larry had been staying at the office so much, and that helped. If only Larry didn't call up sometimes to —

There was a whirr. The clock shuddered and all at once the door opened. The cuckoo came out, sliding swiftly. He paused and looked around solemnly, scrutinizing her, the room, the furniture.

It was the first time he had seen her, she realized, smiling to herself in pleasure. She stood up, coming toward him shyly. "Go on," she said. "I'm waiting."

The cuckoo opened his bill. He whirred and chirped, quickly, rhythmically. Then, after a moment of contemplation, he retired. And the door snapped shut.

She was delighted. She clapped her hands and spun in a little circle. He was marvelous, perfect! And the way he had looked around, studying her, sizing her up. He liked her; she was certain of it. And she, of course, loved him at once, completely. He was just what she had hoped would come out of the little door.

Doris went to the clock. She bent over the little door, her lips close to the wood. "Do you hear me?" she whispered. "I think you're the most wonderful cuckoo in the world." She paused, embarrassed. "I hope you'll like it here."

Then she went downstairs again, slowly, her head high.

Larry and the cuckoo clock really never got along well from the start. Doris said it was because he didn't wind it right, and it didn't like being only half-wound all the time. Larry turned the job of winding over to her; the cuckoo came out every quarter hour and ran the spring down without remorse, and someone had to be ever after it, winding it up again.

Doris did her best, but she forgot a good deal of the time. Then Larry would throw his newspaper down with an elaborate weary motion and stand up. He would go into the dining-room where the clock was mounted on the wall over the fireplace. He would take the clock down and making sure that he had his thumb over the little door, he would wind it up.

"Why do you put your thumb over the door?" Doris asked once.

"You're supposed to."

She raised an eyebrow. "Are you sure? I wonder if it isn't that you don't want him to come out while you're standing so close."

"Why not?"

"Maybe you're afraid of him."

Larry laughed. He put the clock back on the wall and gingerly removed his thumb. When Doris wasn't looking he examined his thumb.

There was still a trace of the nick cut out of the soft part of it. Who-or what-had pecked at him?

* * * * *

One Saturday morning, when Larry was down at the office working over some important special accounts, Bob Chambers came to the front porch and rang the bell.

Doris was taking a quick shower. She dried herself and slipped into her robe. When she opened the door Bob stepped inside, grinning.

"Hi," he said, looking around.

"It's all right. Larry's at the office."

"Fine." Bob gazed at her slim legs below the hem of the robe. "How nice you look today."

She laughed. "Be careful! Maybe I shouldn't let you in after all."

They looked at one another, half amused half frightened. Presently Bob said, "If you want, I'll—"

"No, for God's sake." She caught hold of his sleeve. "Just get out of the doorway so I can close it. Mrs. Peters across the street, you know."

She closed the door. "And I want to show you something," she said. "You haven't seen it."

He was interested. "An antique? Or what?"

She took his arm, leading him toward the dining-room. "You'll love it, Bobby." She stopped, wide-eyed. "I hope you will. You must; you must love it. It means so much to me —he means so much."

"He?" Bob frowned. "Who is he?"

Doris laughed. "You're jealous! Come on." A moment later they stood before the clock, looking up at it. "He'll come out in a few minutes. Wait until you see him. I know you two will get along just fine."

"What does Larry think of him?"

"They don't like each other. Sometimes when Larry's here he won't come out. Larry gets mad if he doesn't come out on time. He says —"

"Says what?"

Doris looked down. "He always says he's been robbed, even if he did get it wholesale." She brightened. "But I know he won't come out because he doesn't like Larry. When I'm here alone he comes right out for me, every fifteen minutes, even though he really only has to come out on the hour."

She gazed up at the clock. "He comes out for me because he wants to. We talk; I tell him things. Of course, I'd like to have him upstairs in my room, but it wouldn't be right."

There was the sound of footsteps on the front porch. They looked at each other, horrified.

Larry pushed the front door open, grunting. He set his briefcase down and took off his hat. Then he saw Bob for the first time.

"Chambers. I'll be damned." His eyes narrowed. "What are you doing here?" He came into the dining-room. Doris drew her robe about her helplessly, backing away.

"I —" Bob began. "That is, we —" He broke off, glancing at Doris. Suddenly the clock began to whirr. The cuckoo came rushing out, bursting into sound. Larry moved toward him.

"Shut that din off," he said. He raised his fist toward the clock. The cuckoo snapped into silence and retreated. The door closed. "That's better." Larry studied Doris and Bob, standing mutely together.

"I came over to look at the clock," Bob said. "Doris told me that it's a rare antique and that —"

"Nuts. I bought it myself." Larry walked up to him. "Get out of here." He turned to Doris. "You too. And take that damn clock with you."

He paused, rubbing his chin. "No. Leave the clock here. It's mine; I bought it and paid for it."

In the weeks that followed after Doris left, Larry and the cuckoo clock got along even worse than before. For one thing, the cuckoo stayed inside most of the time, sometimes even at twelve o'clock when he should have been busiest. And if he did come out at all he usually spoke only once or twice, never the correct number of times. And there was a sullen, uncooperative note in his voice, a jarring sound that made Larry uneasy and a little angry.

But he kept the clock wound, because the house was very still and quiet and it got on his nerves not to hear someone running around, talking and dropping things. And even the whirring of a clock sounded good to him.

But he didn't like the cuckoo at all. And sometimes he spoke to him.

"Listen," he said late one night to the closed little door. "I know you can hear me. I ought to give you back to the Germans-back to the Black Forest." He paced back and forth. "I wonder what they're doing now, the two of them. That young punk with his books and his antiques. A man shouldn't be interested in antiques; that's for women."

He set his jaw. "Isn't that right?"

The clock said nothing. Larry walked up in front of it. "Isn't that right?" he demanded. "Don't you have anything to say?"

He looked at the face of the clock. It was almost eleven, just a few seconds before the hour. "All right. I'll wait until eleven. Then I want to hear what you have to say. You've been pretty quiet the last few weeks since she left."

He grinned wryly. "Maybe you don't like it here since she's gone." He scowled. "Well, I paid for you, and you're coming out whether you like it or not. You hear me?"

Eleven o'clock came. Far off, at the end of town, the great tower clock boomed sleepily to itself. But the little door remained shut. Nothing moved. The minute hand passed on and the cuckoo did not stir. He was someplace inside the clock, beyond the door, silent and remote.

"All right, if that's the way you feel," Larry murmured, his lips twisting. "But it isn't fair. It's your job to come out. We all have to do things we don't like."

He went unhappily into the kitchen and opened the great gleaming refrigerator. As he poured himself a drink he thought about the clock.

There was no doubt about it-the cuckoo should come out, Doris or no Doris. He had always liked her, from the very start. They had got along well, the two of them. Probably he liked

Bob too-probably he had seen enough of Bob to get to know him. They would be quite happy together, Bob and Doris and the cuckoo.

Larry finished his drink. He opened the drawer at the sink and took out the hammer. He carried it carefully into the dining-room. The clock was ticking gently to itself on the wall.

"Look," he said, waving the hammer. "You know what I have here? You know what I'm going to do with it? I'm going to start on you-first." He smiled. "Birds of a feather, that's what you are-the three of you."

The room was silent.

"Are you coming out? Or do I have to come in and get you?"

The clock whirred a little.

"I hear you in there. You've got a lot of talking to do, enough for the last three weeks. As I figure it, you owe me —"

The door opened. The cuckoo came out fast, straight at him. Larry was looking down, his brow wrinkled in thought. He glanced up, and the cuckoo caught him squarely in the eye.

Down he went, hammer and chair and everything, hitting the floor with a tremendous crash. For a moment the cuckoo paused, its small body poised rigidly. Then it went back inside its house. The door snapped tight-shut after it.

The man lay on the floor, stretched out grotesquely, his head bent over to one side. Nothing moved or stirred. The room was completely silent, except, of course, for the ticking of the clock.

* * * * *

"I see," Doris said, her face tight. Bob put his arm around her, steadying her.

"Doctor," Bob said, "can I ask you something?"

"Of course," the doctor said.

"Is it very easy to break your neck, falling from so low a chair? It wasn't very far to fall. I wonder if it might not have been an accident. Is there any chance it might have been —"

"Suicide?" the doctor rubbed his jaw. "I never heard of anyone committing suicide that way. It was an accident; I'm positive."

"I don't mean suicide," Bob murmured under his breath, looking up at the clock on the wall. "I meant *something else.*"

But no one heard him.

Beyond Lies The Wub

They had almost finished with the loading. Outside stood the Optus, his arms folded, his face sunk in gloom. Captain Franco walked leisurely down the gangplank, grinning.

"What's the matter?" he said. "You're getting paid for all this."

The Optus said nothing. He turned away, collecting his robes. The Captain put his boot on the hem of the robe.

"Just a minute. Don't go off. I'm not finished."

"Oh?" The Optus turned with dignity. "I am going back to the village." He looked toward the animals and birds being driven up the gangplank into the spaceship. "I must organize new hunts."

Franco lit a cigarette. "Why not? You people can go out into the veldt and track it all down again. But when we run out halfway between Mars and Earth —"

The Optus went off, wordless. Franco joined the first mate at the bottom of the gangplank. "How's it coming?" he said. He looked at his watch. "We got a good bargain here."

The mate glanced at him sourly. "How do you explain that?"

"What's the matter with you? We need it more than they do."

"I'll see you later, Captain." The mate threaded his way up the plank, between the long-legged Martian go-birds, into the ship. Franco watched him disappear. He was just starting up after him, up the plank toward the port, when he saw *it*.

"My God!" He stood staring, his hands on his hips. Peterson was walking along the path, his face red, leading *it* by a string.

"I'm sorry, Captain," he said, tugging at the string. Franco walked toward him.

"What is it?"

The wub stood sagging, its great body settling slowly. It was sitting down, its eyes half shut. A few flies buzzed about its flank, and it switched its tail.

It sat. There was silence.

"It's a wub," Peterson said. "I got it from a native for fifty cents. He said it was a very unusual animal. Very respected."

"This?" Franco poked the great sloping side of the wub. "It's a pig! A huge dirty pig!"

"Yes sir, it's a pig. The natives call it a wub."

"A huge pig. It must weigh four hundred pounds." Franco grabbed a tuft of the rough hair. The wub gasped. Its eyes opened, small and moist. Then its great mouth twitched.

A tear rolled down the wub's cheek and splashed on the floor.

"Maybe it's good to eat," Peterson said nervously.

"We'll soon find out," Franco said.

* * * * *

The wub survived the take-off, sound asleep in the hold of the ship. When they were out in space and everything was running smoothly, Captain Franco bade his men fetch the wub upstairs so that he might perceive what manner of beast it was.

The wub grunted and wheezed, squeezing up the passageway.

"Come on," Jones grated, pulling at the rope. The wub twisted, rubbing its skin off on the smooth chrome walls. It burst into the ante-room, tumbling down in a heap. The men leaped up.

"Good Lord," French said. "What is it?"

"Peterson says it's a wub," Jones said. "It belongs to him." He kicked at the wub. The wub stood up unsteadily, panting.

"What's the matter with it?" French came over. "Is it going to be sick?"

They watched. The wub rolled its eyes mournfully. It gazed around at the men.

"I think it's thirsty," Peterson said. He went to get some water. French shook his head.

"No wonder we had so much trouble taking off. I had to reset all my ballast calculations."

Peterson came back with the water. The wub began to lap gratefully, splashing the men. Captain Franco appeared at the door.

"Let's have a look at it." He advanced, squinting critically. "You got this for fifty cents?"

"Yes, sir," Peterson said. "It eats almost anything. I fed it on grain and it liked that. And then potatoes, and mash, and scraps from the table, and milk. It seems to enjoy eating. After it eats it lies down and goes to sleep."

"I see," Captain Franco said. "Now, as to its taste. That's the real question. I doubt if there's much point in fattening it up any more. It seems fat enough to me already. Where's the cook? I want him here. I want to find out —"

The wub stopped lapping and looked up at the Captain.

"Really, Captain," the wub said. "I suggest we talk of other matters."

The room was silent.

"What was that?" Franco said. "Just now."

"The wub, sir," Peterson said. "It spoke."

They all looked at the wub.

"What did it say? What did it say?"

"It suggested we talk about other things."

Franco walked toward the wub. He went all around it, examining it from every side. Then he came back over and stood with the men.

"I wonder if there's a native inside it," he said thoughtfully. "Maybe we should open it up and have a look."

"Oh, goodness!" the wub cried. "Is that all you people can think of, killing and cutting?"

Franco clenched his fists. "Come out of there! Whoever you are, come out!"

Nothing stirred. The men stood together, their faces blank, staring at the wub. The wub swished its tail. It belched suddenly.

"I beg your pardon," the wub said.

"I don't think there's anyone in there," Jones said in a low voice. They all looked at each other.

The cook came in.

"You wanted me, Captain?" he said. "What's this thing?"

"This is a wub," Franco said. "It's to be eaten. Will you measure it and figure out —"

"I think we should have a talk," the wub said. "I'd like to discuss this with you, Captain, if I might. I can see that you and I do not agree on some basic issues."

The Captain took a long time to answer. The wub waited good-naturedly, licking the water from its jowls.

"Come into my office," the Captain said at last. He turned and walked out of the room. The wub rose and padded after him. The men watched it go out. They heard it climbing the stairs.

"I wonder what the outcome will be," the cook said. "Well, I'll be in the kitchen. Let me know as soon as you hear."

"Sure," Jones said. "Sure."

* * * * *

The wub eased itself down in the corner with a sigh. "You must forgive me," it said. "I'm afraid I'm addicted to various forms of relaxation. When one is as large as I —"

The Captain nodded impatiently. He sat down at his desk and folded his hands.

"All right," he said. "Let's get started. You're a wub? Is that correct?"

The wub shrugged. "I suppose so. That's what they call us, the natives, I mean We have our own term."

"And you speak English? You've been in contact with Earthmen before?"

"No."

"Then how do you do it?"

"Speak English? Am I speaking English? I'm not conscious of speaking anything in particular. I examined your mind —"

"My mind?"

"I studied the contents, especially the semantic warehouse, as I refer to it —"

"I see," the Captain said. "Telepathy. Of course."

"We are a very old race," the wub said. "Very old and very ponderous. It is difficult for us to move around. You can appreciate that anything so slow and heavy would be at the mercy of more agile forms of life. There was no use in our relying on physical defenses. How could we win? Too heavy to run, too soft to fight, too good-natured to hunt for game —"

"How do you live?"

"Plants. Vegetables. We can eat almost anything. We're very catholic. Tolerant, eclectic, catholic. We live and let live. That's how we've gotten along."

The wub eyed the Captain.

"And that's why I so violently objected to this business about having me boiled. I could see the image in your mind-most of me in the frozen food locker, some of me in the kettle, a bit for your pet cat —"

"So you read minds?" the Captain said. "How interesting. Anything else? I mean, what else can you do along those lines?"

"A few odds and ends," the wub said absently, staring around the room. "A nice apartment you have here, Captain. You keep it quite neat. I respect life-forms that are tidy. Some Martian birds are quite tidy. They throw things out of their nests and sweep them —"

"Indeed." The Captain nodded. "But to get back to the problem —"

"Quite so. You spoke of dining on me. The taste, I am told, is good. A little fatty, but tender. But how can any lasting contact be established between your people and mine if you resort to such barbaric attitudes? Eat me? Rather you should discuss questions with me, philosophy, the arts —"

The Captain stood up. "Philosophy. It might interest you to know that we will be hard put to find something to eat for the next month. An unfortunate spoilage —"

"I know." The wub nodded. "But wouldn't it be more in accord with your principles of democracy if we all drew straws, or something along that line? After all, democracy is to protect the minority from just such infringements. Now, if each of us casts one vote —"

The Captain walked to the door.

"Nuts to you," he said. He opened the door. He opened his mouth.

He stood frozen, his mouth wide, his eyes staring, his fingers still on the knob.

The wub watched him. Presently it padded out of the room, edging past the Captain. It went down the hall, deep in meditation.

* * * * *

The room was quiet.

"So you see," the wub said, "we have a common myth. Your mind contains many familiar myth symbols. Ishtar, Odysseus —"

Peterson sat silently, staring at the floor. He shifted in his chair.

"Go on," he said. "Please go on."

"I find in your Odysseus a figure common to the mythology of most self-conscious races. As I interpret it, Odysseus wanders as an individual, aware of himself as such. This is the idea of separation, of separation from family and country. The process of individuation."

"But Odysseus returns to his home." Peterson looked out the port window, at the stars, endless stars, burning intently in the empty universe. "Finally he goes home."

"As must all creatures. The moment of separation is a temporary period, a brief journey of the soul. It begins, it ends. The wanderer returns to land and race...."

The door opened. The wub stopped, turning its great head.

Captain Franco came into the room, the men behind him. They hesitated at the door.

"Are you all right?" French said.

"Do you mean me?" Peterson said, surprised. "Why me?"

Franco lowered his gun. "Come over here," he said to Peterson. "Get up and come here."

There was silence.

"Go ahead," the wub said. "It doesn't matter."

Peterson stood up. "What for?"

"It's an order."

Peterson walked to the door. French caught his arm.

"What's going on?" Peterson wrenched loose. "What's the matter with you?"

Captain Franco moved toward the wub. The wub looked up from where it lay in the corner, pressed against the wall.

"It is interesting," the wub said, "that you are obsessed with the idea of eating me. I wonder why."

"Get up," Franco said.

"If you wish." The wub rose, grunting. "Be patient. It is difficult for me." It stood, gasping, its tongue lolling foolishly.

"Shoot it now," French said.

"For God's sake!" Peterson exclaimed. Jones turned to him quickly, his eyes gray with fear.

"You didn't see him-like a statue, standing there, his mouth open. If we hadn't come down, he'd still be there."

"Who? The Captain?" Peterson stared around. "But he's all right now."

They looked at the wub, standing in the middle of the room, its great chest rising and falling.

"Come on," Franco said. "Out of the way."

The men pulled aside toward the door.

"You are quite afraid, aren't you?" the wub said. "Have I done anything to you? I am against the idea of hurting. All I have done is try to protect myself. Can you expect me to rush eagerly to my death? I am a sensible being like yourselves. I was curious to see your ship, learn about you. I suggested to the native —"

The gun jerked.

"See," Franco said. "I thought so."

The wub settled down, panting. It put its paw out, pulling its tail around it.

"It is very warm," the wub said. "I understand that we are close to the jets. Atomic power. You have done many wonderful things with it-technically. Apparently, your scientific hierarchy is not equipped to solve moral, ethical —"

Franco turned to the men, crowding behind him, wide-eyed, silent.

"I'll do it. You can watch."

French nodded. "Try to hit the brain. It's no good for eating. Don't hit the chest. If the rib cage shatters, we'll have to pick bones out."

"Listen," Peterson said, licking his lips. "Has it done anything? What harm has it done? I'm asking you. And anyhow, it's still mine. You have no right to shoot it. It doesn't belong to you."

Franco raised his gun.

"I'm going out," Jones said, his face white and sick. "I don't want to see it."

"Me, too," French said. The men straggled out, murmuring. Peterson lingered at the door.

"It was talking to me about myths," he said. "It wouldn't hurt anyone."

He went outside.

Franco walked toward the wub. The wub looked up slowly. It swallowed.

"A very foolish thing," it said. "I am sorry that you want to do it. There was a parable that your Saviour related —"

It stopped, staring at the gun.

"Can you look me in the eye and do it?" the wub said. "Can you do that?"

The Captain gazed down. "I can look you in the eye," he said. "Back on the farm we had hogs, dirty razor-back hogs. I can do it."

Staring down at the wub, into the gleaming, moist eyes, he pressed the trigger.

* * * * *

The taste was excellent.

They sat glumly around the table, some of them hardly eating at all. The only one who seemed to be enjoying himself was Captain Franco.

"More?" he said, looking around. "More? And some wine, perhaps."

"Not me," French said. "I think I'll go back to the chart room."

"Me, too." Jones stood up, pushing his chair back. "I'll see you later."

The Captain watched them go. Some of the others excused themselves.

"What do you suppose the matter is?" the Captain said. He turned to Peterson. Peterson sat staring down at his plate, at the potatoes, the green peas, and at the thick slab of tender, warm meat.

He opened his mouth. No sound came.

The Captain put his hand on Peterson's shoulder.

"It is only organic matter, now," he said. "The life essence is gone." He ate, spooning up the gravy with some bread. "I, myself, love to eat. It is one of the greatest things that a living creature can enjoy. Eating, resting, meditation, discussing things."

Peterson nodded. Two more men got up and went out. The Captain drank some water and sighed.

"Well," he said. "I must say that this was a very enjoyable meal. All the reports I had heard were quite true-the taste of wub. Very fine. But I was prevented from enjoying this pleasure in times past."

He dabbed at his lips with his napkin and leaned back in his chair. Peterson stared dejectedly at the table.

The Captain watched him intently. He leaned over.

"Come, come," he said. "Cheer up! Let's discuss things."

He smiled.

"As I was saying before I was interrupted, the role of Odysseus in the myths —"

Peterson jerked up, staring.

"To go on," the Captain said. "Odysseus, as I understand him —"

The Golden Man

"Is it always hot like this?" the salesman demanded. He addressed everybody at the lunch counter and in the shabby booths against the wall. A middle-aged fat man with a good-natured smile, rumpled gray suit, sweat-stained white shirt, a drooping bowtie, and a Panama hat.

"Only in the summer," the waitress answered.

None of the others stirred. The teen-age boy and girl in one of the booths, eyes fixed intently on each other. Two workmen, sleeves rolled up, arms dark and hairy, eating bean soup and rolls. A lean, weathered farmer. An elderly businessman in a blue-serge suit, vest and pocket watch. A dark rat-faced cab driver drinking coffee. A tired woman who had come in to get off her feet and put down her bundles.

The salesman got out a package of cigarettes. He glanced curiously around the dingy cafe, lit up, leaned his arms on the counter, and said to the man next to him: "What's the name of this town?"

The man grunted. "Walnut Creek."

The salesman sipped at his coke for a while, cigarette held loosely between plump white fingers. Presently he reached in his coat and brought out a leather wallet. For a long time he leafed thoughtfully through cards and papers, bits of notes, ticket stubs, endless odds and ends, soiled fragments — and finally a photograph.

He grinned at the photograph, and then began to chuckle, a low moist rasp. "Look at this," he said to the man beside him.

The man went on reading his newspaper.

"Hey, look at this." The salesman nudged him with his elbow and pushed the photograph at him. "How's that strike you?"

Annoyed, the man glanced briefly at the the photograph. It showed a nude woman, from the waist up. Perhaps thirty-five years old. Face turned away. Body white and flabby. With eight breasts.

"Ever seen anything like that?" the salesman chuckled, his little red eyes dancing. His face broke into lewd smiles and again he nudged the man.

"I've seen that before." Disgusted, the man resumed reading his newspaper.

The salesman noticed the lean old farmer was looking at the picture. He passed it genially over to him. "How's that strike you, pop? Pretty good stuff, eh?"

The farmer examined the picture solemnly. He turned it over, studied the creased back, took a second look at the front, then tossed it to the salesman. It slid from the counter, turned over a couple of times, and fell to the floor face up.

The salesman picked it up and brushed it off. Carefully, almost tenderly, he restored it to his wallet. The waitress' eyes flickered as she caught a glimpse of it.

"Damn nice," the salesman observed, with a wink. "Wouldn't you say so?"

The waitress shrugged indifferently. "I don't know. I saw a lot of them around Denver. A whole colony."

"That's where this was taken. Denver DCA Camp."

"Any still alive?" the farmer asked.

The salesman laughed harshly. "You kidding?" He made a short, sharp swipe with his hand. "Not any more."

They were all listening. Even the high school kids in the booth had stopped holding hands and were sitting up straight, eyes wide with fascination.

"Saw a funny kind down near San Diego," the farmer said. "Last year, some time. Had wings like a bat. Skin, not feathers. Skin and bone wings."

The rat-eyed taxi driver chimed in. "That's nothing. There was a two-headed one in Detroit. I saw it on exhibit."

"Was it alive?" the waitress asked.

"No. They'd already euthed it."

"In sociology," the high school boy spoke up, "we saw tapes of a whole lot of them. The winged kind from down south, the big-headed one they found in Germany, an awful-looking one with sort of cones, like an insect. And —"

"The worst of all," the elderly businessman stated, "are those English ones. That hid out in the coal mines. The ones they didn't find until last year." He shook his head. "Forty years, down there in the mines, breeding and developing. Almost a hundred of them. Survivors from a group that went underground during the War."

"They just found a new kind in Sweden," the waitress said. "I was reading about it. Controls minds at a distance, they said. Only a couple of them. The DCA got there plenty fast."

"That's a variation of the New Zealand type," one of the workmen said. "It read minds."

"Reading and controlling are two different things," the businessman said. "When I hear something like that I'm plenty glad there's the DCA."

"There was a type they found right after the War," the farmer said. "In Siberia. Had the ability to control objects. Psychokinetic ability. The Soviet DCA got it right away. Nobody remembers that any more."

"I remember that," the businessman said. "I was just a kid, then. I remember because that was the first deeve I ever heard of. My father called me into the living room and told me and my brothers and sisters. We were still building the house. That was in the days when the DCA inspected everyone and stamped their arms." He held up his thin, gnarled wrist. "I was stamped there, sixty years ago."

"Now they just have the birth inspection," the waitress said. She shivered. "There was one in San Francisco this month. First in over a year. They thought it was over, around here."

"It's been dwindling," the taxi driver said. "Frisco wasn't too bad hit. Not like some. Not like Detroit."

"They still get ten or fifteen a year in Detroit," the high school boy said. "All around there. Lots of pools still left. People go into them, in spite of the robot signs."

"What kind was this one?" the salesman asked. "The one they found in San Francisco."

The waitress gestured. "Common type. The kind with no toes. Bent-over. Big eyes."

"The nocturnal type," the salesman said.

"The mother had hid it. They say it was three years old. She got the doctor to forge the DCA chit. Old friend of the family."

The salesman had finished his coke. He sat playing idly with his cigarettes, listening to the hum of talk he had set into motion. The high school boy was leaning excitedly toward the girl across from him, impressing her with his fund of knowledge. The lean farmer and the businessman were huddled together, remembering the old days, the last years of the War, before the first Ten-Year Reconstruction Plan. The taxi driver and the two workmen were swapping yarns about their own experiences.

The salesman caught the waitress's attention. "I guess," he said thoughtfully, "that one in Frisco caused quite a stir. Something like that happening so close."

"Yeah," the waitress murmured.

"This side of the Bay wasn't really hit," the salesman continued. "You never get any of them over here."

"No." The waitress moved abruptly. "None in this area. Ever." She scooped up dirty dishes from the counter and headed toward the back.

"Never?" the salesman asked, surprised. "You've never had any deeves on this side of the Bay?"

"No. None." She disappeared into the back, where the fry cook stood by his burners, white apron and tattooed wrists. Her voice was a little too loud, a little too harsh and strained. It made the farmer pause suddenly and glance up.

Silence dropped like a curtain. All sound cut off instantly. They were all gazing down at their food, suddenly tense and ominous.

"None around here," the taxi driver said, loudly and clearly, to no one in particular. "None ever."

"Sure," the salesman agreed genially. "I was only —"

"Make sure you get that straight," one of the workmen said.

The salesman blinked. "Sure, buddy. Sure." He fumbled nervously in his pocket. A quarter and a dime jangled to the floor and he hurriedly scooped them up. "No offense."

For a moment there was silence. Then the high school boy spoke up, aware for the first time that nobody was saying anything. "I heard something," he began eagerly, voice full of importance. "Somebody said they saw something up by the Johnson farm that looked like it was one of those —"

"*Shut up*," the businessman said, without turning his head.

Scarlet-faced, the boy sagged in his seat. His voice wavered and broke off. He peered hastily down at his hands and swallowed unhappily.

The salesman paid the waitress for his coke. "What's the quickest road to Frisco?" he began. But the waitress had already turned her back.

The people at the counter were immersed in their food. None of them looked up. They ate in frozen silence. Hostile, unfriendly faces, intent on their food.

The salesman picked up his bulging briefcase, pushed open the screen door, and stepped out into the blazing sunlight. He moved toward his battered 1978 Buick, parked a few meters up. A blue-shirted traffic cop was standing in the shade of an awning, talking languidly to a young woman in a yellow silk dress that clung moistly to her slim body.

The salesman paused a moment before he got into his car. He waved his hand and hailed the policeman. "Say, you know this town pretty good?"

The policeman eyed the salesman's rumpled gray suit, bowtie, his sweat-stained shirt. The out-of-state license. "What do you want?"

"I'm looking for the Johnson farm," the salesman said. "Here to see him about some litigation." He moved toward the policeman, a small white card between his fingers. "I'm his attorney — from the New York Guild. Can you tell me how to get out there? I haven't been through here in a couple of years."

Nat Johnson gazed up at the noonday sun and saw that it was good. He sat sprawled out on the bottom step of the porch, a pipe between his yellowed teeth, a lithe, wiry man in red-checkered shirt and canvas jeans, powerful hands, iron-gray hair that was still thick despite sixty-five years of active life.

He was watching the children play. Jean rushed laughing in front of him, bosom heaving under her sweatshirt, black hair streaming behind her. She was sixteen, bright-eyed, legs strong and straight, slim young body bent slightly forward with the weight of the two horseshoes. After her scampered Dave, fourteen, white teeth and black hair, a handsome boy, a son to be proud of. Dave caught up with his sister, passed her, and reached the far peg. He stood waiting, legs apart, hands on his hips, his two horseshoes gripped easily. Gasping, Jean hurried toward him.

"Go ahead!" Dave shouted. "You shoot first. I'm waiting for you."

"So you can knock them away?"

"So I can knock them closer."

Jean tossed down one horseshoe and gripped the other with both hands, eyes on the distant peg. Her lithe body bent, one leg slid back, her spine arched. She took careful aim, closed one eye, and then expertly tossed the shoe. With a clang the shoe struck the distant peg, circled briefly around it, then bounced off again and rolled to one side. A cloud of dust rolled up.

"Not bad," Nat Johnson admitted, from his step. "Too hard, though. Take it easy." His chest swelled with pride as the girl's glistening body took aim and again threw. Two powerful, handsome children, almost ripe, on the verge of adulthood. Playing together in the hot sun.

And there was Cris.

Cris stood by the porch, arms folded. He wasn't playing. He was watching. He had stood there since Dave and Jean had begun playing, the same half-intent, half-remote expression on his finely-cut face. As if he were seeing past them, beyond the two of them. Beyond the field, the barn, the creek bed, the rows of cedars.

"Come on, Cris!" Jean called, as she and Dave moved across the field to collect their horseshoes. "Don't you want to play?"

No, Cris didn't want to play. He never played. He was off in a world of his own, a world into which none of them could come. He never joined in anything, games or chores or family activities. He was by himself always. Remote, detached, aloof. Seeing past everyone and everything — that is, until all at once something clicked and he momentarily rephased, reentered their world briefly.

Nat Johnson reached out and knocked his pipe against the step. He refilled it from his leather tobacco pouch, his eyes on his eldest son. Cris was now moving into life. Heading out onto the field. He walked slowly, arms folded calmly, as if he had, for the moment, descended from his own world into theirs. Jean didn't see him; she had turned her back and was getting ready to pitch.

"Hey," Dave said, startled. "Here's Cris."

Cris reached his sister, stopped, and held out his hand. A great dignified figure, calm and impassive. Uncertainly, Jean gave him one of the horseshoes. "You want this? You want to play?"

Cris said nothing. He bent slightly, a supple arc of his incredibly graceful body, then moved his arm in a blur of speed. The shoe sailed, struck the far peg, and dizzily spun around it. Ringer.

The corners of Dave's mouth turned down. "What a lousy darn thing."

"Cris," Jean reproved. "You don't play fair."

No, Cris didn't play fair. He had watched half an hour — then come out and thrown once. One perfect toss, one dead ringer.

"He never makes a mistake," Dave complained.

Cris stood, face blank. A golden statue in the mid-day sun. Golden hair, skin, a light down of gold fuzz on his bare arms and legs —

Abruptly he stiffened. Nat sat up, startled. "What is it?" he barked.

Cris turned in a quick circle, magnificent body alert. "Cris!" Jean demanded. "What —"

Cris shot forward. Like a released energy beam he bounded across the field, over the fence, into the barn and out the other side. His flying figure seemed to skim over the dry grass as he descended into the barren creek bed, between the cedars. A momentary flash of gold — and he was gone. Vanished. There was no sound. No motion. He had utterly melted into the scenery.

"What was it this time?" Jean asked wearily. She came over to her father and threw herself down in the shade. Sweat glowed on her smooth neck and upper lip; her sweat shirt was streaked and damp. "What did he see?"

"He was after something," Dave stated, coming up.

Nat grunted. "Maybe. There's no telling."

"I guess I better tell Mom not to set a place for him," Jean said. "He probably won't be back."

Anger and futility descended over Nat Johnson. No, he wouldn't be back. Not for dinner and probably not the next day — or the one after that. He'd be gone God only knew how long. Or where. Or why. Off by himself, alone some place. "If I thought there was any use," Nat began, "I'd send you two after him. But there's no —"

He broke off. A car was coming up the dirt road toward the farmhouse. A dusty, battered old Buick. Behind the wheel sat a plump red-faced man in a gray suit, who waved cheerfully at them as the car sputtered to a stop and the motor died into silence.

"Afternoon," the man nodded, as he climbed out the car. He tipped his hat pleasantly. He was middle-aged, genial-looking, perspiring freely as he crossed the dry ground toward the porch. "Maybe you folks can help me."

"What do you want?" Nat Johnson demanded hoarsely. He was frightened. He watched the creek bed out of the corner of his eye, praying silently. God, if only he *stayed* away. Jean was breathing quickly, sharp little gasps. She was terrified. Dave's face was expressionless, but all color had drained from it. "Who are you?" Nat demanded.

"Name's Baines. George Baines." The man held out his hand but Johnson ignored it. "Maybe you've heard of me. I own the Pacifica Development Corporation. We built all those little bomb-proof houses just outside town. Those little round ones you see as you come up the main highway from Lafayette."

"What do you want?" Johnson held his hands steady with an effort. He'd never heard of the man, although he'd noticed the housing tract. It couldn't be missed — a great ant-heap of ugly pill-boxes straddling the highway. Baines looked like the kind of man who'd own them. But what did he want here?

"I've bought some land up this way," Baines was explaining. He rattled a sheaf of crisp papers. "This is the deed, but I'll be damned if I can find it." He grinned good-naturedly. "I know it's around this way, someplace, this side of the State road. According to the clerk at the County Recorder's Office, a mile or so this side of that hill over there. But I'm no damn good at reading maps."

"It isn't around here," Dave broke in. "There's only farms around here. Nothing for sale."

"This is a farm, son," Baines said genially. "I bought it for myself and my missus. So we could settle down." He wrinkled his pug nose. "Don't get the wrong idea — I'm not putting up any tracts around here. This is strictly for myself. An old farmhouse, twenty acres, a pump and a few oak trees —"

"Let me see the deed." Johnson grabbed the sheaf of papers, and while Baines blinked in astonishment, he leafed rapidly through them. His face hardened and he handed them back. "What are you up to? This deed is for a parcel fifty miles from here."

"Fifty miles!" Baines was dumbfounded. "No kidding? But the clerk told me —"

Johnson was on his feet. He towered over the fat man. He was in top-notch physical shape — and he was plenty damn suspicious. "Clerk, hell. You get back into your car and drive out of here. I don't know what you're after, or what you're here for, but I want you off my land."

In Johnson's massive fist something sparkled. A metal tube that gleamed ominously in the mid-day sunlight. Baines saw it — and gulped. "No offense, mister." He backed nervously away. "You folks sure are touchy. Take it easy, will you?"

Johnson said nothing. He gripped the lash-tube tighter and waited for the fat man to leave.

But Baines lingered. "Look, buddy. I've been driving around this furnace five hours, looking for my damn place. Any objection to my using your facilities?"

Johnson eyed him with suspicion. Gradually the suspicion turned to disgust. He shrugged. "Dave, show him where the bathroom is."

"Thanks." Baines grinned thankfully. "And if it wouldn't be too much trouble, maybe a glass of water. I'd be glad to pay you for it." He chuckled knowingly. "Never let the city people get away with anything, eh?"

"Christ." Johnson turned away in revulsion as the fat man lumbered after his son, into the house.

"Dad," Jean whispered. As soon as Baines was inside she hurried up onto the porch, eyes wide with fear. "Dad, do you think he —"

Johnson put his arm around her. "Just hold on tight. He'll be gone, soon."

The girl's dark eyes flashed with mute terror. "Every time the man from the water company, or the tax collector, some tramp, children, *anybody* come around, I get a terrible stab of pain — here." She clutched at her heart, hand against her breasts. "It's been that way thirteen years. How much longer can we keep it going? *How long?*"

The man named Baines emerged gratefully from the bathroom. Dave Johnson stood silently by the door, body rigid, youthful face stony.

"Thanks, son," Baines sighed. "Now where can I get a glass of cold water?" He smacked his thick lips in anticipation. "After you've been driving around the sticks looking for a dump some red-hot real estate agent stuck you with —"

Dave headed into the kitchen. "Mom, this man wants a drink of water. Dad said he could have it."

Dave had turned his back. Baines caught a brief glimpse of the mother, gray-haired, small, moving toward the sink with a glass, face withered and drawn, without expression.

Then Baines hurried from the room down a hall. He passed through a bedroom, pulled a door open, found himself facing a closet. He turned and raced back, through the living room, into a dining room, then another bedroom. In a brief instant he had gone through the whole house.

He peered out a window. The back yard. Remains of a rusting truck. Entrance of an underground bomb shelter. Tin cans. Chickens scratching around. A dog, asleep under a shed. A couple of old auto tires.

He found a door leading out. Soundlessly, he tore the door open and stepped outside. No one was in sight. There was the barn, a leaning, ancient wood structure. Cedar trees beyond, a creek of some kind. What had once been an outhouse.

Baines moved cautiously around the side of the house. He had perhaps thirty seconds. He had left the door of the bathroom closed; the boy would think he had gone back in there. Baines looked into the house through a window. A large closet, filled with old clothing, boxes and bundles of magazines.

He turned and started back. He reached the corner of the house and started around it.

Nat Johnson's gaunt shape loomed up and blocked his way. "All right, Baines. You asked for it."

A pink flash blossomed. It shut out the sunlight in a single blinding burst. Baines leaped back and clawed at his coat pocket. The edge of the flash caught him and he half-fell, stunned by the force. His suit-shield sucked in the energy and discharged it, but the power rattled his teeth and for a moment he jerked like a puppet on a string. Darkness ebbed around him. He could feel the mesh of the shield glow white, as it absorbed the energy and fought to control it.

His own tube came out — and Johnson had no shield. "You're under arrest," Baines muttered grimly. "Put down your tube and your hands up. And call your family." He made a motion with the tube. "Come on, Johnson. Make it snappy."

The lash-tube wavered and then slipped from Johnson's fingers. "You're still alive." Dawning horror crept across his face. "Then you must be —"

Dave and Jean appeared. "*Dad!*"

"Come over here," Baines ordered. "Where's your mother?"

Dave jerked his head numbly. "Inside."

"Get her and bring her here."

"You're DCA," Nat Johnson whispered.

Baines didn't answer. He was doing something with his neck, pulling at the flabby flesh. The wiring of a contact mike glittered as he slipped it from a fold between two chins and into his pocket. From the dirt road came the sound of motors, sleek purrs that rapidly grew louder. Two teardrops of black metal came gliding up and parked beside the house. Men swarmed out, in the dark gray-green of the Government Civil Police. In the sky swarms of black dots were descending, clouds of ugly flies that darkened the sun as they spilled out men and equipment. The men drifted slowly down.

"He's not here," Baines said, as the first man reached him. "He got away. Inform Wisdom back at the lab."

"We've got this section blocked off."

Baines turned to Nat Johnson, who stood in dazed silence, uncomprehending, his son and daughter beside him. "How did he know we were coming?" Baines demanded.

"I don't know," Johnson muttered. "He just — knew."

"A telepath?"

"I don't know."

Baines shrugged. "We'll know, soon. A clamp is out, all around here. He can't get past, no matter what the hell he can do. Unless he can dematerialize himself."

"What'll you do with him when you — if you catch him?" Jean asked huskily.

"Study him."

"And then kill him?"

"That depends on the lab evaluation. If you could give me more to work on, I could predict better."

"We can't tell you anything. We don't know anything more." The girl's voice rose with desperation. "He doesn't talk."

Baines jumped. "*What?*"

"He doesn't talk. He never talked to us. Ever."

"How old is he?"

"Eighteen."

"No communication." Baines was sweating. "In eighteen years there hasn't been any semantic bridge between you? Does he have *any* contact? Signs? Codes?"

"He — ignores us. He eats here, stays with us. Sometimes he plays when we play. Or sits with us. He's gone days on end. We've never been able to find out what he's doing — or where. He sleeps in the barn — by himself."

"Is he really gold-colored?"

"Yes. Skin, eyes, hair, nails. Everything."

"And he's large? Well-formed?"

It was a moment before the girl answered. A strange emotion stirred her drawn features, a momentary glow. "He's incredibly beautiful. A god come down to earth." Her lips twisted. "You won't find him. He can do things. Things you have no comprehension of. Powers so far beyond your limited —"

"You don't think we'll get him?" Baines frowned. "More teams are landing all the time. You've never seen an Agency clamp in operation. We've had sixty years to work out all the bugs. If he gets away it'll be the first time —"

Baines broke off abruptly. Three men were quickly approaching the porch. Two green-clad Civil Police. And a third man between them. A man who moved silently, lithely, a faintly luminous shape that towered above them.

"*Cris!*" Jean screamed.

"We got him," one of the police said.

Baines fingered his lash-tube uneasily. "Where? How?"

"He gave himself up," the policeman answered, voice full of awe. "He came to us voluntarily. Look at him. He's like a metal statue. Like some sort of — god."

The golden figure halted for a moment beside Jean. Then it turned slowly, calmly, to face Baines.

"*Cris!*" Jean shrieked. "*Why did you come back?*"

The same thought was eating at Baines, too. He shoved it aside — for the time being. "Is the jet out front?" he demanded quickly.

"Ready to go," one of the CP answered.

"Fine." Baines strode past them, down the steps and onto the dirt field. "Let's go. I want him taken directly to the lab." For a moment he studied the massive figure who stood calmly between the two Civil Policemen. Beside him, they seemed to have shrunk, become ungainly and repellent. Like dwarves... What had Jean said? *A god come to earth.* Baines broke angrily away. "Come on," he muttered brusquely. "This one may be tough; we've never run up against one like it before. We don't know what the hell it can do."

The chamber was empty, except for the seated figure. Four bare walls, floor and ceiling. A steady glare of white light relentlessly etched every corner of the chamber. Near the top of the far wall ran a narrow slot, the view windows through which the interior of the chamber was scanned.

The seated figure was quiet. He hadn't moved since the chamber locks had slid into place, since the heavy bolts had fallen from outside and the rows of bright-faced technicians had taken their places at the view windows. He gazed down at the floor, bent forward, hands clasped together, face calm, almost expressionless. In four hours he hadn't moved a muscle.

"Well?" Baines said. "What have you learned?"

Wisdom grunted sourly. "Not much. If we don't have him doped out in forty-eight hours we'll go ahead with the euth. We can't take any chances."

"You're thinking about the Tunis type," Baines said. He was, too. They had found ten of them, living in the ruins of the abandoned North African town. Their survival method was simple. They killed and absorbed other life forms, then imitated them and took their places. *Chameleons*, they were called. It had cost sixty lives, before the last one was destroyed. Sixty top-level experts, highly trained DCA men.

"Any clues?" Baines asked.

"He's different as hell. This is going to be tough." Wisdom thumbed a pile of tape-spools. "This is the complete report, all the material we got from Johnson and his family. We pumped them with the psych-wash, then let them go home. Eighteen years — and no semantic bridge. Yet, he looks fully developed. Mature at thirteen — a shorter, faster life-cycle than ours. But why the mane? All the gold fuzz? Like a Roman monument that's been gilded."

"Has the report come in from the analysis room? You had a wave-shot taken, of course."

"His brain pattern has been fully scanned. But it takes time for them to plot it out. We're all running around like lunatics while he just sits there!" Wisdom poked a stubby finger at the window. "We caught him easily enough. He can't have *much*, can he? But I'd like to know what it is. Before we euth him."

"Maybe we should keep him alive until we know."

"Euth in forty-eight hours," Wisdom repeated stubbornly. "Whether we know or not. I don't like him. He gives me the creeps."

Wisdom stood chewing nervously on his cigar, a red-haired, beefy-faced man, thick and heavy-set, with a barrel chest and cold, shrewd eyes deep-set in his hard face. Ed Wisdom was Director of DCA's North American Branch. But right now he was worried. His tiny eyes darted back and forth, alarmed flickers of gray in his brutal, massive face.

"You think," Baines said slowly, "this is *it*?"

"I always think so," Wisdom snapped. "I have to think so."

"I mean —"

"I know what you mean." Wisdom paced back and forth, among the study tables, technicians at their benches, equipment and humming computers. Buzzing tape-slots and research hook-ups. "This thing lived eighteen years with his family and *they* don't understand it. *They* don't know what it has. They know what it does, but not how."

"What does it do?"

"It knows things."

"What kind of things?"

Wisdom grabbed his lash-tube from his belt and tossed it on a table. "Here."

"What?"

"Here." Wisdom signaled, and a view window was slid back an inch. "Shoot him."

Baines blinked. "You said forty-eight hours."

With a curse, Wisdom snatched up the tube, aimed it through the window directly at the seated figure's back, and squeezed the trigger.

A blinding flash of pink. A cloud of energy blossomed in the center of the chamber. It sparkled, then died into dark ash.

"Good God!" Baines gasped. "You —"

He broke off. The figure was no longer sitting. As Wisdom fired, it had moved in a blur of speed, away from the blast, to the corner of the chamber. Now it was slowly coming back, face blank, still absorbed in thought.

"Fifth time," Wisdom said, as he put his tube away. "Last time Jamison and I fired together. Missed. He knew exactly when the bolts would hit. And where."

Baines and Wisdom looked at each other. Both of them were thinking the same thing. "But even reading minds wouldn't tell him where they were going to hit," Baines said. "When, maybe. But not where. Could you have called your own shots?"

"Not mine," Wisdom answered flatly. "I fired fast, damn near at random." He frowned. "*Random*. We'll have to make a test of this." He waved a group of technicians over. "Get a construction team up here. On the double." He grabbed paper and pen and began sketching.

While construction was going on, Baines met his fiancee in the lobby outside the lab, the great central lounge of the DCA Building.

"How's it coming?" she asked. Anita Ferris was tall and blonde, blue eyes and a mature, carefully cultivated figure. An attractive, competent-looking woman in her late twenties. She wore a metal foil dress and cape with a red and black stripe on the sleeve, the emblem of the A-Class. Anita was Director of the Semantics Agency, a top-level Government Coordinator. "Anything of interest, this time?"

"Plenty." Baines guided her from the lobby, into the dim recess of the bar. Music played softly in the background, a shifting variety of patterns formed mathematically. Dim shapes moved expertly through the gloom, from table to table. Silent, efficient robot waiters.

As Anita sipped her Tom Collins, Baines outlined what they had found.

"What are the chances," Anita asked slowly, "that he's built up some kind of deflection-cone? There was one kind that warped their environment by direct mental effort. No tools. Direct mind to matter."

"Psychokinetics?" Baines drummed restlessly on the table top. "I doubt it. The thing has ability to predict, not to control. He can't stop the beams, but he can sure as hell get out of the way."

"Does he jump between the molecules?"

Baines wasn't amused. "This is serious. We've handled these things sixty years — longer than you and I have been around added together. Eighty-seven types of deviants have shown up, real mutants that could reproduce themselves, not mere freaks. This is the eighty-eighth. We've been able to handle each of them in turn. But this —"

"Why are you so worried about this one?"

"First, it's eighteen years old. That in itself is incredible. Its family managed to hide it that long."

"Those women around Denver were older than that. Those ones with —"

"They were in a Government camp. Somebody high up was toying with the idea of allowing them to breed. Some sort of industrial use. We withheld euth for years. But Cris Johnson stayed alive *outside our control*. Those things at Denver were under constant scrutiny."

"Maybe he's harmless. You always assume a deeve is a menace. He might even be beneficial. Somebody thought those women might work in. Maybe this thing has something that would advance the race."

"*Which* race? Not the human race. It's the old 'the operation was a success but the patient died' routine. If we introduce a mutant to keep us going it'll be mutants, not us, who'll inherit the earth. It'll be mutants surviving for their own sake. Don't think for a moment we can put padlocks on them and expect them to serve us. If they're really superior to homo sapiens, they'll win out in even competition. To survive, we've got to cold-deck them right from the start."

"In other words, we'll know homo superior when he comes — by definition. He'll be the one we won't be able to euth."

"That's about it," Baines answered. "Assuming there *is* a homo superior. Maybe there's just homo peculiar. Homo with an improved line."

"The Neanderthal probably thought the Cro-Magnon man had merely an improved line. A little more advanced ability to conjure up symbols and shape flint. From your description, this thing is more radical than a mere improvement."

"This thing," Baines said slowly, "has an ability to predict. So far, it's been able to stay alive. It's been able to cope with situations better than you or I could. How long do you think we'd stay alive in that chamber, with energy beams blazing down at us? In a sense it's got the ultimate survival ability. If it can always be accurate —"

A wall-speaker sounded. "Baines, you're wanted in the lab. Get the hell out of the bar and upramp."

Baines pushed back his chair and got to his feet. "Come along. You may be interested in seeing what Wisdom has got dreamed up."

A tight group of top-level DCA officials stood around in a circle, middle-aged, gray-haired, listening to a skinny youth in a white shirt and rolled-up sleeves explaining an elaborate cube of metal and plastic that filled the center of the view-platform. From it jutted an ugly array of tube snouts, gleaming muzzles that disappeared into an intricate maze of wiring.

"This," the youth was saying briskly, "is the first real test. It fires at random — as nearly random as we can make it, at least. Weighted balls are thrown up in an air stream, then dropped free to fall back and cut relays. They can fall in almost any pattern. The thing fires according to their pattern. Each drop produces a new configuration of timing and position. Ten tubes, in all. Each will be in constant motion."

"And *nobody* knows how they'll fire?" Anita asked.

"Nobody." Wisdom rubbed his thick hands together. "Mind reading won't help him, not with this thing."

Anita moved over to the view windows, as the cube was rolled into place. She gasped. "Is that him?"

"What's wrong?" Baines asked.

Anita's cheeks were flushed. "Why, I expected a — a *thing*. My God, he's beautiful! Like a golden statue. Like a deity!"

Baines laughed. "He's eighteen years old, Anita. Too young for you."

The woman was still peering through the view window. "Look at him. Eighteen? I don't believe it."

Cris Johnson sat in the center of the chamber, on the floor. A posture of contemplation, head bowed, arms folded, legs tucked under him. In the stark glare of the overhead lights his powerful body glowed and rippled, a shimmering figure of downy gold.

"Pretty, isn't he?" Wisdom muttered. "All right. Start it going."

"You're going to *kill* him?" Anita demanded.

"We're going to try."

"But he's —" She broke off uncertainly. "He's not a monster. He's not like those others, those hideous things with two heads, or those insects. Or those awful things from Tunis."

"What is he, then?" Baines asked.

"I don't know. But you can't just kill him. It's terrible!"

The cube clicked into life. The muzzles jerked, silently altered position. Three retracted, disappeared into the body of the cube. Others came out. Quickly, efficiently, they moved into position — and abruptly, without warning, opened fire.

A staggering burst of energy fanned out, a complex pattern that altered each moment, different angles, different velocities, a bewildering blur that cracked from the windows down into the chamber.

The golden figure moved. He dodged back and forth, expertly avoiding the bursts of energy that seared around him on all sides. Rolling clouds of ash obscured him; he was lost in a mist of crackling fire and ash.

"Stop it!" Anita shouted. "For God's sake, you'll destroy him!"

The chamber was an inferno of energy. The figure had completely disappeared. Wisdom waited a moment, then nodded to the technicians operating the cube. They touched guide buttons and the muzzles slowed and died. Some sank back into the cube. All became silent. The works of the cube ceased humming.

Cris Johnson was still alive. He emerged from the settling clouds of ash, blackened and singed. But unhurt. He had avoided each beam. He had weaved between them and among them as they came, a dancer leaping over glittering sword-points of pink fire. He had survived.

"No," Wisdom murmured, shaken and grim. "Not a telepath. Those were at random. No prearranged pattern."

The three of them looked at each other, dazed and frightened. Anita was trembling. Her face was pale and her blue eyes were wide. "What, then?" She whispered. "What is it? What does he have?"

"He's a good guesser," Wisdom suggested.

"He's not guessing," Baines answered. "Don't kid yourself. That's the whole point."

"No, he's not guessing." Wisdom nodded slowly. "He *knew*. He predicted each strike. I wonder... *Can* he err? *Can* he make a mistake?"

"We caught him," Baines pointed out.

"You said he came back voluntarily." There was a strange look on Wisdom's face. "Did he come back *after* the clamp was up?"

Baines jumped. "Yes, after."

"He couldn't have got through the clamp. So he came back." Wisdom grinned wryly. "The clamp must actually have been perfect. It was supposed to be."

"If there had been a single hole," Baines murmured, "he would have known it — gone through."

Wisdom ordered a group of armed guards over. "Get him out of there. To the euth stage."

Anita shrieked. "Wisdom, you can't —"

"He's too far ahead of us. We can't compete with him." Wisdom's eyes were bleak. "We can only guess what's going to happen. *He knows.* For him, it's a sure thing. I don't think it'll help him at euth, though. The whole stage is flooded simultaneously. Instantaneous gas, released throughout." He signalled impatiently to the guards. "Get going. Take him down right away. Don't waste any time."

"Can we?" Baines murmured thoughtfully.

The guards took up positions by one of the chamber locks. Cautiously, the tower control slid the lock back. The first two guards stepped cautiously in, lash-tubes ready.

Cris stood in the center of the chamber. His back was to them as they crept toward him. For a moment he was silent, utterly unmoving. The guards fanned out, as more of them entered the chamber. Then —

Anita screamed. Wisdom cursed. The golden figure spun and leaped forward, in a flashing blur of speed. Past the triple line of guards, through the lock and into the corridor.

"Get him!" Baines shouted.

Guards milled everywhere. Flashes of energy lit up the corridor, as the figure raced among them up the ramp.

"No use," Wisdom said calmly. "We can't hit him." He touched a button, then another. "But maybe this will help."

"What —" Baines began. But the leaping figure shot abruptly at him, straight at him, and he dropped to one side. The figure flashed past. It ran effortlessly, face without expression, dodging and jumping as the energy beams seared around it.

For an instant the golden face loomed up before Baines. It passed and disappeared down a side corridor. Guards rushed after it, kneeling and firing, shouting orders excitedly. In the bowels of the building, heavy guns were rumbling up. Locks slid into place as escape corridors were systematically sealed off.

"Good God," Baines gasped, as he got to his feet. "Can't he do anything but run?"

"I gave orders," Wisdom said, "to have the building isolated. There's no way out. Nobody comes and nobody goes. He's loose here in the building — but he won't get out."

"If there's one exit overlooked, he'll know it," Anita pointed out shakily.

"We won't overlook any exit. We got him once; we'll get him again."

A messenger robot had come in. Now it presented its message respectfully to Wisdom. "From analysis, sir."

Wisdom tore the tape open. "Now we'll know how it thinks." His hands were shaking. "Maybe we can figure out its blind spot. It may be able to out-think us, but that doesn't mean it's invulnerable. It only predicts the future — it can't change it. If there's only death ahead, its ability won't..."

Wisdom's voice faded into silence. After a moment he passed the tape to Baines.

"I'll be down in the bar," Wisdom said. "Getting a good stiff drink." His face had turned lead-gray. "All I can say is *I hope to hell this isn't the race to come.*"

"What's the analysis?" Anita demanded impatiently, peering over Baines' shoulder. "How does it think?"

"It doesn't," Baines said, as he handed the tape back to his boss. "It doesn't think at all. Virtually no frontal lobe. It's not a human being — it doesn't use symbols. It's nothing but an animal."

"An animal," Wisdom said. "With a single highly-developed faculty. Not a superior man. Not a man at all."

Up and down the corridors of the DCA Building, guards and equipment clanged. Loads of Civil Police were pouring into the building and taking up positions beside the guards. One by one, the corridors and rooms were being inspected and sealed off. Sooner or later the golden figure of Cris Johnson would be located and cornered.

"We were always afraid a mutant with superior intellectual powers would come along," Baines said reflectively. "A deeve who would be to us what we are to the great apes. Something with a bulging cranium, telepathic ability, a perfect semantic system, ultimate powers of symbolization and calculation. A development along our own path. A better human being."

"He acts by reflex," Anita said wonderingly. She had the analysis and was sitting at one of the desks studying it intently. "Reflex — like a lion. A golden lion." She pushed the tape aside, a strange expression on her face. "The lion god."

"Beast," Wisdom corrected tartly. "Blond beast, you mean."

"He runs fast," Baines said, "and that's all. No tools. He doesn't build anything or utilize anything outside himself. He just stands and waits for the right opportunity and then he runs like hell."

"This is worse than anything we've anticipated," Wisdom said. His beefy face was lead-gray. He sagged like an old man, his blunt hands trembling and uncertain. "To be replaced by an animal! Something that runs and hides. Something without a language!" He spat savagely. "That's why they weren't able to communicate with it. We wondered what kind of semantic system it had. It hasn't got any! No more ability to talk and think than a — dog."

"That means intelligence has failed," Baines went on huskily. "We're the last of our line — like the dinosaur. We've carried intelligence as far as it'll go. Too far, maybe. We've already got to the point where we know so much — think so much — we can't act."

"Men of thought," Anita said. "Not men of action. It's begun to have a paralyzing effect. But this thing —"

"This thing's faculty works better than ours ever did. We can recall past experiences, keep them in mind, learn from them. At best, we can make shrewd guesses about the future, from our memory of what's happened in the past. But we can't be certain. We have to speak of probabilities. Grays. Not blacks and whites. We're only guessing."

"Cris Johnson isn't guessing," Anita added.

"He can look ahead. See what's coming. He can — prethink. Let's call it that. He can see into the future. Probably he doesn't perceive it as the future."

"No," Anita said thoughtfully. "It would seem like the present. He has a broader present. But his present lies ahead, not back. Our present is related to the past. Only the past is certain, to us. To him, the future is certain. And he probably doesn't remember the past, any more than any animal remembers what happened."

"As he develops," Baines said, "as his race evolves, it'll probably expand its ability to prethink. Instead of ten minutes, thirty minutes. Then an hour. A day. A year. Eventually they'll be able to keep ahead a whole lifetime. Each one of them will live in a solid, unchanging world. There'll be no variables, no uncertainty. No motion! They won't have anything to fear. Their world will be perfectly static, a solid block of matter."

"And when death comes," Anita said, "they'll accept it. There won't be any struggle; to them, it'll already have happened."

"*Already have happened*," Baines repeated. "To Cris, our shots had already been fired." He laughed harshly. "Superior survival doesn't mean superior man. If there were another world-wide flood, only fish would survive. If there were another ice age, maybe nothing but polar bears would be left. When we opened the lock, he had already seen the men, seen exactly where they were standing and what they'd do. A neat faculty — but not a development of mind. A pure physical *sense*."

"But if every exit is covered," Wisdom repeated, "he'll see he can't get out. He gave himself up before — he'll give himself up again." He shook his head. "An animal. Without language. Without tools."

"With his new sense," Baines said, "he doesn't need anything else." He examined his watch. "It's after two. Is the building completely sealed off?"

"You can't leave," Wisdom stated. "You'll have to stay here all night — or until we catch the bastard."

"I meant her." Baines indicated Anita. "She's supposed to be back at Semantics by seven in the morning."

Wisdom shrugged. "I have no control over her. If she wants, she can check out."

"I'll stay," Anita decided. "I want to be here when he — when he's destroyed. I'll sleep here." She hesitated. "Wisdom, isn't there some other way? If he's just an animal couldn't we —"

"A zoo?" Wisdom's voice rose in a frenzy of hysteria. "Keep it penned up in the zoo? Christ no! It's got to be killed!"

For a long time the great gleaming shape crouched in the darkness. He was in a store room. Boxes and cartons stretched out on all sides, heaped up in orderly rows, all neatly counted and marked. Silent and deserted.

But in a few moments people burst in and searched the room. He could see this. He saw them in all parts of the room, clear and distinct, men with lash-tubes, grim-faced, stalking with murder in their eyes.

The sight was one of many. One of a multitude of clearly-etched scenes lying tangent to his own. And to each was attached a further multitude of interlocking scenes, that finally grew hazier and dwindled away. A progressive vagueness, each syndrome less distinct.

But the immediate one, the scene that lay closest to him, was clearly visible. He could easily make out the sight of the armed men. Therefore it was necessary to be out of the room before they appeared.

The golden figure got calmly to its feet and moved to the door. The corridor was empty; he could see himself already outside, in the vacant, drumming hall of metal and recessed lights. He pushed the door boldly open and stepped out.

A lift blinked across the hall. He walked to the lift and entered it. In five minutes a group of guards would come running along and leap into the lift. By that time he would have left it and sent it back down. Now he pressed a button and rose to the next floor.

He stepped out into a deserted passage. No one was in sight. That didn't surprise him. He couldn't be surprised. The element didn't exist for him. The positions of things, the space relationships of all matter in the immediate future, were as certain for him as his own body.

The only thing that was unknown was that which had already passed out of being. In a vague, dim fashion, he had occasionally wondered where things went after he had passed them.

He came to a small supply closet. It had just been searched. It would be a half an hour before anyone opened it again. He had that long; he could see that far ahead. And then —

And then he would be able to see another area, a region farther beyond. He was always moving, advancing into new regions he had never seen before. A constantly unfolding panorama of sights and scenes, frozen landscapes spread out ahead. All objects were fixed. Pieces on a vast chess board through which he moved, arms folded, face calm. A detached observer who saw objects that lay ahead of him as clearly as those under foot.

Right now, as he crouched in the small supply closet, he saw an unusually varied multitude of scenes for the next half hour. Much lay ahead. The half hour was divided into an incredibly complex pattern of separate configurations. He had reached a critical region; he was about to move through worlds of intricate complexity.

He concentrated on a scene ten minutes away. It showed, like a three dimensional still, a heavy gun at the end of the corridor, trained all the way to the far end. Men moved cautiously from door to door, checking each room again, as they had done repeatedly. At the end of the half hour they had reached the supply closet. A scene showed them looking inside. By that time he was gone, of course. He wasn't in that scene. He had passed on to another.

The next scene showed an exit. Guards stood in a solid line. No way out. He was in that scene. Off to one side, in a niche just inside the door. The street outside was visible, stars, lights, outlines of passing cars and people.

In the next tableau he had gone back, away from the exit. There was no way out. In another tableau he saw himself at other exits, a legion of golden figures, duplicated again and again, as he explored regions ahead, one after another. But each exit was covered.

In one dim scene he saw himself lying charred and dead; he had tried to run through the line, out the exit.

But that scene was vague. One wavering, indistinct still out of many. The inflexible path along which he moved would not deviate in that direction. It would not turn him that way. The golden figure in that scene, the miniature doll in that room, was only distantly related to him. It was himself, but a far-away self. A self he would never meet. He forgot it and went on to examine the other tableau.

The myriad of tableaux that surrounded him were an elaborate maze, a web which he now considered bit by bit. He was looking down into a doll's house of infinite rooms, rooms without number, each with its furniture, its dolls, all rigid and unmoving. The same dolls and furniture were repeated in many. He, himself, appeared often. The two men on the platform. The woman. Again and again the same combinations turned up; the play was redone frequently, the same actors and props moved around in all possible ways.

Before it was time to leave the supply closet, Cris Johnson had examined each of the rooms tangent to the one he now occupied. He had consulted each, considered its contents thoroughly.

He pushed the door open and stepped calmly out into the hall. He knew exactly where he was going. And what he had to do. Crouched in the stuffy closet, he had quietly and expertly examined each miniature of himself, observed which clearly-etched configuration lay along his inflexible path, the one room of the doll house, the one set out of legions, toward which he was moving.

Anita slipped out of her metal foil dress, hung it over a hanger, then unfastened her shoes and kicked them under the bed. She was just starting to unclip her bra when the door opened.

She gasped. Soundlessly, calmly, the great golden shape closed the door and bolted it after him.

Anita snatched up her lash-tube from the dressing table. Her hand shook; her whole body was trembling. "What do you want?" she demanded. Her fingers tightened convulsively around the tube. "I'll kill you."

The figure regarded her silently, arms folded. It was the first time she had seen Cris Johnson closely. The great dignified face, handsome and impassive. Broad shoulders. The golden mane of hair, golden skin, pelt of radiant fuzz —

"Why?" she demanded breathlessly. Her heart was pounding wildly. "What do you want?"

She could kill him easily. But the lash-tube wavered. Cris Johnson stood without fear; he wasn't at all afraid. Why not? Didn't he understand what it was? What the small metal tube could do to him?

"Of course," she said suddenly, in a choked whisper. "You can see ahead. You know I'm not going to kill you. Or you wouldn't have come here."

She flushed, terrified — and embarrassed. He knew exactly what she was going to do; he could see it as easily as she saw the walls of the room, the wall-bed with its covers folded neatly back, her clothes hanging in the closet, her purse and small things on the dressing table.

"All right." Anita backed away, then abruptly put the tube down on the dressing table. "I won't kill you. Why should I?" She fumbled in her purse and got out her cigarettes. Shakily, she lit up, her pulse racing. She was scared. And strangely fascinated. "Do you expect to stay here? It won't do any good. They've come through the dorm twice, already. They'll be back."

Could he understand her? She saw nothing on his face, only blank dignity. God, he was huge! It wasn't possible he was only eighteen, a boy, a child. He looked more like some great golden god, come down to earth.

She shook the thought off savagely. He wasn't a god. He was a beast. *The blond beast*, come to take the place of man. To drive man from the earth.

Anita snatched up the lash-tube. "Get out of here! You're an animal! A big stupid animal! You can't even understand what I'm saying — you don't even have a language. You're not human."

Cris Johnson remained silent. As if he were waiting. Waiting for what? He showed no sign of fear or impatience, even though the corridor outside rang with the sound of men searching, metal against metal, guns and energy tubes being dragged around, shouts and dim rumbles as section after section of the building was searched and sealed off.

"They'll get you," Anita said. "You'll be trapped here. They'll be searching this wing any moment." She savagely stubbed out her cigarette. "For God's sake, what do you expect me to do?"

Cris moved toward her. Anita shrank back. His powerful hands caught hold of her and she gasped in sudden terror. For a moment she struggled blindly, desperately.

"Let go!" She broke away and leaped back from him. His face was expressionless. Calmly, he came toward her, an impassive god advancing to take her. "Get away!" She groped for the lash-tube, trying to get up. But the tube slipped from her fingers and rolled onto the floor.

Cris bent down and picked it up. He held it out to her, in the open palm of his hand.

"Good God," Anita whispered. Shakily, she accepted the tube, gripped it hesitantly, then put it down again on the dressing table.

In the half-light of the room, the great golden figure seemed to glow and shimmer, outlined against the darkness. A god — no, not a god. An animal. A great golden beast, without a soul. She was confused. Which was he — or was he both? She shook her head, bewildered. It was late, almost four. She was exhausted and confused.

Cris took her in his arms. Gently, kindly, he lifted her face and kissed her. His powerful hands held her tight. She couldn't breathe. Darkness, mixed with the shimmering golden haze, swept around her. Around and around it spiralled, carrying her senses away. She sank down into it gratefully. The darkness covered her and dissolved her in a swelling torrent of sheer force that mounted in intensity each moment, until the roar of it beat against her and at last blotted out everything.

Anita blinked. She sat up and automatically pushed her hair into place. Cris was standing before the closet. He was reaching up, getting something down.

He turned toward her and tossed something on the bed. Her heavy metal foil traveling cape.

Anita gazed down at the cape without comprehension. "What do you want?"

Cris stood by the bed, waiting.

She picked up the cape uncertainly. Cold creepers of fear plucked at her. "You want me to get you out of here," she said softly. "Past the guards and the CP."

Cris said nothing.

"They'll kill you instantly." She got unsteadily to her feet. "You can't run past them. Good God, don't you do anything but run? There must be a better way. Maybe I can appeal to Wisdom. I'm Class A — Director Class. I can go directly to the Full Directorate. I ought to be able to hold them off, keep back the euth indefinitely. The odds are a billion to one against us if we try to break past —"

She broke off.

"But you don't gamble," she continued slowly. "You don't go by odds. You *know* what's coming. You've seen the cards already." She studied his face intently. "No, you can't be cold-decked. It wouldn't be possible."

For a moment she stood deep in thought. Then with a quick, decisive motion, she snatched up the cloak and slipped it around her bare shoulders. She fastened the heavy belt, bent down and got her shoes from under the bed, snatched up her purse, and hurried to the door.

"Come on," she said. She was breathing quickly, cheeks flushed. "Let's go. While there are still a number of exits to choose from. My car is parked outside, in the lot at the side of the building. We can get to my place in an hour. I have a winter home in Argentina. If worse comes to worst we can fly there. It's in the back country, away from the cities. Jungle and swamps. Cut-off from almost everything." Eagerly she started to open the door.

Cris reached out and stopped her. Gently, patiently, he moved in front of her.

He waited a long time, body rigid. Then he turned the knob and stepped boldly out into the corridor.

The corridor was empty. No one was in sight. Anita caught a faint glimpse, the back of a guard hurrying off. If they had come out a second earlier —

Cris started down the corridor. She ran after him. He moved rapidly, effortlessly. The girl had trouble keeping up with him. He seemed to know exactly where to go. Off to the right, down a side hall, a supply passage. Onto an ascent freight-lift. They rose, then abruptly halted.

Cris waited again. Presently he slid the door back and moved out of the lift. Anita followed nervously. She could hear sounds: guns and men, very close.

They were near an exit. A double line of guards stood directly ahead. Twenty men, a solid wall — and a massive heavy-duty robot gun in the center. The men were alert, faces strained and tense. Watching wide-eyed, guns gripped tight. A Civil Police officer was in charge.

"We'll never get past," Anita gasped. "We wouldn't get ten feet." She pulled back. "They'll —"

Cris took her by the arm and continued calmly forward. Blind terror leaped inside her. She fought wildly to get away, but his fingers were like steel. She couldn't pry them loose. Quietly, irresistibly, the great golden creature drew her along beside him toward the double line of guards.

"*There he is!*" Guns went up. Men leaped into action. The barrel of the robot cannon swung around. "*Get him!*"

Anita was paralyzed. She sagged against the powerful body beside her, tugged along helplessly by his inflexible grasp. The lines of guards came nearer, a sheer wall of guns. Anita fought to control her terror. She stumbled, half-fell. Cris supported her effortlessly. She scratched, fought at him, struggled to get loose —

"Don't shoot!" she screamed.

Guns wavered uncertainly. "Who is she?" The guards were moving around, trying to get a sight on Cris without including her. "Who's he got there?"

One of them saw the stripe on her sleeve. Red and black. Director Class. Top-level.

"She's Class A." Shocked, the guards retreated. "Miss, get out of the way!"

Anita found her voice. "Don't shoot. He's — in my custody. You understand? I'm taking him out."

The wall of guards moved back nervously. "No one's supposed to pass. Director Wisdom gave orders —"

"I'm not subject to Wisdom's authority." She managed to edge her voice with a harsh crispness. "Get out of the way. I'm taking him to the Semantics Agency."

For a moment nothing happened. There was no reaction. Then slowly, uncertainly, one guard stepped aside.

Cris moved. A blur of speed, away from Anita, past the confused guards, through the breach in the line, out the exit, and onto the street. Bursts of energy flashed wildly after him. Shouting guards milled out. Anita was left behind, forgotten. The guards, the heavy-duty gun, were pouring out into the early morning darkness. Sirens wailed. Patrol cars roared into life.

Anita stood dazed, confused, leaning against the wall, trying to get her breath.

He was gone. He had left her. Good God — what had she done? She shook her head, bewildered, her face buried in her hands. She had been hypnotized. She had lost her will, her common sense. Her reason! The animal, the great golden beast, had tricked her. Taken advantage of her. And now he was gone, escaped into the night.

Miserable, agonized tears trickled through her clenched fingers. She rubbed at them futilely; but they kept on coming.

"He's gone," Baines said. "We'll never get him, now. He's probably a million miles from here."

Anita sat huddled in the corner, her face to the wall. A little bent heap, broken and wretched.

Wisdom paced back and forth. "But where can he go? Where can he hide? Nobody'll hide him! Everybody knows the law about deeves!"

"He's lived out in the woods most of his life. He'll hunt — that's what he's always done. They wondered what he was up to, off by himself. He was catching game and sleeping under trees." Baines laughed harshly. "And the first woman he meets will be glad to hide him — as *she* was." He indicated Anita with a jerk of his thumb.

"So all that gold, that mane, that god-like stance, was *for* something. Not just ornament." Wisdom's thick lips twisted. "He doesn't have just one faculty — he has two. One is new, the newest thing in survival method. The other is old as life." He stopped pacing to glare at the huddled shape in the corner. "Plumage. Bright feathers, combs for the rooster, swans, birds, bright scales for the fish. Gleaming pelts and manes for the animals. An animal isn't necessarily *bestial*. Lions aren't bestial. Or tigers. Or any of the big cats. They're anything but bestial."

"He'll never have to worry," Baines said. "He'll get by — as long as human women exist to take care of him. And since he can see ahead, into the future, he already knows he's sexually irresistible to human females."

"We'll get him," Wisdom muttered. "I've had the Government declare an emergency. Military and Civil Police will be looking for him. Armies of men — a whole planet of experts, the most advanced machines and equipment. We'll flush him, sooner or later."

"By that time it won't make any difference," Baines said. He put his hand on Anita's shoulder and patted her ironically. "You'll have company, sweetheart. You won't be the only one. You're just the first of a long procession."

"Thanks," Anita grated.

"The oldest survival method and the newest. Combined to form one perfectly adapted animal. How the hell are we going to stop him? We can put *you* through a sterilization tank — but we can't pick them all up, all the women he meets along the way. And if we miss one we're finished."

"We'll have to keep trying," Wisdom said. "Round up as many as we can. Before they can spawn." Faint hope glinted in his tired, sagging face. "Maybe his characteristics are recessive. Maybe ours will cancel his out."

"I wouldn't lay any money on that," Baines said. "I think I know already which of the two strains is going to turn up dominant." He grinned wryly. "I mean, I'm making a good *guess*. It won't be us."

The Gun

The Captain peered into the eyepiece of the telescope. He adjusted the focus quickly.

"It was an atomic fission we saw, all right," he said presently. He sighed and pushed the eyepiece away. "Any of you who wants to look may do so. But it's not a pretty sight."

"Let me look," Tance the archeologist said. He bent down to look, squinting. "Good Lord!" He leaped violently back, knocking against Dorle, the Chief Navigator.

"Why did we come all this way, then?" Dorle asked, looking around at the other men. "There's no point even in landing. Let's go back at once."

"Perhaps he's right," the biologist murmured. "But I'd like to look for myself, if I may." He pushed past Tance and peered into the sight.

He saw a vast expanse, an endless surface of gray, stretching to the edge of the planet. At first he thought it was water but after a moment he realized that it was slag, pitted, fused slag, broken only by hills of rock jutting up at intervals. Nothing moved or stirred. Everything was silent, dead.

"I see," Fomar said, backing away from the eyepiece. "Well, I won't find any legumes there." He tried to smile, but his lips stayed unmoved. He stepped away and stood by himself, staring past the others.

"I wonder what the atmospheric sample will show," Tance said.

"I think I can guess," the Captain answered. "Most of the atmosphere is poisoned. But didn't we expect all this? I don't see why we're so surprised. A fission visible as far away as our system must be a terrible thing."

He strode off down the corridor, dignified and expressionless. They watched him disappear into the control room.

As the Captain closed the door the young woman turned. "What did the telescope show? Good or bad?"

"Bad. No life could possibly exist. Atmosphere poisoned, water vaporized, all the land fused."

"Could they have gone underground?"

The Captain slid back the port window so that the surface of the planet under them was visible. The two of them stared down, silent and disturbed. Mile after mile of unbroken ruin stretched out, blackened slag, pitted and scarred, and occasional heaps of rock.

Suddenly Nasha jumped. "Look! Over there, at the edge. Do you see it?"

They stared. Something rose up, not rock, not an accidental formation. It was round, a circle of dots, white pellets on the dead skin of the planet. A city? Buildings of some kind?

"Please turn the ship," Nasha said excitedly. She pushed her dark hair from her face. "Turn the ship and let's see what it is!"

The ship turned, changing its course. As they came over the white dots the Captain lowered the ship, dropping it down as much as he dared. "Piers," he said. "Piers of some sort of stone. Perhaps poured artificial stone. The remains of a city."

"Oh, dear," Nasha murmured. "How awful." She watched the ruins disappear behind them. In a half-circle the white squares jutted from the slag, chipped and cracked, like broken teeth.

"There's nothing alive," the Captain said at last. "I think we'll go right back; I know most of the crew want to. Get the Government Receiving Station on the sender and tell them what we found, and that we —"

* * * * *

He staggered.

The first atomic shell had struck the ship, spinning it around. The Captain fell to the floor, crashing into the control table. Papers and instruments rained down on him. As he started to his feet the second shell struck. The ceiling cracked open, struts and girders twisted and bent. The ship shuddered, falling suddenly down, then righting itself as automatic controls took over.

The Captain lay on the floor by the smashed control board. In the corner Nasha struggled to free herself from the debris.

Outside the men were already sealing the gaping leaks in the side of the ship, through which the precious air was rushing, dissipating into the void beyond. "Help me!" Dorle was shouting. "Fire over here, wiring ignited." Two men came running. Tance watched helplessly, his eyeglasses broken and bent.

"So there is life here, after all," he said, half to himself. "But how could —"

"Give us a hand," Fomar said, hurrying past. "Give us a hand, we've got to land the ship!"

It was night. A few stars glinted above them, winking through the drifting silt that blew across the surface of the planet.

Dorle peered out, frowning. "What a place to be stuck in." He resumed his work, hammering the bent metal hull of the ship back into place. He was wearing a pressure suit; there were still many small leaks, and radioactive particles from the atmosphere had already found their way into the ship.

Nasha and Fomar were sitting at the table in the control room, pale and solemn, studying the inventory lists.

"Low on carbohydrates," Fomar said. "We can break down the stored fats if we want to, but —"

"I wonder if we could find anything outside." Nasha went to the window. "How uninviting it looks." She paced back and forth, very slender and small, her face dark with fatigue. "What do you suppose an exploring party would find?"

Fomar shrugged. "Not much. Maybe a few weeds growing in cracks here and there. Nothing we could use. Anything that would adapt to this environment would be toxic, lethal."

Nasha paused, rubbing her cheek. There was a deep scratch there, still red and swollen. "Then how do you explain — it? According to your theory the inhabitants must have died in their skins, fried like yams. But who fired on us? Somebody detected us, made a decision, aimed a gun."

"And gauged distance," the Captain said feebly from the cot in the corner. He turned toward them. "That's the part that worries me. The first shell put us out of commission, the second almost destroyed us. They were well aimed, perfectly aimed. We're not such an easy target."

"True." Fomar nodded. "Well, perhaps we'll know the answer before we leave here. What a strange situation! All our reasoning tells us that no life could exist; the whole planet burned dry, the atmosphere itself gone, completely poisoned."

"The gun that fired the projectiles survived," Nasha said. "Why not people?"

"It's not the same. Metal doesn't need air to breathe. Metal doesn't get leukemia from radioactive particles. Metal doesn't need food and water."

There was silence.

"A paradox," Nasha said. "Anyhow, in the morning I think we should send out a search party. And meanwhile we should keep on trying to get the ship in condition for the trip back."

"It'll be days before we can take off," Fomar said. "We should keep every man working here. We can't afford to send out a party."

Nasha smiled a little. "We'll send you in the first party. Maybe you can discover-what was it you were so interested in?"

"Legumes. Edible legumes."

"Maybe you can find some of them. Only —"

"Only what?"

"Only watch out. They fired on us once without even knowing who we were or what we came for. Do you suppose that they fought with each other? Perhaps they couldn't imagine anyone being friendly, under any circumstances. What a strange evolutionary trait, inter-species warfare. Fighting within the race!"

"We'll know in the morning," Fomar said. "Let's get some sleep."

* * * * *

The sun came up chill and austere. The three people, two men and a woman, stepped through the port, dropping down on the hard ground below.

"What a day," Dorle said grumpily. "I said how glad I'd be to walk on firm ground again, but —"

"Come on," Nasha said. "Up beside me. I want to say something to you. Will you excuse us, Tance?"

Tance nodded gloomily. Dorle caught up with Nasha. They walked together, their metal shoes crunching the ground underfoot. Nasha glanced at him.

"Listen. The Captain is dying. No one knows except the two of us. By the end of the day-period of this planet he'll be dead. The shock did something to his heart. He was almost sixty, you know."

Dorle nodded. "That's bad. I have a great deal of respect for him. You will be captain in his place, of course. Since you're vice-captain now —"

"No. I prefer to see someone else lead, perhaps you or Fomar. I've been thinking over the situation and it seems to me that I should declare myself mated to one of you, whichever of you wants to be captain. Then I could devolve the responsibility."

"Well, I don't want to be captain. Let Fomar do it."

Nasha studied him, tall and blond, striding along beside her in his pressure suit. "I'm rather partial to you," she said. "We might try it for a time, at least. But do as you like. Look, we're coming to something."

They stopped walking, letting Tance catch up. In front of them was some sort of a ruined building. Dorle stared around thoughtfully.

"Do you see? This whole place is a natural bowl, a huge valley. See how the rock formations rise up on all sides, protecting the floor. Maybe some of the great blast was deflected here."

They wandered around the ruins, picking up rocks and fragments. "I think this was a farm," Tance said, examining a piece of wood. "This was part of a tower windmill."

"Really?" Nasha took the stick and turned it over. "Interesting. But let's go; we don't have much time."

"Look," Dorle said suddenly. "Off there, a long way off. Isn't that something?" He pointed.

Nasha sucked in her breath. "The white stones."

"What?"

Nasha looked up at Dorle. "The white stones, the great broken teeth. We saw them, the Captain and I, from the control room." She touched Dorle's arm gently. "That's where they fired from. I didn't think we had landed so close."

"What is it?" Tance said, coming up to them. "I'm almost blind without my glasses. What do you see?"

"The city. Where they fired from."

"Oh." All three of them stood together. "Well, let's go," Tance said. "There's no telling what we'll find there." Dorle frowned at him.

"Wait. We don't know what we would be getting into. They must have patrols. They probably have seen us already, for that matter."

"They probably have seen the ship itself," Tance said. "They probably know right now where they can find it, where they can blow it up. So what difference does it make whether we go closer or not?"

"That's true," Nasha said. "If they really want to get us we haven't a chance. We have no armaments at all; you know that."

"I have a hand weapon." Dorle nodded. "Well, let's go on, then. I suppose you're right, Tance."

"But let's stay together," Tance said nervously. "Nasha, you're going too fast."

Nasha looked back. She laughed. "If we expect to get there by nightfall we must go fast."

* * * * *

They reached the outskirts of the city at about the middle of the afternoon. The sun, cold and yellow, hung above them in the colorless sky. Dorle stopped at the top of a ridge overlooking the city.

"Well, there it is. What's left of it."

There was not much left. The huge concrete piers which they had noticed were not piers at all, but the ruined foundations of buildings. They had been baked by the searing heat, baked and charred almost to the ground. Nothing else remained, only this irregular circle of white squares, perhaps four miles in diameter.

Dorle spat in disgust. "More wasted time. A dead skeleton of a city, that's all."

"But it was from here that the firing came," Tance murmured. "Don't forget that."

"And by someone with a good eye and a great deal of experience," Nasha added. "Let's go."

They walked into the city between the ruined buildings. No one spoke. They walked in silence, listening to the echo of their footsteps.

"It's macabre," Dorle muttered. "I've seen ruined cities before but they died of old age, old age and fatigue. This was killed, seared to death. This city didn't die-it was murdered."

"I wonder what the city was called," Nasha said. She turned aside, going up the remains of a stairway from one of the foundations. "Do you think we might find a signpost? Some kind of plaque?"

She peered into the ruins.

"There's nothing there," Dorle said impatiently. "Come on."

"Wait." Nasha bent down, touching a concrete stone. "There's something inscribed on this."

"What is it?" Tance hurried up. He squatted in the dust, running his gloved fingers over the surface of the stone. "Letters, all right." He took a writing stick from the pocket of his pressure suit and copied the inscription on a bit of paper. Dorle glanced over his shoulder. The inscription was:

FRANKLIN APARTMENTS

"That's this city," Nasha said softly. "That was its name."

Tance put the paper in his pocket and they went on. After a time Dorle said, "Nasha, you know, I think we're being watched. But don't look around."

The woman stiffened. "Oh? Why do you say that? Did you see something?"

"No. I can feel it, though. Don't you?"

Nasha smiled a little. "I feel nothing, but perhaps I'm more used to being stared at." She turned her head slightly. "Oh!"

Dorle reached for his hand weapon. "What is it? What do you see?" Tance had stopped dead in his tracks, his mouth half open.

"The gun," Nasha said. "It's the gun."

"Look at the size of it. The size of the thing." Dorle unfastened his hand weapon slowly. "That's it, all right."

The gun was huge. Stark and immense it pointed up at the sky, a mass of steel and glass, set in a huge slab of concrete. Even as they watched the gun moved on its swivel base, whirring underneath. A slim vane turned with the wind, a network of rods atop a high pole.

"It's alive," Nasha whispered. "It's listening to us, watching us."

The gun moved again, this time clockwise. It was mounted so that it could make a full circle. The barrel lowered a trifle, then resumed its original position.

"But who fires it?" Tance said.

Dorle laughed. "No one. No one fires it."

They stared at him. "What do you mean?"

"It fires itself."

They couldn't believe him. Nasha came close to him, frowning, looking up at him. "I don't understand. What do you mean, it fires itself?"

"Watch, I'll show you. Don't move." Dorle picked up a rock from the ground. He hesitated a moment and then tossed the rock high in the air. The rock passed in front of the gun. Instantly the great barrel moved, the vanes contracted.

* * * * *

The rock fell to the ground. The gun paused, then resumed its calm swivel, its slow circling.

"You see," Dorle said, "it noticed the rock, as soon as I threw it up in the air. It's alert to anything that flies or moves above the ground level. Probably it detected us as soon as we entered the gravitational field of the planet. It probably had a bead on us from the start. We don't have a chance. It knows all about the ship. It's just waiting for us to take off again."

"I understand about the rock," Nasha said, nodding. "The gun noticed it, but not us, since we're on the ground, not above. It's only designed to combat objects in the sky. The ship is safe until it takes off again, then the end will come."

"But what's this gun for?" Tance put in. "There's no one alive here. Everyone is dead."

"It's a machine," Dorle said. "A machine that was made to do a job. And it's doing the job. How it survived the blast I don't know. On it goes, waiting for the enemy. Probably they came by air in some sort of projectiles."

"The enemy," Nasha said. "Their own race. It is hard to believe that they really bombed themselves, fired at themselves."

"Well, it's over with. Except right here, where we're standing. This one gun, still alert, ready to kill. It'll go on until it wears out."

"And by that time we'll be dead," Nasha said bitterly.

"There must have been hundreds of guns like this," Dorle murmured. "They must have been used to the sight, guns, weapons, uniforms. Probably they accepted it as a natural thing, part of their lives, like eating and sleeping. An institution, like the church and the state. Men trained to fight, to lead armies, a regular profession. Honored, respected."

Tance was walking slowly toward the gun, peering nearsightedly up at it. "Quite complex, isn't it? All those vanes and tubes. I suppose this is some sort of a telescopic sight." His gloved hand touched the end of a long tube.

Instantly the gun shifted, the barrel retracting. It swung —

"Don't move!" Dorle cried. The barrel swung past them as they stood, rigid and still. For one terrible moment it hesitated over their heads, clicking and whirring, settling into position. Then the sounds died out and the gun became silent.

Tance smiled foolishly inside his helmet. "I must have put my finger over the lens. I'll be more careful." He made his way up onto the circular slab, stepping gingerly behind the body of the gun. He disappeared from view.

"Where did he go?" Nasha said irritably. "He'll get us all killed."

"Tance, come back!" Dorle shouted. "What's the matter with you?"

"In a minute." There was a long silence. At last the archeologist appeared. "I think I've found something. Come up and I'll show you."

"What is it?"

"Dorle, you said the gun was here to keep the enemy off. I think I know why they wanted to keep the enemy off."

They were puzzled.

"I think I've found what the gun is supposed to guard. Come and give me a hand."

"All right," Dorle said abruptly. "Let's go." He seized Nasha's hand. "Come on. Let's see what he's found. I thought something like this might happen when I saw that the gun was —"

"Like what?" Nasha pulled her hand away. "What are you talking about? You act as if you knew what he's found."

"I do." Dorle smiled down at her. "Do you remember the legend that all races have, the myth of the buried treasure, and the dragon, the serpent that watches it, guards it, keeping everyone away?"

She nodded. "Well?"

Dorle pointed up at the gun.

"That," he said, "is the dragon. Come on."

* * * * *

Between the three of them they managed to pull up the steel cover and lay it to one side. Dorle was wet with perspiration when they finished.

"It isn't worth it," he grunted. He stared into the dark yawning hole. "Or is it?"

Nasha clicked on her hand lamp, shining the beam down the stairs. The steps were thick with dust and rubble. At the bottom was a steel door.

"Come on," Tance said excitedly. He started down the stairs. They watched him reach the door and pull hopefully on it without success. "Give a hand!"

"All right." They came gingerly after him. Dorle examined the door. It was bolted shut, locked. There was an inscription on the door but he could not read it.

"Now what?" Nasha said.

Dorle took out his hand weapon. "Stand back. I can't think of any other way." He pressed the switch. The bottom of the door glowed red. Presently it began to crumble. Dorle clicked the weapon off. "I think we can get through. Let's try."

The door came apart easily. In a few minutes they had carried it away in pieces and stacked the pieces on the first step. Then they went on, flashing the light ahead of them.

They were in a vault. Dust lay everywhere, on everything, inches thick. Wood crates lined the walls, huge boxes and crates, packages and containers. Tance looked around curiously, his eyes bright.

"What exactly are all these?" he murmured. "Something valuable, I would think." He picked up a round drum and opened it. A spool fell to the floor, unwinding a black ribbon. He examined it, holding it up to the light.

"Look at this!"

They came around him. "Pictures," Nasha said. "Tiny pictures."

"Records of some kind." Tance closed the spool up in the drum again. "Look, hundreds of drums." He flashed the light around. "And those crates. Let's open one."

Dorle was already prying at the wood. The wood had turned brittle and dry. He managed to pull a section away.

It was a picture. A boy in a blue garment, smiling pleasantly, staring ahead, young and handsome. He seemed almost alive, ready to move toward them in the light of the hand lamp. It was one of them, one of the ruined race, the race that had perished.

For a long time they stared at the picture. At last Dorle replaced the board.

"All these other crates," Nasha said. "More pictures. And these drums. What are in the boxes?"

"This is their treasure," Tance said, almost to himself. "Here are their pictures, their records. Probably all their literature is here, their stories, their myths, their ideas about the universe."

"And their history," Nasha said. "We'll be able to trace their development and find out what it was that made them become what they were."

Dorle was wandering around the vault. "Odd," he murmured. "Even at the end, even after they had begun to fight they still knew, someplace down inside them, that their real treasure was this, their books and pictures, their myths. Even after their big cities and buildings and industries were destroyed they probably hoped to come back and find this. After everything else was gone."

"When we get back home we can agitate for a mission to come here," Tance said. "All this can be loaded up and taken back. We'll be leaving about —"

He stopped.

"Yes," Dorle said dryly. "We'll be leaving about three day-periods from now. We'll fix the ship, then take off. Soon we'll be home, that is, if nothing happens. Like being shot down by that —"

"Oh, stop it!" Nasha said impatiently. "Leave him alone. He's right: all this must be taken back home, sooner or later. We'll have to solve the problem of the gun. We have no choice."

Dorle nodded. "What's your solution, then? As soon as we leave the ground we'll be shot down." His face twisted bitterly. "They've guarded their treasure too well. Instead of being preserved it will lie here until it rots. It serves them right."

"How?"

"Don't you see? This was the only way they knew, building a gun and setting it up to shoot anything that came along. They were so certain that everything was hostile, the enemy, coming to take their possessions away from them. Well, they can keep them."

Nasha was deep in thought, her mind far away. Suddenly she gasped. "Dorle," she said. "What's the matter with us? We have no problem. The gun is no menace at all."

The two men stared at her.

"No menace?" Dorle said. "It's already shot us down once. And as soon as we take off again —"

"Don't you see?" Nasha began to laugh. "The poor foolish gun, it's completely harmless. Even I could deal with it alone."

"You?"

Her eyes were flashing. "With a crowbar. With a hammer or a stick of wood. Let's go back to the ship and load up. Of course we're at its mercy in the air: that's the way it was made. It can fire into the sky, shoot down anything that flies. But that's all! Against something on the ground it has no defenses. Isn't that right?"

Dorle nodded slowly. "The soft underbelly of the dragon. In the legend, the dragon's armor doesn't cover its stomach." He began to laugh. "That's right. That's perfectly right."

"Let's go, then," Nasha said. "Let's get back to the ship. We have work to do here."

* * * * *

It was early the next morning when they reached the ship. During the night the Captain had died, and the crew had ignited his body, according to custom. They had stood solemnly around it until the last ember died. As they were going back to their work the woman and the two men appeared, dirty and tired, still excited.

And presently, from the ship, a line of people came, each carrying something in his hands. The line marched across the gray slag, the eternal expanse of fused metal. When they reached the weapon they all fell on the gun at once, with crowbars, hammers, anything that was heavy and hard.

The telescopic sights shattered into bits. The wiring was pulled out, torn to shreds. The delicate gears were smashed, dented.

Finally the warheads themselves were carried off and the firing pins removed.

The gun was smashed, the great weapon destroyed. The people went down into the vault and examined the treasure. With its metal-armored guardian dead there was no danger any longer. They studied the pictures, the films, the crates of books, the jeweled crowns, the cups, the statues.

At last, as the sun was dipping into the gray mists that drifted across the planet they came back up the stairs again. For a moment they stood around the wrecked gun looking at the unmoving outline of it.

Then they started back to the ship. There was still much work to be done. The ship had been badly hurt, much had been damaged and lost. The important thing was to repair it as quickly as possible, to get it into the air.

With all of them working together it took just five more days to make it spaceworthy.

* * * * *

Nasha stood in the control room, watching the planet fall away behind them. She folded her arms, sitting down on the edge of the table.

"What are you thinking?" Dorle said.

"I? Nothing."

"Are you sure?"

"I was thinking that there must have been a time when this planet was quite different, when there was life on it."

"I suppose there was. It's unfortunate that no ships from our system came this far, but then we had no reason to suspect intelligent life until we saw the fission glow in the sky."

"And then it was too late."

"Not quite too late. After all, their possessions, their music, books, their pictures, all of that will survive. We'll take them home and study them, and they'll change us. We won't be the same afterwards. Their sculpturing, especially. Did you see the one of the great winged creature, without a head or arms? Broken off, I suppose. But those wings — It looked very old. It will change us a great deal."

"When we come back we won't find the gun waiting for us," Nasha said. "Next time it won't be there to shoot us down. We can land and take the treasure, as you call it." She smiled up at Dorle. "You'll lead us back there, as a good captain should."

"Captain?" Dorle grinned. "Then you've decided."

Nasha shrugged. "Fomar argues with me too much. I think, all in all, I really prefer you."

"Then let's go," Dorle said. "Let's go back home."

The ship roared up, flying over the ruins of the city. It turned in a huge arc and then shot off beyond the horizon, heading into outer space.

* * * * *

Down below, in the center of the ruined city, a single half-broken detector vane moved slightly, catching the roar of the ship. The base of the great gun throbbed painfully, straining to turn. After a moment a red warning light flashed on down inside its destroyed works.

And a long way off, a hundred miles from the city, another warning light flashed on, far underground. Automatic relays flew into action. Gears turned, belts whined. On the ground above a section of metal slag slipped back. A ramp appeared.

A moment later a small cart rushed to the surface.

The cart turned toward the city. A second cart appeared behind it. It was loaded with wiring cables. Behind it a third cart came, loaded with telescopic tube sights. And behind came more carts, some with relays, some with firing controls, some with tools and parts, screws and bolts, pins and nuts. The final one contained atomic warheads.

The carts lined up behind the first one, the lead cart. The lead cart started off, across the frozen ground, bumping calmly along, followed by the others. Moving toward the city.

To the damaged gun.

The Defenders

Taylor sat back in his chair reading the morning newspaper. The warm kitchen and the smell of coffee blended with the comfort of not having to go to work. This was his Rest Period, the first for a long time, and he was glad of it. He folded the second section back, sighing with contentment.

"What is it?" Mary said, from the stove.

"They pasted Moscow again last night." Taylor nodded his head in approval. "Gave it a real pounding. One of those R-H bombs. It's about time."

He nodded again, feeling the full comfort of the kitchen, the presence of his plump, attractive wife, the breakfast dishes and coffee. This was relaxation. And the war news was good, good and satisfying. He could feel a justifiable glow at the news, a sense of pride and personal accomplishment. After all, he was an integral part of the war program, not just another factory worker lugging a cart of scrap, but a technician, one of those who designed and planned the nerve-trunk of the war.

"It says they have the new subs almost perfected. Wait until they get *those* going." He smacked his lips with anticipation. "When they start shelling from underwater, the Soviets are sure going to be surprised."

"They're doing a wonderful job," Mary agreed vaguely. "Do you know what we saw today? Our team is getting a leady to show to the school children. I saw the leady, but only for a moment. It's good for the children to see what their contributions are going for, don't you think?"

She looked around at him.

"A leady," Taylor murmured. He put the newspaper slowly down. "Well, make sure it's decontaminated properly. We don't want to take any chances."

"Oh, they always bathe them when they're brought down from the surface," Mary said. "They wouldn't think of letting them down without the bath. Would they?" She hesitated, thinking back. "Don, you know, it makes me remember —"

He nodded. "I know."

* * * * *

He knew what she was thinking. Once in the very first weeks of the war, before everyone had been evacuated from the surface, they had seen a hospital train discharging the wounded, people who had been showered with sleet. He remembered the way they had looked, the expression on their faces, or as much of their faces as was left. It had not been a pleasant sight.

There had been a lot of that at first, in the early days before the transfer to undersurface was complete. There had been a lot, and it hadn't been very difficult to come across it.

Taylor looked up at his wife. She was thinking too much about it, the last few months. They all were.

"Forget it," he said. "It's all in the past. There isn't anybody up there now but the leadys, and they don't mind."

"But just the same, I hope they're careful when they let one of them down here. If one were still hot —"

He laughed, pushing himself away from the table. "Forget it. This is a wonderful moment; I'll be home for the next two shifts. Nothing to do but sit around and take things easy. Maybe we can take in a show. Okay?"

"A show? Do we have to? I don't like to look at all the destruction, the ruins. Sometimes I see some place I remember, like San Francisco. They showed a shot of San Francisco, the bridge broken and fallen in the water, and I got upset. I don't like to watch."

"But don't you want to know what's going on? No human beings are getting hurt, you know."

"But it's so awful!" Her face was set and strained. "Please, no, Don."

Don Taylor picked up his newspaper sullenly. "All right, but there isn't a hell of a lot else to do. And don't forget, *their* cities are getting it even worse."

She nodded. Taylor turned the rough, thin sheets of newspaper. His good mood had soured on him. Why did she have to fret all the time? They were pretty well off, as things went. You couldn't expect to have everything perfect, living undersurface, with an artificial sun and artificial food. Naturally it was a strain, not seeing the sky or being able to go any place or see anything other than metal walls, great roaring factories, the plant-yards, barracks. But it was better than being on surface. And some day it would end and they could return. Nobody *wanted* to live this way, but it was necessary.

He turned the page angrily and the poor paper ripped. Damn it, the paper was getting worse quality all the time, bad print, yellow tint —

Well, they needed everything for the war program. He ought to know that. Wasn't he one of the planners?

He excused himself and went into the other room. The bed was still unmade. They had better get it in shape before the seventh hour inspection. There was a one unit fine —

The vidphone rang. He halted. Who would it be? He went over and clicked it on.

"Taylor?" the face said, forming into place. It was an old face, gray and grim. "This is Moss. I'm sorry to bother you during Rest Period, but this thing has come up." He rattled papers. "I want you to hurry over here."

Taylor stiffened. "What is it? There's no chance it could wait?" The calm gray eyes were studying him, expressionless, unjudging. "If you want me to come down to the lab," Taylor grumbled, "I suppose I can. I'll get my uniform —"

"No. Come as you are. And not to the lab. Meet me at second stage as soon as possible. It'll take you about a half hour, using the fast car up. I'll see you there."

The picture broke and Moss disappeared.

* * * * *

"What was it?" Mary said, at the door.

"Moss. He wants me for something."

"I knew this would happen."

"Well, you didn't want to do anything, anyhow. What does it matter?" His voice was bitter. "It's all the same, every day. I'll bring you back something. I'm going up to second stage. Maybe I'll be close enough to the surface to —"

"Don't! Don't bring me anything! Not from the surface!"

"All right, I won't. But of all the irrational nonsense —"

She watched him put on his boots without answering.

* * * * *

Moss nodded and Taylor fell in step with him, as the older man strode along. A series of loads were going up to the surface, blind cars clanking like ore-trucks up the ramp, disappearing through the stage trap above them. Taylor watched the cars, heavy with tubular machinery of some sort, weapons new to him. Workers were everywhere, in the dark gray uniforms of the labor corps, loading, lifting, shouting back and forth. The stage was deafening with noise.

"We'll go up a way," Moss said, "where we can talk. This is no place to give you details."

They took an escalator up. The commercial lift fell behind them, and with it most of the crashing and booming. Soon they emerged on an observation platform, suspended on the side of the Tube, the vast tunnel leading to the surface, not more than half a mile above them now.

"My God!" Taylor said, looking down the Tube involuntarily. "It's a long way down."

Moss laughed. "Don't look."

They opened a door and entered an office. Behind the desk, an officer was sitting, an officer of Internal Security. He looked up.

"I'll be right with you, Moss." He gazed at Taylor studying him. "You're a little ahead of time."

"This is Commander Franks," Moss said to Taylor. "He was the first to make the discovery. I was notified last night." He tapped a parcel he carried. "I was let in because of this."

Franks frowned at him and stood up. "We're going up to first stage. We can discuss it there."

"First stage?" Taylor repeated nervously. The three of them went down a side passage to a small lift. "I've never been up there. Is it all right? It's not radioactive, is it?"

"You're like everyone else," Franks said. "Old women afraid of burglars. No radiation leaks down to first stage. There's lead and rock, and what comes down the Tube is bathed."

"What's the nature of the problem?" Taylor asked. "I'd like to know something about it."

"In a moment."

They entered the lift and ascended. When they stepped out, they were in a hall of soldiers, weapons and uniforms everywhere. Taylor blinked in surprise. So this was first stage, the closest undersurface level to the top! After this stage there was only rock, lead and rock, and the great tubes leading up like the burrows of earthworms. Lead and rock, and above that, where the tubes opened, the great expanse that no living being had seen for eight years, the vast, endless ruin that had once been Man's home, the place where he had lived, eight years ago.

Now the surface was a lethal desert of slag and rolling clouds. Endless clouds drifted back and forth, blotting out the red Sun. Occasionally something metallic stirred, moving through the remains of a city, threading its way across the tortured terrain of the countryside. A leady, a surface robot, immune to radiation, constructed with feverish haste in the last months before the cold war became literally hot.

Leadys, crawling along the ground, moving over the oceans or through the skies in slender, blackened craft, creatures that could exist where no *life* could remain, metal and plastic figures that waged a war Man had conceived, but which he could not fight himself. Human beings had invented war, invented and manufactured the weapons, even invented the players, the fighters, the actors of the war. But they themselves could not venture forth, could not wage it themselves. In all the world-in Russia, in Europe, America, Africa-no living human being remained. They were under the surface, in the deep shelters that had been carefully planned and built, even as the first bombs began to fall.

It was a brilliant idea and the only idea that could have worked. Up above, on the ruined, blasted surface of what had once been a living planet, the leady crawled and scurried, and fought Man's war. And undersurface, in the depths of the planet, human beings toiled endlessly to produce the weapons to continue the fight, month by month, year by year.

* * * * *

"First stage," Taylor said. A strange ache went through him. "Almost to the surface."

"But not quite," Moss said.

Franks led them through the soldiers, over to one side, near the lip of the Tube.

"In a few minutes, a lift will bring something down to us from the surface," he explained. "You see, Taylor, every once in a while Security examines and interrogates a surface leady, one that has been above for a time, to find out certain things. A vidcall is sent up and contact is made with a field headquarters. We need this direct interview; we can't depend on vidscreen contact alone. The leadys are doing a good job, but we want to make certain that everything is going the way we want it."

Franks faced Taylor and Moss and continued: "The lift will bring down a leady from the surface, one of the A-class leadys. There's an examination chamber in the next room, with a lead wall in the center, so the interviewing officers won't be exposed to radiation. We find this easier than bathing the leady. It is going right back up; it has a job to get back to.

"Two days ago, an A-class leady was brought down and interrogated. I conducted the session myself. We were interested in a new weapon the Soviets have been using, an automatic mine that pursues anything that moves. Military had sent instructions up that the mine be observed and reported in detail.

"This A-class leady was brought down with information. We learned a few facts from it, obtained the usual roll of film and reports, and then sent it back up. It was going out of the chamber, back to the lift, when a curious thing happened. At the time, I thought —"

Franks broke off. A red light was flashing.

"That down lift is coming." He nodded to some soldiers. "Let's enter the chamber. The leady will be along in a moment."

"An A-class leady," Taylor said. "I've seen them on the showscreens, making their reports."

"It's quite an experience," Moss said. "They're almost human."

* * * * *

They entered the chamber and seated themselves behind the lead wall. After a time, a signal was flashed, and Franks made a motion with his hands.

The door beyond the wall opened. Taylor peered through his view slot. He saw something advancing slowly, a slender metallic figure moving on a tread, its arm grips at rest by its sides. The figure halted and scanned the lead wall. It stood, waiting.

"We are interested in learning something," Franks said. "Before I question you, do you have anything to report on surface conditions?"

"No. The war continues." The leady's voice was automatic and toneless. "We are a little short of fast pursuit craft, the single-seat type. We could use also some —"

"That has all been noted. What I want to ask you is this. Our contact with you has been through vidscreen only. We must rely on indirect evidence, since none of us goes above. We can only infer what is going on. We never see anything ourselves. We have to take it all secondhand. Some top leaders are beginning to think there's too much room for error."

"Error?" the leady asked. "In what way? Our reports are checked carefully before they're sent down. We maintain constant contact with you; everything of value is reported. Any new weapons which the enemy is seen to employ —"

"I realize that," Franks grunted behind his peep slot. "But perhaps we should see it all for ourselves. Is it possible that there might be a large enough radiation-free area for a human party to ascend to the surface? If a few of us were to come up in lead-lined suits, would we be able to survive long enough to observe conditions and watch things?"

The machine hesitated before answering. "I doubt it. You can check air samples, of course, and decide for yourselves. But in the eight years since you left, things have continually worsened. You cannot have any real idea of conditions up there. It has become difficult for any moving object to survive for long. There are many kinds of projectiles sensitive to movement. The new mine not only reacts to motion, but continues to pursue the object indefinitely, until it finally reaches it. And the radiation is everywhere."

"I see." Franks turned to Moss, his eyes narrowed oddly. "Well, that was what I wanted to know. You may go."

The machine moved back toward its exit. It paused. "Each month the amount of lethal particles in the atmosphere increases. The tempo of the war is gradually —"

"I understand." Franks rose. He held out his hand and Moss passed him the package. "One thing before you leave. I want you to examine a new type of metal shield material. I'll pass you a sample with the tong."

Franks put the package in the toothed grip and revolved the tong so that he held the other end. The package swung down to the leady, which took it. They watched it unwrap the package and take the metal plate in its hands. The leady turned the metal over and over.

Suddenly it became rigid.

184

"All right," Franks said.

He put his shoulder against the wall and a section slid aside. Taylor gasped-Franks and Moss were hurrying up to the leady!

"Good God!" Taylor said. "But it's radioactive!"

* * * * *

The leady stood unmoving, still holding the metal. Soldiers appeared in the chamber. They surrounded the leady and ran a counter across it carefully.

"Okay, sir," one of them said to Franks. "It's as cold as a long winter evening."

"Good. I was sure, but I didn't want to take any chances."

"You see," Moss said to Taylor, "this leady isn't hot at all. Yet it came directly from the surface, without even being bathed."

"But what does it mean?" Taylor asked blankly.

"It may be an accident," Franks said. "There's always the possibility that a given object might escape being exposed above. But this is the second time it's happened that we know of. There may be others."

"The second time?"

"The previous interview was when we noticed it. The leady was not hot. It was cold, too, like this one."

Moss took back the metal plate from the leady's hands. He pressed the surface carefully and returned it to the stiff, unprotesting fingers.

"We shorted it out with this, so we could get close enough for a thorough check. It'll come back on in a second now. We had better get behind the wall again."

They walked back and the lead wall swung closed behind them. The soldiers left the chamber.

"Two periods from now," Franks said softly, "an initial investigating party will be ready to go surface-side. We're going up the Tube in suits, up to the top-the first human party to leave undersurface in eight years."

"It may mean nothing," Moss said, "but I doubt it. Something's going on, something strange. The leady told us no life could exist above without being roasted. The story doesn't fit."

Taylor nodded. He stared through the peep slot at the immobile metal figure. Already the leady was beginning to stir. It was bent in several places, dented and twisted, and its finish was blackened and charred. It was a leady that had been up there a long time; it had seen war and destruction, ruin so vast that no human being could imagine the extent. It had crawled and slunk in a world of radiation and death, a world where no life could exist.

And Taylor had touched it!

"You're going with us," Franks said suddenly. "I want you along. I think the three of us will go."

* * * * *

Mary faced him with a sick and frightened expression. "I know it. You're going to the surface. Aren't you?"

She followed him into the kitchen. Taylor sat down, looking away from her.

"It's a classified project," he evaded. "I can't tell you anything about it."

"You don't have to tell me. I know. I knew it the moment you came in. There was something on your face, something I haven't seen there for a long, long time. It was an old look."

She came toward him. "But how can they send you to the surface?" She took his face in her shaking hands, making him look at her. There was a strange hunger in her eyes. "Nobody can live up there. Look, look at this!"

She grabbed up a newspaper and held it in front of him.

"Look at this photograph. America, Europe, Asia, Africa-nothing but ruins. We've seen it every day on the showscreens. All destroyed, poisoned. And they're sending you up. Why? No living thing can get by up there, not even a weed, or grass. They've wrecked the surface, haven't they? *Haven't they?*"

Taylor stood up. "It's an order. I know nothing about it. I was told to report to join a scout party. That's all I know."

He stood for a long time, staring ahead. Slowly, he reached for the newspaper and held it up to the light.

"It looks real," he murmured. "Ruins, deadness, slag. It's convincing. All the reports, photographs, films, even air samples. Yet we haven't seen it for ourselves, not after the first months..."

"What are you talking about?"

"Nothing." He put the paper down. "I'm leaving early after the next Sleep Period. Let's turn in."

Mary turned away, her face hard and harsh. "Do what you want. We might just as well all go up and get killed at once, instead of dying slowly down here, like vermin in the ground."

He had not realized how resentful she was. Were they all like that? How about the workers toiling in the factories, day and night, endlessly? The pale, stooped men and women, plodding back and forth to work, blinking in the colorless light, eating synthetics —

"You shouldn't be so bitter," he said.

Mary smiled a little. "I'm bitter because I know you'll never come back." She turned away. "I'll never see you again, once you go up there."

He was shocked. "What? How can you say a thing like that?"

She did not answer.

* * * * *

He awakened with the public newscaster screeching in his ears, shouting outside the building.

"Special news bulletin! Surface forces report enormous Soviet attack with new weapons! Retreat of key groups! All work units report to factories at once!"

Taylor blinked, rubbing his eyes. He jumped out of bed and hurried to the vidphone. A moment later he was put through to Moss.

"Listen," he said. "What about this new attack? Is the project off?" He could see Moss's desk, covered with reports and papers.

"No," Moss said. "We're going right ahead. Get over here at once."

"But —"

"Don't argue with me." Moss held up a handful of surface bulletins, crumpling them savagely. "This is a fake. Come on!" He broke off.

Taylor dressed furiously, his mind in a daze.

Half an hour later, he leaped from a fast car and hurried up the stairs into the Synthetics Building. The corridors were full of men and women rushing in every direction. He entered Moss's office.

"There you are," Moss said, getting up immediately. "Franks is waiting for us at the outgoing station."

They went in a Security Car, the siren screaming. Workers scattered out of their way.

"What about the attack?" Taylor asked.

Moss braced his shoulders. "We're certain that we've forced their hand. We've brought the issue to a head."

They pulled up at the station link of the Tube and leaped out. A moment later they were moving up at high speed toward the first stage.

They emerged into a bewildering scene of activity. Soldiers were fastening on lead suits, talking excitedly to each other, shouting back and forth. Guns were being given out, instructions passed.

Taylor studied one of the soldiers. He was armed with the dreaded Bender pistol, the new snub-nosed hand weapon that was just beginning to come from the assembly line. Some of the soldiers looked a little frightened.

"I hope we're not making a mistake," Moss said, noticing his gaze.

Franks came toward them. "Here's the program. The three of us are going up first, alone. The soldiers will follow in fifteen minutes."

"What are we going to tell the leadys?" Taylor worriedly asked. "We'll have to tell them something."

"We want to observe the new Soviet attack." Franks smiled ironically. "Since it seems to be so serious, we should be there in person to witness it."

"And then what?" Taylor said.

"That'll be up to them. Let's go."

* * * * *

In a small car, they went swiftly up the Tube, carried by anti-grav beams from below. Taylor glanced down from time to time. It was a long way back, and getting longer each moment. He sweated nervously inside his suit, gripping his Bender pistol with inexpert fingers.

Why had they chosen him? Chance, pure chance. Moss had asked him to come along as a Department member. Then Franks had picked him out on the spur of the moment. And now they were rushing toward the surface, faster and faster.

A deep fear, instilled in him for eight years, throbbed in his mind. Radiation, certain death, a world blasted and lethal —

Up and up the car went. Taylor gripped the sides and closed his eyes. Each moment they were closer, the first living creatures to go above the first stage, up the Tube past the lead and rock, up to the surface. The phobic horror shook him in waves. It was death; they all knew that. Hadn't they seen it in the films a thousand times? The cities, the sleet coming down, the rolling clouds —

"It won't be much longer," Franks said. "We're almost there. The surface tower is not expecting us. I gave orders that no signal was to be sent."

The car shot up, rushing furiously. Taylor's head spun; he hung on, his eyes shut. Up and up....

The car stopped. He opened his eyes.

They were in a vast room, fluorescent-lit, a cavern filled with equipment and machinery, endless mounds of material piled in row after row. Among the stacks, leadys were working silently, pushing trucks and handcarts.

"Leadys," Moss said. His face was pale. "Then we're really on the surface."

The leadys were going back and forth with equipment moving the vast stores of guns and spare parts, ammunition and supplies that had been brought to the surface. And this was the receiving station for only one Tube; there were many others, scattered throughout the continent.

Taylor looked nervously around him. They were really there, above ground, on the surface. This was where the war was.

"Come on," Franks said. "A B-class guard is coming our way."

* * * * *

They stepped out of the car. A leady was approaching them rapidly. It coasted up in front of them and stopped, scanning them with its hand-weapon raised.

"This is Security," Franks said. "Have an A-class sent to me at once."

The leady hesitated. Other B-class guards were coming, scooting across the floor, alert and alarmed. Moss peered around.

"Obey!" Franks said in a loud, commanding voice. "You've been ordered!"

The leady moved uncertainly away from them. At the end of the building, a door slid back. Two A-class leadys appeared, coming slowly toward them. Each had a green stripe across its front.

"From the Surface Council," Franks whispered tensely. "This is above ground, all right. Get set."

The two leadys approached warily. Without speaking, they stopped close by the men, looking them up and down.

"I'm Franks of Security. We came from undersurface in order to —"

"This in incredible," one of the leadys interrupted him coldly. "You know you can't live up here. The whole surface is lethal to you. You can't possibly remain on the surface."

"These suits will protect us," Franks said. "In any case, it's not your responsibility. What I want is an immediate Council meeting so I can acquaint myself with conditions, with the situation here. Can that be arranged?"

"You human beings can't survive up here. And the new Soviet attack is directed at this area. It is in considerable danger."

"We know that. Please assemble the Council." Franks looked around him at the vast room, lit by recessed lamps in the ceiling. An uncertain quality came into his voice. "Is it night or day right now?"

"Night," one of the A-class leadys said, after a pause. "Dawn is coming in about two hours."

Franks nodded. "We'll remain at least two hours, then. As a concession to our sentimentality, would you please show us some place where we can observe the Sun as it comes up? We would appreciate it."

A stir went through the leadys.

"It is an unpleasant sight," one of the leadys said. "You've seen the photographs; you know what you'll witness. Clouds of drifting particles blot out the light, slag heaps are everywhere, the whole land is destroyed. For you it will be a staggering sight, much worse than pictures and film can convey."

"However it may be, we'll stay long enough to see it. Will you give the order to the Council?"

* * * * *

"Come this way." Reluctantly, the two leadys coasted toward the wall of the warehouse. The three men trudged after them, their heavy shoes ringing against the concrete. At the wall, the two leadys paused.

"This is the entrance to the Council Chamber. There are windows in the Chamber Room, but it is still dark outside, of course. You'll see nothing right now, but in two hours —"

"Open the door," Franks said.

The door slid back. They went slowly inside. The room was small, a neat room with a round table in the center, chairs ringing it. The three of them sat down silently, and the two leadys followed after them, taking their places.

"The other Council Members are on their way. They have already been notified and are coming as quickly as they can. Again I urge you to go back down." The leady surveyed the three human beings. "There is no way you can meet the conditions up here. Even we survive with some trouble, ourselves. How can you expect to do it?"

The leader approached Franks.

"This astonishes and perplexes us," it said. "Of course we must do what you tell us, but allow me to point out that if you remain here —"

"We know," Franks said impatiently. "However, we intend to remain, at least until sunrise."

"If you insist."

There was silence. The leadys seemed to be conferring with each other, although the three men heard no sound.

"For your own good," the leader said at last, "you must go back down. We have discussed this, and it seems to us that you are doing the wrong thing for your own good."

"We are human beings," Franks said sharply. "Don't you understand? We're men, not machines."

"That is precisely why you must go back. This room is radioactive; all surface areas are. We calculate that your suits will not protect you for over fifty more minutes. Therefore —"

The leadys moved abruptly toward the men, wheeling in a circle, forming a solid row. The men stood up, Taylor reaching awkwardly for his weapon, his fingers numb and stupid. The men stood facing the silent metal figures.

"We must insist," the leader said, its voice without emotion. "We must take you back to the Tube and send you down on the next car. I am sorry, but it is necessary."

"What'll we do?" Moss said nervously to Franks. He touched his gun. "Shall we blast them?"

Franks shook his head. "All right," he said to the leader. "We'll go back."

* * * * *

He moved toward the door, motioning Taylor and Moss to follow him. They looked at him in surprise, but they came with him. The leadys followed them out into the great warehouse. Slowly they moved toward the Tube entrance, none of them speaking.

At the lip, Franks turned. "We are going back because we have no choice. There are three of us and about a dozen of you. However, if —"

"Here comes the car," Taylor said.

There was a grating sound from the Tube. D-class leadys moved toward the edge to receive it.

"I am sorry," the leader said, "but it is for your protection. We are watching over you, literally. You must stay below and let us conduct the war. In a sense, it has come to be *our* war. We must fight it as we see fit."

The car rose to the surface.

Twelve soldiers, armed with Bender pistols, stepped from it and surrounded the three men. Moss breathed a sigh of relief. "Well, this does change things. It came off just right."

The leader moved back, away from the soldiers. It studied them intently, glancing from one to the next, apparently trying to make up its mind. At last it made a sign to the other leadys. They coasted aside and a corridor was opened up toward the warehouse.

"Even now," the leader said, "we could send you back by force. But it is evident that this is not really an observation party at all. These soldiers show that you have much more in mind; this was all carefully prepared."

"Very carefully," Franks said.

They closed in.

"How much more, we can only guess. I must admit that we were taken unprepared. We failed utterly to meet the situation. Now force would be absurd, because neither side can afford to injure the other; we, because of the restrictions placed on us regarding human life, you because the war demands —"

The soldiers fired, quick and in fright. Moss dropped to one knee, firing up. The leader dissolved in a cloud of particles. On all sides D- and B-class leadys were rushing up, some with weapons, some with metal slats. The room was in confusion. Off in the distance a siren was screaming. Franks and Taylor were cut off from the others, separated from the soldiers by a wall of metal bodies.

"They can't fire back," Franks said calmly. "This is another bluff. They've tried to bluff us all the way." He fired into the face of a leady. The leady dissolved. "They can only try to frighten us. Remember that."

* * * * *

They went on firing and leady after leady vanished. The room reeked with the smell of burning metal, the stink of fused plastic and steel. Taylor had been knocked down. He was struggling to find his gun, reaching wildly among metal legs, groping frantically to find it. His fingers strained, a handle swam in front of him. Suddenly something came down on his arm, a metal foot. He cried out.

Then it was over. The leadys were moving away, gathering together off to one side. Only four of the Surface Council remained. The others were radioactive particles in the air. D-class leadys were already restoring order, gathering up partly destroyed metal figures and bits and removing them.

Franks breathed a shuddering sigh.

"All right," he said. "You can take us back to the windows. It won't be long now."

The leadys separated, and the human group, Moss and Franks and Taylor and the soldiers, walked slowly across the room, toward the door. They entered the Council Chamber. Already a faint touch of gray mitigated the blackness of the windows.

"Take us outside," Franks said impatiently. "We'll see it directly, not in here."

A door slid open. A chill blast of cold morning air rushed in, chilling them even through their lead suits. The men glanced at each other uneasily.

"Come on," Franks said. "Outside."

He walked out through the door, the others following him.

They were on a hill, overlooking the vast bowl of a valley. Dimly, against the graying sky, the outline of mountains were forming, becoming tangible.

"It'll be bright enough to see in a few minutes," Moss said. He shuddered as a chilling wind caught him and moved around him. "It's worth it, really worth it, to see this again after eight years. Even if it's the last thing we see —"

"Watch," Franks snapped.

They obeyed, silent and subdued. The sky was clearing, brightening each moment. Some place far off, echoing across the valley, a rooster crowed.

"A chicken!" Taylor murmured. "Did you hear?"

Behind them, the leadys had come out and were standing silently, watching, too. The gray sky turned to white and the hills appeared more clearly. Light spread across the valley floor, moving toward them.

"God in heaven!" Franks exclaimed.

Trees, trees and forests. A valley of plants and trees, with a few roads winding among them. Farmhouses. A windmill. A barn, far down below them.

"Look!" Moss whispered.

Color came into the sky. The Sun was approaching. Birds began to sing. Not far from where they stood, the leaves of a tree danced in the wind.

Franks turned to the row of leadys behind them.

"Eight years. We were tricked. There was no war. As soon as we left the surface —"

"Yes," an A-class leady admitted. "As soon as you left, the war ceased. You're right, it was a hoax. You worked hard undersurface, sending up guns and weapons, and we destroyed them as fast as they came up."

"But why?" Taylor asked, dazed. He stared down at the vast valley below. "Why?"

* * * * *

"You created us," the leady said, "to pursue the war for you, while you human beings went below the ground in order to survive. But before we could continue the war, it was necessary to analyze it to determine what its purpose was. We did this, and we found that it had no purpose, except, perhaps, in terms of human needs. Even this was questionable.

"We investigated further. We found that human cultures pass through phases, each culture in its own time. As the culture ages and begins to lose its objectives, conflict arises within it between those who wish to cast it off and set up a new culture-pattern, and those who wish to retain the old with as little change as possible.

"At this point, a great danger appears. The conflict within threatens to engulf the society in self-war, group against group. The vital traditions may be lost-not merely altered or re-formed, but completely destroyed in this period of chaos and anarchy. We have found many such examples in the history of mankind.

"It is necessary for this hatred within the culture to be directed outward, toward an external group, so that the culture itself may survive its crisis. War is the result. War, to a logical mind, is absurd. But in terms of human needs, it plays a vital role. And it will continue to until Man has grown up enough so that no hatred lies within him."

Taylor was listening intently. "Do you think this time will come?"

"Of course. It has almost arrived now. This is the last war. Man is *almost* united into one final culture —a world culture. At this point he stands continent against continent, one half of the world against the other half. Only a single step remains, the jump to a unified culture. Man has climbed slowly upward, tending always toward unification of his culture. It will not be long —

"But it has not come yet, and so the war had to go on, to satisfy the last violent surge of hatred that Man felt. Eight years have passed since the war began. In these eight years, we have observed and noted important changes going on in the minds of men. Fatigue and disinterest, we have seen, are gradually taking the place of hatred and fear. The hatred is being exhausted gradually, over a period of time. But for the present, the hoax must go on, at least for a while longer. You are not ready to learn the truth. You would want to continue the war."

"But how did you manage it?" Moss asked. "All the photographs, the samples, the damaged equipment —"

"Come over here." The leady directed them toward a long, low building. "Work goes on constantly, whole staffs laboring to maintain a coherent and convincing picture of a global war."

* * * * *

They entered the building. Leadys were working everywhere, poring over tables and desks.

"Examine this project here," the A-class leady said. Two leadys were carefully photographing something, an elaborate model on a table top. "It is a good example."

The men grouped around, trying to see. It was a model of a ruined city.

Taylor studied it in silence for a long time. At last he looked up.

"It's San Francisco," he said in a low voice. "This is a model of San Francisco, destroyed. I saw this on the vidscreen, piped down to us. The bridges were hit —"

"Yes, notice the bridges." The leady traced the ruined span with his metal finger, a tiny spider-web, almost invisible. "You have no doubt seen photographs of this many times, and of the other tables in this building.

"San Francisco itself is completely intact. We restored it soon after you left, rebuilding the parts that had been damaged at the start of the war. The work of manufacturing news goes on all the time in this particular building. We are very careful to see that each part fits in with all the other parts. Much time and effort are devoted to it."

Franks touched one of the tiny model buildings, lying half in ruins. "So this is what you spend your time doing-making model cities and then blasting them."

"No, we do much more. We are caretakers, watching over the whole world. The owners have left for a time, and we must see that the cities are kept clean, that decay is prevented, that everything is kept oiled and in running condition. The gardens, the streets, the water mains, everything must be maintained as it was eight years ago, so that when the owners return, they will not be displeased. We want to be sure that they will be completely satisfied."

Franks tapped Moss on the arm.

"Come over here," he said in a low voice. "I want to talk to you."

He led Moss and Taylor out of the building, away from the leadys, outside on the hillside. The soldiers followed them. The Sun was up and the sky was turning blue. The air smelled sweet and good, the smell of growing things.

Taylor removed his helmet and took a deep breath.

"I haven't smelled that smell for a long time," he said.

"Listen," Franks said, his voice low and hard. "We must get back down at once. There's a lot to get started on. All this can be turned to our advantage."

"What do you mean?" Moss asked.

"It's a certainty that the Soviets have been tricked, too, the same as us. But *we* have found out. That gives us an edge over them."

"I see." Moss nodded. "We know, but they don't. Their Surface Council has sold out, the same as ours. It works against them the same way. But if we could —"

"With a hundred top-level men, we could take over again, restore things as they should be! It would be easy!"

* * * * *

Moss touched him on the arm. An A-class leady was coming from the building toward them.

"We've seen enough," Franks said, raising his voice. "All this is very serious. It must be reported below and a study made to determine our policy."

The leady said nothing.

Franks waved to the soldiers. "Let's go." He started toward the warehouse.

Most of the soldiers had removed their helmets. Some of them had taken their lead suits off, too, and were relaxing comfortably in their cotton uniforms. They stared around them, down the hillside at the trees and bushes, the vast expanse of green, the mountains and the sky.

"Look at the Sun," one of them murmured.

"It sure is bright as hell," another said.

"We're going back down," Franks said. "Fall in by twos and follow us."

Reluctantly, the soldiers regrouped. The leadys watched without emotion as the men marched slowly back toward the warehouse. Franks and Moss and Taylor led them across the ground, glancing alertly at the leadys as they walked.

They entered the warehouse. D-class leadys were loading material and weapons on surface carts. Cranes and derricks were working busily everywhere. The work was done with efficiency, but without hurry or excitement.

The men stopped, watching. Leadys operating the little carts moved past them, signaling silently to each other. Guns and parts were being hoisted by magnetic cranes and lowered gently onto waiting carts.

"Come on," Franks said.

He turned toward the lip of the Tube. A row of D-class leadys was standing in front of it, immobile and silent. Franks stopped, moving back. He looked around. An A-class leady was coming toward him.

"Tell them to get out of the way," Franks said. He touched his gun. "You had better move them."

Time passed, an endless moment, without measure. The men stood, nervous and alert, watching the row of leadys in front of them.

"As you wish," the A-class leady said.

It signaled and the D-class leadys moved into life. They stepped slowly aside.

Moss breathed a sigh of relief.

"I'm glad that's over," he said to Franks. "Look at them all. Why don't they try to stop us? They must know what we're going to do."

Franks laughed. "Stop us? You saw what happened when they tried to stop us before. They can't; they're only machines. We built them so they can't lay hands on us, and they know that."

His voice trailed off.

The men stared at the Tube entrance. Around them the leadys watched, silent and impassive, their metal faces expressionless.

For a long time the men stood without moving. At last Taylor turned away.

"Good God," he said. He was numb, without feeling of any kind.

The Tube was gone. It was sealed shut, fused over. Only a dull surface of cooling metal greeted them.

The Tube had been closed.

* * * * *

Franks turned, his face pale and vacant.

The A-class leady shifted. "As you can see, the Tube has been shut. We were prepared for this. As soon as all of you were on the surface, the order was given. If you had gone back when we asked you, you would now be safely down below. We had to work quickly because it was such an immense operation."

"But why?" Moss demanded angrily.

"Because it is unthinkable that you should be allowed to resume the war. With all the Tubes sealed, it will be many months before forces from below can reach the surface, let alone organize a military program. By that time the cycle will have entered its last stages. You will not be so perturbed to find your world intact.

"We had hoped that you would be undersurface when the sealing occurred. Your presence here is a nuisance. When the Soviets broke through, we were able to accomplish their sealing without —"

"The Soviets? They broke through?"

"Several months ago, they came up unexpectedly to see why the war had not been won. We were forced to act with speed. At this moment they are desperately attempting to cut new Tubes to the surface, to resume the war. We have, however, been able to seal each new one as it appears."

The leady regarded the three men calmly.

"We're cut off," Moss said, trembling. "We can't get back. What'll we do?"

"How did you manage to seal the Tube so quickly?" Franks asked the leady. "We've been up here only two hours."

"Bombs are placed just above the first stage of each Tube for such emergencies. They are heat bombs. They fuse lead and rock."

Gripping the handle of his gun, Franks turned to Moss and Taylor.

"What do you say? We can't go back, but we can do a lot of damage, the fifteen of us. We have Bender guns. How about it?"

He looked around. The soldiers had wandered away again, back toward the exit of the building. They were standing outside, looking at the valley and the sky. A few of them were carefully climbing down the slope.

"Would you care to turn over your suits and guns?" the A-class leady asked politely. "The suits are uncomfortable and you'll have no need for weapons. The Russians have given up theirs, as you can see."

Fingers tensed on triggers. Four men in Russian uniforms were coming toward them from an aircraft that they suddenly realized had landed silently some distance away.

"Let them have it!" Franks shouted.

"They are unarmed," said the leady. "We brought them here so you could begin peace talks."

"We have no authority to speak for our country," Moss said stiffly.

"We do not mean diplomatic discussions," the leady explained. "There will be no more. The working out of daily problems of existence will teach you how to get along in the same world. It will not be easy, but it will be done."

* * * * *

The Russians halted and they faced each other with raw hostility.

"I am Colonel Borodoy and I regret giving up our guns," the senior Russian said. "You could have been the first Americans to be killed in almost eight years."

"Or the first Americans to kill," Franks corrected.

"No one would know of it except yourselves," the leady pointed out. "It would be useless heroism. Your real concern should be surviving on the surface. We have no food for you, you know."

Taylor put his gun in its holster. "They've done a neat job of neutralizing us, damn them. I propose we move into a city, start raising crops with the help of some leadys, and generally make ourselves comfortable." Drawing his lips tight over his teeth, he glared at the A-class leady. "Until our families can come up from undersurface, it's going to be pretty lonesome, but we'll have to manage."

"If I may make a suggestion," said another Russian uneasily. "We tried living in a city. It is too empty. It is also too hard to maintain for so few people. We finally settled in the most modern village we could find."

"Here in this country," a third Russian blurted. "We have much to learn from you."

The Americans abruptly found themselves laughing.

"You probably have a thing or two to teach us yourselves," said Taylor generously, "though I can't imagine what."

The Russian colonel grinned. "Would you join us in our village? It would make our work easier and give us company."

"Your village?" snapped Franks. "It's American, isn't it? It's ours!"

The leady stepped between them. "When our plans are completed, the term will be interchangeable. 'Ours' will eventually mean mankind's." It pointed at the aircraft, which was warming up. "The ship is waiting. Will you join each other in making a new home?"

The Russians waited while the Americans made up their minds.

"I see what the leadys mean about diplomacy becoming outmoded," Franks said at last. "People who work together don't need diplomats. They solve their problems on the operational level instead of at a conference table."

The leady led them toward the ship. "It is the goal of history, unifying the world. From family to tribe to city-state to nation to hemisphere, the direction has been toward unification. Now the hemispheres will be joined and —"

Taylor stopped listening and glanced back at the location of the Tube. Mary was undersurface there. He hated to leave her, even though he couldn't see her again until the Tube was unsealed. But then he shrugged and followed the others.

If this tiny amalgam of former enemies was a good example, it wouldn't be too long before he and Mary and the rest of humanity would be living on the surface like rational human beings instead of blindly hating moles.

"It has taken thousands of generations to achieve," the A-class leady concluded. "Hundreds of centuries of bloodshed and destruction. But each war was a step toward uniting mankind. And now the end is in sight: a world without war. But even that is only the beginning of a new stage of history."

"The conquest of space," breathed Colonel Borodoy.

"The meaning of life," Moss added.

"Eliminating hunger and poverty," said Taylor.

The leady opened the door of the ship. "All that and more. How much more? We cannot foresee it any more than the first men who formed a tribe could foresee this day. But it will be unimaginably great."

The door closed and the ship took off toward their new home.

Tony and the Beetles

Reddish-yellow sunlight filtered through the thick quartz windows into the sleep-compartment. Tony Rossi yawned, stirred a little, then opened his black eyes and sat up quickly. With one motion he tossed the covers back and slid to the warm metal floor. He clicked off his alarm clock and hurried to the closet.

It looked like a nice day. The landscape outside was motionless, undisturbed by winds or dust-shift. The boy's heart pounded excitedly. He pulled his trousers on, zipped up the reinforced mesh, struggled into his heavy canvas shirt, and then sat down on the edge of the cot to tug on his boots. He closed the seams around their tops and then did the same with his gloves. Next he adjusted the pressure on his pump unit and strapped it between his shoulder blades. He grabbed his helmet from the dresser, and he was ready for the day.

In the dining-compartment his mother and father had finished breakfast. Their voices drifted to him as he clattered down the ramp. A disturbed murmur; he paused to listen. What were they talking about? Had he done something wrong, again?

And then he caught it. Behind their voices was another voice. Static and crackling pops. The all-system audio signal from Rigel IV. They had it turned up full blast; the dull thunder of the monitor's voice boomed loudly. The war. Always the war. He sighed, and stepped out into the dining-compartment.

"Morning," his father muttered.

"Good morning, dear," his mother said absently. She sat with her head turned to one side, wrinkles of concentration webbing her forehead. Her thin lips were drawn together in a tight line of concern. His father had pushed his dirty dishes back and was smoking, elbows on the table, dark hairy arms bare and muscular. He was scowling, intent on the jumbled roar from the speaker above the sink.

"How's it going?" Tony asked. He slid into his chair and reached automatically for the ersatz grapefruit. "Any news from Orion?"

Neither of them answered. They didn't hear him. He began to eat his grapefruit. Outside, beyond the little metal and plastic housing unit, sounds of activity grew. Shouts and muffled crashes, as rural merchants and their trucks rumbled along the highway toward Karnet. The reddish daylight swelled; Betelgeuse was rising quietly and majestically.

"Nice day," Tony said. "No flux wind. I think I'll go down to the n-quarter awhile. We're building a neat spaceport, a model, of course, but we've been able to get enough materials to lay out strips for —"

With a savage snarl his father reached out and struck the audio roar immediately died. "I knew it!" He got up and moved angrily away from the table. "I told them it would happen. They shouldn't have moved so soon. Should have built up Class A supply bases, first."

"Isn't our main fleet moving in from Bellatrix?" Tony's mother fluttered anxiously. "According to last night's summary the worst that can happen is Orion IX and X will be dumped."

Joseph Rossi laughed harshly. "The hell with last night's summary. They know as well as I do what's happening."

"What's happening?" Tony echoed, as he pushed aside his grapefruit and began to ladle out dry cereal. "Are we losing the battle?"

"Yes!" His father's lips twisted. "Earthmen, losing to-to *beetles*. I told them. But they couldn't wait. My God, there's ten good years left in this system. Why'd they have to push on? Everybody knew Orion would be tough. The whole damn beetle fleet's strung out around there. Waiting for us. And we have to barge right in."

"But nobody ever thought beetles would fight," Leah Rossi protested mildly. "Everybody thought they'd just fire a few blasts and then —"

"They *have* to fight! Orion's the last jump-off. If they don't fight here, where the hell can they fight?" Rossi swore savagely. "Of course they're fighting. We have all their planets except the inner Orion string–not that they're worth much, but it's the principle of the thing. If we'd built up strong supply bases, we could have broken up the beetle fleet and really clobbered it."

"Don't say 'beetle,'" Tony murmured, as he finished his cereal. "They're Pas-udeti, same as here. The word 'beetle' comes from Betelgeuse. An Arabian word we invented ourselves."

Joe Rossi's mouth opened and closed. "What are you, a goddamn beetle-lover?"

"Joe," Leah snapped. "For heaven's sake."

Rossi moved toward the door. "If I was ten years younger I'd be out there. I'd really show those shiny-shelled insects what the hell they're up against. Them and their junky beat-up old hulks. Converted freighters!" His eyes blazed. "When I think of them shooting down Terran cruisers with *our* boys in them —"

"Orion's their system," Tony murmured.

"*Their* system! When the hell did you get to be an authority on space law? Why, I ought to —" He broke off, choked with rage. "My own kid," he muttered. "One more crack out of you today and I'll hang one on you you'll feel the rest of the week."

Tony pushed his chair back. "I won't be around here today. I'm going into Karnet, with my EEP."

"Yeah, to play with beetles!"

Tony said nothing. He was already sliding his helmet in place and snapping the clamps tight. As he pushed through the back door, into the lock membrane, he unscrewed his oxygen tap and set the tank filter into action. An automatic response, conditioned by a lifetime spent on a colony planet in an alien system.

* * * * *

A faint flux wind caught at him and swept yellow-red dust around his boots. Sunlight glittered from the metal roof of his family's housing unit, one of endless rows of squat boxes set in the sandy slope, protected by the line of ore-refining installations against the horizon. He made an impatient signal, and from the storage shed his EEP came gliding out, catching the sunlight on its chrome trim.

"We're going down into Karnet," Tony said, unconsciously slipping into the Pas dialect. "Hurry up!"

The EEP took up its position behind him, and he started briskly down the slope, over the shifting sand, toward the road. There were quite a few traders out, today. It was a good day for the market; only a fourth of the year was fit for travel. Betelgeuse was an erratic and undependable sun, not at all like Sol (according to the edutapes, fed to Tony four hours a day, six days a week-he had never seen Sol himself).

He reached the noisy road. Pas-udeti were everywhere. Whole groups of them, with their primitive combustion-driven trucks, battered and filthy, motors grinding protestingly. He waved at the trucks as they pushed past him. After a moment one slowed down. It was piled with *tis*, bundled heaps of gray vegetables dried, and prepared for the table. A staple of the Pas-udeti diet. Behind the wheel lounged a dark-faced elderly Pas, one arm over the open window, a rolled leaf between his lips. He was like all other Pas-udeti; lank and hard-shelled, encased in a brittle sheath in which he lived and died.

"You want a ride?" the Pas murmured-required protocol when an Earthman on foot was encountered.

"Is there room for my EEP?"

The Pas made a careless motion with his claw. "It can run behind." Sardonic amusement touched his ugly old face. "If it gets to Karnet we'll sell it for scrap. We can use a few condensers and relay tubing. We're short on electronic maintenance stuff."

"I know," Tony said solemnly, as he climbed into the cabin of the truck. "It's all been sent to the big repair base at Orion I. For your warfleet."

Amusement vanished from the leathery face. "Yes, the warfleet." He turned away and started up the truck again. In the back, Tony's EEP had scrambled up on the load of *tis* and was gripping precariously with its magnetic lines.

Tony noticed the Pas-udeti's sudden change of expression, and he was puzzled. He started to speak to him-but now he noticed unusual quietness among the other Pas, in the other trucks, behind and in front of his own. The war, of course. It had swept through this system a century ago; these people had been left behind. Now all eyes were on Orion, on the battle between the Terran warfleet and the Pas-udeti collection of armed freighters.

"Is it true," Tony asked carefully, "that you're winning?"

The elderly Pas grunted. "We hear rumors."

Tony considered. "My father says Terra went ahead too fast. He says we should have consolidated. We didn't assemble adequate supply bases. He used to be an officer, when he was younger. He was with the fleet for two years."

The Pas was silent a moment. "It's true," he said at last, "that when you're so far from home, supply is a great problem. We, on the other hand, don't have that. We have no distances to cover."

"Do you know anybody fighting?"

"I have distant relatives." The answer was vague; the Pas obviously didn't want to talk about it.

"Have you ever seen your warfleet?"

"Not as it exists now. When this system was defeated most of our units were wiped out. Remnants limped to Orion and joined the Orion fleet."

"Your relatives were with the remnants?"

"That's right."

"Then you were alive when this planet was taken?"

"Why do you ask?" The old Pas quivered violently. "What business is it of yours?"

Tony leaned out and watched the walls and buildings of Karnet grow ahead of them. Karnet was an old city. It had stood thousands of years. The Pas-udeti civilization was stable; it had reached a certain point of technocratic development and then leveled off. The Pas had inter-system ships that had carried people and freight between planets in the days before the Terran Confederation. They had combustion-driven cars, audiophones, a power network of a magnetic type. Their plumbing was satisfactory and their medicine was highly advanced. They had art forms, emotional and exciting. They had a vague religion.

"Who do you think will win the battle?" Tony asked.

"I don't know." With a sudden jerk the old Pas brought the truck to a crashing halt. "This is as far as I go. Please get out and take your EEP with you."

Tony faltered in surprise. "But aren't you going —?"

"No farther!"

Tony pushed the door open. He was vaguely uneasy; there was a hard, fixed expression on the leathery face, and the old creature's voice had a sharp edge he had never heard before. "Thanks," he murmured. He hopped down into the red dust and signaled his EEP. It released its magnetic lines, and instantly the truck started up with a roar, passing on inside the city.

Tony watched it go, still dazed. The hot dust lapped at his ankles; he automatically moved his feet and slapped at his trousers. A truck honked, and his EEP quickly moved him from the road, up to the level pedestrian ramp. Pas-udeti in swarms moved by, endless lines of rural people hurrying into Karnet on their daily business. A massive public bus had stopped by the gate and was letting off passengers. Male and female Pas. And children. They laughed and shouted; the sounds of their voices blended with the low hum of the city.

"Going in?" a sharp Pas-udeti voice sounded close behind him. "Keep moving-you're blocking the ramp."

It was a young female, with a heavy armload clutched in her claws. Tony felt embarrassed; female Pas had a certain telepathic ability, part of their sexual make-up. It was effective on Earthmen at close range.

"Here," she said. "Give me a hand."

Tony nodded his head, and the EEP accepted the female's heavy armload. "I'm visiting the city," Tony said, as they moved with the crowd toward the gates. "I got a ride most of the way, but the driver let me off out here."

"You're from the settlement?"

"Yes."

She eyed him critically. "You've always lived here, haven't you?"

"I was born here. My family came here from Earth four years before I was born. My father was an officer in the fleet. He earned an Emigration Priority."

"So you've never seen your own planet. How old are you?"

"Ten years. Terran."

"You shouldn't have asked the driver so many questions."

They passed through the decontamination shield and into the city. An information square loomed ahead; Pas men and women were packed around it. Moving chutes and transport cars rumbled everywhere. Buildings and ramps and open-air machinery; the city was sealed in a protective dust-proof envelope. Tony unfastened his helmet and clipped it to his belt. The air was stale-smelling, artificial, but usable.

"Let me tell you something," the young female said carefully, as she strode along the foot-ramp beside Tony. "I wonder if this is a good day for you to come into Karnet. I know you've been coming here regularly to play with your friends. But perhaps today you ought to stay at home, in your settlement."

"Why?"

"Because today everybody is upset."

"I know," Tony said. "My mother and father were upset. They were listening to the news from our base in the Rigel system."

"I don't mean your family. Other people are listening, too. These people here. My race."

"They're upset, all right," Tony admitted. "But I come here all the time. There's nobody to play with at the settlement, and anyhow we're working on a project."

"A model spaceport."

"That's right." Tony was envious. "I sure wish I was a telepath. It must be fun."

The female Pas-udeti was silent. She was deep in thought. "What would happen," she asked, "if your family left here and returned to Earth?"

"That couldn't happen. There's no room for us on Earth. C-bombs destroyed most of Asia and North America back in the Twentieth Century."

"Suppose you *had* to go back?"

Tony did not understand. "But we can't. Habitable portions of Earth are overcrowded. Our main problem is finding places for Terrans to live, in other systems." He added, "And anyhow, I don't particularly want to go to Terra. I'm used to it here. All my friends are here."

"I'll take my packages," the female said. "I go this other way, down this third-level ramp."

Tony nodded to his EEP and it lowered the bundles into the female's claws. She lingered a moment, trying to find the right words.

"Good luck," she said.

"With what?"

She smiled faintly, ironically. "With your model spaceport. I hope you and your friends get to finish it."

"Of course we'll finish it," Tony said, surprised. "It's almost done." What did she mean?

The Pas-udeti woman hurried off before he could ask her. Tony was troubled and uncertain; more doubts filled him. After a moment he headed slowly into the lane that took him toward the residential section of the city. Past the stores and factories, to the place where his friends lived.

The group of Pas-udeti children eyed him silently as he approached. They had been playing in the shade of an immense *hengelo*, whose ancient branches drooped and swayed with the air currents pumped through the city. Now they sat unmoving.

"I didn't expect you today," B'prith said, in an expressionless voice.

Tony halted awkwardly, and his EEP did the same. "How are things?" he murmured.

"Fine."

"I got a ride part way."

"Fine."

Tony squatted down in the shade. None of the Pas children stirred. They were small, not as large as Terran children. Their shells had not hardened, had not turned dark and opaque, like horn. It gave them a soft, unformed appearance, but at the same time it lightened their load. They moved more easily than their elders; they could hop and skip around, still. But they were not skipping right now.

"What's the matter?" Tony demanded. "What's wrong with everybody?"

No one answered.

"Where's the model?" he asked. "Have you fellows been working on it?"

After a moment Llyre nodded slightly.

Tony felt dull anger rise up inside him. "Say something! What's the matter? What're you all mad about?"

"Mad?" B'prith echoed. "We're not mad."

Tony scratched aimlessly in the dust. He knew what it was. The war, again. The battle going on near Orion. His anger burst up wildly. "Forget the war. Everything was fine yesterday, before the battle."

"Sure," Llyre said. "It was fine."

Tony caught the edge to his voice. "It happened a hundred years ago. It's not my fault."

"Sure," B'prith said.

"This is my home. Isn't it? Haven't I got as much right here as anybody else? I was born here."

"Sure," Llyre said, tonelessly.

Tony appealed to them helplessly. "Do you have to act this way? You didn't act this way yesterday. I was here yesterday-all of us were here yesterday. What's happened since yesterday?"

"The battle," B'prith said.

"What difference does *that* make? Why does that change everything? There's always war. There've been battles all the time, as long as I can remember. What's different about this?"

B'prith broke apart a clump of dirt with his strong claws. After a moment he tossed it away and got slowly to his feet. "Well," he said thoughtfully, "according to our audio relay, it looks as if our fleet is going to win, this time."

"Yes," Tony agreed, not understanding. "My father says we didn't build up adequate supply bases. We'll probably have to fall back to...." And then the impact hit him. "You mean, for the first time in a hundred years —"

"Yes," Llyre said, also getting up. The others got up, too. They moved away from Tony, toward the near-by house. "We're winning. The Terran flank was turned, half an hour ago. Your right wing has folded completely."

Tony was stunned. "And it matters. It matters to all of you."

"Matters!" B'prith halted, suddenly blazing out in fury. "Sure it matters! For the first time-in a century. The first time in our lives we're beating you. We have you on the run, you —" He choked out the word, almost spat it out. "You white-grubs!"

They disappeared into the house. Tony sat gazing stupidly down at the ground, his hands still moving aimlessly. He had heard the word before, seen it scrawled on walls and in the dust near the settlement. *White-grubs.* The Pas term of derision for Terrans. Because of their softness, their whiteness. Lack of hard shells. Pulpy, doughy skin. But they had never dared say it out loud, before. To an Earthman's face.

Beside him, his EEP stirred restlessly. Its intricate radio mechanism sensed the hostile atmosphere. Automatic relays were sliding into place; circuits were opening and closing.

"It's all right," Tony murmured, getting slowly up. "Maybe we'd better go back."

He moved unsteadily toward the ramp, completely shaken. The EEP walked calmly ahead, its metal face blank and confident, feeling nothing, saying nothing. Tony's thoughts were a wild turmoil; he shook his head, but the crazy spinning kept up. He couldn't make his mind slow down, lock in place.

"Wait a minute," a voice said. B'prith's voice, from the open doorway. Cold and withdrawn, almost unfamiliar.

"What do you want?"

B'prith came toward him, claws behind his back in the formal Pas-udeti posture, used between total strangers. "You shouldn't have come here, today."

"I know," Tony said.

B'prith got out a bit of *tis* stalk and began to roll it into a tube. He pretended to concentrate on it. "Look," he said. "You said you have a right here. But you don't."

"I —" Tony murmured.

"Do you understand why not? You said it isn't your fault. I guess not. But it's not my fault, either. Maybe it's nobody's fault. I've known you a long time."

"Five years. Terran."

B'prith twisted the stalk up and tossed it away. "Yesterday we played together. We worked on the spaceport. But we can't play today. My family said to tell you not to come here any more." He hesitated, and did not look Tony in the face. "I was going to tell you, anyhow. Before they said anything."

"Oh," Tony said.

"Everything that's happened today-the battle, our fleet's stand. We didn't know. We didn't dare hope. You see? A century of running. First this system. Then the Rigel system, all the planets. Then the other Orion stars. We fought here and there-scattered fights. Those that got away joined up. We supplied the base at Orion-you people didn't know. But there was no hope; at least, nobody thought there was." He was silent a moment. "Funny," he said, "what happens when your back's to the wall, and there isn't any further place to go. Then you have to fight."

"If our supply bases —" Tony began thickly, but B'prith cut him off savagely.

"Your supply bases! Don't you understand? We're beating you! Now you'll have to get out! All you white-grubs. Out of our system!"

Tony's EEP moved forward ominously. B'prith saw it. He bent down, snatched up a rock, and hurled it straight at the EEP. The rock clanged off the metal hull and bounced harmlessly away. B'prith snatched up another rock. Llyre and the others came quickly out of the house. An adult Pas loomed up behind them. Everything was happening too fast. More rocks crashed against the EEP. One struck Tony on the arm.

"Get out!" B'prith screamed. "Don't come back! This is our planet!" His claws snatched at Tony. "We'll tear you to pieces if you —"

Tony smashed him in the chest. The soft shell gave like rubber, and the Pas stumbled back. He wobbled and fell over, gasping and screeching.

"*Beetle*," Tony breathed hoarsely. Suddenly he was terrified. A crowd of Pas-udeti was forming rapidly. They surged on all sides, hostile faces, dark and angry, a rising thunder of rage.

More stones showered. Some struck the EEP, others fell around Tony, near his boots. One whizzed past his face. Quickly he slid his helmet in place. He was scared. He knew his EEP's E-signal had already gone out, but it would be minutes before a ship could come. Besides, there were other Earthmen in the city to be taken care of; there were Earthmen all over the planet. In all the cities. On all the twenty-three Betelgeuse planets. On the fourteen Rigel planets. On the other Orion planets.

"We have to get out of here," he muttered to the EEP. "Do something!"

A stone hit him on the helmet. The plastic cracked; air leaked out, and then the autoseal filmed over. More stones were falling. The Pas swarmed close, a yelling, seething mass of black-sheathed creatures. He could smell them, the acrid body-odor of insects, hear their claws snap, feel their weight.

The EEP threw its heat beam on. The beam shifted in a wide band toward the crowd of Pas-udeti. Crude hand weapons appeared. A clatter of bullets burst around Tony; they were firing at the EEP. He was dimly aware of the metal body beside him. A shuddering crash-the EEP was toppled over. The crowd poured over it; the metal hull was lost from sight.

Like a demented animal, the crowd tore at the struggling EEP. A few of them smashed in its head; others tore off struts and shiny arm-sections. The EEP ceased struggling. The crowd moved away, panting and clutching jagged remains. They saw Tony.

As the first line of them reached for him, the protective envelope high above them shattered. A Terran scout ship thundered down, heat beam screaming. The crowd scattered in confusion, some firing, some throwing stones, others leaping for safety.

Tony picked himself up and made his way unsteadily toward the spot where the scout was landing.

* * * * *

"I'm sorry," Joe Rossi said gently. He touched his son on the shoulder. "I shouldn't have let you go down there today. I should have known."

Tony sat hunched over in the big plastic easychair. He rocked back and forth, face pale with shock. The scout ship which had rescued him had immediately headed back toward Karnet; there were other Earthmen to bring out, besides this first load. The boy said nothing. His mind was blank. He still heard the roar of the crowd, felt its hate —a century of pent-up fury and resentment. The memory drove out everything else; it was all around him, even now. And the sight of the floundering EEP, the metallic ripping sound, as its arms and legs were torn off and carried away.

His mother dabbed at his cuts and scratches with antiseptic. Joe Rossi shakily lit a cigarette and said, "If your EEP hadn't been along they'd have killed you. Beetles." He shuddered. "I never should have let you go down there. All this time....They might have done it any time, any day. Knifed you. Cut you open with their filthy goddamn claws."

Below the settlement the reddish-yellow sunlight glinted on gunbarrels. Already, dull booms echoed against the crumbling hills. The defense ring was going into action. Black shapes darted and scurried up the side of the slope. Black patches moved out from Karnet, toward the Terran settlement, across the dividing line the Confederation surveyors had set up a century ago. Karnet was a bubbling pot of activity. The whole city rumbled with feverish excitement.

Tony raised his head. "They-they turned our flank."

"Yeah." Joe Rossi stubbed out his cigarette. "They sure did. That was at one o'clock. At two they drove a wedge right through the center of our line. Split the fleet in half. Broke it up-sent it running. Picked us off one by one as we fell back. Christ, they're like maniacs. Now that they've got the scent, the taste of our blood."

"But it's getting better," Leah fluttered. "Our main fleet units are beginning to appear."

"We'll get them," Joe muttered. "It'll take a while. But by God we'll wipe them out. Every last one of them. If it takes a thousand years. We'll follow every last ship down-we'll get them all." His voice rose in frenzy. "Beetles! Goddamn insects! When I think of them, trying to hurt my kid, with their filthy black claws —"

"If you were younger, you'd be in the line," Leah said. "It's not your fault you're too old. The heart strain's too great. You did your job. They can't let an older person take chances. It's not your fault."

Joe clenched his fists. "I feel so-futile. If there was only something I could do."

"The fleet will take care of them," Leah said soothingly. "You said so yourself. They'll hunt every one of them down. Destroy them all. There's nothing to worry about."

Joe sagged miserably. "It's no use. Let's cut it out. Let's stop kidding ourselves."

"What do you mean?"

"Face it! We're not going to win, not this time. We went too far. Our time's come."

There was silence.

Tony sat up a little. "When did you know?"

"I've known a long time."

"I found out today. I didn't understand, at first. This is-stolen ground. I was born here, but it's stolen ground."

"Yes. It's stolen. It doesn't belong to us."

"We're here because we're stronger. But now we're not stronger. We're being beaten."

"They know Terrans can be licked. Like anybody else." Joe Rossi's face was gray and flabby. "We took their planets away from them. Now they're taking them back. It'll be a while, of course. We'll retreat slowly. It'll be another five centuries going back. There're a lot of systems between here and Sol."

Tony shook his head, still uncomprehending. "Even Llyre and B'prith. All of them. Waiting for their time to come. For us to lose and go away again. Where we came from."

Joe Rossi paced back and forth. "Yeah, we'll be retreating from now on. Giving ground, instead of taking it. It'll be like this today-losing fights, draws. Stalemates and worse."

He raised his feverish eyes toward the ceiling of the little metal housing unit, face wild with passion and misery.

"But, by God, we'll give them a run for their money. All the way back! Every inch!"

The Crystal Crypt

"Attention, Inner-Flight ship! Attention! You are ordered to land at the Control Station on Deimos for inspection. Attention! You are to land at once!"

The metallic rasp of the speaker echoed through the corridors of the great ship. The passengers glanced at each other uneasily, murmuring and peering out the port windows at the small speck below, the dot of rock that was the Martian checkpoint, Deimos.

"What's up?" an anxious passenger asked one of the pilots, hurrying through the ship to check the escape lock.

"We have to land. Keep seated." The pilot went on.

"Land? But why?" They all looked at each other. Hovering above the bulging Inner-Flight ship were three slender Martian pursuit craft, poised and alert for any emergency. As the Inner-Flight ship prepared to land the pursuit ships dropped lower, carefully maintaining themselves a short distance away.

"There's something going on," a woman passenger said nervously. "Lord, I thought we were finally through with those Martians. Now what?"

"I don't blame them for giving us one last going over," a heavy-set business man said to his companion. "After all, we're the last ship leaving Mars for Terra. We're damn lucky they let us go at all."

"You think there really will be war?" A young man said to the girl sitting in the seat next to him. "Those Martians won't dare fight, not with our weapons and ability to produce. We could take care of Mars in a month. It's all talk."

The girl glanced at him. "Don't be so sure. Mars is desperate. They'll fight tooth and nail. I've been on Mars three years." She shuddered. "Thank goodness I'm getting away. If —"

"Prepare to land!" the pilot's voice came. The ship began to settle slowly, dropping down toward the tiny emergency field on the seldom visited moon. Down, down the ship dropped. There was a grinding sound, a sickening jolt. Then silence.

"We've landed," the heavy-set business man said. "They better not do anything to us! Terra will rip them apart if they violate one Space Article."

"Please keep your seats," the pilot's voice came. "No one is to leave the ship, according to the Martian authorities. We are to remain here."

A restless stir filled the ship. Some of the passengers began to read uneasily, others stared out at the deserted field, nervous and on edge, watching the three Martian pursuit ships land and disgorge groups of armed men.

The Martian soldiers were crossing the field quickly, moving toward them, running double time.

This Inner-Flight spaceship was the last passenger vessel to leave Mars for Terra. All other ships had long since left, returning to safety before the outbreak of hostilities. The passengers were the very last to go, the final group of Terrans to leave the grim red planet, business men, expatriates, tourists, any and all Terrans who had not already gone home.

"What do you suppose they want?" the young man said to the girl. "It's hard to figure Martians out, isn't it? First they give the ship clearance, let us take off, and now they radio us to set down again. By the way, my name's Thacher, Bob Thacher. Since we're going to be here awhile —"

* * * * *

The port lock opened. Talking ceased abruptly, as everyone turned. A black-clad Martian official, a Province Leiter, stood framed against the bleak sunlight, staring around the ship. Behind him a handful of Martian soldiers stood waiting, their guns ready.

"This will not take long," the Leiter said, stepping into the ship, the soldiers following him. "You will be allowed to continue your trip shortly."

An audible sigh of relief went through the passengers.

"Look at him," the girl whispered to Thacher. "How I hate those black uniforms!"

"He's just a Provincial Leiter," Thacher said. "Don't worry."

The Leiter stood for a moment, his hands on his hips, looking around at them without expression. "I have ordered your ship grounded so that an inspection can be made of all persons aboard," he said. "You Terrans are the last to leave our planet. Most of you are ordinary and harmless — I am not interested in you. I am interested in finding three saboteurs, three Terrans, two men and a woman, who have committed an incredible act of destruction and violence. They are said to have fled to this ship."

Murmurs of surprise and indignation broke out on all sides. The Leiter motioned the soldiers to follow him up the aisle.

"Two hours ago a Martian city was destroyed. Nothing remains, only a depression in the sand where the city was. The city and all its people have completely vanished. An entire city destroyed in a second! Mars will never rest until the saboteurs are captured. And we know they are aboard this ship."

"It's impossible," the heavy-set business man said. "There aren't any saboteurs here."

"We'll begin with you," the Leiter said to him, stepping up beside the man's seat. One of the soldiers passed the Leiter a square metal box. "This will soon tell us if you're speaking the truth. Stand up. Get on your feet."

The man rose slowly, flushing. "See here —"

"Are you involved in the destruction of the city? Answer!"

The man swallowed angrily. "I know nothing about any destruction of any city. And furthermore —"

"He is telling the truth," the metal box said tonelessly.

"Next person." The Leiter moved down the aisle.

A thin, bald-headed man stood up nervously. "No, sir," he said. "I don't know a thing about it."

"He is telling the truth," the box affirmed.

"Next person! Stand up!"

One person after another stood, answered, and sat down again in relief. At last there were only a few people left who had not been questioned. The Leiter paused, studying them intently.

"Only five left. The three must be among you. We have narrowed it down." His hand moved to his belt. Something flashed, a rod of pale fire. He raised the rod, pointing it steadily at the five people. "All right, the first one of you. What do you know about this destruction? Are you involved with the destruction of our city?"

"No, not at all," the man murmured.

"Yes, he's telling the truth," the box intoned.

"Next!"

"Nothing — I know nothing. I had nothing to do with it."

"True," the box said.

The ship was silent. Three people remained, a middle-aged man and his wife and their son, a boy of about twelve. They stood in the corner, staring white-faced at the Leiter, at the rod in his dark fingers.

"It must be you," the Leiter grated, moving toward them. The Martian soldiers raised their guns. "It *must* be you. You there, the boy. What do you know about the destruction of our city? Answer!"

The boy shook his head. "Nothing," he whispered.

The box was silent for a moment. "He is telling the truth," it said reluctantly.

"Next!"

"Nothing," the woman muttered. "Nothing."

"The truth."

"Next!"

"I had nothing to do with blowing up your city," the man said. "You're wasting your time."

"It is the truth," the box said.

For a long time the Leiter stood, toying with his rod. At last he pushed it back in his belt and signalled the soldiers toward the exit lock.

"You may proceed on your trip," he said. He walked after the soldiers. At the hatch he stopped, looking back at the passengers, his face grim. "You may go — But Mars will not allow her enemies to escape. The three saboteurs will be caught, I promise you." He rubbed his dark jaw thoughtfully. "It is strange. I was certain they were on this ship."

Again he looked coldly around at the Terrans.

"Perhaps I was wrong. All right, proceed! But remember: the three will be caught, even if it takes endless years. Mars will catch them and punish them! I swear it!"

* * * * *

For a long time no one spoke. The ship lumbered through space again, its jets firing evenly, calmly, moving the passengers toward their own planet, toward home. Behind them Deimos and the red ball that was Mars dropped farther and farther away each moment, disappearing and fading into the distance.

A sigh of relief passed through the passengers. "What a lot of hot air that was," one grumbled.

"Barbarians!" a woman said.

A few of them stood up, moving out into the aisle, toward the lounge and the cocktail bar. Beside Thacher the girl got to her feet, pulling her jacket around her shoulders.

"Pardon me," she said, stepping past him.

"Going to the bar?" Thacher said. "Mind if I come along?"

"I suppose not."

They followed the others into the lounge, walking together up the aisle. "You know," Thacher said, "I don't even know your name, yet."

"My name is Mara Gordon."

"Mara? That's a nice name. What part of Terra are you from? North America? New York?"

"I've been in New York," Mara said. "New York is very lovely." She was slender and pretty, with a cloud of dark hair tumbling down her neck, against her leather jacket.

They entered the lounge and stood undecided.

"Let's sit at a table," Mara said, looking around at the people at the bar, mostly men. "Perhaps that table over there."

"But someone's there already," Thacher said. The heavy-set business man had sat down at the table and deposited his sample case on the floor. "Do we want to sit with *him*?"

"Oh, it's all right," Mara said, crossing to the table. "May we sit here?" she said to the man.

The man looked up, half-rising. "It's a pleasure," he murmured. He studied Thacher intently. "However, a friend of mine will be joining me in a moment."

"I'm sure there's room enough for us all," Mara said. She seated herself and Thacher helped her with her chair. He sat down, too, glancing up suddenly at Mara and the business man. They were looking at each other almost as if something had passed between them. The man was middle-aged, with a florid face and tired, grey eyes. His hands were mottled with the veins showing thickly. At the moment he was tapping nervously.

"My name's Thacher," Thacher said to him, holding out his hand. "Bob Thacher. Since we're going to be together for a while we might as well get to know each other."

The man studied him. Slowly his hand came out. "Why not? My name's Erickson. Ralf Erickson."

"Erickson?" Thacher smiled. "You look like a commercial man, to me." He nodded toward the sample case on the floor. "Am I right?"

The man named Erickson started to answer, but at that moment there was a stir. A thin man of about thirty had come up to the table, his eyes bright, staring down at them warmly. "Well, we're on our way," he said to Erickson.

"Hello, Mara." He pulled out a chair and sat down quickly, folding his hands on the table before him. He noticed Thacher and drew back a little. "Pardon me," he murmured.

"Bob Thacher is my name," Thacher said. "I hope I'm not intruding here." He glanced around at the three of them, Mara, alert, watching him intently, heavy-set Erickson, his face blank, and this person. "Say, do you three know each other?" he asked suddenly.

There was silence.

The robot attendant slid over soundlessly, poised to take their orders. Erickson roused himself. "Let's see," he murmured. "What will we have? Mara?"

"Whiskey and water."

"You, Jan?"

The bright slim man smiled. "The same."

"Thacher?"

"Gin and tonic."

"Whiskey and water for me, also," Erickson said. The robot attendant went off. It returned at once with the drinks, setting them on the table. Each took his own. "Well," Erickson said, holding his glass up. "To our mutual success."

* * * * *

All drank, Thacher and the three of them, heavy-set Erickson, Mara, her eyes nervous and alert, Jan, who had just come. Again a look passed between Mara and Erickson, a look so swift that he would not have caught it had he not been looking directly at her.

"What line do you represent, Mr. Erickson?" Thacher asked.

Erickson glanced at him, then down at the sample case on the floor. He grunted. "Well, as you can see, I'm a salesman."

Thacher smiled. "I knew it! You get so you can always spot a salesman right off by his sample case. A salesman always has to carry something to show. What are you in, sir?"

Erickson paused. He licked his thick lips, his eyes blank and lidded, like a toad's. At last he rubbed his mouth with his hand and reached down, lifting up the sample case. He set it on the table in front of him.

"Well?" he said. "Perhaps we might even show Mr. Thacher."

They all stared down at the sample case. It seemed to be an ordinary leather case, with a metal handle and a snap lock. "I'm getting curious," Thacher said. "What's in there? You're all so tense. Diamonds? Stolen jewels?"

Jan laughed harshly, mirthlessly. "Erick, put it down. We're not far enough away, yet."

"Nonsense," Erick rumbled. "We're away, Jan."

"Please," Mara whispered. "Wait, Erick."

"Wait? Why? What for? You're so accustomed to —"

"Erick," Mara said. She nodded toward Thacher. "We don't know him, Erick. Please!"

"He's a Terran, isn't he?" Erickson said. "All Terrans are together in these times." He fumbled suddenly at the catch lock on the case. "Yes, Mr. Thacher. I'm a salesman. We're all salesmen, the three of us."

"Then you do know each other."

"Yes." Erickson nodded. His two companions sat rigidly, staring down. "Yes, we do. Here, I'll show you our line."

He opened the case. From it he took a letter-knife, a pencil sharpener, a glass globe paperweight, a box of thumb tacks, a stapler, some clips, a plastic ashtray, and some things Thacher could not identify. He placed the objects in a row in front of him on the table top. Then he closed the sample case.

"I gather you're in office supplies," Thacher said. He touched the letter-knife with his finger. "Nice quality steel. Looks like Swedish steel, to me."

Erickson nodded, looking into Thacher's face. "Not really an impressive business, is it? Office supplies. Ashtrays, paper clips." He smiled.

"Oh —" Thacher shrugged. "Why not? They're a necessity in modern business. The only thing I wonder —"

"What's that?"

"Well, I wonder how you'd ever find enough customers on Mars to make it worth your while." He paused, examining the glass paperweight. He lifted it up, holding it to the light, staring at the scene within until Erickson took it out of his hand and put it back in the sample case. "And another thing. If you three know each other, why did you sit apart when you got on?"

They looked at him quickly.

"And why didn't you speak to each other until we left Deimos?" He leaned toward Erickson, smiling at him. "Two men and a woman. Three of you. Sitting apart in the ship. Not speaking, not until the check-station was past. I find myself thinking over what the Martian said. Three saboteurs. A woman and two men."

Erickson put the things back in the sample case. He was smiling, but his face had gone chalk white. Mara stared down, playing with a drop of water on the edge of her glass. Jan clenched his hands together nervously, blinking rapidly.

"You three are the ones the Leiter was after," Thacher said softly. "You are the destroyers, the saboteurs. But their lie detector — Why didn't it trap you? How did you get by that? And now you're safe, outside the check-station." He grinned, staring around at them. "I'll be damned! And I really thought you were a salesman, Erickson. You really fooled me."

Erickson relaxed a little. "Well, Mr. Thacher, it's in a good cause. I'm sure you have no love for Mars, either. No Terran does. And I see you're leaving with the rest of us."

"True," Thacher said. "You must certainly have an interesting account to give, the three of you." He looked around the table.

"We still have an hour or so of travel. Sometimes it gets dull, this Mars-Terra run. Nothing to see, nothing to do but sit and drink in the lounge." He raised his eyes slowly. "Any chance you'd like to spin a story to keep us awake?"

Jan and Mara looked at Erickson. "Go on," Jan said. "He knows who we are. Tell him the rest of the story."

"You might as well," Mara said.

Jan let out a sigh suddenly, a sigh of relief. "Let's put the cards on the table, get this weight off us. I'm tired of sneaking around, slipping —"

"Sure," Erickson said expansively. "Why not?" He settled back in his chair, unbuttoning his vest. "Certainly, Mr. Thacher. I'll be glad to spin you a story. And I'm sure it will be interesting enough to keep you awake."

* * * * *

They ran through the groves of dead trees, leaping across the sun-baked Martian soil, running silently together. They went up a little rise, across a narrow ridge. Suddenly Erick stopped, throwing himself down flat on the ground. The others did the same, pressing themselves against the soil, gasping for breath.

"Be silent," Erick muttered. He raised himself a little. "No noise. There'll be Leiters nearby, from now on. We don't dare take any chances."

Between the three people lying in the grove of dead trees and the City was a barren, level waste of desert, over a mile of blasted sand. No trees or bushes marred the smooth, parched surface. Only an occasional wind, a dry wind eddying and twisting, blew the sand up into little rills. A faint odor came to them, a bitter smell of heat and sand, carried by the wind.

Erick pointed. "Look. The City — There it is."

They stared, still breathing deeply from their race through the trees. The City was close, closer than they had ever seen it before. Never had they gotten so close to it in times past. Terrans were never allowed near the great Martian cities, the centers of Martian life. Even in ordinary times, when there was no threat of approaching war, the Martians shrewdly kept all Terrans away from their citadels, partly from fear, partly from a deep, innate sense of hostility toward the white-skinned visitors whose commercial ventures had earned them the respect, and the dislike, of the whole system.

"How does it look to you?" Erick said.

The City was huge, much larger than they had imagined from the drawings and models they had studied so carefully back in New York, in the War Ministry Office. Huge it was, huge and stark, black towers rising up against the sky, incredibly thin columns of ancient metal, columns that had stood wind and sun for centuries. Around the City was a wall of stone, red stone, immense bricks that had been lugged there and fitted into place by slaves of the early Martian dynasties, under the whiplash of the first great Kings of Mars.

An ancient, sun-baked City, a City set in the middle of a wasted plain, beyond groves of dead trees, a City seldom seen by Terrans-but a City studied on maps and charts in every War Office on Terra. A City that contained, for all its ancient stone and archaic towers, the ruling group of all Mars, the Council of Senior Leiters, black-clad men who governed and ruled with an iron hand.

The Senior Leiters, twelve fanatic and devoted men, black priests, but priests with flashing rods of fire, lie detectors, rocket ships, intra-space cannon, many more things the Terran Senate could only conjecture about. The Senior Leiters and their subordinate Province Leiters — Erick and the two behind him suppressed a shudder.

"We've got to be careful," Erick said again. "We'll be passing among them, soon. If they guess who we are, or what we're here for —"

He snapped open the case he carried, glancing inside for a second. Then he closed it again, grasping the handle firmly. "Let's go," he said. He stood up slowly. "You two come up beside me. I want to make sure you look the way you should."

* * * * *

Mara and Jan stepped quickly ahead. Erick studied them critically as the three of them walked slowly down the slope, onto the plain, toward the towering black spires of the City.

"Jan," Erick said. "Take hold of her hand! Remember, you're going to marry her; she's your bride. And Martian peasants think a lot of their brides."

Jan was dressed in the short trousers and coat of the Martian farmer, a knotted rope tied around his waist, a hat on his head to keep off the sun. His skin was dark, colored by dye until it was almost bronze.

"You look fine," Erick said to him. He glanced at Mara. Her black hair was tied in a knot, looped through a hollowed-out yuke bone. Her face was dark, too, dark and lined with colored ceremonial pigment, green and orange stripes across her cheeks. Earrings were strung through her ears. On her feet were tiny slippers of perruh hide, laced around her ankles, and she wore long translucent Martian trousers with a bright sash tied around her waist. Between her small breasts a chain of stone beads rested, good-luck charms for the coming marriage.

"All right," Erick said. He, himself, wore the flowing grey robe of a Martian priest, dirty robes that were supposed to remain on him all his life, to be buried around him when he died. "I think we'll get past the guards. There should be heavy morning traffic on the road."

They walked on, the hard sand crunching under their feet. Against the horizon they could see specks moving, other persons going toward the City, farmers and peasants and merchants, bringing their crops and goods to market.

"See the cart!" Mara exclaimed.

They were nearing a narrow road, two ruts worn into the sand. A Martian hufa was pulling the cart, its great sides wet with perspiration, its tongue hanging out. The cart was piled high with bales of cloth, rough country cloth, hand dipped. A bent farmer urged the hufa on.

"And there." She pointed, smiling.

A group of merchants riding small animals were moving along behind the cart, Martians in long robes, their faces hidden by sand masks. On each animal was a pack, carefully tied on with rope. And beyond the merchants, plodding dully along, were peasants and farmers in an endless procession, some riding carts or animals, but mostly on foot.

Mara and Jan and Erick joined the line of people, melting in behind the merchants. No one noticed them; no one looked up or gave any sign. The march continued as before. Neither Jan nor Mara said anything to each other. They walked a little behind Erick, who paced with a certain dignity, a certain bearing becoming his position.

Once he slowed down, pointing up at the sky. "Look," he murmured, in the Martian hill dialect. "See that?"

Two black dots circled lazily. Martian patrol craft, the military on the outlook for any sign of unusual activity. War was almost ready to break out with Terra. Any day, almost any moment.

"We'll be just in time," Erick said. "Tomorrow will be too late. The last ship will have left Mars."

"I hope nothing stops us," Mara said. "I want to get back home when we're through."

* * * * *

Half an hour passed. They neared the City, the wall growing as they walked, rising higher and higher until it seemed to blot out the sky itself. A vast wall, a wall of eternal stone that had felt the wind and sun for centuries. A group of Martian soldiers were standing at the entrance, the single passage-gate hewn into the rock, leading to the City. As each person went through the soldiers examined him, poking his garments, looking into his load.

Erick tensed. The line had slowed almost to a halt. "It'll be our turn, soon," he murmured. "Be prepared."

"Let's hope no Leiters come around," Jan said. "The soldiers aren't so bad."

Mara was staring up at the wall and the towers beyond. Under their feet the ground trembled, vibrating and shaking. She could see tongues of flame rising from the towers, from the deep underground factories and forges of the City. The air was thick and dense with particles of soot. Mara rubbed her mouth, coughing.

"Here they come," Erick said softly.

The merchants had been examined and allowed to pass through the dark gate, the entrance through the wall into the City. They and their silent animals had already disappeared inside. The leader of the group of soldiers was beckoning impatiently to Erick, waving him on.

"Come along!" he said. "Hurry up there, old man."

Erick advanced slowly, his arms wrapped around his body, looking down at the ground.

"Who are you and what's your business here?" the soldier demanded, his hands on his hips, his gun hanging idly at his waist. Most of the soldiers were lounging lazily, leaning against the wall, some even squatting in the shade. Flies crawled on the face of one who had fallen asleep, his gun on the ground beside him.

"My business?" Erick murmured. "I am a village priest."

"Why do you want to enter the City?"

"I must bring these two people before the magistrate to marry them." He indicated Mara and Jan, standing a little behind him. "That is the Law the Leiters have made."

The soldier laughed. He circled around Erick. "What do you have in that bag you carry?"

"Laundry. We stay the night."

"What village are you from?"

"Kranos."

"Kranos?" The soldier looked to a companion. "Ever heard of Kranos?"

"A backward pig sty. I saw it once on a hunting trip."

The leader of the soldiers nodded to Jan and Mara. The two of them advanced, their hands clasped, standing close together. One of the soldiers put his hand on Mara's bare shoulder, turning her around.

"Nice little wife you're getting," he said. "Good and firm-looking." He winked, grinning lewdly.

Jan glanced at him in sullen resentment. The soldiers guffawed. "All right," the leader said to Erick. "You people can pass."

Erick took a small purse from his robes and gave the soldier a coin. Then the three of them went into the dark tunnel that was the entrance, passing through the wall of stone, into the City beyond.

They were within the City!

"Now," Erick whispered. "Hurry."

Around them the City roared and cracked, the sound of a thousand vents and machines, shaking the stones under their feet. Erick led Mara and Jan into a corner, by a row of brick warehouses. People were everywhere, hurrying back and forth, shouting above the din, merchants, peddlers, soldiers, street women. Erick bent down and opened the case he carried. From the case he quickly took three small coils of fine metal, intricate meshed wires and vanes worked together into a small cone. Jan took one and Mara took one. Erick put the remaining cone into his robe and snapped the case shut again.

"Now remember, the coils must be buried in such a way that the line runs through the center of the City. We must trisect the main section, where the largest concentration of buildings is. Remember the maps! Watch the alleys and streets carefully. Talk to no one if you can help it. Each of you has enough Martian money to buy your way out of trouble. Watch especially for cut-purses, and for heaven's sake, don't get lost."

* * * * *

Erick broke off. Two black-clad Leiters were coming along the inside of the wall, strolling together with their hands behind their backs. They noticed the three who stood in the corner by the warehouses and stopped.

"Go," Erick muttered. "And be back here at sundown." He smiled grimly. "Or never come back."

Each went off a different way, walking quickly without looking back. The Leiters watched them go. "The little bride was quite lovely," one Leiter said. "Those hill people have the stamp of nobility in their blood, from the old times."

"A very lucky young peasant to possess her," the other said. They went on. Erick looked after them, still smiling a little. Then he joined the surging mass of people that milled eternally through the streets of the City.

At dusk they met outside the gate. The sun was soon to set, and the air had turned thin and frigid. It cut through their clothing like knives.

Mara huddled against Jan, trembling and rubbing her bare arms.

"Well?" Erick said. "Did you both succeed?"

Around them peasants and merchants were pouring from the entrance, leaving the City to return to their farms and villages, starting the long trip back across the plain toward the hills beyond. None of them noticed the shivering girl and the young man and the old priest standing by the wall.

212

"Mine's in place," Jan said. "On the other side of the City, on the extreme edge. Buried by a well."

"Mine's in the industrial section," Mara whispered, her teeth chattering. "Jan, give me something to put over me! I'm freezing."

"Good," Erick said. "Then the three coils should trisect dead center, if the models were correct." He looked up at the darkening sky. Already, stars were beginning to show. Two dots, the evening patrol, moved slowly toward the horizon. "Let's hurry. It won't be long."

They joined the line of Martians moving along the road, away from the City. Behind them the City was losing itself in the sombre tones of night, its black spires disappearing into darkness.

They walked silently with the country people until the flat ridge of dead trees became visible on the horizon. Then they left the road and turned off, walking toward the trees.

"Almost time!" Erick said. He increased his pace, looking back at Jan and Mara impatiently. "Come on!"

They hurried, making their way through the twilight, stumbling over rocks and dead branches, up the side of the ridge. At the top Erick halted, standing with his hands on his hips, looking back.

"See," he murmured. "The City. The last time we'll ever see it this way."

"Can I sit down?" Mara said. "My feet hurt me."

Jan pulled at Erick's sleeve. "Hurry, Erick! Not much time left." He laughed nervously. "If everything goes right we'll be able to look at it-forever."

"But not like this," Erick murmured. He squatted down, snapping his case open. He took some tubes and wiring out and assembled them together on the ground, at the peak of the ridge. A small pyramid of wire and plastic grew, shaped by his expert hands.

At last he grunted, standing up. "All right."

"Is it pointed directly at the City?" Mara asked anxiously, looking down at the pyramid.

Erick nodded. "Yes, it's placed according —" He stopped, suddenly stiffening. "Get back! It's time! *Hurry!*"

Jan ran, down the far side of the slope, away from the City, pulling Mara with him. Erick came quickly after, still looking back at the distant spires, almost lost in the night sky.

"Down."

Jan sprawled out, Mara beside him, her trembling body pressed against his. Erick settled down into the sand and dead branches, still trying to see. "I want to see it," he murmured. "A miracle. I want to see —"

A flash, a blinding burst of violet light, lit up the sky. Erick clapped his hands over his eyes. The flash whitened, growing larger, expanding. Suddenly there was a roar, and a furious hot wind rushed past him, throwing him on his face in the sand. The hot dry wind licked and seared at them, crackling the bits of branches into flame. Mara and Jan shut their eyes, pressed tightly together.

"God —" Erick muttered.

The storm passed. They opened their eyes slowly. The sky was still alive with fire, a drifting cloud of sparks that was beginning to dissipate with the night wind. Erick stood up unsteadily, helping Jan and Mara to their feet. The three of them stood, staring silently across the dark waste, the black plain, none of them speaking.

The City was gone.

At last Erick turned away. "That part's done," he said. "Now the rest! Give me a hand, Jan. There'll be a thousand patrol ships around here in a minute."

"I see one already," Mara said, pointing up. A spot winked in the sky, a rapidly moving spot. "They're coming, Erick." There was a throb of chill fear in her voice.

"I know." Erick and Jan squatted on the ground around the pyramid of tubes and plastic, pulling the pyramid apart. The pyramid was fused, fused together like molten glass. Erick tore the pieces away with trembling fingers. From the remains of the pyramid he pulled something forth, something he held up high, trying to make it out in the darkness. Jan and Mara came close to see, both staring up intently, almost without breathing.

"There it is," Erick said. "There!"

* * * * *

In his hand was a globe, a small transparent globe of glass. Within the glass something moved, something minute and fragile, spires almost too small to be seen, microscopic, a complex web swimming within the hollow glass globe. A web of spires. A City.

Erick put the globe into the case and snapped it shut. "Let's go," he said. They began to lope back through the trees, back the way they had come before. "We'll change in the car," he said as they ran. "I think we should keep these clothes on until we're actually inside the car. We still might encounter someone."

"I'll be glad to get my own clothing on again," Jan said. "I feel funny in these little pants."

"How do you think I feel?" Mara gasped. "I'm freezing in this, what there is of it."

"All young Martian brides dress that way," Erick said. He clutched the case tightly as they ran. "I think it looks fine."

"Thank you," Mara said, "but it is cold."

"What do you suppose they'll think?" Jan asked. "They'll assume the City was destroyed, won't they? That's certain."

"Yes," Erick said. "They'll be sure it was blown up. We can count on that. And it will be damn important to us that they think so!"

"The car should be around here, someplace," Mara said, slowing down.

"No. Farther on," Erick said. "Past that little hill over there. In the ravine, by the trees. It's so hard to see where we are."

"Shall I light something?" Jan said.

"No. There may be patrols around who —"

He halted abruptly. Jan and Mara stopped beside him. "What —" Mara began.

A light glimmered. Something stirred in the darkness. There was a sound.

"Quick!" Erick rasped. He dropped, throwing the case far away from him, into the bushes. He straightened up tensely.

A figure loomed up, moving through the darkness, and behind it came more figures, men, soldiers in uniform. The light flashed up brightly, blinding them. Erick closed his eyes. The light left him, touching Mara and Jan, standing silently together, clasping hands. Then it flicked down to the ground and around in a circle.

A Leiter stepped forward, a tall figure in black, with his soldiers close behind him, their guns ready. "You three," the Leiter said. "Who are you? Don't move. Stand where you are."

He came up to Erick, peering at him intently, his hard Martian face without expression. He went all around Erick, examining his robes, his sleeves.

"Please —" Erick began in a quavering voice, but the Leiter cut him off.

"I'll do the talking. Who are you three? What are you doing here? Speak up."

"We-we are going back to our village," Erick muttered, staring down, his hands folded. "We were in the City, and now we are going home."

One of the soldiers spoke into a mouthpiece. He clicked it off and put it away.

"Come with me," the Leiter said. "We're taking you in. Hurry along."

"In? Back to the City?"

One of the soldiers laughed. "The City is gone," he said. "All that's left of it you can put in the palm of your hand."

"But what happened?" Mara said.

"No one knows. Come on, hurry it up!"

There was a sound. A soldier came quickly out of the darkness. "A Senior Leiter," he said. "Coming this way." He disappeared again.

* * * * *

"A Senior Leiter." The soldiers stood waiting, standing at a respectful attention. A moment later the Senior Leiter stepped into the light, a black-clad old man, his ancient face thin and hard, like a bird's, eyes bright and alert. He looked from Erick to Jan.

"Who are these people?" he demanded.

"Villagers going back home."

"No, they're not. They don't stand like villagers. Villagers slump-diet, poor food. These people are not villagers. I myself came from the hills, and I know."

He stepped close to Erick, looking keenly into his face. "Who are you? Look at his chin-he never shaved with a sharpened stone! Something is wrong here."

In his hand a rod of pale fire flashed. "The City is gone, and with it at least half the Leiter Council. It is very strange, a flash, then heat, and a wind. But it was not fission. I am puzzled. All at once the City has vanished. Nothing is left but a depression in the sand."

"We'll take them in," the other Leiter said. "Soldiers, surround them. Make certain that —"

"Run!" Erick cried. He struck out, knocking the rod from the Senior Leiter's hand. They were all running, soldiers shouting, flashing their lights, stumbling against each other in the darkness. Erick dropped to his knees, groping frantically in the bushes. His fingers closed over the handle of the case and he leaped up. In Terran he shouted to Mara and Jan.

"Hurry! To the car! Run!" He set off, down the slope, stumbling through the darkness. He could hear soldiers behind him, soldiers running and falling. A body collided against him and he struck out. Someplace behind him there was a hiss, and a section of the slope went up in flames. The Leiter's rod —

"Erick," Mara cried from the darkness. He ran toward her. Suddenly he slipped, falling on a stone. Confusion and firing. The sound of excited voices.

"Erick, is that you?" Jan caught hold of him, helping him up. "The car. It's over here. Where's Mara?"

"I'm here," Mara's voice came. "Over here, by the car."

A light flashed. A tree went up in a puff of fire, and Erick felt the singe of the heat against his face. He and Jan made their way toward the girl. Mara's hand caught his in the darkness.

"Now the car," Erick said. "If they haven't got to it." He slid down the slope into the ravine, fumbling in the darkness, reaching and holding onto the handle of the case. Reaching, reaching —

He touched something cold and smooth. Metal, a metal door handle. Relief flooded through him. "I've found it! Jan, get inside. Mara, come on." He pushed Jan past him, into the car. Mara slipped in after Jan, her small agile body crowding in beside him.

"Stop!" a voice shouted from above. "There's no use hiding in that ravine. We'll get you! Come up and —"

The sound of voices was drowned out by the roar of the car's motor. A moment later they shot into the darkness, the car rising into the air. Treetops broke and cracked under them as Erick turned the car from side to side, avoiding the groping shafts of pale light from below, the last furious thrusts from the two Leiters and their soldiers.

Then they were away, above the trees, high in the air, gaining speed each moment, leaving the knot of Martians far behind.

"Toward Marsport," Jan said to Erick. "Right?"

Erick nodded. "Yes. We'll land outside the field, in the hills. We can change back to our regular clothing there, our commercial clothing. Damn it-we'll be lucky if we can get there in time for the ship."

"The last ship," Mara whispered, her chest rising and falling. "What if we don't get there in time?"

Erick looked down at the leather case in his lap. "We'll have to get there," he murmured. "We must!"

For a long time there was silence. Thacher stared at Erickson. The older man was leaning back in his chair, sipping a little of his drink. Mara and Jan were silent.

"So you didn't destroy the City," Thacher said. "You didn't destroy it at all. You shrank it down and put it in a glass globe, in a paperweight. And now you're salesmen again, with a sample case of office supplies!"

Erickson smiled. He opened the briefcase and reaching into it he brought out the glass globe paperweight. He held it up, looking into it. "Yes, we stole the City from the Martians. That's how we got by the lie detector. It was true that we knew nothing about a *destroyed* City."

"But why?" Thacher said. "Why steal a City? Why not merely bomb it?"

"Ransom," Mara said fervently, gazing into the globe, her dark eyes bright. "Their biggest City, half of their Council-in Erick's hand!"

"Mars will have to do what Terra asks," Erickson said. "Now Terra will be able to make her commercial demands felt. Maybe there won't even be a war. Perhaps Terra will get her way without fighting." Still smiling, he put the globe back into the briefcase and locked it.

"Quite a story," Thacher said. "What an amazing process, reduction of size — A whole City reduced to microscopic dimensions. Amazing. No wonder you were able to escape. With such daring as that, no one could hope to stop you."

He looked down at the briefcase on the floor. Underneath them the jets murmured and vibrated evenly, as the ship moved through space toward distant Terra.

"We still have quite a way to go," Jan said. "You've heard our story, Thacher. Why not tell us yours? What sort of line are you in? What's your business?"

"Yes," Mara said. "What do you do?"

"What do I do?" Thacher said. "Well, if you like, I'll show you." He reached into his coat and brought out something. Something that flashed and glinted, something slender. A rod of pale fire.

The three stared at it. Sickened shock settled over them slowly.

Thacher held the rod loosely, calmly, pointing it at Erickson. "We knew you three were on this ship," he said. "There was no doubt of that. But we did not know what had become of the City. My theory was that the City had not been destroyed at all, that something else had happened to it. Council instruments measured a sudden loss of mass in that area, a decrease equal to the mass of the City. Somehow the City had been spirited away, not destroyed. But I could not convince the other Council Leiters of it. I had to follow you alone."

Thacher turned a little, nodding to the men sitting at the bar. The men rose at once, coming toward the table.

"A very interesting process you have. Mars will benefit a great deal from it. Perhaps it will even turn the tide in our favor. When we return to Marsport I wish to begin work on it at once. And now, if you will please pass me the briefcase —"

Upon the Dull Earth

Silvia ran laughing through the night brightness, between the roses and cosmos and Shasta daisies, down the gravel path and beyond the heaps of sweet-tasting grass swept from the lawns. Stars, caught in pools of water, glittered everywhere, as she brushed through them to the slope beyond the brick wall. Cedars supported the sky and ignored the slim shape squeezing past, her brown hair flying, her eyes flashing.

"Wait for me," Rick complained, as he cautiously threaded his way after her, along the half familiar path. Silvia danced on without stopping. "Slow down!" he shouted angrily.

"Can't -- we're late." Without warning, Silvia appeared in front of him, blocking the path. "Empty your pockets," she gasped, her gray eyes sparkling. "Throw away all metal. You know they can't stand metal."

Rick searched his pockets. In his overcoat were two dimes and a fifty-cent piece. "Do these count?"

"*Yes!*" Silvia snatched the coins and threw them into the dark heaps of calla lilies. The bits of metal hissed into the moist depths and were gone. "Anything else?" She caught hold of his arm anxiously. "They're already on their way. Anything else, Rick?"

"Just my watch." Rick pulled his wrist away as Silvia's wild fingers snatched for the watch. "*That's* not going in the bushes."

"Then lay it on the sundial -- or the wall. Or in a hollow tree." Silvia raced off again. Her excited, rapturous voice danced back to him. "Throw away your cigarette case. And your keys, your belt buckle -- everything metal. You know how they hate metal. Hurry, we're late!"

Rick followed sullenly after her. "All right, *witch.*"

Silvia snapped at him furiously from the darkness. "Don't *say* that! It isn't true. You've been listening to my sisters and my mother and --"

Her words were drowned out by the sound. Distant flapping, a long way off, like vast leaves rustling in a winter storm. The night sky was alive with the frantic poundings; they were coming very quickly this time. They were too greedy, too desperately eager to wait. Flickers of fear touched the man and he ran to catch up with Silvia.

Silvia was a tiny column of green skirt and blouse in the center of the thrashing mass. She was pushing them away with one arm and trying to manage the faucet with the other. The churning activity of wings and bodies twisted her like a reed. For a time she was lost from sight.

"Rick!" she called faintly. "Come here and help!" She pushed them away and struggled up. "They're suffocating me!"

Rick fought his way through the wall of flashing white to the edge of the trough. They were drinking greedily at the blood that spilled from the wooden faucet. He pulled Silvia close against him; she was terrified and trembling. He held her tight until some of the violence and fury around them had died down.

"They're hungry," Silvia gasped feebly.

"You're a little cretin for coming ahead. They can sear you to ash!"

"I know. They can do anything." She shuddered, excited and frightened. "Look at them," she whispered, her voice husky with awe. "Look at the size of them -- their wing-spread. And they're *white*, Rick. Spotless -- perfect. There's nothing in our world as spotless as that. Great and clean and wonderful."

"They certainly wanted the lamb's blood."

Silvia's soft hair blew against his face as the wings fluttered on all sides. They were leaving now, roaring up into the sky. Not up, really -- away. Back to their own world whence they had scented the blood. But it was not only the blood -- they had come because of Silvia. *She* had attracted them.

The girl's gray eyes were wide. She reached up towards the rising white creatures. One of them swooped close. Grass and flowers sizzled as blinding white flames roared in a brief fountain.

Rick scrambled away. The flaming figure hovered momentarily over Silvia and then there was a hollow *pop*. The last of the white-winged giants was gone. The air, the ground, gradually cooled into darkness and silence.

"I'm sorry," Silvia whispered.

"Don't do it again," Rick managed. He was numb with shock. "It isn't safe."

"Sometimes I forget. I'm sorry, Rick. I didn't mean to draw them so close." She tried to smile. "I haven't been that careless in months. Not since that other time, when I first brought you out here." The avid, wild look slid across her face. "Did you *see him?* Power and flames! And he didn't even touch us. He just -- looked at us. That was all. And everything's burned up, all around."

Rick grabbed hold of her. "Listen," he grated. "You mustn't call them again. It's wrong. This isn't their world."

"It's not wrong -- it's beautiful."

"It's not safe!" His fingers dug into her flesh until she gasped. "Stop tempting them down here!"

Silvia laughed hysterically. She pulled away from him, out into the blasted circle that the horde of angels had seared behind them as they rose into the sky. "I can't *help* it," she cried. "I belong with them. They're my family, my people. Generations of them, back into the past."

"What do you mean?"

"They're my ancestors. And some day I'll join them."

"You are a little witch!" Rick shouted furiously.

"No," Silvia answered. "Not a witch, Rick. Don't you see? I'm a saint."

The kitchen was warm and bright. Silvia plugged in the Silex and got a big red can of coffee down from the cupboards over the sink. "You mustn't listen to them," she said, as she set out plates and cups and got cream from the refrigerator. "You know they don't understand. Look at them in there."

Silvia's mother and her sisters, Betty Lou and Jean, stood huddled together in the living room, fearful and alert, watching the young couple in the kitchen. Walter Everett was standing by the fireplace, his face blank, remote.

"Listen to *me,*" Rick said. "You have this power to attract them. You mean you're not -- isn't Walter your real father?"

"Oh, yes -- of course he is. I'm completely human. Don't I look human?"

"But you're the only one who has the power."

"I'm not physically different," Silvia said thoughtfully. "I have the ability to see, that's all. Others have had it before me -- saints, martyrs. When I was a child, my mother read to me about St. Bernadette. Remember where her cave was? Near a hospital. They were hovering there and she saw one of them."

"But the blood! It's grotesque. There never was anything like that."

"Oh, yes. The blood draws them, lamb's blood especially. They hover over battlefields. Valkyries -- carrying off the dead to Valhalla. That's why saints and martyrs cut and mutilate themselves. You know where I got the idea?"

Silvia fastened a little apron around her waist and filled the Silex with coffee. "When I was nine years old, I read of it in Homer, in the Odyssey. Ulysses dug a trench in the ground and filled it with blood to attract the spirits. The shades from the netherworld."

"That's right," Rick admitted reluctantly. "I remember."

"The ghosts of people who died. They had lived once. Everybody lives here, then dies and goes there." Her face glowed. "We're all going to have wings! We're all going to fly. We'll all be filled with fire and power. We won't be worms any more."

"Worms! That's what you always call me."

"Of course you're a worm. We're all worms -- grubby worms creeping over the crust of the Earth, through dust and dirt."

"Why should blood bring them?"

"Because it's life and they're attracted by life. Blood is *uisge beatha* -- the water of life."

"Blood means death! A trough of spilled blood. . ."

"It's *not* death. When you see a caterpillar crawl into its cocoon, do you think it's dying?"

Walter Everett was standing in the doorway. He stood listening to his daughter, his face dark. "One day," he said hoarsely, "they're going to grab her and carry her off. She wants to go with them. She's waiting for that day."

"You see?" Silvia said to Rick. "He doesn't understand either." She shut off the Silex and poured coffee. "Coffee for you?" she asked her father.

"No," Everett said.

"Silvia," Rick said, as if speaking to a child, "if you went away with them, you know you couldn't come back to us."

"We all have to cross sooner or later. It's all part of our life."

"But you're only nineteen," Rick pleaded. "You're young and healthy and beautiful. And our marriage -- what about our marriage?" He half rose from the table. "Silvia, you've got to stop this!"

"I *can't* stop it. I was seven when I saw them first." Silvia stood by the sink, gripping the Silex, a faraway look in her eyes. "Remember, Daddy? We were living back in Chicago. It was winter. I fell, walking home from school." She held up a slim arm. "See the scar? I fell and cut myself on the gravel and slush. I came home crying -- it was sleeting and the wind was howling around me. My arm was bleeding and my mitten was soaked with blood. And then I looked up and saw them."

There was silence.

"They want you," Everett said wretchedly. "They're flies -- bluebottles, hovering around, waiting for you. Calling you to come along with them."

"Why not?" Silvia's gray eyes were shining and her cheeks radiated joy and anticipation. "You've seen them, Daddy. You know what it means. Transfiguration -- from clay into gods!"

Rick left the kitchen. In the living-room, the two sisters stood together, curious and uneasy. Mrs. Everett stood by herself, her face granite-hard, eyes bleak behind her steel-rimmed glasses. She turned away as Rick passed them.

"What happened out there?" Betty Lou asked him in a taut whisper. She was fifteen, skinny and plain, hollow cheeked, with mousy, sand-colored hair. "Silvia never lets us come out with her."

"Nothing happened," Rick answered.

Anger stirred the girl's barren face. "That's not true. You were both out in the garden, in the dark, and --"

"Don't talk to him!" her mother snapped. She yanked the two girls away and shot Rick a glare of hatred and misery. Then she turned quickly from him.

Rick opened the door to the basement and switched on the light. He descended slowly into the cold, damp room of concrete and dirt, with its unwinking yellow light hanging from the dust-covered wires overhead.

In one corner loomed the big floor furnace with its mammoth hot air pipes. Beside it stood the water heater and discarded bundles, boxes of books, newspapers and old furniture, thick with dust, encrusted with strings of spider webs.

At the far end were the washing machine and spin dryer. And Silvia's pump and refrigeration system.

From the work bench Rick selected a hammer and two heavy pipe wrenches. He was moving towards the elaborate tanks and pipes when Silvia appeared abruptly at the top of the stairs, her coffee cup in one hand.

She hurried quickly down to him. "What are you doing down here?" she asked, studying him intently. "Why that hammer and those two wrenches?"

Rick dropped the tools back onto the bench. "I thought maybe this could be solved on the spot."

Silvia moved between him and the tanks. "I thought you understood. They've always been a part of my life. When I brought you with me the first time, you seemed to see what --"

"I don't want to lose you," Rick said harshly, "to anybody or anything -- in this world or any other. *I'm not going to give you up.*"

"It's not giving me up!" Her eyes narrowed. "You came down here to destroy and break everything. The moment I'm not looking you'll smash all this, won't you?"

"That's right."

Fear replaced anger on the girl's face. "Do you want me to be chained here? I have to go on -- I'm through with this part of the journey. I've stayed here long enough."

"Can't you wait?" Rick demanded furiously. He couldn't keep the ragged edge of despair out of his voice. "Doesn't it come soon enough anyhow?"

Silvia shrugged and turned away, her arms folded, her red lips tight together. "You want to be a worm always. A fuzzy, little creeping caterpillar."

"I want *you.*"

"You can't *have* me!" She whirled angrily. "I don't have any time to waste with this."

"You have higher things in mind," Rick said savagely.

"Of course." She softened a little. "I'm sorry, Rick. Remember Icarus? You want to fly, too. I know it."

"In my time."

"Why not now? Why wait? You're afraid." She slid lithely away from him, cunning twisting her red lips. "Rick, I want to show you something. Promise me first -- you won't tell anybody."

"What is it?"

"Promise?" She put her hand to his mouth. "I have to be careful. It cost a lot of money. Nobody knows about it. It's what they do in China -- everything goes towards it."

"I'm curious," Rick said. Uneasiness flicked at him. "Show it to me."

Trembling with excitement, Silvia disappeared behind the huge lumbering refrigerator, back into the darkness behind the web of frost-hard freezing coils. He could hear her tugging and pulling at something. Scraping sounds, sounds of something large being dragged out.

"See?" Silvia gasped. "Give me a hand, Rick. It's heavy. Hardwood and brass -- and metal lined. It's hand-stained and polished. And the carving -- see the carving! Isn't it beautiful?"

"What is it?" Rick demanded huskily.

"It's my cocoon," Silvia said simply. She settled down in a contented heap on the floor, and rested her head happily against the polished oak coffin.

Rick grabbed her by the arm and dragged her to her feet. "You can't sit with that coffin, down here in the basement with --" He broke off. "What's the matter?"

Silvia's face was twisting with pain. She backed away from him and put her finger quickly to her mouth. "I cut myself -- when you pulled me up -- on a nail or something." A thin trickle of blood oozed down her fingers. She groped in her pocket for a handkerchief.

"Let me see it." He moved towards her, but she avoided him. "Is it bad?" he demanded.

"Stay away from me," Silvia whispered.

"What's wrong? Let me see it!"

"Rick," Silvia said in a low intense voice, "get some water and adhesive tape. As quickly as possible!" She was trying to keep down her rising terror. "I have to stop the bleeding."

"Upstairs?" He moved awkwardly away. "It doesn't look too bad. Why don't you. . ."

"Hurry." The girl's voice was suddenly bleak with fear. "Rick, *hurry!*"

Confused, he ran a few steps.

Silvia's terror poured after him. "No, it's too late," she called thinly. "Don't come back -- keep away from me. It's my own fault. I trained them to come. *Keep away!* I'm sorry, Rick. *Oh --*" Her voice was lost to him, as the wall of the basement burst and shattered. A cloud of luminous white forced its way through and blazed out into the basement.

It was Silvia they were after. She ran a few hesitant steps towards Rick, halted uncertainly, then the white mass of bodies and wings settled around her. She shrieked once. Then a violent explosion blasted the basement into a shimmering dance of furnace heat.

He was thrown to the floor. The cement was hot and dry -- the whole basement crackled with heat. Windows shattered as pulsing white shapes pushed out again. Smoke and flames licked up the walls. The ceiling sagged and rained plaster down.

Rick struggled to his feet. The furious activity was dying away. The basement was a littered chaos. All surfaces were scorched black, seared and crusted with smoking ash. Splintered wood, torn cloth and broken concrete were strewn everywhere. The furnace and washing machine were in ruins. The elaborate pumping and refrigeration system -- now were a glittering mass of slag. One whole wall had been twisted aside. Plaster was rubbled over everything.

Silvia was a twisted heap, arms and legs doubled grotesquely. Shriveled, carbonized remains of fire-scorched ash, settling in a vague mound. What had been left were charred fragments, a brittle burned-out husk.

It was a dark night, cold and intense. A few stars glittered like ice from above his head. A faint, dank wind stirred through the dripping calla lilies and whipped gravel up in a frigid mist along the path between the black roses.

He crouched for a long time, listening and watching. Behind the cedars, the big house loomed against the sky. At the bottom of the slope a few cars slithered along the highway. Otherwise, there was no sound. Ahead of him jutted the squat outline of the porcelain trough and the pipe that had carried blood from the refrigerator in the basement. The trough was empty and dry, except for a few leaves that had fallen in it.

Rick took a deep breath of thin night air and held it. Then he got stiffly to his feet. He scanned the sky, but saw no movement. They were there, though, watching and waiting -- dim shadows, echoing into the legendary past, a line of god-figures.

He picked up the heavy gallon drums, dragged them to the trough and poured blood from a New Jersey abattoir, cheap-grade steer refuse, thick and clotted. It splashed against his clothes and he backed away nervously. But nothing stirred in the air above. The garden was silent, drenched with night fog and darkness.

He stood beside the trough, waiting and wondering if they were coming. They had come for Silvia, not merely for the blood. Without her there was no attraction but the raw food. He carried the empty metal cans over to the bushes and kicked them down the slope. He searched his pockets carefully, to make sure there was no metal in them.

Over the years, Silvia had nourished their habit of coming. Now she was on the other side. Did that mean they wouldn't come? Somewhere in the damp bushes something rustled. An animal or a bird?

In the trough the blood glistened, heavy and dull, like old lead. It was their time to come, but nothing stirred the great trees above. He picked out the rows of nodding black roses, the gravel path down which he and Silvia had run -- violently he shut out the recent memory of her flashing eyes and deep red lips. The highway beyond the slope -- the empty, deserted garden -- the silent house in which her family huddled and waited. After a time, there was a dull, swishing sound. He tensed, but it was only a diesel truck lumbering along the highway, headlights blazing.

He stood grimly, his feet apart, his heels dug into the soft black ground. He wasn't leaving. He was staying there until they came. He wanted her back -- at any cost.

Overhead, foggy webs of moisture drifted across the moon. The sky was a vast barren plain, without life or warmth. The deathly cold of deep space, away from suns and living things. He gazed up until his neck ached. Cold stars, sliding in and out of the matted layer of fog. Was there anything else? Didn't they want to come, or weren't they interested in him? It had been Silvia who had interested them -- now they had her.

Behind him there was a movement without sound. He sensed it and started to turn, but suddenly, on all sides, the trees and undergrowth shifted. Like cardboard props they wavered and ran together, blending dully in the night shadows. Something moved through them, rapidly, silently, then was gone.

They had come. He could feel them. They had shut off their power and flame. Cold, indifferent statues, rising among the trees, dwarfing the cedars -- remote from him and his world, attracted by curiosity and mild habit.

"Silvia," he said clearly. "Which are you?"

There was no response. Perhaps she wasn't among them. He felt foolish. A vague flicker of white drifted past the trough, hovered momentarily and then went on without stopping. The air above the trough vibrated, then died into immobility, as another giant inspected briefly and withdrew.

Panic breathed through him. They were leaving again, receding back into their own world. The trough had been rejected; they weren't interested.

"Wait," he muttered thickly.

Some of the white shadows lingered. He approached them slowly, wary of their flickering immensity. If one of them touched him, he would sizzle briefly and puff into a dark heap of ash. A few feet away he halted.

"You know what I want," he said. "I want her back. She shouldn't have been taken yet."

Silence.

"You were too greedy," he said. "You did the wrong thing. She was going to come over to you, eventually. She had it all worked out."

The dark fog rustled. Among the trees the flickering shapes stirred and pulsed, responsive to his voice. *"True,"* came a detached impersonal sound. The sound drifted around him, from tree to tree, without location or direction. It was swept off by the night wind to die into dim echoes.

Relief settled over him. They had paused -- they were aware of him -- listening to what he had to say.

"You think it's right?" he demanded. "She had a long life here. We were to marry, have children."

There was no answer, but he was conscious of a growing tension. He listened intently, but he couldn't make out anything. Presently he realized a struggle was taking place, a conflict among them. The tension grew -- more shapes flickered -- the clouds, the icy stars, were obscured by the vast presence swelling around him.

"Rick!" A voice spoke close by. Wavering, drifting back into the dim regions of the trees and dripping plants. He could hardly hear it -- the words were gone as soon as they were spoken. "Rick -- help me get back."

"Where are you?" He couldn't locate her. "What can I do?"

"I don't know." Her voice was wild with bewilderment and pain. "I don't understand. Something went wrong. They must have thought I-wanted to come right away. I *didn't!*"

"I know," Rick said. "It was an accident."

"They were waiting. The cocoon, the trough -- but it was too soon." Her terror came across to him, from the vague distances of another universe. "Rick, I've changed my mind. I want to come back."

"It's not as simple as that."

"I know. Rick, time is different on this side. I've been gone so long -- your world seems to creep along. It's been years, hasn't it?"

"One week," Rick said.

"It was their fault. You don't blame me, do you? They know they did the wrong thing. Those who did it have been punished, but that doesn't help me." Misery and panic distorted her voice so he could hardly understand her. "How can I come back?"

"Don't they know?"

"They say it can't be done." Her voice trembled. "They say they destroyed the clay part -- it was incinerated. There's nothing for me to go back to."

Rick took a deep breath. "Make them find some other way. It's up to them. Don't they have the power? They took you over too soon -- they must send you back. It's *their* responsibility."

The white shapes shifted uneasily. The conflict rose sharply; they couldn't agree. Rick warily moved back a few paces.

"They say it's dangerous," Silvia's voice came from no particular spot. "They say it was attempted once." She tried to control her voice. "The nexus between this world and yours is unstable. There are vast amounts of free-floating energy. The power we -- on this side -- have isn't really our own. It's a universal energy, tapped and controlled."

"Why can't they. . ."

"This is a higher continuum. There's a natural process of energy from lower to higher regions. But the reverse process is risky. The blood -- it's a sort of guide to follow -- a bright marker."

"Like moths around a light bulb," Rick said bitterly.

"If they send me back and something goes wrong --" She broke off and then continued, "If they make a mistake, I might be lost between the two regions. I might be absorbed by the free energy. It seems to be partly alive. It's not understood. Remember Prometheus and the fire. . ."

"I see," Rick said, as calmly as he could.

"Darling, if they try to send me back, I'll have to find some shape to enter. You see, I don't exactly have a shape any more. There's no real material form on this side. What you see, the wings and the whiteness, are not really there. If I succeeded in making the trip back to your side. . ."

"You'd have to mold something," Rick said.

"I'd have to take something there -- something of clay. I'd have to enter it and reshape it. As He did a long time ago, when the original form was put on your world."

"If they did it once, they can do it again."

"The One who did that is gone. He passed on upward." There was unhappy irony in her voice. "There are regions beyond this. The ladder doesn't stop here. Nobody knows where it ends, it just seems to keep on going up and up. World after world."

"Who decides about you?" Rick demanded.

"It's up to me," Silvia said faintly. "They say, if I want to take the chance, they'll try it."

"What do you think you'll do?" he asked.

"I'm afraid. What if something goes wrong? You haven't seen it, the region between. The possibilities there are incredible -- they terrify me. He was the only one with enough courage. Everyone else has been afraid."

"It was their fault. They have to take responsibility."

"They know that." Silvia hesitated miserably. "Rick, darling, please tell me what to do."

"Come back!"

Silence. Then her voice, thin and pathetic. "All right, Rick. If you think that's the right thing."

"It is," he said firmly. He forced his mind not to think, not to picture or imagine anything. *He had to have her back.* "Tell them to get started now. Tell them --"

A deafening crack of heat burst in front of him. He was lifted up and tossed into a flaming sea of pure energy. They were leaving and the scalding lake of sheer power bellowed and thundered around him. For a split second he thought he glimpsed Silvia, her hands reaching imploringly towards him.

Then the fire cooled and he lay blinded in dripping, night-moistened darkness. Alone in the silence.

Walter Everett was helping him up. "You damn fool!" he was saying, again and again. "You shouldn't have brought them back. They've got enough from us."

Then he was in the big, warm living room. Mrs. Everett stood silently in front of him, her face hard and expressionless. The two daughters hovered anxiously around him, fluttering and curious, eyes wide with morbid fascination.

"I'll be all right," Rick muttered. His clothing was charred and blacked. He rubbed black ash from his face. Bits of dried grass stuck to his hair -- they had seared a circle around him as they'd ascended. He lay back against the couch and closed his eyes. When he opened them, Betty Lou Everett was forcing a glass of water into his hands.

"Thanks," he muttered.

"You should never have gone out there," Walter Everett repeated. "Why? Why'd you do it? You know what happened to her. You want the same thing to happen to you?"

"I want her back," Rick said quietly.

"Are you mad? You can't get her back. She's gone." His lips twitched convulsively. "You saw her."

Betty Lou was gazing at Rick intently. "What happened out there?" she demanded. "You saw her."

Rick got heavily to his feet and left the living room. In the kitchen he emptied the water in the sink and poured himself a drink. While he was leaning wearily against the sink, Betty Lou appeared in the doorway.

"What do you want?" Rick demanded.

The girl's face was flushed an unhealthy red. "I know something happened out there. You were feeding them, weren't you?" She advanced towards him. "You're trying to get her back?"

"That's right," Rick said.

Betty Lou giggled nervously. "But you can't. She's dead -- her body's been cremated -- I saw it." Her face worked excitedly. "Daddy always said that something bad would happen to her, and it did." She leaned close to Rick. "She was a witch! She got what she deserved!"

"She's coming back," Rick said.

"*No!*" Panic stirred the girl's drab features. "She *can't* come back. She's dead -- like she always said -- worm into butterfly -- she's a butterfly!"

"Go inside," Rick said.

"You can't order me around," Betty Lou answered. Her voice rose hysterically. "This is *my* house. We don't want you around here any more. Daddy's going to tell you. He doesn't want you and I don't want you and my mother and sister. . ."

The change came without warning. Like a film gone dead, Betty Lou froze, her mouth half open, one arm raised, her words dead on her tongue. She was suspended, an instantly lifeless thing raised off the floor, as if caught between two slides of glass. A vacant insect, without speech or sound, inert and hollow. Not dead, but abruptly thinned back to primordial inanimacy.

Into the captured shell filtered new potency and being. It settled over her, a rainbow of life that poured into place eagerly -- like hot fluid -- into every part of her. The girl stumbled and moaned; her body jerked violently and pitched against the wall. A china teacup tumbled from an overhead shelf and smashed on the floor. The girl retreated numbly, one hand to her mouth, her eyes wide with pain and shock.

"Oh!" she gasped. "I cut myself." She shook her head and gazed up mutely at him, appealing to him. "On a nail or something."

"*Silvia!*" He caught hold of her and dragged her to her feet, away from the wall. It was *her* arm he gripped, warm and full and mature. Stunned gray eyes, brown hair, quivering breasts -- she was now as she had been those last moments in the basement.

"Let's see it," he said. He tore her hand from her mouth and shakily examined her finger. There was no cut, only a thin white line rapidly dimming. "It's all right, honey. You're all right. There's nothing wrong with you!"

"Rick, I was over *there*." Her voice was husky and faint. "They came and dragged me across with them." She shuddered violently. "Rick, am I actually *back?*"

He crushed her tight. "Completely back."

"It was so long. I was over there a century. Endless ages. I thought --" Suddenly she pulled away. "Rick. . ."

"What is it?"

Silvia's face was wild with fear. "There's something wrong."

"There's nothing wrong. You've come back home and that's all that matters."

Silvia retreated from him. "But they took a living form, didn't they? Not discarded clay. They don't have the power, Rick. They altered His work instead." Her voice rose in panic. "A mistake -- they should have known better than to alter the balance. It's unstable and none of them can control the. . ."

Rick blocked the doorway. "Stop talking like that!" he said fiercely. "It's worth it -- any-thing's worth it. If they set things out of balance, it's their own fault."

"We can't turn it back!" Her voice rose shrilly, thin and hard, like drawn wire. "We've set it in motion, started the waves lapping out. The balance He set up is *altered.*"

"Come on, darling," Rick said. "Let's go and sit in the living room with your family. You'll feel better. You'll have to try to recover from this."

They approached the three seated figures, two on the couch, one in the traight chair by the fireplace. The figures sat motionless, their faces blank, their bodies limp and waxen, dulled forms that did not respond as the couple entered the room.

Rick halted, uncomprehending. Walter Everett was slumped forward, newspaper in one hand, slippers on his feet; his pipe was still smoking in the deep ashtray on the arm of his chair. Mrs. Everett sat with a lapful of sewing, her face grim and stern, but strangely vague. An unformed face, as if the material were melting and running together. Jean sat huddled in a shapeless heap, a ball of clay wadded up, more formless each moment.

Abruptly Jean collapsed. Her arms fell loose beside her. Her head sagged. Her body, her arms and legs filled out. Her features altered rapidly. Her clothing changed. Colors flowed in her hair, her eyes, her skin. The waxen pallor was gone.

Pressing her fingers to her lips she gazed up at Rick mutely. She blinked and her eyes focused. "Oh," she gasped. Her lips moved awkwardly; the voice was faint and uneven, like a poor soundtrack. She struggled up jerkily, with uncoordinated movements that propelled her stiffly to her feet and towards him -- one awkward step at a time -- like a wire dummy.

"Rick, I cut myself," she said. "On a nail or something."

What had been Mrs. Everett stirred. Shapeless and vague, it made dull sounds and flopped grotesquely. Gradually it hardened and shaped itself. "My finger," its voice gasped feebly. Like mirror echoes dimming off into darkness, the third figure in the easy chair took up the words. Soon, they were all of them repeating the phrase, four fingers, their lips moving in unison.

"My finger. I cut myself, Rick."

Parrot reflections, receding mimicries of words and movement. And the settling shapes were familiar in every detail. Again and again, repeated around him, twice on the couch, in the easy chair, close beside him -- so close he could hear her breath and see her trembling lips.

"What is it?" the Silvia beside him asked.

On the couch one Silvia resumed its sewing -- she was sewing methodically, absorbed in her work. In the deep chair another took up its newspapers, its pipe and continued reading. One huddled, nervous and afraid. The one beside him followed as he retreated to the door. She was panting with uncertainty, her gray eyes wide, her nostrils flaring.

"Rick. . ."

He pulled the door open and made his way out onto the dark porch. Machine-like, he felt his way down the steps, through the pools of night collected everywhere, toward the driveway. In the yellow square of light behind him, Silvia was outlined, peering unhappily after him. And behind her, the other figures, identical, pure repetitions, nodding over their tasks.

He found his coupe and pulled out onto the road.

Gloomy trees and houses flashed past. He wondered how far it would go. Lapping waves spreading out -- a widening circle as the imbalance spread.

He turned onto the main highway; there were soon more cars around him. He tried to see into them, but they moved too swiftly. The car ahead was a red Plymouth. A heavyset man in a blue business suit was driving, laughing merrily with the woman beside him. He pulled his own coupe up close behind the Plymouth and followed it. The man flashed gold teeth, grinned, waved his plump hands. The girl was dark-haired, pretty. She smiled at the man, adjusted her white gloves, smoothed down her hair, then rolled up the window on her side.

He lost the Plymouth. A heavy diesel truck cut in between them. Desperately he swerved around the truck and nosed in beyond the swift-moving red sedan. Presently it passed him and, for a moment, the two occupants were clearly framed. The girl resembled Silvia. The same delicate line of her small chin -- the same deep lips, parting slightly when she smiled -- the same slender arms and hands. It was Silvia. The Plymouth turned off and there was no other car ahead of him.

He drove for hours through the heavy night darkness. The gas gauge dropped lower and lower. Ahead of him dismal rolling countryside spread out, blank fields between towns and unwinking stars suspended in the bleak sky. Once, a cluster of red and yellow lights gleamed. An intersection -- filling stations and a big neon sign. He drove on past it.

At a single-pump stand, he pulled the car off the highway, onto the oil-soaked gravel. He climbed out, his shoes crunching the stone underfoot, as he grabbed the gas hose and unscrewed the cap of his car's tank. He had the tank almost full when the door of the drab station building opened and a slim woman in white overalls and navy shirt, with a little cap lost in her brown curls, stepped out.

"Good evening, Rick," she said quietly.

He put back the gas hose. Then he was driving out onto the highway. Had he screwed the cap back on again? He didn't remember. He gained speed. He had gone over a hundred miles. He was nearing the state line.

At a little roadside cafe, warm, yellow light glowed in the chill gloom of early morning. He slowed the car down and parked at the edge of the highway in the deserted parking lot. Bleary-eyed he pushed the door open and entered.

Hot, thick smells of cooking ham and black coffee surrounded him, the comfortable sight of people eating. A jukebox blared in the corner. He threw himself onto a stool and hunched over, his head in his hands. A thin farmer next to him glanced at him curiously and then returned to his newspaper. Two hard-faced women across from him gazed at him momentarily. A handsome youth in denim jacket and jeans was eating red beans and rice, washing it down with steaming coffee from a heavy mug.

"What'll it be?" the pert blonde waitress asked, a pencil behind her ear, her hair tied back in a tight bun. "Looks like you've got some hangover, mister."

He ordered coffee and vegetable soup. Soon he was eating, his hands working automatically. He found himself devouring a ham and cheese sandwich; had he ordered it? The jukebox blared and people came and went. There was a little town sprawled beside the road, set back in some gradual hills. Gray sunlight, cold and sterile, filtered down as morning came. He ate hot apple pie and sat wiping dully at his mouth with a napkin.

The cafe was silent. Outside nothing stirred. An uneasy calm hung over everything. The jukebox had ceased. None of the people at the counter stirred or spoke. An occasional truck roared past, damp and lumbering, windows rolled up tight.

When he looked up, Silvia was standing in front of him. Her arms were folded and she gazed vacantly past him. A bright yellow pencil was behind her ear. Her brown hair was tied back in a hard bun. At the corner others were sitting, other Silvias, dishes in front of them, half dozing or eating, some of them reading. Each the same as the next, except for their clothing.

He made his way back to his parked car. In half an hour he had crossed the state line. Cold, bright sunlight sparkled off dew-moist roofs and pavements as he sped through tiny unfamiliar towns.

Along the shiny morning streets he saw them moving -- early risers, on their way to work. In twos and threes they walked, their heels echoing in sharp silence. At bus stops he saw groups of them collected together. In the houses, rising from their beds, eating breakfast, bathing, dressing, were more of them -- hundreds of them, legions without number. A town of them preparing for the day, resuming their regular tasks, as the circle widened and spread.

He left the town behind. The car slowed under him as his foot slid heavily from the gas pedal. Two of them walked across a level field together. They carried books -- children on their way to school. Repetition, unvarying and identical. A dog circled excitedly after them, unconcerned, his joy untainted.

He drove on. Ahead a city loomed, its stern columns of office buildings sharply outlined against the sky. The streets swarmed with noise and activity as he passed through the main business section. Somewhere, near the center of the city, he overtook the expanding periphery of the circle and emerged beyond. Diversity took the place of the endless figures of Silvia. Gray eyes and , brown hair gave way to countless varieties of men and women, children and adults, of all ages and appearances. He increased his speed and raced out on the far side, onto the wide four-lane highway.

He finally slowed down. He was exhausted. He had driven for hours; his body was shaking with fatigue.

Ahead of him a carrot-haired youth was cheerfully thumbing a ride, a thin bean-pole in brown slacks and light camel's-hair sweater. Rick pulled to a halt and opened the front door. "Hop in," he said.

"Thanks, buddy." The youth hurried to the car and climbed in as Rick gathered speed. He slammed the door and settled gratefully back against the seat. "It was getting hot, standing there."

"How far are you going?" Rick demanded.

"All the way to Chicago." The youth grinned shyly. "Of course, I don't expect you to drive me that far. Anything at all is appreciated." He eyed Rick curiously. "Which way you going?"

"Anywhere," Rick said. "I'll drive you to Chicago."

"It's two hundred miles!"

"Fine," Rick said. He steered over into the left lane and gained speed. "If you want to go to New York, I'll drive you there."

"You feel all right?" The youth moved away uneasily. "I sure appreciate a lift, but. . ." He hesitated. "I mean, I don't want to take you out of your way."

Rick concentrated on the road ahead, his hands gripping hard around the rim of the wheel. "I'm going fast. I'm not slowing down or stopping."

"You better be careful," the youth warned, in a troubled voice. "I don't want to get in an accident."

"I'll do the worrying."

"But it's dangerous. What if something happens? It's too risky."

"You're wrong," Rick muttered grimly, eyes on the road. "It's worth the risk."

"But if something goes wrong --" The voice broke off uncertainly and then continued, "I might be lost. It would be so easy. It's all so unstable." The voice trembled with worry and fear. "Rick, please. . ."

Rick whirled. "How do you know my name?"

The youth was crouched in a heap against the door. His face had a soft, molten look, as if it were losing its shape and sliding together in an unformed mass. "I want to come back," he was saying, from within himself, "but I'm afraid. You haven't seen it -- the region between. It's nothing but energy, Rick. He tapped it a long time ago, but nobody else knows how."

The voice lightened, became clear and treble. The hair faded to a rich brown. Gray, frightened eyes flickered up at Rick. Hands frozen, he hunched over the wheel and forced himself not to move. Gradually he decreased speed and brought the car over into the right-hand lane.

"Are we stopping?" the shape beside him asked. It was Silvia's voice now. Like a new insect, drying in the sun, the shape hardened and locked into firm reality. Silvia struggled up on the seat and peered out. "Where are we? We're between towns."

He jammed on the brakes, reached past her and threw open the door. "Get out!"

Silvia gazed at him uncomprehendingly. "What do you mean?" she faltered. "Rick, what is it? What's wrong?"

"*Get out!*"

"Rick, I don't understand." She slid over a little. Her toes touched the pavement. "Is there something wrong with the car? I thought everything was all right."

He gently shoved her out and slammed the door. The car leaped ahead, out into the stream of mid-morning traffic. Behind him the small, dazed figure was pulling itself up, bewildered and injured. He forced his eyes from the rearview mirror and crushed down the gas pedal with all his weight.

The radio buzzed and clicked in vague static when he snapped it briefly on. He turned the dial and, after a time, a big network station came in. A faint, puzzled voice, a woman's voice. For a time he couldn't make out the words. Then he recognized it and, with a pang of panic, switched the thing off.

Her voice. Murmuring plaintively. Where was the station? Chicago. The circle had already spread that far.

He slowed down. There was no point hurrying. It had already passed him by and gone on. Kansas farms -- sagging stores in little old Mississippi towns -- along the bleak streets of New England manufacturing cities swarms of brown-haired gray-eyed women would be hurrying.

It would cross the ocean. Soon it would take in the whole world. Africa would be strange -- kraals of white-skinned young women, all exactly alike, going about the primitive chores of hunting and fruit-gathering, mashing grain, skinning animals. Building fires and weaving cloth and carefully shaping razor-sharp knives.

In China. . . he grinned inanely. She'd look strange there, too. In the austere high-collar suit, the almost monastic robe of the young communist cadres. Parade marching up the main streets of Peiping. Row after row of slim-legged full-breasted girls, with heavy Russian-made rifles. Carrying spades, picks, shovels. Columns of cloth-booted soldiers. Fast-moving workers with their precious tools. Reviewed by an identical figure on the elaborate stand overlooking the street, one slender arm raised, her gentle, pretty face expressionless and wooden.

He turned off the highway onto a side road. A moment later he was on his way back, driving slowly, listlessly, the way he had come.

At an intersection a traffic cop waded out through traffic to his car. He sat rigid, hands on the wheel, waiting numbly.

"Rick" she whispered pleadingly as she reached the window. "Isn't everything all right?"

"Sure," he answered dully.

She reached in through the open window and touched him imploringly on the arm. Familiar fingers, red nails, the hand he knew so well, "I want to be with you so badly. Aren't we together again? Aren't I back?"

"Sure." -

She shook her head miserably. "I don't understand," she repeated. "I thought it was all right again."

Savagely he put the car into motion and hurtled ahead. The intersection was left behind.

It was afternoon. He was exhausted, riddled with fatigue. He guided the car towards his own town automatically. Along the streets she hurried everywhere, on all sides. She was omnipresent. He came to his apartment building and parked.

The janitor greeted him in the empty hall. Rick identified him by the greasy rag clutched in one hand, the big push-broom, the bucket of wood shavings. "Please," she implored, "tell me what it is, Rick. Please tell me."

He pushed past her, but she caught at him desperately. "Rick, *I'm back.* Don't you understand? They took me too soon and then they sent me back again. It was a mistake. I won't ever call them again -- that's all in the past." She followed after him, down the hall to the stairs. "I'm never going to call them again."

He climbed the stairs. Silvia hesitated, then settled down on the bottom step in a wretched, unhappy heap, a tiny figure in thick workman's clothing and huge cleated boots.

He unlocked his apartment door and entered.

The late afternoon sky was a deep blue beyond the windows. The roofs of nearby apartment buildings sparkled white in the sun.

His body ached. He wandered clumsily into the bathroom -- it seemed alien and unfamiliar, a difficult place to find. He filled the bowl with hot water, rolled up his sleeves and washed his face and hands in the swirling hot stream. Briefly, he glanced up.

It was a terrified reflection that showed out of the mirror above the bowl, a face, tear-stained and frantic. The face was difficult to catch -- it seemed to waver and slide. Gray eyes, bright with terror. Trembling red mouth, pulse-fluttering throat, soft brown hair. The face gazed out pathetically -- and then the girl at the bowl bent to dry herself.

She turned and moved wearily out of the bathroom into the living room.

Confused, she hesitated, then threw herself onto a chair and closed her eyes, sick with misery and fatigue.

"Rick," she murmured pleadingly. "Try to help me. I'm back, aren't I?" She shook her head, bewildered. "Please, Rick, I thought everything was all right."

Piper in the Woods

"Well, Corporal Westerburg," Doctor Henry Harris said gently, "just why do you think you're a plant?"

As he spoke, Harris glanced down again at the card on his desk. It was from the Base Commander himself, made out in Cox's heavy scrawl: *Doc, this is the lad I told you about. Talk to him and try to find out how he got this delusion. He's from the new Garrison, the new check-station on Asteroid Y-3, and we don't want anything to go wrong there. Especially a silly damn thing like this!*

Harris pushed the card aside and stared back up at the youth across the desk from him. The young man seemed ill at ease and appeared to be avoiding answering the question Harris had put to him. Harris frowned. Westerburg was a good-looking chap, actually handsome in his Patrol uniform, a shock of blond hair over one eye. He was tall, almost six feet, a fine healthy lad, just two years out of Training, according to the card. Born in Detroit. Had measles when he was nine. Interested in jet engines, tennis, and girls. Twenty-six years old.

"Well, Corporal Westerburg," Doctor Harris said again. "Why do you think you're a plant?"

The Corporal looked up shyly. He cleared his throat. "Sir, I *am* a plant, I don't just think so. I've been a plant for several days, now."

"I see." The Doctor nodded. "You mean that you weren't always a plant?"

"No, sir. I just became a plant recently."

"And what were you before you became a plant?"

"Well, sir, I was just like the rest of you."

There was silence. Doctor Harris took up his pen and scratched a few lines, but nothing of importance came. A plant? And such a healthy-looking lad! Harris removed his steel-rimmed glasses and polished them with his handkerchief. He put them on again and leaned back in his chair. "Care for a cigarette, Corporal?"

"No, sir."

The Doctor lit one himself, resting his arm on the edge of the chair. "Corporal, you must realize that there are very few men who become plants, especially on such short notice. I have to admit you are the first person who has ever told me such a thing."

"Yes, sir, I realize it's quite rare."

"You can understand why I'm interested, then. When you say you're a plant, you mean you're not capable of mobility? Or do you mean you're a vegetable, as opposed to an animal? Or just what?"

The Corporal looked away. "I can't tell you any more," he murmured. "I'm sorry, sir."

"Well, would you mind telling me *how* you became a plant?"

Corporal Westerburg hesitated. He stared down at the floor, then out the window at the spaceport, then at a fly on the desk. At last he stood up, getting slowly to his feet. "I can't even tell you that, sir," he said.

"You can't? Why not?"

"Because-because I promised not to."

*   *   *   *   *

The room was silent. Doctor Harris rose, too, and they both stood facing each other. Harris frowned, rubbing his jaw. "Corporal, just *who* did you promise?"

"I can't even tell you that, sir. I'm sorry."

The Doctor considered this. At last he went to the door and opened it. "All right, Corporal. You may go now. And thanks for your time."

"I'm sorry I'm not more helpful." The Corporal went slowly out and Harris closed the door after him. Then he went across his office to the vidphone. He rang Commander Cox's letter. A moment later the beefy good-natured face of the Base Commander appeared.

"Cox, this is Harris. I talked to him, all right. All I could get is the statement that he's a plant. What else is there? What kind of behavior pattern?"

"Well," Cox said, "the first thing they noticed was that he wouldn't do any work. The Garrison Chief reported that this Westerburg would wander off outside the Garrison and just sit, all day long. Just sit."

"In the sun?"

"Yes. Just sit in the sun. Then at nightfall he would come back in. When they asked why he wasn't working in the jet repair building he told them he had to be out in the sun. Then he said —" Cox hesitated.

"Yes? Said what?"

"He said that work was unnatural. That it was a waste of time. That the only worthwhile thing was to sit and contemplate-outside."

"What then?"

"Then they asked him how he got that idea, and then he revealed to them that he had become a plant."

"I'm going to have to talk to him again, I can see," Harris said. "And he's applied for a permanent discharge from the Patrol? What reason did he give?"

"The same, that he's a plant now, and has no more interest in being a Patrolman. All he wants to do is sit in the sun. It's the damnedest thing I ever heard."

"All right. I think I'll visit him in his quarters." Harris looked at his watch. "I'll go over after dinner."

"Good luck," Cox said gloomily. "But who ever heard of a man turning into a plant? We told him it wasn't possible, but he just smiled at us."

"I'll let you know how I make out," Harris said.

* * * * *

Harris walked slowly down the hall. It was after six; the evening meal was over. A dim concept was coming into his mind, but it was much too soon to be sure. He increased his pace, turning right at the end of the hall. Two nurses passed, hurrying by. Westerburg was quartered with a buddy, a man who had been injured in a jet blast and who was now almost recovered. Harris came to the dorm wing and stopped, checking the numbers on the doors.

"Can I help you, sir?" the robot attendant said, gliding up.

"I'm looking for Corporal Westerburg's room."

"Three doors to the right."

Harris went on. Asteroid Y-3 had only recently been garrisoned and staffed. It had become the primary check-point to halt and examine ships entering the system from outer space. The Garrison made sure that no dangerous bacteria, fungus, or what-not arrived to infect the system. A nice asteroid it was, warm, well-watered, with trees and lakes and lots of sunlight. And the most modern Garrison in the nine planets. He shook his head, coming to the third door. He stopped, raising his hand and knocking.

"Who's there?" sounded through the door.

"I want to see Corporal Westerburg."

The door opened. A bovine youth with horn-rimmed glasses looked out, a book in his hand. "Who are you?"

"Doctor Harris."

"I'm sorry, sir. Corporal Westerburg is asleep."

"Would he mind if I woke him up? I want very much to talk to him." Harris peered inside. He could see a neat room, with a desk, a rug and lamp, and two bunks. On one of the bunks was Westerburg, lying face up, his arms folded across his chest, his eyes tightly closed.

"Sir," the bovine youth said, "I'm afraid I can't wake him up for you, much as I'd like to."

"You can't? Why not?"

"Sir, Corporal Westerburg won't wake up, not after the sun sets. He just won't. He can't be wakened."

"Cataleptic? Really?"

"But in the morning, as soon as the sun comes up, he leaps out of bed and goes outside. Stays the whole day."

"I see," the Doctor said. "Well, thanks anyhow." He went back out into the hall and the door shut after him. "There's more to this than I realized," he murmured. He went on back the way he had come.

* * * * *

It was a warm sunny day. The sky was almost free of clouds and a gentle wind moved through the cedars along the bank of the stream. There was a path leading from the hospital building down the slope to the stream. At the stream a small bridge led over to the other side, and a few patients were standing on the bridge, wrapped in their bathrobes, looking aimlessly down at the water.

It took Harris several minutes to find Westerburg. The youth was not with the other patients, near or around the bridge. He had gone farther down, past the cedar trees and out onto a strip of bright meadow, where poppies and grass grew everywhere. He was sitting on the stream bank, on a flat grey stone, leaning back and staring up, his mouth open a little. He did not notice the Doctor until Harris was almost beside him.

"Hello," Harris said softly.

Westerburg opened his eyes, looking up. He smiled and got slowly to his feet, a graceful, flowing motion that was rather surprising for a man of his size. "Hello, Doctor. What brings you out here?"

"Nothing. Thought I'd get some sun."

"Here, you can share my rock." Westerburg moved over and Harris sat down gingerly, being careful not to catch his trousers on the sharp edges of the rock. He lit a cigarette and gazed silently down at the water. Beside him, Westerburg had resumed his strange position, leaning back, resting on his hands, staring up with his eyes shut tight.

"Nice day," the Doctor said.

"Yes."

"Do you come here every day?"

"Yes."

"You like it better out here than inside."

"I can't stay inside," Westerburg said.

"You can't? How do you mean, 'can't'?"

"You would die without *air*, wouldn't you?" the Corporal said.

"And you'd die without sunlight?"

Westerburg nodded.

"Corporal, may I ask you something? Do you plan to do this the rest of your life, sit out in the sun on a flat rock? Nothing else?"

Westerburg nodded.

"How about your job? You went to school for years to become a Patrolman. You wanted to enter the Patrol very badly. You were given a fine rating and a first-class position. How do you feel, giving all that up? You know, it won't be easy to get back in again. Do you realize that?"

"I realize it."

"And you're really going to give it all up?"

"That's right."

* * * * *

Harris was silent for a while. At last he put his cigarette out and turned toward the youth. "All right, let's say you give up your job and sit in the sun. Well, what happens, then? Someone else has to do the job instead of you. Isn't that true? The job has to be done, *your* job has to be done. And if you don't do it someone else has to."

"I suppose so."

"Westerburg, suppose everyone felt the way you do? Suppose everyone wanted to sit in the sun all day? What would happen? No one would check ships coming from outer space. Bacteria and toxic crystals would enter the system and cause mass death and suffering. Isn't that right?"

"If everyone felt the way I do they wouldn't be going into outer space."

"But they have to. They have to trade, they have to get minerals and products and new plants."

"Why?"

"To keep society going."

"Why?"

"Well —" Harris gestured. "People couldn't live without society."

Westerburg said nothing to that. Harris watched him, but the youth did not answer.

"Isn't that right?" Harris said.

"Perhaps. It's a peculiar business, Doctor. You know, I struggled for years to get through Training. I had to work and pay my own way. Washed dishes, worked in kitchens. Studied at night, learned, crammed, worked on and on. And you know what I think, now?"

"What?"

"I wish I'd become a plant earlier."

Doctor Harris stood up. "Westerburg, when you come inside, will you stop off at my office? I want to give you a few tests, if you don't mind."

"The shock box?" Westerburg smiled. "I knew that would be coming around. Sure, I don't mind."

Nettled, Harris left the rock, walking back up the bank a short distance. "About three, Corporal?"

The Corporal nodded.

Harris made his way up the hill, to the path, toward the hospital building. The whole thing was beginning to become more clear to him. A boy who had struggled all his life. Financial insecurity. Idealized goal, getting a Patrol assignment. Finally reached it, found the load too great. And on Asteroid Y-3 there was too much vegetation to look at all day. Primitive identification and projection on the flora of the asteroid. Concept of security involved in immobility and permanence. Unchanging forest.

He entered the building. A robot orderly stopped him almost at once. "Sir, Commander Cox wants you urgently, on the vidphone."

"Thanks." Harris strode to his office. He dialed Cox's letter and the Commander's face came presently into focus. "Cox? This is Harris. I've been out talking to the boy. I'm beginning to get this lined up, now. I can see the pattern, too much load too long. Finally gets what he wants and the idealization shatters under the —"

"Harris!" Cox barked. "Shut up and listen. I just got a report from Y-3. They're sending an express rocket here. It's on the way."

"An express rocket?"

"Five more cases like Westerburg. All say they're plants! The Garrison Chief is worried as hell. Says we *must* find out what it is or the Garrison will fall apart, right away. Do you get me, Harris? Find out what it is!"

"Yes, sir," Harris murmured. "Yes, sir."

* * * * *

By the end of the week there were twenty cases, and all, of course, were from Asteroid Y-3.

Commander Cox and Harris stood together at the top of the hill, looking gloomily down at the stream below. Sixteen men and four women sat in the sun along the bank, none of them moving, none speaking. An hour had gone by since Cox and Harris appeared, and in all that time the twenty people below had not stirred.

"I don't get it," Cox said, shaking his head. "I just absolutely don't get it. Harris, is this the beginning of the end? Is everything going to start cracking around us? It gives me a hell of a strange feeling to see those people down there, basking away in the sun, just sitting and basking."

"Who's that man there with the red hair?"

"That's Ulrich Deutsch. He was Second in Command at the Garrison. Now look at him! Sits and dozes with his mouth open and his eyes shut. A week ago that man was climbing, going right up to the top. When the Garrison Chief retires he was supposed to take over. Maybe another year, at the most. All his life he's been climbing to get up there."

"And now he sits in the sun," Harris finished.

"That woman. The brunette, with the short hair. Career woman. Head of the entire office staff of the Garrison. And the man beside her. Janitor. And that cute little gal there, with the bosom. Secretary, just out of school. All kinds. And I got a note this morning, three more coming in sometime today."

Harris nodded. "The strange thing is-they really *want* to sit down there. They're completely rational; they could do something else, but they just don't care to."

"Well?" Cox said. "What are you going to do? Have you found anything? We're counting on you. Let's hear it."

"I couldn't get anything out of them directly," Harris said, "but I've had some interesting results with the shock box. Let's go inside and I'll show you."

"Fine," Cox turned and started toward the hospital. "Show me anything you've got. This is serious. Now I know how Tiberius felt when Christianity showed up in high places."

* * * * *

Harris snapped off the light. The room was pitch black. "I'll run this first reel for you. The subject is one of the best biologists stationed at the Garrison. Robert Bradshaw. He came in yesterday. I got a good run from the shock box because Bradshaw's mind is so highly differentiated. There's a lot of repressed material of a non-rational nature, more than usual."

He pressed a switch. The projector whirred, and on the far wall a three-dimensional image appeared in color, so real that it might have been the man himself. Robert Bradshaw was a man of fifty, heavy-set, with iron grey hair and a square jaw. He sat in the chair calmly, his hands resting on the arms, oblivious to the electrodes attached to his neck and wrist. "There I go," Harris said. "Watch."

His film-image appeared, approaching Bradshaw. "Now, Mr. Bradshaw," his image said, "this won't hurt you at all, and it'll help us a lot." The image rotated the controls on the shock box. Bradshaw stiffened, and his jaw set, but otherwise he gave no sign. The image of Harris regarded him for a time and then stepped away from the controls.

"Can you hear me, Mr. Bradshaw?" the image asked.

"Yes."

"What is your name?"

"Robert C. Bradshaw."

"What is your position?"

"Chief Biologist at the check-station on Y-3."

"Are you there now?"

"No, I'm back on Terra. In a hospital."

"Why?"

"Because I admitted to the Garrison Chief that I had become a plant."

"Is that true? That you are a plant."

"Yes, in a non-biological sense. I retain the physiology of a human being, of course."

"What do you mean, then, that you're a plant?"

"The reference is to attitudinal response, to Weltanschauung."

"Go on."

"It is possible for a warm-blooded animal, an upper primate, to adopt the psychology of a plant, to some extent."

"Yes?"

"I refer to this."

"And the others? They refer to this also?"

"Yes."

"How did this occur, your adopting this attitude?"

Bradshaw's image hesitated, the lips twisting. "See?" Harris said to Cox. "Strong conflict. He wouldn't have gone on, if he had been fully conscious."

"I —"

"Yes?"

"I was taught to become a plant."

The image of Harris showed surprise and interest. "What do you mean, you were *taught* to become a plant?"

"They realized my problems and taught me to become a plant. Now I'm free from them, the problems."

"Who? Who taught you?"

"The Pipers."

"Who? The Pipers? Who are the Pipers?"

There was no answer.

"Mr. Bradshaw, who are the Pipers?"

After a long, agonized pause, the heavy lips parted. "They live in the woods...."

Harris snapped off the projector, and the lights came on. He and Cox blinked. "That was all I could get," Harris said. "But I was lucky to get that. He wasn't supposed to tell, not at all. That was the thing they all promised not to do, tell who taught them to become plants. The Pipers who live in the woods, on Asteroid Y-3."

"You got this story from all twenty?"

"No." Harris grimaced. "Most of them put up too much fight. I couldn't even get *this* much from them."

Cox reflected. "The Pipers. Well? What do you propose to do? Just wait around until you can get the full story? Is that your program?"

"No," Harris said. "Not at all. I'm going to Y-3 and find out who the Pipers are, myself."

* * * * *

The small patrol ship made its landing with care and precision, its jets choking into final silence. The hatch slid back and Doctor Henry Harris found himself staring out at a field, a brown, sun-baked landing field. At the end of the field was a tall signal tower. Around the field on all sides were long grey buildings, the Garrison check-station itself. Not far off a huge Venusian cruiser was parked, a vast green hulk, like an enormous lime. The technicians from the station were swarming all over it, checking and examining each inch of it for lethal life-forms and poisons that might have attached themselves to the hull.

"All out, sir," the pilot said.

Harris nodded. He took hold of his two suitcases and stepped carefully down. The ground was hot underfoot, and he blinked in the bright sunlight. Jupiter was in the sky, and the vast planet reflected considerable sunlight down onto the asteroid.

Harris started across the field, carrying his suitcases. A field attendant was already busy opening the storage compartment of the patrol ship, extracting his trunk. The attendant lowered the trunk into a waiting dolly and came after him, manipulating the little truck with bored skill.

As Harris came to the entrance of the signal tower the gate slid back and a man came forward, an older man, large and robust, with white hair and a steady walk.

"How are you, Doctor?" he said, holding his hand out. "I'm Lawrence Watts, the Garrison Chief."

They shook hands. Watts smiled down at Harris. He was a huge old man, still regal and straight in his dark blue uniform, with his gold epaulets sparkling on his shoulders.

"Have a good trip?" Watts asked. "Come on inside and I'll have a drink fixed for you. It gets hot around here, with the Big Mirror up there."

"Jupiter?" Harris followed him inside the building. The signal tower was cool and dark, a welcome relief. "Why is the gravity so near Terra's? I expected to go flying off like a kangaroo. Is it artificial?"

"No. There's a dense core of some kind to the asteroid, some kind of metallic deposit. That's why we picked this asteroid out of all the others. It made the construction problem much simpler, and it also explains why the asteroid has natural air and water. Did you see the hills?"

"The hills?"

"When we get up higher in the tower we'll be able to see over the buildings. There's quite a natural park here, a regular little forest, complete with everything you'd want. Come in here, Harris. This is my office." The old man strode at quite a clip, around the corner and into a large, well-furnished apartment. "Isn't this pleasant? I intend to make my last year here as amiable as possible." He frowned. "Of course, with Deutsch gone, I may be here forever. Oh, well." He shrugged. "Sit down, Harris."

"Thanks." Harris took a chair, stretching his legs out. He watched Watts as he closed the door to the hall. "By the way, any more cases come up?"

"Two more today," Watts was grim. "Makes almost thirty, in all. We have three hundred men in this station. At the rate it's going —"

"Chief, you spoke about a forest on the asteroid. Do you allow the crew to go into the forest at will? Or do you restrict them to the buildings and grounds?"

* * * * *

Watts rubbed his jaw. "Well, it's a difficult situation, Harris. I have to let the men leave the grounds sometimes. They can *see* the forest from the buildings, and as long as you can see a nice place to stretch out and relax that does it. Once every ten days they have a full period of rest. Then they go out and fool around."

"And then it happens?"

"Yes, I suppose so. But as long as they can see the forest they'll want to go. I can't help it."

"I know. I'm not censuring you. Well, what's your theory? What happens to them out there? What do they do?"

"What happens? Once they get out there and take it easy for a while they don't want to come back and work. It's boondoggling. Playing hookey. They don't want to work, so off they go."

"How about this business of their delusions?"

Watts laughed good-naturedly. "Listen, Harris. You know as well as I do that's a lot of poppycock. They're no more plants than you or I. They just don't want to work, that's all. When I was a cadet we had a few ways to make people work. I wish we could lay a few on their backs, like we used to."

"You think this is simple goldbricking, then?"

"Don't you think it is?"

"No," Harris said. "They really believe they're plants. I put them through the high-frequency shock treatment, the shock box. The whole nervous system is paralyzed, all inhibitions stopped cold. They tell the truth, then. And they said the same thing-and more."

Watts paced back and forth, his hands clasped behind his back. "Harris, you're a doctor, and I suppose you know what you're talking about. But look at the situation here. We have a garrison, a good modern garrison. We're probably the most modern outfit in the system. Every new device and gadget is here that science can produce. Harris, this garrison is one vast machine. The men are parts, and each has his job, the Maintenance Crew, the Biologists, the Office Crew, the Managerial Staff.

"Look what happens when one person steps away from his job. Everything else begins to creak. We can't service the bugs if no one services the machines. We can't order food to feed the crews if no one makes out reports, takes inventories. We can't direct any kind of activity if the Second in Command decides to go out and sit in the sun all day.

"Thirty people, one tenth of the Garrison. But we can't run without them. The Garrison is built that way. If you take the supports out the whole building falls. No one can leave. We're all tied here, and these people know it. They know they have no right to do that, run off on their own. No one has that right anymore. We're all too tightly interwoven to suddenly start doing what we want. It's unfair to the rest, the majority."

* * * * *

Harris nodded. "Chief, can I ask you something?"

"What is it?"

"Are there any inhabitants on the asteroid? Any natives?"

"Natives?" Watts considered. "Yes, there's some kind of aborigines living out there." He waved vaguely toward the window.

"What are they like? Have you seen them?"

"Yes, I've seen them. At least, I saw them when we first came here. They hung around for a while, watching us, then after a time they disappeared."

"Did they die off? Diseases of some kind?"

"No. They just-just disappeared. Into their forest. They're still there, someplace."

"What kind of people are they?"

"Well, the story is that they're originally from Mars. They don't look much like Martians, though. They're dark, a kind of coppery color. Thin. Very agile, in their own way. They hunt and fish. No written language. We don't pay much attention to them."

"I see." Harris paused. "Chief, have you ever heard of anything called-The Pipers?"

"The Pipers?" Watts frowned. "No. Why?"

"The patients mentioned something called The Pipers. According to Bradshaw, the Pipers taught him to become a plant. He learned it from them, a kind of teaching."

"The Pipers. What are they?"

"I don't know," Harris admitted. "I thought maybe you might know. My first assumption, of course, was that they're the natives. But now I'm not so sure, not after hearing your description of them."

"The natives are primitive savages. They don't have anything to teach anybody, especially a top-flight biologist."

Harris hesitated. "Chief, I'd like to go into the woods and look around. Is that possible?"

"Certainly. I can arrange it for you. I'll give you one of the men to show you around."

"I'd rather go alone. Is there any danger?"

"No, none that I know of. Except —"

"Except the Pipers," Harris finished. "I know. Well, there's only one way to find them, and that's it. I'll have to take my chances."

"If you walk in a straight line," Chief Watts said, "you'll find yourself back at the Garrison in about six hours. It's a damn small asteroid. There's a couple of streams and lakes, so don't fall in."

"How about snakes or poisonous insects?"

"Nothing like that reported. We did a lot of tramping around at first, but it's grown back now, the way it was. We never encountered anything dangerous."

"Thanks, Chief," Harris said. They shook hands. "I'll see you before nightfall."

"Good luck." The Chief and his two armed escorts turned and went back across the rise, down the other side toward the Garrison. Harris watched them go until they disappeared inside the building. Then he turned and started into the grove of trees.

The woods were very silent around him as he walked. Trees towered up on all sides of him, huge dark-green trees like eucalyptus. The ground underfoot was soft with endless leaves that had fallen and rotted into soil. After a while the grove of high trees fell behind and he found himself crossing a dry meadow, the grass and weeds burned brown in the sun. Insects buzzed around him, rising up from the dry weed-stalks. Something scuttled ahead, hurrying through the undergrowth. He caught sight of a grey ball with many legs, scampering furiously, its antennae weaving.

The meadow ended at the bottom of a hill. He was going up, now, going higher and higher. Ahead of him an endless expanse of green rose, acres of wild growth. He scrambled to the top finally, blowing and panting, catching his breath.

He went on. Now he was going down again, plunging into a deep gully. Tall ferns grew, as large as trees. He was entering a living Jurassic forest, ferns that stretched out endlessly ahead of him. Down he went, walking carefully. The air began to turn cold around him. The floor of the gully was damp and silent; underfoot the ground was almost wet.

He came out on a level table. It was dark, with the ferns growing up on all sides, dense growths of ferns, silent and unmoving. He came upon a natural path, an old stream bed, rough and rocky, but easy to follow. The air was thick and oppressive. Beyond the ferns he could see the side of the next hill, a green field rising up.

Something grey was ahead. Rocks, piled-up boulders, scattered and stacked here and there. The stream bed led directly to them. Apparently this had been a pool of some kind, a stream emptying from it. He climbed the first of the boulders awkwardly, feeling his way up. At the top he paused, resting again.

As yet he had had no luck. So far he had not met any of the natives. It would be through them that he would find the mysterious Pipers that were stealing the men away, if such really existed. If he could find the natives, talk to them, perhaps he could find out something. But as yet he had been unsuccessful. He looked around. The woods were very silent. A slight breeze moved through the ferns, rustling them, but that was all. Where were the natives? Probably they had a settlement of some sort, huts, a clearing. The asteroid was small; he should be able to find them by nightfall.

* * * * *

He started down the rocks. More rocks rose up ahead and he climbed them. Suddenly he stopped, listening. Far off, he could hear a sound, the sound of water. Was he approaching a pool of some kind? He went on again, trying to locate the sound. He scrambled down rocks and up rocks, and all around him there was silence, except for the splashing of distant water. Maybe a waterfall, water in motion. A stream. If he found the stream he might find the natives.

The rocks ended and the stream bed began again, but this time it was wet, the bottom muddy and overgrown with moss. He was on the right track; not too long ago this stream had flowed, probably during the rainy season. He went up on the side of the stream, pushing through the ferns and vines. A golden snake slid expertly out of his path. Something glinted ahead, something sparkling through the ferns. Water. A pool. He hurried, pushing the vines aside and stepping out, leaving them behind.

He was standing on the edge of a pool, a deep pool sunk in a hollow of grey rocks, surrounded by ferns and vines. The water was clear and bright, and in motion, flowing in a waterfall at the far end. It was beautiful, and he stood watching, marveling at it, the undisturbed quality of it. Untouched, it was. Just as it had always been, probably. As long as the asteroid existed. Was he the first to see it? Perhaps. It was so hidden, so concealed by the ferns. It gave him a strange feeling, a feeling almost of ownership. He stepped down a little toward the water.

And it was then he noticed her.

The girl was sitting on the far edge of the pool, staring down into the water, resting her head on one drawn-up knee. She had been bathing; he could see that at once. Her coppery body was still wet and glistening with moisture, sparkling in the sun. She had not seen him. He stopped, holding his breath, watching her.

She was lovely, very lovely, with long dark hair that wound around her shoulders and arms. Her body was slim, very slender, with a supple grace to it that made him stare, accustomed as he was to various forms of anatomy. How silent she was! Silent and unmoving, staring down at the water. Time passed, strange, unchanging time, as he watched the girl. Time might even have ceased, with the girl sitting on the rock staring into the water, and the rows of great ferns behind her, as rigid as if they had been painted there.

All at once the girl looked up. Harris shifted, suddenly conscious of himself as an intruder. He stepped back. "I'm sorry," he murmured. "I'm from the Garrison. I didn't mean to come poking around."

She nodded without speaking.

"You don't mind?" Harris asked presently.

"No."

So she spoke Terran! He moved a little toward her, around the side of the pool. "I hope you don't mind my bothering you. I won't be on the asteroid very long. This is my first day here. I just arrived from Terra."

She smiled faintly.

"I'm a doctor. Henry Harris." He looked down at her, at the slim coppery body, gleaming in the sunlight, a faint sheen of moisture on her arms and thighs. "You might be interested in why I'm here." He paused. "Maybe you can even help me."

She looked up a little. "Oh?"

"Would you like to help me?"

She smiled. "Yes. Of course."

"That's good. Mind if I sit down?" He looked around and found himself a flat rock. He sat down slowly, facing her. "Cigarette?"

"No."

"Well, I'll have one." He lit up, taking a deep breath. "You see, we have a problem at the Garrison. Something has been happening to some of the men, and it seems to be spreading. We have to find out what causes it or we won't be able to run the Garrison."

* * * * *

He waited for a moment. She nodded slightly. How silent she was! Silent and unmoving. Like the ferns.

"Well, I've been able to find out a few things from them, and one very interesting fact stands out. They keep saying that something called-called The Pipers are responsible for their condition. They say the Pipers taught them —" He stopped. A strange look had flitted across her dark, small face. "Do you know the Pipers?"

She nodded.

Acute satisfaction flooded over Harris. "You do? I was sure the natives would know." He stood up again. "I was sure they would, if the Pipers really existed. Then they do exist, do they?"

"They exist."

Harris frowned. "And they're here, in the woods?"

"Yes."

"I see." He ground his cigarette out impatiently. "You don't suppose there's any chance you could take me to them, do you?"

"Take you?"

"Yes. I have this problem and I have to solve it. You see, the Base Commander on Terra has assigned this to me, this business about the Pipers. It has to be solved. And I'm the one assigned to the job. So it's important to me to find them. Do you see? Do you understand?"

She nodded.

"Well, will you take me to them?"

The girl was silent. For a long time she sat, staring down into the water, resting her head against her knee. Harris began to become impatient. He fidgeted back and forth, resting first on one leg and then on the other.

"Well, will you?" he said again. "It's important to the whole Garrison. What do you say?" He felt around in his pockets. "Maybe I could give you something. What do I have...." He brought out his lighter. "I could give you my lighter."

The girl stood up, rising slowly, gracefully, without motion or effort. Harris' mouth fell open. How supple she was, gliding to her feet in a single motion! He blinked. Without effort she had stood, seemingly without *change*. All at once she was standing instead of sitting, standing and looking calmly at him, her small face expressionless.

"Will you?" he said.

"Yes. Come along." She turned away, moving toward the row of ferns.

Harris followed quickly, stumbling across the rocks. "Fine," he said. "Thanks a lot. I'm very interested to meet these Pipers. Where are you taking me, to your village? How much time do we have before nightfall?"

The girl did not answer. She had entered the ferns already, and Harris quickened his pace to keep from losing her. How silently she glided!

"Wait," he called. "Wait for me."

The girl paused, waiting for him, slim and lovely, looking silently back.

He entered the ferns, hurrying after her.

* * * * *

"Well, I'll be damned!" Commander Cox said. "It sure didn't take you long." He leaped down the steps two at a time. "Let me give you a hand."

Harris grinned, lugging his heavy suitcases. He set them down and breathed a sigh of relief. "It isn't worth it," he said. "I'm going to give up taking so much."

"Come on inside. Soldier, give him a hand." A Patrolman hurried over and took one of the suitcases. The three men went inside and down the corridor to Harris' quarters. Harris unlocked the door and the Patrolman deposited his suitcase inside.

"Thanks," Harris said. He set the other down beside it. "It's good to be back, even for a little while."

"A little while?"

"I just came back to settle my affairs. I have to return to Y-3 tomorrow morning."

"Then you didn't solve the problem?"

"I solved it, but I haven't *cured* it. I'm going back and get to work right away. There's a lot to be done."

"But you found out what it is?"

"Yes. It was just what the men said. The Pipers."

"The Pipers do exist?"

"Yes." Harris nodded. "They do exist." He removed his coat and put it over the back of the chair. Then he went to the window and let it down. Warm spring air rushed into the room. He settled himself on the bed, leaning back.

"The Pipers exist, all right-in the minds of the Garrison crew! To the crew, the Pipers are real. The crew created them. It's a mass hypnosis, a group projection, and all the men there have it, to some degree."

"How did it start?"

"Those men on Y-3 were sent there because they were skilled, highly-trained men with exceptional ability. All their lives they've been schooled by complex modern society, fast tempo and high integration between people. Constant pressure toward some goal, some job to be done.

"Those men are put down suddenly on an asteroid where there are natives living the most primitive of existence, completely vegetable lives. No concept of goal, no concept of purpose, and hence no ability to plan. The natives live the way the animals live, from day to day, sleeping, picking food from the trees. A kind of Garden-of-Eden existence, without struggle or conflict."

"So? But —"

"Each of the Garrison crew sees the natives and *unconsciously* thinks of his own early life, when he was a child, when *he* had no worries, no responsibilities, before he joined modern society. A baby lying in the sun.

"But he can't admit this to himself! He can't admit that he might *want* to live like the natives, to lie and sleep all day. So he invents The Pipers, the idea of a mysterious group living in the woods who trap him, lead him into their kind of life. Then he can blame *them*, not himself. They 'teach' him to become a part of the woods."

"What are you going to do? Have the woods burned?"

"No." Harris shook his head. "That's not the answer; the woods are harmless. The answer is psychotherapy for the men. That's why I'm going right back, so I can begin work. They've got to be made to see that the Pipers are inside them, their own unconscious voices calling to them to give up their responsibilities. They've got to be made to realize that there are no Pipers, at least, not outside themselves. The woods are harmless and the natives have nothing to teach anyone. They're primitive savages, without even a written language. We're seeing a psychological projection by a whole Garrison of men who want to lay down their work and take it easy for a while."

The room was silent.

"I see," Cox said presently. "Well, it makes sense." He got to his feet. "I hope you can do something with the men when you get back."

"I hope so, too," Harris agreed. "And I think I can. After all, it's just a question of increasing their self-awareness. When they have that the Pipers will vanish."

Cox nodded. "Well, you go ahead with your unpacking, Doc. I'll see you at dinner. And maybe before you leave, tomorrow."

"Fine."

* * * * *

Harris opened the door and the Commander went out into the hall. Harris closed the door after him and then went back across the room. He looked out the window for a moment, his hands in his pockets.

It was becoming evening, the air was turning cool. The sun was just setting as he watched, disappearing behind the buildings of the city surrounding the hospital. He watched it go down.

Then he went over to his two suitcases. He was tired, very tired from his trip. A great weariness was beginning to descend over him. There were so many things to do, so terribly many. How could he hope to do them all? Back to the asteroid. And then what?

He yawned, his eyes closing. How sleepy he was! He looked over at the bed. Then he sat down on the edge of it and took his shoes off. So much to do, the next day.

He put his shoes in the corner of the room. Then he bent over, unsnapping one of the suitcases. He opened the suitcase. From it he took a bulging gunnysack. Carefully, he emptied the contents of the sack out on the floor. Dirt, rich soft dirt. Dirt he had collected during his last hours there, dirt he had carefully gathered up.

When the dirt was spread out on the floor he sat down in the middle of it. He stretched himself out, leaning back. When he was fully comfortable he folded his hands across his chest and closed his eyes. So much work to do-But later on, of course. Tomorrow. How warm the dirt was....

He was sound asleep in a moment.

Of Withered Apples

SOMETHING was tapping on the window. Blowing up against the pane, again and again. Carried by the wind. Tapping faintly, insistently.

Lori, sitting on the couch, pretended not to hear. She gripped her book tightly and turned a page. The tapping came again, louder and more imperative. It could not be ignored.

"Darn!" Lori said, throwing her book down on the coffee table and hurrying to the window. She grasped the heavy brass handles and lifted.

For a moment the window resisted. Then, with a protesting groan, it reluctantly rose. Cold autumn air, rushed into the room. The bit of leaf ceased tapping and swirled against the woman's throat, dancing to the floor.

Lori picked the leaf up. It was old and brown. Her heart skipped a beat as she slipped the leaf into the pocket of her jeans. Against her loins the leaf cut and tingled, a little hard point piercing her smooth skin and sending exciting shudders up and down her spine. She stood at the open window a moment, sniffing the air. The air was full of the presence of trees and rocks, of great boulders and remote places. It was time-time to go again. She touched the leaf. She was *wanted*.

Quickly Lori left the big living-room, hurrying through the hall into the dining-room. The dining-room was empty. A few chords of laughter drifted from the kitchen. Lori pushed the kitchen door open. "Steve?"

Her husband and his father were siting around the kitchen table, smoking their cigars and drinking steaming black coffee. "What is it?" Steve demanded, frowning at his young wife. "Ed and I are in the middle of business."

"I—I want to ask you something."

The two men gazed at her, brown-haired Steven, his dark eyes full of the stubborn dignity of New England men, and his father, silent and withdrawn in her presence. Ed Patterson scarcely noticed her. He rustled through a sheaf of feed bills, his broad back turned toward her.

"What is it?" Steve demanded impatiently. "What do you want? Can't it wait?"

"I have to go," Lori blurted.

"Go where?"

"Outside." Anxiety flooded over her. "This is the last time. I promise. I won't go again, after this. Okay?" She tried to smile, but her heart was pounding too hard. "Please let me, Steve."

"Where does she go?" Ed rumbled.

Steve grunted in annoyance. "Up in the hills. Some old abandoned place up there."

Ed's gray eyes flickered. "Abandoned farm?"

"Yes. You know it?"

"The old Rickley farm. Rickley moved away years ago. Couldn't get anything to grow, not up there. Ground's all rocks. Bad soil. A lot of clay and stones. The place is all overgrown, tumbled down."

"What kind of farm was it?"

"Orchard. Fruit orchard. Never yielded a damn thing. Thin old trees. Waste of effort."

Steve looked at his pocket watch. "You'll be back in time to fix dinner?"

"Yes!" Lori moved toward the door. "Then I can go?"

Steve's face twisted as he made up his mind. Lori waited impatiently, scarcely breathing. She had never got used to Vermont men and their slow, deliberate way. Boston people were quite different. And her group had been more the college youths, dances and talk, and late laughter.

"Why do you go up there?" Steve grumbled.

"Don't ask me, Steve. Just let me go. This is the last time." She writhed in agony. She clenched her fists. "Please!"

Steve looked out the window. The cold autumn wind swirled through the trees. "All right. But it's going to snow. I don't see why you want to —"

Lori ran to get her coat from the closet. "I'll be back to fix dinner!" she shouted joyfully. She hurried to the front porch buttoning her coat, her heart racing. Her cheeks were flushed a deep, excited red as she closed the door behind her, her blood pounding in her veins.

Cold wind whipped against her, rumpling her hair, plucking at her body. She took a deep breath of the wind and started down the steps.

She walked rapidly onto the field, toward the bleak line of hills beyond. Except for the wind there was no sound. She patted her pocket. The dry leaf broke and dug hungrily into her.

"I'm coming..." she whispered, a little awed and frightened. "I'm on my way..."

HIGHER and higher the woman climbed. She passed through a deep cleft between two rocky ridges. Huge roots from old stumps spurted out on all sides. She followed a dried-up creek bed, winding and turning.

After a time low mists began to blow about her. At the top of the ridge she halted, breathing deeply, looking back the way she had come.

A few drops of rain stirred the leaves around her. Again the wind moved through the great dead trees along the ridge. Lori turned and started on, her head down, hands in her coat pockets.

She was on a rocky field, overgrown with weeds and dead grass. After a time she came to a ruined fence, broken and rotting. She stepped over it. She passed a tumbled-down well, half filled with stones and earth.

Her heart beat quickly, fluttering with nervous excitement. She was almost there. She passed the remains of a building, sagging timbers and broken glass, a few ruined pieces of furniture strewn nearby. An old automobile tire caked and cracked. Some damp rags heaped over rusty, bent bed-springs.

And there it was-directly ahead.

Along the edge of the field was a grove of ancient trees. Lifeless trees, withered and dead, their thin, blackened stalks rising up leaflessly. Broken sticks stuck in the hard ground. Row after row of dead trees, some bent and leaning, torn loose from the rocky soil by the unending wind.

Lori crossed the field to the trees, her lungs laboring painfully. The wind surged against her without respite, whipping the foul-smelling mists into her nostrils and face. Her smooth skin was damp and shiny with the mist. She coughed and hurried on, stepping over the rocks and clods of earth, trembling with fear and anticipation.

She circled around the grove of trees, almost to the edge of the ridge. Carefully, she stepped among the sliding heaps of rocks. Then —

She stopped, rigid. Her chest rose and fell with the effort of breathing. "I came," she gasped.

For a long time she gazed at the withered old apple tree. She could not take her eyes from it. The sight of the ancient tree fascinated and repelled her. It was the only one alive, the only tree of all the grove still living. All the others were dead, dried-up. They had lost the struggle. But this tree still clung to life.

The tree was hard and barren. Only a few dark leaves hung from it-and some withered apples, dried and seasoned by wind and mists. They had stayed there, on the branches, forgotten and abandoned. The ground around the tree was cracked and bleak. Stones and decayed heaps of old leaves in ragged clumps.

"I came," Lori said again. She took the leaf from her pocket and held it cautiously out. "This tapped at the window. I knew when I heard it." She smiled mischievously, her red lips curling. "It tapped and tapped, trying to get in. I ignored it. It was so-so impetuous. It annoyed me."

The tree swayed ominously. Its gnarled branches rubbed together. Something in the sound made Lori pull away. Terror rushed through her. She hurried back along the ridge, scrambling frantically out of reach.

"Don't," she whispered. *"Please."*

The wind ceased. The tree became silent. For a long time Lori watched it apprehensively.

Night was coming. The sky was darkening rapidly. A burst of frigid wind struck her, half turning her around. She shuddered, bracing herself against it, pulling her long coat around her. Far below, the floor of the valley was disappearing into shadow, into the vast cloud of night.

In the darkening mists the tree was stern and menacing, more ominous than usual. A few leaves blew from it, drifting and swirling with the wind. A leaf blew past her and she tried to catch it. The leaf escaped, dancing back toward the tree. Lori followed a little way and then stopped, gasping and laughing.

"No," she said firmly, her hands on her hips. "I won't."

There was silence. Suddenly the heaps of decayed leaves blew up in a furious circle around the tree. They quieted down, settling back.

"No," Lori said. "I'm not afraid of you. You can't hurt me." But her heart was hammering with fear. She moved back farther away.

The tree remained silent. Its wiry branches were motionless.

Lori regained her courage. "This is the last time I can come," she said. "Steve says I can't come any more. He doesn't like it."

She waited, but the tree did not respond.

"They're sitting in the kitchen. The two of them. Smoking cigars and drinking coffee. Adding up feed bills." She wrinkled her nose." That's all they ever do. Add and subtract feed bills. Figure and figure. Profit and loss. Government taxes. Depreciation on the equipment."

The tree did not stir.

Lori shivered. A little more rain fell, big icy drops that slid down her cheeks, down the back of her neck and inside her heavy coat.

She moved closer to the tree. "I won't be back. I won't see you again. This is the last time. I wanted to tell you. . . ."

The tree moved. Its branches whipped into sudden life. Lori felt something hard and thin cut across her shoulder. Something caught her around the waist, tugging her forward.

She struggled desperately, trying to pull herself free. Suddenly the tree released her. She stumbled back, laughing and trembling with fear. "No!" she gasped. "You can't have me!" She hurried to the edge of the ridge. "You'll never get me again. Understand? And I'm not afraid of you!"

She stood, waiting and watching, trembling with cold and fear. Suddenly she turned and fled, down the side of the ridge, sliding and falling on the loose stones. Blind terror gripped her. She ran on and on, down the steep slope, grabbing at roots and weeds —

Something rolled beside her shoe. Something small and hard. She bent down and picked it up.

It was a little dried apple.

Lori gazed back up the slope at the tree. The tree was almost lost in the swirling mists. It stood, jutting up against the black sky, a hard unmoving pillar.

Lori put the apple in her coat pocket and continued down the side of the hill. When she reached the floor of the valley she took the apple out of her pocket.

It was late. A deep hunger began to gnaw inside her. She thought suddenly of dinner, the warm kitchen, the white tablecloth. Steaming stew and biscuits.

As she walked she nibbled on the little apple.

Lori sat up in bed, the covers falling away from her. The house was dark and silent. A few night noises sounded faintly, far off. It was past midnight. Beside her Steven slept quietly, turned over on his side.

What had wakened her? Lori pushed her dark hair back out of her eyes, shaking her head. What —

A spasm of pain burst loose inside her. She gasped and put her hand to her stomach. For a time she wrestled silently, jaws locked, swaying back and forth.

The pain went away. Lori sank back. She cried out, a faint, thin cry. "Steve —"

Steven stirred. He turned over a little, grunting in his sleep.

The pain came again. Harder. She fell forward on her face, writhing in agony. The pain ripped at her, tearing at her belly. She screamed, a shrill wail of fear and pain.

Steve sat up. "For God's sake —" He rubbed his eyes and snapped on the lamp. "What the hell —"

Lori lay on her side, gasping and moaning, her eyes staring, knotted fists pressed into her stomach. The pain twisted and seared, devouring her, eating into her.

"Lori!" Steven grated. "What is it?"

She screamed. Again and again. Until the house rocked with echoes. She slid from the bed, onto the floor, her body writhing and jerking, her face unrecognizable.

Ed came hurrying into the room, pulling his bathrobe around him. "What's going on?"

The two men stared helplessly down at the woman on the floor.

"Good God," Ed said. He closed his eyes.

The day was cold and dark. Snow fell silently over the streets and houses, over the red brick county hospital building. Doctor Blair walked slowly up the gravel path to his Ford car. He slid inside and turned the ignition key. The motor leaped alive, and he let the brake out.

"I'll call you later," Doctor Blair said. "There are certain particulars."

"I know," Steve muttered. He was still dazed. His face was gray and puffy from lack of sleep.

"I left some sedatives for you. Try to get a little rest."

"You think," Steve asked suddenly, "if we had called you earlier —"

"No." Blair glanced up at him sympathetically. "I don't. In a thing like that, there's not much chance. Not after it's burst."

"Then it *was* appendicitis?"

Blair nodded. "Yes."

"If we hadn't been so damn far out," Steve said bitterly. "stuck out in the country. No hospital. Nothing. Miles from town. And we didn't realize at first —"

"Well, it's over now." The upright Ford moved forward a little. All at once a thought came to the Doctor. "One more thing."

"What is it?" Steve said dully.

Blair hesitated. "Post mortems-very unfortunate. I don't think there's any reason for one in this case. I'm certain in my own mind. . . . But I wanted to ask —"

"What is it?"

"Is there anything the girl might have swallowed? Did she put things in her mouth? Needles-while she was sewing? Pins, coins, anything like that? Seeds? Did she ever eat watermelon? Sometimes the appendix —"

"No."

Steve shook his head wearily. "I don't know."

"It was just a thought." Doctor Blair drove slowly off down the narrow tree-lined street, leaving two dark streaks, two soiled lines that marred the pale, glistening snow.

SPRING came, warm and sunny. The ground turned black and rich. Overhead the sun shone, a hot white orb, full of strength.

"Stop here," Steve murmured.

Ed Patterson brought the car to a halt at the side of the street. He turned off the motor. The two men sat in silence, neither of them speaking.

At the end of the street children were playing. A high school boy was mowing a lawn, pushing the machine over the wet grass. The street was dark in the shade of the great trees growing along each side.

"Nice," Ed said.

Steve nodded without answering. Moodily, he watched a young girl walking by, a shopping bag under her arm. The girl climbed the stairs of a porch and disappeared into an old-fashioned yellow house.

Steve pushed the car door open. "Come on. Let's get it over with."

Ed lifted the wreath of flowers from the back seat and put them in his son's lap. "You'll have to carry it. It's your job."

"All right." Steve grabbed the flowers and stepped out onto the pavement.

The two men walked up the street together, silent and thoughtful.

"It's been seven or eight months, now," Steve said abruptly.

"At least." Ed lit the cigar as they walked along, puffing clouds of gray smoke around them. "Maybe a little more."

"I never should have brought her up here. She lived in town all her life. She didn't know anything about the country."

"It would have happened anyhow."

"If we had been closer to a hospital —"

The doctor said it wouldn't have made any difference. Even if we'd called him right away instead of waiting until morning." They came to the corner and turned. "And as you know —"

"Forget it," Steve said, suddenly tense.

The sounds of the children had fallen behind them. The houses had thinned out. Their footsteps rang out against the pavement as they walked along.

"We're almost there," Steve said.

They came to a rise. Beyond the rise was a heavy brass fence, running the length of a small field. A green field, neat and even. With carefully placed plaques of white marble criss-crossing it.

"Here we are," Steve said tightly.

"They keep it nice."

"Can we get in from this side?"

"We can try." Ed started along the brass fence, looking for a gate.

Suddenly Steve halted, grunting. He stared across the field, his face white. *"Look."*

"What is it?" Ed took off his glasses to see. "What you looking at?"

"I was right." Steve's voice was low and indistinct. "I thought there was something. Last time we were here. . . . I saw. . . . You see it?"

"I'm not sure. I see the tree, if that's what you mean."

In the center of the neat green field the lime apple tree rose proudly. Its bright leaves sparkled in the warm sunlight. The young tree was strong and very healthy. It swayed confidently with the wind, its supple trunk moist with sweet spring sap.

"They're *red,*" Steve said softly. "They're already red. How the hell can they be red? It's only April. How the hell can they be red so soon?"

"I don't know," Ed said. "I don't know anything about apples. A strange chill moved through him. But graveyards always made him uncomfortable. "Maybe we ought to go."

"Her cheeks were that color," Steve said, his voice low. "When she had been running. Remember?"

The two men gazed uneasily at the little apple tree, its shiny red fruit glistening in the spring sunlight, branches moving gently with the wind.

"I remember, all right," Ed said grimly. "Come on." He took his son's arm insistently, the wreath of flowers forgotten. "Come on, Steve. Let's get out of here."

The Unreconstructed M

1

The machine was a foot wide and two feet long; it looked like an oversized box of crackers. Silently, with great caution, it climbed the side of a concrete building; it had lowered two rubberized rollers and was now beginning the first phase of its job.

From its rear, a flake of blue enamel was exuded. The machine pressed the flake firmly against the rough concrete and then continued on. Its upward path carried it from vertical concrete to vertical steel: it had reached a window. The machine paused and produced a microscopic fragment of cloth fabric. The cloth, with great care, was embedded in the fitting of the steel window frame.

In the chill darkness, the machine was virtually invisible. The glow of a distant tangle of traffic briefly touched it, illuminated its polished hull, and departed. The machine resumed its work.

It projected a plastic pseudopodium and incinerated the pane of window glass. There was no response from within the gloomy apartment: nobody was home. The machine, now dulled with particles of glass-dust, crept over the steel frame and raised an inquisitive receptor.

While it received, it exerted precisely two hundred pounds pressure on the steel window frame; the frame obediently bent. Satisfied, the machine descended the inside of the wall to the moderately thick carpet. There it began the second phase of its job.

One single human hair -- follicle and speck of scalp included -- was deposited on the hardwood floor by the lamp. Not far from the piano, two dried grains of tobacco were ceremoniously laid out. The machine waited an interval of ten seconds and then, as an internal section of magnetic tape clicked into place, it suddenly said, "Ugh! Damn it. . ."

Curiously, its voice was husky and masculine.

The machine made its way to the closet door, which was locked. Climbing the wood surface, the machine reached the lock mechanism, and, inserting a thin section of itself, caressed the tumblers back. Behind the row of coats was a small mound of batteries and wires: a self-powered video recorder. The machine destroyed the reservoir of film -- which was vital -- and then, as it left the closet, expelled a drop of blood on the jagged tangle that had been the lens-scanner. The drop of blood was even more vital.

While the machine was pressing the artificial outline of a heel mark into the greasy film that covered the flooring of the closet, a sharp sound came from the hallway. The machine ceased its work and became rigid. A moment later a small, middle-aged man entered the apartment, coat over one arm, briefcase in the other.

"Good God," he said, stopping instantly as he saw the machine. "What are you?"

The machine lifted the nozzle of its front section and shot an explosive pellet at the man's half-bald head. The pellet traveled into the skull and detonated. Still clutching his coat and briefcase, bewildered expression on his face, the man collapsed to the rug. His glasses, broken, lay twisted beside his ear. His body stirred a little, twitched, and then was satisfactorily quiet.

Only two steps remained to the job, now that the main part was done. The machine deposited a bit of burnt match in one of the spotless ashtrays resting on the mantel, and entered the kitchen to search for a water glass. It was starting up the side of the sink when the noise of human voices startled it.

"This is the apartment," a voice said, clear and close.

"Get ready -- he ought to still be here." Another voice, a man's voice, like the first. The hall door was pushed open and two individuals in heavy overcoats sprinted purposefully into the apartment. At their approach, the machine dropped to the kitchen floor, the water glass forgotten. Something had gone wrong. Its rectangular outline flowed and wavered; pulling itself into an upright package it fused its shape into that of a conventional TV unit.

It was holding that emergency form when one of the men -- tall, red-haired -- peered briefly into the kitchen.

"Nobody in here," the man declared, and hurried on.

"The window," his companion said, panting. Two more figures entered the apartment, an entire crew. "The glass is gone -- missing. He got in that way."

"But he's gone." The red-haired man reappeared at the kitchen door; he snapped on the light and entered, a gun visible in his hand. "Strange ... we got here right away, as soon as we picked up the rattle." Suspiciously, he examined his wristwatch. "Rosenburg's been dead only a few seconds . . . how could he have got out again so fast?"

Standing in the street entrance, Edward Ackers listened to the voice. During the last half hour the voice had taken on a carping, nagging whine; sinking almost to inaudibility, it plodded along, mechanically turning out its message of complaint.

"You're tired," Ackers said. "Go home. Take a hot bath."

"No," the voice said, interrupting its tirade. The locus of the voice was a large illuminated blob on the dark sidewalk, a few yards to Acker's right. The revolving neon sign read:

BANISH IT!

Thirty times -- he had counted -- within the last few minutes the sign had captured a passerby and the man in the booth had begun his harangue. Beyond the booth were several theaters and restaurants: the booth was well-situated.

But it wasn't for the crowd that the booth had been erected. It was for Ackers and the offices behind him; the tirade was aimed directly at the Interior Department. The nagging racket had gone on so many months that Ackers was scarcely aware of it. Rain on the roof. Traffic noises. He yawned, folded his arms, and waited.

"Banish it," the voice complained peevishly. "Come on, Ackers. Say something; do something."

"I'm waiting," Ackers said complacently.

A group of middle-class citizens passed the booth and were handed leaflets. The citizens scattered the leaflets after them, and Ackers laughed.

"Don't laugh," the voice muttered. "It's not funny; it costs us money to print those."

"Your personal money?" Ackers inquired.

"Partly." Garth was lonely, tonight. "What are you waiting for? What's happened? I saw a police team leave your roof a few minutes ago . . . ?

"We may take in somebody," Ackers said, "there's been a killing."

Down the dark sidewalk the man stirred in his dreary propaganda booth. "Oh?" Harvey Garth's voice came. He leaned forward and the two looked directly at each other: Ackers, carefully-groomed, well-fed, wearing a respectable overcoat. . . Garth, a thin man, much younger, with a lean, hungry face composed mostly of nose and forehead.

"So you see," Ackers told him, "we do need the system. Don't be Utopian."

"A man is murdered; and you rectify the moral imbalance by killing the killer." Garth's protesting voice rose in a bleak spasm. "Banish it! Banish the system that condemns men to certain extinction!"

"Get your leaflets here," Ackers parodied dryly. "And your slogans. Either or both. What would you suggest in place of the system?"

Garth's voice was proud with conviction. "Education."

Amused, Ackers asked: "Is that all? You think that would stop anti-social activity? Criminals just don't -- know better?"

"And psychotherapy, of course." His projected face bony and intense, Garth peered out of his booth like an aroused turtle. "They're sick . . . that's why they commit crimes, healthy men don't commit crimes. And you compound it; you create a sick society of punitive cruelty." He waggled an accusing finger. "You're the real culprit, you and the whole Interior Department. You and the whole Banishment System."

Again and again the neon sign blinked BANISH it! Meaning, of course, the system of compulsory ostracism for felons, the machinery that projected a condemned human being into some random backwater region of the sidereal universe, into some remote and out-of-the-way corner where he would be of no harm.

"No harm to us, anyhow," Ackers mused aloud.

Garth spoke the familiar argument. "Yes, but what about the local inhabitants?"

Too bad about the local inhabitants. Anyhow, the banished victim spent his energy and time trying to find a way back to the Sol System. If he got back before old age caught up with him he was readmitted by society. Quite a challenge . . . especially to some cosmopolite who had never set foot outside Greater New York. There were -- probably -- many involuntary expatriates cutting grain in odd fields with primitive sickles. The remote sections of the universe seemed composed mostly of dank rural cultures, isolated agrarian enclaves typified by small-time bartering of fruit and vegetables and handmade artifacts.

"Did you know," Ackers said, "that in the Age of Monarchs, a pickpocket was usually hanged?"

"Banish it," Garth continued monotonously, sinking back into his booth. The sign revolved; leaflets were passed out. And Ackers impatiently watched the late-evening street for sign of the hospital truck.

He knew Heimie Rosenburg. A sweeter little guy there never was. . . although Heimie had been mixed up in one of the sprawling slave combines that illegally transported settlers to outsystem fertile planets. Between them, the two largest slavers had settled virtually the entire Sirius System. Four out of six emigrants were hustled out in carriers registered as "freighters." It was hard to picture gentle little Heimie Rosenburg as a business agent for Tirol Enterprises, but there it was.

As he waited, Ackers conjectured on Heimie's murder. Probably one element of the incessant subterranean war going on between Paul Tirol and his major rival, David Lantano, was a brilliant and energetic newcomer . . . but murder was anybody's game. It all depended on how it was done; it could be commercial hack or the purest art.

"Here comes something," Garth's voice sounded, carried to his inner ear by the delicate output transformers of the booth's equipment. "Looks like a freezer."

It was; the hospital truck had arrived. Ackers stepped forward as the truck halted and the back was let down.

"How soon did you get there?" he asked the cop who jumped heavily to the pavement.

"Right away," the cop answered, "but no sign of the killer. I don't think we're going to get Heimie back . . . they got him dead-center, right in the cerebellum. Expert work, no amateur stuff."

Disappointed, Ackers clambered into the hospital truck to inspect for himself.

Very tiny and still, Heimie Rosenburg lay on his back, arms at his sides, gazing sightlessly up at the roof of the truck. On his face remained the expression of bewildered wonder. Somebody -- one of the cops -- had placed his bent glasses in his clenched hand. In falling he had cut his cheek. The destroyed portion of his skull was covered by a moist plastic web.

"Who's back at the apartment?" Ackers asked presently.

"The rest of my crew," the cop answered. "And an independent researcher. Leroy Beam."

"Him," Ackers said, with aversion. "How is it he showed up?"

"Caught the rattle, too, happened to be passing with his rig. Poor Heimie had an awful big booster on that rattle . . . I'm surprised it wasn't picked up here at the main offices."

"They say Heimie had a high anxiety level," Ackers said. "Bugs all over his apartment. You're starting to collect evidence?"

"The teams are moving in," the cop said. "We should begin getting specifications in half an hour. The killer knocked out the vid bug set up in the closet. But --" He grinned. "He cut himself breaking the circuit. A drop of blood, right on the wiring; it looks promising."

At the apartment, Leroy Beam watched the Interior police begin their analysis. They worked smoothly and thoroughly, but Beam was dissatisfied.

His original impression remained: he was suspicious. Nobody could have gotten away so quickly. Heimie had died, and his death -- the cessation of his neural pattern -- had triggered off an automatic squawk. A rattle didn't particularly protect its owner, but its existence ensured (or usually ensured) detection of the murderer. Why had it failed Heimie?

Prowling moodily, Leroy Beam entered the kitchen for the second time. There, on the floor by the sink, was a small portable TV unit, the kind popular with the sporting set: a gaudy little packet of plastic and knobs and multi-tinted lenses.

"Why this?" Beam asked, as one of the cops plodded past him. "This TV unit sitting here on the kitchen floor. It's out of place."

The cop ignored him. In the living room, elaborate police detection equipment was scraping the various surfaces inch by inch. In the half hour since Heimie's death, a number of specifications had been logged. First, the drop of blood on the damaged vid wiring. Second, a hazy heel mark where the murderer had stepped. Third, a bit of burnt match in the ashtray. More were expected; the analysis had only begun.

It usually took nine specifications to delineate the single individual. Leroy Beam glanced cautiously around him. None of the cops was watching, so he bent down and picked up the TV unit; it felt ordinary. He clicked the *on* switch and waited. Nothing happened; no image formed. Strange.

He was holding it upside down, trying to see the inner chassis, when Edward Ackers from Interior entered the apartment. Quickly, Beam stuffed the TV unit into the pocket of his heavy overcoat.

"What are you doing here?" Ackers said.

"Seeking," Beam answered, wondering if Ackers noticed his tubby bulge. "I'm in business, too."

"Did you know Heimie?"

"By reputation," Beam answered vaguely. "Tied in with Tirol's combine, I hear; some sort of front man. Had an office on Fifth Avenue."

"Swank place, like the rest of those Fifth Avenue feather merchants." Ackers went on into the living room to watch detectors gather up evidence.

There was a vast nearsightedness to the wedge grinding ponderously across the carpet. It was scrutinizing at a microscopic level, and its field was sharply curtailed. As fast as material was obtained, it was relayed to the Interior offices, to the aggregate file banks where the civil population was represented by a series of punch cards, cross-indexed infinitely.

Lifting the telephone, Ackers called his wife. "I won't be home," he told her. "Business."

A lag and then Ellen responded. "Oh?" she said distantly. "Well, thanks for letting me know."

Over in the corner, two members of the police crew were delightedly examining a new discovery, valid enough to be a specification. "I'll call you again," he said hurriedly to Ellen, "before I leave. Goodbye."

"Goodbye," Ellen said curtly, and managed to hang up before he did. The new discovery was the undamaged aud bug, which was mounted under the floor lamp. A continuous magnetic tape -- still in motion -- gleamed amiably; the murder episode had been recorded sound-wise in its entirety.

"Everything," a cop said gleefully to Ackers. "It was going before Heimie got home."

"You played it back?"

"A portion. There's a couple words spoken by the murderer, should be enough."

Ackers got in touch with Interior. "Have the specifications on the Rosenburg case been fed, yet?"

"Just the first," the attendant answered. "The file discriminates the usual massive category -- about six billion names."

Ten minutes later the second specification was fed to the files. Persons with type O blood, with size 11 1/2 shoes, numbered slightly over a billion. The third specification brought in the element of smoker-nonsmoker. That dropped the number to less than a billion, but not much less. Most adults smoked.

"The aud tape will drop it fast," Leroy Beam commented, standing beside Ackers, his arms folded to conceal his bulging coat. "Ought to be able to get age, at least."

The aud tape, analyzed, gave thirty to forty years as the conjectured age. And -- timbre analysis -- a man of perhaps two hundred pounds. A little later the bent steel window frame was examined, and the warp noted. It jibed with the specification of the aud tape. There were now six specifications, including that of sex (male). The number of persons in the in-group was falling rapidly.

"It won't be long," Ackers said genially. "And if he tacked one of those little buckets to the building side, we'll have a paint scrape."

Beam said: "I'm leaving. Good luck."

"Stick around."

"Sorry." Beam moved toward the hall door. "This is yours, not mine. I've got my own business to attend to. . . I'm doing research for a hot-shot nonferrous mining concern."

Ackers eyed his coat. "Are you pregnant?"

"Not that I know of," Beam said, coloring. "I've led a good clean life." Awkwardly, he patted his coat. "You mean this?"

By the window, one of the police gave a triumphant yap. The two bits of pipe tobacco had been discovered: a refinement for the third specification. "Excellent," Ackers said, turning away from Beam and momentarily forgetting him.

Beam left.

Very shortly he was driving across town toward his own labs, the small and independent research outfit that he headed, unsupported by a government grant. Resting on the seat beside him was the portable TV unit; it was still silent.

"First of all," Beam's gowned technician declared, "it has a power supply approximately seventy times that of a portable TV pack. We picked up the Gamma radiation." He displayed the usual detector. "So you're right, it's not a TV set"

Gingerly, Beam lifted the small unit from the lab bench. Five hours had passed, and still he knew nothing about it. Taking firm hold of the back he pulled with all his strength. The back refused to come off. It wasn't stuck: there were no seams. The back was not a back; it only looked like a back.

"Then what is it?" he asked.

"Could be lots of things," the technician said noncommittally; he had been roused from the privacy of his home, and it was now two-thirty in the morning. "Could be some sort of scanning equipment. A bomb. A weapon. Any kind of gadget." Laboriously, Beam felt the unit all over, searching for a flaw in the surface. "It's uniform," he murmured. "A single surface."

"You bet. The breaks are false -- it's a poured substance. And," the technician added, "it's hard. I tried to chip off a representative sample but --" He gestured. "No results."

"Guaranteed not to shatter when dropped," Beam said absently. "New extra-tough plastic." He shook the unit energetically; the muted noise of metal parts in motion reached his ear. "It's full of guts."

"We'll get it open," the technician promised, "but not tonight."

Beam replaced the unit on the bench. He could, with bad luck, work days on this one item -- to discover, after all, that it had nothing to do with the murder of Heimie Rosenburg. On the other hand . . .

"Drill me a hole in it," he instructed. "So we can see it."

His technician protested: "I drilled; the drill broke. I've sent out for an improved density. This substance is imported; somebody hooked it from a white dwarf system. It was conceived under stupendous pressure."

"You're stalling," Beam said, irritated. "That's how they talk in the advertising media."

The technician shrugged. "Anyhow, it's extra hard. A naturally-evolved element, or an artificially-processed product from somebody's labs. Who has funds to develop a metal like this?"

"One of the big slavers," Beam said. "That's where the wealth winds up. And they hop around to various systems . . . they'd have access to raw materials. Special ores."

"Can't I go home?" the technician asked. "What's so important about this?"

"This device either killed or helped kill Heimie Rosenburg. We'll sit here, you and I, until we get it open." Beam seated himself and began examining the check sheet showing which tests had been applied. "Sooner or later it'll fly open like a clam -- if you can remember that far back."

Behind them, a warning bell sounded.

"Somebody in the anteroom," Beam said, surprised and wary. "At two-thirty?" He got up and made his way down the dark hall to the front of the building. Probably it was Ackers. His conscience stirred guiltily: somebody had logged the absence of the TV unit.

But it was not Ackers.

Waiting humbly in the cold, deserted anteroom was Paul Tirol; with him was an attractive young woman unknown to Beam. Tirol's wrinkled face broke into smiles, and he extended a hearty hand. "Beam," he said. They shook. "Your front door said you were down here. Still working?"

Guardedly, wondering who the woman was and what Tirol wanted, Beam said: "Catching up on some slipshod errors. Whole firm's going broke."

Tirol laughed indulgently. "Always a japer." His deep-set eyes darted; Tirol was a powerfully-built person, older than most, with a somber, intensely-creased face. "Have room for a few contracts? I thought I might slip a few jobs your way. . . if you're open."

"I'm always open," Beam countered, blocking Tirol's view of the lab proper. The door, anyhow, had slid itself shut. Tirol had been Heimie's boss . . . he no doubt felt entitled to all extant information on the murder. Who did it? When? How? Why? But that didn't explain why he was *here*.

"Terrible thing," Tirol said crudely. He made no move to introduce the woman; she had retired to the couch to light a cigarette. She was slender, with mahogany-colored hair; she wore a blue coat, and a kerchief tied around her head.

"Yes," Beam agreed. "Terrible."

"You were there, I understand."

That explained some of it. "Well," Beam conceded, "I showed up."

"But you didn't actually see it?"

"No," Beam admitted, "nobody saw it. Interior is collecting specification material. They should have it down to one card before morning."

Visibly, Tirol relaxed. "I'm glad of that. I'd hate to see the vicious criminal escape. Banishment's too good for him. He ought to be gassed."

"Barbarism," Beam murmured dryly. "The days of the gas chamber. Medieval."

Tirol peered past him. "You're working on --" Now he was overtly beginning to pry. "Come now, Leroy. Heimie Rosenburg -- God bless his soul -- was killed tonight and tonight I find you burning the midnight oil. You can talk openly with me; you've got something relevant to his death, haven't you?"

"That's Ackers you're thinking of."

Tirol chuckled. "Can I take a look?"

"Not until you start paying me; I'm not on your books yet."

In a strained, unnatural voice, Tirol bleated: "I want it."

Puzzled, Beam said: "You want what?"

With a grotesque shudder, Tirol blundered forward, shoved Beam aside, and groped for the door. The door flew open and Tirol started noisily down the dark corridor, feeling his way by instinct toward the research labs.

"Hey!" Beam shouted, outraged. He sprinted after the older man, reached the inner door, and prepared to fight it out. He was shaking, partly with amazement, partly with anger. "What the hell?" he demanded breathlessly. "You don't own me!"

Behind him the door mysteriously gave way. Foolishly, he sprawled backward, half-falling into the lab. There, stricken with helpless paralysis, was his technician. And, coming across the floor of the lab was something small and metallic. It looked like an oversized box of crackers, and it was going lickety-split toward Tirol. The object -- metal and gleaming -- hopped up into Tirol's arms, and the old man turned and lumbered back up the hall to the anteroom.

"What was it?" the technician said, coming to life.

Ignoring him, Beam hurried after Tirol. "He's got it!" he yelled futilely.

"It --" the technician mumbled. "It was the TV set. And it *ran.*"

2

The file banks at Interior were in agitated flux.

The process of creating a more and more restricted category was tedious, and it took time. Most of the Interior staff had gone home to bed; it was almost three in the morning, and the corridors and offices were deserted. A few mechanical cleaning devices crept here and there in the darkness. The sole source of life was the study chamber of the file banks. Edward Ackers sat patiently waiting for the results, waiting for specifications to come in, and for the file machinery to process them.

To his right a few Interior police played a benign lottery and waited stoically to be sent out for the pick-up. The lines of communication to Heimie Rosenburg's apartment buzzed ceaselessly. Down the street, along the bleak sidewalk, Harvey Garth was still at his propaganda booth, still flashing his BANISH it! sign and muttering in people's ears. There were virtually no passersby, now, but Garth went on. He was tireless; he never gave up.

"Psychopath," Ackers said resentfully. Even where he sat, six floors up, the tinny, carping voice reached his middle ear.

"Take him in," one of the game-playing cops suggested. The game, intricate and devious, was a version of a Centaurian III practice. "We can revoke his vendor's license."

Ackers had, when there was nothing else to do, concocted and refined an indictment of Garth, a sort of lay analysis of the man's mental aberrations. He enjoyed playing the psychoanalytic game; it gave him a sense of power.

Garth, Harvey

Prominent compulsive syndrome. Has assumed role of ideological anarchist, opposing legal and social system. No rational expression, only repetition of key words and phrases. Idee fixe is *Banish the banishment system.* Cause dominates life. Rigid fanatic, probably of manic type, since. . .

Ackers let the sentence go, since he didn't really know what the structure of the manic type was. Anyhow, the analysis was excellent, and someday it would be resting in an official slot instead of merely drifting through his mind. And, when that happened, the annoying voice would conclude.

"Big turmoil," Garth droned. "Banishment system in vast upheaval. . . crisis moment has arrived."

"Why crisis?" Ackers asked aloud.

Down below on the pavement Garth responded. "All your machines are humming. Grand excitement reigns. Somebody's head will be in the basket before sun-up." His voice trailed off in a weary blur. "Intrigue and murder. Corpses . . . the police scurry and a beautiful woman lurks." To his analysis Ackers added an amplifying clause.

. . .Garth's talents are warped by his compulsive sense of *mission.* Having designed an ingenious communication device he sees only its propaganda possibility. Whereas Garth's voice-ear mechanism could be put to work for All Humanity.

That pleased him. Ackers got up and wandered over to the attendant operating the file. "How's it coming?" he asked.

"Here's the situation," the attendant said. There was a line of gray stubble smeared over his chin, and he was bleary-eyed. "We're gradually paring it down."

Ackers, as he resumed his seat, wished he were back in the days of the almighty fingerprint. But a print hadn't shown up in months; a thousand techniques existed for print-removal and print alteration. There was no single specification capable, in itself, of delineating the individual. A composite was needed, a gestalt of the assembled data.

1) blood sample (type O) 6,139,481,601
2) shoe size (11 1/2) 1,268,303,431
3) smoker 791,992,386
3a) smoker (pipe) 52,774,853

4) sex (male) 26,449,094
5) age (30-40 years) 9,221,397
6) weight (200 lbs) 488,290
7) fabric of clothing 17,459
8) hair variety 866
9) ownership of utilized weapon 40

A vivid picture was emerging from the data. Ackers could see him clearly. The man was practically standing there, in front of his desk. A fairly young man, somewhat heavy, a man who smoked a pipe and wore an extremely expensive tweed suit. An individual created by nine specifications; no tenth had been listed because no more data of specification level had been found.

Now, according to the report, the apartment had been thoroughly searched. The detection equipment was going outdoors.

"One more should do it," Ackers said, returning the report to the attendant. He wondered if it would come in and how long it would take.

To waste time he telephoned his wife, but instead of getting Ellen he got the automatic response circuit. "Yes, sir," it told him. "Mrs. Ackers has retired for the night. You may state a thirty-second message which will be transcribed for her attention tomorrow morning. Thank you."

Ackers raged at the mechanism futilely and then hung up. He wondered if Ellen were really in bed; maybe she had, as often before, slipped out. But, after all, it was almost three o'clock in the morning. Any sane person would be asleep: only he and Garth were still at their little stations, performing their vital duties.

What had Garth meant by a *"beautiful woman"?*

"Mr. Ackers," the attendant said, "there's a tenth specification coming in over the wires."

Hopefully, Ackers gazed up at the file bank. He could see nothing, of course; the actual mechanism occupied the underground levels of the building, and all that existed here was the input receptors and throw-out slots. But just looking at the machinery was in itself comforting. At this moment the bank was accepting the tenth piece of material. In a moment he would know how many citizens fell into the ten categories . . . he would know if already he had a group small enough to be sorted one by one.

"Here it is," the attendant said, pushing the report to him.

Type of utilized vehicle (color) 7

"My God," Ackers said mildly. "That's low enough. Seven persons -- we can go to work."

"You want the seven cards popped?"

"Pop them," Ackers said.

A moment later, the throw-out slot deposited seven neat white cards in the tray. The attendant passed them to Ackers and he quickly riffled them. The next step was personal motive and proximity: items that had to be gotten from the suspects themselves.

Of the seven names six meant nothing to him. Two lived on Venus, one in the Centaurus System, one was somewhere in Sirius, one was in the hospital, and one lived in the Soviet Union. The seventh, however, lived within a few miles, on the outskirts of New York.

LANTANO, DAVID

That clinched it. The gestalt, in Ackers' mind, locked clearly in place; the image hardened to reality. He had half expected, even prayed to see Lantano's card brought up.

"Here's your pick-up," he said shakily to the game-playing cops. "Better get as large a team together as possible, this one won't be easy." Momentously, he added: "Maybe I'd better come along."

Beam reached the anteroom of his lab as the ancient figure of Paul Tirol disappeared out the street door and onto the dark sidewalk. The young woman, trotting ahead of him, had climbed into a parked car and started it forward; as Tirol emerged, she swept him up and at once departed.

Panting, Beam stood impotently collecting himself on the deserted pavement. The ersatz TV unit was gone; now he had nothing. Aimlessly, he began to run down the street. His heels echoed loudly in the cold silence. No sign of them; no sign of anything.

"I'll be damned," he said, with almost religious awe. The unit -- a robot device of obvious complexity -- clearly belonged to Paul Tirol; as soon as it had identified his presence it had sprinted gladly to him. For. . . protection?

It had killed Heimie; and it belonged to Tirol. So, by a novel and indirect method, Tirol had murdered his employee, his Fifth Avenue front man. At a rough guess, such a highly-organized robot would cost in the neighborhood of a hundred thousand dollars.

A lot of money, considering that murder was the easiest of criminal acts. Why not hire an itinerant goon with a crowbar?

Beam started slowly back toward his lab. Then, abruptly, he changed his mind and turned in the direction of the business area. When a free-wheeling cab came by, he hailed it and clambered in.

"Where to, sport?" the starter at cab relay asked. City cabs were guided by remote control from one central source.

He gave the name of a specific bar. Settling back against the seat he pondered. Anybody could commit a murder; an expensive, complicated machine wasn't necessary.

The machine had been built to do something else. The murder of Heimie Rosenburg was incidental.

Against the nocturnal skyline, a huge stone residence loomed. Ackers inspected it from a distance. There were no lights burning; everything was locked up tight. Spread out before the house was an acre of grass. David Lantano was probably the last person on Earth to own an acre of grass outright; it was less expensive to buy an entire planet in some other system.

"Let's go," Ackers commanded; disgusted by such opulence, he deliberately trampled through a bed of roses on his way up the wide porch steps. Behind him flowed the team of shock-police.

"Gosh," Lantano rumbled, when he had been roused from his bed. He was a kindly-looking, rather youthful fat man, wearing now an abundant silk dressing robe. He would have seemed more in place as director of a boys' summer camp; there was an expression of perpetual good humor on his soft, sagging face. "What's wrong, officer?"

Ackers loathed being called officer. "You're under arrest," he stated.

"Me?" Lantano echoed feebly. "Hey, officer, I've got lawyers to take care of these things." He yawned voluminously. "Care for some coffee?" Stupidly, he began puttering around his front room, fixing a pot.

It had been years since Ackers had splurged and bought himself a cup of coffee. With Terran land covered by dense industrial and residential installations there was no room for crops, and coffee had refused to "take" in any other system. Lantano probably grew his somewhere on an illicit plantation in South America -- the pickers probably believed they had been transported to some remote colony.

"No thanks," Ackers said. "Let's get going."

Still dazed, Lantano plopped himself down in an easy chair and regarded Ackers with alarm. "You're serious." Gradually his expression faded; he seemed to be drifting back to sleep. "Who?" he murmured distantly.

"Heimie Rosenburg."

"No kidding." Lantano shook his head listlessly. "I always wanted him in my company. Heimie's got real charm. Had, I mean."

It made Ackers nervous to remain here in the vast lush mansion. The coffee was heating, and the smell of it tickled his nose. And, heaven forbid -- there on the table was a basket *of apricots.*

"Peaches," Lantano corrected, noticing his fixed stare. "Help yourself."

"Where -- did you get them?"

Lantano shrugged. "Synthetic dome. Hydroponics. I forget where . . . I don't have a technical mind."

"You know what the fine is for possessing natural fruit?"

"Look," Lantano said earnestly, clasping his mushy hands together. "Give me the details on this affair, and I'll prove to you I had nothing to do with it. Come on, officer."

"Ackers," Ackers said.

"Okay, Ackers. I thought I recognized you, but I wasn't sure; didn't want to make a fool of myself. When was Heimie killed?"

Grudgingly, Ackers gave him the pertinent information.

For a time Lantano was silent. Then, slowly, gravely, he said: "You better look at those seven cards again. One of those fellows isn't in the Sirius System . . . he's back here."

Ackers calculated the chances of successfully banishing a man of David Lantano's importance. His organization -- Interplay Export -- had fingers all over the galaxy; there'd be search crews going out like bees. But nobody went out banishment distance. The condemned, temporarily ionized, rendered in terms of charged particles of energy, radiated outward at the velocity of light. This was an experimental technique that had failed; it worked only one way.

"Consider," Lantano said thoughtfully. "If I *was* going to kill Heimie -- *would I do it myself?* You're not being logical, Ackers. I'd send somebody." He pointed a fleshy finger at Ackers. "You imagine I'd risk my own life? I know you pick up everybody . . . you usually turn up enough specifications."

"We have ten on you," Ackers said briskly.

"So you're going to banish me?"

"If you're guilty, you'll have to face banishment like anyone else. Your particular prestige has no bearing."

Nettled, Ackers added, "Obviously, you'll be released. You'll have plenty of opportunity to prove your innocence; you can question each of the ten specifications in turn."

He started to go on and describe the general process of court procedure employed in the twenty-first century, but something made him pause. David Lantano and his chair seemed to be gradually sinking into the floor. Was it an illusion? Blinking, Ackers rubbed his eyes and peered. At the same time, one of the policemen yelped a warning of dismay; Lantano was quietly leaving them.

"Come back!" Ackers demanded; he leaped forward and grabbed hold of the chair. Hurriedly, one of his men shorted out the power supply of the building; the chair ceased descending and groaned to a halt. Only Lantano's head was visible above the floor level. He was almost entirely submerged in a concealed escape shaft.

"What seedy, useless -- " Ackers began.

"I know," Lantano admitted, making no move to drag himself up. He seemed resigned; his mind was again off in clouds of contemplation. "I hope we can clear all this up. Evidently I'm being framed. Tirol got somebody who looks like me, somebody to go in and murder Heimie."

Ackers and the police crew helped him up from his depressed chair. He gave no resistance; he was too deep in his brooding.

The cab let Leroy Beam off in front of the bar. To his right, in the next block, was the Interior Building. . . and, on the sidewalk, the opaque blob that was Harvey Garth's propaganda booth.

Entering the bar, Beam found a table in the back and seated himself. Already he could pick up the faint, distorted murmur of Garth's reflections. Garth, speaking to himself in a directionless blur, was not yet aware of him.

"Banish it," Garth was saying. "Banish all of them. Bunch of crooks and thieves." Garth, in the miasma of his booth, was rambling vitriolically.

"What's going on?" Beam asked. "What's the latest?"

Garth's monologue broke off as he focussed his attention on Beam. "You in there? In the bar?"

"I want to find out about Heimie's death."

"Yes," Garth said. "He's dead; the files are moving, kicking out cards."

"When I left Heimie's apartment," Beam said, "they had turned up six specifications." He punched a button on the drink selector and dropped in a token.

"That must have been earlier," Garth said; "they've got more."

"How many?"

"Ten in all."

Ten. That was usually enough. And all ten of them laid out by a robot device . . . a little procession of hints strewn along its path: between the concrete side of the building and the dead body of Heimie Rosenburg.

"That's lucky," he said speculatively. "Helps out Ackers."

"Since you're paying me," Garth said, "I'll tell you the rest. They've already gone out on their pick-up: Ackers went along."

Then the device had been successful. Up to a point, at least. He was sure of one thing: the device should have been out of the apartment. Tirol hadn't known about Heimie's death rattle; Heimie had been wise enough to do the installation privately.

Had the rattle not brought persons into the apartment, the device would have scuttled out and returned to Tirol. Then, no doubt, Tirol would have detonated it. Nothing would remain to indicate that a machine could lay down a trail of synthetic clues: blood type, fabric, pipe tobacco, hair... all the rest, and all spurious.

"Who's the pick-up on?" Beam asked.

"David Lantano."

Beam winced. "Naturally. That's what the whole thing's about; he's being framed!"

Garth was indifferent; he was a hired employee, stationed by the pool of independent researchers to siphon information from the Interior Department. He had no actual interest in politics; his *Banish It!* was sheer window-dressing.

"I know it's a frame," Beam said, "and so does Lantano. But neither of us can prove it. . . unless Lantano has an absolutely airtight alibi."

"Banish it," Garth murmured, reverting to his routine. A small group of late-retiring citizens had strolled past his booth, and he was masking his conversation with Beam. The conversation, directed to the one listener, was inaudible to everyone else; but it was better not to take risks. Sometimes, very close to the booth, there was an audible feedback of the signal.

Hunched over his drink, Leroy Beam contemplated the various items he could try. He could inform Lantano's organization, which existed relatively intact. . . but the result would be epic civil war. And, in addition, he didn't really care if Lantano was framed; it was all the same to him. Sooner or later one of the big slavers had to absorb the other: cartel is the natural conclusion of big business. With Lantano gone, Tirol would painlessly swallow his organization; everybody would be working at his desk as always.

On the other hand, there might someday be a device -- now half-completed in Tirol's basement -- that left a trail of *Leroy Beam* clues. Once the idea caught on, there was no particular end.

"And I had the damn thing," he said fruitlessly. "I hammered on it for five hours. It was a TV unit, then, but it was still the device that killed Heimie."

"You're positive it's gone?"

"It's not only gone -- it's out of existence. Unless she wrecked the car driving Tirol home."

"She?" Garth asked.

"The woman." Beam pondered. "She saw it. Or she knew about it; she was with him." But, unfortunately, he had no idea who the woman might be.

"What'd she look like?" Garth asked.

"Tall, mahogany hair. Very nervous mouth."

"I didn't realize she was working with him openly. They must have really needed the device." Garth added: "You didn't identify her? I guess there's no reason why you should; she's kept out of sight."

"Who is she?"

"That's Ellen Ackers."

Beam laughed sharply. "And she's driving Paul Tirol around?"

"She's -- well, she's driving Tirol around, yes. You can put it that way."

"How long?"

"I thought you were in on it. She and Ackers split up; that was last year. But he wouldn't let her leave; he wouldn't give her a divorce. Afraid of the publicity. Very important to keep up respectability. . . keep the shirt fully stuffed."

"He knows about Paul Tirol and her?"

"Of course not. He knows she's -- spiritually hooked up. But he doesn't care . . . as long as she keeps it quiet. It's his position he's thinking about."

"If Ackers found out," Beam murmured. "If he saw the link between his wife and Tirol. . . he'd ignore his ten interoffice memos. He'd *want* to haul in Tirol. The hell with the evidence; he could always collect that later." Beam pushed away his drink; the glass was empty anyhow. "Where is Ackers?"

"I told you. Out at Lantano's place, picking him up."

"He'd come back here? He wouldn't go home?"

"Naturally he'd come back here." Garth was silent a moment. "I see a couple of Interior vans turning into the garage ramp. That's probably the pick-up crew returning."

Beam waited tensely. "Is Ackers along?"

"Yes, he's there. *Banish It!*" Garth's voice rose in stentorian frenzy. "*Banish the system of Banishment! Root out the crooks and pirates!*"

Sliding to his feet, Beam left the bar.

A dull light showed in the rear of Edward Ackers' apartment: probably the kitchen light. The front door was locked. Standing in the carpeted hallway, Beam skillfully tilted with the door mechanism. It was geared to respond to specific neural patterns: those of its owners and a limited circle of friends. For him there was no activity.

Kneeling down, Beam switched on a pocket oscillator and started sine wave emission. Gradually, he increased the frequency. At perhaps 150,000 cps the lock guiltily clicked; that was all he needed. Switching the oscillator off, he rummaged through his supply of skeleton patterns until he located the closet cylinder. Slipped into the turret of the oscillator, the cylinder emitted a synthetic neural pattern close enough to the real thing to affect the lock.

The door swung open. Beam entered.

In half-darkness the living room seemed modest and tasteful. Ellen Ackers was an adequate housekeeper. Beam listened. Was she home at all? And if so, where? Awake? Asleep?

He peeped into the bedroom. There was the bed, but nobody was in it.

If she wasn't here she was at Tirol's. But he didn't intend to follow her; this was as far as he cared to risk.

He inspected the dining room. Empty. The kitchen was empty, too. Next came an upholstered general-purpose rumpus room; on one side was a gaudy bar and on the other a wall-to-wall couch. Tossed on the couch was a woman's coat, purse, gloves. Familiar clothes: Ellen Ackers had worn them. So she had come here after leaving his research lab.

The only room left was the bathroom. He fumbled with the knob; it was locked from the inside. There was no sound, but somebody was on the other side of the door. He could sense her in there.

"Ellen," he said, against the panelling. "Mrs. Ellen Ackers; is that you?"

No answer. He could sense her not making any sound at all: a stifled, frantic silence.

While he was kneeling down, fooling with his pocketful of magnetic lock-pullers, an explosive pellet burst through the door at head level and splattered into the plaster of the wall beyond.

Instantly the door flew open; there stood Ellen Ackers, her face distorted with fright. One of her husband's government pistols was clenched in her small, bony hand. She was less than a foot from him. Without getting up, Beam grabbed her wrist, she fired over his head, and then the two of them deteriorated into harsh, labored breathing.

"Come on," Beam managed finally. The nozzle of the gun was literally brushing the top of his head. To kill him, she would have to pull the pistol back against her. But he didn't let her; he kept hold of her wrist until finally, reluctantly, she dropped the gun. It clattered to the floor and he got stiffly up.

"You were sitting down," she whispered, in a stricken, accusing voice.

"Kneeling down: picking the lock. I'm glad you aimed for my brain." He picked up the gun and succeeded in getting it into his overcoat pocket; his hands were shaking.

Ellen Ackers gazed at him starkly; her eyes were huge and dark, and her face was an ugly white. Her skin had a dead cast, as if it were artificial, totally dry, thoroughly sifted with talc. She seemed on the verge of hysteria; a harsh, muffled shudder struggled up inside her, lodging finally in her throat. She tried to speak but only a rasping noise came out.

"Gee, lady," Beam said, embarrassed. "Come in the kitchen and sit down."

She stared at him as if he had said something incredible or obscene or miraculous; he wasn't sure which.

"Come on." He tried to take hold of her arm but she jerked frantically away. She had on a simple green suit, and in it she looked very nice; a little too thin and terribly tense, but still attractive. She had on expensive earrings, an imported stone that seemed always in motion . . . but otherwise her outfit was austere.

"You -- were the man at the lab," she managed, in a brittle, choked voice.

"I'm Leroy Beam. An independent." Awkwardly guiding her, he led her into the kitchen and seated her at the table. She folded her hands in front of her and studied them fixedly; the bleak boniness of her face seemed to be increasing rather than receding. He felt uneasy.

"Are you all right?" he asked.

She nodded.

"Cup of coffee?" He began searching the cupboards for a bottle of Venusian-grown coffee substitute. While he was looking, Ellen Ackers said tautly: "You better go in there. In the bathroom. I don't think he's dead, but he might be."

Beam raced into the bathroom. Behind the plastic shower curtain was an opaque shape. It was Paul Tirol, lying wadded up in the tub, fully clothed. He was not dead but he had been struck behind the left ear and his scalp was leaking a slow, steady trickle of blood. Beam took his pulse, listened to his breathing, and then straightened up.

At the doorway Ellen Ackers materialized, still pale with fright. "Is he? Did I kill him?"

"He's fine."

Visibly, she relaxed. "Thank God. It happened so fast -- he stepped ahead of me to take the M inside his place, and then I did it. I hit him as lightly as I could. He was so interested in it. . . he forgot about me." Words spilled from her, quick, jerky sentences, punctuated by rigid tremors of her hands. "I lugged him back in the car and drove here; it was all I could think of."

"What are you in this for?"

Her hysteria rose in a spasm of convulsive muscle-twitching. "It was all planned -- I had everything worked out. As soon as I got hold of it I was going to --" She broke off.

"Blackmail Tirol?" he asked, fascinated.

She smiled weakly. "No, not Paul. It was Paul who gave me the idea . . . it was his first idea, when his researchers showed him the thing. The M, he calls it. M stands for machine. He means it can't be educated, morally corrected."

Incredulous, Beam said: "You were going to blackmail your husband."

Ellen Ackers nodded. "So he'd let me leave."

Suddenly Beam felt sincere respect for her. "My God -- the rattle. Heimie didn't arrange that; you did. So the device would be trapped in the apartment."

"Yes," she agreed. "I was going to pick it up. But Paul showed up with other ideas; he wanted it, too."

"What went haywire? You have it, don't you?"

Silently she indicated the linen closet. "I stuffed it away when I heard you."

Beam opened the linen closet. Resting primly on the neatly-folded towels was a small, familiar, portable TV unit.

"It's reverted," Ellen said, from behind him, in an utterly defeated monotone. "As soon as I hit Paul it changed. For half an hour I've been trying to get it to shift. It won't. It'll stay that way forever."

3

Beam went to the telephone and called a doctor. In the bathroom, Tirol groaned and feebly thrashed his arms. He was beginning to return to consciousness.

"Was that necessary?" Ellen Ackers demanded. "The doctor -- did you have to call?"

Beam ignored her. Bending, he lifted the portable TV unit and held it in his hands; he felt its weight move up his arms like a slow, leaden fatigue. The ultimate adversary, he thought; too stupid to be defeated. It was worse than an animal. It was a rock, solid and dense, lacking all qualities. Except, he thought, the quality of determination. It was determined to persist, to survive; a rock with will. He felt as if he were holding up the universe, and he put the unreconstructed M down.

From behind him Ellen said: "It drives you crazy." Her voice had regained tone. She lit a cigarette with a silver cigarette lighter and then shoved her hands in the pockets of her suit.

"Yes," he said.

"There's nothing you can do, is there? You tried to get it open before. They'll patch Paul up, and he'll go back to his place, and Lantano will be banished --" She took a deep shuddering breath. "And the Interior Department will go on as always."

"Yes," he said. Still kneeling, he surveyed the M. Now, with what he knew, he did not waste time struggling with it. He considered it impassively; he did not even bother to touch it.

In the bathroom, Paul Tirol was trying to crawl from the tub. He slipped back, cursed and moaned, and started his laborious ascent once again.

"Ellen?" his voice quavered, a dim and distorted sound, like dry wires rubbing.

"Take it easy," she said between her teeth; not moving she stood smoking rapidly on her cigarette.

"Help me, Ellen," Tirol muttered. "Something happened to me . . . I don't remember what. Something hit me."

"He'll remember," Ellen said.

Beam said: "I can take this thing to Ackers as it is. You can tell him what it's for -- what it did. That ought to be enough; he won't go through with Lantano."

But he didn't believe it, either. Ackers would have to admit a mistake, a basic mistake, and if he had been wrong to pick up Lantano, he was ruined. And so, in a sense, was the whole system of delineation. It could be fooled; it had been fooled. Ackers was rigid, and he would go right on in a straight line: the hell with Lantano. The hell with abstract justice. Better to preserve cultural continuity and keep society running on an even keel.

"Tirol's equipment," Beam said. "Do you know where it is?"

She shrugged wildly. "What equipment?"

"This thing -- " he jabbed at the M -- "was made somewhere."

"Not here, Tirol didn't make it."

"All right," he said reasonably. They had perhaps six minutes more before the doctor and the emergency medical carrier arrived on rooftop. "Who did make it?"

"The alloy was developed on Bellatrix." She spoke jerkily, word by word. "The rind . . . forms a skin on the outside, a bubble that gets sucked in and out of a reservoir. That's its rind, the TV shape. It sucks it back and becomes the M; it's ready to act."

"What made it?" he repeated.

"A Bellatrix machine tool syndicate . . . a subsidiary of Tirol's organization. They're made to be watchdogs. The big plantations on outplanets use them; they patrol. They get poachers."

Beam said: "Then originally they're not set for one person."

"No."

"Then *who* set this for Heimie? Not a machine tool syndicate."

"That was done here."

He straightened up and lifted the portable TV unit. "Let's go. Take me there, where Tirol had it altered."

For a moment the woman did not respond. Grabbing her arm he hustled her to the door. She gasped and stared at him mutely.

"Come on," he said, pushing her out into the hall. The portable TV unit bumped against the door as he shut it; he held the unit tight and followed after Ellen Ackers.

The town was slatternly and run-down, a few retail stores, fuel station, bars and dance halls. It was two hours' flight from Greater New York and it was called Olum.

"Turn right," Ellen said listlessly. She gazed out at the neon signs and rested her arm on the window sill of the ship.

They flew above warehouses and deserted streets. Lights were few. At an intersection Ellen nodded and he set the ship down on a roof.

Below them was a sagging, fly-specked wooden frame store. A peeling sign was propped up in the window: FULTON BROTHERS locksmiths. With the sign were doorknobs, locks, keys, saws, and spring-wound alarm clocks. Somewhere in the interior of the store a yellow night light burned fitfully.

"This way," Ellen said. She stepped from the ship and made her way down a flight of rickety wooden stairs. Beam laid the portable TV unit on the floor of the ship, locked the doors, and then followed after the woman. Holding onto the railing, he descended to a back porch on which were trash cans and a pile of sodden newspapers tied with string. Ellen was unlocking a door and feeling her way inside.

First he found himself in a musty, cramped storeroom. Pipe and rolls of wire and sheets of metal were heaped everywhere; it was like a junkyard. Next came a narrow corridor and then he was standing in the entrance of a workshop. Ellen reached overhead and groped to find the hanging string of a light. The light clicked on. To the right was a long and littered workbench with a hand grinder at one end, a vise, a keyhole saw; two wooden stools were before the bench and half-assembled machinery was stacked on the floor in no apparent order. The workshop was chaotic, dusty, and archaic. On the wall was a threadbare blue coat hung from a nail: the workcoat of a machinist.

"Here," Ellen said, with bitterness. "This is where Paul had it brought. This outfit is owned by the Tirol organization; this whole slum is part of their holdings."

Beam walked to the bench. "To have altered it," he said, "Tirol must have had a plate of Heimie's neural pattern." He overturned a heap of glass jars; screws and washers poured onto the pitted surface of the bench.

"He got it from Heimie's door," Ellen said. "He had Heimie's lock analyzed and Heimie's pattern inferred from the setting of the tumblers."

"And he had the M opened?"

"There's an old mechanic," Ellen said. "A little dried-up old man; he runs this shop. Patrick Fulton. He installed the bias on the M."

"A bias," Beam said, nodding.

"A bias against killing people. Heimie was the exception, for everybody else it took its protective form. Out in the wilds they would have set it for something else, not a TV unit." She laughed, a sudden ripple close to hysteria. "Yes, that would have looked odd, it sitting out in a forest somewhere, a TV unit. They would have made it into a rock or a stick."

"A rock," Beam said. He could imagine it. The M waiting, covered with moss, waiting for months, years, and then weathered and corroded, finally picking up the presence of a human being. Then the M ceasing to be a rock, becoming, in a quick blur of motion, a box one foot wide and two feet long. An oversized cracker box that started forward --

But there was something missing. "The fakery," he said. "Emitting flakes of paint and hair and tobacco. How did that come in?"

In a brittle voice Ellen said: "The landowner murdered the poacher, and he was culpable in the eyes of the law. So the M left clues. Claw marks. Animal blood. Animal hair."

"God," he said, revolted. "Killed by an animal."

"A bear, a wildcat -- whatever was indigenous, it varied. The predator of the region, a natural death." With her toe she touched a cardboard carton under the workbench. "It's in there, it used to be, anyhow. The neural plate, the transmitter, the discarded parts of the M, the schematics."

The carton had been a shipping container for power packs. Now the packs were gone, and in their place was a carefully-wrapped inner box, sealed against moisture and insect infestation. Beam tore away the metal foil and saw that he had found what he wanted. He gingerly carried the contents out and spread them on the workbench among the soldering irons and drills.

"It's all there," Ellen said, without emotion.

"Maybe," he said, "I can leave you out of this. I can take this and the TV unit to Ackers and try it without your testimony."

"Sure," she said wearily.

"What are you going to do?"

"Well," she said, "I can't go back to Paul, so I guess there's not much I can do."

"The blackmail bit was a mistake," he said.

Her eyes glowed. "Okay."

"If he releases Lantano," Beam said, "he'll be asked to resign. Then he'll probably give you your divorce, it won't be important to him one way or another."

"I --" she began. And then she stopped. Her face seemed to fade, as if the color and texture of her flesh was vanishing from within. She lifted one hand and half-turned, her mouth open and the sentence still unfinished.

Beam, reaching, slapped the overhead light out; the workroom winked into darkness. He had heard it too, had heard it at the same time as Ellen Ackers. The rickety outside porch had creaked and now the slow, ponderous motion was past the storeroom and into the hall.

A heavy man, he thought. A slow-moving man, sleepy, making his way step by step, his eyes almost shut, his great body sagging beneath his suit. Beneath, he thought, his expensive tweed suit. In the darkness the man's shape was looming; Beam could not see it but he could sense it there, filling up the doorway as it halted. Boards creaked under its weight. In a daze he wondered if Ackers already knew, if his order had already been rescinded. Or had the man got out on his own, worked through his own organization?

The man, starting forward again, spoke in a deep, husky voice. "Ugh," Lantano said. "Damn it."

Ellen began to shriek. Beam still did not realize what it was; he was still fumbling for the light and wondering stupidly why it did not come on. He had smashed the bulb, he realized. He lit a match; the match went out and he grabbed for Ellen Ackers' cigarette lighter. It was in her purse, and it took him an agonized second to get it out.

The unreconstructed M was approaching them slowly, one receptor stalk extended. Again it halted, swiveled to the left until it was facing the workbench. It was not now in the shape of a portable TV unit; it had retaken its cracker-box shape.

"The plate," Ellen Ackers whispered. "It responded to the plate."

The M had been roused by Heimie Rosenburg's looking for it. But Beam still felt the presence of David Lantano. The big man was still here in the room; the sense of heaviness, the proximity of weight and ponderousness had arrived with the machine, as it moved, sketching Lantano's existence. As he fixedly watched, the machine produced a fragment of cloth fabric and pressed it into a nearby heap of grid-mesh. Other elements, blood and tobacco and hair, were being produced, but they were too small for him to see. The machine pressed a heel mark into the dust of the floor and then projected a nozzle from its anterior section.

Her arm over her eyes, Ellen Ackers ran away. But the machine was not interested in her; revolving in the direction of the workbench it raised itself and fired. An explosive pellet, released by the nozzle, traveled across the workbench and entered the debris heaped across the bench. The pellet detonated; bits of wire and nails showered in particles.

Heimie's dead, Beam thought, and went on watching. The machine was searching for the plate, trying to locate and destroy the synthetic neural emission. It swiveled, lowered its nozzle hesitantly, and then fired again. Behind the workbench, the wall burst and settled into itself.

Beam, holding the cigarette lighter, walked toward the M. A receptor stalk waved toward him and the machine retreated. Its lines wavered, flowed, and then painfully reformed. For an interval, the device struggled with itself; then, reluctantly, the portable TV unit again became visible. From the machine a high-pitched whine emerged, an anguished squeal. Conflicting stimuli were present; the machine was unable to make a decision.

The machine was developing a situation neurosis and the ambivalence of its response was destroying it. In a way its anguish had a human quality, but he could not feel sorry for it. It was a mechanical contraption trying to assume a posture of disguise and attack at the same time; the breakdown was one of relays and tubes, not of a living brain. And it had been a living brain into which it had fired its original pellet. Heimie Rosenburg was dead, and there were no more like him and no possibility that more could be assembled. He went over to the machine and nudged it onto its back with his foot.

The machine whirred snake-like and spun away. "Ugh, damn it!" it said. It showered bits of tobacco as it rolled off; drops of blood and flakes of blue enamel fell from it as it disappeared into the corridor. Beam could hear it moving about, bumping into the walls like a blind, damaged organism. After a moment he followed after it.

In the corridor, the machine was traveling in a slow circle. It was erecting around itself a wall of particles: cloth and hairs and burnt matches and bits of tobacco, the mass cemented together with blood.

"Ugh, damn it," the machine said in its heavy masculine voice. It went on working, and Beam returned to the other room.

"Where's a phone?" he said to Ellen Ackers.

She stared at him vacantly.

"It won't hurt you," he said. He felt dull and worn-out. "It's in a closed cycle. It'll go on until it runs down."

"It went crazy," she said. She shuddered.

"No," he said. "Regression. It's trying to hide."

From the corridor the machine said, "Ugh. Damn it." Beam found the phone and called Edward Ackers.

Banishment for Paul Tirol meant first a procession of bands of darkness and then a protracted, infuriating interval in which empty matter drifted randomly around him, arranging itself into first one pattern and then another.

The period between the time Ellen Ackers attacked him and the time banishment sentence had been pronounced was vague and dim in his mind. Like the present shadows, it was hard to pin down.

He had -- he thought -- awakened in Ackers' apartment. Yes, that was it; and Leroy Beam was there, too. A sort of transcendental Leroy Beam who hovered robustly around, arranging everybody in configurations of his choice. A doctor had come. And finally Edward Ackers had shown up to face his wife and the situation.

Bandaged, and on his way into Interior, he had caught a glimpse of a man going out. The ponderous, bulbous shape of David Lantano, on his way home to his luxurious stone mansion and acre of grass.

At sight of him Tirol had felt a goad of fear. Lantano hadn't even noticed him; an acutely thoughtful expression on his face, Lantano padded into a waiting car and departed.

"You have one thousand dollars," Edward Ackers was saying wearily, during the final phase. Distorted, Ackers' face bloomed again in the drifting shadows around Tirol, an image of the man's last appearance. Ackers, too, was ruined, but in a different way. "The law supplies you with one thousand dollars to meet your immediate needs, also you'll find a pocket dictionary of representative out-system dialects."

Ionization itself was painless. He had no memory of it; only a blank space darker than the blurred images on either side.

"You hate me," he had declared accusingly, his last words to Ackers. "I destroyed you. But. . . it wasn't you." He had been confused. "Lantano. Maneuvered but not. How? You did . . ."

But Lantano had had nothing to do with it. Lantano had shambled off home, a withdrawn spectator throughout. The hell with Lantano. The hell with Ackers and Leroy Beam and -- reluctantly -- the hell with Mrs. Ellen Ackers.

"Wow," Tirol babbled, as his drifting body finally collected physical shape. "We had a lot of good times . . . didn't we, Ellen?"

And then a roaring hot field of sunlight was radiating down on him. Stupefied, he sat slumped over, limp and passive. Yellow, scalding sunlight. . . everywhere. Nothing but the dancing heat of it, blinding him, cowing him into submission.

He was sprawled in the middle of a yellow clay road. To his right was a baking, drying field of corn wilted in the midday heat. A pair of large, disreputable-looking birds wheeled silently overhead. A long way off was a line of blunted hills: ragged troughs and peaks that seemed nothing more than heaps of dust. At their base was a meager lump of man-made buildings.

At least he *hoped* they were man-made.

As he climbed shakily to his feet, a feeble noise drifted to his ears. Coming down the hot, dirty road was a car of some sort. Apprehensive and cautious, Tirol walked to meet it.

The driver was human, a thin, almost emaciated youth with pebbled black skin and a heavy mass of weed-colored hair. He wore a stained canvas shirt and overalls. A bent, unlit cigarette hung from his lower lip. The car was a combustion-driven model and had rolled out of the twentieth century; battered and twisted, it rattled to a halt as the driver critically inspected Tirol. From the car's radio yammered a torrent of tinny dance music.

"You a tax collector?" the driver asked.

"Certainly not," Tirol said, knowing the bucolic hostility toward tax collectors. But -- he floundered. He couldn't confess that he was a banished criminal from Earth; that was an invitation to be massacred, usually in some picturesque way. "I'm an inspector," he announced, "Department of Health."

Satisfied, the driver nodded. "Lots of scuttly cutbeede, these days. You fellows got a spray, yet? Losing one crop after another."

Tirol gratefully climbed into the car. "I didn't realize the sun was so hot," he murmured.

"You've got an accent," the youth observed, starting up the engine. "Where you from?"

"Speech impediment," Tirol said cagily. "How long before we reach town?"

"Oh, maybe an hour," the youth answered, as the car wandered lazily forward.

Tirol was afraid to ask the name of the planet. It would give him away. But he was consumed with the need to know. He might be two star-systems away or two million; he might be a month out of Earth or seventy years. Naturally, he had to get back; he had no intention of becoming a sharecropper on some backwater colony planet.

"Pretty swip," the youth said, indicating the torrent of noxious jazz pouring from the car radio. "That's Calamine Freddy and his Woolybear Creole Original Band. Know that tune?"

"No," Tirol muttered. The sun and dryness and heat made his head ache, and he wished to God he knew where he was.

The town was miserably tiny. The houses were dilapidated; the streets were dirt. A kind of domestic chicken roamed here and there, pecking in the rubbish. Under a porch a bluish quasi-dog lay sleeping. Perspiring and unhappy, Paul Tirol entered the bus station and located a schedule. A series of meaningless entries flashed by: names of towns. The name of the planet, of course, was not listed.

"What's the fare to the nearest port?" he asked the indolent official behind the ticket window.

The official considered. "Depends on what sort of port you want. Where you planning to go?"

"Toward Center," Tirol said. "Center" was the term used in out-systems for the Sol Group.

Dispassionately, the official shook his head. "No inter-system port around here."

Tirol was baffled. Evidently, he wasn't on the hub planet of this particular system. "Well," he said, "then the nearest interplan port."

The official consulted a vast reference book. "You want to go to which system-member?"

"Whichever one has the inter-system port," Tirol said patiently. He would leave from there.

"That would be Venus."

Astonished, Tirol said: "Then this system -- " He broke off, chagrined, as he remembered. It was the parochial custom in many out-systems, especially those a long way out, to name their member planets after the original nine. This one was probably called "Mars" or "Jupiter" or "Earth," depending on its position in the group. "Fine," Tirol finished. "One-way ticket to -- Venus."

Venus, or what passed for Venus, was a dismal orb no larger than an asteroid. A bleak cloud of metallic haze hung over it, obscuring the sun. Except for mining and smelting operations the planet was deserted. A few dreary shacks dotted the barren countryside. A perpetual wind blew, scattering debris and trash.

But the inter-system port was here, the field which linked the planet to its nearest star-neighbor and, ultimately, with the balance of the universe. At the moment a giant freighter was taking ore.

Tirol entered the ticket office. Spreading out most of his remaining money he said: "I want a one-way ticket taking me toward Center. As far as I can go."

The clerk calculated. "You care what class?"

"No," he said, mopping his forehead.

"How fast?"

"No."

The clerk said: "That'll carry you as far as the Betelgeuse System."

"Good enough," Tirol said, wondering what he did then. But at least he could contact his organization from there; he was already back in the charted universe. But now he was almost broke. He felt a prickle of icy fear, despite the heat.

The hub planet of the Betelgeuse System was called Plantagenet III. It was a thriving junction for passenger carriers transporting settlers to undeveloped colony planets. As soon as Tirol's ship landed he hurried across the field to the taxi stand.

"Take me to Tirol Enterprises," he instructed, praying there was an outlet here. There had to be, but it might be operating under a front name. Years ago he lost track of the particulars of his sprawling empire.

"Tirol Enterprises," the cab driver repeated thoughtfully. "Nope, no such outfit, mister."

Stunned, Tirol said: "Who does the slaving around here?"

The driver eyed him. He was a wizened, dried-up little man with glasses; he peered turtle-wise, without compassion. "Well," he said, "I've been told you can get carried out-system without papers. There's a shipping contractor. . . called --" He reflected. Tirol, trembling, handed him a last bill.

"The Reliable Export-Import," the driver said.

That was one of Lantano's fronts. In horror Tirol said: "And that's it?"

The driver nodded.

Dazed, Tirol moved away from the cab. The buildings of the field danced around him; he settled down on a bench to catch his breath. Under his coat his heart pounded unevenly. He tried to breathe, but his breath caught painfully in his throat. The bruise on his head where Ellen Ackers had hit him began to throb. It was true, and he was gradually beginning to understand and believe it. He was not going to get to Earth; he was going to spend the rest of his life here on this rural world, cut off from his organization and everything he had built up over the years.

And, he realized, as he sat struggling to breathe, the rest of his life was not going to be very long.

He thought about Heimie Rosenburg.

"Betrayed," he said, and coughed wrackingly. "You betrayed me. You hear that? Because of you I'm here. It's your fault; I never should have hired you."

He thought about Ellen Ackers. "You too," he gasped, coughing. Sitting on the bench he alternately coughed and gasped and thought about the people who had betrayed him. There were hundreds of them.

The living room of David Lantano's house was furnished in exquisite taste. Priceless late nineteenth century Blue Willow dishes lined the walls in a rack of wrought iron. At his antique yellow plastic and chrome table, David Lantano was eating dinner, and the spread of food amazed Beam even more than the house.

Lantano was in good humor and he ate with enthusiasm. His linen napkin was tucked under his chin and once, as he sipped coffee, he dribbled and belched. His brief period of confinement was over; he ate to make up for the ordeal.

He had been informed, first by his own apparatus and now by Beam, that banishment had successfully carried Tirol past the point of return. Tirol would not be coming back and for that Lantano was thankful. He felt expansive toward Beam; he wished Beam would have something to eat.

Moodily, Beam said: "It's nice here."

"You could have something like this," Lantano said.

On the wall hung a framed folio of ancient paper protected by helium-filled glass. It was the first printing of a poem of Ogden Nash, a collector's item that should have been in a museum. It aroused in Beam a mixed feeling of longing and aversion.

"Yes," Beam said. "I could have this." This, he thought, or Ellen Ackers or the job at Interior or perhaps all three at once. Edward Ackers had been retired on pension and he had given his wife a divorce. Lantano was out of jeopardy. Tirol had been banished. He wondered what he did want.

"You could go a long way," Lantano said sleepily.

"As far as Paul Tirol?"

Lantano chuckled and yawned.

"I wonder if he left any family," Beam said. "Any children." He was thinking about Heimie.

Lantano reached across the table toward the bowl of fruit. He selected a peach and carefully brushed it against the sleeve of his robe. "Try a peach," he said.

"No thanks," Beam said irritably.

Lantano examined the peach but he did not eat it. The peach was made of wax; the fruit in the bowl was imitation. He was not really as rich as he pretended, and many of the artifacts about the living room were fakes. Each time he offered fruit to a visitor he took a calculated risk. Returning the peach to the bowl he leaned back in his chair and sipped his coffee.

If Beam did not have plans, at least *he* had, and with Tirol gone the plans had a better than even chance of working out. He felt peaceful. Someday, he thought, and not too far off, the fruit in the bowl would be real.

The Turning Wheel

Bard Chai said thoughtfully, "Cults." He examined a tape-report grinding from the receptor. The receptor was rusty and unoiled; it whined piercingly and sent up an acrid wisp of smoke. Chai shut it off as its pitted surface began to heat ugly red. Presently he finished with the tape and tossed it with a heap of refuse jamming the mouth of a disposal slot.

"What about cults?" Bard Sung-wu asked faintly. He brought himself back with an effort, and forced a smile of interest on his plump olive-yellow face. "You were saying?"

"Any stable society is menaced by cults; our society is no exception." Chai rubbed his finely-tapered fingers together reflectively. "Certain lower strata are axiomatically dissatisfied. Their hearts burn with envy of those the wheel has placed above them; in secret they form fanatic, rebellious bands. They meet in the dark of the night; they insidiously express inversions of accepted norms; they delight in flaunting basic mores and customs."

"Ugh," Sung-wu agreed. "I mean," he explained quickly, "it seems incredible people could practice such fanatic and disgusting rites." He got nervously to his feet. "I must go, if it's permitted."

"Wait," snapped Chai. "You are familiar with the Detroit area?"

Uneasily, Sung-wu nodded. "Very slightly."

With characteristic vigor, Chai made his decision. "I'm sending you; investigate and make a blue-slip report. If this group is dangerous, the Holy Arm should know. It's of the worst elements -- the Techno class." He made a wry face. "Caucasians, hulking, hairy things. We'll give you six months in Spain, on your return; you can poke over ruins of abandoned cities."

"Caucasians!" Sung-wu exclaimed, his face turning green. "But I haven't been well; please, if somebody else could go --"

"You, perhaps, hold to the Broken Feather theory?" Chai raised an eyebrow. "An amazing philologist, Broken Feather; I took partial instruction from him. He held, you know, the Caucasian to be descended of Neanderthal stock. Their extreme size, thick body hair, their general brutish cast, reveal an innate inability to comprehend anything but a purely animalistic horizontal; proselytism is a waste of time."

He affixed the younger man with a stern eye. "I wouldn't send you, if I didn't have unusual faith in your devotion."

Sung-wu fingered his beads miserably. "Elron be praised," he muttered; "you are too kind."

Sung-wu slid into a lift and was raised, amid great groans and whirrings and false stops, to the top level of the Central Chamber building. He hurried down a corridor dimly lit by occasional yellow bulbs. A moment later he approached the doors of the scanning offices and flashed his identification at the robot guard. "Is Bard Fei-p'ang within?" he inquired.

"Verily," the robot answered, stepping aside.

Sung-wu entered the offices, bypassed the rows of rusted, discarded machines, and entered the still-functioning wing. He located his brother-in-law, hunched over some graphs at one of the desks, laboriously copying material by hand. "Clearness be with you," Sung-wu murmured.

Fei-p'ang glanced up in annoyance. "I told you not to come again; if the Arm finds out I'm letting you use the scanner for a personal plot, they'll stretch me on the rack."

"Gently," Sung-wu murmured, his hand on his relation's shoulder. "This is the last time. I'm going away; one more look, a final look." His olive face took on a pleading, piteous cast. "The turn comes for me very soon; this will be our last conversation."

Sung-wu's piteous look hardened into cunning. "You wouldn't want it on your soul; no restitution will be possible at this late date."

Fei-p'ang snorted. "All right; but for Elron's sake, do it quickly."

Sung-wu hurried to the mother-scanner and seated himself in the rickety basket. He snapped on the controls, clamped his forehead to the viewpiece, inserted his identity tab, and set the space-time finger into motion. Slowly, reluctantly, the ancient mechanism coughed into life and began tracing his personal tab along the future track.

Sung-wu's hands shook; his body trembled; sweat dripped from his neck, as he saw himself scampering in miniature. *Poor Sung-wu*, he thought wretchedly. The mite of a thing hurried about its duties; this was but eight months hence. Harried and beset, it performed its tasks -- and then, in a subsequent continuum, fell down and died.

Sung-wu removed his eyes from the viewpiece and waited for his pulse to slow. He could stand that part, watching the moment of death; it was what came next that was too jangling for him.

He breathed a silent prayer. Had he fasted enough? In the four-day purge and self-flagellation, he had used the whip with metal points, the heaviest possible. He had given away all his money; he had smashed a lovely vase his mother had left him, a treasured heirloom; he had rolled in the filth and mud in the center of town. Hundreds had seen him. Now, surely, all this was enough. But time was so short!

Faint courage stirring, he sat up and again put his eyes to the viewpiece. He was shaking with terror. What if it hadn't changed? What if his mortification weren't enough? He spun the controls, sending the finger tracing his time-track past the moment of death.

Sung-wu shrieked and scrambled back in horror. His future was the same, exactly the same; there had been no change at all. His guilt had been too great to be washed away in such short a time; it would take ages -- and he didn't have ages.

He left the scanner and passed by his brother-in-law. "Thanks," he muttered shakily.

For once, a measure of compassion touched Fei-p'ang's efficient brown features. "Bad news? The next turn brings an unfortunate manifestation?"

"Bad scarcely describes it."

Fei-p'ang's pity turned to righteous rebuke. "Who do you have to blame but yourself?" he demanded sternly. "You know your conduct in this manifestation determines the next; if you look forward to a future life as a lower animal, it should make you glance over your behavior and repent your wrongs. The cosmic law that governs us is impartial. It is true justice: cause and effect; what you do determines what you next become -- there can be no blame and no sorrow. There can be only understanding and repentence." His curiosity overcame him. "What is it? A snake? A squirrel?"

"It's no affair of yours," Sung-wu said, as he moved unhappily toward the exit doors.

"I'll look myself."

"Go ahead." Sung-wu pushed moodily out into the hall. He was dazed with despair: it hadn't changed; it was still the same.

In eight months he would die, stricken by one of the numerous plagues that swept over the inhabited parts of the world. He would become feverish, break out with red spots, turn and twist in an anguish of delirium. His bowels would drop out; his flesh would waste away; his eyes would roll up; and after an interminable time of suffering, be would die. His body would lie in a mass heap, with hundreds of others -- a whole streetful of dead, to be carted away by one of the robot sweepers, happily immune. His mortal remains would be burned in a common rubbish incinerator at the outskirts of the city.

Meanwhile, the eternal spark, Sung-wu's divine soul, would hurry from this space-time manifestation to the next in order. But it would not rise; it would sink; he had watched its descent on the scanner many times. There was always the same hideous picture -- a sight beyond endurance -- of his soul, as it plummeted down like a stone, into one of the lowest continua, a sinkhole of a manifestation at the very bottom of the ladder.

He had sinned. In his youth, Sung-wu had got mixed up with a black-eyed wench with long flowing hair, a glittering waterfall down her back and shoulders. Inviting red lips, plump breasts, hips that undulated and beckoned unmistakably. She was the wife of a friend, from the Warrior class, but he had taken her as his mistress; he had been certain time remained to rectify his venality.

But he was wrong: the wheel was soon to turn for him. The plague -- not enough time to fast and pray and do good works. He was determined to go down, straight down to a wallowing, foul-aired planet in a stinking red-sun system, an ancient pit of filth and decay and unending slime -- a jungle world of the lowest type.

In it, he would be a shiny-winged fly, a great blue-bottomed, buzzing carrion-eater that hummed and guzzled and crawled through the rotting carcasses of great lizards, slain in combat.

From this swamp, this pest-ridden planet in a diseased, contaminated system, he would have to rise painfully up the endless rungs of the cosmic ladder he had already climbed. It had taken eons to climb this far, to the level of a human being on the planet Earth, in the bright yellow Sol system; now he would have to do it all over again.

Chai beamed, "Elron be with you," as the corroded observation ship was checked by the robot crew, and finally okayed for limited flight. Sung-wu slowly entered the ship and seated himself at what remained of the controls. He waved listlessly, then slammed the lock and bolted it by hand.

As the ship limped into the late afternoon sky, he reluctantly consulted the reports and records Chai had transferred to him.

The Tinkerists were a small cult; they claimed only a few hundred members, all drawn from the Techno class, which was the most despised of the social castes. The Bards, of course, were at the top; they were the teachers of society, the holy men who guided man to clearness. Then the Poets; they turned into saga the great legends of Elron Hu, who lived (according to legend) in the hideous days of the Time of Madness. Below the Poets were the Artists; then the Musicians; then the Workers, who supervised the robot crews. After them the Businessmen, the Warriors, the Farmers, and finally, at the bottom, the Technos.

Most of the Technos were Caucasians -- immense white-skinned things, incredibly hairy, like apes; their resemblance to the great apes was striking. Perhaps Broken Feather was right; perhaps they did have Neanderthal blood and were outside the possibility of clearness. Sung-wu had always considered himself an anti-racist; he disliked those who maintained the Caucasians were a race apart. Extremists believed eternal damage would result to the species if the Caucasians were allowed to intermarry. In any case, the problem was academic; no decent, self-respecting woman of the higher classes -- of Indian or Mongolian, or Bantu stock -- would allow herself to be approached by a *Cauc*.

Below his ship, the barren countryside spread out, ugly and bleak. Great red spots that hadn't yet been overgrown, and slag surfaces were still visible -- but by this time most ruins were covered by soil and crabgrass. He could see men and robots fanning; villages, countless tiny brown circles in the green fields; occasional ruins of ancient cities -- gaping sores like blind mouths, eternally open to the sky. They would never close, not now.

Ahead was the Detroit area, named, so it ran, for some now-forgotten spiritual leader. There were more villages, here. Off to his left, the leaden surface of a body of water, a lake of some kind. Beyond that -- only Elron knew. No one went that far; there was no human life there, only wild animals and deformed things spawned from radiation infestation still lying heavy in the north.

He dropped his ship down. An open field lay to his right; a robot farmer was plowing with a metal hook welded to its waist, a section torn off some discarded machine. It stopped dragging the hook and gazed up in amazement, as Sung-wu landed the ship awkwardly and bumped to a halt.

"Clearness be with you," the robot rasped obediently, as Sung-wu climbed out.

Sung-wu gathered up his bundle of reports and papers and stuffed them in a briefcase. He snapped the ship's lock and hurried off toward the ruins of the city. The robot went back to dragging the rusty metal hook through the hard ground, its pitted body bent double with the strain, working slowly, silently, uncomplaining.

The little boy piped, "Whither, Bard?" as Sung-wu pushed wearily through the tangled debris and slag. He was a little black-faced Bantu, in red rags sewed and patched together. He ran alongside Sung-wu like a puppy, leaping and bounding and grinning white-teethed.

Sung-wu became immediately crafty; his intrigue with the black-haired girl had taught him elemental dodges and evasions. "My ship broke down," he answered cautiously; it was certainly common enough. "It was the last ship still in operation at our field."

The boy skipped and laughed and broke off bits of green weeds that grew along the trail. "I know somebody who can fix it," he cried carelessly.

Sung-wu's pulse-rate changed. "Oh?" he murmured, as if uninterested. "There are those around here who practice the questionable art of repairing."

The boy nodded solemnly.

"Technos?" Sung-wu pursued. "Are there many of them here, around these old ruins?"

More black-faced boys, and some little dark-eyed Bantu girls, came scampering through the slag and ruins. "What's the matter with your ship?" one hollered at Sung-wu. "Won't it run?"

They all ran and shouted around him, as he advanced slowly -- an unusually wild bunch, completely undisciplined. They rolled and fought and tumbled and chased each other around madly.

"How many of you," Sung-wu demanded, "have taken your first instruction?"

There was a sudden uneasy silence. The children looked at each other guiltily; none of them answered.

"Good Elron!" Sung-wu exclaimed in horror. "Are you all untaught?"

Heads hung guiltily.

"How do you expect to phase yourselves with the cosmic will? How can you expect to know the divine plan? This is really too much!"

He pointed a plump finger at one of the boys. "Are you constantly preparing yourself for the life to come? Are you constantly purging and purifying yourself? Do you deny yourself meat, sex, entertainment, financial gain, education, leisure?"

But it was obvious; their unrestrained laughter and play proved they were still jangled, far from clear -- And clearness is the only road by which a person can gain understanding of the eternal plan, the cosmic wheel which turns endlessly, for all living things.

"Butterflies!" Sung-wu snorted with disgust. "You are no better than the beasts and birds of the field, who take no heed of the morrow. You play and game for today, thinking tomorrow won't come. Like insects --"

But the thought of insects reminded him of the shiny-winged blue-rumped fly, creeping over a rotting lizard carcass, and Sung-wu's stomach did a flip-flop; he forced it back in place and strode on, toward the line of villages emerging ahead.

Farmers were working the barren fields on all sides. A thin layer of soil over slag; a few limp wheat stalks waved, thin and emaciated. The ground was terrible, the worst he had seen. He could feel the metal under his feet; it was almost to the surface. Bent men and women watered their sickly crops with tin cans, old metal containers picked from the ruins. An ox was pulling a crude cart.

In another field, women were weeding by hand; all moved slowly, stupidly, victims of hookworm, from the soil. They were all barefoot. The children hadn't picked it up yet, but they soon would.

Sung-wu gazed up at the sky and gave thanks to Elron; here, suffering was unusually severe; trials of exceptional vividness lay on every hand. These men and women were being tempered in a hot crucible; their souls were probably purified to an astonishing degree. A baby lay in the shade, beside a half-dozing mother. Flies crawled over its eyes; its mother breathed heavily, hoarsely, her mouth open. An unhealthy flush discolored her brown cheeks. Her belly bulged; she was already pregnant again. Another eternal soul to be raised from a lower level. Her great breasts sagged and wobbled as she stirred in her sleep, spilling out over her dirty wraparound.

"Come here," Sung-wu called sharply to the gang of black-faced children who followed along after him. "I'm going to talk to you."

The children approached, eyes on the ground, and assembled in a silent circle around him. Sung-wu sat down, placed his briefcase beside him and folded his legs expertly under him in the traditional posture outlined by Elron in his seventh book of teaching.

"I will ask and you will answer," Sung-wu stated. "You know the basic catechisms?" He peered sharply around. "Who knows the basic catechisms?"

One or two hands went up. Most of the children looked away unhappily.

"First!" snapped Sung-wu. "*Who are you?* You are a minute fragment of the cosmic plan.

"Second! *What are you?* A mere speck in a system so vast as to be beyond comprehension.

"Third! *What is the way of life?* To fulfill what is required by the cosmic forces

"Fourth! *Where are you?* On one step of the cosmic ladder.

"Fifth! *Where have you been?* Through endless steps; each turn of the wheel advances or depresses you.

"Sixth! *What determines your direction at the next turn?* Your conduct in this manifestation.

"Seventh! *What is right conduct?* Submitting yourself to the eternal forces, the cosmic elements that make up the divine plan.

"Eighth! *What is the significance of suffering?* To purify the soul.

"Ninth! *What is the significance of death?* To release the person from this manifestation, so he may rise to a new rung of the ladder.

"Tenth --"

But at that moment Sung-wu broke off. Two quasi-human shapes were approaching him. Immense white-skinned figures striding across the baked fields, between the sickly rows of wheat.

Technos -- coming to meet him; his flesh crawled. Caucs. Their skins glittered pale and unhealthy, like nocturnal insects, dug from under rocks.

He rose to his feet, conquered his disgust, and prepared to greet them.

Sung-wu said, "Clearness!" He could smell them, a musky sheep smell, as they came to a halt in front of him. Two bucks, two immense sweating males, skin damp and sticky, with beards, and long disorderly hair. They wore sailcloth trousers and boots. With horror Sung-wu perceived a thick body-hair, on their chests, like woven mats -- tufts in their armpits, on their arms, wrists, even the backs of their hands. Maybe Broken Feather was right; perhaps, in these great lumbering blond-haired beasts, the archaic Neanderthal stock -- the false men -- still survived. He could almost see the ape, peering from behind their blue eyes.

"Hi," the first Cauc said. After a moment he added reflectively, "My name's Jamison."

"Pete Ferris," the other grunted. Neither of them observed the customary deferences; Sung-wu winced but managed not to show it. Was it deliberate, a veiled insult, or perhaps mere ignorance? This was hard to tell; in lower classes there was, as Chai said, an ugly undercurrent of resentment and envy, and hostility.

"I'm making a routine survey," Sung-wu explained, "on birth and death rates in rural areas. I'll be here a few days. Is there some place I can stay? Some public inn or hostel?"

The two Cauc bucks were silent. "Why?" one of them demanded bluntly.

Sung-wu blinked. "Why? Why what?"

"Why are you making a survey? If you want any information we'll supply it."

Sung-wu was incredulous. "Do you know to whom you're talking? I'm a Bard! Why, you're ten classes down; how dare you --" He choked with rage. In these rural areas the Technos had utterly forgotten their place. What was ailing the local Bards? Were they letting the system break apart?

He shuddered violently at the thought of what it would mean if Technos and Farmers and Businessmen were allowed to intermingle -- even intermarry, and eat, and drink, in the same places. The whole structure of society would collapse. If all were to ride the same carts, use the same outhouses; it passed belief. A sudden nightmare picture loomed up before Sung-wu, of

Technos living and mating with women of the Bard and Poet classes. He visioned a horizontally-oriented society, all persons on the same level, with horror. It went against the very grain of the cosmos, against the divine plan; it was the Time of Madness all over again. He shuddered.

"Where is the Manager of this area?" he demanded. 'Take me to him; I'll deal directly with him."

The two Caucs turned and headed back the way they had come, without a word. After a moment of fury, Sung-wu followed behind them.

They led him through withered fields and over barren, eroded hills on which nothing grew; the ruins increased. At the edge of the city, a line of meager villages had been set up; he saw leaning, rickety wood huts, and mud streets. From the villages a thick stench rose, the smell of offal and death.

Dogs lay sleeping under the huts; children poked and played in the filth and rotting debris. A few old people sat on porches, vacant-faced, eyes glazed and dull. Chickens pecked around, and he saw pigs and skinny cats -- and the eternal rusting piles of metal, sometimes thirty feet high. Great towers of red slag were heaped up everywhere.

Beyond the villages were the ruins proper -- endless miles of abandoned wreckage; skeletons of buildings; concrete walls; bathtubs and pipe; overturned wrecks that had been cars. All these were from the Time of Madness, the decade that had finally rung the curtain down on the sorriest interval in man's history. The five centuries of madness and jangledness were now known as the Age of Heresy, when man had gone against the divine plan and taken his destiny in his own hands.

They came to a larger hut, a two-story wood structure. The Caucs climbed a decaying flight of steps; boards creaked and gave ominously under their heavy boots. Sung-wu followed them nervously; they came out on a porch, a kind of open balcony.

On the balcony sat a man, an obese copper-skinned official in unbuttoned breeches, his shiny black hair pulled back and tied with a bone against his bulging red neck. His nose was large and prominent, his face, flat and wide, with many chins. He was drinking lime juice from a tin cup and gazing down at the mud street below. As the two Caucs appeared he rose slightly, a prodigious effort.

"This man," the Cauc named Jamison said, indicating Sung-wu, "wants to see you."

Sung-wu pushed angrily forward. "I am a Bard, from the Central Chamber; do you people recognize this?" He tore open his robe and flashed the symbol of the Holy Arm, gold worked to form a swath of flaming red. "I insist you accord me proper treatment! I'm not here to be pushed around by any --"

He had said too much; Sung-wu forced his anger down and gripped his briefcase. The fat Indian was studying him calmly; the two Caucs had wandered to the far end of the balcony and were squatting down in the shade. They lit crude cigarettes and turned their backs.

"Do you permit this?" Sung-wu demanded, incredulous. "This -- mingling?"

The Indian shrugged and sagged down even more in his chair. "Clearness be with you," he murmured; "will you join me?" His calm expression remained unchanged; he seemed not to have noticed. "Some lime juice? Or perhaps coffee? Lime juice is good for these." He tapped his mouth; his soft gums were lined with caked sores.

"Nothing for me," Sung-wu muttered grumpily, as he took a seat opposite the Indian; "I'm here on an official survey."

The Indian nodded faintly. "Oh?"

"Birth and death rates." Sung-wu hesitated, then leaned toward the Indian. "I insist you send those two Caucs away; what I have to say to you is private."

The Indian showed no change of expression; his broad face was utterly impassive. After a time he turned slightly. "Please go down to the street level," he ordered. "As you will."

The two Caucs got to their feet, grumbling, and pushed past the table, scowling and darting resentful glances at Sung-wu. One of them hawked and elaborately spat over the railing, an obvious insult.

"Insolence!" Sung-wu choked. "How can you allow it? Did you see them? By Elron, it's beyond belief!"

The Indian shrugged indifferently -- and belched. "All men are brothers on the wheel. Didn't Elron Himself teach that, when He was on Earth?"

"Of course. But --"

"Are not even these men our brothers?"

"Naturally," Sung-wu answered haughtily, "but they must know their place; they're an insignificant class. In the rare event some object wants fixing, they called; but in the last year I do not recall a single incident when it was deemed advisable to repair anything. The need of such a class diminishes yearly; eventually such a class and the elements composing it --"

"You perhaps advocate sterilization?" the Indian inquired, heavy-lidded and sly.

"I advocate something. The lower classes reproduce like rabbits; spawning all the time -- much faster than we Bards. I always see some swollen-up Cauc woman, but hardly a single Bard is born these days; the lower classes must fornicate constantly."

"That's about all that's left them," the Indian murmured mildly. He sipped a little lime juice. "You should try to be more tolerant."

"Tolerant? I have nothing against them, as long as they --"

"It is said," the Indian continued softly, "that Elron Hu, Himself, was a Cauc."

Sung-wu spluttered indignantly and started to rejoin, but the hot words stuck fast in his mouth; down the mud street something was coming.

Sung-wu demanded, "What is it?" He leaped up excitedly and hurried to the railing.

A slow procession was advancing with solemn step. As if at a signal, men and women poured from their rickety huts and excitedly lined the street to watch. Sung-wu was transfixed, as the procession neared; his senses reeled. More and more men and women were collecting each moment; there seemed to be hundreds of them. They were a dense, murmuring mob, packed tight, swaying back and forth, faces avid. An hysterical moan passed through them, a great wind that stirred them like leaves of a tree. They were a single collective whole, a vast primitive organism, held ecstatic and hypnotized by the approaching column.

The marchers wore a strange costume: white shirts, with the sleeves roiled up; dark gray trousers of an incredibly archaic design, and black shoes. All were dressed exactly alike. They formed a dazzling double line of white shirts, gray trousers, marching calmly and solemnly, faces up, nostrils flared, jaws stern. A glazed fanaticism stamped each man and woman, such a ruthless expression that Sung-wu shrank back in terror. On and on they came, figures of grim stone in their primordial white shirts and gray trousers, a frightening breath from the past. Their heels struck the ground in a dull, harsh beat that reverberated among the rickety huts. The dogs woke; the children began to wail. The chickens flew squawking.

"Elron!" Sung-wu cried. "What's happening?"

The marchers carried strange symbolic implements, ritualistic images with esoteric meaning that of necessity escaped Sung-wu. There were tubes and poles, and shiny webs of what looked like metal. *Metal!* But it was not rusty; it was shiny and bright. He was stunned; they looked -- new.

The procession passed directly below. After the marchers came a huge rumbling cart. On it was mounted an obvious fertility symbol, a corkscrew-bore as long as a tree; it jutted from a square cube of gleaming steel; as the cart moved forward the bore lifted and fell.

After the cart came more marchers, also grim-faced, eyes glassy, loaded down with pipes and tubes and armfuls of glittering equipment. They passed on, and then the street was filled by surging throngs of awed men and women, who followed after them, utterly dazed. And then came children and barking dogs.

The last marcher carried a pennant that fluttered above her as she strode along, a tall pole, hugged tight to her chest. At the top, the bright pennant fluttered boldly. Sung-wu made its marking out, and for a moment consciousness left him. There it was, directly below; it had passed under his very nose, out in the open for all to see -- unconcealed. The pennant had a great T emblazoned on it.

"They --" he began, but the obese Indian cut him off.

"The Tinkerists," he rumbled, and sipped his lime juice.

Sung-wu grabbed up his briefcase and scrambled toward the stairs. At the bottom, the two hulking Caucs were already moving into motion. The Indian signaled quickly to them. "Here!" They started grimly up, little blue eyes mean, red-rimmed and cold as stone; under their pelts their bulging muscles rippled.

Sung-wu fumbled in his cloak. His shiver-gun came out; he squeezed the release and directed it toward the two Caucs. But nothing happened; the gun had stopped functioning. He shook it wildly; flakes of rust and dried insulation fluttered from it. It was useless, worn out; he tossed it away and then, with the resolve of desperation, jumped through the railing.

He, and a torrent of rotten wood, cascaded to the street. He hit, rolled, struck his head against the corner of a hut, and shakily pulled himself to his feet.

He ran. Behind him, the two Caucs pushed after him through the throngs of men and women milling aimlessly along. Occasionally he glimpsed their white, perspiring faces. He turned a corner, raced between shabby huts, leaped over a sewage ditch, climbed heaps of sagging debris, slipping and rolled and at last lay gasping behind a tree, his briefcase still clutched.

The Caucs were nowhere in sight. He had evaded them; for the moment, he was safe.

He peered around. Which way was his ship? He shielded his eyes against the late-afternoon sun until he managed to make out its bent, tubular outline. It was far off to his right, barely visible in the dying glare that hung gloomily across the sky. Sung-wu got unsteadily to his feet and began walking cautiously in that direction.

He was in a terrible spot; the whole region was pro-Tinkerist -- even the Chamber-appointed Manager. And it wasn't along class lines; the cult had knifed to the top level. And it wasn't just Caucs, anymore; he couldn't count on Bantu or Mongolian or Indian, not in this area. An entire countryside was hostile, and lying in wait for him.

Elron, it was worse than the Arm had thought! No wonder they wanted a report. A whole area had swung over to a fanatic cult, a violent extremist group of heretics, teaching a most diabolical doctrine. He shuddered -- and kept on, avoiding contact with the farmers in their fields, both human and robot. He increased his pace, as alarm and horror pushed him suddenly faster.

If the thing were to spread, if it were to hit a sizable portion of mankind, it might bring back the Time of Madness.

The ship was taken. Three or four immense Caucs stood lounging around it, cigarettes dangling from their slack mouths, white-faced and hairy. Stunned, Sung-wu moved back down the hillside, prickles of despair numbing him. The ship was lost; they had got there ahead of him. What was he supposed to do now?

It was almost evening. He'd have to walk fifty miles through the darkness, over unfamiliar, hostile ground, to reach the next inhabited area. The sun was already beginning to set, the air turning cool; and in addition, he was sopping wet with filth and slimy water. He had slipped in the gloom and fallen in a sewage ditch.

He retraced his steps, mind blank. What could he do? He was helpless; his shiver-gun had been useless. He was alone, and there was no contact with the Arm. Tinkerists swarming on all sides; they'd probably gut him and sprinkle his blood over the crops -- or worse.

He skirted a farm. In the fading twilight, a dim figure was working, a young woman. He eyed her cautiously, as he passed; she had her back to him. She was bending over, between rows of corn. What was she doing? Was she -- good Elron!

He stumbled blindly across the field toward her, caution forgotten. "Young woman! *Stop!* In the name of Elron, stop at once!"

The girl straightened up. "Who are you?"

Breathless, Sung-wu arrived in front of her, gripping his battered briefcase and gasping. "Those are our *brothers!* How can you destroy them? They may be close relatives, recently deceased." He struck out and knocked the jar from her hand; it hit the ground and the imprisoned beetles scurried off in all directions.

The girl's cheeks flushed with anger. "It took me an hour to collect those!"

"You were killing them! Crushing them!" He was speechless with horror. "I saw you!"

"Of course." The girl raised her black eyebrows. "They gnaw the corn."

"They're our brothers!" Sung-wu repeated wildly. "Of course they gnaw the corn; because of certain sins committed, the cosmic forces have --" He broke off, appalled. "Don't you know? You've never been told?"

The girl was perhaps sixteen. In the fading light she was a small, slender figure, the empty jar in one hand, a rock in the other. A tide of black hair tumbled down her neck. Her eyes were large and luminous; her lips full and deep red; her skin a smooth copper-brown -- Polynesian, probably. He caught a glimpse of firm brown breasts as she bent to grab a beetle that had landed on its back. The sight made his pulse race; in a flash he was back three years.

"What's your name?" he asked, more kindly.

"Frija."

"How old are you?"

"Seventeen."

"I am a Bard; have you ever spoken to a Bard before?"

"No," the girl murmured. "I don't think so."

She was almost invisible in the darkness. Sung-wu could scarcely see her, but what he saw sent his heart into an agony of paroxysms; the same cloud of black hair, the same deep red lips. This girl was younger, of course -- a mere child, and from the Farmer class, at that. But she had Liu's figure, and in time she'd ripen -- probably in a matter of months.

Ageless, honeyed craft worked his vocal cords. "I have landed in this area to make a survey. Something has gone wrong with my ship and I must remain the night. I know no one here, however. My plight is such that --"

"Oh," Frija said, immediately sympathetic. "Why don't you stay with us, tonight? We have an extra room, now that my brother's away."

"Delighted," Sung-wu answered instantly. "Will you lead the way? I'll gladly repay you for your kindness." The girl moved off toward a vague shape looming up in the darkness. Sung-wu hurried quickly after her. "I find it incredible you haven't been instructed. This whole area has deteriorated beyond belief. What ways have you fallen in? We'll have to spend much time together; I can see that already. Not one of you even approaches clearness -- you're jangled, every one of you."

"What does that mean?" Frija asked, as she stepped up on the porch and opened the door.

"Jangled?" Sung-wu bunked in amazement. "We *will* have to study much together." In his eagerness, he tripped on the top step, and barely managed to catch himself. "Perhaps you need complete instruction; it may be necessary to start from the very bottom. I can arrange a stay at the Holy Arm for you -- under my protection, of course. Jangled means out of harmony with the cosmic elements. How can you live this way? My dear, you'll have to be brought back in line with the divine plan!"

"What plan is that?" She led him into a warm living room; a crackling fire burned in the grate. Two or three men sat around a rough wood table, an old man with long white hair and two younger men. A frail, withered old woman sat dozing in a rocker in the corner. In the kitchen, a buxom young woman was fixing the evening meal.

"Why, *the* plan!" Sung-wu answered, astounded. His eyes darted around. Suddenly his briefcase fell to the floor. "Caucs," he said.

They were all Caucasians, even Frija. She was deeply tanned; her skin was almost black; but she was a Cauc, nonetheless. He recalled: Caucs, in the sun, turned dark, sometimes even darker than Mongolians. The girl had tossed her work robe over a door hook; in her household shorts her thighs were as white as milk. And the old man and woman --

"This is my grandfather," Frija said, indicating the old man. "Benjamin Tinker."

Under the watchful eyes of the two younger Tinkers, Sung-wu was washed and scrubbed, given clean clothes, and then fed. He ate only a little; he didn't feel very well.

"I can't understand it," he muttered, as he listlessly pushed his plate away. "The scanner at the Central Chamber said I had eight months left. The plague will --" He considered. "But it can always change. The scanner goes on prediction, not certainty; multiple possibilities; free will. . . Any overt act of sufficient significance --"

Ben Tinker laughed. "You want to stay alive?"

"Of course!" Sung-wu muttered indignantly.

They all laughed -- even Frija, and the old woman in her shawl, snow-white hair and mild blue eyes. They were the first Cauc women he had ever seen. They weren't big and lumbering like the male Caucs; they didn't seem to have the same bestial characteristics. The two young Cauc bucks looked plenty tough, though; they and their father were poring over an elaborate series of papers and reports, spread out on the dinner table, among the empty plates.

"This area," Ben Tinker murmured. "Pipes should go here. And here. Water's the main need. Before the next crop goes in, we'll dump a few hundred pounds of artificial fertilizers and plow it in. The power plows should be ready, then."

"After that?" one of the tow-headed sons asked.

"Then spraying. If we don't have the nicotine sprays, we'll have to try the copper dusting again. I prefer the spray, but we're still behind on production. The bore has dug us up some good storage caverns, though. It ought to start picking up."

"And here," a son said, "there's going to be need of draining. A lot of mosquito breeding going on. We can try the oil, as we did over here. But I suggest the whole thing be filled in. We can use the dredge and scoop, if they're not tied up."

Sung-wu had taken this all in. Now he rose unsteadily to his feet, trembling with wrath. He pointed a shaking finger at the elder Tinker.

"You're -- meddling!" he gasped.

They looked up. "Meddling?"

"With the plan! With the cosmic plan! Good Elron -- you're interfering with the divine processes. Why --" He was staggered by a realization so alien it convulsed the very core of his being. "You're actually going to set back turns of the wheel."

"That," said old Ben Tinker, "is right."

Sung-wu sat down again, stunned. His mind refused to take it all in. "I don't understand; what'll happen? If you slow the wheel, if you disrupt the divine plan --"

"He's going to be a problem," Ben Tinker murmured thoughtfully. "If we kill him, the Arm will merely send another; they have hundreds like him. And if we don't kill him, if we send him back, he'll raise a hue and cry that'll bring the whole Chamber down here. It's too soon for this to happen. We're gaining support fast, but we need another few months."

Sweat stood out on Sung-wu's plump forehead. He wiped it away shakily. "If you kill me," he muttered, "you will sink down many rungs of the cosmic ladder. You have risen this far; why undo the work accomplished in endless ages past?"

Ben Tinker fixed one powerful blue eye on him. "My friend," he said slowly, "isn't it true one's next manifestation is determined by one's moral conduct in this?"

Sung-wu nodded. "Such is well known."

"And what is right conduct?"

"Fulfilling the divine plan," Sung-wu responded immediately.

"Maybe our whole Movement is part of the plan," Ben Tinker said thoughtfully. "Maybe the cosmic forces want us to drain the swamps and kill the grasshoppers and inoculate the children; after all, the cosmic forces put us all here."

"If you kill me," Sung-wu wailed, "I'll be a carrion-eating fly. I *saw* it, a shiny-winged blue-rumped fly crawling over the carcass of a dead lizard -- In a rotting, steaming jungle in a filthy cesspool of a planet." Tears came; he dabbed at them futilely. "In an out-of-the-way system, at the bottom of the ladder!"

Tinker was amused. "Why this?"

"I've sinned." Sung-wu sniffed and flushed. "I committed adultery."

"Can't you purge yourself?"

"There's no time!" His misery rose to wild despair. "My mind is *still* impure!" He indicated Frija, standing in the bedroom doorway, a supple white and tan shape in her household shorts. "I continue to think carnal thoughts; I can't rid myself. In eight months the plague will turn the wheel on me -- and it'll be done! If I lived to be an old man, withered and toothless -- no more appetite --" His plump body quivered in a frenzied convulsion. "There's no *time* to purge and atone. According to the scanner, I'm going to die a young man!"

After this torrent of words, Tinker was silent, deep in thought. "The plague," he said, at last. "What, exactly, are the symptoms?"

Sung-wu described them, his olive face turning to a sickly green. When he had finished, the three men looked significantly at each other.

Ben Tinker got to his feet. "Come along," he commanded briskly, taking the Bard by the arm. "I have something to show you. It is left from the old days. Sooner or later we'll advance enough to turn out our own, but right now we have only these remaining few. We have to keep them guarded and sealed."

"This is for a good cause," one of the sons said. "It's worth it." He caught his brother's eye and grinned.

Bard Chai finished reading Sung-wu's blue-slip report; he tossed it suspiciously down and eyed the younger Bard.

"You're sure? There's no further need of investigation?"

"The cult will wither away," Sung-wu murmured indifferently. "It lacks any real support; it's merely an escape valve, without intrinsic validity."

Chai wasn't convinced. He reread parts of the report again. "I suppose you're right; but we've heard so many --"

"Lies," Sung-wu said vaguely. "Rumors. Gossip. May I go?" He moved toward the door.

"Eager for your vacation?" Chai smiled understandingly. "I know how you feel. This report must have exhausted you. Rural areas, stagnant backwaters. We must prepare a better program of rural education. I'm convinced whole regions are in a jangled state. We've got to bring clearness to these people. It's our historic role; our class function."

"Verily," Sung-wu murmured, as he bowed his way out of the office and down the hall.

As he walked he fingered his beads thankfully. He breathed a silent prayer as his fingers moved over the surface of the little red pellets, shiny spheres that glowed freshly in place of the faded old -- the gift of the Tinkerists. The beads would come in handy; he kept his hand on them tightly. Nothing must happen to them, in the next eight months. He had to watch them carefully, while he poked around the ruined cities of Spain -- and finally came down with the plague.

He was the first Bard to wear a rosary of penicillin capsules.

The Last of the Masters

Consciousness collected around him. He returned with reluctance; the weight of centuries, an unbearable fatigue, lay over him. The ascent was painful. He would have shrieked if there were anything to shriek with. And anyhow, he was beginning to feel glad.

Eight thousand times he had crept back thus, with ever-increasing difficulty. Someday he wouldn't make it. Someday the black pool would remain. But not this day. He was still alive; above the aching pain and reluctance came joyful triumph.

"Good morning," a bright voice said. "Isn't it a nice day? I'll pull the curtains and you can look out."

He could see and hear. But he couldn't move. He lay quietly and allowed the various sensations of the room to pour in on him. Carpets, wallpaper, tables, lamps, pictures. Desk and vidscreen. Gleaming yellow sunlight streamed through the window. Blue sky. Distant hills. Fields, buildings, roads, factories. Workers and machines.

Peter Green was busily straightening things, his young face wreathed with smiles. "Lots to do today. Lots of people to see you. Bills to sign. Decisions to make. This is Saturday. There will be people coming in from the remote sectors. I hope the maintenance crew has done a good job." He added quickly, "They have, of course. I talked to Fowler on my way over here. Everything's fixed up fine."

The youth's pleasant tenor mixed with the bright sunlight. Sounds and sights, but nothing else. He could feel nothing. He tried to move his arm but nothing happened.

"Don't worry," Green said, catching his terror. "They'll soon be along with the rest. You'll be all right. You *have* to be. How could we survive without you?"

He relaxed. God knew, it had happened often enough before. Anger surged dully. Why couldn't they coordinate? Get it up all at once, not piecemeal. He'd have to change their schedule. Make them organize better.

Past the bright window a squat metal car chugged to a halt. Uniformed men piled out, gathered up heavy armloads of equipment, and hurried toward the main entrance of the building.

"Here they come," Green exclaimed with relief. "A little late, eh?"

"Another traffic tie-up," Fowler snorted, as he entered. "Something wrong with the signal system again. Outside flow got mixed up with the urban stuff; tied up on all sides. I wish you'd change the law."

Now there was motion all around him. The shapes of Fowler and McLean loomed, two giant moons abruptly ascendant. Professional faces that peered down at him anxiously. He was turned over on his side. Muffled conferences. Urgent whispers. The clank of tools.

"Here," Fowler muttered. "Now here. No, that's later. Be careful. Now run it up through here."

The work continued in taut silence. He was aware of their closeness. Dim outlines occasionally cut off his light. He was turned this way and that, thrown around like a sack of meal.

"Okay," Fowler said. "Tape it."

A long silence. He gazed dully at the wall, at the slightly-faded blue and pink wallpaper. An old design that showed a woman in hoopskirts, with a little parasol over her dainty shoulder. A frilly white blouse, tiny tips of shoes. An astoundingly clean puppy at her side.

Then he was turned back, to face upward. Five shapes groaned and strained over him. Their fingers flew, their muscles rippled under their shirts. At last they straightened up and retreated. Fowler wiped sweat from his face; they were all tense and bleary eyed.

"Go ahead," Fowler rasped. "Throw it."

Shock hit him. He gasped. His body arched, then settled slowly down.

His body. He could feel. He moved his arms experimentally. He touched his face, his shoulder, the wall. The wall was real and hard. All at once the world had become three-dimensional again.

Relief showed on Fowler's face. "Thank God." He sagged wearily. "How do you feel?"

After a moment he answered, "All right."

Fowler sent the rest of the crew out. Green began dusting again, off in the corner. Fowler sat down on the edge of the bed and lit his pipe. "Now listen to me," he said. "I've got bad news. I'll give it to you the way you always want it, straight from the shoulder."

"What is it?" he demanded. He examined his fingers. He already knew.

There were dark circles under Fowler's eyes. He hadn't shaved. His square-jawed face was drawn and unhealthy. "We were up all night. Working on your motor system. We've got it jury-rigged, but it won't hold. Not more than another few months. The thing's climbing. The basic units can't be replaced. When they wear out they're gone. We can weld in relays and wiring, but we can't fix the five synapsis-coils. There were only a few men who could make those, and they've been dead two centuries. If the coils burn out --"

"Is there any deterioration in the synapsis-coils?" he interrupted.

"Not yet. Just motor areas. Arms, in particular. What's happening to your legs will happen to your arms and finally all your motor system. You'll be paralyzed by the end of the year. You'll be able to see, hear, and think. And broadcast. But that's all." He added, "Sorry, Bors. We're doing all we can."

"All right," Bors said. "You're excused. Thanks for telling me straight. I guessed."

"Ready to go down? A lot of people with problems, today. They're stuck until you get there."

"Let's go." He focused his mind with an effort and turned his attention to the details of the day. "I want the heavy metals research program speeded. It's lagging, as usual. I may have to pull a number of men from related work and shift them to the generators. The water level will be dropping soon. I want to start feeding power along the lines while there's still power to feed. As soon as I turn my back everything starts falling apart."

Fowler signalled Green and he came quickly over. The two of them bent over Bors and, grunting, hoisted him up and carried him to the door. Down the corridor and outside.

They deposited him in the squat metal car, the new little service truck. Its polished surface was a startling contrast to his pitted, corroded hull, bent and splotched and eaten away. A dull, patina-covered machine of archaic steel and plastic that hummed faintly, rustily, as the men leaped in the front seat and raced the car out onto the main highway.

Edward Tolby perspired, pushed his pack up higher, hunched over, tightened his gun belt, and cursed.

"Daddy," Silvia reproved. "Cut that."

Tolby spat furiously in the grass at the side of the road. He put his arm around his slim daughter. "Sorry, Silv. Nothing personal. The damn heat."

Mid-morning sun shimmered down on the dusty road. Clouds of dust rose and billowed around the three as they pushed slowly along. They were dead tired. Tolby's heavy face was flushed and sullen. An unlit cigarette dangled between his lips. His big, powerfully built body was hunched resentfully forward. His daughter's canvas shirt clung moistly to her arms and breasts. Moons of sweat darkened her back. Under her jeans her thigh muscles rippled wearily.

Robert Penn walked a little behind the two Tolby's, hands deep in his pockets, eyes on the road ahead. His mind was blank; he was half asleep from the double shot of hexobarb he had swallowed at the last League camp. And the heat lulled him. On each side of the road fields stretched out, pastures of grass and weeds, a few trees here and there. A tumbled-down farmhouse. The ancient rusting remains of a bomb shelter, two centuries old. Once, some dirty sheep.

"Sheep," Penn said. "They eat the grass too far down. It won't grow back."

"Now he's a farmer," Tolby said to his daughter.

"Daddy," Silvia snapped. "Stop being nasty."

"It's this heat. This damn heat." Tolby cursed again, loudly and futilely. "It's not worth it. For ten pinks I'd go back and tell them it was a lot of pig swill."

"Maybe it is, at that," Penn said mildly.

"All right, you go back," Tolby grunted. "You go back and tell them it's a lot of pig swill. They'll pin a medal on you. Maybe raise you up a grade."

Penn laughed. "Both of you shut up. There's some kind of town ahead."

Tolby's massive body straightened eagerly. "Where?" He shielded his eyes. "By God, he's right. A village. And it isn't a mirage. You see it, don't you?" His good humor returned and he rubbed his big hands together. "What say, Penn. A couple of beers, a few games of throw with some of the local peasants -- maybe we can stay overnight." He licked his thick lips with anticipation. "Some of those village wenches, the kind that hang around the grog shops --"

"I know the kind you mean," Penn broke in. "The kind that are tired of doing nothing. Want to see the big commercial centers. Want to meet some guy that'll buy them mecho-stuff and take them places."

At the side of the road a farmer was watching them curiously. He had halted his horse and stood leaning on his crude plow, hat pushed back on his head.

"What's the name of this town?" Tolby yelled.

The farmer was silent a moment. He was an old man, thin and weathered. "This town?" he repeated.

"Yeah, the one ahead."

"That's a nice town." The farmer eyed the three of them. "You been through here before?"

"No, sir," Tolby said. "Never."

"Team break down?"

"No, we're on foot."

"How far you come?"

"About a hundred and fifty miles."

The farmer considered the heavy packs strapped on their backs. Their cleated hiking shoes. Dusty clothing and weary, sweat-streaked faces. Jeans and canvas shirts. Ironite walking staffs. "That's a long way," he said. "How far you going?"

"As far as we feel like it," Tolby answered. "Is there a place ahead we can stay? Hotel? Inn?"

"That town," the farmer said, "is Fairfax. It has a lumber mill, one of the best in the world. A couple of pottery works. A place where you can get clothes put together by machines. Regular mecho-clothing. A gun shop where they pour the best shot this side of the Rockies. And a bakery. Also there's an old doctor living there, and a lawyer. And some people with books to teach the kids. They came with t.b. They made a school house out of an old barn."

"How large a town?" Penn asked.

"Lot of people. More born all the time. Old folks die. Kids die. We had a fever last year. About a hundred kids died. Doctor said it came from the water hole. We shut the water hole down. Kids died anyhow. Doctor said it was the milk. Drove off half the cows. Not mine. I stood out there with my gun and I shot the first of them came to drive off my cow. Kids stopped dying as soon as fall came. I think it was the heat."

"Sure is hot," Tolby agreed.

"Yes, it gets hot around here. Water's pretty scarce." A crafty look slid across his old face. "You folks want a drink? The young lady looks pretty tired. Got some bottles of water down under the house. In the mud. Nice and cold." He hesitated. "Pink a glass."

Tolby laughed. "No, thanks."

"Two glasses a pink," the farmer said.

"Not interested," Penn said. He thumped his canteen and the three of them started on. "So long."

The farmer's face hardened. "Damn foreigners," he muttered. He turned angrily back to his plowing.

The town baked in silence. Flies buzzed and settled on the backs of stupefied horses, tied up at posts. A few cars were parked here and there. People moved listlessly along the sidewalks. Elderly lean-bodied men dozed on porches. Dogs and chickens slept in the shade under houses. The houses were small, wooden, chipped and peeling boards, leaning and angular -- and old.

Warped and split by age and heat. Dust lay over everything. A thick blanket of dry dust over the cracking houses and the dull-faced men and animals.

Two lank men approached them from an open doorway. "Who are you? What do you want?"

They stopped and got out their identification. The men examined the sealed-plastic cards. Photographs, fingerprints, data. Finally they handed them back.

"AL," one said. "You really from the Anarchist League?"

"That's right," Tolby said.

"Even the girl?" The men eyed Silvia with languid greed. "Tell you what. Let us have the girl a while and we'll skip the head tax."

"Don't kid me," Tolby grunted. "Since when does the League pay head tax or any other tax?" He pushed past them impatiently. "Where's the grog shop? I'm dying!"

A two-story white building was on their left. Men lounged on the porch, watching them vacantly. Penn headed toward it and the Tolby's followed. A faded, peeling sign lettered across the front read: *Beer, Wine on Tap.*

"This is it," Penn said. He guided Silvia up the sagging steps, past the men, and inside. Tolby followed; he unstrapped his pack gratefully as he came.

The place was cool and dark. A few men and women were at the bar; the rest sat around tables. Some youths were playing throw in the back. A mechanical tune-maker wheezed and composed in the corner, a shabby, half-ruined machine only partially functioning. Behind the bar a primitive scene-shifter created and destroyed vague phantasmagoria: seascapes, mountain peaks, snowy valleys, great rolling hills, a nude woman that lingered and then dissolved into one vast breast. Dim, uncertain processions that no one noticed or looked at. The bar itself was an incredibly ancient sheet of transparent plastic, stained and chipped and yellow with age. Its n-grav coat had faded from one end; bricks now propped it up. The drink mixer had long since fallen apart. Only wine and beer were served. No living man knew how to mix the simplest drink.

Tolby moved up to the bar. "Beer," he said. "Three beers." Penn and Silvia sank down at a table and removed their packs, as the bartender served Tolby three mugs of thick, dark beer. He showed his card and carried the mugs over to the table.

The youths in the back had stopped playing. They were watching the three as they sipped their beer and unlaced their hiking boots. After a while one of them came slowly over.

"Say," he said. "You're from the League."

"That's right," Tolby murmured sleepily.

Everyone in the place was watching and listening. The youth sat down across from the three; his companions flocked excitedly around and took seats on all sides. The juveniles of the town. Bored, restless, dissatisfied. Their eyes took in the ironite staffs, the guns, the heavy metal-cleated boots. A murmured whisper rustled through them. They were about eighteen. Tanned, rangy.

"How do you get in?" one demanded bluntly.

"The League?" Tolby leaned back in his chair, found a match, and lit his cigarette. He unfastened his belt, belched loudly, and settled back contentedly. "You get in by examination."

"What do you have to know?"

Tolby shrugged. "About everything." He belched again and scratched thoughtfully at his chest, between two buttons. He was conscious of the ring of people around on all sides. A little old man with a beard and horn-rimmed glasses. At another table, a great tub of a man in a red shirt and blue-striped trousers, with a bulging stomach.

Youths. Farmers. A Negro in a dirty white shirt and trousers, a book under his arm. A hard-jawed blonde, hair in a net, red nails and high heels, tight yellow dress. Sitting with a gray-haired businessman in a dark brown suit. A tall young man holding hands with a young black-haired girl, huge eyes, in a soft white blouse and skirt, little slippers kicked under the table. Under the table her bare, tanned feet twisted; her slim body was bent forward with interest

"You have to know," Tolby said, "how the League was formed. You have to know how we pulled down the governments that day. Pulled them down and destroyed them. Burned all the buildings. And all the records. Billions of microfilms and papers. Great bonfires that burned for weeks. And the swarms of little white things that poured out when we knocked the buildings over."

"You killed them?" the great tub of a man asked, lips twitching avidly.

"We let them go. They were harmless. They ran and hid. Under rocks." Tolby laughed. "Funny little scurrying things. Insects. Then we went in and gathered up all the records and equipment for making records. By God, we burned everything."

"And the robots," a youth said.

"Yeah, we smashed all the government robots. There weren't many of them. They were used only at high levels. When a lot of facts had to be integrated."

The youth's eyes bulged. "You saw them? You were there when they smashed the robots?"

Penn laughed. "Tolby means the League. That was two hundred years ago."

The youth grinned nervously. "Yeah. Tell us about the marches."

Tolby drained his mug and pushed it away. "I'm out of beer."

The mug was quickly refilled. He grunted his thanks and continued, voice deep and furry, dulled with fatigue. "The marches. That was really something, they say. All over the world, people getting up, throwing down what they were doing --"

"It started in East Germany," the hard-jawed blonde said. "The riots."

"Then it spread to Poland," the Negro put in shyly. "My grandfather used to tell me how everybody sat and listened to the television. His grandfather used to tell him. It spread to Czechoslovakia and then Austria and Roumania and Bulgaria. Then France. And Italy."

"France was first!" the little old man with beard and glasses cried violently. "They were without a government a whole month. The people saw they could live without a government!"

"The marches started it," the black-haired girl corrected. "That was the first time they started pulling down the government buildings. In East Germany and Poland. Big mobs of unorganized workers."

"Russia and America were the last," Tolby said. "When the march on Washington came there was close to twenty million of us. We were big in those days! They couldn't stop us when we finally moved."

"They shot a lot," the hard-faced blonde said.

"Sure. But the people kept coming. And yelling to the soldiers. 'Hey, Bill! Don't shoot!' 'Hey, Jack! It's me, Joe.' 'Don't shoot -- we're your friends!' 'Don't kill us, join us!' And by God, after a while they did. They couldn't keep shooting their own people. They finally threw down their guns and got out of the way."

"And then you found the place," the little black-haired girl said breathlessly.

"Yeah. We found the place. *Six* places. Three in America. One in Britain. Two in Russia. It took us ten years to find the last place -- and make sure it was the last place."

"What then?" the youth asked, bug-eyed.

"Then we busted every one of them." Tolby raised himself up, a massive man, beer mug clutched, heavy face flushed dark red. "Every damn A-bomb in the whole world."

There was an uneasy silence.

"Yeah," the youth murmured. "You sure took care of those war people."

"Won't be any more of them," the great tub of a man said. "They're gone for good."

Tolby fingered his ironite staff. "Maybe so. And maybe not. There just might be a few of them left."

"What do you mean?" the tub of a man demanded.

Tolby raised his hard gray eyes. "It's time you people stopped kidding us. You know damn well what I mean. We've heard rumors. Someplace around this area there's a bunch of them. Hiding out."

Shocked disbelief, then anger hummed to a roar. "That's a lie!" the tub of a man shouted.

"Is it?"

The little man with beard and glasses leaped up. "There's nobody here has anything to do with governments! We're all good people!"

"You better watch your step," one of the youths said softly to Tolby. "People around here don't like to be accused."

Tolby got unsteadily to his feet, his ironite staff gripped. Penn got up beside him and they stood together. "If any of you knows something," Tolby said, "you better tell it. Right now."

"Nobody knows anything," the hard-faced blonde said. "You're talking to honest folks."

"That's so," the Negro said, nodding his head. "Nobody here's doing anything wrong."

"You saved our lives," the black-haired girl said. "If you hadn't pulled down the governments we'd all be dead in the war. Why should we hold back something?"

"That's true," the great tub of a man grumbled. "We wouldn't be alive if it wasn't for the League. You think we'd do anything against the League?"

"Come on," Silvia said to her father. "Let's go." She got to her feet and tossed Penn his pack.

Tolby grunted belligerently. Finally he took his own pack and hoisted it to his shoulder. The room was deathly silent. Everyone stood frozen, as the three gathered their things and moved toward the door.

The little dark-haired girl stopped them. "The next town is thirty miles from here," she said.

"The road's blocked," her tall companion explained. "Slides closed it years ago."

"Why don't you stay with us tonight? There's plenty of room at our place. You can rest up and get an early start tomorrow."

"We don't want to impose," Silvia murmured.

Tolby and Penn glanced at each other, then at the girl. "If you're sure you have plenty of room --"

The great tub of a man approached them. "Listen. I have ten yellow slips. I want to give them to the League. I sold my farm last year. I don't need any more slips; I'm living with my brother and his family." He pushed the slips at Tolby. "Here."

Tolby pushed them back. "Keep them."

"This way," the tall young man said, as they clattered down the sagging steps, into a sudden blinding curtain of heat and dust. "We have a car. Over this way. An old gasoline car. My dad fixed it so it burns oil."

"You should have taken the slips," Penn said to Tolby, as they got into the ancient, battered car. Flies buzzed around them. They could hardly breathe; the car was a furnace. Silvia fanned herself with a rolled-up paper. The black-haired girl unbuttoned her blouse.

"What do we need money for?" Tolby laughed good-naturedly. "I haven't paid for anything in my life. Neither have you."

The car sputtered and moved slowly forward, onto the road. It began to gain speed. Its motor banged and roared. Soon it was moving surprisingly fast.

"You saw them," Silvia said, over the racket. "They'd give us anything they had. We saved their lives." She waved at the fields, the farmers and their crude teams, the withered crops, the sagging old farmhouses. "They'd all be dead, if it hadn't been for the League." She smashed a fly peevishly. "They depend on us."

The black-haired girl turned toward them, as the car rushed along the decaying road. Sweat streaked her tanned skin. Her half-covered breasts trembled with the motion of the car. "I'm Laura Davis. Pete and I have an old farmhouse his dad gave us when we got married."

"You can have the whole downstairs," Pete said.

"There's no electricity, but we've got a big fireplace. It gets cold at night. It's hot in the day, but when the sun sets it gets terribly cold."

"We'll be all right," Penn murmured. The vibration of the car made him a little sick.

"Yes," the girl said, her black eyes flashing. Her crimson lips twisted. She leaned toward Penn intently, her small face strangely alight. "Yes, we'll take good care of you."

At that moment the car left the road.

Silvia shrieked. Tolby threw himself down, head between his knees, doubled up in a ball. A sudden curtain of green burst around Penn. Then a sickening emptiness, as the car plunged down. It struck with a roaring crash that blotted out everything. A single titanic cataclysm of fury that picked Penn up and flung his remains in every direction.

"Put me down," Bors ordered. "On this railing for a moment before I go inside."

The crew lowered him onto the concrete surface and fastened magnetic grapples into place. Men and women hurried up the wide steps, in and out of the massive building that was Bors' main offices.

The sight from these steps pleased him. He liked to stop here and look around at his world. At the civilization he had carefully constructed. Each piece added painstakingly, scrupulously with infinite care, throughout the years.

It wasn't big. The mountains ringed it on all sides. The valley was a level bowl, surrounded by dark violet hills. Outside, beyond the hills, the regular world began. Parched fields. Blasted, poverty-stricken towns. Decayed roads. The remains of houses, tumbled-down farm buildings. Ruined cars and machinery. Dust-covered people creeping listlessly around in hand-made clothing, dull rags and tatters.

He had seen the outside. He knew what it was like. At the mountains the blank faces, the disease, the withered crops, the crude plows and ancient tools all ended here. Here, within the ring of hills, Bors had constructed an accurate and detailed reproduction of a society two centuries gone. The world as it had been in the old days. The time of governments. The time that had been pulled down by the Anarchist League.

Within his five synapsis-coils the plans, knowledge, information, blueprints of a whole world existed. In the two centuries he had carefully recreated that world, had made this miniature society that glittered and hummed on all sides of him. The roads, buildings, houses, industries of a dead world, all a fragment of the past, built with his hands, his own metal fingers and brain.

"Fowler," Bors said.

Fowler came over. He looked haggard. His eyes were red-rimmed and swollen. "What is it? You want to go inside?"

Overhead, the morning patrol thundered past. A string of black dots against the sunny, cloudless sky. Bors watched with satisfaction. "Quite a sight."

"Right on the nose," Fowler agreed, examining his wristwatch. To their right, a column of heavy tanks snaked along a highway between green fields. Their gun-snouts glittered. Behind them a column of foot soldiers marched, faces hidden behind bacteria masks.

"I'm thinking," Bors said, "that it may be unwise to trust Green any longer."

"Why the hell do you say that?"

"Every ten days I'm inactivated. So your crew can see what repairs are needed." Bors twisted restlessly. "For twelve hours I'm completely helpless. Green takes care of me. Sees nothing happens. But --"

"But what?"

"It occurs to me perhaps there'd be more safety in a squad of troops. It's too much of a temptation for one man, alone."

Fowler scowled. "I don't see that. How about me? I have charge of inspecting you. I could switch a few leads around. Send a load through your synapsis-coils. Blow them out."

Bors whirled wildly, then subsided. "True. You could do that." After a moment he demanded, "But what would you gain? You know I'm the only one who can keep all this together. I'm the only one who knows how to maintain a planned society, not a disorderly chaos! If it weren't for me, all this would collapse, and you'd have dust and ruins and weeds. The whole outside would come rushing in to take over!"

"Of course. So why worry about Green?"

Trucks of workers rumbled past. Loads of men in blue-green, sleeves rolled up, armloads of tools. A mining team, heading for the mountains.

"Take me inside," Bors said abruptly.

Fowler called McLean. They hoisted Bors and carried him past the throngs of people, into the building, down the corridor and to his office. Officials and technicians moved respectfully out of the way as the great pitted, corroded tank was carried past.

"All right," Bors said impatiently. "That's all. You can go."

Fowler and McLean left the luxurious office, with its lush carpets, furniture, drapes and rows of books. Bors was already bent over his desk, sorting through heaps of reports and papers.

Fowler shook his head, as they walked down the hall. "He won't last much longer."

"The motor system? Can't we reinforce the --"

"I don't mean that. He's breaking up mentally. He can't take the strain any longer."

"None of us can," McLean muttered.

"Running this thing is too much for him. Knowing it's all dependent on him. Knowing as soon as he turns his back or lets down it'll begin to come apart at the seams. A hell of a job, trying to shut out the real world. Keeping his model universe running."

"He's gone on a long time," McLean said.

Fowler brooded. "Sooner or later we're going to have to face the situation." Gloomily, he ran his fingers along the blade of a large screwdriver. "He's wearing out. Sooner or later somebody's going to have to step in. As he continues to decay. . ." He stuck the screwdriver back in his belt, with his pliers and hammer and soldering iron. "One crossed wire."

"What's that?"

Fowler laughed. "Now he's got me doing it. One crossed wire and -- *poof!* But what then? That's the big question."

"Maybe," McLean said softly, "you and I can then get off this rat race. You and I and all the rest of us. And live like human beings."

"*Rat race,*" Fowler murmured. "Rats in a maze. Doing tricks. Performing chores thought up by somebody else."

McLean caught Fowler's eye. "By somebody of another species."

Tolby struggled vaguely. Silence. A faint dripping close by. A beam pinned his body down. He was caught on all sides by the twisted wreck of the car. He was head down. The car was turned on its side. Off the road in a gully, wedged between two huge trees. Bent struts and smashed metal all around him. And bodies.

He pushed up with all his strength. The beam gave, and he managed to get to a sitting position. A tree branch had burst in the windshield. The black-haired girl, still turned toward the back seat, was impaled on it. The branch had driven through her spine, out her chest, and into the seat; she clutched at it with both hands, head limp, mouth half-open. The man beside her was also dead. His hands were gone; the windshield had burst around him. He lay in a heap among the remains of the dashboard and the bloody shine of his own internal organs.

Penn was dead. Neck snapped like a rotten broom handle. Tolby pushed his corpse aside and examined his daughter. Silvia didn't stir. He put his ear to her shirt and listened. She was alive. Her heart beat faintly. Her bosom rose and fell against his ear.

He wound a handkerchief around her arm, where the flesh was ripped open and oozing blood. She was badly cut and scratched; one leg was doubled under her, obviously broken. Her clothes were ripped, her hair matted with blood. But she was alive. He pushed the twisted door open and stumbled out. A fiery tongue of afternoon sunlight struck him and he winced. He began to ease her limp body out of the car, past the twisted door-frame.

A sound.

Tolby glanced up, rigid. Something was coming. A whirring insect that rapidly descended. He let go of Silvia, crouched, glanced around, then lumbered awkwardly down the gully. He slid and fell and rolled among the green vines and jagged gray boulders. His gun gripped, he lay gasping in the moist shadows, peering, upward.

The insect landed. A small air-ship, jet-driven. The sight stunned him. He had heard about jets, seen photographs of them. Been briefed and lectured in the history indoctrination courses at the League Camps. But to *see* a jet!

Men swarmed out. Uniformed men who started from the road, down the side of the gully, bodies crouched warily as they approached the wrecked car. They lugged heavy rifles. They looked grim and experienced, as they tore the car doors open and scrambled in.

"One's gone," a voice drifted to him.

"Must be around somewhere."

"Look, this one's alive! This woman. Started to crawl out. The rest all dead."

Furious cursing. "Damn Laura! She should have leaped! The fanatic little fool!"

"Maybe she didn't have time. God's sake, the thing's all the way through her." Horror and shocked dismay. "We won't hardly be able to get her loose."

"Leave her." The officer directing things waved the men back out of the car. "Leave them all."

"How about this wounded one?"

The leader hesitated. "Kill her," he said finally. He snatched a rifle and raised the butt. "The rest of you fan out and try to get the other one. He's probably --"

Tolby fired, and the leader's body broke in half. The lower part sank down slowly; the upper dissolved in ashy fragments. Tolby turned and began to move in a slow circle, firing as he crawled. He got two more of them before the rest retreated in panic to their jet-powered insect and slammed the lock.

He had the element of surprise. Now that was gone. They had strength and numbers. He was doomed. Already, the insect was rising. They'd be able to spot him easily from above. But he had saved Silvia. That was something.

He stumbled down a dried-up creek bed. He ran aimlessly; he had no place to go. He didn't know the countryside, and he was on foot. He slipped on a stone and fell headlong. Pain and billowing darkness beat at him as he got unsteadily to his knees. His gun was gone, lost in the shrubbery. He spat broken teeth and blood. He peered wildly up at the blazing afternoon sky.

The insect was leaving. It hummed off toward the distant hills. It dwindled, became a black ball, a fly-speck, then disappeared.

Tolby waited a moment. Then he struggled up the side of the ravine to the wrecked car. They had gone to get help. They'd be back. Now was his only chance. If he could get Silvia out and down the road, into hiding. Maybe to a farmhouse. Back to town.

He reached the car and stood, dazed and stupefied. Three bodies remained, the two in the front seat, Penn in the back. But Silvia was gone.

They had taken her with them. Back where they came from. She had been dragged to the jet-driven insect; a trail of blood led from the car up the side of the gully to the highway.

With a violent shudder Tolby pulled himself together. He climbed into the car and pried loose Penn's gun from his belt. Silvia's ironite staff rested on the seat; he took that, too. Then he started off down the road, walking without haste, carefully, slowly.

An ironic thought plucked at his mind. He had found what they were after. The men in uniform. They were organized, responsible to a central authority. In a newly-assembled jet. Beyond the hills was a government.

"Sir," Green said. He smoothed his short blond hair anxiously, his young face twisting.

Technicians and experts and ordinary people in droves were everywhere. The offices buzzed and echoed with the business of the day. Green pushed through the crowd and to the desk where Bors sat, propped up by two magnetic frames.

"Sir," Green said. "Something's happened."

Bors looked up. He pushed a metal-foil slate away and laid down his stylus. His eye cells clicked and flickered; deep inside his battered trunk motor gears whined. "What is it?"

Green came close. There was something in his face, an expression Bors had never seen before. A look of fear and glassy determination. A glazed, fanatic cast, as if his flesh had hardened to rock. "Sir, scouts contacted a League team moving North. They met the team outside Fairfax. The incident took place directly beyond the first road block."

Bors said nothing. On all sides, officials, experts, farmers, workmen, industrial managers, soldiers, people of all kinds buzzed and murmured and pushed forward impatiently. Trying to get to Bors' desk. Loaded down with problems to be solved, situations to be explained. The pressing business of the day. Roads, factories, disease control. Repairs. Construction. Manufacture. Design. Planning. Urgent problems for Bors to consider and deal with. Problems that couldn't wait.

"Was the League team destroyed?" Bors said.

"One was killed. One was wounded and brought here." Green hesitated. "One escaped."

For a long time Bors was silent. Around him the people murmured and shuffled; he ignored them. All at once he pulled the vidscanner to him and snapped the circuit open. "One escaped? I don't like the sound of that."

"He shot three members of our scout unit. Including the leader. The others got frightened. They grabbed the injured girl and returned here."

Bors' massive head lifted. "They made a mistake. They should have located the one who escaped."

"This was the first time the situation --"

"I know," Bors said. "But it was an error. Better not to have touched them at all, than to have taken two and allowed the third to get away." He turned to the vidscanner. "Sound an emergency alert. Close down the factories. Arm the work crews and any male farmers capable of using weapons. Close every road. Remove the women and children to the undersurface shelters. Bring up the heavy guns and supplies. Suspend all non-military production and --" He considered. "Arrest everyone we're not sure of. On the C sheet. Have them shot." He snapped the scanner off.

"What'll happen?" Green demanded, shaken.

"The thing we've prepared for. Total war."

"We have weapons!" Green shouted excitedly. "In an hour there'll be ten thousand men ready to fight. We have jet-driven ships. Heavy artillery. Bombs. Bacteria pellets. What's the League? A lot of people with packs on their backs!"

"Yes," Bors said. "A lot of people with packs on their backs."

"How can they do anything? How can a bunch of anarchists organize? They have no structure, no control, no central power."

"They have the whole world. A billion people."

"Individuals! A club, not subject to law. Voluntary membership. We have disciplined organization. Every aspect of our economic life operates at maximum efficiency. We -- you -- have your thumb on everything. All you have to do is give the order. Set the machine in motion."

Bors nodded slowly. "It's true the anarchist can't coordinate. The League can't organize. It's a paradox. Government by anarchists. . . Anti-government, actually. Instead of governing the world they tramp around to make sure no one else does."

"Dog in the manger."

"As you say, they're actually a voluntary club of totally unorganized individuals. Without law or central authority. They maintain no society -- they can't govern. All they can do is interfere with anyone else who tries. Troublemakers. But --"

"But what?"

"It was this way before. Two centuries ago. They were unorganized. Unarmed. Vast mobs, without discipline or authority. Yet they pulled down all the governments. All over the world."

"We've got a whole army. All the roads are mined. Heavy guns. Bombs. Pellets. Every one of us is a soldier. We're an armed camp!"

Bors was deep in thought. "You say one of them is here? One of the League agents?"

"A young woman."

Bors signalled the nearby maintenance crew. "Take me to her. I want to talk to her in the time remaining."

Silvia watched silently, as the uniformed men pushed and grunted their way into the room. They staggered over to the bed, pulled two chairs together, and carefully laid down their massive armload.

Quickly they snapped protective struts into place, locked the chairs together, threw magnetic grapples into operation, and then warily retreated.

"All right," the robot said. "You can go." The men left. Bors turned to face the woman on the bed.

"A machine," Silvia whispered, white-faced. "You're a machine."

Bors nodded slightly without speaking.

Silvia shifted uneasily on the bed. She was weak. One leg was in a transparent plastic cast. Her face was bandaged and her right arm ached and throbbed. Outside the window, the late afternoon sun sprinkled through the drapes. Flowers bloomed. Grass. Hedges. And beyond the hedges, buildings and factories.

For the last hour the sky had been filled with jet-driven ships. Great flocks that raced excitedly across the sky toward distant hills. Along the highway cars hurtled, dragging guns and heavy military equipment. Men were marching in close rank, rows of gray-clad soldiers, guns and helmets and bacteria masks. Endless lines of figures, identical in their uniforms, stamped from the same matrix.

"There are a lot of them," Bors said, indicating the marching men.

"Yes." Silvia watched a couple of soldiers hurry by the window. Youths with worried expressions on their smooth faces. Helmets bobbing at their waists. Long rifles. Canteens. Counters. Radiation shields. Bacteria masks wound awkwardly around their necks, ready to go into place. They were scared. Hardly more than kids. Others followed. A truck roared into life. The soldiers were swept off to join the others.

"They're going to fight," Bors said, "to defend their homes and factories."

"All this equipment. You manufacture it, don't you?"

"That's right. Our industrial organization is perfect. We're totally productive. Our society here is operated rationally. Scientifically. We're fully prepared to meet this emergency."

Suddenly Silvia realized what the emergency was. "The League! One of us must have got away." She pulled herself up. "Which of them? Penn or my father?"

"I don't know," the robot murmured indifferently.

Horror and disgust choked Silvia. "My God," she said softly. "You have no understanding of us. You run all this, and you're incapable of empathy. You're nothing but a mechanical computer. One of the old government integration robots."

"That's right. Two centuries old."

She was appalled. "And you've been alive all this time. We thought we destroyed all of you!"

"I was missed. I had been damaged. I wasn't in my place. I was in a truck, on my way out of Washington. I saw the mobs and escaped."

"Two hundred years ago. Legendary times. You actually saw the events they tell us about. The old days. The great marches. The day the governments fell."

"Yes. I saw it all. A group of us formed in Virginia. Experts, officials, skilled workmen. Later we came here. It was remote enough, off the beaten path."

"We heard rumors. A fragment. . . still maintaining itself. But we didn't know where or how."

"I was fortunate," Bors said. "I escaped by a fluke. All the others were destroyed. It's taken a long time to organize what you see here. Fifteen miles from here is a ring of hills. This valley is a bowl -- mountains on all sides. We've set up road blocks in the form of natural slides. Nobody comes here. Even in Fairfax, thirty miles off, they know nothing."

"That girl. Laura."

"Scouts. We keep scout teams in all inhabited regions within a hundred mile radius. As soon as you entered Fairfax, word was relayed to us. An air unit was dispatched. To avoid questions, we arranged to have you killed in an auto Wreck. But one of you escaped."

Silvia shook her head, bewildered. "How?" she demanded. "How do you keep going? Don't the people revolt?" She struggled to a sitting position. "They must know what's happened everywhere else. How do you control them? They're going out now, in their uniforms. But -- *will they fight? Can you count on them?*"

Bors answered slowly. "They trust me," he said. "I brought with me a vast amount of knowledge. Information and techniques lost to the rest of the world. Are jet-ships and vidscanners and power cables made anywhere else in the world? I retain all that knowledge. I have memory units, synapsis-coils. Because of me they have these things. Things you know only as dim memories, vague legends."

"What happens when you die?"

"I won't die! I'm eternal!"

"You're wearing out. You have to be carried around. And your right arm. You can hardly move it!" Silvia's voice was harsh, ruthless. "Your whole tank is pitted and rusty."

The robot whirred; for a moment he seemed unable to speak. "My knowledge remains," he grated finally. "I'll always be able to communicate. Fowler has arranged a broadcast system. Even when I talk --" He broke off. "Even then. Everything is under control. I've organized every aspect of the situation. I've maintained this system for two centuries. It's got to be kept going!"

Silvia lashed out. It happened in a split second. The boot of her cast caught the chairs on which the robot rested. She thrust violently with her foot and hands; the chairs teetered, hesitated --

"Fowler!" the robot screamed.

Silvia pushed with all her strength. Blinding agony seared through her leg; she bit her lip and threw her shoulder against the robot's pitted hulk. He waved his arms, whirred wildly, and then the two chairs slowly collapsed. The robot slid quietly from them, over on his back, his arms still waving helplessly.

Silvia dragged herself from the bed. She managed to pull herself to the window; her broken leg hung uselessly, a dead weight in its transparent plastic cast. The robot lay like some futile bug, arms waving, eye lens clicking, its rusty works whirring in fear and rage.

"Fowler!" it screamed again. "Help me!"

Silvia reached the window. She tugged at the locks; they were sealed. She grabbed up a lamp from the table and threw it against the glass. The glass burst around her, a shower of lethal fragments. She stumbled forward -- and then the repair crew was pouring into the room.

Fowler gasped at the sight of the robot on its back. A strange expression crossed his face. "Look at him!"

"Help me!" the robot shrilled. "Help me!"

One of the men grabbed Silvia around the waist and lugged her back to the bed. She kicked and bit, sunk her nails into the man's cheek. He threw her on the bed, face down, and drew his pistol. "Stay there," he gasped.

The others were bent over the robot, getting him to an upright position.

"What happened?" Fowler said. He came over to the bed, his face twisting. "Did he fall?"

Silvia's eyes glowed with hatred and despair. "I pushed him over. I almost got there." Her chest heaved. "The window. But my leg --"

"Get me back to my quarters!" Bors cried.

The crew gathered him up and carried him down the hall, to his private office. A few moments later he was sitting shakily at his desk, his mechanism pounding wildly, surrounded by his papers and memoranda.

He forced down his panic and tried to resume his work. He had to keep going. His vidscreen was alive with activity. The whole system was in motion. He blankly watched a subcommander sending up a cloud of black dots, jet bombers that shot up like flies and headed quickly off.

The system had to be preserved. He repeated it again and again. He had to save it. Had to organize the people and make *them* save it. If the people didn't fight, wasn't everything doomed?

Fury and desperation overwhelmed him. The system couldn't preserve itself; it wasn't a thing apart, something that could be separated from the people who lived it. Actually it *was* the people. They were identical; when the people fought to preserve the system they were fighting to preserve nothing less than themselves.

They existed only as long as the system existed.

He caught sight of a marching column of white-faced troops, moving toward the hills. His ancient synapsis-coils radiated and shuddered uncertainly, then fell back into pattern. He was two centuries old. He had come into existence a long time ago, in a different world. That world had created him; through him that world still lived. As long as he existed, that world existed. In miniature, it still functioned. His model universe, his recreation. His rational, controlled world, in which each aspect was fully organized, fully analyzed and integrated.

He kept a rational, progressive world alive. A humming oasis of productivity on a dusty, parched planet of decay and silence.

Bors spread out his papers and went to work on the most pressing problem. The transformation from a peace-time economy to full military mobilization. Total military organization of every man, woman, child, piece of equipment and dyne of energy under his direction.

Edward Tolby emerged cautiously. His clothes were torn and ragged. He had lost his pack, crawling through the brambles and vines. His face and hands were bleeding. He was utterly exhausted.

Below him lay a valley. A vast bowl. Fields, houses, highways. Factories. Equipment. Men.

He had been watching the men three hours. Endless streams of them, pouring from the valley into the hills, along the roads and paths. On foot, in trucks, in cars, armored tanks, weapons carriers. Overhead, in fast little jet-fighters and great lumbering bombers. Gleaming ships that took up positions above the troops and prepared for battle.

Battle in the grand style. The two-centuries-old full-scale war that was supposed to have disappeared. But here it was, a vision from the past. He had seen this in the old tapes and records, used in the camp orientation courses. A ghost army resurrected to fight again. A vast host of men and guns, prepared to fight and die.

Tolby climbed down cautiously. At the foot of a slope of boulders a soldier had halted his motorcycle and was setting up a communications antenna and transmitter. Tolby circled, crouched, expertly approached him. A blond-haired youth, fumbling nervously with the wires and relays, licking his lips uneasily, glancing up and grabbing for his rifle at every sound

Tolby took a deep breath. The youth had turned his back; he was tracing a power circuit. It was now or never. With one stride Tolby stepped out, raised his pistol and fired. The clump of equipment and the soldier's rifle vanished.

"Don't make a sound," Tolby said. He peered around. No one had seen; the main line was half a mile to his right. The sun was setting. Great shadows were falling over the hills. The fields were rapidly fading from brown-green to a deep violet. "Put your hands up over your head, clasp them, and get down on your knees."

The youth tumbled down in a frightened heap. "What are you going to do?" He saw the ironite staff, and the color left his face. "You're a League agent!"

"Shut up," Tolby ordered. "First, outline your system of responsibility. *Who's your superior?*"

The youth stuttered forth what he knew. Tolby listened intently. He was satisfied. The usual monolithic structure. Exactly what he wanted.

"At the top," he broke in. "At the top of the pillar. Who has ultimate responsibility?"

"Bors."

"Bors!" Tolby scowled. "That doesn't sound like a name. Sounds like --" He broke off, staggered. "We should have guessed! An old government robot. Still functioning."

The youth saw his chance. He leaped up and darted frantically away.

Tolby shot him above the left ear. The youth pitched over on his face and lay still. Tolby hurried to him and quickly pulled off his dark gray uniform. It was too small for him of course.

But the motorcycle was just right. He'd seen tapes of them; he'd wanted one since he was a child. A fast little motorcycle to propel his weight around. Now he had it.

Half an hour later he was roaring down a smooth, broad highway toward the center of the valley and the buildings that rose against the dark sky. His headlights cut into the blackness; he still wobbled from side to side, but for all practical purposes he had the hang of it. He increased speed; the road shot by, trees and fields, haystacks, stalled farm equipment. All traffic was going against him, troops hurrying to the front.

The front. Lemmings going out into the ocean to drown. A thousand, ten thousand, metal-clad figures, armed and alert. Weighted down with guns and bombs and flame throwers and bacteria pellets.

There was only one hitch. No army opposed them. A mistake had been made. It took two sides to make a war, and only one had been resurrected.

A mile outside the concentration of buildings he pulled his motorcycle off the road and carefully hid it in a haystack. For a moment he considered leaving his ironite staff. Then he shrugged and grabbed it up, along with his pistol. He always carried his staff, it was the League symbol. It represented the walking Anarchists who patrolled the world on foot, the world's protection agency.

He loped through the darkness toward the outline ahead. There were fewer men here. He saw no women or children. Ahead, charged wire was set up. Troops crouched behind it, armed to the teeth. A searchlight moved back and forth across the road. Behind it, radar vanes loomed and behind them an ugly square of concrete. The great offices from which the government was run.

For a time he watched the searchlight. Finally he had its motion plotted. In its glare, the faces of the troops stood out, pale and drawn. Youths. They had never fought. This was their first encounter. They were terrified.

When the light was off him, he stood up and advanced toward the wire. Automatically, a breach was slid back for him. Two guards raised up and awkwardly crossed bayonets ahead of him.

"Show your papers!" one demanded. Young lieutenants. Boys, white-lipped, nervous. Playing soldier.

Pity and contempt made Tolby laugh harshly and push forward. "Get out of my way."

One anxiously flashed a pocket light. "Halt! What's the code-key for this watch?" He blocked Tolby's way with his bayonet, hands twisting convulsively.

Tolby reached in his pocket, pulled out his pistol, and as the searchlight started to swerve back, blasted the two guards. The bayonets clattered down and he dived forward. Yells and shapes rose on all sides. Anguished, terrified shouts. Random firing. The night was lit up, as he dashed and crouched, turned a corner past a supply warehouse, raced up a flight of stairs and into the massive building ahead.

He had to work fast. Gripping his ironite staff, he plunged down a gloomy corridor. His boots echoed. Men poured into the building behind him. Bolts of energy thundered past him; a whole section of the ceiling burst into ash and collapsed behind him.

He reached stairs and climbed rapidly. He came to the next floor and groped for the door handle. Something flickered behind him. He half-turned, his gun quickly up --

A stunning blow sent him sprawling. He crashed against the wall; his gun flew from his fingers. A shape bent over him, rifle gripped. "Who are you? What are you doing here?"

Not a soldier. A stubble-chinned man in stained shirt and rumpled trousers. Eyes puffy and red. A belt of tools, hammer, pliers, screwdriver, a soldering iron, around his waist.

Tolby raised himself up painfully. "If you didn't have that rifle --"

Fowler backed warily away. "Who are you? This floor is forbidden to troops of the line. You know this -" Then he saw the ironite staff. "By God," he said softly. "You're the one they didn't get." He laughed shakily. "You're the one who got away."

Tolby's fingers tightened around the staff, but Fowler reacted instantly. The snout of the rifle jerked up, on a line with Tolby's face.

"Be careful," Fowler warned. He turned slightly; soldiers were hurrying up the stairs, boots drumming, echoing shouts ringing. For a moment he hesitated, then waved his rifle toward the stairs ahead. "Up. Get going."

Toby blinked. "What --"

"Up!" The rifle snout jabbed into Tolby. "Hurry!"

Bewildered, Tolby hurried up the stairs, Fowler close behind him. At the third floor Fowler pushed him roughly through the doorway, the snout of his rifle digging urgently into his back. He found himself in a corridor of doors. Endless offices.

"Keep going," Fowler snarled. "Down the hall. Hurry!"

Tolby hurried, his mind spinning. "What the hell are you --"

"I could never do it," Fowler gasped, close to his ear. "Not in a million years. But it's got to be done."

Tolby halted.

"What is this?"

They faced each other defiantly, faces contorted, eyes blazing. "He's in there," Fowler snapped, indicating a door with his rifle. "You have one chance. Take it."

For a fraction of a second Tolby hesitated. Then he broke away. "Okay. I'll take it."

Fowler followed after him. "Be careful. Watch your step. There's a series of check points. Keep going straight, in all the way. As far as you can go. And for God's sake, hurry!"

His voice faded, as Tolby gained speed. He reached the door and tore it open.

Soldiers and officials ballooned. He threw himself against them; they sprawled and scattered. He scrambled on, as they struggled up and stupidly fumbled for their guns. Through another door, into an inner office, past a desk where a frightened girl sat, eyes wide, mouth open. Then a third door, into an alcove.

A wild-faced youth leaped up and snatched frantically for his pistol. Tolby was unarmed, trapped in the alcove. Figures already pushed against the door behind him. He gripped his ironite staff and backed away as the blond-haired fanatic fired blindly. The bolt burst a foot away; it flicked him with a tongue of heat.

"You dirty anarchist!" Green screamed. His face distorted, he fired again and again. "You murdering anarchist spy!"

Tolby hurled his ironite staff. He put all his strength in it; the staff leaped through the air in a whistling arc, straight at the youth's head. Green saw it coming and ducked. Agile and quick, he jumped away, grinning humorlessly. The staff crashed against the wall and rolled clanging to the floor.

"Your walking staff!" Green gasped and fired.

The bolt missed him on purpose. Green was playing games with him. Tolby bent down and groped frantically for the staff. He picked it up. Green watched, face rigid, eyes glittering. "Throw it again!" he snarled.

Tolby leaped. He took the youth by surprise. Green grunted, stumbled back from the impact, then suddenly fought with maniacal fury.

Tolby was heavier. But he was exhausted. He had crawled hours, beat his way through the mountains, walked endlessly. He was at the end of his strength. The car wreck, the days of walking. Green was in perfect shape. His wiry, agile body twisted away. His hands came up. Fingers dug into Tolby's windpipe; he kicked the youth in the groin. Green staggered back, convulsed and bent over with pain.

"All right," Green gasped, face ugly and dark. His hand fumbled with his pistol. The barrel came up.

Half of Green's head dissolved. His hands opened and his gun fell to the floor. His body stood for a moment, then settled down in a heap, like an empty suit of clothes.

Tolby caught a glimpse of a rifle snout pushed past him -- and the man with the tool belt. The man waved him on frantically. "Hurry!"

Tolby raced down a carpeted hall, between two great flickering yellow lamps. A crowd of officials and soldiers stumbled uncertainly after him, shouting and firing at random. He tore open a thick oak door and halted.

He was in a luxurious chamber. Drapes, rich wallpaper. Lamps. Bookcases. A glimpse of the finery of the past. The wealth of the old days. Thick carpets. Warm radiant heat. A vidscreen. At the far end, a huge mahogany desk.

At the desk a figure sat. Working on heaps of papers and reports, piled masses of material. The figure contrasted starkly with the lushness of the furnishings. It was a great pitted, corroded tank of metal. Bent and greenish, patched and repaired. An ancient machine.

"Is that you, Fowler?" the robot demanded.

Tolby advanced, his ironite staff gripped.

The robot turned angrily. "Who is it? Get Green and carry me down into the shelter. One of the roadblocks has reported a League agent already --" The robot broke off. Its cold, mechanical eye lens bored up at the man. It clicked and whirred in uneasy astonishment. "I don't know you."

It saw the ironite staff.

"League agent," the robot said. "You're the one who got through." Comprehension came. *"The third one.* You came here. You didn't go back." Its metal fingers fumbled clumsily at the objects on the desk, then in the drawer. It found a gun and raised it awkwardly.

Tolby knocked the gun away; it clattered to the floor.

"Run!" he shouted at the robot. "Start running!"

It remained. Tolby's staff came down. The fragile, complex brain-unit of the robot burst apart. Coils, wiring, relay fluid, spattered over his arms and hands. The robot shuddered. Its machinery thrashed. It half-rose from its chair, then swayed and toppled. It crashed full length on the floor, parts and gears rolling in all directions.

"Good God," Tolby said, suddenly seeing it for the first time. Shakily, he bent over its remains. "It was crippled."

Men were all around him. "He's killed Bors!" Shocked, dazed faces. "Bors is dead!"

Fowler came up slowly. "You got him, all right. There's nothing left now."

Tolby stood holding his ironite staff in his hands. "The poor blasted thing," he said softly. "Completely helpless. Sitting there and I came and killed him. He didn't have a chance."

The building was bedlam. Soldiers and officials scurried crazily about, grief-stricken, hysterical. They bumped into each other, gathered in knots, shouted and gave meaningless orders.

Tolby pushed past them; nobody paid any attention to him. Fowler was gathering up the remains of the robot. Collecting the smashed pieces and bits. Tolby stopped beside him. Like Humpty-Dumpty, pulled down off his wall he'd never be back together, not now.

"Where's the woman?" he asked Fowler. "The League agent they brought in."

Fowler straightened up slowly. "I'll take you." He led Tolby down the packed, surging hall, to the hospital wing of the building.

Silvia sat up apprehensively as the two men entered the room. "What's going on?" She recognized her father. "Dad! Thank God! It was you who got out."

Tolby slammed the door against the chaos of sound hammering up and down the corridor. "How are you? How's your leg?"

"Mending. What happened?"

"I got him. The robot. He's dead."

For a moment the three of them were silent. Outside, in the halls, men ran frantically back and forth. Word had already leaked out. Troops gathered in huddled knots outside the building. Lost men, wandering away from their posts. Uncertain. Aimless.

"It's over," Fowler said.

Tolby nodded. "I know."

"They'll get tired of crouching in their foxholes," Fowler said. "They'll come filtering back. As soon as the news reaches them, they'll desert and throw away their equipment."

"Good," Tolby grunted. "The sooner the better." He touched Fowler's rifle. "You, too, I hope."

Silvia hesitated. "Do you think --"

"Think what?"

"Did we make a mistake?"

Tolby grinned wearily. "Hell of a time to think about that."

"He was doing what he thought was right. They built up their homes and factories. This whole area. . . They turn out a lot of goods. I've been watching through the window. It's made me think. They've done so much. Made so much."

"Made a lot of guns," Tolby said.

"We have guns, too. We kill and destroy. We have all the disadvantages and none of the advantages."

"We don't have war," Tolby answered quietly. "To defend this neat little organization there are ten thousand men up there in those hills. All waiting to fight. Waiting to drop their bombs and bacteria pellets, to keep this place running. But they won't. Pretty soon they'll give up and start to trickle back."

"This whole system will decay rapidly," Fowler said. "He was already losing his control. He couldn't keep the clock back much longer."

"Anyhow, it's done," Silvia murmured. "We did our job." She smiled a little. "Bors did his job and we did ours. But the times were against him and with us."

"That's right," Tolby agreed. "We did our job. And we'll never be sorry."

Fowler said nothing. He stood with his hands in his pockets, gazing silently out the window. His fingers were touching something. Three undamaged synapsis-coils. Intact memory elements from the dead robot, snatched from the scattered remains.

Just in case, he said to himself. *Just in case the times change.*

James P. Crow

"You're a nasty little *human being*," the newly-formed Z Type robot shrilled peevishly.

Donnie flushed and slunk away. It was true. He was a human being, a human child. And there was nothing science could do. He was stuck with it. A human being in a robot's world.

He wished he were dead. He wished he lay under the grass and the worms were eating him up and crawling through him and devouring his brain, his poor miserable human's brain. The Z-236r, his robot companion, wouldn't have anybody to play with and it would be sorry.

"Where are you going?" Z-236r demanded.

"Home."

"Sissy."

Donnie didn't reply. He gathered up his set of fourth dimensional chess, stuffed it in his pocket, and walked off between the rows of ecarda trees, toward the human quarter. Behind him, Z236r stood gleaming in the late afternoon sun, a pale tower of metal and plastic.

"See if I care," Z-236r shouted sullenly. "Who wants to play with a human being, anyhow? Go on home. You you smell."

Donnie said nothing. But he hunched over a little more. And his chin sank lower against his chest.

"Well, it happened," Edgar Parks said gloomily to his wife, across the kitchen table.

Grace looked quickly up. "It?"

"Donnie learned his place today. He told me while I was changing my clothes. One of the new robots he was playing with. Called him a human being. Poor kid. Why the hell do they have to rub it in? Why can't they let us alone?"

"So that's why he didn't want any dinner. He's in his room. I knew something had happened." Grace touched her husband's hand. "He'll get over it. We all have to learn the hard way. He's strong. He'll snap back."

Ed Parks got up from the table and moved into the living-room of his modest five-room dwelling unit, located in the section of the city set aside for humans. He didn't feel like eating. "Robots." He clenched his fists futilely. "I'd like to get hold of one of them. Just once. Get my hands into their guts. Rip out handfuls of wires and parts. Just once before I die."

"Maybe you'll get your chance."

"No. No, it'll never come to that. Anyhow, humans wouldn't be able to run things without robots. It's true, honey. Humans haven't got the integration to maintain a society. The Lists prove that twice a year. Let's face it. Humans are inferior to robots. But it's their damn holding it up to us! Like today with Donnie. Holding it up to our faces. I don't mind being a robot's body servant. It's a good job. Pays well and the work is light. But when my kid gets told he's"

Ed broke off. Donnie had come out of his room slowly, into the living-room. "Hi, Dad."

"Hi, son." Ed thumped the boy gently on the back. "How you doing? Want to take in a show tonight?"

Humans entertained nightly on the vid-screens. Humans made good entertainers. That was one area the robots couldn't compete in. Human beings painted and wrote and danced and sang and acted for the amusement of robots. They cooked better, too, but robots didn't eat. Human beings had their place. They were understood and wanted: as body servants, entertainers, clerks, gardeners, construction workers, repairmen, odd-jobbers and factory workers.

But when it came to something like civic control coordinator or traffic supervisor for the usone tapes that fed energy into the planet's twelve hydrosystems

"Dad," Donnie said, "can I ask you something?"

"Sure." Ed sat down on the couch with a sigh. He leaned back and crossed his legs. "What is it?"

Donnie sat quietly beside him, his little round face serious. "Dad, I want to ask you about the Lists."

"Oh, yeah." Ed rubbed his jaw. "That's right. Lists in a few weeks. Time to start boning up for your entry. We'll get out some of the sample tests and go over them. Maybe between the two of us we can get you ready for Class Twenty."

"Listen." Donnie leaned close to his father, his voice low and intense. "Dad, how many humans have ever passed their Lists?"

Ed got up abruptly and paced around the room, filling his pipe and frowning. "Well, son, that's hard to say. I mean, humans don't have access to the C-Bank records. So I can't check to see. The law says any human who gets a score in the top forty per cent is eligible for classification with a gradual upward gradation according to subsequent showing. I don't know how many humans have been able to"

"Has *any* human ever passed his List?" Ed swallowed nervously.

"Gosh, kid. I don't know. I mean, I don't honestly know of any, when you put it like that. Maybe not. The Lists have been conducted only three hundred years. Before that the Government was reactionary and forbade humans to compete with robots. Nowadays, we have a liberal Government and we can compete on the Lists and if we get high enough scores. . ." His voice wavered and faded. "No, kid," he said miserably. "No human ever passed a List. We're just not smart enough."

The room was silent. Donnie nodded faintly, expressionless. Ed didn't look at him. He concentrated on his pipe, hands shaking.

"It's not so bad," Ed said huskily. "I have a good job. I'm body servant to a hell of a fine N Type robot. I get big tips at Christmas and Easter. It gives me time off when I'm sick." He cleared his throat noisily. "It's not so bad."

Grace was standing at the door. Now she came into the room, eyes bright. "No, not bad. Not at all. You open doors for it, bring its instruments to it, make calls for it, run errands for it, oil it, repair it, sing to it, talk to it, scan tapes for it"

"Shut up," Ed muttered irritably. "What the hell should I do? Quit? Maybe I should mow lawns like John Hollister and Pete Klein. At least my robot calls me by name. Like a living thing. It calls me Ed."

"Will a human ever pass a List?" Donnie asked.

"Yes," Grace said sharply.

Ed nodded. "Sure, kid. Of course. Someday maybe humans and robots will live together in equality. There's an Equality Party among the robots. Holds ten seats in the Congress. They think humans should be admitted without Lists. Since it's obvious" He broke off. "I mean, since no humans have ever been able to pass their Lists so far"

"Donnie," Grace said fiercely, bending down over her son, "Listen to me. I want you to pay attention. Nobody knows this. The robots don't talk about it. Humans don't know. But it's true."

"What is it?"

"I know of a human being who who's classified. He passed his Lists. Ten years ago. And he's gone up. He's up to Class Two. Someday he'll be Class One. Do you hear? A human being. And he's going up."

Donnie's face showed doubt. "Really?" The doubt turned to wistful hope. "Class Two? No kidding?"

"It's just a story," Ed grunted. "I've heard that all my life."

"It's true! I heard two robots talking about it when I was cleaning up one of the Engineering Units. They stopped when they noticed me."

"What's his name?" Donnie asked, wide-eyed.

"James P. Crow," Grace said proudly.

"Strange name," Ed murmured.

"That's his name. I know. It's not a story. It's true! And sometime, someday, he'll be on the top level. On the Supreme Council."

Bob McIntyre lowered his voice. "Yeah, it's true, all right. James P. Crow is his name."

"It's not a legend?" Ed demanded eagerly.

"There really is such a human. And he's Class Two. Gone all the way up. Passed his Lists like *that*." McIntyre snapped his fingers. "The robots hush it up, but it's a fact. And the news is spreading. More and more humans know."

The two men had stopped by the service entrance of the enormous Structural Research Building. Robot officials moved busily in and out through the main doors, at the front of the building. Robot planners who guided Terran society with skill and efficiency.

Robots ran Earth. It had always been that way. The history tapes said so. Humans had been invented during the Total War of the Eleventh Millibar. All types of weapons had been tested and used; humans were one of many. The War had utterly wrecked society. For decades after, anarchy and ruin lay everywhere. Only gradually had society reformed under the patient guidance of robots. Humans had been useful in the reconstruction. But why they had originally been made, what they had been used for, how they had served in the War all knowledge had perished in the hydrogen bomb blasts. The historians had to fill in with conjecture. They did so.

"Why such a strange name?" Ed asked.

McIntyre shrugged. "All I know is he's sub-Advisor to the Northern Security Conference. And in line for the Council when he makes Class One."

"What do the robs think?"

"They don't like it. But there's nothing they can do. The law says they have to let a human hold a job if he's qualified. They never thought a human would be qualified, of course. But this Crow passed his Lists."

"It certainly is strange. A human, smarter than the robs. I wonder why."

"He was an ordinary repairman. A mechanic, fixing machinery and designing circuits. Unclassified, of course. Then suddenly he passed his first List. Entered Class Twenty. He rose the next bi-annual to Class Nineteen. They had to put him to work." McIntyre chuckled. "Too damn bad, isn't it? They have to sit with a human being."

"How do they react?"

"Some quit. Walk out, rather than sit with a human. But most stay. A lot of robs are decent. They try hard."

"I'd sure like to meet this fellow Crow."

McIntyre frowned. "Well"

"What is it?"

"I understand he doesn't like to be seen with humans too much."

"Why not?" Ed bristled. "What's wrong with humans? Is he too high and mighty, sitting up there with robots"

"It's not that." There was a strange look in McIntyre's eyes. A yearning, distant look. "It's not just that, Ed. He's up to something. Something important. I shouldn't be saying. But it's big. Big as hell."

"What is it?"

"I can't say. But wait until he gets on the Council. Wait." McIntyre's eyes were feverish. "It's so big it'll shake the world. The stars and the sun'll shake."

"What is it?"

"I don't know. But Crow's got something up his sleeve. Something incredibly big. We're all waiting for it. Waiting for the day. . ."

James P. Crow sat at his polished mahogany desk, thinking. That wasn't his real name, of course. He had taken it after the first experiments, grinning to himself as he did so. Nobody would ever know what it meant; it would remain a private joke, personal and unannounced. But it was a good joke nonetheless. Biting and appropriate.

He was a small man. Irish-German. A little lean light-skinned man with blue eyes and sandy hair that fell down in his face and had to be brushed back. He wore unpressed baggy pants and rolled-up sleeves. He was nervous, high-strung. He smoked all day and drank black coffee and usually couldn't sleep at night. But there was a lot on his mind.

A hell of a lot. Crow got abruptly to his feet and paced over to the vidsender. "Send in the Commissioner of Colonies," he ordered.

The Commissioner's metal and plastic body pushed through the door, into the office. An R Type robot, patient and efficient. "You wished to" It broke off, seeing a human. For a second its pale eye lens flickered doubtfully. A faint sheen of distaste spread across its features. "You wished to see me?"

Crow had seen that expression before. Endless times. He was used to it almost. The surprise, and then the lofty withdrawal, the cold, clipped formality. He was "Mister Crow." Not Jim. The law made them address him as an equal. It hurt some of them more than others. Some showed it without restraint. This one held its feelings back a trifle; Crow was its official superior.

"Yes, I wished to see you," Crow said calmly. "I want your report. Why hasn't it come in?"

The robot stalled, still lofty and withdrawn. "Such a report takes time. We're doing the best we can."

"I want it within two weeks. No later."

The robot struggled with itself, life-long prejudices versus the requirements of Governmental codes. "All right, sir. The report will be ready in two weeks." It moved out of the office. The door formed behind it.

Crow let his breath out with a rush. Doing the best they could? Hardly. Not to please a human being. Even if he was at Advisory Level, Class Two. They all dragged their feet, all the way down the line. Little things here and there.

His door melted and a robot wheeled quickly into the office. "I say there, Crow. Got a minute?"

"Of course." Crow grinned. "Come in and sit down. I'm always glad to talk to you."

The robot dumped some papers on Crow's desk. "Tapes and such. Business trifles." He eyed Crow intently. "You look upset. Anything happen?"

"A report I want. Overdue. Somebody taking its time."

L-87t grunted. "Same old stuff. By the way. . . We're having a meeting tonight. Want to come over and make a speech? Should have a good turn out."

"Meeting?"

"Party meeting. Equality." L-87t made a quick sign with its right gripper, a sort of half-arc in the air. The Equality sign. "We'd be glad to have you, Jim. Want to come?"

"No. I'd like to, but I have things to do."

"Oh." The robot moved toward the door. "All right. Thanks anyhow." It lingered at the door. "You'd give us a shot in the arm, you know. Living proof of our contention that a human being is the equal of a robot and should be afforded such recognition."

Crow smiled faintly. "But a human isn't the equal of a robot."

L-87t sputtered indignantly. "What are you saying? Aren't you the living proof? Look at your List scores. Perfect. Not a mistake. And in a couple of weeks you'll be Class One. Highest there is."

Crow shook his head. "Sorry. A human isn't the equal of a robot anymore than he's the equal of a stove. Or a diesel motor. Or a snowplow. There are a lot of things a human can't do. Let's face facts."

L-87t was baffled. "But"

"I mean it. You're ignoring reality. Humans and robots are completely different. We humans can sing, act, write plays, stories, operas, paint, design sets, flower gardens, buildings, cook delicious meals, make love, scratch sonnets on menus and robots can't. But robots can build elaborate cities and machines that function perfectly, work for days without rest, think without emotional interruption, gestalt complex data without a time lag.

"Humans excel in some fields, robots in others. Humans have highly developed emotions and feelings. Esthetic awareness. We're sensitive to colors and sounds and textures and soft music mixed with wine. All very fine things. Worthwhile. But realms totally beyond robots. Robots are purely intellectual. Which is fine, too. Both realms are fine. Emotional humans, sensitive to art and music and drama. Robots who think and plan and design machinery. But that doesn't mean we're both the same."

L-87t shook its head sadly. "I don't understand you, Jim. Don't you want to help your race?"

"Of course. But realistically. Not by ignoring facts and making an illusionary assertion that men and robots are interchangeable. Identical elements."

A curious look slid across L-87t's eye lens. "What's your solution, then?"

Crow clamped his jaw tight. "Stick around another few weeks and maybe you'll see."

Crow headed out of the Terran Security Building and along the street. Around him robots streamed, bright hulls of metal and plastic and d/n fluid. Except for body servants, humans never came to this area. This was the managerial section of the city, the core, the nucleus, where the planning and organization went on. From this area the life of the city was controlled. Robots were everywhere. In the surface cars, on the moving ramps, the balconies, entering buildings, streaming out, standing in pale glowing knots here and there like Roman Senators, talking and discussing business.

A few greeted him, faintly, formally, with a nod of their metal heads. And then turned their backs. Most robots ignored him or pulled aside to avoid contact. Sometimes a clump of talking robots would become abruptly silent, as Crow pushed past. Robot eye lenses fixed on him, solemn and half astonished. They noticed his arm color, Class Two. Surprise and indignation. And after he had passed, a quick angry buzz of resentment. Backward glances at him as he threaded his way toward the human quarter.

A pair of humans stood in front of the Domestic Control Offices, armed with pruning shears and rakes. Gardeners, weeding and watering the lawns of the big public building. They watched Crow pass with excited stares. One waved nervously at him, feverish and hopeful. A menial human waving at the only human ever to reach classification.

Crow waved back briefly.

The two humans' eyes grew wide with awe and reverence. They were still looking after him when he turned the corner at the main intersection and mixed with the business crowds shopping at the trans-planet marts.

Goods from the wealthy colonies of Venus and Mars and Ganymede filled the open-air marts. Robots drifted in swarms, sampling and pricing and discussing and gossiping. A few humans were visible, mostly household servants in charge of maintenance, stocking up on supplies. Crow edged his way through and beyond the marts. He was approaching the human quarter of the city. He could smell it already. The faint pungent scent of humans.

The robots, of course, were odorless. In a world of odorless machines the human scent stood out in bold relief. The human quarter was a section of the city once prosperous. Humans had moved in and property values had dropped. Gradually the houses had been abandoned by robots and now humans exclusively lived there. Crow, in spite of his position, was obliged to live in the human quarter. His house, a uniform five-room dwelling, identical with the others, was located to the rear of the quarter. One house of many.

He held his hand up to the front door and the door melted. Crow entered quickly and the door reformed. He glanced at his watch. Plenty of time. An hour before he was due back at his desk.

He rubbed his hands. It was always a thrilling moment to come here, to his personal quarters, where he had grown up, lived as an ordinary unclassified human being before he had come across *it* and begun his meteoric ascent into the upper-class regions.

Crow passed through the small silent house, to the work shed in back. He unlocked the bolted doors and slid them aside. The shed was hot and dry. He clicked off the alarm system. Complex tangles of bells and wires that were really unnecessary: robots never entered the human section, and humans seldom stole from each other.

Locking the doors behind him, Crow seated himself before a bank of machinery assembled in the center of the shed. He snapped on the power and the machinery hummed into life. Dials and meters swung into activity. Lights glowed.

Before him, a square window of gray faded to light pink and shimmered slightly. The Window. Crow's pulse throbbed painfully. He flicked a key. The Window clouded and showed a scene. He slid a tape scanner before the Window and activated it. The scanner clicked as the Window gained shape. Forms moved, dim forms that wavered and hesitated. He steadied the picture.

Two robots were standing behind a table. They moved quickly, jerkily. He slowed them down. The two robots were handling something. Crow increased the power of the image and the objects bloated up, to be caught by the scanning lens and preserved on tape.

The robots were sorting Lists. Class One Lists. Grading and dividing them into groups. Several hundred packets of questions and answers. Before the table a restless crowd waited, eager robots waiting to hear their scores. Crow speeded the image up. The two robots leaped into activity, tossing and arranging Lists in a blur of energy. Then the master Class One List was held up

The List. Crow caught it in the Window, dropping the velocity to zero. The List was held, fixed tight like a specimen on a slide. The tape scanner hummed away, recording the questions and answers.

He felt no guilt. No sting of conscience at using a Time Window to see the results of future Lists. He had been doing it ten years, all the way up from the bottom, from unclassified up to the top List, to Class One. He had never kidded himself. Without advance sight of the answers, he could never have passed. He would still be unclassified, at the bottom of the pile, along with the great undifferentiated mass of humans.

The Lists were geared to robot minds. Made up by robots, phased to a robot culture. A culture which was alien to humans, to which humans had to make difficult adjustment. No wonder only robots passed their Lists.

Crow wiped the scene from the Window and threw the scanner aside. He sent the Window back into time, spinning back through the centuries into the past. He never tired of seeing the early days, the days before the Total War wrecked human society and destroyed all human tradition. The days when man lived without robots.

He fiddled with the dials, capturing a moment. The Window showed robots building up their post-war society, swarming over their ruined planet, erecting vast cities and buildings, clearing away the debris. With humans as slaves. Second-class servant citizens.

He saw the Total War, the rain of death from the sky. The blossoming pale funnels of destruction. He saw man's society dissolve into radioactive particles. All human knowledge and culture lost in the chaos.

And once again, he caught his favorite of all scenes. A scene he had examined repeatedly, enjoying with acute satisfaction this unique sight. A scene of human beings in an undersurface lab, in the early days of the war. Designing and building the first robots, the original A Type robots, four centuries before.

Ed Parks walked home slowly, holding his son's hand. Donnie gazed down at the ground. He said nothing. His eyes were red and puffy. He was pale with misery.

"I'm sorry, Dad," he muttered.

Ed's grip tightened. "It's okay, kid. You did your best. Don't worry about it. Maybe next time. We'll get started practicing sooner." He cursed under his breath. "Those lousy metal tubs. Damn soul-less heaps of tin!"

It was evening. The sun was setting. The two of them climbed the porch steps slowly and entered the house. Grace met them at the door. "No luck?" She studied their faces. "I can see. Same old story."

"Same old story," Ed said bitterly. "He didn't have a chance. Hopeless."

From the dining-room came a murmur of sound. Voices, men and women.

"Who's in there?" Ed demanded irritably. "Do we have to have company? For God's sake, today of all days"

"Come on." Grace pulled him toward the kitchen. "Some news. Maybe it'll make you feel better. Come along, Donnie. This will interest you, too."

Ed and Donnie entered the kitchen. It was full of people. Bob McIntyre and his wife Pat. John Hollister and his wife Joan and their two daughters. Pete Klein and Rose Klein. Neighbors, Nat Johnson and Tim Davis and Barbara Stanley. An eager murmur buzzed through the room. Everybody was grouped around the table, excited and nervous. Sandwiches and beer bottles were piled up in heaps. The men and women were laughing and grinning happily, eyes bright with agitation.

"What's up?" Ed grumbled. "Why the party?"

Bob McIntyre clapped him on the shoulder. "How you doing, Ed? We've got news." He rattled a public news tape. "Get ready. Brace yourself."

"Read it to him," Pete Klein said excitedly.

"Go on! Read it!" They all grouped around McIntyre. "Let's hear it again!"

McIntyre's face was alive with emotion. "Well, Ed. This is it. He made it. He's there."

"Who? Who made what?"

"Crow. Jim Crow. He made Class One." The tape spool trembled in McIntyre's hand. "He's been named to the Supreme Council. Understand? He's in. A human being. A member of the supreme governing body of the planet."

"Gosh," Donnie said, awed.

"Now what?" Ed asked. "What's he going to do?"

McIntyre grinned shakily. "We'll know, soon. He's got something. We know. We can feel it. And we should start seeing it in action any time, now."

Crow strode briskly into the Council Chamber, his portfolio under his arm. He wore a slick new suit. His hair was combed. His shoes were shined. "Good day," he said politely.

The five robots regarded him with mixed feelings. They were old, over a century old. The powerful N Type that had dominated the social scene since its construction. And an incredibly ancient D Type, almost three centuries old. As Crow advanced toward his seat the five robots stepped away, leaving a wide path for him.

"You," one of the N Types said. "You are the new Council member?"

"That's right." Crow took his seat. "Care to examine my credentials?"

"Please."

Crow passed over the card plate given him by the Lists Committee. The five robots studied it intently. Finally they passed it back.

"It appears to be in order," the D admitted reluctantly.

"Of course." Crow unzipped his portfolio. "I wish to begin work at once. There's quite a lot of material to cover. I have some reports and tapes you'll find worth your while."

The robots took their places slowly, eyes still on Jim Crow. "This is incredible," the D said. "Are you serious? Can you really expect to sit with us?"

"Of course," Crow snapped. "Let's forgo this and get down to business."

One of the N Types leaned toward him, massive and contemptuous, its patina-encrusted hull glinting dully. "Mr Crow," it said icily. "You must understand this is utterly impossible. In spite of the legal ruling and your technical right to sit on this"

Crow smiled calmly back. "I suggest you check my Listing scoring. You'll discover I've made no errors in all twenty Lists. A perfect score. To my knowledge, none of you has achieved a perfect score. Therefore, according to the Governmental ruling contained in the official Lists Committee decree, I'm your superior."

The word fell like a bomb shell. The five robots slumped down in their seats, stricken. Their eye lenses flickered uneasily. A worried hum rose in pitch, filling the chamber.

"Let's see," an N murmured, extending his gripper. Crow tossed his List sheets over and the five robots each scanned them rapidly.

"It's true," the D stated. "Incredible. No robot has ever achieved a perfect score. This human outranks us, according to our own laws."

"Now," Crow said. "Let's get down to business." He spread out his tapes and reports. "I won't waste any time. I have a proposal to make. An important proposal bearing on the most critical problem of this society."

"What problem is that?" an X asked apprehensively.

Crow was tense. "The problem of humans. Humans occupying an inferior position in a robot world. Menials in an alien culture. Servants of robots."

Silence.

The five robots sat frozen. It had happened. The thing they had feared. Crow sat back in his chair, lighting a cigarette. The robots watched each motion, his hands, the cigarette, the smoke, the match as he ground it out underfoot. The moment had come.

"What do you propose?" the D asked at last, with metallic dignity. "What is this proposal of yours?"

"I propose you robots evacuate Earth at once. Pack up and leave. Emigrate to the colonies. Ganymede, Mars, Venus. Leave Earth to us humans."

The robots got instantly up. "Incredible! We built this world. This is our world! Earth belongs to us. It has always belonged to us."

"Has it?" Crow said grimly.

An uneasy chill moved through the robots. They hesitated, strangely alarmed. "Of course," the D murmured.

Crow reached toward his heap of tapes and reports. The robots watched his movement with fear. "What is that?" an N demanded nervously. "What do you have there?"

"Tapes," Crow said.

"What kind of tapes?"

"History tapes." Crow signaled and a gray-clad human servant hurried into the chamber with a tape scanner. "Thanks," Crow said. The human started out. "Wait. You might like to stay and watch this, my friend."

The servant's eyes bulged. He found a place in the back and stood trembling and watching.

"Highly irregular," the D protested. "What are you doing? What is this?"

"Watch." Crow snapped on the scanner, feeding the first tape into it. In the air in the center of the Council table, a three-dimensional image formed. "Keep your eyes on this. You'll remember this moment for a long time."

The image hardened. They were looking into the Time Window. A scene from the Total War was in motion. Men, human technicians, working frantically in an undersurface lab. Assembling something. Assembling

The human servant squawked wildly. "An A! It's a Type A robot! They're making it!"

The five Council robots buzzed in consternation. "Get that servant out of here!" the D ordered.

The scene changed. It showed the first robots, the original Type A, rising to the surface to fight the war. Other early robots appeared, snaking through the ruins and ash, approaching warily. The robots clashed. Bursts of white light. Gleaming clouds of particles.

"Robots were originally designed as soldiers," Crow explained. "Then more advanced types were produced to act as technicians and lab workers and machinists."

The scene showed an undersurface factory. Rows of robots worked presses and stampers. The robots worked rapidly, efficiently supervised by human foremen.

"These tapes are fake!" an N cried angrily. "Do you expect us to believe this?"

A new scene formed. Robots, more advanced, types more complex and elaborate. Taking over more and more economic and industrial functions as humans were destroyed by the War.

"At first robots were simple," Crow explained. "They served simple needs. Then, as the War progressed, more advanced types were created. Finally, humans were making Types D and E. Equal to humans and in conceptual faculties, superior to humans."

"This is insane!" an N stated. "Robots evolved. The early types were simple because they were original stages, primitive forms that gave rise to more complex forms. The law of evolution fully explains this process."

A new scene formed. The last stages of the War. Robots fighting men. Robots eventually winning. The complete chaos of the latter years. Endless wastes of rolling ash and radioactive particles. Miles of ruin.

"All cultural records were destroyed," Crow said. "Robots emerged masters without knowing how or why, or in what manner they came into being. But now you see the facts. Robots were created as human tools. During the War they got out of hand."

He snapped off the tape scanner. The image faded. The five robots sat in stunned silence.

Crow folded his arms. "Well? What do you say?" He jerked his thumb at the human servant crouching in the rear of the chamber, dazed and astonished. "Now you know and now he knows. What do you imagine he's thinking? I can tell you. He's thinking"

"How did you get these tapes?" the D demanded. "They can't be genuine. They must be fakes."

"Why weren't they found by our archeologists?" an N shouted shrilly.

"I took them personally," Crow said.

"You took them? What do you mean?"

"Through a Time Window." Crow tossed a thick package onto the table. "Here are the schematics. You can build a Time Window yourself if you want."

"A time machine." The D snatched up the package and leafed through the contents. "You saw into the past." Dawning realization showed on its ancient face. "Then"

"He saw ahead!" an N searched wildly. "Into the future! That explains his perfect Lists. He scanned them in advance."

Crow rattled his papers impatiently. "You've heard my proposal. You've seen the tapes. If you vote down the proposal I'll release the tapes publicly. And the schematics. Every human in the world will know the true story of his origin, and yours."

"So?" an N said nervously. "We can handle humans. If there's an uprising we'll put it down."

"Will you?" Crow got suddenly to his feet, his face hard. "Consider. Civil war raging over the whole planet. Men on one side, centuries of pent-up hatred. On the other side robots suddenly deprived of their myth. Knowing they were originally mechanical tools. Are you sure you'll come out on top this time? Are you positive?"

The robots were silent.

"If you'll evacuate Earth I'll suppress the tapes. The two races can go on, each with its own culture and society. Humans here on Earth. Robots on the colonies. Neither one master. Neither one slave."

The five robots hesitated, angry and resentful. "But we worked centuries to build up this planet! It won't make sense. Our leaving. What'll we say? What'll we give as our reason?"

Crow smiled harshly. "You can say Earth isn't adequate for the great original master race."

There was silence. The four Type N robots looked at each other nervously, drawing together in a whispered huddle. The massive D sat silent, its archaic brass eye lens fixed intently on Crow, a baffled, defeated expression on its face.

Calmly, Jim Crow waited.

"Can I shake your hand?" L-87t asked timidly. "I'll be going soon. I'm in one of the first loads."

Crow stuck out his hand briefly and L-87t shook, a little embarrassed.

"I hope it works out," L-87t ventured. "Vid us from time to time. Keep us posted."

Outside the Council Buildings the blaring voices of the street speakers were beginning to disturb the late afternoon gloom. All up and down the city the speakers roared out their message, the Council Directive.

Men, scurrying home from work, paused to listen. In the uniform houses in the human quarter men and women glanced up, pausing in their routine of living, curious and attentive.

Everywhere, in all cities of Earth, robots and human beings ceased their activities and looked up as the Government speakers roared into life.

"This is to announce that the Supreme Council has decreed the rich colony planets Venus, Mars, and Ganymede, are to be set aside exclusively for the use of robots. No humans will be permitted outside of Earth. In order to take advantage of the superior resources and living conditions of these colonies, all robots now on Earth are to be transferred to the colony of their choice.

"The Supreme Council has decided that Earth is no fit place for robots. Its wasted and still partly-devastated condition renders it unworthy of the robot race. All robots are to be conveyed to their new homes in the colonies as quickly as adequate transportation can be arranged.

"In no case can humans enter the colony areas. The colonies are exclusively for the use of robots. The human population will be permitted to remain on Earth.

"This is to announce that the Supreme Council had decreed that the rich colony planets of Venus"

Crow moved away from the window, satisfied.

He returned to his desk and continued assembling papers and reports in neat piles, glancing at them briefly as he classified them and laid them aside.

"I hope you humans will get along all right," L-87t repeated. Crow continued checking the heaps of top-level reports, marking them with his writing stick. Working rapidly, with absorbed attention, deep in his work. He scarcely noticed the robot lingering at the door. "Can you give me some idea of the government you'll set up?"

Crow glanced up impatiently. "What?"

"Your form of government. How will your society be ruled, now that you've maneuvered us off Earth? What sort of government will take the place of our Supreme Council and Congress?"

Crow didn't answer. He had already returned to his work. There was a strange granite cast to his face, a peculiar hardness L-87t had never seen.

"Who'll run things?" L-87t asked. "Who'll be the Government now that we're gone? You said yourself humans show no ability to manage a complex modern society. Can you find a human capable of keeping the wheels turning? Is there a human being capable of leading mankind?"

Crow smiled thinly. And continued working.

Prominent Author

"My husband," said Mary Ellis, "although he is a very prompt man, and hasn't been late to work in twenty-five years, is actually still some place around the house." She sipped at her faintly scented hormone and carbohydrate drink. "As a matter of fact, he won't be leaving for another ten minutes."

"Incredible," said Dorothy Lawrence, who had finished *her* drink, and now basked in the dermalmist spray that descended over her virtually unclad body from an automatic jet above the couch. "What they won't think of next!"

Mrs Ellis beamed proudly, as if she personally were an employee of Terran Development. "Yes, it is incredible. According to somebody down at the office, the whole history of civilization can be explained in terms of transportation techniques. Of course, I don't know anything about history. That's for Government research people. But from what this man told Henry --"

"Where's my briefcase?" came a fussy voice from the bedroom. "Good Lord, Mary. I know I left it on the clothes-cleaner last night."

"You left it upstairs," Mary replied, raising her voice slightly. "Look in the closet."

"Why would it be in the closet?" Sounds of angry stirring around. "You'd think a man's own briefcase would be safe." Henry Ellis stuck his head into the living-room briefly. "I found it. Hello, Mrs Lawrence."

"Good morning," Dorothy Lawrence replied. "Mary was explaining that you're still here."

"Yes, I'm still here." Ellis straightened his tie, as the mirror revolved slowly around him. "Anything you want me to pick up downtown, honey?"

"No," Mary replied. "Nothing I can think of. I'll vid you at the office if I remember something."

"Is it true," Mrs Lawrence asked, "that *as soon as you step into it* you're all the way downtown?"

"Well, almost all the way."

"A hundred and sixty miles! It's beyond belief. Why, it takes my husband two and a half hours to get his monojet through the commercial lanes and down at the parking lot then walk all the way up to his office."

"I know," Ellis muttered, grabbing his hat and coat. "Used to take me about that long. But no more." He kissed his wife good-bye. "So long. See you tonight. Nice to have seen you again, Mrs Lawrence."

"Can I -- watch?" Mrs Lawrence asked hopefully.

"Watch? Of course, of course." Ellis hurried through the house, out the back door and down the steps into the yard. "Come along!" he shouted impatiently. "I don't want to be late. It's nine-fifty-nine and I have to be at my desk by ten."

Mrs Lawrence hurried eagerly after Ellis. In the backyard stood a big circular hoop that gleamed brightly in the mid-morning sun. Ellis turned some controls at the base. The hoop changed color, from silver to a shimmering red.

"Here I go!" Ellis shouted. He stepped briskly into the hoop. The hoop fluttered about him. There was a faint *pop*. The glow died.

"Good Heavens!" Mrs Lawrence gasped. "He's gone!"

"He's in downtown N'York," Mary Ellis corrected. "I wish *my* husband had a Jiffi-scuttler. When they show up on the market commercially maybe I can afford to get him one."

"Oh, they're very handy," Mary Ellis agreed. "He's probably saying hello to the boys right this minute."

Henry Ellis was in a sort of tunnel. All round him a gray, formless tube stretched out in both directions, a sort of hazy sewer-pipe.

Framed in the opening behind him, he could see the faint outline of his own house. His back porch and yard, Mary standing on the steps in her red bra and slacks. Mrs Lawrence beside her in green-checkered shorts. The cedar tree and rows of petunias. A hill. The neat little houses of Cedar Groves, Pennsylvania. And in front of him --

New York City. A wavering glimpse of the busy street-corner in front of his office. The great building itself, a section of concrete and glass and steel. People moving. Skyscrapers. Monojets landing in swarms. Aerial signs. Endless white-collar workers hurrying everywhere, rushing to their offices.

Ellis moved leisurely toward the New York end. He had taken the Jiffi-scuttler often enough to know just exactly how many steps it was. Five steps. Five steps along the wavery gray tunnel and he had gone a hundred and sixty miles. He halted, glancing back. So far he had gone three steps. Ninety-six miles. More than half way.

The fourth dimension was a wonderful thing. Ellis lit his pipe, leaning his briefcase against his trouser-leg and groping in his coat pocket for his tobacco. He still had thirty seconds to get to work. Plenty of time. The pipe-lighter flared and he sucked in expertly. He snapped the lighter shut and restored it to his pocket.

A wonderful thing, all right. The Jiffi-scuttler had already revolutionized society. It was now possible to go anywhere in the world *instantly*, with no time lapse. And without wading through endless lanes of other monojets, also going places. The transportation problem had been a major headache since the middle of the twentieth century. Every year more families moved from the cities out into the country, adding numbers to the already swollen swarms that choked the roads and jetlanes. But it was all solved now. An *infinite* number of Jiffi-scuttlers could be set up; there was no interference between them. The Jiffi-scuttler bridged distances non-spacially, through another dimension of some kind (they hadn't explained that part too clearly to him). For a flat thousand credits any Terran family could have Jiffi-scuttler hoops set up, one in the back yard -- the other in Berlin, or Bermuda, or San Francisco, or Port Said. Anywhere in the world. Of course, there was one drawback. The hoop had to be anchored in one specific spot. You picked your destination and that was that. But for an office worker, it was perfect. Step in one end, step out the other. Five steps -- a hundred and sixty miles. A hundred and sixty miles that had been a two-hour nightmare of grinding gears and sudden jolts, monojets cutting in and out, speeders, reckless flyers, alert cops waiting to pounce, ulcers and bad tempers. It was all over now. All over for him, at least, as an employee of Terran Development, the manufacturer of the Jiffi-scuttler. And soon for everybody, when they were commercially on the market.

Ellis sighed. Time for work. He could see Ed Hall racing up the steps of the TD building two at a time. Tony Franklin hurrying after him. Time to get moving. He bent down and reached for his briefcase --

It was then he saw them.

The wavery gray haze was thin there. A sort of thin spot where the shimmer wasn't so strong. Just a bit beyond his foot and past the corner of his briefcase.

Beyond the thin spot were three tiny figures. Just beyond the gray waver. Incredibly small men, no larger than insects. Watching him with incredulous astonishment.

Ellis gazed down intently, his briefcase forgotten. The three tiny men were equally dumbfounded. None of them stirred, the three tiny figures, rigid with awe. Henry Ellis bent over, his mouth open, eyes wide.

A fourth little figure joined the others. They all stood rooted to the spot, eyes bulging. They had on some kind of robes. Brown robes and sandals. Strange, unTerran costumes. Everything about them was unTerran. Their size, their oddly colored dark faces, their clothing -- and their voices.

Suddenly the tiny figures were shouting shrilly at each other, squeaking a strange gibberish. They had broken out of their freeze and now ran about in queer, frantic circles. They raced with incredible speed, scampering like ants on a hot griddle. They raced jerkily, their arms and legs pumping wildly. And all the time they squeaked in their shrill high-pitched voices.

Ellis found his briefcase. He picked it up slowly. The figures watched in mixed wonder and terror as the huge bag rose, only a short distance from them. An idea drifted through Ellis's brain. Good Lord -- could they come into the Jiffi-scuttler, through the gray haze?

But he had no time to find out. He was already late as it was. He pulled away and hurried towards the New York end of the tunnel. A second later he stepped out in the blinding sunlight, abruptly finding himself on the busy street-corner in front of his office.

"Hey, there, Hank!" Donald Potter shouted, as he raced through the doors into the TD building. "Get with it!"

"Sure, sure." Ellis followed after him automatically. Behind the entrance to the Jiffi-scuttler was a vague circle above the pavement, like the ghost of a soap-bubble.

He hurried up the steps and inside the offices of Terran Development, his mind already on the hard day ahead.

As they were locking up the office and getting ready to go home, Ellis stopped coordinator Patrick Miller in his office. "Say, Mr Miller. You're also in charge of the research end, aren't you?"

"Yeah. So?"

"Let me ask you something. Just where does the Jiffi-scuttler go? It must go somewhere."

"It goes out of this continuum completely." Miller was impatient to get home. "Into another dimension."

"I know that. But -- *where?*"

Miller unfolded his breast-pocket handkerchief rapidly and spread it out on his desk. "Maybe I can explain it to you this way. Suppose you're a two dimensional creature and this handkerchief represents your --"

"I've seen that a million times," Ellis said, disappointed. "That's merely an analogy, and I'm not interested in an analogy. I want a factual answer. Where does my Jiffi-scuttler go, between here and Cedar Groves?"

Miller laughed. "What the hell do you care?"

Ellis became abruptly guarded. He shrugged indifferently. "Just curious. It certainly must go *some place.*"

Miller put his hand on Ellis's shoulder in a friendly big-brother fashion. "Henry, old man, you just leave that up to us. Okay? We're the designers, you're the consumer. Your job is to use the 'scuttler, try it out for us, report any defects or failure so when we put it on the market next year we'll be sure there's nothing wrong with it."

"As a matter of fact --" Ellis began.

"What is it?"

Ellis clamped his sentence off. "Nothing." He picked up his briefcase. "Nothing at all. I'll see you tomorrow. Thanks, Mr Miller. Goodnight."

He hurried downstairs and out of the TD building. The faint outline of his Jiffi-scuttler was visible in the fading late-afternoon sunlight. The sky was already full of mono jets taking off. Weary workers beginning their long trip back to their homes in the country. The endless commute. Ellis made his way to the hoop and stepped into it. Abruptly the bright sunlight dimmed and faded.

Again he was in the wavery gray tunnel. At the far end flashed a circle of green and white. Rolling green hills and his own house. His backyard. The cedar tree and flower beds. The town of Cedar Groves.

Two steps down the tunnel. Ellis halted, bending over. He studied the floor of the tunnel intently. He studied the misty gray wall, where it rose and flickered -- and the thin place. The place he had noticed.

They were still there. *Still?* It was a different bunch. This time ten or eleven of them. Men and women and children. Standing together, gazing up at him with awe and wonder. No more than a half-inch high, each. Tiny distorted figures, shifting and changing shape oddly. Altering colors and hues.

Ellis hurried on. The tiny figures watched him go. A brief glimpse of their microscopic astonishment -- and then he was stepping out into his backyard.

He clicked off the Jiffi-scuttler and mounted the back steps. He entered his house, deep in thought.

"Hi," Mary cried, from the kitchen. She rustled towards him in her hip-length mesh shirt, her arms out. "How was work today?"

"Fine."

"Is anything wrong? You look -- strange."

"No. No, nothing's wrong." Ellis kissed his wife absently on the forehead. "What's for dinner?"

"Something choice. Siriusian mole steak. One of your favorites. Is that all right?"

"Sure." Ellis tossed his hat and coat down on the chair. The chair folded them up and put them away. His thoughtful, preoccupied look still remained. "Fine, honey."

"Are you *sure* there's nothing wrong? You didn't get into another argument with Pete Taylor, did you?"

"No. Of course not." Ellis shook his head in annoyance. "Everything's all right, honey. Stop needling me."

"Well, I *hope* so," Mary said, with a sigh.

The next morning they were waiting for him.

He saw them the first step into the Jiffi-scuttler. A small group waiting within the wavering gray, like bugs caught in a block of jello. They moved jerkily, rapidly, arms and legs pumping in a blur of motion. Trying to attract his attention. Piping wildly in their pathetically faint voices.

Ellis stopped and squatted down. They were putting something through the wall of the tunnel, through the thin place in the gray. It was small, so incredibly small he could scarcely see it. A square of white at the end of a microscopic pole. They were watching him eagerly, faces alive with fear and hope. Desperate, pleading hope.

Ellis took the tiny square. It came loose like some fragile rose petal from its stalk. Clumsily, he let it drop and had to hunt all round for it. The little figures watched in an agony of dismay as his huge hands moved blindly around the floor of the tunnel. At last he found it and gingerly lifted it up.

It was too small to make out. *Writing?* Some tiny lines -- but he couldn't read them. Much too small to read. He got out his wallet and carefully placed the square between the two cards. He restored his wallet to his pocket.

"I'll look at it later," he said.

His voice boomed and echoed up and down the tunnel. At the sound the tiny creatures scattered. They all fled, shrieking in their shrill, piping voices, away from the gray shimmer, into the dimness beyond. In a flash they were gone. Like startled mice. He was alone. Ellis knelt down and put his eye against the gray shimmer, where it was thin. Where they had stood waiting. He could see something dim and distorted, lost in a vague haze. A landscape of some sort. Indistinct. Hard to make out.

Hills. Trees and crops. But so tiny. And dim. . .

He glanced at his watch. God, it was ten! Hastily he scrambled to his feet and hurried out of the tunnel, on to the blazing New York pavement.

Late. He raced up the stairs of the Terran Development building and down the long corridor to his office.

At lunchtime he stopped in at the Research Labs. "Hey," he called, as Jim Andrews brushed past, loaded down with reports and equipment. "Got a second?"

"What do you want, Henry?"

"I'd like to borrow something. A magnifying glass." He considered. "Maybe a photon-microscope would be better. One- or two-hundred power."

"Kids' stuff." Jim found him a small microscope. "Slides?"

"Yeah, a couple of blank slides."

He carried the microscope back to his office. He set it up on his desk, clearing away his paper. As a precaution he sent Miss Nelson, his secretary, out of the room and off to lunch. Then carefully, cautiously, he got the tiny wisp from his wallet and slipped it between two slides.

It was writing, all right. But nothing he could read. Utterly unfamiliar. Complex, interlaced little characters.

For a time he sat thinking. Then he dialed his inter-department vidphone. "Give me the Linguistics Department."

After a moment Earl Peterson's good-natured face appeared. "Hi, there, Ellis. What can I do for you?"

Ellis hesitated. He had to do this right. "Say, Earl, old man. Got a little favor to ask you."

"Like what? Anything to oblige an old pal."

"You, uh -- you have that Machine down there, don't you? That translating business you use for working over documents from non-Terran cultures?"

"Sure. So?"

"Think I could use it?" He talked fast. "It's a screwy sort of a deal, Earl. I got this pal living on -- uh -- Centaurus VI, and he writes me in -- uh -- you know the Centauran native semantic system, and I --"

"You want the Machine to translate a letter? Sure, I think we could manage it. This once, at least. Bring it down."

He brought it down. He got Earl to show him how the intake feed worked, and as soon as Earl had turned his back he fed in the tiny square of material. The Linguistics Machine clicked and whirred. Ellis prayed silently that the paper wasn't too small. Wouldn't fall out between the relay-probes of the Machine.

But sure enough, after a couple of seconds, a tape unreeled from the output slot. The tape cut itself off and dropped into a basket. The Linguistics Machine turned promptly to other stuff, more vital material from TD's various export branches.

With trembling fingers Ellis spread out the tape. The words danced before his eyes.

Questions. They were asking him questions. God, it was getting complicated. He read the questions intently, his lips moving. What was he getting himself into? They were expecting answers. He had taken their paper, gone off with it. Probably they would be waiting for him, on his way home.

He returned to his office and dialed his vidphone. "Give me outside," he ordered.

The regular vid monitor appeared. "Yes, sir?"

"I want the Federal Library of Information," Ellis said. "Cultural Research Division."

That night they were waiting, all right. But not the same ones. It was odd -- each time a different group. Their clothing was slightly different, too. A new hue. And in the background the landscape had also altered slightly. The trees he had seen were gone. The hills were still there, but a different shade. A hazy gray-white. Snow?

He squatted down. He had worked it out with care. The answers from the Federal Library of Information had gone back to the Linguistics Machine for re-translation. The answers were now in the original tongue of the questions -- but on a trifle larger piece of paper.

Ellis made like a marble game and flicked the wad of paper through the gray shimmer. It bowled over six or seven of the watching figures and rolled down the side of the hill on which they were standing. After a moment of terrified immobility the figures scampered frantically after it. They disappeared into the vague and invisible depths of their world and Ellis got stiffly to his feet again.

"Well," he muttered to himself, "that's that."

But it wasn't. The next morning there was a new group -- and a new list of questions. The tiny figures pushed their microscopic square of paper through the thin spot in the wall of the tunnel and stood waiting and trembling as Ellis bent over and felt around for it.

He found it -- finally. He put it in his wallet and continued on his way, stepping out at New York, frowning. This was getting serious. Was this going to be a full-time job?

But then he grinned. It was the damn oddest thing he had ever heard of. The little rascals were cute, in their own way. Tiny intent faces, screwed up with serious concern. And terror. They were scared of him, really scared. And why not? Compared to them he was a giant.

He conjectured about their world. What kind of planet was theirs? Odd to be so small. But size was a relative matter. Small, though, compared to him. Small and reverent. He could read fear and yearning, gnawing hope, as they pushed up their papers. They were depending on him. Praying he'd give them answers.

Ellis grinned. "Damn unusual job," he said to himself.

"What's this?" Peterson said, when he showed up in the Linguistics Lab at noontime.

"Well, you see, I got another letter from my friend on Centaurus VI."

"Yeah?" A certain suspicion flickered across Peterson's face. "You're not ribbing me, are you, Henry? This Machine has a lot to do, you know. Stuff's coming in all the time. We can't afford to waste any time with --"

"This is really serious stuff, Earl." Ellis patted his wallet. "Very important business. Not just gossip."

"Okay. If you say so." Peterson gave the nod to the team operating the Machine. "Let this guy use the Translator, Tommie."

"Thanks," Ellis murmured.

He went through the routine, getting a translation and then carrying the questions up to his vidphone and passing them over to the Library research staff. By nightfall the answers were back in the original tongue and with them carefully in his wallet, Ellis headed out of the Terran Development building and into his Jiffi-scuttler.

As usual, a new group was waiting.

"Here you go, boys," Ellis boomed, flicking the wad through the thin place in the shimmer. The wad rolled down the microscopic countryside, bouncing from hill to hill, the little people tumbling jerkily after it in their funny stiff-legged fashion. Ellis watched them go, grinning with interest -- and pride.

They really hurried; no doubt about that. He could make them out only vaguely, now. They had raced wildly off away from the shimmer. Only a small portion of their world was tangent to the Jiffi-scuttler, apparently. Only the one spot, where the shimmer was thin. He peered intently through.

They were getting the wad open, now. Three or four of them, unprying the paper and examining the answers.

Ellis swelled with pride as he continued along the tunnel and out into his own backyard. He couldn't read their questions -- and when translated, he couldn't answer them. The Linguistics Department did the first part, the Library research staff the rest. Nevertheless, Ellis felt pride. A deep, glowing spot of warmth far down inside him. The expression on their faces. The look they gave him when they saw the answer-wad in his hand. When they realized he was going to answer their questions. And the way they scampered after it. It was sort of -- satisfying. It made him feel damn good.

"Not bad," he murmured, opening the back door and entering the house. "Not bad at all."

"What's not bad, dear?" Mary asked, looking quickly up from the table. She laid down her magazine and got to her feet. "Why, you look so *happy!* What is it?"

"Nothing. Nothing at all!" He kissed her warmly on the mouth. "You're looking pretty good tonight yourself, kid."

"Oh, Henry!" Much of Mary blushed prettily. "How sweet."

He surveyed his wife in her two-piece wraparound of clear plastic with appreciation. "Nice looking fragments you have on."

"Why, Henry! What's come over you? You seem so -- so *spirited?*"

Ellis grinned. "Oh, I guess I enjoy my job. You know, there's nothing like taking pride in your work. A job well done, as they say. Work you can be proud of."

"I thought you always said you were nothing but a cog in a great impersonal machine. Just a sort of cipher."

"Things are different," Ellis said firmly. "I'm doing a -- uh -- a new project. A new assignment."

"A new assignment?"

"Gathering information. A sort of -- creative business. So to speak."

By the end of the week he had turned over quite a body of information to them.

He began starting for work about nine-thirty. That gave him a whole thirty minutes to spend squatting down on his hands and knees, peering through the thin place in the shimmer. He got so he was pretty good at seeing them and what they were doing in their microscopic world.

Their civilization was somewhat primitive. No doubt of that. By Terran standards it was scarcely a civilization at all. As near as he could tell, they were virtually without scientific techniques; a kind of agrarian culture, rural communism, a monolithic tribal-based organization apparently without too many members.

At least, not at one time. That was the part he didn't understand. Every time he came past there was a different group of them. No familiar faces. And their world changed, too. The trees, the crops, fauna. The weather, apparently.

Was their time rate different? They moved rapidly, jerkily. Like a vidtape speeded up. And their shrill voices. Maybe that was it. A totally different universe in which the whole time structure was radically different.

As to their attitude towards him, there was no mistaking it. After the first couple of times they began assembling offerings, unbelievably small bits of smoking food, prepared in ovens and on open brick hearths. If he got down with his nose against the gray shimmer he could get a faint whiff of the food. It smelled good. Strong and pungent. Highly spiced. Meat, probably.

On Friday he brought a magnifying glass along and watched them through it. It was meat, all right. They were bringing ant-sized animals to be killed and cooked, leading them up to the ovens. With the magnifying glass he could see more of their faces. They had strange faces. Strong and dark, with a peculiar firm look.

Of course, there was only one look *he* got from them. A combination of fear, reverence, and hope. The look made him feel good. It was a look for him, only. Between themselves they shouted and argued -- and sometimes stabbed and fought each other furiously, rolling in their brown robes in a wild tangle. They were a passionate and strong species. He got so he admired them.

Which was good -- because it made him feel better. To have the reverent awe of such a proud, sturdy face was really something. There was nothing craven about them.

About the fifth time he came there was a rather attractive structure built. Some kind of temple. A place of religious worship.

To him! They were developing a real religion about him. No doubt of it. He began going to work at nine o'clock, to give himself a full hour with them. They had, by the middle of the second week, a full-sized ritual evolved. Processions, lighted tapers, what seemed to be songs or chants. Priests in long robes. And the spiced offerings.

No idols, though. Apparently he was so big they couldn't make out his appearance. He tried to imagine what it looked like to be on their side of the shimmer. An immense shape looming up above them, beyond a wall of gray haze. An indistinct being, something like themselves, yet not like them at all. A different kind of being, obviously. Larger -- but different in other ways. And when he spoke -- booming echoes up and down the Jiffi-scuttler. Which still sent them fleeing in panic.

An evolving religion. He was changing them. Through his actual presence and through his answers, the precise, correct responses he obtained from the Federal Library of Information and had the Linguistics Machine translate into their language. Of course, by *their* time-rate they had to wait generations for the answers. But they had become accustomed to it, by now.

They waited. They expected. They passed up questions and after a couple of centuries he passed down answers, answers which they no doubt put to good use.

"What in the world?" Mary demanded, as he got home from work an hour late one night. "Where have you been?"

"Working," Ellis said carelessly, removing his hat and coat. He threw himself on the couch. "I'm tired. Really tired." He sighed with relief and motioned for the couch-arm to bring him a whiskey sour.

Mary came over by the couch. "Henry, I'm a little worried."

"Worried?"

"You shouldn't work so hard. You ought to take it easy, more. How long since you've had a real vacation? A trip off Terra. Out of the System. You know, I'd just like to call that fellow Miller and ask him why it's necessary for a man your age to put in so much --"

"A man my age!" Ellis bristled indignantly. "I'm not so old."

"Of course not." Mary sat down beside him and put her arms around him affectionately. "But you shouldn't have to do so much. You deserve a rest. Don't you think?"

"This is different. You don't understand. This isn't the same old stuff. Reports and statistics and the damn filing. This is --"

"What is it?"

"This is *different*. I'm not a cog. This gives me something. I can't explain it to you, I guess. But it's something I have to do."

"If you could tell me more about it --"

"I can't tell you any more about it," Ellis said. "But there's nothing in the world like it. I've worked twenty-five years for Terran Development. Twenty-five years at the same reports, again and again. Twenty-five years -- and I never felt this way."

"Oh, yeah?" Miller roared. "Don't give me that! Come clean, Ellis!"

Ellis opened and closed his mouth. "What are you talking about?" Horror rolled through him. "What's happened?"

"Don't try to give *me* the runaround." On the vidscreen Miller's face was purple. "Come into my office."

The screen went dead.

Ellis sat stunned at his desk. Gradually, he collected himself and got shakily to his feet. "Good Lord." Weakly, he wiped cold sweat from his forehead. All at once. Everything in ruins. He was dazed with the shock.

"Anything wrong?" Miss Nelson asked sympathetically.

"No." Ellis moved numbly towards the door. He was shattered. What had Miller found out? Good God! Was it possible he had --

"Mr Miller looked angry."

"Yeah." Ellis moved blindly down the hall, his mind reeling. Miller looked angry all right. Somehow he had found out. But why was he mad? Why did he care? A cold chill settled over Ellis. It looked bad. Miller was his superior -- with hiring and firing powers. Maybe he'd done something wrong. Maybe he had somehow broken a law. Committed a crime. But what?

What did Miller care about *them*! What concern was it of Terran Development?

He opened the door to Miller's office. "Here I am, Mr Miller," he muttered. "What's the trouble?"

Miller glowered at him with rage. "All this goofy stuff about your cousin on Proxima."

"It's -- uh -- you mean a business friend on Centaurus VI."

"You -- you swindler!" Miller leaped up. "And after all the Company's done for you."

"I don't understand," Ellis muttered. "What have --"

"Why do you think we gave you the Jiffi-scuttler in the first place?"

"Why?"

"To *test!* To try out, you wall-eyed Venusian stink-cricket! The Company magnanimously consented to allow you to operate a Jiffi-scuttler in advance of market presentation, and what do you do? Why, you --"

Ellis started to get indignant. After all, he had been with TD twenty-five years. "You don't have to be so offensive. I plunked down my thousand gold credits for it."

"Well, you can just mosey down to the accountant's office and get your money back. I've already sent out a directive for a construction team to crate up your Jiffi-scuttler and bring it back to receiving."

Ellis was dumbfounded. "But *why?*"

"Why indeed! Because it's defective. Because it doesn't work. That's why." Miller's eyes blazed with technological outrage. "The inspection crew found a leak a mile wide in it." His lip curled. "As if you didn't know."

Ellis's heart sank. "Leak?" he croaked apprehensively.

"Leak. It's a damn good thing I authorized a periodic inspection. If we depended on people like you to --"

"Are you *sure?* It seemed all right to me. That is, it got me here without any trouble," Ellis floundered. "Certainly no complaints from my end."

"No. No complaints from your end. That's exactly why you're not getting another one. That's why you're taking the monojet transport back home tonight. Because you didn't report the leak! And if you ever try to put something over on this office again --"

"How do you know I was aware of the -- defect?"

Miller sank down in his chair, overcome with fury. "Because," he said carefully, "of your daily pilgrimage to the Linguistic Machine. With your alleged letter from your grandmother on Betelgeuse II. Which wasn't any such thing. Which was an utter fraud. Which you got through the leak in the Jiffi-scuttler!"

"How do you know?" Ellis squeaked boldly, driven to the wall. "So maybe there was a defect. But you can't prove there's any connection between your badly constructed Jiffi-scuttler and my --"

"Your missive," Miller stated, "which you foisted on our Linguistics Machine, was not a non-Terran script. It was not from Centaurus VI. It was not from any non-Terran system. It was ancient Hebrew. And there's only one place you could have got it, Ellis. So don't try to kid me."

"Hebrew!" Ellis exclaimed, startled. He turned white as a sheet. "Good Lord. The other continuum -- the fourth dimension. Time, of course." He trembled. "And the expanding universe. That would explain their size. And it explains why a new group, a new generation --"

"We're taking enough of a chance as it is, with these Jiffi-scuttlers. Warping a tunnel through other space-time continua." Miller shook his head warily. "You meddler. You *knew* you were supposed to report any defect."

"I don't think I did any harm, did I?" Ellis was suddenly terribly nervous. "They seemed pleased, even grateful. Gosh, I'm sure I didn't cause any trouble."

Miller shrieked in insane rage. For a time he danced around the room. Finally he threw something down on his desk, directly in front of Ellis. "No trouble. No, none. *Look* at this. I got this from the Ancient Artifacts Archives."

"What is it?"

"Look at it! I compared one of your question sheets to this. The same. *Exactly* the same. All your sheets, questions and answers, every one of them's in here. You multi-legged Ganymedean mange beetle!"

Ellis picked up the book and opened it. As he read the pages a strange look came slowly over his face. "Good Heavens. So they kept a record of what I gave them. They put it all together in a book. Every word of it. And some commentaries, too. It's all here -- every single word. It *did* have an effect, then. They passed it on. Wrote all of it down."

"Go back to your office. I'm through looking at you for today. I'm through looking at you forever. Your severance check will come through regular channels."

In a trance, his face flushed with a strange excitement, Ellis gripped the book and moved dazedly towards the door. "Say, Mr Miller. Can I have this? Can I take it along?"

"Sure," Miller said wearily. "Sure, you can take it. You can read it on your way home tonight. On the public monojet transport."

"Henry has something to show you," Mary Ellis whispered excitedly, gripping Mrs Lawrence's arm. "Make sure you say the right thing."

"The right thing?" Mrs Lawrence faltered nervously, a trifle uneasy. "What is it? Nothing alive, I hope."

"No, no." Mary pushed her towards the study door. "Just smile." She raised her voice. "Henry, Dorothy Lawrence is here."

Henry Ellis appeared at the door of his study. He bowed slightly, a dignified figure in silk dressing gown, pipe in his mouth, fountain pen in one hand. "Good evening, Dorothy," he said in a low, well-modulated voice. "Care to step into my study a moment?"

"Study?" Mrs Lawrence came hesitantly in. "What do you study? I mean, Mary says you've been doing something very interesting recently, now that you're not with -- I mean, now that you're home more. She didn't give me any idea what it was, though."

Mrs Lawrence's eyes roved curiously around the study. The study was full of reference volumes, charts, a huge mahogany desk, an atlas, globe, leather chairs, an unbelievably ancient electric typewriter.

"Good Heavens!" she exclaimed. "How odd. All these old things."

Ellis lifted something carefully from the bookcase and held it out to her casually. "By the way -- you might glance at this."

"What is it? A book?" Mrs Lawrence took the book and examined it eagerly. "My goodness. Heavy, isn't it?" She read the back, her lips moving. "What does it mean? It looks old. What strange letters! I've never seen anything like it. *Holy Bible.*" She glanced up brightly. "What is this?"

Ellis smiled faintly. "Well --"

A light dawned. Mrs Lawrence gasped in revelation. "Good Heavens! You didn't *write* this, did you?"

Ellis's smile broadened into a deprecating blush. A dignified hue of modesty. "Just a little thing I threw together," he murmured indifferently. "My first, as a matter of fact." Thoughtfully, he fingered his fountain pen. "And now, if you'll excuse me, I really should be getting back to my work. . ."

Small Town

Verne Haskel crept miserably up the front steps of his house, his overcoat dragging behind him. He was tired. Tired and discouraged. And his feet ached.

"My God," Madge exclaimed, as he closed the door and peeled off his coat and hat. "You home already?"

Haskel dumped his briefcase and began untying his shoes. His body sagged. His face was drawn and gray.

"Say something!"

"Dinner ready?"

"No, dinner isn't ready. What's wrong this time? Another fight with Larson?"

Haskel stumped into the kitchen and filled a glass with warm water and soda. "Let's move," he said.

"Move?"

"Away from Woodland. To San Francisco. Anywhere." Haskel drank his soda, his middle-aged flabby body supported by the gleaming sink. "I feel lousy. Maybe I ought to see Doc Barnes again. I wish this was Friday and tomorrow was Saturday."

"What do you want for dinner?"

"Nothing. I don't know." Haskel shook his head wearily. "Anything." He sank down at the kitchen table. "All I want is rest. Open a can of stew. Pork and beans. Anything."

"I suggest we go out to Don's Steakhouse. On Monday they have good sirloins."

"No. I've seen enough human faces today."

"I suppose you're too tired to drive me over to Helen Grant's."

"The car's in the garage. Busted again."

"If you took better care of it --"

"What the hell do you want me to do? Carry it around in a cellophane bag?"

"Don't shout at me, Verne Haskel!" Madge flushed with anger. "Maybe you want to fix your own dinner."

Haskel got wearily to his feet. He shuffled toward the cellar door. "I'll see you."

"Where are you going?"

"Downstairs in the basement."

"Oh, Lord!" Madge cried wildly. "Those trains! Those toys! How can a grown man, a middle-aged man --"

Haskel said nothing. He was already half way down the stairs, feeling around for the basement light.

The basement was cool and moist. Haskel took his engineer's cap from the hook and fitted it on his head. Excitement and a faint surge of renewed energy filled his tired body. He approached the great plywood table with eager steps.

Trains ran everywhere. Along the floor, under the coal bin, among the steam pipes of the furnace. The tracks converged at the table, rising up on carefully graded ramps. The table itself was littered with transformers and signals and switches and heaps of equipment and wiring. And -- And the town.

The detailed, painfully accurate model of Woodland. Every tree and house, every store and building and street and fireplug. A minute town, each facet in perfect order. Constructed with elaborate care throughout the years. As long as he could remember. Since he was a kid, building and glueing and working after school.

Haskel turned on the main transformer. All along the track signal lights glowed. He fed power to the heavy Lionel engine parked with its load of freight cars. The engine sped smoothly into life, gliding along the track. A flashing dark projectile of metal that made his breath catch in his throat. He opened an electric switch and the engine headed down the ramp, through a tunnel and off the table. It raced under the workbench.

His trains. And his town. Haskel bent over the miniature houses and streets, his heart glowing with pride. He had built it -- himself. Every inch. Every perfect inch. The whole town. He touched the corner of Fred's Grocery Store. Not a detail lacking. Even the windows. The displays of food. The signs. The counters.

The Uptown Hotel. He ran his hand over its flat roof. The sofas and chairs in the lobby. He could see them through the window.

Green's Drugstore. Bunion pad displays. Magazines. Frazier's Auto Parts. Mexico City Dining. Sharpstein's Apparel. Bob's Liquor Store. Ace Billiard Parlor.

The whole town. He ran his hands over it. He had built it; the town was his.

The train came rushing back, out from under the workbench. Its wheels passed over an automatic switch and a drawbridge lowered itself obediently. The train swept over and beyond, dragging its cars behind it.

Haskel turned up the power. The train gained speed. Its whistle sounded. It turned a sharp curve and grated across a cross-track. More speed. Haskel's hands jerked convulsively at the transformer. The train leaped and shot ahead. It swayed and bucked as it shot around a curve. The transformer was turned up to maximum. The train was a clattering blur of speed, rushing along the track, across bridges and switches, behind the big pipes of the floor furnace.

It disappeared into the coal bin. A moment later it swept out the other side, rocking wildly.

Haskel slowed the train down. He was breathing hard, his chest rising painfully. He sat down on the stool by the workbench and lit a cigarette with shaking fingers.

The train, the model town, gave him a strange feeling. It was hard to explain. He had always loved trains, model engines and signals and buildings. Since he was a little kid, maybe six or seven. His father had given him his first train. An engine and a few pieces of track. An old wind-up train. When he was nine he got his first real electric train. And two switches.

He added to it, year after year. Track, engines, switches, cars, signals. More powerful transformers. And the beginnings of the town.

He had built the town up carefully. Piece by piece. First, when he was in junior high, a model of the Southern Pacific Depot. Then the taxi stand next door. The cafe where the drivers ate. Broad Street.

And so on. More and more. Houses, buildings, stores. A whole town, growing under his hands, as the years went by. Every afternoon he came home from school and worked. Glued and cut and painted and sawed.

Now it was virtually complete. Almost done. He was forty-three years old and the town was almost done.

Haskel moved around the big plywood table, his hands extended reverently. He touched a miniature store here and there. The flower shop. The theater. The Telephone Company. Larson's Pump and Valve Works.

That, too. Where he worked. His place of business. A perfect miniature of the plant, down to the last detail.

Haskel scowled. Jim Larson. For twenty years he had worked there, slaved day after day. For what? To see others advanced over him. Younger men. Favorites of the boss. Yes-men with bright ties and pressed pants and wide, stupid grins.

Misery and hatred welled up in Haskel. All his life Woodland had got the better of him. He had never been happy. The town had always been against him. Miss Murphy in high school. The frats in college. Clerks in the snooty department stores. His neighbors. Cops and mailmen and bus drivers and delivery boys. Even his wife. Even Madge.

He had never meshed with the town. The rich, expensive little suburb of San Francisco, down the peninsula beyond the fog belt. Woodland was too damn upper-middle class. Too many big houses and lawns and chrome cars and deck chairs. Too stuffy and sleek. As long as he could remember. In school. His job -- Larson. The Pump and Valve Works. Twenty years of hard work.

Haskel's fingers closed over the tiny building, the model of the Larson's Pump and Valve Works. Savagely, he ripped it loose and threw it to the floor. He crushed it underfoot, grinding the bits of glass and metal and cardboard into a shapeless mass.

God, he was shaking all over. He stared down at the remains, his heart pounding wildly. Strange emotions, crazy emotions, twisted through him. Thoughts he never had had before. For a long time he gazed down at the crumpled wad by his hose. What had once been the model of Larson's Pump and Valve Works.

Abruptly he pulled away. In a trance he returned to his workbench and sat stiffly down on the stool. He pulled his tools and materials together, clicking the power drill on.

It took only a few moments. Working rapidly, with quick, expert fingers, Haskel assembled a new model. He painted, glued, fitted pieces together. He lettered a microscopic sign and sprayed a green lawn into place.

Then he carried the new model carefully over to the table and glued it in the correct spot. The place where Larson's Pump and Valve Works had been. The new building gleamed in the overhead light, still moist and shiny.

WOODLAND MORTUARY

Haskel rubbed his hands in an ecstasy of satisfaction. The Valve Works was gone. He had destroyed it. Obliterated it. Removed it from the town. Below him was Woodland -- without the Valve Works. A mortuary instead.

His eyes gleamed. His lips twitched. His surging emotions swelled. He had got rid of it. In a brief flurry of action. In a second. The whole thing was simple -- amazingly easy.

Odd he hadn't thought of it before.

Sipping a tall glass of ice-cold beer thoughtfully, Madge Haskel said, "There's something wrong with Verne. I noticed it especially last night. When he came home from work."

Doctor Paul Tyler grunted absently. "A highly neurotic type. Sense of inferiority. Withdrawal and introversion."

"But he's getting worse. Him and his trains. Those damn model trains. My God, Paul! Do you know he has a whole town down there in the basement?"

Tyler was curious. "Really? I never knew that."

"All the time I've known him he's had them down there. Started when he was a kid. Imagine a grown man playing with trains! It's -- it's disgusting. Every night the same thing."

"Interesting." Tyler rubbed his jaw. "He keeps at them continually? An unvarying pattern?"

"Every night. Last night he didn't even eat dinner. He just came home and went directly down."

Paul Tyler's polished features twisted into a frown. Across from him Madge sat languidly sipping her beer. It was two in the afternoon. The day was warm and bright. The living-room was attractive in a lazy, quiet way. Abruptly Tyler got to his feet. "Let's take a look at them. The models. I didn't know it had gone so far."

"Do you really want to?" Madge slid back the sleeve of her green silk lounge pajamas and consulted her wristwatch. "He won't be home until five." She jumped to her feet, setting down her glass. "All right. We have time."

"Fine. Let's go down." Tyler caught hold of Madge's arm and they hurried down into the basement, a strange excitement flooding through them. Madge clicked on the basement light and they approached the big plywood table, giggling and nervous, like mischievous children.

"See?" Madge said, squeezing Tyler's arm. "Look at it. Took years. All his life."

Tyler nodded slowly. "Must have." There was awe in his voice. "I've never seen anything like it. The detail. . . He has skill."

"Yes, Verne is good with his hands." Madge indicated the workbench. "He buys tools all the time."

Tyler walked slowly around the big table, bending over and peering. "Amazing. Every building. The whole town is here. Look! There's my place."

He indicated his luxurious apartment building, a few blocks from the Haskel residence.

"I guess it's all there," Madge said. "Imagine a grown man coming down here and playing with model trains!"

"Power." Tyler pushed an engine along a track. "That's why it appeals to boys. Trains are big things. Huge and noisy. Power-sex symbols. The boy sees the train rushing along the track. It's so huge and ruthless it scares him. Then he gets a toy train. A model, like these. He controls it. Makes it start, stop. Go slow. Fast. He runs it. It responds to him."

Madge shivered. "Let's go upstairs where it's warm. It's so cold down here."

"But as the boy grows up, he gets bigger and stronger. He can shed the model-symbol. Master the real object, the real train. Get genuine control over things. Valid mastery." Tyler shook his head. "Not this substitute thing. Unusual, a grown person going to such lengths." He frowned. "I never noticed a mortuary on State Street."

"A mortuary?"

"And this, Steuben Pet Shop. Next door to the radio repair shop. There's no pet shop there." Tyler cudgeled his brain. "What *is* there? Next to the radio repair place."

"Paris Furs." Madge clasped her arms. "Brrrrr. Come on, Paul. Let's go upstairs before I freeze."

Tyler laughed. "Okay, sissy." He headed toward the stairs, frowning again. "I wonder why. Steuben Pets. Never heard of it. Everything is so detailed. He must know the town by heart. To put a shop there that isn't --" He clicked off the basement light. "And the mortuary. What's supposed to be there? Isn't the --"

"Forget it," Madge called back, hurrying past him, into the warm living-room. "You're practically as bad as he is. Men are such children."

Tyler didn't respond. He was deep in thought. His suave confidence was gone; he looked nervous and shaken.

Madge pulled the Venetian blinds down. The living-room sank into amber gloom. She flopped down on the couch and pulled Tyler down beside her. "Stop looking like that," she ordered. "I've never seen you this way." Her slim arms circled his neck and her lips brushed close to his ear. "I wouldn't have let you in if I thought you were going to worry about *him*."

Tyler grunted, preoccupied. "Why *did* you let me in?"

The pressure of Madge's arms increased. Her silk pajamas rustled as she moved against him. "Silly," she said.

Big red-headed Jim Larson gaped in disbelief. "What do you mean? What's the matter with you?"

"I'm quitting." Haskel shoveled the contents of his desk into his briefcase. "Mail the check to my house."

"But --"

"Get out of the way." Haskel pushed past Larson, out into the hall. Larson was stunned with amazement. There was a fixed expression on Haskel's face. A glazed look. A rigid look Larson had never seen before.

"Are you -- all right?" Larson asked.

"Sure." Haskel opened the front door of the plant and disappeared outside. The door slammed after him. "Sure I'm all right," he muttered to himself. He made his way through the crowds of late-afternoon shoppers, his lips twitching. "You're damn right I'm all right."

"Watch it, buddy," a laborer muttered ominously, as Haskel shoved past him.

"Sorry." Haskel hurried on, gripping his briefcase. At the top of the hill he paused a moment to get his breath. Behind him was Larson's Pump and Valve Works. Haskel laughed shrilly. Twenty years -- cut short in a second. It was over. No more Larson. No more dull, grinding job, day after day. Without promotion or future. Routine and boredom, months on end. It was over and done for. A new life and beginning.

He hurried on. The sun was setting. Cars streaked by him, businessmen going home from work. Tomorrow they would be going back but not him. Not ever again.

He reached his own street. Ed Tildon's house rose up, a great stately structure of concrete and glass. Tildon's dog came rushing out to bark. Haskel hastened past. Tildon's dog. He laughed wildly.

"Better keep away!" he shouted at the dog. He reached his own house and leaped up the front steps two at a time. He tore the door open. The living-room was dark and silent. There was a sudden stir of motion. Shapes untangling themselves, getting quickly up from the couch.

"Verne!" Madge gasped. "What are you doing home so early?" Verne Haskel threw his briefcase down and dropped his hat and coat over a chair. His lined face was twisted with emotion, pulled out of shape by violent inner forces.

"What in the world!" Madge fluttered, hurrying toward him nervously, smoothing down her lounge pajamas. "Has something happened? I didn't expect you so --" She broke off, blushing. "I mean, I --"

Paul Tyler strolled leisurely toward Haskel. "Hi there, Verne," he murmured, embarrassed. "Dropped by to say hello and return a book to your wife."

Haskel nodded curtly. "Afternoon." He turned and headed toward the basement door, ignoring the two of them. "I'll be downstairs."

"But Verne!" Madge protested. "What's happened?"

Verne halted briefly at the door. "I quit my job."

"You *what?*"

"I quit my job. I finished Larson off. There won't be any more of him." The basement door slammed.

"Good Lord!" Madge shrieked, clutching at Tyler hysterically. "He's gone out of his mind!"

Down in the basement, Verne Haskel snapped on the light impatiently. He put on his engineer's cap and pulled his stool up beside the great plywood table.

What next?

Morris Home Furnishings. The big plush store. Where the clerks all looked down their noses at him.

He rubbed his hands gleefully. No more of them. No more snooty clerks, lifting their eyebrows when he came in. Only hair and bow ties and folded handkerchiefs.

He removed the model of Morris Home Furnishings and disassembled it. He worked feverishly, with frantic haste. Now that he had really begun he wasted no time. A moment later he was glueing two small buildings in its place. Ritz Shoeshine. Pete's Bowling Alley.

Haskel giggled excitedly. Fitting extinction for the luxurious, exclusive furniture store. A shoeshine parlor and a bowling alley. Just what it deserved.

The California State Bank. He had always hated the Bank. They had once refused him a loan. He pulled the Bank loose.

Ed Tildon's mansion. His damn dog. The dog had bit him on the ankle one afternoon. He ripped the model off. His head spun. He could do anything.

Harrison Appliance. They had sold him a bum radio. Off came Harrison Appliance.

Joe's Cigar and Smoke Shop. Joe had given him a lead quarter in May, 1949. Off came Joe's.

The Ink Works. He loathed the smell of ink. Maybe a bread factory, instead. He loved baking bread. Off came the Ink Works.

Elm Street was too dark at night. A couple of times he had stumbled. A few more streetlights were in order.

Not enough bars along High Street. Too many dress shops and expensive hat and fur shops and ladies' apparel. He ripped a whole handful loose and carried them to the workbench.

At the top of the stairs the door opened slowly. Madge peered down, pale and frightened. "Verne?"

He scowled up impatiently. "What do you want?"

Madge came downstairs hesitantly. Behind her Doctor Tyler followed, suave and handsome in his gray suit. "Verne -- is everything all right?"

"Of course."

"Did -- did you really quit your job?"

Haskel nodded. He began to disassemble the Ink Works, ignoring his wife and Doctor Tyler. "But *why?*"

Haskel grunted impatiently. "No time."

Doctor Tyler had begun to look worried. "Do I understand you're too busy for your job?"

"That's right."

"Too busy doing *what?*" Tyler's voice rose; he was trembling nervously. "Working down here on this town of yours? Changing things?"

"Go away," Haskel muttered. His deft hands were assembling a lovely little Langendorf Bread Factory. He shaped it with loving care, sprayed it with white paint, brushed a gravel walk and shrubs in front of it. He put it aside and began on a park. A big green park. Woodland had always needed a park. It would go in place of State Street Hotel.

Tyler pulled Madge away from the table, off in a corner of the basement. "Good God." He lit a cigarette shakily. The cigarette flipped out of his hands and rolled away. He ignored it and fumbled for another. "You see? You see what he's doing?"

Madge shook her head mutely. "What is it? I don't --"

"How long has he been working on this? All his life?"

Madge nodded, white-faced. "Yes, all his life."

Tyler's features twisted. "My God, Madge. It's enough to drive you out of your mind. I can hardly believe it. We've got to do something."

"What's happening?" Madge moaned. "What --"

"He's losing himself into it." Tyler's face was a mask of incredulous disbelief. "Faster and faster."

"He's always come down here," Madge faltered. "It's nothing new. He's always wanted to get away."

"Yes. Get away." Tyler shuddered, clenched his fists and pulled himself together. He advanced across the basement and stopped by Verne Haskel.

"What do you want?" Haskel muttered, noticing him.

Tyler licked his lips. "You're adding some things, aren't you? New buildings."

Haskel nodded.

Tyler touched the little bread factory with shaking fingers. "What's this? Bread? Where does it go?" He moved around the table. "I don't remember any bread factory in Woodland." He whirled. "You aren't by any chance *improving* on the town? Fixing it up here and there?"

"Get the hell out of here," Haskel said, with ominous calm. "Both of you."

"Verne!" Madge squeaked.

"I've got a lot to do. You can bring sandwiches down about eleven. I hope to finish sometime tonight."

"Finish?" Tyler asked.

"Finish," Haskel answered, returning to his work.

"Come on, Madge." Tyler grabbed her and pulled her to the stairs. "Let's get out of here." He strode ahead of her, up to the stairs and into the hall. "Come on!" As soon as she was up he closed the door tightly after them.

Madge dabbed at her eyes hysterically. "He's gone crazy, Paul! What'll we do?"

Tyler was in deep thought. "Be quiet. I have to think this out." He paced back and forth, a hard scowl on his features. "It'll come soon. It won't be long, not at this rate. Sometime tonight."

"*What?* What do you mean?"

"His withdrawal. Into his substitute world. The improved model he controls. Where he can get away."

"Isn't there something we can do?"

"Do?" Tyler smiled faintly. "Do we want to do something?"

Madge gasped. "But we can't just --"

"Maybe this will solve our problem. This may be what we've been looking for." Tyler eyed Mrs Haskel thoughtfully. "This may be just the thing."

It was after midnight, almost two o'clock in the morning, when he began to get things into final shape. He was tired -- but alert. Things were happening fast. The job was almost done. Virtually perfect.

He halted work a moment, surveying what he had accomplished. The town had been radically changed. About ten o'clock he had begun basic structural alterations in the layout of the streets. He had removed most of the public buildings, the civic center and the sprawling business district around it.

He had erected a new city hall, police station, and an immense park with fountains and indirect lighting. He had cleared the slum area, the old run-down stores and houses and streets. The streets were wider and well-lit. The houses were now small and clean. The stores modern and attractive -- without being ostentatious.

All advertising signs had been removed. Most of the filling stations were gone. The immense factory area was gone, too. Rolling countryside took its place. Trees and hills and green grass.

The wealthy district had been altered. There were now only a few of the mansions left -- belonging to persons he looked favorably on. The rest had been cut down, turned into uniform two-bedroom dwellings, one story, with a single garage each.

The city hall was no longer an elaborate, rococo structure. Now it was low and simple, modeled after the Parthenon, a favorite of his.

There were ten or twelve persons who had done him special harm. He had altered their houses considerably. Given them war-time housing unit apartments, six to a building, at the far edge of town. Where the wind came off the bay, carrying the smell of decaying mud-flats.

Jim Larson's house was completely gone. He had erased Larson utterly. He no longer existed, not in this new Woodland -- which was now almost complete.

Almost. Haskel studied his work intently. All the changes had to be made *now*. Not later. This was the time of creation. Later, when it had been finished, it could not be altered. He had to catch all the necessary changes now -- or forget them.

The new Woodland looked pretty good. Clean and neat -- and simple. The rich district had been toned down. The poor district had been improved. Glaring ads, signs, displays, had all been changed or removed. The business community was smaller. Parks and countryside took the place of factories. The civic center was lovely.

He added a couple of playgrounds for smaller kids. A small theater instead of the enormous Uptown with its flashing neon sign. After some consideration he removed most of the bars he had previously constructed. The new Woodland was going to be moral. Extremely moral. Few bars, no billiards, no red light district. And there was an especially fine jail for undesirables.

The most difficult part had been the microscopic lettering of the main office door of the city hall. He had left it until last, and then painted the words with agonizing care:

MAYOR VERNON R. HASKEL

A few last changes. He gave the Edwardses a '39 Plymouth instead of a new Cadillac. He added more trees in the downtown district. One more fire department. One less dress shop. He had never liked taxis. On impulse, he removed the taxi stand and put in a flower shop.

Haskel rubbed his hands. Anything more? Or was it complete. . . Perfect. . . He studied each part intently. What had he overlooked?

The high school. He removed it and put in two smaller high schools, one at each end of town. Another hospital. That took almost half an hour. He was getting tired. His hands were less swift. He mopped his forehead shakily. Anything else? He sat down on his stool wearily, to rest and think.

All done. It was complete. Joy welled up in him. A bursting cry of happiness. His work was over. "Finished!" Verne Haskel shouted.

He got unsteadily to his feet. He closed his eyes, held his arms out, and advanced toward the plywood table. Reaching, grasping, fingers extended, Haskel headed toward it, a look of radiant exaltation on his seamed, middle-aged face.

Upstairs, Tyler and Madge heard the shout. A distant booming that rolled through the house in waves. Madge winced in terror. "What was that?"

Tyler listened intently. He heard Haskel moving below them, in the basement. Abruptly, he stubbed out his cigarette. "I think it's happened. Sooner than I expected."

"It? You mean he's --"

Tyler got quickly to his feet. "He's gone, Madge. Into his other world. We're finally free."

Madge caught his arm. "Maybe we're making a mistake. It's so terrible. Shouldn't we -- try to do something? Bring him out of it -- try to pull him back."

"Bring him back?" Tyler laughed nervously. "I don't think we could, now. Even if we wanted to. It's too late." He hurried toward the basement door. "Come on."

"It's horrible." Madge shuddered and followed reluctantly. "I wish we had never got started."

Tyler halted briefly at the door. "Horrible? He's happier where he is now. And you're happier. The way it was, nobody was happy. This is the best thing."

He opened the basement door. Madge followed him. They moved cautiously down the stairs, into the dark, silent basement, damp with the faint night mists. The basement was empty.

Tyler relaxed. He was overcome with dazed relief. "He's gone. Everything's okay. It worked out exactly right."

"But I don't understand," Madge repeated hopelessly, as Tyler's Buick purred along the dark, deserted streets. "Where did he go?"

"You know where he went," Tyler answered. "Into his substitute world, of course." He screeched around a corner on two wheels. "The rest should be fairly simple. A few routine forms. There really isn't much left, now."

The night was frigid and bleak. No lights showed, except an occasional lonely streetlamp. Far off, a train whistle sounded mournfully, a dismal echo. Rows of silent houses flickered by on both sides of them.

"Where are we going?" Madge asked. She sat huddled against the door, face pale with shock and terror, shivering under her coat.

"To the police station."

"Why?"

"To report him, naturally. So they'll know he's gone. We'll have to wait; it'll be several years before he'll be declared legally dead." Tyler reached over and hugged her briefly. "We'll make out in the meantime, I'm sure."

"What if -- they find him?"

Tyler shook his head angrily. He was still tense, on edge. "Don't you understand? They'll never find him -- he doesn't exist. At least, not in our world. He's in his own world. You saw it. The model. The improved substitute."

"He's there?"

"All his life he's worked on it. Built it up. Made it real. He brought that world into being -- and now he's in it. That's what he wanted. That's why he built it. He didn't merely dream about an escape world. He actually constructed it -- every bit and piece. Now he's warped himself right out of our world, into it. Out of our lives."

Madge finally began to understand. "Then he really *did* lose himself in his substitute world. You meant that, what you said about him -- getting away."

"It took me awhile to realize it. The mind constructs reality. Frames it. Creates it. We all have a common reality, a common dream. But Haskel turned his back on our common reality and created his own. And he had a unique capacity -- far beyond the ordinary. He devoted his whole life, his whole skill to building it. He's there now."

Tyler hesitated and frowned. He gripped the wheel tightly and increased speed. The Buick hissed along the dark street, through the silent, unmoving bleakness that was the town.

"There's only one thing," he continued presently. "One thing I don't understand."

"What is it?"

"The model. It was also gone. I assumed he'd -- shrink, I suppose. Merge with it. But the model's gone, too." Tyler shrugged. "It doesn't matter." He peered into the darkness. "We're almost there. This is Elm."

It was then Madge screamed. *"Look!"*

To the right of the car was a small, neat building. And a sign. The sign was easily visible in the darkness.

WOODLAND MORTUARY

Madge was sobbing in horror. The car roared forward, automatically guided by Tyler's numb hands. Another sign flashed by briefly, as they coasted up before the city hall.

STEUBEN PET SHOP

The city hall was lit by recessed, hidden illumination. A low, simple building, a square of glowing white. Like a marble Greek temple.

Tyler pulled the car to a halt. Then suddenly shrieked and started up again. But not soon enough.

The two shiny-black police cars came silently up around the Buick, one on each side. The four stern cops already had their hands on the door. Stepping out and coming toward him, grim and efficient.

Survey Team

Halloway came up through six miles of ash to see how the rocket looked in landing. He emerged from the lead-shielded bore and joined Young, crouching down with a small knot of surface troops.

The surface of the planet was dark and silent. The air stung his nose. It smelled foul. Halloway shivered uneasily. "Where the hell are we?"

A soldier pointed into the blackness. "The mountains are over there. See them? The Rockies, and this is Colorado."

Colorado. . . The old name awakened vague emotion in Halloway. He fingered his blast rifle. "When will it get here?" he asked. Far off, against the horizon, he could see the Enemy's green and yellow signal flares. And an occasional flash of fission white.

"Any time now. It's mechanically controlled all the way, piloted by robot. When it comes it really comes."

An Enemy mine burst a few dozen miles away. For a brief instant the landscape was outlined in jagged lightning. Halloway and the troops dropped to the ground automatically. He caught the dead burned smell of the surface of Earth as it was now, thirty years after the war began.

It was a lot different from the way he remembered it when he was a kid in California. He could remember the valley country, grape orchards and walnuts and lemons. Smudge pots under the orange trees. Green mountains and sky the color of a woman's eyes. And the fresh smell of the soil . . .

That was all gone now. Nothing remained but gray ash pulverized with the white stones of buildings. Once a city had been in this spot. He could see the yawning cavities of cellars, filled now with slag, dried rivers of rust that had once been buildings. Rubble strewn everywhere, aimlessly . . .

The mine flare faded out and the blackness settled back. They got cautiously to their feet. "Quite a sight," a soldier murmured.

"It was a lot different before," Halloway said.

"Was it? I was born undersurface."

"In those days we grew our food right in the ground, on the surface. In the soil. Not in underground tanks. We --"

Halloway broke off. A great rushing sound filled the air suddenly, cutting off his words. An immense shape roared past them in the blackness, struck someplace close, and shook the earth.

"The rocket!" a soldier shouted. They all began running, Halloway lumbering awkwardly along.

"Good news, I hope," Young said, close by him.

"I hope, too," Halloway gasped. "Mars is our last chance. If this doesn't work we're finished. The report on Venus was negative; nothing there but lava and steam."

Later they examined the rocket from Mars.

"It'll do," Young murmured.

"You're sure?" Director Davidson asked tensely. "Once we get there we can't come running back."

"We're sure." Halloway tossed the spools across the desk to Davidson. "Examine them yourself. The air on Mars will be thin, and dry. The gravity is much weaker than ours. But we'll be able to live there, which is more than you can say for this God-forsaken Earth."

Davidson picked up the spools. The unblinking recessed lights gleamed down on the metal desk, the metal walls and floor of the office. Hidden machinery wheezed in the walls, maintaining the air and temperature. "I'll have to rely on you experts, of course. If some vital factor is not taken into account --"

"Naturally, it's a gamble," Young said. "We can't be sure of all factors at this distance." He tapped the spools. "Mechanical samples and photos. Robots creeping around, doing the best they can. We're lucky to have *anything* to go on."

"There's no radiation at least," Halloway said. "We can count on that. But Mars will be dry and dusty and cold. It's a long way out."Weak sun. Deserts and wrinkled hills."

"Mars is old," Young agreed.

"It was cooled a long time ago. Look at it this way: We have eight planets, excluding Earth. Pluto to Jupiter is *out*. No chance of survival there. Mercury is nothing but liquid metal. Venus is still volcano and steam -- pre-Cambrian. That's seven of the eight. Mars is the only possibility *a priori*."

"In other words," Davidson said slowly, "Mars *has* to be okay because there's nothing else for us to try."

"We could stay here. Live on here in the undersurface systems like gophers."

"We could not last more than another year. You've seen the recent psych graphs."

They had. The tension index was up. Men weren't made to live in metal tunnels, living on tank-grown food, working and sleeping and dying without seeing the sun.

It was the children they were really thinking about. Kids that had never been up to the surface. Wan-faced pseudo mutants with eyes like blind fish. A generation born in the subterranean world. The tension index was up because men were seeing their children alter and meld in with a world of tunnels and slimy darkness and dripping luminous rocks.

"Then it's agreed?" Young said.

Davidson searched the faces of the two technicians. "Maybe we could reclaim the surface, revive Earth again, renew its soil. It hasn't really gone that far, has it?"

"No chance," Young said flatly. "Even if we could work an arrangement with the Enemy there'll be particles in suspension for another fifty years. Earth will be too hot for life the rest of this century. *And we can't wait.*"

"All right," Davidson said. "I'll authorize the survey team. We'll risk that, at least. You want to go? Be the first humans to land on Mars?"

"You bet," Halloway said grimly. "It's in our contract that I go."

The red globe that was Mars grew steadily larger. In the control room Young and van Ecker, the navigator, watched it intently.

"We'll have to bail," van Ecker said. "No chance of landing at this velocity."

Young was nervous. "That's all right for us, but how about the first load of settlers? We can't expect women and children to jump."

"By then we'll know more." Van Ecker nodded and Captain Mason sounded the emergency alarm. Throughout the ship relay bells clanged ominously. The ship throbbed with scampering feet as crew members grabbed their jump-suits and hurried to the hatches.

"Mars," Captain Mason murmured, still at the viewscreen. "Not like Luna. This is the real thing."

Young and Halloway moved toward the hatch. "We better get going."

Mars was swelling rapidly. An ugly bleak globe, dull red. Halloway fitted on his jump helmet. Van Ecker came behind him.

Mason remained in the control cabin. "I'll follow," he said, "after the crew's out."

The hatch slid back and they moved out onto the jump shelf. The crew were already beginning to leap.

"Too bad to waste a ship," Young said.

"Can't be helped." Van Ecker clamped his helmet on and jumped. His brake-units sent him spinning upward, rising like a balloon into the blackness above them. Young and Halloway followed. Below them the ship plunged on, downward toward the surface of Mars. In the sky tiny luminous dots drifted -- the crew members.

"I've been thinking," Halloway said into his helmet speaker.

"What about?" Young's voice came in his earphones.

"Davidson was talking about overlooking some vital factor. There is one we haven't considered."

"What's that?"

"The Martians."

"Good God!" van Ecker chimed in. Halloway could see him drifting off to his right, settling slowly toward the planet below. "You think there *are* Martians?"

"It's possible. Mars will sustain life. If we can live there other complex forms could exist, too."

"We'll know soon enough," Young said.

Van Ecker laughed. "Maybe they trapped one of our robot rockets. Maybe they're expecting us."

Halloway was silent. It was too close to be funny. The red planet was growing rapidly. He could see white spots at the poles. A few hazy blue-green ribbons that had once been called *canals.* Was there a civilization down there, an organized culture waiting for them, as they drifted slowly down? He groped at his pack until his fingers closed over the butt of his pistol.

"Better get your guns out," he said.

"If there's a Martian defense system waiting for us we won't have a chance," Young said. "Mars cooled millions of years ahead of Earth. It's a cinch they'll be so advanced we won't even be --"

"Too late now," Mason's voice came faintly. "You experts should have thought of that before."

"Where are you?" Halloway demanded.

"Drifting below you. The ship is empty. Should strike any moment. I got all the equipment out, attached it to automatic jump units."

A faint flash of light exploded briefly below, winked out. The ship, striking the surface. . .

"I'm almost down," Mason said nervously. "I'll be the first. . ."

Mars had ceased to be a globe. Now it was a great red dish, a vast plain of dull rust spread out beneath them. They fell slowly, silently, toward it. Mountains became visible. Narrow trickles of water that were rivers. A vague checker-board pattern that might have been fields and pastures. . .

Halloway gripped his pistol tightly. His brake-units shrieked as the air thickened. He was almost down. A muffled *crunch* sounded abruptly in his earphones.

"Mason!" Young shouted.

"I'm down," Mason's voice came faintly.

"You all right?"

"Knocked the wind out of me. But I'm all right."

"How does it look?" Halloway demanded.

For a moment there was silence. Then: "Good God!" Mason gasped. "A *city!*"

"A city?" Young yelled. "What kind? What's it like?"

"Can you see them?" van Ecker shouted. "What are they like? Are there a lot of them?"

They could hear Mason breathing. His breath rasped hoarsely in their phones. "No," he gasped at last. "No sign of life. No activity. The city is -- it looks deserted."

"Deserted?"

"Ruins. Nothing but ruins. Miles of wrecked columns and walls and rusting scaffolding."

"Thank God," Young breathed. "They must have died out. We're safe. They must have evolved and finished their cycle a long time ago."

"Did they leave us anything?" Fear clutched at Halloway. "Is there anything left for *us?*" He clawed wildly at his brake-units, struggling frantically to hurry his descent. "Is it all gone?"

"You think they used up everything?" Young said. "You think they exhausted all the --"

"I can't tell." Mason's weak voice came, tinged with uneasiness. "It looks bad. Big pits. Mining pits. I can't tell, but it looks bad. . ."

Halloway struggled desperately with his brake-units.

The planet was a shambles.

"Good God," Young mumbled. He sat down on a broken column and wiped his face. "Not a damn thing left. Nothing."

Around them the crew were setting up emergency defense units. The communications team was assembling a battery-driven transmitter. A bore team was drilling for water. Other teams were scouting around, looking for food.

"There won't be any signs of life," Halloway said. He waved at the endless expanse of debris and rust. "They're gone, finished a long time ago."

"I don't understand," Mason muttered. "How could they wreck a whole planet?"

"We wrecked Earth in thirty years."

"Not this way. They've *used* Mars up. Used up everything. Nothing left. Nothing at all. It's one vast scrap-heap."

Shakily Halloway tried to light a cigarette. The match burned feebly, then sputtered out. He felt light and dopey. His heart throbbed heavily. The distant sun beat down, pale and small. Mars was a cold, lonely dead world.

Halloway said, "They must have had a hell of a time, watching their cities rot away. No water or minerals, finally no soil." He picked up a handful of dry sand, let it trickle through his fingers.

"Transmitter working," a crew member said.

Mason got to his feet and lumbered awkwardly over to the transmitter. "I'll tell Davidson what we've found." He bent over the microphone.

Young looked across at Halloway. "Well, I guess we're stuck. How long will our supplies carry us?"

"Couple of months."

"And then --" Young snapped his fingers. "Like the Martians." He squinted at the long corroded wall of a ruined house. "I wonder what they were like."

"A semantics team is probing the ruins. Maybe they'll turn up something."

Beyond the ruined city stretched out what had once been an industrial area. Fields of twisted installations, towers and pipes and machinery. Sand-covered and partly rusted. The surface of the land was pocked with great gaping sores. Yawning pits where scoops had once dredged. Entrances of underground mines. Mars was honeycombed. Termite-ridden. A whole race had burrowed and dug in trying to stay alive. The Martians had sucked Mars dry, then fled it.

"A graveyard," Young said. "Well, they got what they deserved."

"You blame them? What should they have done? Perished a few thousand years sooner and left their planet in better shape?"

"They could have left us *something,*" Young said stubbornly. "Maybe we can dig up their bones and boil them. I'd like to get my hands on one of them long enough to --"

A pair of crewmen came hurrying across the sand. "Look at these!" They carried armloads of metal tubes, glittering cylinders heaped up in piles. "Look what we found buried!"

Halloway roused himself. "What is it?"

"Records. Written documents. Get these to the semantics team!" Carmichael spilled his armload at Halloway's feet. "And this isn't all. We found something else -- installations."

"Installations? What kind?"

"Rocket launchers. Old towers, rusty as hell. There are fields of them on the other side of the town." Carmichael wiped perspiration from his red face. "They didn't die, Halloway. They took off. They used up this place, then left."

Doctor Judde and Young pored over the gleaming tubes. "It's coming," Judde murmured, absorbed in the shifting pattern undulating across the scanner.

"Can you make anything out?" Halloway asked tensely.

"They left, all right. Took off. The whole lot of them."

Young turned to Halloway. "What do you think of that? So they didn't die out."

"Can't you tell where they went?"

Judde shook his head. "Some planet their scout ships located. Ideal climate and temperature." He pushed the scanner aside. "In their last period the whole Martian civilization was oriented around this escape planet. Big project, moving a society lock, stock and barrel. It took them three or four hundred years to get everything of value off Mars and on its way to the other planet."

"How did the operation come out?"

"Not so good. The planet was beautiful. But they had to adapt. Apparently they didn't anticipate all the problems arising from colonization on a strange planet." Judde indicated a cylinder. "The colonies deteriorated rapidly. Couldn't keep the traditions and techniques going. The society broke apart. Then came war, barbarism."

"Then their migration was a failure." Halloway pondered. "Maybe it can't be done. Maybe it's impossible."

"Not a failure," Judde corrected. "They lived, at least. This place was no good any more. Better to live as savages on a strange world than stay here and die. So they say, on these cylinders."

"Come along," Young said to Halloway. The two men stepped outside the semantics hut. It was night. The sky was littered with glowing stars. The two moons had risen. They glimmered coldly, two dead eyes in the chilly sky.

"This place won't do," Young stated. "We can't migrate here. That's settled."

Halloway eyed him. "What's on your mind?"

"This was the last of the nine planets. We tested every one of them." Young's face was alive with emotion. "None of them will support life. All of them are lethal or useless, like this rubbish heap. The whole damn solar system is out."

"So?"

"We'll have to leave the solar system."

"And go where? *How?*"

Young pointed toward the Martian ruins, to the city and the rusted, bent rows of towers. "Where *they* went. They found a place to go. An untouched world outside the solar system. And they developed some kind of outer-space drive to get them there."

"You mean --"

"Follow them. This solar system is dead. But outside, someplace in some other system, they found an escape world. And they were able to get there."

"We'd have to fight with them if we land on their planet. They won't want to share it."

Young spat angrily on the sand. "Their colonies deteriorated. Remember? Broke down into barbarism. We can handle them. We've got everything in the way of war weapons -- weapons that can wipe a planet clean."

"We don't want to do that."

"What *do* we want to do? Tell Davidson we're stuck on Terra? Let the human race turn into underground moles? Blind crawling things. . ."

"If we follow the Martians we'll be competing for their world. They found it; the damn thing belongs to them, not us. And maybe we can't work out their drive. Maybe the schematics are lost."

Judde emerged from the semantics hut. "I've some more information. The whole story is here. Details on the escape planet. Fauna and flora. Studies of its gravity, air density, mineral possessions, soil layer, climate, temperature -- everything."

"How about their drive?"

"Breakdown on that, too. Everything." Judde was shaking with excitement. "I have an idea. Let's get the designs team on these drive schematics and see if they can duplicate it. If they can, we could follow the Martians. We could sort of *share* their planet with them."

"See?" Young said to Halloway. "Davidson will say the same thing. It's obvious."

Halloway turned and walked off.

"What's wrong with him?" Judde asked.

"Nothing. He'll get over it." Young scratched out a quick message on a piece of paper. "Have this transmitted to Davidson back on Terra."

Judde peered at the message. He whistled. "You're telling him about the Martian migration. And about the escape planet?"

"We want to get started. It'll take a long time to get things under way."

"Will Halloway come around?"

"He'll come around," Young said. "Don't worry about him."

Halloway gazed up at the towers. The leaning, sagging towers from which the Martian transports had been launched thousands of years before.

Nothing stirred. No sign of life. The whole dried-up planet was dead.

Halloway wandered among the towers. The beam from his helmet cut a white path in front of him. Ruins, heaps of rusting metal. Bales of wire and building material. Parts of uncompleted equipment. Half-buried construction sections sticking up from the sand.

He came to a raised platform and mounted the ladder cautiously. He found himself in an observation mount, surrounded by the remains of dials and meters. A telescopic sight stuck up, rusted in place, frozen tight.

"Hey," a voice came from below. "Who's up there?"

"Halloway."

"God, you scared me." Carmichael slid his blast rifle away and climbed the ladder. "What are you doing?"

"Looking around."

Carmichael appeared beside him, puffing and red-faced. "Interesting, these towers. This was an automatic sighting station. Fixed the take-off for supply transports. The population was already gone." Carmichael slapped at the ruined control board. "These supply ships continued to take off, loaded by machines and dispatched by machines, after all the Martians were gone."

"Lucky for them they had a place to go."

"Sure was. The minerals team says there's not a damn thing left here. Nothing but dead sand and rock and debris. Even the water's no good. They took everything of value."

"Judde says their escape world is pretty nice."

"Virgin." Carmichael smacked his fat lips. "Never touched. Trees and meadows and blue oceans. He showed me a scanner translation of a cylinder."

"Too bad we don't have a place like that to go. A virgin world for ourselves."

Carmichael was bent over the telescope. "This here sighted for them. When the escape planet swam into view a relay delivered a trigger charge to the control tower. The tower launched the ships. When the ships were gone a new flock came up into position." Carmichael began to polish the encrusted lenses of the telescope, wiping the accumulated rust and debris away. "Maybe we'll see their planet."

In the ancient lenses a vague luminous globe was swimming. Halloway could make it out, obscured by the filth of centuries, hidden behind a curtain of metallic particles and dirt.

Carmichael was down on his hands and knees, working with the focus mechanism. "See anything?" he demanded.

Halloway nodded. "Yeah."

Carmichael pushed him away. "Let me look." He squinted into the lens. "Aw, for God's sake!"

"What's wrong? Can't you see it?"

"I see it," Carmichael said, getting down on his hands and knees again. "The thing must have slipped. Or the time shift is too great. But this is supposed to adjust automatically. Of course, the gear box has been frozen for --"

"What's wrong?" Halloway demanded.

"That's Earth. Don't you recognize it?"

"Earth!"

Carmichael sneered with disgust. "This fool thing must be busted. I wanted to get a look at their dream planet. That's just old Terra, where we came from. All my work trying to fix this wreck up, and what do we see?"

"*Earth!*" Halloway murmured.

He had just finished telling Young about the telescope.

"I can't believe it," Young said. "But the description fitted Earth thousands of years ago. . ."

"How long ago did they take off?" Halloway asked.

"About six hundred thousand years ago," Judde said.

"And their colonies descended into barbarism on the new planet."

The four men were silent. They looked at each other, tight-lipped.

"We've destroyed two worlds," Halloway said at last. "Not one. Mars first. We finished up here, then we moved to Terra. And we destroyed Terra as systematically as we did Mars."

"A closed circle," Mason said. "We're back where we started. Back to reap the crop our ancestors sowed. They left Mars this way. Useless. And now we're back here poking around the ruins like ghouls."

"Shut up," Young snapped. He paced angrily back and forth. "I can't believe it."

"We're Martians. Descendants of the original stock that left here. We're back from the colonies. Back home." Mason's voice rose hysterically. "We're home again, where we belong!"

Judde pushed aside the scanner and got to his feet. "No doubt about it. I checked their analysis with our own archeological records. It fits. Their escape world was Terra, six hundred thousand years ago."

"What'll we tell Davidson?" Mason demanded. He giggled wildly. "We've found a perfect place. A word untouched by human hands. Still in the original cellophane wrapper."

Halloway moved to the door of the hut, stood gazing silently out. Judde joined him. "This is catastrophic. We're really stuck. What the hell are you looking at?"

Above them, the cold sky glittered. In the bleak light the barren plains of Mars stretched out, mile after mile of empty, wasted ruin.

"At that," Halloway said. "You know what it reminds me of?"

"A picnic site."

"Broken bottles and tin cans and wadded up plates. After the picnickers have left. Only, the picnickers are back. They're back -- and they have to live in the mess they made."

"What'll we tell Davidson?" Mason demanded.

"I've already called him," Young said wearily. "I told him there was a planet, out of the solar system. Someplace we could go. The Martians had a drive."

"A drive." Judde pondered. "Those towers." His lips twisted. "Maybe they did have an outer space drive. Maybe it's worth going on with the translation."

They looked at each other.

"Tell Davidson we're going on," Halloway ordered. "We'll keep on until we find it. We're not staying on this God-forsaken junkyard." His gray eyes glowed. "We'll find it, yet. A virgin world. A world that's unspoiled."

"*Unspoiled,*" Young echoed. "Nobody there ahead of us."

"We'll be the first," Judde muttered avidly.

"It's wrong!" Mason shouted. "Two are enough! Let's not destroy a third world!"

Nobody listened to him. Judde and Young and Halloway gazed up, faces eager, hands clenching and unclenching. As if they were already there. As if they were already holding onto the new world, clutching it with all their strength. Tearing it apart, atom by atom. . .

Sales Pitch

Commute ships roared on all sides, as Ed Morris made his way wearily home to Earth at the end of a long hard day at the office. The Ganymede-Terra lanes were choked with exhausted, grim-faced businessmen; Jupiter was in opposition to Earth and the trip was a good two hours. Every few million miles the great flow slowed to a grinding, agonized halt; signal-lights flashed as streams from Mars and Saturn fed into the main traffic-arteries.

"Lord," Morris muttered. "How tired can you *get?*" He locked the autopilot and momentarily turned from the control-board to light a much-needed cigarette. His hands shook. His head swam. It was past six; Sally would be fuming; dinner would be spoiled. The same old thing. Nerve-wracking driving, honking horns and irate drivers zooming past his little ship, furious gesturing, shouting, cursing. . .

And the ads. That was what really did it. He could have stood everything else -- but the ads, the whole long way from Ganymede to Earth. And on Earth, the swarms of sales robots; it was too much. And they were everywhere.

He slowed to avoid a fifty-ship smashup. Repair-ships were scurrying around trying to get the debris out of the lane. His audio-speaker wailed as police rockets hurried up. Expertly, Morris raised his ship, cut between two slow-moving commercial transports, zipped momentarily into the unused left lane, and then sped on, the wreck left behind. Horns honked furiously at him; he ignored them.

"Trans-Solar Products greets you!" an immense voice boomed in his ear. Morris groaned and hunched down in his seat. He was getting near Terra; the barrage was increasing. "Is your tension-index pushed over the safety-margin by the ordinary frustrations of the day? Then you need an Id-Persona Unit. So small it can be worn behind the ear, close to the frontal lobe --"

Thank God, he was past it. The ad dimmed and receded behind, as his fast-moving ship hurtled forward. But another was right ahead.

"Drivers! Thousands of unnecessary deaths each year from inter-planet driving. Hypno-Motor Control from an expert source-point insures your safety. Surrender your body and save your life!" The voice roared louder. "Industrial experts say -- "

Both audio ads, the easiest to ignore. But now a visual ad was forming; he winced, closed his eyes, but it did no good.

"Men!" an unctuous voice thundered on all sides of him. "Banish internally-caused obnoxious odors *forever.* Removal by modern painless methods of the gastrointestinal tract and substitution system will relieve you of the most acute cause of social rejection." The visual image locked; a vast nude girl, blonde hair disarranged, blue eyes half shut, lips parted, head tilted back in sleep-drugged ecstasy. The features ballooned as the lips approached his own. Abruptly the orgiastic expression on the girl's face vanished. Disgust and revulsion swept across, and then the image faded out.

"Does this happen to you?" the voice boomed. "During erotic sex-play do you offend your love-partner by the presence of gastric processes which --" The voice died, and he was past. His mind his own again, Morris kicked savagely at the throttle and sent the little ship leaping. The pressure, applied directly to the audio-visual regions of his brain, had faded below spark point. He groaned and shook his head to clear it. All around him the vague half-defined echoes of ads glittered and gibbered, like ghosts of distant video-stations. Ads waited on all sides; he steered a careful course, dexterity born of animal desperation, but not all could be avoided. Despair seized him. The outline of a new visual-audio ad was already coming into being.

"You, mister wage-earner!" it shouted into the eyes and ears, noses and throats, of a thousand weary commuters. "Tired of the same old job? Wonder Circuits Inc. has perfected a marvelous long-range thoughtwave scanner. Know what others are thinking and saying. Get the edge on fellow employees. Learn facts, figures about your employer's personal existence. Banish uncertainty!"

343

Morris' despair swept up wildly. He threw the throttle on full blast; the little ship bucked and rolled as it climbed from the traffic-lane into the dead zone beyond. A shrieking roar, as his fender whipped through the protective wall -- and then the ad faded behind him.

He slowed down, trembling with misery and fatigue. Earth lay ahead. He'd be home, soon. Maybe he could get a good night's sleep. He shakily dropped the nose of the ship and prepared to hook onto the tractor beam of the Chicago commute field.

"The best metabolism adjuster on the market," the salesrobot shrilled. "Guaranteed to maintain a perfect endocrine-balance, or your money refunded in full."

Morris pushed wearily past the salesrobot, up the sidewalk toward the residential-block that contained his living-unit. The robot followed a few steps, then forgot him and hurried after another grim-faced commuter.

"All the news while it's news," a metallic voice dinned at him. "Have a retinal vidscreen installed in your least-used eye. Keep in touch with the world; don't wait for out-of-date hourly summaries."

"Get out of the way," Morris muttered. The robot stepped aside for him and he crossed the street with a pack of hunched-over men and women.

Robot-salesmen were everywhere, gesturing, pleading, shrilling. One started after him and he quickened his pace. It scurried along, chanting its pitch and trying to attract his attention, all the way up the hill to his living-unit. It didn't give up until he stooped over, snatched up a rock, and hurled it futilely. He scrambled in the house and slammed the doorlock after him. The robot hesitated, then turned and raced after a woman with an armload of packages toiling up the hill. She tried vainly to elude it, without success.

"Darling!" Sally cried. She hurried from the kitchen, drying her hands on her plastic shorts, bright-eyed and excited. "Oh, you poor thing! You look so tired!"

Morris peeled off his hat and coat and kissed his wife briefly on her bare shoulder. "What's for dinner?"

Sally gave his hat and coat to the closet. "We're having Uranian wild pheasant; your favorite dish."

Morris' mouth watered, and a tiny surge of energy crawled back into his exhausted body. "No kidding? What the hell's the occasion?"

His wife's brown eyes moistened with compassion. "Darling, it's your birthday; you're thirty-seven years old today. Had you forgotten?"

"Yeah," Morris grinned a little. "I sure had." He wandered into the kitchen. The table was set; coffee was steaming in the cups and there was butter and white bread, mashed potatoes and green peas. "My golly. A real occasion."

Sally punched the stove controls and the container of smoking pheasant was slid onto the table and neatly sliced open. "Go wash your hands and we're ready to eat. Hurry -- before it gets cold."

Morris presented his hands to the wash slot and then sat down gratefully at the table. Sally served the tender, fragrant pheasant, and the two of them began eating.

"Sally," Morris said, when his plate was empty and he was leaning back and sipping slowly at his coffee. "I can't go on like this. Something's got to be done."

"You mean the drive? I wish you could get a position on Mars like Bob Young. Maybe if you talked to the Employment Commission and explained to them how all the strain --"

"It's not just the drive. *They're right out front.* Everywhere. Waiting for me. All day and night."

"Who are, dear?"

"Robots selling things. As soon as I set down the ship. Robots and visual-audio ads. They dig right into a man's brain. They follow people around until they die."

"I know." Sally patted his hand sympathetically. "When I go shopping they follow me in clusters. All talking at once. It's really a panic -- you can't understand half what they're saying."

"We've got to break out."

"Break out?" Sally faltered. "What do you mean?"

"We've got to get away from them. They're destroying us."

Morris fumbled in his pocket and carefully got out a tiny fragment of metal-foil. He unrolled it with painstaking care and smoothed it out on the table. "Look at this. It was circulated in the office, among the men; it got to me and I kept it."

"What does it mean?" Sally's brow wrinkled as she made out the words. "Dear, I don't think you got all of it. There must be more than this."

"A new world," Morris said softly. "Where they haven't got to, yet. It's a long way off, out beyond the solar system. Out in the stars."

"Proxima?"

"Twenty planets. Half of them habitable. Only a few thousand people out there. Families, workmen, scientists, some industrial survey teams. Land free for the asking."

"But it's so --" Sally made a face. "Dear, isn't it sort of under-developed? They say it's like living back in the twentieth century. Flush toilets, bathtubs, gasoline driven cars --"

"That's right." Morris rolled up the bit of crumpled metal, his face grim and dead-serious. "It's a hundred years behind times. None of this." He indicated the stove and the furnishings in the living room. "We'll have to do without. We'll have to get used to a simpler life. The way our ancestors lived." He tried to smile but his face wouldn't cooperate. "You think you'd like it? No ads, no salesrobots, traffic moving at sixty miles an hour instead of sixty million. We could raise passage on one of the big trans-system liners. I could sell my commute rocket. . ."

There was a hesitant, doubtful silence.

"Ed," Sally began. "I think we should think it over more. What about your job? What would you do out there?"

"I'd find something."

"But what? Haven't you got that part figured out?" A shrill tinge of annoyance crept into her voice. "It seems to me we should consider that part just a little more before we throw away everything and just -- take off."

"If we don't go," Morris said slowly, trying to keep his voice steady, "they'll get us. There isn't much time left. I don't know how much longer I can hold them off."

"Really, Ed! You make it sound so melodramatic. If you feel that bad why don't you take some time off and have a complete inhibition check? I was watching a vidprogram and I saw them going over a man whose psychosomatic system was much worse than yours. A much older man."

She leaped to her feet. "Let's go out tonight and celebrate. Okay?" Her slim fingers fumbled at the zipper of her shorts. "I'll put on my new plasti-robe, the one I've never had nerve enough to wear."

Her eyes sparkled with excitement as she hurried into the bedroom. "You know the one I mean? When you're up close it's translucent but as you get farther off it becomes more and more sheer until --"

"I know the one," Morris said wearily. "I've seen them advertised on my way home from work." He got slowly to his feet and wandered into the living room. At the door of the bedroom he halted. "Sally --"

"Yes?"

Morris opened his mouth to speak. He was going to ask her again, talk to her about the metal-foil fragment he had carefully wadded up and carried home. He was going to talk to her about the frontier. About Proxima Centauri. Going away and never coming back. But he never had a chance.

The doorchimes sounded.

"Somebody's at the door!" Sally cried excitedly. "Hurry up and see who it is!"

In the evening darkness the robot was a silent, unmoving figure. A cold wind blew around it and into the house. Morris shivered and moved back from the door. "What do you want?" he demanded. A strange fear licked at him. "What is it?"

The robot was larger than any he had seen. Tall and broad, with heavy metallic grippers and elongated eye-lenses. Its upper trunk was a square tank instead of the usual cone. It rested on four treads, not the customary two. It towered over Morris, almost seven feet high. Massive and solid.

"Good evening," it said calmly. Its voice was whipped around by the night wind; it mixed with the dismal noises of evening, the echoes of traffic and the clang of distant street signals. A few vague shapes hurried through the gloom. The world was black and hostile.

"Evening," Morris responded automatically. He found himself trembling. "What are you selling?"

"I would like to show you a fasrad," the robot said.

Morris' mind was numb; it refused to respond. What was a *fasrad?* There was something dreamlike and nightmarish going on. He struggled to get his mind and body together. "A what?" he croaked.

"A fasrad." The robot made no effort to explain. It regarded him without emotion, as if it was not its responsibility to explain anything. "It will take only a moment."

"I --" Morris began. He moved back, out of the wind. And the robot, without change of expression, glided past him and into the house.

"Thank you," it said. It halted in the middle of the living room. "Would you call your wife, please? I would like to show her the fasrad, also."

"Sally," Morris muttered helplessly. "Come here."

Sally swept breathlessly into the living room, her breasts quivering with excitement. "What is it? Oh!" She saw the robot and halted uncertainly. "Ed, did you order something? Are we buying something?"

"Good evening," the robot said to her. "I am going to show you the fasrad. Please be seated. On the couch, if you will. Both together."

Sally sat down expectantly, her cheeks flushed, eyes bright with wonder and bewilderment. Numbly, Ed seated himself beside her. "Look," he muttered thickly. "What the hell is a fasrad? *What's going on?* I don't want to buy anything!"

"What is your name?" the robot asked him.

"Morris." He almost choked. "Ed Morris."

The robot turned to Sally. "Mrs. Morris." It bowed slightly. "I'm glad to meet you, Mr. and Mrs. Morris. You are the first persons in your neighborhood to see the fasrad. This is the initial demonstration in this area." Its cold eyes swept the room. "Mr. Morris, you are employed, I assume. Where are you employed?"

"He works on Ganymede," Sally said dutifully, like a little girl in school. "For the Terran Metals Development Co."

The robot digested this information. "A fasrad will be of value to you." It eyed Sally. "What do you do?"

"I'm a tape transcriber at Histo-Research."

"A fasrad will be of no value in your professional work, but it will be helpful here in the home." It picked up a table in its powerful steel grippers. "For example, sometimes an attractive piece of furniture is damaged by a clumsy guest." The robot smashed the table to bits; fragments of wood and plastic rained down. "A fasrad is needed."

Morris leaped helplessly to his feet. He was powerless to halt events; a numbing weight hung over him, as the robot tossed the fragments of table away and selected a heavy floor lamp.

"Oh dear," Sally gasped. "That's my best lamp."

"When a fasrad is possessed, there is nothing to fear." The robot seized the lamp and twisted it grotesquely. It ripped the shade, smashed the bulbs, then threw away the remnants. "A situation of this kind can occur from some violent explosion, such as an H-Bomb."

"For God's sake," Morris muttered. "We --"

"An H-Bomb attack may never occur," the robot continued, "but in such an event a fasrad is indispensable." It knelt down and pulled an intricate tube from its waist. Aiming the tube

346

at the floor it atomized a hole five feet in diameter. It stepped back from the yawning pocket. "I have not extended this tunnel, but you can see a fasrad would save your life in case of attack."

The word *attack* seemed to set off a new train of reactions in its metal brain.

"Sometimes a thug or hood will attack a person at night," it continued. Without warning it whirled and drove its fist through the wall. A section of the wall collapsed in a heap of powder and debris. "That takes care of the thug." The robot straightened out and peered around the room. "Often you are too tired in the evening to manipulate the buttons on the stove." It strode into the kitchen and began punching the stove controls; immense quantities of food spilled in all directions.

"Stop!" Sally cried. "Get away from my stove!"

"You may be too weary to run water for your bath." The robot tripped the controls of the tub and water poured down. "Or you may wish to go right to bed." It yanked the bed from its concealment and threw it flat. Sally retreated in fright as the robot advanced toward her. "Sometimes after a hard day at work you are too tired to remove your clothing. In that event --"

"Get out of here!" Morris shouted at it. "Sally, run and get the cops. The thing's gone crazy. *Hurry.*"

"The fasrad is a necessity in all modern homes," the robot continued. "For example, an appliance may break down. The fasrad repairs it instantly." It seized the automatic humidity control and tore the wiring and replaced it on the wall. "Sometimes you would prefer not to go to work. The fasrad is permitted by law to occupy your position for a consecutive period not to exceed ten days. If, after that period --"

"Good God," Morris said, as understanding finally came. "You're the fasrad."

"That's right," the robot agreed. "Fully Automatic Self-Regulating Android (Domestic). There is also the fasrac (Construction), the fasram (Managerial), the fasras (Soldier), and the fasrab (Bureaucrat). I am designed for home use."

"You --" Sally gasped. "You're for sale. You're selling yourself."

"I am demonstrating myself," the fasrad, the robot, answered. Its impassive metal eyes were fixed intently on Morris as it continued, "I am sure, Mr. Morris, you would like to own me. I am reasonably priced and fully guaranteed. A full book of instructions is included. I cannot conceive of taking *no* for an answer."

At half past twelve, Ed Morris still sat at the foot of the bed, one shoe on, the other in his hand. He gazed vacantly ahead. He said nothing.

"For heaven's sake," Sally complained. "Finish untying that knot and get into bed; you have to be up at five-thirty."

Morris fooled aimlessly with the shoelace. After a while he dropped the shoe and tugged at the other one. The house was cold and silent. Outside, the dismal night-wind whipped and lashed at the cedars that grew along the side of the building. Sally lay curled up beneath the radiant-lens, a cigarette between her lips, enjoying the warmth and half-dozing.

In the living room stood the fasrad. It hadn't left. It was still there, was waiting for Morris to buy it.

"Come on!" Sally said sharply. "What's wrong with you? It fixed all the things it broke; it was just demonstrating itself." She sighed drowsily. "It certainly gave me a scare. I thought something had gone wrong with it. They certainly had an inspiration, sending it around to sell itself to people."

Morris said nothing.

Sally rolled over on her stomach and languidly stubbed out her cigarette. "That's not so much, is it? Ten thousand gold units, and if we get our friends to buy one we get a five per cent commission. All we have to do is show it. It isn't as if we had to *sell* it. It sells itself." She giggled. "They always wanted a product that sold itself, didn't they?"

Morris untied the knot in his shoelace. He slid his shoe back on and tied it tight.

"What are you doing?" Sally demanded angrily. "You come to bed!" She sat up furiously, as Morris left the room and moved slowly down the hall. "Where are you going?"

In the living room, Morris switched on the light and sat down facing the fasrad. "Can you hear me?" he said.

"Certainly," the fasrad answered. "I'm never inoperative. Sometimes an emergency occurs at night: a child is sick or an accident takes place. You have no children as yet, but in the event --"

"Shut up," Morris said, "I don't want to hear you."

"You asked me a question. Self-regulating androids are plugged in to a central information exchange. Sometimes a person wishes immediate information; the fasrad is always ready to answer any theoretical or factual inquiry. Anything not metaphysical."

Morris picked up the book of instructions and thumbed it. The fasrad did thousands of things; it never wore out; it was never at a loss; it couldn't make a mistake. He threw the book away. "I'm not going to buy you," he said to it. "Never. Not in a million years."

"Oh, yes you are," the fasrad corrected. "This is an opportunity you can't afford to miss." There was calm, metallic confidence in its voice. "You can't turn me down, Mr. Morris. A fasrad is an indispensable necessity in the modern home."

"Get out of here," Morris said evenly. "Get out of my house and don't come back."

"I'm not your fasrad to order around. Until you've purchased me at the regular list price, I'm responsible only to Self-Regulating Android Inc. Their instructions were to the contrary; I'm to remain with you until you buy me."

"Suppose I never buy you?" Morris demanded, but in his heart ice formed even as he asked. Already he felt the cold terror of the answer that was coming; there could be no other.

"I'll continue to remain with you," the fasrad said, "eventually you'll buy me." It plucked some withered roses from a vase on the mantel and dropped them into its disposal slot. "You will see more and more situations in which a fasrad is indispensible. Eventually you'll wonder how you ever existed without one."

"Is there anything you can't do?"

"Oh, yes; there's a great deal I can't do. But I can do anything *you* can do -- and considerably better."

Morris let out his breath slowly. "I'd be insane to buy you."

"You've got to buy me," the impassive voice answered. The fasrad extended a hollow pipe and began cleaning the carpet. "I am useful in all situations. Notice how fluffy and free of dust this rug is." It withdrew the pipe and extended another. Morris coughed and staggered quickly away; clouds of white particles billowed out and filled every part of the room.

"I am spraying for moths," the fasrad explained.

The white cloud turned to an ugly blue-black. The room faded into ominous darkness; the fasrad was a dim shape moving methodically about in the center. Presently the cloud lifted and the furniture emerged.

"I sprayed for harmful bacteria," the fasrad said.

It painted the walls of the room and constructed new furniture to go with them. It reinforced the ceiling in the bathroom. It increased the number of heat-vents from the furnace. It put in new electrical wiring. It tore out all the fixtures in the kitchen and assembled more modern ones. It examined Morris' financial accounts and computed his income tax for the following year. It sharpened all the pencils; it caught hold of his wrist and quickly diagnosed his high blood-pressure as psychosomatic.

"You'll feel better after you've turned responsibility over to me," it explained. It threw out some old soup Sally had been saving. "Danger of botulism," it told him. "Your wife is sexually attractive, but not capable of a high order of intellectualization."

Morris went to the closet and got his coat.

"Where are you going?" the fasrad asked.

"To the office."

"At this time of night?"

Morris glanced briefly into the bedroom. Sally was sound asleep under the soothing radiant-lens. Her slim body was rosy pink and healthy, her face free of worry. He closed the front door and hurried down the steps into the darkness. Cold night wind slashed at him as he approached the parking lot. His little commute ship was parked with hundreds of others; a quarter sent the attendant robot obediently after it.

In ten minutes he was on his way to Ganymede.

The fasrad boarded his ship when he stopped at Mars to refuel.

"Apparently you don't understand," the fasrad said. "My instructions are to demonstrate myself until you're satisfied. As yet, you're not wholly convinced; further demonstration is necessary." It passed an intricate web over the controls of the ship until all the dials and meters were in adjustment. "You should have more frequent servicing."

It retired to the rear to examine the drive jets. Morris numbly signalled the attendant, and the ship was released from the fuel pumps. He gained speed and the small sandy planet fell behind. Ahead, Jupiter loomed.

"Your jets aren't in good repair," the fasrad said, emerging from the rear. "I don't like that knock to the main brake drive. As soon as you land I'll make extensive repair."

"The Company doesn't mind your doing favors for me?" Morris asked, with bitter sarcasm.

"The Company considers me your fasrad. An invoice will be mailed to you at the end of the month." The robot whipped out a pen and a pad of forms. "I'll explain the four easy-payment plans. Ten thousand gold units cash means a three per cent discount. In addition, a number of household items may be traded in -- items you won't have further need for. If you wish to divide the purchase in four parts, the first is due at once, and the last in ninety days."

"I always pay cash," Morris muttered. He was carefully resetting the route positions on the control board.

"There's no carrying charge for the ninety day plan. For the six month plan there's a six per cent per annum charge which will amount to approximately --" It broke off. "We've changed course."

"We've left the official traffic lane." The fasrad stuck its pen and pad away and hurried to the control board. "What are you doing? There's a two unit fine for this."

Morris ignored it. He hung on grimly to the controls and kept his eyes on the viewscreen. The ship was gaining speed rapidly. Warning buoys sounded angrily as he shot past them and into the bleak darkness of space beyond. In a few seconds they had left all traffic behind. They were alone, shooting rapidly away from Jupiter, out into deep space.

The fasrad computed the trajectory. "We're moving out of the solar system. Toward Centaurus."

"You guessed it."

"Hadn't you better call your wife?"

Morris grunted and notched the drive bar farther up. The ship bucked and pitched, then managed to right itself. The jets began to whine ominously. Indicators showed the main turbines were beginning to heat. He ignored them and threw on the emergency fuel supply.

"I'll call Mrs. Morris," the fasrad offered. "We'll be beyond range in a short while."

"Don't bother."

"She'll worry." The fasrad hurried to the back and examined the jets again. It popped back into the cabin buzzing with alarm. "Mr. Morris, this ship is not equipped for inter-system travel. It's a Class D four-shaft domestic model for home consumption only. It was never made to stand this velocity."

"To get to Proxima," Morris answered, "we need this velocity."

The fasrad connected its power cables to the control board. "I can take some of the strain off the wiring system. But unless you rev her back to normal I can't be responsible for the deterioration of the jets."

"The hell with the jets."

The fasrad was silent. It was listening intently to the growing whine under them. The whole ship shuddered violently. Bits of paint drifted down. The floor was hot from the grinding shafts. Morris' foot stayed on the throttle. The ship gained more velocity as Sol fell behind. They were out of the charted area. Sol receded rapidly.

"It's too late to vid your wife," the fasrad said. "There are three emergency-rockets in the stern; if you want, I'll fire them off in the hope of attracting a passing military transport."

"Why?"

"They can take us in tow and return us to the Sol system. There's a six hundred gold unit fine, but under the circumstances it seems to me the best policy."

Morris turned his back to the fasrad and jammed down the throttle with all his weight. The whine had grown to a violent roar. Instruments smashed and cracked. Fuses blew up and down the board. The lights dimmed, faded, then reluctantly came back.

"Mr. Morris," the fasrad said, "you must prepare for death. The statistical probabilities of turbine explosion are seventy-thirty. I'll do what I can, but the danger-point has already passed."

Morris returned to the viewscreen. For a time he gazed hungrily up at the growing dot that was the twin star Centaurus. "They look all right, don't they? Prox is the important one. Twenty planets." He examined the wildly fluttering instruments. "How are the jets holding up? I can't tell from these; most of them are burned out."

The fasrad hesitated. It started to speak, then changed its mind. "I'll go back and examine them," it said. It moved to the rear of the ship and disappeared down the short ramp into the thundering, vibrating engine chamber.

Morris leaned over and put out his cigarette. He waited a moment longer, then reached out and yanked the drives full up, the last possible notch on the board.

The explosion tore the ship in half. Sections of hull hurtled around him. He was lifted weightless and slammed into the control board. Metal and plastic rained down on him. Flashing incandescent points winked, faded, and finally died into silence, and there was nothing but cold ash.

The dull *swish-swish* of emergency air-pumps brought consciousness back. He was pinned under the wreckage of the control board; one arm was broken and bent under him. He tried to move his legs but there was no sensation below his waist.

The splintered debris that had been his ship was still hurling toward Centaurus. Hull-sealing equipment was feebly trying to patch the gaping holes. Automatic temperature and grav feeds were thumping spasmodically from self-contained batteries. In the viewscreen the vast flaming bulk of the twin suns grew quietly, inexorably.

He was glad. In the silence of the ruined ship he lay buried beneath the debris, gratefully watching the growing bulk. It was a beautiful sight. He had wanted to see it for a long time. There it was, coming closer each moment. In a day or two the ship would plunge into the fiery mass and be consumed. But he could enjoy this interval; there was nothing to disturb his happiness -- He thought about Sally, sound asleep under the radiant-lens. Would Sally have liked Proxima? Probably not. Probably she would have wanted to go back home as soon as possible. This was something he had to enjoy alone. This was for him only. A vast peace descended over him. He could lie here without stirring, and the flaming magnificence would come nearer and nearer. . .

A sound. From the heaps of fused wreckage something was rising. A twisted, dented shape dimly visible in the flickering glare of the viewscreen. Morris managed to turn his head.

The fasrad staggered to a standing position. Most of its trunk was gone, smashed and broken away. It tottered, then pitched forward on its face with a grinding crash. Slowly it inched its way toward him, then settled to a dismal halt a few feet off. Gears whirred creakily. Relays popped open and shut. Vague, aimless life animated its devastated hulk.

"Good evening," its shrill, metallic voice grated.

Morris screamed. He tried to move his body but the ruined beams held him tight. He shrieked and shouted and tried to crawl away from it. He spat and wailed and wept.

"I would like to show you a fasrad," the metallic voice continued. "Would you call your wife, please? I would like to show her a fasrad, too."

"Get away!" Morris screamed. "Get away from me!"

"Good evening," the fasrad continued, like a broken tape. "Good evening. Please be seated. I am happy to meet you. What is your name? Thank you. You are the first persons in your neighborhood to see the fasrad. Where are you employed?"

Its dead eye-lenses gaped at him empty and vacant.

"Please be seated," it said again. "This will take only a second. Only a second. This demonstration will take only a --"

Breakfast at Twilight

"Dad?" Earl asked, hurrying out of the bathroom, "you going to drive us to school today?"

Tim McLean poured himself a second cup of coffee. "You kids can walk for a change. The car's in the garage."

Judy pouted. "It's raining."

"No it isn't," Virginia corrected her sister. She drew the shade back. "It's all foggy, but it isn't raining."

"Let me look." Mary McLean dried her hands and came over from the sink. "What an odd day. Is that fog? It looks more like smoke. I can't make out a thing. What did the weatherman say?"

"I couldn't get anything on the radio," Earl said. "Nothing but static."

Tim stirred angrily. "That darn thing on the blink again? Seems like I just had it fixed." He got up and moved sleepily over to the radio. He fiddled idly with the dials. The three children hurried back and forth, getting ready for school. "Strange," Tim said.

"I'm going." Earl opened the front door.

"Wait for your sisters," Mary ordered absently.

"I'm ready," Virginia said. "Do I look all right?"

"You look fine," Mary said, kissing her.

"I'll call the radio repair place from the office," Tim said.

He broke off. Earl stood at the kitchen door, pale and silent, his eyes wide with terror.

"What is it?"

"I -- I came back."

"What is it? Are you sick?"

"I can't go to school."

They stared at him. "What is wrong?" Tim grabbed his son's arm. "Why can't you go to school?"

"They -- they won't let me."

"*Who?*"

"The soldiers." It came tumbling out with a rush. "They're all over. Soldiers and guns. And they're coming here."

"Coming? Coming here?" Tim echoed, dazed.

"They're coming here and they're going to --" Earl broke off, terrified. From the front porch came the sound of heavy boots. A crash. Splintering wood. Voices.

"Good Lord," Mary gasped. "What is it, Tim?"

Tim entered the living-room, his heart laboring painfully. Three men stood inside the door. Men in gray-green uniforms, weighted with guns and complex tangles of equipment. Tubes and hoses. Meters on thick cords. Boxes and leather straps and antennae. Elaborate masks locked over their heads. Behind the masks Tim saw tired, whisker-stubbled faces, red-rimmed eyes that gazed at him in brutal displeasure.

One of the soldiers jerked up his gun, aiming at McLean's middle. Tim peered at it dumbly. *The gun.* Long and thin. Like a needle. Attached to a coil of tubes.

"What in the name of --" he began, but the soldier cut him off savagely.

"Who are you?" His voice was harsh, guttural. "What are you doing here?" He pushed his mask aside. His skin was dirty. Cuts and pocks lined his sallow flesh. His teeth were broken and missing.

"Answer!" a second soldier demanded. "What are you doing here?"

"Show your blue card," the third said. "Let's see your Sector number." His eyes strayed to the children and Mary standing mutely at the dining-room door. His mouth fell open.

"A woman?"

The three soldiers gazed in disbelief.

"What the hell is this?" the first demanded. "How long has this woman been here?"

Tim found his voice. "She's my wife. What is this? What --"

"Your *wife?*" They were incredulous.

"My wife and children. For God's sake --"

"Your wife? And you'd bring her here? You must be out of your head!"

"He's got ash sickness," one said. He lowered his gun and strode across the living-room to Mary. "Come on, sister. You're coming with us."

Tim lunged.

A wall of force hit him. He sprawled, clouds of darkness rolling around him. His ears sang. His head throbbed. Everything receded. Dimly, he was aware of shapes moving. Voices. The room. He concentrated.

The soldiers were herding the children back. One of them grabbed Mary by the arm. He tore her dress away, ripping it from her shoulders. "Gee," he snarled. "He'd bring her here, and she's not even strung!"

"Take her along."

"Okay, Captain." The soldier dragged Mary toward the front door. "We'll do what we can with her."

"The kids." The captain waved the other soldier over with the children. "Take them along. I don't get it. No masks. No cards. How'd this house miss getting hit? Last night was the worst in months!"

Tim struggled painfully to his feet. His mouth was bleeding. His vision blurred. He hung on tight to the wall. "Look," he muttered. "For God's sake --"

The captain was staring into the kitchen. "Is that -- is that *food?*" He advanced slowly through the dining-room. "Look!"

The other soldiers came after him, Mary and the children forgotten. They stood around the table, amazed.

"Look at it!"

"Coffee." One grabbed up the pot and drank it greedily down. He choked, black coffee dripping down his tunic. "Hot. Jeez. Hot coffee."

"Cream!" Another soldier tore open the refrigerator. "Look. Milk. Eggs. Butter. Meat." His voice broke. "It's full of food."

The captain disappeared into the pantry. He came out, lugging a case of canned peas. "Get the rest. Get it all. We'll load it in the snake."

He dropped the case on the table with a crash. Watching Tim intently, he fumbled in his dirty tunic until he found a cigarette.

He lit it slowly, not taking his eyes from Tim. "All right," he said. "Let's hear what you have to say."

Tim's mouth opened and closed. No words came. His mind was blank. Dead. He couldn't think.

"This food. Where'd you get it? And these things." The captain waved around the kitchen. "Dishes. Furniture. How come this house hasn't been hit? How did you survive last night's attack?"

"I --" Tim gasped.

The captain came toward him ominously. "The woman. And the kids. All of you. What are you doing here?" His voice was hard. "You better be able to explain, mister. You better be able to explain what you're doing here -- or we'll have to burn the whole damn lot of you."

Tim sat down at the table. He took a deep, shuddering breath, trying to focus his mind. His body ached. He rubbed blood from his mouth, conscious of a broken molar and bits of loose tooth. He got out a handkerchief and spat the bits into it. His hands were shaking.

"Come on," the captain said.

Mary and the children slipped into the room. Judy was crying. Virginia's face was blank with shock. Earl stared wide-eyed at the soldiers, his face white.

"Tim," Mary said, putting her hand on his arm. "Are you all right?"

Tim nodded. "I'm all right."

Mary pulled her dress around her. "Tim, they can't get away with it. Somebody'll come. The mailman. The neighbors. They can't just --"

"Shut up," the captain snapped. His eyes flickered oddly. "The mailman? What are you talking about?" He held out his hand. "Let's see your yellow slip, sister."

"Yellow slip?" Mary faltered.

The captain rubbed his jaw. "No yellow slip. No masks. No cards."

"They're geeps," a soldier said.

"Maybe. And maybe not."

"They're geeps, Captain. We better burn 'em. We can't take any chances."

"There's something funny going on here," the captain said. He plucked at his neck, lifting up a small box on a cord. "I'm getting a polic here."

"A polic?" A shiver moved through the soldiers. "Wait, Captain. We can handle this. Don't get a polic. He'll put us on 4 and then we'll never --"

The captain spoke into the box. "Give me Web B."

Tim looked up at Mary. "Listen, honey. I --"

"Shut up." A soldier prodded him. Tim lapsed into silence.

The box squawked. "Web B."

"Can you spare a polic? We've run into something strange. Group of five. Man, woman, three kids. No masks, no cards, the woman not strung, dwelling completely intact. Furniture, fixtures, about two hundred pounds of food."

The box hesitated. "All right. Polic on the way. Stay there. Don't let them escape."

"I won't." The captain dropped the box back in his shirt. "A polic will be here any minute. Meanwhile, let's get the food loaded."

From outside came a deep thundering roar. It shook the house, rattling the dishes in the cupboard.

"Jeez," a soldier said. That was close."

"I hope the screens hold until nightfall." The captain grabbed up the case of canned peas. "Get the rest. We want it loaded before the polic comes."

The two soldiers filled their arms and followed him through the house, out the front door. Their voices diminished as they strode down the path.

Tim got to his feet. "Stay here," he said thickly.

"What are you doing?" Mary asked nervously.

"Maybe I can get out." He ran to the back door and unlatched it, hands shaking. He pulled the door wide and stepped out on the back porch. "I don't see any of them. If we can only. . ."

He stopped.

Around him gray clouds blew. Gray ash, billowing as far as he could see. Dim shapes were visible. Broken shapes, silent and unmoving in the grayness.

Ruins.

Ruined buildings. Heaps of rubble. Debris everywhere. He walked slowly down the back steps. The concrete walk ended abruptly. Beyond it, slag and heaps of rubble were strewn. Nothing else. Nothing as far as the eye could see.

Nothing stirred. Nothing moved. In the gray silence there was no life. No motion. Only the clouds of drifting ash. The slag and the endless heaps.

The city was gone. The buildings were destroyed. Nothing remained. No people. No life. Jagged walls, empty and gaping. A few dark weeds growing among the debris. Tim bent down, touching a weed. Rough, thick stalk. And the slag. It was a metal slag. Melted metal. He straightened up --

"Come back inside," a crisp voice said.

He turned numbly. A man stood on the porch, behind him, hands on his hips. A small man, hollow-cheeked. Eyes small and bright, like two black coals. He wore a uniform different from the soldiers'. His mask was pushed back, away from his face. His skin was yellow, faintly luminous, clinging to his cheekbones. A sick face, ravaged by fever and fatigue.

"Who are you?" Tim said.

"Douglas. Political Commissioner Douglas."

"You're -- you're the police," Tim said.

"That's right. Now come inside. I expect to hear some answers from you. I have quite a few questions."

"The first thing I want to know," Commissioner Douglas said, "is how this house escaped destruction."

Tim and Mary and the children sat together on the couch, silent and unmoving, faces blank with shock.

"Well?" Douglas demanded.

Tim found his voice. "Look," he said. "I don't know. I don't know anything. We woke up this morning like every other morning. We dressed and ate breakfast --"

"It was foggy out," Virginia said. "We looked out and saw the fog."

"And the radio wouldn't work," Earl said.

"The radio?" Douglas's thin face twisted. "There haven't been any audio signals in months. Except for government purposes. This house. All of you. I don't understand. If you were geeps --"

"Geeps. What does that mean?" Mary murmured.

"Soviet general-purpose troops."

"Then the war has begun."

"North America was attacked two years ago," Douglas said. "In 1978."

Tim sagged. "1978. Then this is 1980." He reached suddenly into his pocket. He pulled out his wallet and tossed it to Douglas. "Look in there."

Douglas opened the wallet suspiciously. "Why?"

"The library card. The parcel receipts. Look at the dates." Tim turned to Mary. "I'm beginning to understand now. I had an idea when I saw the ruins."

"Are we winning?" Earl piped.

Douglas studied Tim's wallet intently. "Very interesting. These are all old. Seven and eight years." His eyes flickered. "What are you trying to say? That you came from the past? That you're time travelers?"

The captain came back inside. "The snake is all loaded, sir."

Douglas nodded curtly. "All right. You can take off with your patrol."

The captain glanced at Tim. "Will you be --"

"I'll handle them."

The captain saluted. "Fine, sir." He quickly disappeared through the door. Outside, he and his men climbed aboard a long thin truck, like a pipe mounted on treads. With a faint hum the truck leaped forward.

In a moment only gray clouds and the dim outline of ruined buildings remained.

Douglas paced back and forth, examining the living-room, the wallpaper, the light fixture and chairs. He picked up some magazines and thumbed through them. "From the past. But not far in the past."

"Seven years?"

"Could it be? I suppose. A lot of things have happened in the last few months. Time travel." Douglas grinned ironically. "You picked a bad spot, McLean. You should have gone farther on."

"I didn't pick it. It just happened."

"You must have done *something.*"

Tim shook his head. "No. Nothing. We got up. And we were -- here."

Douglas was deep in thought. "Here. Seven years in the future. Moved forward through time. We know nothing about time travel. No work has been done with it. There seem to be evident military possibilities."

"How did the war begin?" Mary asked faintly.

"Begin? It didn't begin. You remember. There was war seven years ago."

"The real war. This."

"There wasn't any point when it became -- this. We fought in Korea. We fought in China. In Germany and Yugoslavia and Iran. It spread, farther and farther. Finally the bombs were falling here. It came like the plague. The war *grew*. It didn't begin." Abruptly he put his notebook away. "A report on you would be suspect. They might think that I had the ash sickness."

"What's that?" Virginia asked.

"Radioactive particles in the air. Carried to the brain. Causes insanity. Everybody has a touch of it, even with the masks."

"I'd sure like to know who's winning," Earl repeated. "What was that outside? That truck. Was it rocket propelled?"

"The snake? No. Turbines. Boring snout. Cuts through the debris."

"Seven years," Mary said. "So much has changed. It doesn't seem possible."

"So much?" Douglas shrugged. "I suppose so. I remember what I was doing seven years ago. I was still in school. Learning. I had an apartment and a car. I went out dancing. I bought a TV set. But these things were there. The twilight. This. Only I didn't know. None of us knew. But they were there."

"You're a Political Commissioner?" Tim asked.

"I supervise the troops. Watch for political deviation. In a total war we have to keep people under constant surveillance. One Commie down in the Webs could wreck the whole business. We can't take chances."

Tim nodded. "Yes. It was there. The twilight. Only we didn't understand it."

Douglas examined the books in the bookcase. "I'll take a couple of these along. I haven't seen fiction in months. Most of it disappeared. Burned back in '77."

"Burned?"

Douglas helped himself. "Shakespeare. Milton. Dryden. I'll take the old stuff. It's safer. None of the Steinbeck and Dos Passos. Even a polic can get in trouble. If you stay here, you better get rid of *that*." He tapped a volume of Dostoevski, *The Brothers Karamazov*.

"If we stay! What else can we do?"

"You want to stay?"

"No," Mary said quietly.

Douglas shot her a quick glance. "No, I suppose not. If you stay you'll be separated, of course. Children to the Canadian Relocation Centers. Women are situated down in the under-surface factory-labor camps. Men are automatically a part of Military."

"Like those there who left," Tim said.

"Unless you can qualify for the id block."

"What's that?"

"Industrial Designing and Technology. What training have you had? Anything along scientific lines?"

"No. Accounting."

Douglas shrugged. "Well, you'll be given a standard test. If your IQ is high enough you could go in the Political Service. We use a lot of men." He paused thoughtfully, his arms loaded with books. "You better go back, McLean. You'll have trouble getting accustomed to this. I'd go back, if I could. But I can't."

"Back?" Mary echoed. "How?"

"The way you came."

"We just came."

Douglas halted at the front door. "Last night was the worst rom attack so far. They hit this whole area."

"Rom?"

"Robot operated missiles. The Soviets are systematically destroying continental America, mile by mile. Roms are cheap. They make them by the million and fire them off. The whole process is automatic. Robot factories turn them out and fire them at us. Last night they came over here -- waves of them. This morning the patrol came in and found nothing. Except you, of course."

Tim nodded slowly. "I'm beginning to see."

"The concentrated energy must have tipped some unstable time fault. Like a rock fault. We're always starting earthquakes. But a *time quake*. . . Interesting. That's what happened, I think. The release of energy, the destruction of matter, sucked your house into the future. Carried the house seven years ahead. This street, everything here, this very spot, was pulverized. Your house, seven years back, was caught in the undertow. The blast must have lashed back through time."

"Sucked into the future," Tim said. "During the night. While we were asleep."

Douglas watched him carefully. "Tonight," he said, "there will be another rom attack. It should finish off what is left." He looked at his watch. "It is now four in the afternoon. The attack will begin in a few hours. You should be undersurface. Nothing will survive up here. I can take you down with me, if you want. But if you want to take a chance, if you want to stay here --"

"You think it might tip us back?"

"Maybe. I don't know. It's a gamble. It might tip you back to your own time, or it might not. If not --"

"If not we wouldn't have a chance of survival."

Douglas flicked out a pocket map and spread it open on the couch. "A patrol will remain in this area another half-hour. If you decide to come undersurface with us, go down the street this way." He traced a line on the map. "To this open field here. The patrol is a Political unit. They'll take you the rest of the way down. You think you can find the field?"

"I think so," Tim said, looking at the map. His lips twisted. "That open field used to be the grammar school my kids went to. That's where they were going when the troops stopped them. Just a little while ago."

"Seven years ago," Douglas corrected. He snapped the map shut and restored it to his pocket. He pulled his mask down and moved out the front door onto the porch. "Maybe I'll see you again. Maybe not. It's your decision. You'll have to decide one way or the other. In any case -- good luck."

He turned and walked briskly from the house.

"Dad," Earl shouted, "are you going in the Army? Are you going to wear a mask and shoot one of those guns?" His eyes sparkled with excitement. "Are you going to drive a *snake?*"

Tim McLean squatted down and pulled his son to him. "You want that? *You want to stay here?* If I'm going to wear a mask and shoot one of those guns we can't go back."

Earl looked doubtful. "Couldn't we go back later?"

Tim shook his head. "Afraid not. We've got to decide now, whether we're going back or not."

"You heard Mr Douglas," Virginia said disgustedly. "The attack's going to start in a couple hours."

Tim got to his feet and paced back and forth. "If we stay in the house we'll get blown to bits. Let's face it. There's only a faint chance we'll be tipped back to our own time. A slim possibility -- a long shot. Do we want to stay here with roms falling all around us, knowing any second it may be the end -- hearing them come closer, hitting nearer -- lying on the floor, waiting, listening --"

"Do you really want to go back?" Mary demanded.

"Of course, but the risk --"

"I'm not asking you about the risk. I'm asking you if you really want to go back. Maybe you want to stay here. Maybe Earl's right. You in a uniform and a mask, with one of those needle guns. Driving a snake."

"With you in a factory-labor camp! And the kids in a Government Relocation Center! How do you think that would be? What do you think they'd teach them? What do you think they'd grow up like? And believe. . ."

"They'd probably teach them to be very useful."

"Useful! To what? To themselves? To mankind? Or to the war effort. . .?"

"They'd be alive," Mary said. "They'd be safe. This way, if we stay in the house, wait for the attack to come --"

"Sure," Tim grated. "They would be alive. Probably quite healthy. Well fed. Well clothed and cared for." He looked down at his children, his face hard. "They'd stay alive, all right. They'd live to grow up and become adults. But what kind of adults? You heard what he said! Book burnings in '77. What'll they be taught from? What kind of ideas are left, since '77? What kind of beliefs can they get from a Government Relocation Center? What kind of values will they have?"

"There's the id block," Mary suggested.

"Industrial Designing and Technology. For the bright ones. The clever ones with imagination. Busy slide rules and pencils. Drawing and planning and making discoveries. The girls could go into that. They could design the guns. Earl could go into the Political Service. He could make sure the guns were used. If any of the troops deviated, didn't want to shoot, Earl could report them and have them hauled off for reeducation. To have their political faith strengthened -- in a world where those *with* brains design weapons and those *without* brains fire them."

"But they'd be alive," Mary repeated.

"You've got a strange idea of what being alive is! You call that alive? Maybe it is." Tim shook his head wearily. "Maybe you're right. Maybe we should go undersurface with Douglas. Stay in this world. Stay alive."

"I didn't say that," Mary said softly. "Tim, I had to find out if you *really* understood why it's worth it. Worth staying in the house, taking the chance we won't be tipped back."

"Then you want to take the chance?"

"Of course! We *have* to. We can't turn our children over to them -- to the Relocation Center. To be taught how to hate and kill and destroy." Mary smiled up wanly. "Anyhow, they've always gone to the Jefferson School. And here, in this world, it's only an open field."

"Are we going back?" Judy piped. She caught hold of Tim's sleeve imploringly. "Are we going back now?"

Tim disengaged her arm. "Very soon, honey."

Mary opened the supply cupboards and rooted in them. "Everything's here. What did they take?"

"The case of canned peas. Everything we had in the refrigerator. And they smashed the front door."

"I'll bet we're beating them!" Earl shouted. He ran to the window and peered out. The sight of the rolling ash disappointed him. "I can't see anything! Just the fog!" He turned questioningly to Tim. "Is it always like this, here?"

"Yes," Tim answered.

Earl's face fell. "Just fog? Nothing else. Doesn't the sun shine ever?"

"I'll fix some coffee," Mary said.

"Good." Tim went into the bathroom and examined himself in the mirror. His mouth was cut, caked with dried blood. His head ached. He felt sick at his stomach.

"It doesn't seem possible," Mary said, as they sat down at the kitchen table.

Tim sipped his coffee. "No. It doesn't." Where he sat he could see out the window. The clouds of ash. The dim, jagged outline of ruined buildings.

"Is the man coming back?" Judy piped. "He was all thin and funny-looking. He isn't coming back, is he?"

Tim looked at his watch. It read ten o'clock. He reset it, moving the hands to four-fifteen. "Douglas said it would begin at nightfall. That won't be long."

"Then we're really staying in the house," Mary said.

"That's right."

"Even though there's only a little chance?"

"Even though there's only a little chance we'll get back. Are you glad?"

"I'm glad," Mary said, her eyes bright. "It's worth it, Tim. You know it is. Anything's worth it, any chance. *To get back.* And something else. We'll all be here together. . . We can't be -- broken up. Separated."

Tim poured himself more coffee. "We might as well make ourselves comfortable. We have maybe three hours to wait. We might as well try to enjoy them."

At six-thirty the first rom fell. They felt the shock, a deep rolling wave of force that lapped over the house.

Judy came running in from the dining-room, face white with fear. "Daddy! What is it?"

"Nothing. Don't worry."

"Come on back," Virginia called impatiently. "It's your turn." They were playing Monopoly.

Earl leaped to his feet. "I want to see." He ran excitedly to the window. "I can see where it hit!"

Tim lifted the shade and looked out. Far off, in the distance, a white glare burned fitfully. A towering column of luminous smoke rose from it.

A second shudder vibrated through the house. A dish crashed from the shelf, into the sink.

It was almost dark outside. Except for the two spots of white Tim could make out nothing. The clouds of ash were lost in the gloom. The ash and the ragged remains of buildings.

"That was closer," Mary said.

A third rom fell. In the living-room windows burst, showering glass across the rug.

"We better get back," Tim said.

"Where?"

"Down in the basement. Come on." Tim unlocked the basement door and they trooped nervously downstairs.

"Food," Mary said. "We better bring the food that's left."

"Good idea. You kids go on down. We'll come along in a minute."

"I can carry something," Earl said.

"Go on down." The fourth rom hit, farther off than the last. "And stay away from the window."

"I'll move something over the window," Earl said. "The big piece of plywood we used for my train."

"Good idea." Tim and Mary returned to the kitchen. "Food. Dishes. What else?"

"Books." Mary looked nervously around. "I don't know. Nothing else. Come on."

A shattering roar drowned out her words. The kitchen window gave, showering glass over them. The dishes over the sink tumbled down in a torrent of breaking china. Tim grabbed Mary and pulled her down.

From the broken window rolling clouds of ominous gray drifted into the room. The evening air stank, a sour, rotten smell. Tim shuddered.

"Forget the food. Let's get back down."

"But --"

"Forget it." He grabbed her and pulled her down the basement stairs. They tumbled in a heap, Tim slamming the door after them.

"Where's the food?" Virginia demanded.

Tim wiped his forehead shakily. "Forget it. We won't need it."

"Help me," Earl gasped. Tim helped him move the sheet of plywood over the window above the laundry tubs. The basement was cold and silent. The cement floor under them was faintly moist.

Two roms struck at once. Tim was hurled to the floor. The concrete hit him and he grunted. For a moment blackness swirled around him. Then he was on his knees, groping his way up.

"Everybody all right?" he muttered.

"I'm all right," Mary said. Judy began to whimper. Earl was feeling his way across the room.

"I'm all right," Virginia said. "I guess."

The lights flickered and dimmed. Abruptly they went out. The basement was pitch-black.

"Well," Tim said. "There they go."

"I have my flashlight." Earl winked the flashlight on. "How's that?"

"Fine," Tim said.

More roms hit. The ground leaped under them, bucking and heaving. A wave of force shuddering the whole house.

"We better lie down," Mary said.

"Yes. Lie down." Tim stretched himself out awkwardly. A few bits of plaster rained down around them.

"When will it stop?" Earl asked uneasily.

"Soon," Tim said.

"Then we'll be back?"

"Yes. We'll be back."

The next blast hit them almost at once. Tim felt the concrete rise under him. It grew, swelling higher and higher. He was going up. He shut his eyes, holding on tight. Higher and higher he went, carried up by the ballooning concrete. Around him beams and timbers cracked. Plaster poured down. He could hear glass breaking. And a long way off, the licking crackles of fire.

"Tim," Mary's voice came faintly.

"Yes."

"We're not going to -- to make it."

"I don't know."

"We're not. I can tell."

"Maybe not." He grunted in pain as a board struck his back, settling over him. Boards and plaster, covering him, burying him. He could smell the sour smell, the night air and ash. It drifted and rolled into the cellar, through the broken window.

"Daddy," Judy's voice came faintly.

"What?"

"Aren't we going back?"

He opened his mouth to answer. A shattering roar cut his words off. He jerked, tossed by the blast. Everything was moving around him. A vast wind tugged at him, a hot wind, licking at him, gnawing at him. He held on tight. The wind pulled, dragging him with it. He cried out as it seared his hands and face.

"Mary --"

Then silence. Only blackness and silence.

Cars.

Cars were stopping nearby. Then voices. And the noise of footsteps. Tim stirred, pushing the boards from him. He struggled to his feet.

"Mary." He looked around. "We're back."

The basement was in ruins. The walls were broken and sagging. Great gaping holes showed a green line of grass beyond. A concrete walk. The small rose garden. The white stucco house next door.

Lines of telephone poles. Roofs. Houses. The city. As it had always been. Every morning.

"We're back!" Wild joy leaped through him. *Back.* Safe. It was over. Tim pushed quickly through the debris of his ruined house. "Mary, are you all right?"

"Here." Mary sat up, plaster dust raining from her. She was white all over, her hair, her skin, her clothing. Her face was cut and scratched. Her dress was torn. "Are we really back?"

"Mr McLean! You all right?"

A blue-clad policeman leaped down into the cellar. Behind him two white-clad figures jumped. A group of neighbors collected outside, peering anxiously to see.

"I'm okay," Tim said. He helped Judy and Virginia up. "I think we're all okay."

"What happened?" The policeman pushed boards aside, coming over. "A bomb? Some kind of a bomb?"

"The house is a shambles," one of the white-clad interns said. "You sure nobody's hurt?"

"We were down here. In the basement."

"You all right, Tim?" Mrs Hendricks called, stepping down gingerly into the cellar.

"What happened?" Frank Foley shouted. He leaped down with a crash. "God, Tim! What the hell were you doing?"

The two white-clad interns poked suspiciously around the ruins. "You're lucky, mister. Damn lucky. There's nothing left upstairs."

Foley came over beside Tim. "Damn it man! I *told* you to have that hot water heater looked at!"

"What?" Tim muttered.

"The hot water heater! I told you there was something wrong with the cut-off. It must've kept heating up, not turned off. . ." Foley winked nervously. "But I won't say anything, Tim. The insurance. You can count on me."

Tim opened his mouth. But the words didn't come. What could he say? -- No, it wasn't a defective hot water heater that I forgot to have repaired. No, it wasn't a faulty connection in the stove. It wasn't any of those things. It wasn't a leaky gas line, it wasn't a plugged furnace, it wasn't a pressure cooker we forgot to turn off.

It's war. Total war. And not just war for me. For my family. For my house.

It's for your house, too. Your house and my house and all the houses. Here and in the next block, in the next town, the next state and country and continent. The whole world, like this. Shambles and ruins. Fog and dank weeds growing in the rusting slag. War for all of us. For everybody crowding down into the basement, white-faced, frightened, somehow sensing something terrible.

And when it really came, when the five years were up, there'd be no escape. No going back, tipping back into the past, away from it. When it came for them all, it would have them for eternity; there would be no one climbing back out, as he had.

Mary was watching him. The policeman, the neighbors, the white-clad interns -- all of them were watching him. Waiting for him to explain. To tell them what it was.

"Was it the hot water heater?" Mrs Hendricks asked timidly. "That was it, wasn't it, Tim? Things like that do happen. You can't be sure. . ."

"Maybe it was home brew," a neighbor suggested, in a feeble attempt at humor. "Was that it?"

He couldn't tell them. They wouldn't understand, because they didn't want to understand. They didn't want to know. They needed reassurance. He could see it in their eyes. Pitiful, pathetic fear. They sensed something terrible -- and they were afraid. They were searching his face, seeking his help. Words of comfort. Words to banish their fear.

"Yeah," Tim said heavily. "It was the hot water heater."

"I thought so!" Foley breathed. A sigh of relief swept through them all. Murmurs, shaky laughs. Nods, grins.

"I should have got it fixed," Tim went on. "I should have had it looked at a long time ago. Before it got in such bad shape." Tim looked around at the circle of anxious people, hanging on his words. "I should have had it looked at. Before it was too late."

The Crawlers

He built , and the more he built the more he enjoyed building. Hot sunlight filtered down; summer breezes stirred around him as he toiled joyfully. When he ran out of material he paused awhile and rested. His edifice wasn't large; it was more a practice model than the real thing. One part of his brain told him that, and another part thrilled with excitement and pride. It was at least large enough to enter. He crawled down the entrance tunnel and curled up inside in a contented heap.

Through a rent in the roof a few bits of dirt rained down. He oozed binder fluid and reinforced the weak place. In his edifice the air was clean and cool, almost dust-free. He crawled over the inner walls one last time, leaving a quick-drying coat of binder over everything. What else was needed? He was beginning to feel drowsy; in a moment he'd be asleep.

He thought about it, and then he extended a part of himself up through the still-open entrance. That part watched and listened warily, as the rest of him dozed off in a grateful slumber. He was peaceful and content, conscious that from a distance all that was visible was a light mound of dark clay. No one would notice it: no one would guess what lay beneath.

And if they did notice, he had methods of taking care of them.

The farmer halted his ancient Ford truck with a grinding shriek of brakes. He cursed and backed up a few yards. "There's one. Hop down and take a look at it. Watch the cars -- they go pretty fast along here."

Ernest Gretry pushed the cabin door open and stepped down gingerly onto the hot midmorning pavement. The air smelled of sun and drying grass. Insects buzzed around him as he advanced cautiously up the highway, hands in his trouser pockets, lean body bent forward. He stopped and peered down.

The thing was well mashed. Wheel marks crossed it in four places and its internal organs had ruptured and burst through. The whole thing was snail-like, a gummy elongated tube with sense organs at one end and a confusing mass of protoplasmic extensions at the other.

What got him most was the face. For a time he couldn't look directly at it: he had to contemplate the road, the hills, the big cedar trees, anything else. There was something in the little dead eyes, a glint that was rapidly fading. They weren't the lusterless eyes of a fish, stupid and vacant. The life he had seen haunted him, and he had got only a brief glimpse, as the truck bore down on it and crushed it flat.

"They crawl across here every once in a while," the farmer said quietly. "Sometimes they get as far as town. The first one I saw was heading down the middle of Grant Street, about fifty yards an hour. They go pretty slow. Some of the teenage kids like to run them down. Personally I avoid them, if I see them."

Gretry kicked aimlessly at the thing. He wondered vaguely how many more there were in the bushes and hills. He could see farmhouses set back from the road, white gleaming squares in the hot Tennessee sun. Horses and sleeping cattle. Dirty chickens scratching. A sleepy, peaceful countryside, basking in the late-summer sun.

"Where's the radiation lab from here?" he asked.

The farmer indicated. "Over there, on the other side of those hills. You want to collect the remains? They have one down at the Standard Oil Station in a big tank. Dead, of course. They filled the tank with kerosene to try to preserve it. That one's in pretty good shape, compared to this. Joe Jackson cracked its head with a two-by-four. He found it crawling across his property one night."

Gretry got shakily back into the truck. His stomach turned over and he had to take some long deep breaths. "I didn't realize there were so many. When they sent me out from Washington they just said a few had been seen."

"There's been quite a lot." The farmer started up the truck and carefully skirted the remains on the pavement. "We're trying to get used to them, but we can't. It's not nice stuff. A lot of people are moving away. You can feel it in the air, a sort of heaviness. We've got this problem and we have to meet it." He increased speed, leathery hands tight around the wheel. "It seems like there's more of *them* born all the time, and almost no normal children."

Back in town, Gretry called Freeman long distance from the booth in the shabby hotel lobby. "We'll have to do something. They're all around here. I'm going out at three to see a colony of them. The fellow who runs the taxi stand knows where they are. He says there must be eleven or twelve of them together."

"How do the people around there feel?" ;

"How the hell do you expect? They think it's God's Judgment. Maybe they're right."

"We should have made them move earlier. We should have cleaned out the whole area for miles around. Then we wouldn't have this problem." Freeman paused. "What do you suggest?"

"That island we took over for the H-bomb tests."

"It's a damn big island. There was a whole group of natives we moved off and resettled." Freeman choked. "Good God, are there *that* many of them?"

"The staunch citizens exaggerate, of course. But I get the impression there must be at least a hundred."

Freeman was silent a long time. "I didn't realize," he said finally. "I'll have to put it through channels, of course. We were going to make further tests on that island. But I see your point."

"I'd like it," Gretry said. "This is a bad business. We can't have things like this. People can't live with this sort of thing. You ought to drop out here and take a look. It's something to remember."

"I'll -- see what I can do. I'll talk to Gordon. Give me a ring tomorrow."

Gretry hung up and wandered out of the drab, dirty lobby onto the blazing sidewalk. Dingy stores and parked cars. A few old men hunched over on steps and sagging cane-bottom chairs. He lit a cigarette and shakily examined his watch. It was almost three. He moved slowly toward the taxi stand.

The town was dead. Nothing stirred. Only the motionless old men in their chairs and the out-of-town cars zipping along the highway. Dust and silence lay over everything. Age, like a gray spider web, covered all the houses and stores. No laughter. No sounds of any kind.

No children playing games.

A dirty blue taxicab pulled up silently beside him. "Okay, mister," the driver said, a rat-faced man in his thirties, toothpick hanging between his crooked teeth. He kicked the bent door open. "Here we go."

"How far is it?" Gretry asked, as he climbed in.

"Just outside town." The cab picked up speed and hurtled noisily along, bouncing and bucking. "You from the FBI?"

"No."

"I thought from your suit and hat you was." The driver eyed him curiously. "How'd you hear about the crawlers?"

"From the radiation lab."

"Yeah, it's that hot stuff they got there." The driver turned off the highway and onto a dirt side-road. "It's up here on the Higgins farm. The crazy damn things picked the bottom of old lady Higgins' place to build their houses."

"Houses?"

"They've got some sort of city, down under the ground. You'll see it -- the entrances, at least. They work together, building and fussing." He twisted the cab off the dirt road, between two huge cedars, over a bumpy field; and finally brought it to rest at the edge of a rocky gully. "This is it."

It was the first time Gretry had seen one alive.

He got out of the cab awkwardly, his legs numb and unresponding. The things were moving slowly between the woods and the entrance tunnels in the center of the clearing. They were bringing building material, clay and weeds. Smearing it with some kind of ooze and plastering it in rough forms which were carefully carried beneath the ground. The crawlers were two or three feet long; some were older than others, darker and heavier. All of them moved with agonizing slowness, a silent flowing motion across the sun-baked ground. They were soft, shell-less, and looked harmless.

Again, he was fascinated and hypnotized by their faces. The weird parody of human faces. Wizened little baby features, tiny shoebutton eyes, slit of a mouth, twisted ears, and a few wisps of damp hair. What should have been arms were elongated pseudopods that grew and receded like soft dough. The crawlers seemed incredibly flexible; they extended themselves, then snapped their bodies back, as their feelers made contact with obstructions. They paid no attention to the two men; they didn't even seem to be aware of them.

"How dangerous are they?" Gretry asked finally.

"Well, they have some sort of stinger. They stung a dog, I know. Stung him pretty hard. He swelled up and his tongue turned black. He had fits and got hard. He died." The driver added half-apologetically, "He was nosing around. Interrupting their building. They work all the time. Keep busy."

"Is this most of them?"

"I guess so. They sort of congregate here. I see them crawling this way." The driver gestured. "See, they're born in different places. One or two at each farmhouse, near the radiation lab."

"Which way is Mrs. Higgins' farmhouse?" Gretry asked.

"Up there. See it through the trees? You want to --"

"I'll be right back," Gretry said, and started abruptly off. "Wait here."

The old woman was watering the dark red geraniums that grew around her front porch, when Gretry approached. She looked up quickly, her ancient wrinkled face shrewd and suspicious, the sprinkling can poised like a blunt instrument.

"Afternoon," Gretry said. He tipped his hat and showed her his credentials. "I'm investigating the -- crawlers. At the edge of your land."

"Why?" Her voice was empty, bleak, cold. Like her withered face and body.

"We're trying to find a solution." Gretry felt awkward and uncertain. "It's been suggested we transport them away from here, out to an island in the Gulf of Mexico. They shouldn't be here. It's too hard on people. It isn't right," he finished lamely.

"No. It isn't right."

"And we've already begun moving everybody away from the radiation lab. I guess we should have done that a long time ago."

The old woman's eyes flashed. "You people and your machines. See what you've done!" She jabbed a bony finger at him excitedly. "Now you have to fix it. You have to do something."

"We're taking them away to an island as soon as possible. But there's one problem. We have to be sure about the parents. They have complete custody of them. We can't just --" He broke off futilely. "How do they feel? Would they let us cart up their -- children, and haul them away?"

Mrs. Higgins turned and headed into the house. Uncertainly, Gretry followed her through the dim, dusty interior rooms. Musty chambers full of oil lamps and faded pictures, ancient sofas and tables She led him through a great kitchen of immense cast iron pots and pans down a flight of wooden stairs to a painted white door. She knocked sharply.

Flurry and movement on the other side. The sound of people whispering and moving things hurriedly.

"Open the door," Mrs. Higgins commanded. After an agonized pause the door opened slowly. Mrs. Higgins pushed it wide and motioned Gretry to follow her.

In the room stood a young man and woman. They backed away as Gretry came in. The woman hugged a long pasteboard carton which the man had suddenly passed to her.

"Who are you?" the man demanded. He abruptly grabbed the carton back; his wife's small hands were trembling under the shifting weight.

Gretry was seeing the parents of one of them. The young woman, brown-haired, not more than nineteen. Slender and small in a cheap green dress, a full-breasted girl with dark frightened eyes. The man was bigger and stronger, a handsome dark youth with massive arms and competent hands gripping the pasteboard carton tight.

Gretry couldn't stop looking at the carton. Holes had been punched in the top; the carton moved slightly in the man's arms, and there was a faint shudder that rocked it back and forth.

"This man," Mrs. Higgins said to the husband, "has come to take it away."

The couple accepted the information in silence. The husband made no move except to get a better grip on the box.

"He's going to take all of them to an island," Mrs. Higgins said. "It's all arranged. Nobody'll harm them. They'll be safe and they can do what they want. Build and crawl around where nobody has to look at them."

The young woman nodded blankly.

"Give it to him," Mrs. Higgins ordered impatiently. "Give him the box and let's get it over with once and for all."

After a moment the husband carried the box over to a table and put it down. "You know anything about them?" he demanded. "You know what they eat?"

"We --" Gretry began helplessly.

"They eat leaves. Nothing but leaves and grass. We've been bringing in the smallest leaves we could find."

"It's only a month old," the young woman said huskily. "It already wants to go down with the others, but we keep it here. We don't want it to go down here. Not yet. Later, maybe, we thought. We didn't know what to do. We weren't sure." Her large dark eyes flashed briefly in mute appeal, then faded out again. "It's a hard thing to know."

The husband untied the heavy brown twine and took the lid from the carton. "Here. You can see it."

It was the smallest Gretry had seen. Pale and soft, less than a foot long. It had crawled in a corner of the box and was curled up in a messy web of chewed leaves and some kind of wax. A translucent covering spun clumsily around it, behind which it lay asleep. It paid no attention to them; they were out of its scope. Gretry felt a strange helpless horror rise up in him. He moved away, and the young man replaced the lid.

"We knew what it was," he said hoarsely. "Right away, as soon as it was born. Up the road, there was one we saw. One of the first. Bob Douglas made us come over and look at it. It was his and Julie's. That was before they started coming down and collecting together by the gully."

"Tell him what happened," Mrs. Higgins said.

"Douglas mashed its head with a rock. Then he poured gasoline on it and burned it up. Last week he and Julie packed and left."

"Have many of them been destroyed?" Gretry managed to ask.

"A few. A lot of men, they see something like that and they go sort of wild. You can't blame them." The man's dark eyes darted hopelessly. "I guess I almost did the same thing."

"Maybe we should have," his wife murmured. "Maybe I should have let you."

Gretry picked up the pasteboard carton and moved toward the door. "We'll get this done as quickly as we can. The trucks are on the way. It should be over in a day."

"Thank God for that," Mrs. Higgins exclaimed in a clipped, emotionless voice. She held the door open, and Gretry carried the carton through the dim, musty house, down the sagging front steps and out into the blazing mid-afternoon sun.

Mrs. Higgins stopped at the red geraniums and picked up her sprinkling can. "When you take them, take them all. Don't leave any behind. Understand?"

"Yes," Gretry muttered.

"Keep some of your men and trucks here. Keep checking. Don't let any stay where we have to look at them."

"When we get the people near the radiation lab moved away there shouldn't be any more of--"

He broke off. Mrs. Higgins had turned her back and was watering the geraniums. Bees buzzed around her. The flowers swayed dully with the hot wind. The old woman passed on around the side of the house, still watering and stooping over. In a few moments she was gone and Gretry was alone with his carton.

Embarrassed and ashamed, he carried the carton slowly down the hill and across the field to the ravine. The taxi driver was standing by his cab, smoking a cigarette and waiting patiently for him. The colony of crawlers was working steadily on its city. There were streets and passages. On some of the entrance-mounds he noticed intricate scratches that might have been words. Some of the crawlers were grouped together, setting up involved things he couldn't make out.

"Let's go," he said wearily to the driver.

The driver grinned and yanked the back door. "I left the meter running," he said, his ratty face bright with craft. "You guys all have a swindle sheet -- you don't care."

He built, and the more he built the more he enjoyed building. By now the city was over eighty miles deep and five miles in diameter. The whole island had been converted into a single vast city that honeycombed and interlaced farther each day. Eventually it would reach the land beyond the ocean; then the work would begin in earnest.

To his right, a thousand methodically moving companions toiled silently on the structural support that was to reinforce the main breeding chamber. As soon as it was in place everyone would feel better; the mothers were just now beginning to bring forth their young.

That was what worried him. It took some of the joy out ot building. He had seen one of the first born -- before it was quickly hidden and the thing hushed up. A brief glimpse of a bulbous head, foreshortened body, incredibly rigid extensions. It shrieked and wailed and turned red in the face. Gurgled and plucked aimlessly and kicked its feet.

In horror, somebody had finally mashed the throwback with a rock. And hoped there wouldn't be any more.

Exhibit Piece

"That's a strange suit you have on," the robot pubtrans driver observed. It slid back its door and came to rest at the curb. "What are the little round things?"

"Those are buttons," George Miller explained. "They are partly functional, partly ornamental. This is an archaic suit of the twentieth century. I wear it because of the nature of my employment."

He paid the robot, grabbed up his briefcase, and hurried along the ramp to the History Agency. The main building was already open for the day; robed men and women wandered everywhere. Miller entered a private lift, squeezed between two immense controllers from the pre-Christian division, and in a moment was on his way to his own level, the Middle Twentieth Century.

"Gorning," he murmured, as Controller Fleming met him at the atomic engine exhibit.

"Gorning," Fleming responded brusquely. "Look here, Miller. Let's have this out once and for all. What if everyone dressed like you? The Government sets up strict rules for dress. Can't you forget your damn anachronisms once in a while? What in God's name is that thing in your hand? It looks like a squashed Jurassic lizard."

"This is an alligator hide briefcase," Miller explained. "I carry my study spools in it. The briefcase was an authority symbol of the managerial class of the later twentieth century." He unzipped the briefcase. "Try to understand, Fleming. By accustoming myself to everyday objects of my research period I transform my relation from mere intellectual curiosity to genuine empathy. You have frequently noticed I pronounce certain words oddly. The accent is that of an American businessman of the Eisenhower administration. Dig me?"

"Eh?" Fleming muttered.

"Dig me was a twentieth-century expression." Miller laid out his study spools on his desk. "Was there anything you wanted? If not I'll begin today's work. I've uncovered fascinating evidence to indicate that although twentieth-century Americans laid their own floor tiles, they did not weave their own clothing. I wish to alter my exhibits on this matter."

"There's no fanatic like an academician," Fleming grated. "You're two hundred years behind times. Immersed in your relics and artifacts. Your damn authentic replicas of discarded trivia."

"I love my work," Miller answered mildly.

"Nobody complains about your work. But there are other things than work. You're a political-social unit here in this society. Take warning, Miller! The Board has reports on your eccentricities. They approve devotion to work. . ." His eyes narrowed significantly. "But you go too far."

"My first loyalty is to my art," Miller said.

"Your what? What does that mean?"

"A twentieth-century term." There was undisguised superiority on Miller's face. "You're nothing but a minor bureaucrat in a vast machine. You're a function of an impersonal cultural totality. You have no standards of your own. In the twentieth century men had personal standards of workmanship. Artistic craft. Pride of accomplishment. These words mean nothing to you. You have no soul -- another concept from the golden days of the twentieth century when men were free and could speak their minds."

"Beware, Miller!" Fleming blanched nervously and lowered his voice. "You damn scholars. Come up out of your tapes and face reality. You'll get us all in trouble, talking this way. Idolize the past, if you want. But remember -- it's gone and buried. Times change. Society progresses." He gestured impatiently at the exhibits that occupied the level. "That's only an imperfect replica."

"You impugn my research?" Miller was seething. "This exhibit is absolutely accurate! I correct it to all new data. There isn't anything I don't know about the twentieth century."

Fleming shook his head. "It's no use." He turned and stalked wearily off the level, onto the descent ramp.

Miller straightened his collar and bright hand-painted necktie. He smoothed down his blue pin stripe coat, expertly lit a pipeful of two-century-old tobacco, and returned to his spools.

Why didn't Fleming leave him alone? Fleming, the officious representative of the great hierarchy that spread like a sticky gray web over the whole planet. Into each industrial, professional, and residential unit. Ah, the freedom of the twentieth century! He slowed his tape scanner a moment, and a dreamy look slid over his features. The exciting age of virility and individuality, when men were men --

It was just about then, just as he was settling deep in the beauty of his research, that he heard the inexplicable sounds. They came from the center of his exhibit, from within the intricate, carefully regulated interior.

Somebody was in his exhibit.

He could hear them back there, back in the depths. Somebody or something had gone past the safety barrier set up to keep the public out. Miller snapped off his tape scanner and got slowly to his feet. He was shaking all over as he moved cautiously toward the exhibit. He killed the barrier and climbed the railing on to a concrete pavement. A few curious visitors blinked, as the small, oddly dressed man crept among the authentic replicas of the twentieth century that made up the exhibit and disappeared within.

Breathing hard, Miller advanced up the pavement and on to a carefully tended gravel path. Maybe it was one of the other theorists, a minion of the Board, snooping around looking for something with which to discredit him. An inaccuracy here -- a trifling error of no consequence there. Sweat came out of his forehead; anger became terror. To his right was a flower bed. Paul Scarlet roses and low-growing pansies. Then the moist green lawn. The gleaming white garage, with its door half up. The sleek rear of a 1954 Buick -- and then the house itself.

He'd have to be careful. If this *was* somebody from the Board he'd be up against official hierarchy. Maybe it was somebody big. Maybe even Edwin Carnap, President of the Board, the highest ranking official in the N'York branch of the World Directorate. Shakily, Miller climbed the three cement steps. Now he was on the porch of the twentieth-century house that made up the center of the exhibit.

It was a nice little house; if he had lived back in those days he would have wanted one of his own. Three bedrooms, a ranch style California bungalow. He pushed open the front door and entered the living room. Fireplace at one end. Dark wine-colored carpets. Modern couch and easy chair. Low hardwood glass-topped coffee table. Copper ashtrays. A cigarette lighter and a stack of magazines. Sleek plastic and steel floor lamps. A bookcase. Television set. Picture window overlooking the front garden. He crossed the room to the hall.

The house was amazingly complete. Below his feet the floor furnace radiated a faint aura of warmth. He peered into the first bedroom. A woman's boudoir. Silk bedcover. White starched sheets. Heavy drapes. A vanity table. Bottles and jars. Huge round mirror. Clothes visible within the closet. A dressing gown thrown over the back of a chair. Slippers. Nylon hose carefully placed at the foot of the bed.

Miller moved down the hall and peered into the next room. Brightly painted wallpaper: clowns and elephants and tight-rope walkers. The children's room. Two little beds for the two boys. Model airplanes. A dresser with a radio on it, pair of combs, school books, pennants, a No Parking sign, snapshots stuck in the mirror. A postage stamp album. Nobody there, either.

Miller peered in the modern bathroom, even in the yellow-tiled shower. He passed through the dining room, glanced down the basement stairs where the washing machine and dryer were. Then he opened the back door and examined the back yard. A lawn, and the incinerator. A couple of small trees and then the three-dimensional projected backdrop of other houses receding off into incredibly convincing blue hills. And still no one. The yard was empty -- deserted. He closed the door and started back.

From the kitchen came laughter.

A woman's laugh. The clink of spoons and dishes. And smells. It took him a moment to identify them, scholar that he was. Bacon and coffee. And hot cakes. Somebody was eating breakfast. A twentieth-century breakfast.

He made his way down the hall, past a man's bedroom, shoes and clothing strewn about, to the entrance of the kitchen.

A handsome late-thirtyish woman and two teenage boys were sitting around the little chrome and plastic breakfast table. They had finished eating; the two boys were fidgeting impatiently. Sunlight filtered through the window over the sink. The electric clock read half past eight. The radio was chirping merrily in the corner. A big pot of black coffee rested in the center of the table, surrounded by empty plates and milk glasses and silverware.

The woman had on a white blouse and checkered tweed skirt. Both boys wore faded blue jeans, sweatshirts, and tennis shoes. As yet they hadn't noticed him. Miller stood frozen at the doorway, while laughter and small talk bubbled around him.

"You'll have to ask your father," the woman was saying, with mock sternness. "Wait until he comes back."

"He already said we could," one of the boys protested.

"Well, ask him again."

"He's always grouchy in the morning."

"Not today. He had a good night's sleep. His hay fever didn't bother him. The new anti-hist the doctor gave him." She glanced up at the clock. "Go see what's keeping him, Don. He'll be late for work."

"He was looking for the newspaper." One of the boys pushed back his chair and got up. "It missed the porch again and fell in the flowers." He turned towards the door, and Miller found himself confronting him face to face. Briefly, the observation flashed through his mind that the boy looked familiar. Damn familiar -- like somebody he knew, only younger. He tensed himself for the impact, as the boy abruptly halted.

"Gee," the boy said. "You scared me."

The woman glanced quickly up at Miller. "What are you doing out there, George?" she demanded. "Come on back in here and finish you coffee."

Miller came slowly into the kitchen. The woman was finishing her coffee; both boys were on their feet and beginning to press around him.

"Didn't you tell me I could go camping over the weekend up at Russian River with the group from school?" Don demanded. "You said I could borrow a sleeping bag from the gym because the one I had you gave to the Salvation Army because you were allergic to the kapok in it."

"Yeah," Miller muttered uncertainly. Don. That was the boy's name. And his brother, Ted. But how did he know that? At the table the woman had got up and was collecting the dirty dishes to carry over to the sink. "They said you already promised them," she said over her shoulder. The dishes clattered into the sink and she began sprinkling soap flakes over them. "But you remember that time they wanted to drive the car and the way they said it, you'd think they had got your okay. And they hadn't, of course."

Miller sank weakly down at the table. Aimlessly, he fooled with his pipe. He set it down in the copper ashtray and examined the cuff of his coat. What was happening? His head spun. He got up abruptly and hurried to the window, over the sink.

Houses, streets. The distant hills beyond the town. The sights and sounds of people. The three dimensional projected backdrop was utterly convincing; or was it the projected backdrop? How could he be sure. *What was happening?*

"George, what's the matter?" Marjorie asked, as she tied a pink plastic apron around her waist and began running hot water in the sink. "You better get the car out and get started to work. Weren't you saying last night old man Davidson was shouting about employees being late for work and standing around the water cooler talking and having a good time on company time?"

Davidson. The word stuck in Miller's mind. He knew it, of course. A clear picture leaped up; a tall, white-haired old man, thin and stern. Vest and pocket watch. And the whole office, United Electronic Supply. The twelve-story building in downtown San Francisco. The newspaper and cigar stand in the lobby. The honking cars. Jammed parking lots. The elevator, packed with bright-eyed secretaries, tight sweaters and perfume.

He wandered out of the kitchen, through the hall, past his own bedroom, his wife's, and into the living room. The front door was open and he stepped out on to the porch.

The air was cool and sweet. It was a bright April morning. The lawns were still wet. Cars moved down Virginia Street, towards Shattuck Avenue. Early morning commuting traffic, businessmen on their way to work. Across the street Earl Kelly cheerfully waved his Oakland Tribune as he hurried down the pavement towards the bus stop.

A long way off Miller could see the Bay Bridge, Yerba Buena Island, and Treasure Island. Beyond that was San Francisco itself. In a few minutes he'd be shooting across the bridge in his Buick, on his way to the office. Along with thousands of other businessmen in blue pinstripe suits.

Ted pushed past him and out on the porch. "Then it's okay? You don't care if we go camping?"

Miller licked his dry lips. "Ted, listen to me. There's something strange."

"Like what?"

"I don't know." Miller wandered nervously around on the porch. "This is Friday, isn't it?"

"Sure."

"I thought it was." But how did he know it was Friday? How did he know anything? But of course it was Friday. A long hard week -- old man Davidson breathing down his neck. Wednesday, especially, when the General Electric order was slowed down because of a strike.

"Let me ask you something," Miller said to his son. "This morning -- I left the kitchen to get the newspaper."

Ted nodded. "Yeah. So?"

"I got up and went out of the room. *How long was I gone?* Not long, was I?" He searched for words, but his mind was a maze of disjointed thoughts. "I was sitting at the breakfast table with you all, and then I got up and went to look for the paper. Right? And then I came back in. Right?" His voice rose desperately. "I got up and shaved and dressed this morning. I ate breakfast. Hot cakes and coffee. Bacon. *Right?*"

"Right," Ted agreed. "So?"

"Like I always do."

"We only have hot cakes on Friday."

Miller nodded slowly. "That's right. Hot cakes on Friday. Because your uncle Frank eats with us Saturday and Sunday and he can't stand hot cakes, so we stopped having them on weekends. Frank is Marjorie's brother. He was in the Marines in the First World War. He was a corporal."

"Good-bye," Ted said, as Don came out to join him. "We'll see you this evening."

School books clutched, the boys sauntered off towards the big modern high school in the center of Berkeley.

Miller re-entered the house and automatically began searching the closet for his briefcase. Where was it? Damn it, he needed it. The whole Throckmorton account was in it; Davidson would be yelling his head off if he left it anywhere, like in the True Blue Cafeteria that time they were all celebrating the Yankees' winning the series. Where the hell was it?

He straightened up slowly, as memory came. Of course. He had left it by his work desk, where he had tossed it after taking out the research tapes. While Fleming was talking to him. Back at the History Agency.

He joined his wife in the kitchen. "Look," he said huskily. "Marjorie, I think maybe I won't go down to the office this morning."

Marjorie spun in alarm. "George, is anything wrong?"

"I'm -- completely confused."

372

"Your hay fever again?"

"No. My mind. What's the name of that psychiatrist the PTA recommended when Mrs. Bentley's kid had that fit?" He searched his disorganized brain. "Grunberg, I think. In the Medical-Dental building." He moved towards the door. "I'll drop by and see him. Something's wrong -- really wrong. And I don't know what it is."

Adam Grunberg was a large heavy-set man in his late forties, with curly brown hair and horn-rimmed glasses. After Miller had finished, Grunberg cleared his throat, brushed at the sleeve of his Brooks Bros, suit, and asked thoughtfully, "Did anything happen while you were out looking for the newspaper? Any sort of accident? You might try going over that part in detail. You got up from the breakfast table, went out on the porch, and started looking around in the bushes. And then what?"

Miller rubbed his forehead vaguely. "I don't know. It's all confused. I don't remember looking for any newspaper. I remember coming back in the house. Then it gets clear. But before that it's all tied up with the History Agency and my quarrel with Fleming."

"What was that again about your briefcase? Go over that."

"Fleming said it looked like a squashed Jurassic lizard. And I said --"

"No. I mean, about looking for it in the closet and not finding it."

"I looked in the closet and it wasn't there, of course. It's sitting beside my desk at the History Agency. On the Twentieth Century level. By my exhibits." A strange expression crossed Miller's face. "Good God, Grunberg. You realize this may be nothing but an *exhibit?* You and everybody else -- maybe you're not real. Just pieces of this exhibit."

"That wouldn't be very pleasant for us, would it?" Grunberg said, with a faint smile.

"People in dreams are always secure until the dreamer wakes up," Miller retorted.

"So you're dreaming me," Grunberg laughed tolerantly. "I suppose I should thank you."

"I'm not here because I especially like you. I'm here because I can't stand Fleming and the whole History Agency."

Grunberg protested. "This Fleming. Are you aware of thinking about him before you went out looking for the newspaper?"

Miller got to his feet and paced around the luxurious office, between the leather-covered chairs and the huge mahogany desk. "I want to face this thing. I'm an exhibit. An artificial replica of the past. Fleming said something like this would happen to me."

"Sit down, Mr. Miller," Grunberg said, in a gentle but commanding voice.

When Miller had taken his chair again, Grunberg continued, "I understand what you say. You have a general feeling that everything around you is unreal. A sort of stage."

"An exhibit."

"Yes, an exhibit in a museum."

"In the N'York History Agency. Level R, the Twentieth Century level."

"And in addition to this general feeling of -- insubstantiality, there are specific projected memories of persons and places beyond this world. Another realm in which this one is contained. Perhaps I should say, the reality within which this is only a sort of shadow world."

"This world doesn't look shadowy to me." Miller struck the leather arm of the chair savagely. "This world is completely real. That's what's wrong. I came in to investigate the noises and now I can't get back out. Good God, do I have to wander around this replica the rest of my life?"

"You know, of course, that your feeling is common to most of mankind. Especially during periods of great tension. Where -- by the way -- was the newspaper? Did you find it?"

"As far as I'm concerned --"

"Is that a source of irritation with you? I see you react strongly to a mention of the newspaper."

Miller shook his head wearily. "Forget it."

"Yes, a trifle. The paperboy carelessly throws the newspaper in the bushes, not on the porch. It makes you angry. It happens again and again. Early in the day, just as you're starting to work. It seems to symbolize in a small way the whole petty frustrations and defeats of your job. Your whole life."

"Personally, I don't give a damn about the newspaper." Miller examined his wristwatch. "I'm going -- it's almost noon. Old man Davidson will be yelling his head off if I'm not at the office by --" He broke off. "There it is again."

"There what is?"

"All this!" Miller gestured impatiently out the window. "This whole place. This damn world. This *exhibition.*"

"I have a thought," Doctor Grunberg said slowly. "I'll put it to you for what it's worth. Feel free to reject it if it doesn't fit." He raised his shrewd, professional eyes. "Ever see kids playing with rocket ships?"

"Lord," Miller said wretchedly. "I've seen commercial rocket freighters hauling cargo between Earth and Jupiter, landing at La Guardia Spaceport."

Grunberg smiled slightly. "Follow me through on this. A question. Is it job tension?"

"What do you mean?"

"It would be nice," Grunberg said blandly, "to live in the world of tomorrow. With robots and rocket ships to do all the work. You could just sit back and take it easy. No worries, no cares. No frustrations."

"My position in the History Agency has plenty of cares and frustrations." Miller rose abruptly. "Look, Grunberg. Either this is an exhibit on R level of the History Agency, or I'm a middle-class businessman with an escape fantasy. Right now I can't decide which. One minute I think this is real, and the next minute --"

"We can decide easily," Grunberg said.

"How?"

"You were looking for the newspaper. Down the path, on to the lawn. *Where did it happen?* Was it on the path? On the porch? Try to remember."

"I don't have to try. I was still on the pavement. I had just jumped over the rail past the safety screens."

"On the pavement. Then go back there. Find the exact place."

"Why?"

"So you can prove to yourself there's nothing on the other side."

Miller took a deep slow breath. "Suppose there is?"

"There can't be. You said yourself: only one of the worlds can be real. This world is real --" Grunberg thumped his massive mahogany desk. "Ergo, you won't find anything on the other side."

"Yes," Miller said, after a moment's silence. A peculiar expression cut across his face and stayed there. "You've found the mistake."

"What mistake?" Grunberg was puzzled. "What --"

Miller moved towards the door of the office. "I'm beginning to get it. I've been putting up a false question. Trying to decide which world is real." He grinned humorlessly back at Doctor Grunberg. "They're both real, of course."

He grabbed a taxi and headed back to the house. No one was home. The boys were in school and Marjorie had gone downtown to shop. He waited indoors until he was sure nobody was watching along the street, and then started down the path to the pavement.

He found the spot without any trouble. There was a faint shimmer in the air, a weak place just at the edge of the parking strip. Through it he could see faint shapes.

He was right. There it was -- complete and real. As real as the pavement under him.

A long metallic bar was cut off by the edges of the circle. He recognized it; the safety railing he had leaped over to enter the exhibit. Beyond it was the safety screen system. Turned off, of course. And beyond that, the rest of the level and the far walls of the History building.

He took a cautious step into the weak haze. It shimmered around him, misty and oblique. The shapes beyond became clearer. A moving figure in a dark blue robe. Some curious person examining the exhibits. The figure moved on and was lost. He could see his own work desk now. His tape scanner and heaps of study spools. Beside the desk was his briefcase, exactly where he had expected it.

While he was considering stepping over the railing to get the briefcase, Fleming appeared.

Some inner instinct made Miller step back through the weak spot, as Fleming approached. Maybe it was the expression on Fleming's face. In any case, Miller was back and standing firmly on the concrete pavement, when Fleming halted just beyond the juncture, face red, lips twisted with indignation.

"Miller," he said thickly. "Come out of there."

Miller laughed. "Be a good fellow, Fleming. Toss me my briefcase. It's that strange looking thing over by the desk. I showed it to you -- remember?"

"Stop playing games and listen to me!" Fleming snapped. "This is serious. *Carnap knows.* I had to inform him."

"Good for you. The loyal bureaucrat."

Miller bent over to light his pipe. He inhaled and puffed a great cloud of gray tobacco smoke through the weak spot, out into the R level. Fleming coughed and retreated.

"What's that stuff?" he demanded.

"Tobacco. One of the things they have around here. Very common substance in the twentieth century. You wouldn't know about that -- your period is the second century, B.C. The Hellenistic world. I don't know how well you'd like that. They didn't have very good plumbing back there. Life expectancy was damn short."

"What are you talking about?"

"In comparison, the life expectancy of *my* research period is quite high. And you should see the bathroom I've got. Yellow tile. And a shower. We don't have anything like that at the Agency leisure-quarters."

Fleming grunted sourly. "In other words, you're going to stay in there."

"It's a pleasant place," Miller said easily. "Of course, my position is better than average. Let me describe it for you. I have an attractive wife: marriage is permitted, even sanctioned in this era. I have two fine kids -- both boys -- who are going up to the Russian River this weekend. They live with me and my wife -- we have complete custody of them. The State has no power of that, yet. I have a brand new Buick --"

"Illusions," Fleming spat. "Psychotic delusions."

"Are you sure?"

"You damn fool! I always knew you were too ego-recessive to face reality. You and your anachronistic retreats. Sometimes I'm ashamed I'm a theoretician. I wish I had gone into engineering." Fleming's lips twitched. "You're insane, you know. You're standing in the middle of an artificial exhibit, which is owned by the History Agency, a bundle of plastic and wire and struts. A replica of a past age. An imitation. And you'd rather be there than in the real world."

"Strange," Miller said thoughtfully. "Seems to me I've heard the same thing very recently. You don't know a Doctor Grunberg, do you? A psychiatrist."

Without formality, Director Carnap arrived with his company of assistants and experts. Fleming quickly retreated. Miller found himself facing one of the most powerful figures of the twenty-second century. He grinned and held out his hand.

"You insane imbecile," Carnap rumbled. "Get out of there before we drag you out. If we have to do that, you're through. You know what they do with advanced psychotics. It'll be euthanasia for you. I'll give you one last chance to come out of that fake exhibit --"

"Sorry," Miller said. "It's not an exhibit."

Carnap's heavy face registered sudden surprise. For a brief instant his massive pose vanished. "You still try to maintain --"

"This is a time gate," Miller said quietly. "You can't get me out, Carnap. You can't reach me. I'm in the past, two hundred years back. I've crossed back to a previous existence-coordinate.

I found a bridge and escaped from your continuum to this. And there's nothing you can do about it."

Carnap and his experts huddled together in a quick technical conference. Miller waited patiently. He had plenty of time; he had decided not to show up at the office until Monday.

After a while Carnap approached the juncture again, being careful not to step over the safety rail. "An interesting theory, Miller. That's the strange part about psychotics. They rationalize their delusions into a logical system. *A priori,* your concept stands up well. It's internally consistent. Only --"

"Only what?"

"Only it doesn't happen to be true." Carnap had regained his confidence; he seemed to be enjoying the interchange. "You think you're really back in the past. Yes, this exhibit is extremely accurate. Your work has always been good. The authenticity of detail is unequalled by any of the other exhibits."

"I tried to do my work well," Miller murmured.

"You wore archaic clothing and affected archaic speech mannerisms. You did everything possible to throw yourself back. You devoted yourself to your work." Carnap tapped the safety railing with his fingernail. "It would be a shame, Miller. A terrible shame to demolish such an authentic replica."

"I see your point," Miller said, after a time. "I agree with you, certainly. I've been very proud of my work -- I'd hate to see it all torn down. But that really won't do you any good. All you'll succeed in doing is closing the time gate."

"You're sure?"

"Of course. The exhibit is only a bridge, a link with the past. I passed *through* the exhibit, but I'm not there now. I'm beyond the exhibit." He grinned tightly. "Your demolition can't reach me. But seal me off, if you want. I don't think I'll be wanting to come back. I wish you could see this side, Carnap. It's a nice place here. Freedom, opportunity. Limited government, responsible to the people. If you don't like a job here you quit. There's no euthanasia, here. Come on over. I'll introduce you to my wife."

"We'll get you," Carnap said. "And all your psychotic figments along with you."

"I doubt if any of my 'psychotic figments' are worried. Grunberg wasn't. I don't think Marjorie is --"

"We've already begun demolition preparations," Carnap said calmly. "We'll do it piece by piece, not all at once. So you may have the opportunity to appreciate the scientific and -- *artistic* way we take your imaginary world apart."

"You're wasting your time," Miller said. He turned and walked off, down the pavement, to the gravel path and up on to the front porch of the house.

In the living room he threw himself down in the easy chair and snapped on the television set. Then he went to the kitchen and got a can of ice cold beer. He carried it happily back into the safe, comfortable living room.

As he was seating himself in front of the television set he noticed something rolled up on the low coffee table.

He grinned wryly. It was the morning newspaper, which he had looked so hard for. Marjorie had brought it in with the milk, as usual. And of course forgotten to tell him. He yawned contentedly and reached over to pick it up. Confidently, he unfolded it -- and read the big black headlines.

RUSSIA REVEALS COBALT BOMB
TOTAL WORLD DESTRUCTION AHEAD

Meddler

They entered the great chamber. At the far end, technicians hovered around an immense illuminated board, following a complex pattern of lights that shifted rapidly, flashing through seemingly endless combinations. At long tables machines whirred -- computers, human-operated and robot. Wall-charts covered every inch of vertical space. Hasten gazed around him in amazement.

Wood laughed. "Come over here and I'll really show you something. You recognize *this,* don't you?" He pointed to a hulking machine surrounded by silent men and women in white lab robes.

"I recognize it," Hasten said slowly. "It's something like our own Dip, but perhaps twenty times larger. What do you haul up? And *when* do you haul?" He fingered the surface-plate of the Dip, then squatted down, peering into the maw. The maw was locked shut; the Dip was in operation. "You know, if we had any idea this existed, Histo-Research would have --"

"You know now." Wood bent down beside him. "Listen. Hasten, you're the first man from outside the Department ever to get into this room. You saw the guards. No one gets in here unauthorized; the guards have orders to kill anyone trying to enter illegally."

"To hide this? A machine? You'd shoot to --"

They stood, Wood facing him, his jaw hard. "*Your* Dip digs back into antiquity. Rome. Greece. Dust and old volumes." Wood touched the big Dip beside them. "This Dip is different. We guard it with our lives, and anyone else's lives; do you know why?"

Hasten stared at it.

"This Dip is set, not for antiquity, but -- for the future." Wood looked directly into Hasten's face. "Do you understand? The future."

"You're dredging the future? But you can't! It's forbidden by law; you know that!" Hasten drew back. "If the Executive Council knew this they'd break this building apart. You know the dangers. Berkowsky himself demonstrated them in his original thesis."

Hasten paced angrily. "I can't understand you, using a future oriented Dip. When you pull material from the future you automatically introduce new factors into the present; the future is altered -- you start a never-ending shift. The more you dip the more new factors are brought in. You create unstable conditions for centuries to come. That's why the law was passed."

Wood nodded. "I know."

"And you still keep dipping?" Hasten gestured at the machine and the technicians. "Stop, for God's sake! Stop before you introduce some lethal element that can't be erased. Why do you keep --"

Wood sagged suddenly. "All right, Hasten, don't lecture us. It's too late; it's already happened. A lethal factor was introduced in our first experiments. We thought we knew what we were doing. . ." He looked up. "And that's why you were brought here. Sit down -- you're going to hear all about it."

They faced each other across the desk. Wood folded his hands. "I'm going to put it straight on the line. You are considered an expert, *the* expert at Histo-Research. You know more about using a Time Dip than anyone alive; that's why you've been shown our work, our illegal work."

"And you've already got into trouble?"

"Plenty of trouble, and every attempt to meddle further makes it that much worse. Unless we do something, we'll be the most culpable organization in history."

"Please start at the beginning," Hasten said.

"The Dip was authorized by the Political Science Council; they wanted to know the results of some of their decisions. At first we objected, giving Berkowsky's theory; but the idea is hypnotic, you know. We gave in, and the Dip was built -- secretly, of course.

"We made our first dredge about one year hence. To protect ourselves against Berkowsky's factor we tried a subterfuge; we actually brought nothing back. This Dip is geared to pick up nothing. No object is scooped; it merely photographs from a high altitude. The film comes back to us and we make enlargements and try to gestalt the conditions.

"Results were all right, at first. No more wars, cities growing, much better looking. Blow-ups of street scenes show many people, well-content, apparently. Pace a little slower.

"Then we went ahead fifty years. Even better: cities on the decrease. People not so dependent on machines. More grass, parks. Same general conditions, peace, happiness, much leisure. Less frenetic waste, hurry.

"We went on, skipping ahead. Of course, with such an indirect viewing method we couldn't be certain of anything, but it all looked fine. We relayed our information to the Council and they went ahead with their planning. And then it happened."

"What, exactly?" Hasten said, leaning forward.

"We decided to revisit a period we had already photographed, about a hundred years hence. We sent out the Dip, got it back with a full reel. The men developed it and we watched the run." Wood paused.

"And?"

"And it wasn't the same. It was different. Everything was changed. War -- war and destruction everywhere." Wood shuddered. "We were appalled; we sent the Dip back at once to make absolutely certain."

"And what did you find this time?"

Wood's fists clenched. "Changed again, and for worse! Ruins, vast ruins. People poking around. Ruin and death everywhere. Slag. The *end* of war, the last phase."

"I see," Hasten said, nodding.

"That's not the worst! We conveyed the news to the Council. It ceased all activity and went into a two-week conference; it canceled all ordinances and withdrew every plan formed on the basis of our reports. It was a month before the Council got in touch with us again. The members wanted us to try once more, take one more Dip to the same period. We said no, but they insisted. It could be no worse, they argued.

"So we sent the Dip out again. It came back and we ran the film. Hasten, there are things worse than war. You wouldn't believe what we saw. There was no human life; none at all, not a single human being."

"Everything was destroyed?"

"No! No destruction, cities big and stately, roads, buildings, lakes, fields. But no human life; the cities empty, functioning mechanically, every machine and wire untouched. But no living people."

"What was it?"

"We sent the Dip on ahead, at fifty year leaps. Nothing. Nothing each time. Cities, roads, buildings, but no human life. Everyone dead. Plague, radiation, or what, we don't know. But *something* killed them. Where did it come from? We don't know. It wasn't there at first, not in our original dips.

"Somehow, *we* introduced it, the lethal factor. *We* brought it, with our meddling. It wasn't there when we started; it was done by us, Hasten." Wood stared at him, his face a white mask. "We brought it and now we've got to find what it is and get rid of it."

"How are you going to do that?"

"We've built a Time Car, capable of carrying one human observer into the future. We're sending a man there to see what it is. Photographs don't tell us enough; we have to know more! When did it first appear? How? What were the first signs? *What is it?* Once we know, maybe we can eliminate it, the factor, trace it down and remove it. Someone must go into the future and find out what it was we began. It's the only way."

Woods stood up, and Hasten rose, too.

"You're that person," Wood said. "You're going, the most competent person available. The Time Car is outside, in an open square, carefully guarded." Wood gave a signal. Two soldiers came toward the desk.

"Sir?"

"Come with us," Wood said. "We're going outside to the square; make sure no one follows after us." He turned to Hasten. "Ready?"

Hasten hesitated. "Wait a minute. I'll have to go over your work, study what's been done. Examine the Time Car itself. I can't --"

The two soldiers moved closer, looking to Wood. Wood put his hand on Hasten's shoulder. "I'm sorry," he said, "we have no time to waste; come along with me."

All around him blackness moved, swirling toward him and then receding. He sat down on the stool before the bank of controls, wiping the perspiration from his face. He was on his way, for better or worse. Briefly, Wood had outlined the operation of the Time Car. A few moments of instruction, the controls set for him, and then the metal door slammed behind him.

Hasten looked around him. It was cold in the sphere; the air was thin and chilly. He watched the moving dials for a while, but presently the cold began to make him uncomfortable. He went over to the equipment-locker and slid the door back. A jacket, a heavy jacket, and a flash gun. He held the gun for a minute, studying it. And tools, all kinds of tools and equipment. He was just putting the gun away when the dull chugging under him suddenly ceased. For one terrible second he was floating, drifting aimlessly, then the feeling was gone.

Sunlight flowed through the window, spreading out over the floor. He snapped the artificial lights off and went to the window to see. Wood had set the controls for a hundred years hence; bracing himself, he looked out.

A meadow, flowers and grass, rolling off into the distance. Blue sky and ' wandering clouds. Some animals grazed a long way off, standing together in the shade of a tree. He went to the door and unlocked it, stepping out. Warmy sunlight struck him, and he felt better at once. Now he could see the animal were cows.

He stood for a long time at the door, his hands on his hips. Could the plague have been bacterial? Air-carried? If it *were* a plague. He reached feeling the protective helmet on his shoulders. Better to keep it on.

He went back and got the gun from the locker. Then he returned to the lip of the sphere, checked the door-lock to be certain it would remain closed during his absence. Only then, Hasten stepped down onto the grass of the meadow. He closed the door and looked around him. Presently he began to walk quickly away from the sphere, toward the top of a long hill that stretched out half a mile away. As he strode along, he examined the click-band on his wrist which would guide him back to the metal sphere, the Time Car, if he could not find the way himself.

He came to the cows, passing by their tree. The cows got up and moved away from him. He noticed something that gave him a sudden chill; their udders were small and wrinkled. Not herd cows.

When he reached the top of the hill he stopped, lifting his glasses from his waist. The earth fell away, mile after mile of it, dry green fields without pattern or design, rolling like waves as far as the eye could see. Nothing else? He turned, sweeping the horizon.

He stiffened, adjusting the sight. Far off to the left, at the very limit of vision, the vague perpendiculars of a city rose up. He lowered the glasses and hitched up his heavy boots. Then he walked down the other side of the hill, taking big steps; he had a long way to go.

Hasten had not walked more than half an hour when he saw butterflies. They rose up suddenly a few yards in front of him, dancing and fluttering in the sunlight. He stopped to rest, watching them. They were all colors, red and blue, with splashes of yellow and green. They were the largest butterflies he had ever seen. Perhaps they had come from some zoo, escaped and bred wild after man left the scene. The butterflies rose higher and higher in the air. They took no notice of him but struck out toward the distant spires of the city; in a moment they were gone.

Hasten started up again. It was hard to imagine the death of man in such circumstances, butterflies and grass and cows in the shade. What a quiet and lovely world was left, without the human race!

Suddenly one last butterfly fluttered up, almost in his face, rising quickly from the grass. He put his arm up automatically, batting at it. The butterfly dashed against his hand. He began to laugh --

Pain made him sick; he fell half to his knees, gasping and retching. He rolled over on his face, hunching himself up, burying his face in the ground. His arm ached, and pain knotted him up; his head swam and he closed his eyes.

When Hasten turned over at last, the butterfly was gone; it had not lingered.

He lay for a time in the grass, then he sat up slowly, getting shakily to his feet. He stripped off his shirt and examined his hand and wrist. The flesh was black, hard and already swelling. He glanced down at it and then at the distant city. The butterflies had gone there. . .

He made his way back to the Time Car.

Hasten reached the sphere a little after the sun had begun to drop into evening darkness. The door slid back to his touch and he stepped inside. He dressed his hand and arm with salve from the medicine kit and then sat down on the stool, deep in thought, staring at his arm. A small sting, accidental, in fact. The butterfly had not even noticed. Suppose the whole pack --

He waited until the sun had completely set and it was pitch black outside the sphere. At night all the bees and butterflies disappeared; or at least, those he knew did. Well, he would have to take a chance. His arm still ached dully, throbbing without respite. The salve had done no good; he felt dizzy, and there was a fever taste in his mouth.

Before he went out he opened the locker and brought all the things out. He examined the flash gun but put it aside. A moment later he found what he wanted. A blowtorch, and a flashlight. He put all the other things back and stood up. Now he was ready -- if that were the word for it. As ready as he would ever be.

He stepped out into the darkness, flashing the light ahead of him. He walked quickly. It was a dark and lonely night; only a few stars shone above him, and his was the only earthly light. He passed up the hill and down the other side. A grove of trees loomed up, and then he was on a level plain, feeling his way toward the city by the beam of the flashlight.

When he reached the city he was very tired. He had gone a long way, and his breath was beginning to come hard. Huge ghostly outlines rose up ahead of him, disappearing above, vanishing into darkness. It was not a large city, apparently, but its design was strange to Hasten, more vertical and slim than he was used to.

He went through the gate. Grass was growing from the stone pavement of the streets. He stopped, looking down. Grass and weeds everywhere; and in the corners, by the buildings were bones, little heaps of bones and dust. He walked on, flashing his light against the sides of the slender buildings. His footsteps echoed hollowly. There was no light except his own.

The buildings began to thin out. Soon he found himself entering a great tangled square, overgrown with bushes and vines. At the far end a building larger than the others rose. He walked toward it, across the empty, desolate square, flashing his light from side to side. He walked up a half-buried step and onto a concrete plaza. All at once he stopped. To his right, another building reared up, catching his attention. His heart thudded. Above the doorway his light made out a word cut expertly into the arch:

Bibliotheca

This was what he wanted, the library. He went up the steps toward the dark entrance. Wood boards gave under his feet. He reached the entrance and found himself facing a heavy wood door with metal handles. When he took hold of the handles the door fell toward him, crashing past him, down the steps and into the darkness. The odor of decay and dust choked him.

He went inside. Spider webs brushed against his helmet as he passed along silent halls. He chose a room at random and entered it. Here were more heaps of dust and gray bits of bones. Low tables and shelves ran along the walls. He went to the shelves and took down a handful of books. They powdered and broke in his hands, showering bits of paper and thread onto him. Had only a century passed since his own time?

Hasten sat down at one of the tables and opened one of the books that was in better condition. The words were no language he knew, a Romance language that he knew must be artificial. He turned page after page. At last he took a handful of books at random and moved back toward the door. Suddenly his heart jumped. He went over to the wall, his hands trembling. Newspapers.

He took the brittle, cracking sheets carefully down, holding them to the light. The same language, of course. Bold, black headlines. He managed to roll some of the papers together and add them to his load of books. Then he went through the door, out into the corridor, back the way he had come.

When he stepped out onto the steps cold fresh air struck him, tingling his nose. He looked around at the dim outlines rising up on all sides of the square. Then he walked down and across the square, feeling his way carefully along. He came to the gate of the city, and a moment later he was outside, on the flat plain again, heading back toward the Time Car.

For an endless time he walked, his head bent down, plodding along. Finally fatigue made him stop, swaying back and forth, breathing deeply. He set down his load and looked around him. Far off, at the edge of the horizon, a long streak of gray had appeared, silently coming into existence while he was walking. Dawn. The sun coming up.

A cold wind moved through the air, eddying against him. In the forming gray light the trees and hills were beginning to take shape, a hard, unbending outline. He turned toward the city. Bleak and thin, the shafts of the deserted buildings stuck up. For a moment he watched, fascinated by the first color of day as it struck the shafts and towers. Then the color faded, and a drifting mist moved between him and the city. All at once he bent down and grabbed up his load. He began to walk, hurrying as best he could, chill fear moving through him.

From the city a black speck had leaped up into the sky and was hovering over it.

After a time, a long time, Hasten looked back. The speck was still there -- but it had grown. And it was no longer black; in the clear light of day the speck was beginning to flash, shining with many colors.

He increased his pace; he went down the side of a hill and up another. For a second he paused to snap on his click-band. It spoke loudly; he was not far from the sphere. He waved his arm and the clicks rose and fell. To the right. Wiping the perspiration from his hands he went on.

A few minutes later he looked down from the top of a ridge and saw a gleaming metal sphere resting silently on the grass, dripping with cold dew from the night. The Time Car; sliding and running, he leaped down the hill toward it.

He was just pushing the door open with his shoulder when the first cloud of butterflies appeared at the top of the hill, moving quietly toward him.

He locked the door and set his armload down, flexing his muscles. His hand ached, burning now with an intense pain. He had no time for that -- he hurried to the window and peered out. The butterflies were swarming toward the sphere, darting and dancing above him, flashing with color. They began to settle down onto the metal, even onto the window. Abruptly, his gaze was cut off by gleaming bodies, soft and pulpy, their beating wings mashed together. He listened. He could hear them, a muffled, echoing sound that came from all sides of him. The interior of the sphere dimmed into darkness as the butterflies sealed off the window. He lit the artificial lights.

Time passed. He examined the newspapers, uncertain of what to do. Go back? Or ahead? Better jump ahead fifty years or so. The butterflies were dangerous, but perhaps not the real thing, the lethal factor that he was looking for. He looked at his hand. The skin was black and hard, a dead area was increasing. A faint shadow of worry went through him; it was getting worse, not better.

The scratching sound on all sides of him began to annoy him, filling him with an uneasy restlessness. He put down the books and paced back and forth. How could insects, even immense insects such as these, destroy the human race? Surely human beings could combat them. Dusts, poisons, sprays.

A bit of metal, a little particle drifted down onto his sleeve. He brushed it off. A second particle fell, and then some tiny fragments. He leaped, his head jerking up.

A circle was forming above his head. Another circle appeared to the right of it, and then a third. All around him circles were forming in the walls and roof of the sphere. He ran to the control board and closed the safety switch. The board hummed into life. He began to set the indicator panel, working rapidly, frantically. Now pieces of metal were dropping down, a rain of metal fragments onto the floor. Corrosive, some kind of substance exuded from them. Acid? Natural secretion of some sort. A large piece of metal fell; he turned.

Into the sphere the butterflies came, fluttering and dancing toward him. The piece that had fallen was a circle of metal, cut cleanly through. He did not have time even to notice it; he snatched up the blowtorch and snapped it on. The flame sucked and gurgled. As the butterflies came toward him he pressed the handle and held the spout up. The air burst alive with burning particles that rained down all over him, and a furious odor reeked through the sphere.

He closed the last switches. The indicator lights flickered, the floor chugged under him. He threw the main lever. More butterflies were pushing in, crowding each other eagerly, struggling to get through. A second circle of metal crashed to the floor suddenly, emitting a new horde. Hasten cringed, backing away, the blowtorch up, spouting flame. The butterflies came on, more and more of them.

Then sudden silence settled over everything, a quiet so abrupt that he blinked. The endless, insistent scratching had ceased. He was alone, except for a cloud of ashes and particles over the floor and walls, the remains of the butterflies that had got into the sphere. Hasten sat down on the stool, trembling, he was safe, on his way back to his own time; and there was no doubt, no possible doubt that he had found the lethal factor. It was there, in the heap of ashes on the floor, in the circles neatly cut in the hull of the car. Corrosive secretion? He smiled grimly.

His last vision of them, of the swelling horde had told him what he wanted to know. Clutched carefully against the first butterflies through the circles were tools, tiny cutting tools. They had cut their way in, bored through; they had come carrying their own equipment.

He sat down, waiting for the Time Car to complete its journey.

Department guards caught hold of him, helping him from the Car. He stepped down unsteadily, leaning against them. "Thanks," he murmured.

Wood hurried up. "Hasten, you're all right?"

He nodded. "Yes. Except my hand."

"Let's get inside at once." They went through the door, into the great chamber. "Sit down." Wood waved his hand impatiently, and a soldier hurried a chair over. "Get him some hot coffee."

Coffee was brought. Hasten sat sipping. At last he pushed the cup away and leaned back.

"Can you tell us now?" Wood asked.

"Yes."

"Fine." Wood sat down across from him. A tape recorder whirred into life and a camera began to photograph Hasten's face as he talked. "Go on. What did you find?"

When he had finished the room was silent. None of the guards or technicians spoke.

Wood stood up, trembling. "God. So it's a form of toxic life that got them. I thought it was something like that. But butterflies? And intelligent. Planning attacks. Probably rapid breeding, quick adaptation."

"Maybe the books and newspapers will help us."

"But where did they come from? Mutation of some existing form? Or from some other planet. Maybe space travel brought them in. We've got to find out."

"They attacked only human beings," Hasten said. "They left the cows. Just people."

"Maybe we can stop them." Wood snapped on the vidphone. "I'll have the Council convene an emergency session. We'll give them your description and recommendations. We'll start a program, organize units all over the planet. Now that we know what it is, we have a chance. Thanks to you, Hasten, maybe we can stop them in time!"

The operator appeared and Wood gave the Council's code letter. Hasten watched dully. At last he got to his feet and wandered around the room. His arm throbbed unmercifully. Presently he went back outside, through the doorway into the open square. Some soldiers were examining the Time Car curiously. Hasten watched them without feeling, his mind blank.

"What is it, sir?" one asked.

"That?" Hasten roused himself, going slowly over. "That's a Time Car."

"No, I mean this." The soldier pointed to something on the hull. "This, sir; it wasn't on there when the Car went out."

Hasten's heart stopped beating. He pushed past them, staring up. At first he saw nothing on the metal hull, only the corroded metal surface. Then chill fright rushed through him.

Something small and brown and furry was there, on the surface. He reached out, touching it. A sack, a stiff little brown sack. It was dry, dry and empty. There was nothing in it; it was open at one end. He stared up. All across the hull of the Car were little brown sacks, some still full, but most of them already empty.

Cocoons.

Souvenir

"Here we go, sir," the robot pilot said. The words startled Rogers and made him look up sharply. He tensed his body and adjusted the trace web inside his coat as the bubble ship started dropping, swiftly and silently, toward the planet's surface.

This -- his heart caught -- was Williamson's World. The legendary lost planet -- found, after three centuries. By accident, of course. This blue and green planet, the holy grail of the Galactic System, had been almost miraculously discovered by a routine charting mission.

Frank Williamson had been the first Terran to develop an outer-space drive -- the first to hop from the Solar System toward the universe beyond. He had never come back. He -- his world, his colony -- had never been found. There had been endless rumors, false leads, fake legends -- and nothing more.

"I'm receiving field clearance." The robot pilot raised the gain on the control speaker, and clicked to attention.

"Field ready," came a ghostly voice from below. "Remember, your drive mechanism is unfamiliar to us. How much run is required? Emergency brake-walls are up."

Rogers smiled. He could hear the pilot telling them that no run would be required. Not with this ship. The brake-walls could be lowered with perfect safety.

Three hundred years! It had taken a long time to find Williamson's World. Many authorities had given him up. Some believed he had never landed, had died out in space. Perhaps there was *no* Williamson's World. Certainly there had been no real clues, nothing tangible to go on. Frank Williamson and three families had utterly disappeared in the trackless void, never to be heard from again.

Until now. . .

The young man met him at the field. He was thin and red-haired and dressed in a colorful suit of bright material. "You're from the Galactic Relay Center?" he asked.

"That's right," Rogers said huskily. "I'm Edward Rogers."

The young man held out his hand. Rogers shook it awkwardly. "My name is Williamson," the young man said. "Gene Williamson."

The name thundered in Rogers' ears. "Are you --"

The young man nodded, his gaze enigmatical. "I'm his great-great-great-great-grandson. His tomb is here. You may see it, if you wish."

"I almost expected to see him. He's -- well, almost a god-figure to us. The first man to break out of the Solar System."

"He means a lot to us, too," the young man said. "He brought us here. They searched a long time before they found a planet that was habitable." Williamson waved at the city stretched out beyond the field. "This one proved satisfactory. It's the System's tenth planet."

Rogers' eyes began to shine. Williamson's World. Under his feet. He stamped hard as they walked down the ramp together, away from the field. How many men in the Galaxy had dreamed of striding down a landing ramp onto Williamson's World with a young descendant of Frank Williamson beside them?

"They'll all want to come here," Williamson said, as if aware of his thoughts. "Throw rubbish around and break off the flowers. Pick up handfuls of dirt to take back." He laughed a little nervously. "The Relay will control them, of course."

"Of course," Rogers assured him.

At the ramp-end Rogers stopped short. For the first time he saw the city.

"What's wrong?" Gene Williamson asked, with a faint trace of amusement.

They had been cut off, of course. Isolated -- so perhaps it wasn't so surprising. It was a wonder they weren't living in caves, eating raw meat. But Williamson had always symbolized progress -- development. He had been a man *ahead* of other men.

True, his space-drive by modern standards had been primitive, a curiosity. But the concept remained unaltered; Williamson the pioneer, and inventor. The man who built.

Yet the city was nothing more than a village, with a few dozen houses, and some public buildings and industrial units at its perimeter. Beyond the city stretched green fields, hills, and broad prairies. Surface vehicles crawled leisurely along the narrow streets and most of the citizens walked on foot. An incredible anachronism it seemed, dragged up from the past.

"I'm accustomed to the uniform Galactic culture," Rogers said. "Relay keeps the technocratic and ideological level constant throughout. It's hard to adjust to such a radically different social stage. But you've been cut off."

"Cut off?" asked Williamson.

"From Relay. You've had to develop without help."

In front of them a surface vehicle crept to a halt. The driver opened the doors manually.

"Now that I recall these factors, I can adjust," Rogers assured him.

"On the contrary," Williamson said, entering the vehicle. "We've been receiving your Relay coordinates for over a century." He motioned Rogers to get in beside him.

Rogers was puzzled. "I don't understand. You mean you hooked onto the web and yet made no attempt to --"

"We receive your coordinates," Gene Williamson said, "but our citizens are not interested in using them."

The surface vehicle hurried along the highway, past the rim of an immense red hill. Soon the city lay behind them -- a faintly glowing place reflecting the rays of the sun. Bushes and plants appeared along the highway. The sheer side of the cliff rose, a towering wall of deep red sandstone; ragged, untouched.

"Nice evening," Williamson said.

Rogers nodded in disturbed agreement.

Williamson rolled down the window. Cool air blew into the car. A few gnatlike insects followed. Far off, two tiny figures were plowing a field -- a man and a huge lumbering beast.

"When will we be there?" Rogers asked.

"Soon. Most of us live away from the cities. We live in the country -- in isolated self-sufficient farm units. They're modeled on the manors of the Middle Ages."

"Then you maintain only the most rudimentary subsistence level. How many people live on each farm?"

"Perhaps a hundred men and women."

"A hundred people can't manage anything more complex than weaving and dyeing and paper pressing."

"We have special industrial units -- manufacturing systems. This vehicle is a good example of what we can turn out. We have communication and sewage and medical agencies. We have technological advantages equal to Terra's."

"Terra of the twenty-first century," Rogers protested. "But that was three hundred years ago. You're purposely maintaining an archaic culture in the face of the Relay coordinates. It doesn't make any sense."

"Maybe we prefer it."

"But you're not free to prefer an inferior cultural stage. Every culture has to keep pace with the general trend. Relay makes actual a uniformity of development. It integrates the valid factors and rejects the rest."

They were approaching the farm, Gene Williamson's "manor." It consisted of a few simple buildings clustered together in a valley, to the side of the highway, surrounded by fields and pastures. The surface vehicle turned down a narrow side road and spiraled cautiously toward the floor of the valley. The air became darker. Cold wind blew into the car, and the driver clicked his headlights on.

"No robots?" Rogers asked.

"No," Williamson replied. "We do all our own work."

"You're making a purely arbitrary distinction," Rogers pointed out. "A robot is a machine. You don't dispense with machines as such. This car is a machine."

"True," Williamson acknowledged.

"The machine is a development of the tool," Rogers went on. "The ax is a simple machine. A stick becomes a tool, a simple machine, in the hands of a man reaching for something. A machine is merely a multi-element tool that increases the power ratio. Man is the tool-making animal. The history of man is the history of tools into machines, greater and more efficient functioning elements. If you reject machinery you reject man's essential key."

"Here we are," Williamson said. The vehicle came to a halt and the driver opened the doors for them.

Three or four wooden buildings loomed up in the darkness. A few dim shapes moved around - - human shapes.

"Dinner's ready," Williamson said, sniffing. "I can smell it."

They entered the main building. Several men and women were sitting at a long rough table. Plates and dishes had been set in front of them. They were waiting for Williamson.

"This is Edward Rogers," Williamson announced. The people studied Rogers curiously, then turned back to their food.

"Sit down," a dark-eyed girl urged. "By me."

They made a place for him near the end of the table. Rogers started forward, but Williamson restrained him. "Not there. You're *my* guest. You're expected to sit with me."

The girl and her companion laughed. Rogers sat down awkwardly by Williamson. The bench was rough and hard under him. He examined a handmade wooden drinking cup. The food was piled in huge wooden bowls. There was a stew and a salad and great loaves of bread.

"We could be back in the fourteenth century," Rogers said.

"Yes," Williamson agreed. "Manor life goes back to Roman times and to the classical world. The Gauls. Britons."

"These people here. Are they --"

Williamson nodded. "My family. We're divided up into small units arranged according to the traditional patriarch basis. I'm the oldest male and titular head."

The people were eating rapidly, intent on their food -- boiled meat, vegetables, scooped up with hunks of bread and butter and washed down with milk. The room was lit by fluorescent lighting.

"Incredible," Rogers murmured. "You're still using electric power."

"Oh, yes. There are plenty of waterfalls on this planet. The vehicle was electric. It was run by a storage battery."

"Why are there no older men?" Rogers saw several dried-up old women, but Williamson was the oldest man. And he couldn't have been over thirty.

"The fighting," Williamson replied, with an expressive gesture.

"Fighting?"

"Clan wars between families are a major part of our culture." Williamson nodded toward the long table. "We don't live long."

Rogers was stunned. "Clan wars? But --"

"We have pennants, and emblems -- like the old Scottish tribes."

He touched a bright ribbon on his sleeve, the representation of a bird. "There are emblems and colors for each family and we fight over them. The Williamson family no longer controls this planet. There is no central agency, now. For a major issue we have the plebiscite -- a vote by all the clans. Each family on the planet has a vote."

"Like the American Indians."

Williamson nodded. "It's a tribal system. In time we'll be distinct tribes, I suppose. We still retain a common language, but we're breaking up -- decentralizing. And each family to its own ways, its own customs and manners."

"Just what do you fight for?"

Williamson shrugged. "Some real things like land and women. Some imaginary. Prestige for instance. When honor is at stake we have an official semi-annual public battle. A man from each family takes part. The best warrior and his weapons."

"Like the medieval joust."

"We've drawn from all traditions. Human tradition as a whole."

"Does each family have its separate deity?"

Williamson laughed. "No. We worship in common a vague animism. A sense of the general positive vitality of the universal process." He held up a loaf of bread. "Thanks for all this."

"Which you grew yourselves."

"On a planet provided for us." Williamson ate his bread thoughtfully. "The old records say the ship was almost finished. Fuel just about gone -- one dead, and waste after another. If this planet hadn't turned up, the whole expedition would have perished."

"Cigar?" Williamson said, when the empty bowls had been pushed back.

"Thanks." Rogers accepted a cigar noncommittally. Williamson lit his own, and settled back against the wall.

"How long are you staying?" he asked presently.

"Not long," Rogers answered.

"There's a bed fixed up for you," Williamson said. "We retire early, but there'll be some kind of dancing, also singing and dramatic acts. We devote a lot of time to staging, and producing drama."

"You place an emphasis on psychological release?"

"We enjoy making and doing things, if that's what you mean."

Rogers stared about him. The walls were covered with murals painted directly on the rough wood. "So I see," he said. "You grind your own colors from clay and berries?"

"Not quite," Williamson replied. "We have a big pigment industry. Tomorrow I'll show you our kiln where we fire our own things. Some of our best work is with fabrics and screen processes."

"Interesting. A decentralized society, moving gradually back into primitive tribalism. A society that voluntarily rejects the advanced technocratic and cultural products of the Galaxy, and thus deliberately withdraws from contact with the rest of mankind."

"From the uniform Relay-controlled society only," Williamson insisted.

"Do you know why Relay maintains a uniform level for all worlds?" Rogers asked. "I'll tell you. There are two reasons. First, the body of knowledge which men have amassed doesn't permit duplication of experiment. There's no time.

"When a discovery has been made it's absurd to repeat it on countless planets throughout the universe. Information gained on any of the thousand worlds is flashed to Relay Center and then out again to the whole Galaxy. Relay studies and selects experiences and coordinates them into a rational, functional system with contradictions. Relay orders the total experience of mankind into a coherent structure."

"And the second reason?"

"If uniform culture is maintained, controlled from a central source, there won't be war."

"True," Williamson admitted.

"We've abolished war. It's as simple as that. We have a homogeneous culture like that of ancient Rome -- a common culture for all mankind which we maintain throughout the Galaxy. Each planet is as involved in it as any other. There are no backwaters of culture to breed envy and hatred."

"Such as this."

Rogers let out his breath slowly. "Yes -- you've confronted us with a strange situation. We've searched for Williamson's World for three centuries. We've wanted it, dreamed of finding it. It has seemed like Prester John's Empire -- a fabulous world, cut off from the rest of humanity. Maybe not real at all. Frank Williamson might have crashed."

"But he didn't."

"He didn't, and Williamson's World is alive with a culture of its own. Deliberately set apart, with its own way of life, its own standards. Now contact has been made, and our dream has come true. The people of the Galaxy will soon be informed that Williamson's World has been found. We can now restore the first colony outside the Solar System to its rightful place in the Galactic culture."

Rogers reached into his coat, and brought out a metal packet. He unfastened the packet and laid a clean, crisp document on the table.

"What's this?" Williamson asked.

"The Articles of Incorporation. For you to sign, so that Williamson's World can become a part of the Galactic culture."

Williamson and the rest of the people in the room fell silent. They gazed down at the document, none of them speaking.

"Well?" Rogers said. He was tense. He pushed the document toward Williamson. "Here it is."

Williamson shook his head. "Sorry." He pushed the document firmly back toward Rogers. "We've already taken a plebiscite. I hate to disappoint you, but we've already decided not to join. That's our *final* decision."

The Class-One battleship assumed an orbit outside the gravity belt of Williamson's World. Commander Ferris contacted the Relay Center. "We're here. What next?"

"Send down a wiring team. Report back to me as soon as it has made surface contact."

Ten minutes later Corporal Pete Matson was dropped overboard in a pressurized gravity suit. He drifted slowly toward the blue and green globe beneath, turning and twisting as he neared the surface of the planet.

Matson landed and bounced a couple of times. He got shakily to his feet. He seemed to be at the edge of a forest. In the shadow of the huge trees he removed his crash helmet. Holding his blast rifle tightly he made his way forward, cautiously advancing among the trees.

His earphones clicked. "Any sign of activity?"

"None, Commander," he signaled back.

"There's what appears to be a village to your right. You may run into someone. Keep moving, and watch out. The rest of the team is dropping, now. Instructions will follow from your Relay web."

"I'll watch out," Matson promised, cradling his blast rifle. He sighted it experimentally at a distant hill and squeezed the trigger. The hill disintegrated into dust, a rising column of waste particles.

Matson climbed a long ridge and shielded his eyes to peer around him.

He could see the village. It was small, like a country town on Terra. It looked interesting. For a moment he hesitated. Then he stepped quickly down from the ridge and headed toward the village, moving rapidly, his supple body alert.

Above him, from the Class-One battleship, three more of the team were already falling, clutching their guns and tumbling gently toward the surace of the planet. . .

Rogers folded up the Incorporation papers and returned them slowly to his coat. "You understand what you're doing?" he asked.

The room was deathly silent. Williamson nodded. "Of course. We're refusing to join your Relay system."

Rogers' fingers touched the trace web. The web warmed into life. "I'm sorry to hear that," he said.

"Does it surprise you?"

"Not exactly. Relay submitted our scout's report to the computers. There was always the possibility you'd refuse. I was given instructions in case of such an event."

"What are your instructions?"

Rogers examined his wristwatch. "To inform you that you have six hours to join us -- or be blasted out of the universe." He got abruptly to his feet. "I'm sorry this had to happen.

Williamson's World is one of our most precious legends. But nothing must destroy the unity of the Galaxy."

Williamson had risen. His face was ash white, the color of death. They faced each other defiantly.

"We'll fight," Williamson said quietly. His fingers knotted together violently, clenching and unclenching.

"That's unimportant. You've received Relay coordinates on weapons development. You know what our war fleet has."

The other people sat quietly at their places, staring rigidly down at their empty plates. No one moved.

"Is it necessary?" Williamson said harshly.

"Cultural variation must be avoided if the Galaxy is to have peace," Rogers replied firmly.

"You'd destroy us to avoid war?"

"We'd destroy anything to avoid war. We can't permit our society to degenerate into bickering provinces, forever quarreling and fighting -- like your clans. We're stable because we lack the very concept of variation. Uniformity must be preserved and separation must be discouraged. The idea itself must remain unknown."

Williamson was thoughtful. "Do you think you can keep the idea unknown? There are so many semantic correlatives, hints, verbal leads. Even if you blast us, it may arise somewhere else."

"We'll take that chance." Rogers moved toward the door. "I'll return to my ship and wait there. I suggest you take another vote. Maybe knowing how far we're prepared to go will change the results."

"I doubt it."

Rogers' web whispered suddenly. "This is North at Relay."

Rogers fingered the web in acknowledgment.

"A Class-One Battleship is in your area. A team has already been landed. Keep your ship grounded until it can fall back. I've ordered the team to lay out its fission-mine terminals."

Rogers said nothing. His fingers tightened around the web convulsively.

"What's wrong?" Williamson asked.

"Nothing." Rogers pushed the door open. "I'm in a hurry to return to my ship. Let's go."

Commander Ferris contacted Rogers as soon as his ship had left Williamson's World.

"North tells me you've already informed them," Ferris said.

"That's right. He also contacted your team directly. Had it prepare to attack."

"So I'm informed. How much time did you offer them?"

"Six hours."

"Do you think they'll give in?"

"I don't know," Rogers said. "I hope so. But I doubt it."

Williamson's World turned slowly in the viewscreen with its green and blue forest, rivers and oceans. Terra might have looked that way, once. He could see the Class-One battleship, a great silvery globe moving slowly in its orbit around the planet.

The legendary world had been found and contacted. Now it would be destroyed. He had tried to prevent it, but without success. He couldn't prevent the inevitable.

If Williamson's World refused to join the Galactic culture its destruction became a necessity -- grim, axiomatic. It was either Williamson's World or the Galaxy. To preserve the greater, the lesser had to be sacrificed.

He made himself as comfortable as possible by the view-screen, and waited.

At the end of six hours a line of black dots rose from the planet and headed slowly toward the Class-One battleship. He recognized them for what they were -- old-fashioned jet-driven rocket ships. A formation of antiquated war vessels, rising up to give battle.

The planet had not changed its mind. It was going to fight. It was willing to be destroyed, rather than give up its way of life. The black dots grew swiftly larger, became roaring blazing metal disks puffing awkwardly along. A pathetic sight. Rogers felt strangely moved, watching the jet-driven ships divide up for the contact. The Class-One battleship had secured its orbit, and was swinging in a lazy, efficient arc. Its banks of energy tubes were slowly rising, lining up to meet the attack.

Suddenly the formation of the ancient rocketships dived. They rumbled over the Class-One, firing jerkily. The Class-One's tubes followed their path. They began to reform clumsily, gaining distance for a second try, and another run.

A tongue of colorless energy flicked out. The attackers vanished.

Commander Ferris contacted Rogers. "The poor tragic fools." His heavy face was gray. "Attacking us with those things."

"Any damage?"

"None whatever." Ferris wiped his forehead shakily. "No damage to me at all."

"What next?" Rogers asked stonily.

"I've declined the mine operation and passed it back to Relay. They'll have to do it. The impulse should already be --" Below them, the green and blue globe shuddered convulsively. Soundlessly, effortlessly, it flew apart. Fragments rose, bits of debris and the planet dissolved in a cloud of white flame, a blazing mass of incandescent fire. For an instant it remained a miniature sun, lighting up the void. Then it faded into ash.

The screens of Rogers' ship hummed into life, as the debris struck. Particles rained against them, and were instantly disintegrated.

"Well," Ferris said. "It's over. North will report the original scout mistaken. Williamson's World wasn't found. The legend will remain a legend."

Rogers continued to watch until the last bits of debris had ceased flying, and only a vague, discolored shadow remained. The screens clicked off automatically. To his right, the Class-One battleship picked up speed and headed toward the Riga System.

Williamson's World was gone. The Galactic Relay culture had been preserved. The idea, the concept of a separate culture with its own ways, its own customs, had been disposed of in the most effective possible way.

"Good job," the Relay trace web whispered. North was pleased. "The fission mines were perfectly placed. Nothing remains."

"No," Rogers agreed. "Nothing remains."

Corporal Pete Matson pushed the front door open, grinning from ear to ear. "Hi, honey! Surprise!"

"Pete!" Gloria Matson came running, throwing her arms around her husband. "What are you doing home? Pete --"

"Special leave. Forty-eight hours." Pete tossed down his suitcase triumphantly. "Hi there, kid."

His son greeted him shyly. "Hello."

Pete squatted down and opened his suitcase. "How have things been going? How's school?"

"He's had another cold," Gloria said. "He's almost over it. But what happened? Why did they --"

"Military secret." Pete fumbled in his suitcase. "Here." He held something out to his son. "I brought you something. A souvenir."

He handed his son a handmade wooden drinking cup. The boy took it shyly and turned it around, curious and puzzled. "What's a -- a *souvenir?*"

Matson struggled to express the difficult concept. "Well, it's something that reminds you of a different place. Something you don't have, where you are. You know." Matson tapped the cup. "That's to drink out of. It's sure not like our plastic cups, is it?"

"No," the child said.

"Look at this, Gloria." Pete shook out a great folded cloth from his suitcase, printed with multi-colored designs. "Picked this up cheap. You can make a shirt out of it. What do you say? Ever seen anything like it?"

"No," Gloria said, awed. "I haven't." She took the cloth and fingered it reverently.

Pete Matson beamed, as his wife and child stood clutching the souvenirs he had brought them, reminders of his excursion to distant places. Foreign lands.

"Gee," his son whispered, turning the cup around and around. A strange light glowed in his eyes. Thanks a lot, Dad. For the -- *souvenir.*"

The strange light grew.

Progeny

Ed Doyle hurried. He caught a surface car, waved fifty credits in the robot driver's face, mopped his florid face with a red pocket-handkerchief, unfastened his collar, perspired and licked his lips and swallowed piteously all the way to the hospital.

The surface car slid up to a smooth halt before the great white-domed hospital building. Ed leaped out and bounded up the steps three at a time, pushing through the visitors and convalescent patients standing on the broad terrace. He threw his weight against the door and emerged in the lobby, astonishing the attendants and persons of importance moving about their tasks.

"Where?" Ed demanded, gazing around, his feet wide apart, his fists clenched, his chest rising and falling. His breath came hoarsely, like an animal's. Silence fell over the lobby. Everyone turned toward him, pausing in their work. "Where?" Ed demanded again. "Where is she? *They?*"

It was fortunate Janet had been delivered of a child on this of all days. Proxima Centauri was a long way from Terra and the service was bad. Anticipating the birth of his child, Ed had left Proxima some weeks before. He had just arrived in the city. While stowing his suitcase in the luggage tread at the station the message had been handed to him by a robot courier: *Los Angeles Central Hospital. At once.*

Ed hurried, and fast. As he hurried he couldn't help feeling pleased he had hit the day exactly right, almost to the hour. It was a good feeling. He had felt it before, during years of business dealings in the "colonies," the frontier, the fringe of Terran civilization where the streets were still lit by electric lights and doors opened by hand.

That was going to be hard to get used to. Ed turned toward the door behind him, feeling suddenly foolish. He had shoved it open, ignoring the eye. The door was just now closing, sliding slowly back in place. He calmed down a little, putting his handkerchief away in his coat pocket. The hospital attendants were resuming their work, picking up their activities where they had left off. One attendant, a strapping late-model robot, coasted over to Ed and halted.

The robot balanced his noteboard expertly, his photocell eyes appraising Ed's flushed features. "May I inquire whom you are looking for, sir? Whom do you wish to find?"

"My wife."

"Her name, sir?"

"Janet. Janet Doyle. She's just had a child."

The robot consulted his board. "This way, sir." He coasted off down the passage.

Ed followed nervously. "Is she okay? Did I get here in time?" His anxiety was returning.

"She is quite well, sir." The robot raised his metal arm and a side door slid back. "In here, sir."

Janet, in a chic blue-mesh suit, was sitting before a mahogany desk, a cigarette between her fingers, her slim legs crossed, talking rapidly. On the other side of the desk a well-dressed doctor sat listening.

"Janet!" Ed said, entering the room.

"Hi, Ed." She glanced up at him. "You just now get in?"

"Sure. It's -- it's all over? You -- I mean, it's *happened?*"

Janet laughed, her even white teeth sparkling. "Of course. Come in and sit. This is Doctor Bish."

"Hello, Doc." Ed sat down nervously across from them. "Then it's all over?"

"The event has happened," Doctor Bish said. His voice was thin and metallic. Ed realized with a sudden shock that the doctor was a robot. A top-level robot, made in humanoid form, not like the ordinary metal-limbed workers. It had fooled him -- he had been away so long. Doctor Bish appeared plump and well fed, with kindly features and eyeglasses. His large fleshy hands rested on the desk, a ring on one finger. Pinstripe suit and necktie. Diamond tie clasp. Nails carefully manicured. Hair black and evenly parted.

But his voice had given him away. They never seemed to be able to get a really human sound into the voice. The compressed air and whirling disc system seemed to fall short. Otherwise, it was very convincing.

"I understand you've been situated near Promixa, Mr Doyle," Doctor Bish said pleasantly.

Ed nodded. "Yeah."

"Quite a long way, isn't it? I've never been out there. I have always wanted to go. Is it true they're almost ready to push on to Sirius?"

"Look, Doc --"

"Ed, don't be impatient." Janet stubbed out her cigarette, glancing reprovingly up at him. She hadn't changed in six months. Small blond face, red mouth, cold eyes like little blue rocks. And now, her perfect figure back again. "They're bringing him here. It takes a few minutes. They have to wash him off and put drops in his eyes and take a wave shot of his brain."

"He? Then it's a boy?"

"Of course. Don't you remember? You were with me when I had the shots. We agreed at the time. You haven't changed your mind, have you?"

"Too late to change your mind now, Mr Doyle," Doctor Bish's toneless voice came, high-pitched and calm. "Your wife has decided to call him Peter."

"Peter." Ed nodded, a little dazed. "That's right. We did decide, didn't we? Peter." He let the word roll around in his mind. "Yeah. That's fine. I like it."

The wall suddenly faded, turning from opaque to transparent. Ed spun quickly. They were looking into a brightly lit room, filled with hospital equipment and white-clad attendant robots. One of the robots was moving toward them, pushing a cart. On the cart was a container, a big metal pot.

Ed's breathing increased. He felt a wave of dizziness. He went up to the transparent wall and stood gazing at the metal pot on the cart.

Doctor Bish rose. "Don't you want to see, too, Mrs Doyle?"

"Of course." Janet crossed to the wall and stood beside Ed. She watched critically, her arms folded.

Doctor Bish made a signal. The attendant reached into the pot and lifted out a wire tray, gripping the handles with his magnetic clamps. On the tray, dripping through the wire, was Peter Doyle, still wet from his bath, his eyes wide with astonishment. He was pink all over, except for a fringe of hair on the top of his head, and his great blue eyes. He was little and wrinkled and toothless, like an ancient withered sage.

"Golly," Ed said.

Doctor Bish made a second signal. The wall slid back. The attendant robot advanced into the room, holding his dripping tray out. Doctor Bish removed Peter from the tray and held him up for inspection. He turned him around and around, studying him from every angle.

"He looks fine," he said at last.

"What was the result of the wave photo?" Janet asked.

"Result was good. Excellent tendencies indicated. Very promising. High development of the --" The doctor broke off. "What is it, Mr Doyle?"

Ed was holding out his hands. "Let me have him, Doc. I want to hold him." He grinned from ear to ear. "Let's see how heavy he is. He sure looks big."

Doctor Bish's mouth fell open in horror. He and Janet gasped.

"Ed!" Janet exclaimed sharply. "What's the matter with you?"

"Good heavens, Mr Doyle," the doctor murmured.

Ed blinked. "What?"

"If I had thought you had any such thing in mind --" Doctor Bish quickly returned Peter to the attendant. The attendant rushed Peter from the room, back to the metal pot. The cart and robot and pot hurriedly vanished, and the wall banged back in place.

Janet grabbed Ed's arm angrily. "Good Lord, Ed! Have you lost your mind? Come on. Let's get out of here before you do something else."

"But --"

"Come on." Janet smiled nervously at Doctor Bish. "We'll run along now, Doctor. Thanks so much for everything. Don't pay any attention to him. He's been out there so long, you know."

"I understand," Doctor Bish said smoothly. He had regained his poise. "I trust we'll hear from you later, Mrs Doyle."

Janet pulled Ed out into the hall. "Ed, what's the matter with you? I've never been so embarrassed in all my life." Two spots of red glowed in Janet's cheeks. "I could have kicked you."

"But what --"

"You know we aren't allowed to touch him. What do you want to do, ruin his whole life?"

"But --"

"Come on." They hurried outside the hospital, on to the terrace. Warm sunlight streamed down on them. "There's no telling what harm you've done. He may already be hopelessly warped. If he grows up all warped and -- and neurotic and emotional, it'll be your fault."

Suddenly Ed remembered. He sagged, his features drooping with misery. "That's right. I forgot. Only robots can come near the children. I'm sorry, Jan. I got carried away. I hope I didn't do anything they can't fix."

"How *could* you forget?"

"It's so different out at Prox." Ed waved to a surface car, crestfallen and abashed. The driver drew up in front of them. "Jan, I'm sorry as hell. I really am. I was all excited. Let's go have a cup of coffee some place and talk. I want to know what the doctor said."

Ed had a cup of coffee and Janet sipped at a brandy frappe. The Nymphite Room was pitch black except for a vague light oozing up from the table between them. The table diffused a pale illumination that spread over everything, a ghostly radiation seemingly without source. A robot waitress moved back and forth soundlessly with a tray of drinks. Recorded music played softly in the back of the room.

"Go on," Ed said.

"Go on?" Janet slipped her jacket off and laid it over the back of her chair. In the pale light her breasts glowed faintly. "There's not much to tell. Everything went all right. It didn't take long. I chatted with Doctor Bish most of the time."

"I'm glad I got here."

"How was your trip?"

"Fine."

"Is the service getting any better? Does it still take as long as it did?"

"About the same."

"I can't see why you want to go all the way out there. It's so -- so cut off from things. What do you find out there? Are plumbing fixtures really that much in demand?"

"They need them. Frontier area. Everyone wants the refinements." Ed gestured vaguely. "What did he tell you about Peter? What's he going to be like? Can he tell? I guess it's too soon."

"He was going to tell me when you started acting the way you did. I'll call him on the vidphone when we get home. His wave pattern should be good. He comes from the best eugenic stock."

Ed grunted. "On your side, at least."

"How long are you going to be here?"

"I don't know. Not long. I'll have to go back. I'd sure like to see him again, before I go." He glanced up hopefully at his wife. "Do you think I can?"

"I suppose."

"How long will he have to stay there?"

"At the hospital? Not long. A few days."

Ed hesitated. "I didn't mean at the hospital, exactly. I mean with *them*. How long before we can have him? How long before we can bring him home?"

There was silence. Janet finished her brandy. She leaned back, lighting a cigarette. Smoke drifted across to Ed, blending with the pale light. "Ed, I don't think you understand. You've been out there so long. A lot has happened since you were a child. New methods, new techniques. They've found so many things they didn't know. They're making progress, for the first time. They know what to do. They're developing a real methodology for dealing with children. For the growth period. Attitude development. Training." She smiled brightly at Ed. "I've been reading all about it."

"How long before we get him?"

"In a few days he'll be released from the hospital. He'll go to a child guidance center. He'll be tested and studied. They'll determine his various capacities and his latent abilities. The direction his development seems to be taking."

"And then?"

"Then he's put in the proper educational division. So he'll get the right training. Ed, you know, I think he's really going to be something! I could tell by the way Doctor Bish looked. He was studying the wave pattern charts when I came in. He had a look on his face. How can I describe it?" She searched for the word. "Well, almost -- almost a greedy look. Real excitement. They take so much interest in what they're doing. He --"

"Don't say he. Say *it*."

"Ed, really! What's got into you?"

"Nothing." Ed glared sullenly down. "Go on."

"They make sure he's trained in the right direction. All the time he's there ability tests are given. Then, when he's about nine, he'll be transferred to --"

"Nine! You mean nine *years?*"

"Of course."

"But when do we get him?"

"Ed, I thought you knew about this. Do I have to go over the whole thing?"

"My God, Jan! We can't wait nine years!" Ed jerked himself upright. "I never heard of such a thing. Nine years? Why, he'll be half grown up then."

"That's the point." Janet leaned towards him, resting her bare elbow against the table. "As long as he's growing he has to be with them. Not with us. Afterwards, when he's finished growing, when he's no longer so plastic, then we can be with him all we want."

"Afterwards? When he's eighteen?" Ed leaped up, pushing his chair back. "I'm going down there and get him."

"Sit down, Ed." Janet gazed up calmly, one supple arm thrown lightly over the back of her chair. "Sit down and act like an adult for a change."

"Doesn't it matter to you? Don't you care?"

"Of course I care." Janet shrugged. "But it's necessary. Otherwise he won't develop correctly. It's for *his* good. Not ours. He doesn't exist for us. Do you want him to have conflicts?"

Ed moved away from the table. "I'll see you later."

"Where are you going?"

"Just around. I can't stand this kind of place. It bothers me. I'll see you later." Ed pushed across the room to the door. The door opened and he found himself on the shiny noonday street. Hot sunlight beat down on him. He blinked, adjusting himself to the blinding light. People streamed around him. People and noise. He moved with them.

He was dazed. He had known, of course. It was there in the back of his mind. The new developments in child care. But it had been abstract, general. Nothing to do with him. With *his* child.

He calmed himself, as he walked along. He was getting all upset about nothing. Janet was right, of course. It was for Peter's good. Peter didn't exist for them, like a dog or cat. A pet to have around the house. He was a human being, with his own life. The training was for him, not for them. It was to develop him, his abilities, his powers. He was to be molded, realized, brought out.

Naturally, robots could do the best job. Robots could train him scientifically, according to a rational technique. Not according to emotional whim. Robots didn't get angry. Robots didn't nag and whine. They didn't spank a child or yell at him. They didn't give conflicting orders. They didn't quarrel among themselves or use the child for their own ends. And there could be no *Oedipus Complex,* with only robots around.

No complexes at all. It had been discovered long ago that neurosis could be traced to child-hood training. To the way parents brought up the child. The inhibitions he was taught, the manners, the lessons, the punishments, the rewards. Neuroses, complexes, warped develop-ment, all stemmed from the subjective relationship existing between the child and the parent. If perhaps the parent could be eliminated as a factor. . .

Parents could never become objective about their children. It was always a biased, emotional projection the parent held toward the child. Inevitably, the parent's view was distorted. No parent could be a fit instructor for his child.

Robots could study the child, analyze his needs, his wants, test his abilities and interests. Robots would not try to force the child to fit a certain mold. The child would be trained along his own lines; wherever scientific study indicated his interest and need lay.

Ed came to the corner. Traffic whirred past him. He stepped absently forward.

A clang and crash. Bars dropped in front of him, stopping him. A robot safety control.

"Sir, be more careful!" the strident voice came, close by him.

"Sorry." Ed stepped back. The control bars lifted. He waited for the lights to change. It was for Peter's own good. Robots could train him right. Later on, when he was out of growth stage, when he was not so pliant, responsive -- "It's better for him," Ed murmured. He said it again, half aloud. Some people glanced at him and he colored. Of course it was better for him. No doubt about it.

Eighteen. He couldn't be with his son until he was eighteen. Practically grown up.

The lights changed. Deep in thought, Ed crossed the street with the other pedestrians, keep-ing carefully inside the safety lane. It was best for Peter. But eighteen years was a long time.

"A hell of a long time," Ed murmured, frowning. "Too damn long a time."

Doctor 2g-Y Bish carefully studied the man standing in front of him. His relays and mem-ory banks clicked, narrowing down the image identification, flashing a variety of comparison possibilities past the scanner.

"I recall you, sir," Doctor Bish said at last. "You're the man from Proxima. From the colonies. Doyle, Edward Doyle. Let's see. It was some time ago. It must have been --"

"Nine years ago," Ed Doyle said grimly. "Exactly nine years ago, practically to the day."

Doctor Bish folded his hands. "Sit down, Mr Doyle. What can I do for you? How is Mrs Doyle? Very engaging wife, as I recall. We had a delightful conversation during her delivery. How --"

"Doctor Bish, do you know where my son is?"

Doctor Bish considered, tapping his fingers on the desk top, the polished mahogany surface. He closed his eyes slightly, gazing off into the distance. "Yes. Yes, I know where your son is, Mr Doyle."

Ed Doyle relaxed. "Fine." He nodded, letting his breath out in relief.

"I know exactly where your son is. I placed him in the Los Angeles Biological Research Station about a year ago. He's undergoing specialized training there. Your son, Mr Doyle, has shown exceptional ability. He is, shall I say, one of the few, the very few we have found with real possibilities."

"Can I see him?"

"See him? How do you mean?"

Doyle controlled himself with an effort. "I think the term is clear."

Doctor Bish rubbed his chin. His photocell brain whirred, operating at maximum velocity. Switches routed power surges, building up loads and leaping gaps rapidly, as he contemplated the man before him. "You wish to *view* him? That's one meaning of the term. Or do you wish to talk to him? Sometimes the term is used to cover a more direct contact. It's a loose word."

"I want to talk to him."

"I see." Bish slowly drew some forms from the dispenser on his desk. "There are a few routine papers that have to be filled out first, of course. Just how long did you want to speak to him?"

Ed Doyle gazed steadily into Doctor Bish's bland face. "I want to talk to him several hours. *Alone.*"

"Alone?"

"No robots around."

Doctor Bish said nothing. He stroked the papers he held, creasing the edges with his nail. "Mr Doyle," he said carefully, "I wonder if you're in a proper emotional state to visit your son. You have recently come in from the colonies?"

"I left Proxima three weeks ago."

"Then you have just arrived here in Los Angeles?"

"That's right."

"And you've come to see your son? Or have you other business?"

"I came for my son."

"Mr Doyle, Peter is at a very critical stage. He has just recently been transferred to the Biology Station for his higher training. Up to now his training has been general. What we call the non-differentiated stage. Recently he has entered a new period. Within the last six months Peter has begun advanced work along his specific line, that of organic chemistry. He will --"

"What does Peter think about it?"

Bish frowned. "I don't understand, sir."

"How does *he* feel? Is it what he wants?"

"Mr Doyle, your son has the possibility of becoming one of the world's finest bio-chemists. In all the time we have worked with human beings, in their training and development, we have never come across a more alert and integrated faculty for the assimilation of data, construction of theory, formulation of material, than that which your son possesses. All tests indicate he will rapidly rise to the top of his chosen field. He is still only a child, Mr Doyle, but it is the children who must be trained."

Doyle stood up. "Tell me where I can find him. I'll talk to him for two hours and then the rest is up to him."

"The rest?"

Doyle clamped his jaw shut. He shoved his hands in his pockets. His face was flushed and set grim with determination. In the nine years he had grown much heavier, more stocky and florid. His thinning hair had turned iron-gray. His clothes were dumpy and unpressed. He looked stubborn.

Doctor Bish sighed. "All right, Mr Doyle. Here are your papers. The law allows you to observe your boy whenever you make proper application. Since he is out of his non-differentiated stage, you may also speak to him for a period of ninety minutes."

"Alone?"

"You can take him away from the Station grounds for that length of time." Doctor Bish pushed the papers over to Doyle. "Fill these out, and I'll have Peter brought here."

He looked up steadily at the man standing before him.

"I hope you'll remember that any emotional experience at this crucial stage may do much to inhibit his development. He has chosen his field, Mr Doyle. He must be permitted to grow along his selected lines, unhindered by situational blocks. Peter has been in contact with our technical staff throughout his entire training period. He is not accustomed to contact with other human beings. So please be careful."

Doyle said nothing. He grabbed up the papers and plucked out his fountain pen.

He hardly recognized his son when the two robot attendants brought him out of the massive concrete Station building and deposited him a few yards from Ed's parked surface car.

Ed pushed the door open. "Pete!" His heart was thumping heavily, painfully. He watched his son come toward the car, frowning in the bright sunlight. It was late afternoon, about four. A faint breeze blew across the parking lot, rustling a few papers and bits of debris.

Peter stood slim and straight. His eyes were large, deep brown, like Ed's. His hair was light, almost blond. More like Janet's. He had Ed's jaw, though, the firm line, clean and well chiseled. Ed grinned at him. Nine years it had been. Nine years since the robot attendant had lifted the rack up from the conveyor pot to show him the little wrinkled baby, red as a boiled lobster.

Peter had grown. He was not a baby any longer. He was a young boy, straight and proud, with firm features and wide, clear eyes.

"Pete," Ed said. "How the hell are you?"

The boy stopped by the door of the car. He gazed at Ed calmly. His eyes flickered, taking in the car, the robot driver, the heavy set man in the rumpled tweed suit grinning nervously at him.

"Get in. Get inside." Ed moved over. "Come on. We have places to go."

The boy was looking at him again. Suddenly Ed was conscious of his baggy suit, his un-shined shoes, his gray stubbled chin. He flushed, yanking out his red pocket-handkerchief and mopping his forehead uneasily. "I just got off the ship, Pete. From Proxima. I haven't had time to change. I'm a little dusty. Long trip."

Peter nodded. "4.3 light years, isn't it?"

"Takes three weeks. Get in. Don't you want to get in?"

Peter slid in beside him. Ed slammed the door.

"Let's go." The car started up. "Drive --" Ed peered out the window. "Drive up there. By the hill. Out of town." He turned to Pete. "I hate big cities. I can't get used to them."

"There are no large cities in the colonies, are there?" Pete murmured. "You're unused to urban living."

Ed settled back. His heart had begun to slow down to its normal beat. "No, as a matter of fact it's the other way around, Pete."

"How do you mean?"

"I went to Prox *because* I couldn't stand cities."

Peter said nothing. The surface car was climbing, going up a steel highway into the hills. The Station, huge and impressive, spread out like a heap of cement bricks directly below them. A few cars moved along the road, but not many. Most transportation was by air, now. Surface cars had begun to disappear.

The road leveled off. They moved along the ridge of the hills. Trees and bushes rose on both sides of them. "It's nice up here," Ed said.

"Yes."

"How -- how have you been? I haven't seen you for a long time. Just once. Just after you were born."

"I know. Your visit is listed in the records."

"You been getting along all right?"

"Yes. Quite well."

"They treating you all right?"

"Of course."

After a while Ed leaned forward. "Stop here," he said to the robot driver.

The car slowed down, pulling over to the side of the road. "Sir, there is nothing --"

"This is fine. Let us out. We'll walk from here."

The car stopped. The door slid reluctantly open. Ed stepped quickly out of the car, on to the pavement. Peter got out slowly after him, puzzled. "Where are we?"

"No place." Ed slammed the door. "Go on back to town," he said to the driver. "We won't need you."

The car drove off. Ed walked to the side of the road. Peter came after him. The hill dropped away, falling down to the beginnings of the city below. A vast panorama stretched out, the great metropolis in the late afternoon sun. Ed took a deep breath, throwing his arms out. He took off his coat and tossed it over his shoulder.

"Come on." He started down the hillside. "Here we go."

"Where?"

"For a walk. Let's get off this damn road."

They climbed down the side of the hill, walking carefully, holding on to the grass and roots jutting out from the soil. Finally they came to a level place by a big sycamore tree. Ed threw himself down on the ground, grunting and wiping sweat from his neck.

"Here. Let's sit here."

Peter sat down carefully, a little way off. Ed's blue shirt was stained with sweat. He unfastened his tie and loosened his collar. Presently he searched through his coat pockets. He brought out his pipe and tobacco.

Peter watched him fill the pipe and light it with a big sulphur match. "What's that?" he murmured.

"This? My pipe." Ed grinned, sucking at the pipe. "Haven't you ever seen a pipe?"

"No."

"This is a good pipe. I got this when I first went out to Proxima. That was a long time ago, Pete. It was twenty-five years ago. I was just nineteen, then. Only about twice as old as you."

He put his tobacco away and leaned back, his heavy face serious, preoccupied.

"Just nineteen. I went out there as a plumber. Repair and sales, when I could make a sale. Terran Plumbing. One of those big ads you used to see. Unlimited opportunities. Virgin lands. Make a million. Gold in the streets." Ed laughed.

"How did you make out?"

"Not bad. Not bad at all. I own my own line, now, you know. I service the whole Proxima system. We do repairing, maintenance, building, construction. I've got six hundred people working for me. It took a long time. It didn't come easy."

"No."

"Hungry?"

Peter turned. "What?"

"Are you hungry?" Ed pulled a brown paper parcel from his coat and unwrapped it. "I still have a couple of sandwiches from the trip. When I come in from Prox I bring some food along with me. I don't like to buy in the diner. They skin you." He held out the parcel. "Want one?"

"No thank you."

Ed took a sandwich and began to eat. He ate nervously, glancing at his son. Peter sat silently, a short distance off, staring ahead without expression. His smooth handsome face was blank.

"Everything all right?" Ed said.

"Yes."

"You're not cold, are you?"

"No."

"You don't want to catch cold."

A squirrel crossed in front of them, hurrying toward the sycamore tree. Ed threw it a piece of his sandwich. The squirrel ran off a way, then came back slowly. It scolded at them, standing up on its hind feet, its great gray tail flowing out behind it.

Ed laughed. "Look at him. Ever see a squirrel before?"

"I don't think so."

"It's good to come back to Terra once in a while. See some of the old things. They're going, though."

"Going?"

"Away. Destroyed. Terra is always changing." Ed waved around at the hillside. "This will be gone, some day. They'll cut down the trees. Then they'll level it. Some day they'll carve the whole range up and carry it off. Use it for fill, some place along the coast."

"That's beyond our scope," Peter said.

400

"What?"

"I don't receive that type of material. I think Doctor Bish told you. I'm working with bio-chemistry."

"I know," Ed murmured. "Say, how the hell did you ever get mixed up with that stuff? Bio-chemistry?"

"The tests showed that my abilities lie along those lines."

"You enjoy what you're doing?"

"What a strange thing to ask. Of course I enjoy what I'm doing. It's the work I'm fitted for."

"It seems funny as hell to me, starting a nine-year-old kid off on something like that."

"Why?"

"My God, Pete. When I was nine I was bumming around town. In school sometimes, outside mostly, wandering here and there. Playing. Reading. Sneaking into the rocket launching yards all the time." He considered. "Doing all sorts of things. When I was sixteen I hopped over to Mars. I stayed there a while. Worked as a hasher. I went on to Ganymede. Ganymede was all sewed up tight. Nothing doing there. From Ganymede I went out to Prox. Got a work-away all the way out. Big freighter."

"You stayed at Proxima?"

"I sure did. I found what I wanted. Nice place, out there. Now we're starting on to Sirius, you know." Ed's chest swelled. "I've got an outlet in the Sirius system. Little retail and service place."

"Sirius is 8.8 light years from Sol."

"It's a long way. Seven weeks from here. Rough grind. Meteor swarms. Keeps things hot all the way out."

"I can imagine."

"You know what I thought I might do?" Ed turned toward his son, his face alive with hope and enthusiasm. "I've been thinking it over. I thought maybe I'd go out there. To Sirius. It's a fine little place we have. I drew up the plans myself. Special design to fit with the characteristics of the system."

Peter nodded.

"Pete --"

"Yes?"

"Do you think maybe you'd be interested? Like to hop out to Sirius and take a look? It's a good place. Four clean planets. Never touched. Lots of room. Miles and miles of room. Cliffs and mountains. Oceans. Nobody around. Just a few colonists, families, some construction. Wide, level plains."

"How do you mean, interested?"

"In going all the way out." Ed's face was pale. His mouth twitched nervously. "I thought maybe you'd like to come along and see how things are. It's a lot like Prox was, twenty-five years ago. It's good and clean out there. No cities."

Peter smiled.

"Why are you smiling?"

"No reason." Peter stood up abruptly. "If we have to walk back to the Station we'd better start. Don't you think? It's getting late."

"Sure." Ed struggled to his feet. "Sure, but --"

"When are you going to be back in the Sol system again?"

"Back?" Ed followed after his son. Peter climbed up the hill toward the road. "Slow down, will you?"

Peter slowed down. Ed caught up with him.

"I don't know when I'll be back. I don't come here very often. No ties. Not since Jan and I separated. As a matter of fact I came here this time to --"

"This way." Peter started down the road.

Ed hurried along beside him, fastening his tie and putting his coat on, gasping for breath. "Peter, what do you say? You want to hop out to Sirius with me? Take a look? It's a nice place out there. We could work together. The two of us. If you want."

"But I already have my work."

"That stuff? That damn chemistry stuff?"

Peter smiled again.

Ed scowled, his face dark red. "Why are you smiling?" he demanded. His son did not answer. "What's the matter? What's so damn funny?"

"Nothing," Peter said. "Don't become excited. We have a long walk down." He increased his pace slightly, his supple body swinging in long, even strides. "It's getting late. We have to hurry."

Doctor Bish examined his wristwatch, pushing back his pinstriped coat sleeve. "I'm glad you're back."

"He sent the surface car away," Peter murmured. "We had to walk down the hill on foot."

It was dark outside. The Station lights were coming on automatically, along the rows of buildings and laboratories.

Doctor Bish rose from his desk. "Sign this, Peter. Bottom of this form."

Peter signed. "What is it?"

"Certifies you saw him in accord with the provisions of the law. We didn't try to obstruct you in any way."

Peter handed the paper back. Bish filed it away with the others. Peter moved toward the door of the doctor's office. "I'll go. Down to the cafeteria for dinner."

"You haven't eaten?"

"No."

Doctor Bish folded his arms, studying the boy. "Well?" he said. "What do you think of him? This is the first time you've seen your father. It must have been strange for you. You've been around us so much, in all your training and work."

"It was -- unusual."

"Did you gain any impressions? Was there anything you particularly noticed?"

"He was very emotional. There was a distinct bias through everything he said and did. A distortion present, virtually uniform."

"Anything else?"

Peter hesitated, lingering at the door. He broke into a smile. "One other thing."

"What was it?"

"I noticed --" Peter laughed. "I noticed a distinct odor about him. A constant pungent smell, all the time I was with him."

"I'm afraid that's true of all of them," Doctor Bish said. "Certain skin glands. Waste products thrown off from the blood. You'll get used to it, after you've been around them more."

"Do I have to be around them?"

"They're your own race. How else can you work with them? Your whole training is designed with that in mind. When we've taught you all we can, then you will --"

"It reminded me of something. The pungent odor. I kept thinking about it, all the time I was with him. Trying to place it."

"Can you identify it now?"

Peter reflected. He thought hard, concentrating deeply. His small face wrinkled up. Doctor Bish waited patiently by his desk, arms folded. The automatic heating system clicked on for the night, warming the room with a soft glow that drifted gently around them.

"I know!" Peter exclaimed suddenly.

"What was it?"

"The animals in the biology lab. It was the same smell. The same smell as the experimental animals."

They glanced at each other, the robot doctor and the promising young boy. Both of them smiled, a secret, private smile. A smile of complete understanding.

"I believe I know what you mean," Doctor Bish said. "In fact, I know exactly what you mean."

Strange Eden

Captain Johnson was the first man out of the ship. He scanned the planet's great rolling forests, its miles of green that made your eyes ache. The sky overhead that was pure blue. Off beyond the trees lapped the edges of an ocean, about the same color as the sky, except for a bubbling surface of incredibly bright seaweed that darkened the blue almost to purple.

He had only four feet to go from the control board to the automatic hatch, and from there down the ramp to the soft black soil dug up by the jet blast and strewn everywhere, still steaming. He shaded his eyes against the golden sun, and then, after a moment, removed his glasses and polished them on his sleeve. He was a small man, thin and sallow-faced. He blinked nervously without his glasses and quickly fitted them back in place. He took a deep breath of the warm air, held it in his lungs, let it roll through his system, then reluctantly let it escape.

"Not bad," Brent rumbled, from the open hatch.

"If this place were closer to Terra there'd be empty beer cans and plastic plates strewn around. The trees would be gone. There'd be old jet motors in the water. The beaches would stink to high heaven. Terran Development would have a couple of million little plastic houses set up everywhere."

Brent grunted indifferently. He jumped down, a huge barrel-chested man, sleeves rolled up, arms dark and hairy.

"What's that over there? Some kind of trail?"

Captain Johnson uneasily got out a star chart and studied it. "No ship ever reported this area, before us. According to this chart the whole system's uninhabited."

Brent laughed. "Ever occur to you there might already be culture here? Non-Terran?"

Captain Johnson fingered his gun. He had never used it; this was the first time he had been assigned to an exploring survey outside the patrolled area of the galaxy. "Maybe we ought to take off. Actually, we don't have to map this place. We've mapped the three bigger planets, and this one isn't really required."

Brent strode across the damp ground, toward the trail. He squatted down and ran his hands over the broken grass. "Something comes along here. There's a rut worn in the soil." He gave a startled exclamation. "Footprints!"

"People?"

"Looks like some kind of animal. Large -- maybe a big cat." Brent straightened up, his heavy face thoughtful. "Maybe we could get ourselves some fresh game. And if not, maybe a little sport."

Captain Johnson fluttered nervously. "How do we know what sort of defenses these animals have? Let's play it safe and stay in the ship. We can make the survey by air; the usual processes ought to be enough for a little place like this. I hate to stick around here." He shivered. "It gives me the creeps."

"The creeps?" Brent yawned and stretched, then started along the trail, toward the rolling miles of green forest. "I like it. A regular national park -- complete with wildlife. You stay in the ship. I'll have a little fun."

Brent moved cautiously through the dark woods, one hand on his gun. He was an old-time surveyor; he had wandered around plenty of remote places in his time, enough to know what he was doing. He halted from time to time, examining the trail and feeling the soil. The large prints continued and were joined by others. A whole group of animals had come along this way, several species, all large. Probably flocking to a water source. A stream or pool of some kind.

He climbed a rise -- then abruptly crouched. Ahead of him an animal was curled up on a flat stone, eyes shut, obviously sleeping. Brent moved around in a wide circle, carefully keeping his face to the animal. It was a cat, all right. But not the kind of cat he had ever seen before. Something like a lion -- but larger. As large as a Terran rhino. Long tawny fur, great pads, a tail like a twisted spare-rope. A few flies crawled over its flanks; muscles rippled and the flies darted off. Its mouth was slightly open; he could see gleaming white fangs that sparkled moistly in the sun. A vast pink tongue. It breathed heavily, slowly, snoring in its slumber.

Brent toyed with his r-pistol. As a sportsman he couldn't shoot it sleeping: he'd have to chuck a rock at it and wake it up. But as a man looking at a beast twice his weight, he was tempted to blast its heart out and lug the remains back to the ship. The head would look fine; the whole damn pelt would look fine. He could make up a nice story to go along with it -- the thing dropping on him from a branch, or maybe springing out of a thicket, roaring and snarling.

He knelt down, rested his right elbow on his right knee, clasped the butt of his pistol with his left hand, closed one eye, and carefully aimed. He took a deep breath, steadied the gun, and released the safety catch.

As he began squeezing the trigger, two more of the great cats sauntered past him along the trail, nosed briefly at their sleeping relation, and continued on into the brush.

Feeling foolish, Brent lowered his gun. The two beasts had paid no attention to him. One had glanced his way slightly, but neither had paused or taken any notice. He got unsteadily to his feet, cold sweat breaking out on his forehead. Good God, if they had wanted they could have torn him apart. Crouching there with his back turned --

He'd have to be more careful. Not stop and stay in one place. Keep moving, or go back to the ship. No, he wouldn't go back to the ship. He still needed something to show pipsqueak Johnson. The little Captain was probably sitting nervously at the controls, wondering what had happened to him. Brent pushed carefully through the shrubs and regained the trail on the far side of the sleeping cat. He'd explore some more, find something worth bringing back, maybe camp the night in a sheltered spot. He had a pack of hard rations, and in an emergency he could raise Johnson with his throat transmitter.

He came out on a flat meadow. Flowers grew everywhere, yellow and red and violet blossoms; he strode rapidly through them. The planet was virgin -- still in its primitive stage. No humans had come here; as Johnson said, in a while there'd be plastic plates and beer cans and rotting debris. Maybe he could take out a lease. Form a corporation and claim the whole damn thing. Then slowly subdivide, only to the best people. Promise them no commercialization; only the most exclusive homes. A garden retreat for wealthy Terrans who had plenty of leisure. Fishing and hunting: all the game they wanted. Completely tame, too. Unfamiliar with humans.

His scheme pleased him. As he came out of the meadow and plunged into dense trees, he considered how he'd raise the initial investment. He might have to cut others in on it; get somebody with plenty of loot to back him. They'd need good promotion and advertising; really push the thing good. Untouched planets were getting scarce; this might well be the last. If he missed this, it might be a long time before he had another chance to. . .

His thoughts died. His scheme collapsed. Dull resentment choked him and he came to an abrupt halt.

Ahead the trail broadened. The trees were farther apart; bright sunlight sifted down into the silent darkness of the ferns and bushes and flowers. On a little rise was a building. A stone house, with steps, a front porch, solid white walls like marble. A garden grew around it. Windows. A path. Smaller buildings in the back. All neat and pretty -- and extremely modern-looking. A small fountain sprinkled blue water into a basin. A few birds moved around the gravel paths, pecking and scratching.

The planet was inhabited.

Brent approached warily. A wisp of gray smoke trailed out of the stone chimney. Behind the house were chicken pens, a cow-like thing dozing in the shade by its water trough. Other animals, some dog-like, and a group that might have been sheep. A regular little farm -- but not like any farm he had seen. The buildings were of marble, or what looked like marble. And the animals were penned in by some kind of force-field. Everything was clean; in one corner a disposal tube sucked exhausted water and refuse into a half-buried tank.

He came to steps leading up to a back porch and, after a moment of thought, climbed them. He wasn't especially frightened. There was a serenity about the place, an orderly calm. It was hard to imagine any harm coming from it. He reached the door, hesitated, and then began looking for a knob.

There wasn't any knob. At his touch the door swung open. Feeling foolish, Brent entered. He found himself in a luxurious hall; recessed lights flickered on at the pressure of his boots on the thick carpets. Long glowing drapes hid the windows. Massive furniture -- he peered into a room. Strange machines and objects. Pictures on the walls. Statues in the corners. He turned a corner and emerged into a large foyer. And still no one.

A huge animal, as large as a pony, moved out of a doorway, sniffed at him curiously, licked his wrist, and wandered off. He watched it go, heart in his mouth.

Tame. All the animals were tame. What kind of people had built this place? Panic stabbed at him. Maybe not people. Maybe some other race. Something alien, from beyond the galaxy. Maybe this was the frontier of an alien empire, some kind of advanced station.

While he was thinking about it, wondering if he should try to get out, run back to the ship, vid the cruiser station at Orion IX, there was a faint rustle behind him. He turned quickly, hand on his gun.

"Who --" he gasped. And froze.

A girl stood there, face calm, eyes large and dark, a cloudy black. She was tall, almost as tall as he, a little under six feet. Cascades of black hair spilled down her shoulders, down to her waist. She wore a glistening robe of some oddly-metallic material; countless facets glittered and sparkled and reflected the overhead lights. Her lips were deep red and full. Her arms were folded beneath her breasts; they stirred faintly as she breathed. Beside her stood the pony-like animal that had nosed him and gone on.

"Welcome, Mr. Brent," the girl said. She smiled at him; he caught a flash of her tiny white teeth. Her voice was gentle and lilting, remarkably pure. Abruptly she turned; her robe fluttered behind her as she passed through the doorway and into the room beyond. "Come along. I've been expecting you."

Brent entered cautiously. A man stood at the end of the long table, watching him with obvious dislike. He was huge, over six feet, broad shoulders and arms that rippled as he buttoned his cloak and moved toward the door. The table was covered with dishes and bowls of food; robot servants were clearing away the things silently. Obviously, the girl and man had been eating.

"This is my brother," the girl said, indicating the dark-faced giant. He bowed slightly to Brent, exchanged a few words with the girl in an unfamiliar, liquid tongue, and then abruptly departed. His footsteps died down the hall.

"I'm sorry," Brent muttered. "I didn't mean to bust in here and break up anything."

"Don't worry. He was going. Actually, we don't get along very well." The girl drew the drapes aside to reveal a wide window overlooking the forest. "You can watch him go. His ship is parked out there. See it?"

It took a moment for Brent to make out the ship. It blended into the scenery perfectly. Only when it abruptly shot upward at a ninety-degree angle did he realize it had been there all the time. He had walked within yards of it.

"He's quite a person," the girl said, letting the drapes fall back in place. "Are you hungry? Here, sit down and eat with me. Now that Aeetes is gone and I'm all alone."

Brent sat down cautiously. The food looked good. The dishes were some kind of semi-transparent metal. A robot set places in front of him, knives, forks, spoons, then waited to be instructed. The girl gave it orders in her strange liquid tongue. It promptly served Brent and retired.

He and the girl were alone. Brent began to eat greedily; the food was delicious. He tore the wings from a chicken-like fowl and gnawed at it expertly. He gulped down a tumbler of dark red wine, wiped his mouth on his sleeve, and attacked a bowl of ripe fruit. Vegetables, spiced meats, seafood, warm bread -- he gobbled down everything with pleasure. The girl ate a few dainty bites; she watched him curiously, until finally he was finished and had pushed his empty dishes away.

"Where's your Captain?" she asked. "Didn't he come?"

"Johnson? He's back at the ship." Brent belched noisily. "How come you speak Terran? It's not your natural language. And how did you know there's somebody with me?"

The girl laughed, a tinkling musical peal. She wiped her slim hands on a napkin and drank from a dark red glass. "We watched you on the scanner. We were curious. This is the first time one of your ships has penetrated this far. We wondered what your intentions were."

"You didn't learn Terran by watching our ship on a scanner."

"No. I learned your language from people of your race. That was a long time ago. I've spoken your language as long as I can remember."

Brent was baffled. "But you said our ship was the first to come here."

The girl laughed. "True. But we've often visited your little world. We know all about it. It's a stop-over point when we travel in that direction. I've been there many times -- not for a while, but in the old days when I traveled more.

A strange chill settled over Brent. "Who are you people? Where are you from?"

"I don't know where we're from originally," the girl answered. "Our civilization is all over the universe, by now. It probably started from one place, back in legendary times. By now it's practically everywhere."

"Why haven't we run into your people before?"

The girl smiled and continued eating. "Didn't you hear what I said? You *have* met us. Often. We've even brought Terrans here. I remember one time very clearly, a few thousand years ago --"

"How long are your years?" Brent demanded.

"We don't have years." The girl's dark eyes bored into him, luminous with amusement. "I mean *Terran* years."

It took a minute for the full impact to hit him. "Thousand years," he murmured. "You've been alive a thousand years?"

"Eleven thousand," the girl answered simply. She nodded, and a robot cleared away the dishes. She leaned back in her chair, yawned, stretched like a small, lithe cat, then abruptly sprang to her feet. "Come on. We've finished eating. I'll show you my house."

Brent scrambled up and hurried after her, his confidence shattered. "You're immortal, aren't you?" He moved between her and the door, breathing rapidly, heavy face flushed. "You don't age."

"Age? No, of course not."

Brent managed to find words. "You're gods."

The girl smiled up at him, dark eyes flashing merrily. "Not really. You have just about everything we have -- almost as much knowledge, science, culture. Eventually you'll catch up with us. We're an old race. Millions of years ago our scientists succeeded in slowing down the processes of decay; since then we've ceased to die."

"Then your race stays constant. None die, none are born."

The girl pushed past him, through the doorway and down the hall. "Oh, people are born all the time. Our race grows and expands." She halted at a doorway. "We haven't given up any of our pleasures." She eyed Brent thoughtfully, his shoulders, arms, his dark hair, heavy face. "We're about like you, except that we're eternal. You'll probably solve that, too, sometime."

"You've moved among us?" Brent demanded. He was beginning to understand. "Then all those old religions and myths were true. Gods. Miracles. You've had contact with us, given us things. Done things for us." He followed her wonderingly into the room.

"Yes. I suppose we've done things for you. As we pass through." The girl moved about the room, letting down massive drapes. Soft darkness fell over the couches and bookcases and statues. "Do you play chess?"

"CHESS?"

"It's our national game. We introduced it to some of your Brahmin ancestors." Disappointment showed on her sharp little face. "You don't play? Too bad. What do you do? What about your companion? He looked as if his intellectual capacity was greater than yours. Does he play chess? Maybe you ought to go back and get him."

"I don't think so," Brent said. He moved toward her. "As far as I know he doesn't do anything." He reached out and caught her by the arm. The girl pulled away, astonished. Brent gathered her up in his big arms and drew her tight against him. "I don't think we need him," he said.

He kissed her on the mouth. Her red lips were warm and sweet; she gasped and fought wildly. He could feel her slim body struggling against him. A cloud of fragrant scent billowed from her dark hair. She tore at him with her sharp nails, breasts heaving violently. He let go and she slid away, wary and bright-eyed, breathing quickly, body tense, drawing her luminous robe about her.

"I could kill you," she whispered. She touched her jeweled belt. "You don't understand, do you?"

Brent came forward. "You probably can. But I bet you won't."

She backed away from him. "Don't be a fool." Her red lips twisted and a smile flickered briefly. "You're brave. But not very smart. Still, that's not such a bad combination in a man. Stupid and brave." Agilely, she avoided his grasp and slipped out of his reach. "You're in good physical shape, too. How do you manage it aboard that little ship?"

"Quarterly fitness courses," Brent answered. He moved between her and the door. "You must get pretty damn bored here, all by yourself. After the first few thousand years it must get trying."

"I find things to do," she said. "Don't come any closer to me. As much as I admire your daring, it's only fair to warn you that --"

Brent grabbed her. She fought wildly; he pinned her hands together behind her back with one paw, arched her body taut, and kissed her half-parted lips. She sank her tiny white teeth into him; he grunted and jerked away. She was laughing, black eyes dancing, as she struggled. Her breath came rapidly, cheeks flushed, half-covered breasts quivering, body twisting like a trapped animal. He caught her around the waist and grabbed her up in his arms.

A wave of force hit him.

He dropped her; she landed easily on her feet and danced back. Brent was doubled up, face gray with agony. Cold sweat stood out on his neck and hands. He sank down on a couch and closed his eyes, muscles knotted, body writhing with pain.

"Sorry," the girl said. She moved around the room, ignoring him, "It's your own fault -- I told you to be careful. Maybe you better get out of here. Back to your little ship. I don't want anything to happen to you. It's against our policy to kill Terrans."

"What -- was that?"

"Nothing much. A form of repulsion, I suppose. This belt was constructed on one of our industrial planets; it protects me but I don't know the operational principle."

Brent manage to get to his feet. "You're pretty tough for a little girl."

"A little girl? I'm pretty *old* for a little girl. I was old before you were born. I was old before your people had rocket ships. I was old before you knew how to weave clothing and write your thoughts down with symbols. I've watched your race advance and fall back into barbarism and advance again. Endless nations and empires. I was alive when the Egyptians first began spreading out into Asia Minor. I saw the city builders of the Tigris Valley begin putting up their brick houses. I saw the Assyrian war chariots roll out to fight. I and my friends visited Greece and Rome and Minos and Lydia and the great kingdoms of the red-skinned Indians. We were gods to the ancients, saints to the Christians. We come and go. As your people advanced we came less often. We have other way-stations; yours isn't the only stop-over point."

Brent was silent. Color was beginning to come back to his face. The girl had thrown herself down on one of the soft couches; she leaned back against a pillow and gazed up at him calmly, one arm outstretched, the other across her lap. Her long legs were tucked under her, tiny feet pressed together. She looked like a small, contented kitten resting after a game. It was hard for him to believe what she had told him. But his body still ached; he had felt a minute portion of her power-field, and it had almost killed him. That was something to think about.

"Well?" the girl asked, presently. "What are you going to do? It's getting late. I think you ought to go back to your ship. Your Captain will be wondering what happened to you."

Brent moved over to the window and drew aside the heavy drapes. The sun had set. Darkness was settling over the forests outside. Stars had already begun to come out, tiny dots of white in the thickening violet. A distant line of hills jutted up black and ominous.

"I can contact him," Brent said. He tapped at his neck. "In case of emergency. Tell him I'm all right."

"*Are you all right?* You shouldn't be here. You think you know what you're doing? You think you can handle me." She raised herself up slightly and tossed her black hair back over her shoulders. "I can see what's going on in your mind. I'm so much like a girl you had an affair with, a young brunette you used to wrap around your finger -- and boast about to your companions."

Brent flushed. "You're a telepath. You should have told me."

"A partial telepath. All I need. Toss me your cigarettes. We don't have such things."

Brent fumbled in his pocket, got his pack out and tossed it to her. She lit up and inhaled gratefully. A cloud of gray smoke drifted around her; it mixed with the darkening shadows of the room. The corners dissolved into gloom. She became an indistinct shape, curled up on the couch, the glowing cigarette between her dark red lips.

"I'm not afraid," Brent said.

"No, you're not. You're not a coward. If you were as smart as you are brave -- but then I guess you wouldn't be brave. I admire your bravery, stupid as it is. Man has a lot of courage. Even though it's based on ignorance, it's impressive." After a moment, she said, "Come over here and sit with me."

"What do I have to be worried about?" Brent asked after a while. "If you don't turn on that damn belt, I'll be all right."

In the darkness, the girl stirred. "There's more than that." She sat up a little, arranged her hair, pulled a pillow behind her head. "You see, we're of totally different races. My race is millions of years advanced over yours. Contact with us -- close contact -- is lethal. Not to us, of course. To you. You can't be with me and remain a human being."

"What do you mean?"

"You'll undergo changes. Evolutionary changes. There's pull which we exert. We're fully charged; close contact with us will exert influence on the cells of your body. Those animals outside. They've evolved slightly; they're no longer wild beasts. They're able to understand simple commands and follow basic routines. As yet, they have no language. With such low animals it's a long process; and my contact with them hasn't really been close. But with you --"

"I see."

"We're not supposed to let humans near us. Aeetes cleared out of here. I'm too lazy to go -- I don't especially care. I'm not mature and responsible, I suppose." She smiled slightly. "And my kind of close contact is a little closer than most."

Brent could barely make out her slim form in the darkness. She lay back against the pillows, lips parted, arms folded beneath her breasts, head tilted back. She was lovely. The most beautiful woman he had ever seen. After a moment he leaned toward her. This time she didn't move away. He kissed her gently. Then he put his arms around her slender body and drew her tight against him. Her robe rustled. Her soft hair brushed against him, warm and fragrant.

"It's worth it," he said.

"You're sure? You can't turn back, once it's begun. Do you understand? You won't be human any more. You'll have evolved. Along lines your race will take millions of years from now. You'll be an outcast, a forerunner of things to come. Without companions."

"I'll stay." He caressed her cheek, her hair, her neck. He could feel the blood pulsing beneath the downy skin; a rapid pounding in the hollow of her throat. She was breathing rapidly; her breasts rose and fell against him. "If you'll let me."

"Yes," she murmured. "I'll let you. If it's what you really want. But don't blame me." A half-sad, half-mischievous smile flitted across her sharp features; her dark eyes sparkled. "Promise you won't blame me? It's happened before -- I hate people to reproach me. I always say never again. No matter what."

"Has it happened before?"

The girl laughed, softly and close to his ear. She kissed him warmly and hugged him hard against her. "In eleven thousand years," she whispered, "it's happened quite often."

Captain Johnson had a bad night. He tried to raise Brent on the emergency com, but there was no response. Only faint static and a distant echo of a vid program from Orion X. Jazz music and sugary commercials.

The sounds of civilization reminded him that they had to keep moving. Twenty-four hours was all the time allotted to this planet, smallest of its system.

"Damn," he muttered. He fixed a pot of coffee and checked his wrist-watch. Then he got out of the ship and wandered around in the early-morning sunlight. The sun was beginning to come up. The air turned from dark violet to gray. It was cold as hell. He shivered and stamped his feet and watched some small bird-like things fly down to peck around the bushes.

He was just beginning to think of notifying Orion XI when he saw her.

She walked quickly toward the ship. Tall and slim in a heavy fur jacket, her arms buried in the deep pelt. Johnson stood rooted to the spot, dumbfounded. He was too astonished even to touch his gun. His mouth fell open as the girl halted a little way off, tossed her dark hair back, blew a cloud of silvery breath at him and then said, "I'm sorry you had a bad night. It's my fault. I should have sent him right back."

Captain Johnson's mouth opened and shut. "Who are you?" he managed finally. Fear seized him. "Where's Brent? What happened?"

"He'll be along." She turned back toward the forest and made a sign. "I think you'd better leave, now. He wants to stay here and that is best -- for he's changed. He'll be happy in my forest with the other -- men. It's strange how all you humans come out exactly alike. Your race is moving along an unusual path. It might be worth our while to study you, sometime. It must have something to do with your low esthetic plateau. You seem to have an innate vulgarity, which eventually will dominate you."

From out of the woods came a strange shape. For a moment, Captain Johnson thought his eyes were playing tricks on him. He blinked, squinted, then grunted in disbelief. Here, on this remote planet -- but there was no mistake. It was definitely an immense cat-like beast that came slowly and miserably out of the woods after the girl.

The girl moved away, then halted to wave to the beast, who whined wretchedly around the ship.

Johnson stared at the animal and felt a sudden fear. Instinctively he knew that Brent was not coming back to the ship. Something had happened on this strange planet -- that girl. . .

Johnson slammed the airlock shut and hurried to the control panel. He had to get back to the nearest base and make a report. This called for an elaborate investigation.

As the rockets blasted Johnson glanced through the viewplate. He saw the animal shaking a huge paw futilely in the air after the departing ship.

Johnson shuddered. That was too much like a man's angry gesture. . .

Human Is

Jill Herrick's blue eyes filled with tears. She gazed at her husband in unspeakable horror. "You're -- you're hideous!" she wailed.

Lester Herrick continued working, arranging heaps of notes and graphs in precise piles.

"Hideous," he stated, "is a value judgment. It contains no factual information." He sent a report tape on Centauran parasitic life whizzing through the desk scanner. "Merely an opinion. An expression of emotion, nothing more."

Jill stumbled back to the kitchen. Listlessly, she waved her hand to trip the stove into activity. Conveyor belts in the wall hummed to life, hurrying the food from the underground storage lockers for the evening meal.

She turned to face her husband one last time. "Not even a *little* while?" she begged. "Not even --"

"Not even for a month. When he comes you can tell him. If you haven't the courage, I'll do it. I can't have a child running around here. I have too much work to do. This report on Betelgeuse XI is due in ten days." Lester dropped a spool on Fomalhautan fossil implements into the scanner. "What's the matter with your brother? Why can't he take care of his own child?"

Jill dabbed at swollen eyes. "Don't you understand? I *want* Gus here! I begged Frank to let him come. And now you --"

"I'll be glad when he's old enough to be turned over to the Government." Lester's thin face twisted in annoyance. "Damn it, Jill, isn't dinner ready yet? It's been ten minutes! What's wrong with that stove?"

"It's almost ready." The stove showed a red signal light. The robant waiter had come out of the wall and was waiting expectantly to take the food.

Jill sat down and blew her small nose violently. In the living-room, Lester worked on unperturbed. His work. His research. Day after day. Lester was getting ahead; there was no doubt of that. His lean body was bent like a coiled spring over the tape scanner, cold gray eyes taking in the information feverishly, analyzing, appraising, his conceptual faculties operating like well-greased machinery.

Jill's lips trembled in misery and resentment. Gus -- little Gus. How could she tell him? Fresh tears welled up in her eyes. Never to see the chubby little fellow again. He could never come back -- because his childish laughter and play bothered Lester. Interfered with his research.

The stove clicked to green. The food slid out, into the arms of the robant. Soft chimes sounded to announce dinner.

"I hear it," Lester grated. He snapped off the scanner and got to his feet. "I suppose he'll come while we're eating."

"I can vid Frank and ask --"

"No. Might as well get it over with." Lester nodded impatiently to the robant. "All right. Put it down." His thin lips set in an angry line. "Damn it, don't dawdle! I want to get back to my work!"

Jill bit back the tears.

Little Gus came trailing into the house as they were finishing dinner.

Jill gave a cry of joy. "Gussie!" She ran to sweep him up in her arms. "I'm so glad to see you!"

"Watch out for my tiger," Gus muttered. He dropped his little gray kitten onto the rug and it rushed off, under the couch. "He's hiding."

Lester's eyes flickered as he studied the little boy and the tip of gray tail extending from under the couch.

"Why do you call it a tiger? It's nothing but an alley cat."

Gus looked hurt. He scowled. "He's a tiger. He's got stripes."

"Tigers are yellow and a great deal bigger. You might as well learn to classify things by their correct names."

"Lester, please --" Jill pleaded.

"Be quiet," her husband said crossly. "Gus is old enough to shed childish illusions and develop a realistic orientation. What's wrong with the psych testers? Don't they straighten this sort of nonsense out?"

Gus ran and snatched up his tiger. "You leave him alone!"

Lester contemplated the kitten. A strange, cold smile played about his lips. "Come down to the lab some time, Gus. We'll show you lots of cats. We use them in our research. Cats, guinea pigs, rabbits --"

"Lester!" Jill gasped. "How can you!"

Lester laughed thinly. Abruptly he broke off and returned to his desk. "Now clear out of here. I have to finish these reports. And don't forget to tell Gus."

Gus got excited. "Tell me what?" His cheeks flushed. His eyes sparkled. "What is it? Something for me? A *secret*?"

Jill's heart was like lead. She put her hand heavily on the child's shoulder. "Come on, Gus. We'll go sit out in the garden and I'll tell you. Bring -- bring your tiger."

A click. The emergency vidsender lit up. Instantly Lester was on his feet. "Be quiet!" He ran to the sender, breathing rapidly. "Nobody speak!"

Jill and Gus paused at the door. A confidential message was sliding from the slot into the dish. Lester grabbed it up and broke the seal. He studied it intently.

"What is it?" Jill asked. "Anything bad?"

"Bad?" Lester's face shone with a deep inner glow. "No, not bad at all." He glanced at his watch. "Just time. Let's see, I'll need --"

"What is it?"

"I'm going on a trip. I'll be gone two or three weeks. Rexor IV is into the charted area."

"Rexor IV? You're going there?" Jill clasped her hands eagerly. "Oh, I've always wanted to see an old system, old ruins and cities! Lester, can I come along? Can I go with you? We never took a vacation, and you always promised --"

Lester Herrick stared at his wife in amazement. "You?" he said. "*You* go along?" He laughed unpleasantly. "Now hurry and get my things together. I've been waiting for this a long time." He rubbed his hands together in satisfaction. "You can keep the boy here until I'm back. But no longer. Rexor IV! I can hardly wait!"

"You have to make allowances," Frank said. "After all, he's a scientist."

"I don't care," Jill said. "I'm leaving him. As soon as he gets back from Rexor IV. I've made up my mind."

Her brother was silent, deep in thought. He stretched his feet out, onto the lawn of the little garden. "Well, if you leave him you'll be free to marry again. You're still classed as sexually adequate, aren't you?"

Jill nodded firmly. "You bet I am. I wouldn't have any trouble. Maybe I can find somebody who likes children."

"You think a lot of children," Frank perceived. "Gus loves to visit you. But he doesn't like Lester. Les needles him."

"I know. This past week has been heaven, with him gone." Jill patted her soft blonde hair, blushing prettily. "I've had fun. Makes me feel alive again."

"When'll he be back?"

"Any day." Jill clenched her small fists. "We've been married five years and every year it's worse. He's so -- so inhuman. Utterly cold and ruthless. Him and his work. Day and night."

"Les is ambitious. He wants to get to the top in his field." Frank lit a cigarette lazily. "A pusher. Well, maybe he'll do it. What's he in?"

"Toxicology. He works out new poisons for Military. He invented the copper sulphate skin-lime they used against Callisto."

"It's a small field. Now take me." Frank leaned contentedly against the wall of the house. "There are thousands of Clearance lawyers. I could work for years and never create a ripple. I'm content just to be. I do my job. I enjoy it."

"I wish Lester felt that way."

"Maybe he'll change."

"He'll *never* change," Jill said bitterly. "I know that, now. That's why I've made up my mind to leave him. He'll always be the same."

Lester Herrick came back from Rexor IV a different man. Beaming happily, he deposited his anti-grav suitcase in the arms of the waiting robant. "Thank you."

Jill gasped speechlessly. "Les! What --"

Lester removed his hat, bowing a little. "Good day, my dear. You're looking lovely. Your eyes are clear and blue. Sparkling like some virgin lake, fed by mountain streams." He sniffed. "Do I smell a delicious repast warming on the hearth?"

"Oh, Lester." Jill blinked uncertainly, faint hope swelling in her bosom. "Lester, what's happened to you? You're so -- so different."

"Am I, my dear?" Lester moved about the house, touching things and sighing. "What a dear little house. So sweet and friendly. You don't know how wonderful it is to be here. Believe me."

"I'm afraid to believe it," Jill said.

"Believe what?"

"That you mean all this. That you're not the way you were. The way you've always been."

"What way is that?"

"Mean. Mean and cruel."

"I?" Lester frowned, rubbing his lip. "Hmm. Interesting." He brightened. "Well, that's all in the past. What's for dinner? I'm faint with hunger."

Jill eyed him uncertainly as she moved into the kitchen. "Anything you want, Lester. You know our stove covers the maximum select-list."

"Of course." Lester coughed rapidly. "Well, shall we try sirloin steak, medium, smothered in onions? With mushroom sauce. And white rolls. With hot coffee. Perhaps ice cream and apple pie for dessert."

"You never seemed to care much about food," Jill said thoughtfully.

"Oh?"

"You always said you hoped eventually they'd make intravenous intake universally applicable." She studied her husband intently. "Lester, what's happened?"

"Nothing. Nothing at all." Lester carelessly took his pipe out and lit it rapidly, somewhat awkwardly. Bits of tobacco drifted to the rug. He bent nervously down and tried to pick them up again. "Please go about your tasks and don't mind me. Perhaps I can help you prepare -- that is, can I do anything to help?"

"No," Jill said. "I can do it. You go ahead with your work, if you want."

"Work?"

"Your research. In toxins."

"Toxins!" Lester showed confusion. "Well, for heaven's sake! Toxins. Devil take it!"

"What dear?"

"I mean, I really feel too tired, just now. I'll work later." Lester moved vaguely around the room. "I think I'll sit and enjoy being home again. Off that awful Rexor IV."

"Was it awful?"

"Horrible." A spasm of disgust crossed Lester's face. "Dry and dead. Ancient. Squeezed to a pulp by wind and sun. A dreadful place, my dear."

"I'm sorry to hear that. I always wanted to visit it."

"Heaven forbid!" Lester cried feelingly. "You stay right here, my dear. With me. The -- the two of us." His eyes wandered around the room. "Two, yes. Terra is a wonderful planet. Moist and full of life." He beamed happily. "Just right."

"I don't understand it," Jill said.

"Repeat all the things you remember," Frank said. His robot pencil poised itself alertly. "The changes you've noticed in him. I'm curious."

"Why?"

"No reason. Go on. You say you sensed it right away? That he was different?"

"I noticed it at once. The expression on his face. Not that hard, practical look. A sort of mellow look. Relaxed. Tolerant. A sort of calmness."

"I see," Frank said. "What else?"

Jill peered nervously through the back door into the house. "He can't hear us, can he?"

"No. He's inside playing with Gus. In the living-room. They're Venusian otter-men today. Your husband built an otter slide down at his lab. I saw him unwrapping it."

"His talk."

"His what?"

The way he talks. His choice of words. Words he never used before. Whole new phrases. Metaphors. I never heard him use a metaphor in all our five years together. He said metaphors were inexact. Misleading. And --"

"And what?" The pencil scratched busily.

"And they're *strange* words. Old words. Words you don't hear any more."

"Archaic phraseology?" Frank asked tensely.

"Yes." Jill paced back and forth across the small lawn, her hands in the pockets of her plastic shorts. "Formal words. Like something --"

"Something out of a book?"

"Exactly! You've noticed it?"

"I noticed it." Frank's face was grim. "Go on."

Jill stopped pacing. "What's on your mind? Do you have a theory?"

"I want to know more facts."

She reflected. "He plays. With Gus. He plays and jokes. And he -- he eats."

"Didn't he eat before?"

"Not like he does now. Now he *loves* food. He goes into the kitchen and tries endless combinations. He and the stove get together and cook up all sorts of weird things."

"I thought he'd put on weight."

"He's gained ten pounds. He eats, smiles and laughs. He's constantly polite." Jill glanced away coyly. "He's even -- romantic! He always said *that* was irrational. And he's not interested in his work. His research in toxins."

"I see." Frank chewed his lip. "Anything more?"

"One thing puzzles me very much. I've noticed it again and again."

"What is it?"

"He seems to have strange lapses of --"

A burst of laughter. Lester Herrick, eyes bright with merriment, came rushing out of the house, little Gus close behind.

"We have an announcement!" Lester cried.

"An announzelmen," Gus echoed.

Frank folded his notes up and slid them into his coat pocket. The pencil hurried after them. He got slowly to his feet. "What is it?"

"You make it," Lester said, taking little Gus's hand and leading him forward.

Gus's plump face screwed up in concentration. "I'm going to come live with you," he stated. Anxiously he watched Jill's expression. "Lester says I can. Can I? Can I, Aunt Jill?"

Her heart flooded with incredible joy. She glanced from Gus to Lester. "Do you -- do you really mean it?" Her voice was almost inaudible.

Lester put his arm around her, holding her close to him. "Of course, we mean it," he said gently. His eyes were warm and understanding. "We wouldn't tease you, my dear."

"No teasing!" Gus shouted excitedly. "No more teasing!" He and Lester and Jill drew close together. "Never again!"

Frank stood a little way off, his face grim. Jill noticed him and broke away abruptly. "What is it?" she faltered. "Is anything --"

"When you're quite finished," Frank said to Lester Herrick, "I'd like you to come with me." A chill clutched Jill's heart. "What is it? Can I come, too?"

Frank shook his head. He moved toward Lester ominously. "Come on, Herrick. Let's go. You and I are going to take a little trip."

The three Federal Clearance Agents took up positions a few feet from Lester Herrick, vibro-tubes gripped alertly.

Clearance Director Douglas studied Herrick for a long time. "You're sure?" he said finally.

"Absolutely," Frank stated.

"When did he get back from Rexor IV?"

"A week ago."

"And the change was noticeable at once?"

"His wife noticed it as soon as she saw him. There's no doubt it occurred on Rexor." Frank paused significantly. "And you know what that means."

"I know." Douglas walked slowly around the seated man, examining him from every angle.

Lester Herrick sat quietly, his coat neatly folded across his knee. He rested his hands on his ivory-topped cane, his face calm and expressionless. He wore a soft gray suit, a subdued necktie, French cuffs, and shiny black shoes. He said nothing.

"Their methods are simple and exact," Douglas said. "The original psychic contents are re-moved and stored -- in some sort of suspension. The interjection of the substitute contents is instantaneous. Lester Herrick was probably poking around the Rexor city ruins, ignoring the safety precautions -- shield or manual screen -- and they got him."

The seated man stirred. "I'd like very much to communicate with Jill," he murmured. "She surely is becoming anxious."

Frank turned away, face choked with revulsion. "God. It's still pretending."

Director Douglas restrained himself with the greatest effort. "It's certainly an amazing thing. No physical changes. You could look at it and never know." He moved toward the seated man, his face hard. "Listen to me, whatever you call yourself. Can you understand what I say?"

"Of course," Lester Herrick answered.

"Did you really think you'd get away with it? We caught the others -- the ones before you. All ten of them. Even before they got here." Douglas grinned coldly. "Vibro-rayed them one after another."

The color left Lester Herrick's face. Sweat came out on his forehead. He wiped it away with a silk handkerchief from his breast pocket. "Oh?" he murmured.

"You're not fooling us. All Terra is alerted for you Rexorians. I'm surprised you got off Rexor at all. Herrick must have been extremely careless. We stopped the others aboard ship. Fried them out in deep space."

"Herrick had a private ship," the seated man murmured. "He bypassed the check station going in. No record of his arrival existed. He was never checked."

"*Fry it!*" Douglas grated. The three Clearance agents lifted their tubes, moving forward.

"No." Frank shook his head. "We can't. It's a bad situation."

"What do you mean? Why can't we? We fried the others --"

"They were caught in deep space. This is Terra. Terran law, not military law, applies." Frank waved toward the seated man. "And it's in a human body. It comes under regular civil laws. We've got to *prove* it's not Lester Herrick -- that it's a Rexorian infiltrator. It's going to be tough. But it can be done."

"How?"

"His wife. Herrick's wife. Her testimony. Jill Herrick can assert the difference between Lester Herrick and this thing. She knows -- and I think we can make it stand up in court."

It was late afternoon. Frank drove his surface cruiser slowly along. Neither he nor Jill spoke.

"So that's it," Jill said at last. Her face was gray. Her eyes dry and bright, without emotion. "I knew it was too good to be true." She tried to smile. "It seemed so wonderful."

"I know," Frank said. "It's a terrible damn thing. If only --"

"*Why?*" Jill said. "Why did he -- did it do this? Why did it take Lester's body?"

"Rexor IV is old. Dead. A dying planet. Life is dying out."

"I remember, now. He -- it said something like that. Something about Rexor. That it was glad to get away."

"The Rexorians are an old race. The few that remain are feeble. They've been trying to migrate for centuries. But their bodies are too weak. Some tried to migrate to Venus -- and died instantly. They worked out this system about a century ago."

"But it knows so much. About us. It speaks our language."

"Not quite. The changes you mentioned. The odd diction. You see, the Rexorians have only a vague knowledge of human beings. A sort of ideal abstraction, taken from Terran objects that have found their way to Rexor. Books mostly. Secondary data like that. The Rexorian idea of Terra is based on centuries-old Terran literature. Romantic novels from our past. Language, customs, manners from old Terran books. That accounts for the strange archaic quality to it. It had studied Terra, all right. But in an indirect and misleading way." Frank grinned wryly. "The Rexorians are two hundred years behind the times -- which is a break for us. That's how we're able to detect them."

"Is this sort of thing -- common? Does it happen often? It seems unbelievable." Jill rubbed her forehead wearily. "Dreamlike. It's hard to realize that it's actually happened. I'm just beginning to understand what it means."

"The galaxy is full of alien life forms. Parasitic and destructive entities. Terran ethics don't extend to them. We have to guard constantly against this sort of thing. Lester went in unsuspectingly -- and this thing ousted him and took over his body."

Frank glanced at his sister. Jill's face was expressionless. A stern little face, wide-eyed, but composed. She sat up straight, staring fixedly ahead, her small hands folded quietly in her lap.

"We can arrange it so you won't actually have to appear in court," Frank went on. "You can vid a statement and it'll be presented as evidence. I'm certain your statement will do. The Federal courts will help us all they can, but they have to have *some* evidence to go on."

Jill was silent.

"What do you say?" Frank asked.

"What happens after the court makes its decision?"

"Then we vibro-ray it. Destroy the Rexorian mind. A Terran patrol ship on Rexor IV sends out a party to locate the -- er -- original contents."

Jill gasped. She turned toward her brother in amazement. "You mean --"

"Oh, yes. Lester is alive. In suspension, somewhere on Rexor. In one of the old city ruins. We'll have to force them to give him up. They won't want to, but they'll do it. They've done it before. Then he'll be back with you. Safe and sound. Just like before. And this horrible nightmare you've been living will be a thing of the past."

"I see."

"Here we are." The cruiser pulled to a halt before the imposing Federal Clearance Building. Frank got quickly out, holding the door for his sister. Jill stepped down slowly. "Okay?" Frank said.

"Okay."

When they entered the building, Clearance agents led them through the check screens, down the long corridors. Jill's high heels echoed in the ominous silence.

"Quite a place," Frank observed.

"It's unfriendly."

"Consider it a glorified police station." Frank halted. Before them was a guarded door. "Here we are."

"Wait." Jill pulled back, her face twisting in panic. "I --"

"We'll wait until you're ready." Frank signaled to the Clearance agent to leave. "I understand. It's a bad business."

Jill stood for a moment, her head down. She took a deep breath, her small fists clenched. Her chin came up, level and steady. "All right."

"You ready?"

"Yes."

Frank opened the door. "Here we are."

Director Douglas and the three Clearance agents turned expectantly as Jill and Frank entered. "Good," Douglas murmured, with relief. "I was beginning to get worried."

The sitting man got slowly to his feet, picking up his coat. He gripped his ivory-headed cane tightly, his hands tense. He said nothing. He watched silently as the woman entered the room, Frank behind her. "This is Mrs Herrick," Frank said. "Jill, this is Clearance Director Douglas."

"I've heard of you," Jill said faintly.

"Then you know our work."

"Yes. I know your work."

"This is an unfortunate business. It's happened before. I don't know what Frank has told you --"

"He explained the situation."

"Good." Douglas was relieved. "I'm glad of that. It's not easy to explain. You understand, then, what we want. The previous cases were caught in deep space. We vibro-tubed them and got the original contents back. But this time we must work through legal channels." Douglas picked up a vidtape recorder. "We will need your statement, Mrs Herrick. Since no physical change has occurred we'll have no direct evidence to make our case. We'll have only your testimony of character alteration to present to the court."

He held the vidtape recorder out. Jill took it slowly.

"Your statement will undoubtedly be accepted by the court. The court will give us the release we want and then we can go ahead. If everything goes correctly we hope to be able to set things exactly as they were before."

Jill was gazing silently at the man standing in the corner with his coat and ivory-headed cane. "Before?" she said. "What do you mean?"

"Before the change."

Jill turned toward Director Douglas. Calmly, she laid the vidtape recorder down on the table. "What change are you talking about?"

Douglas paled. He licked his lips. All eyes in the room were on Jill. "The change in *him*." He pointed at the man.

"Jill!" Frank barked. "What's the matter with you?" He came quickly toward her. "What the hell are you doing? You know damn well what change we mean!"

"That's odd," Jill said thoughtfully. "I haven't noticed any change."

Frank and Director Douglas looked at each other. "I don't get it," Frank muttered, dazed.

"Mrs Herrick --" Douglas began.

Jill walked over to the man standing quietly in the corner. "Can we go now, dear?" she asked. She took his arm. "Or is there some reason why my husband has to stay here?"

The man and woman walked silently along the dark street.

"Come on," Jill said. "Let's go home."

The man glanced at her. "It's a nice afternoon," he said. He took a deep breath, filling his lungs. "Spring is coming -- I think. Isn't it?"

Jill nodded.

"I wasn't sure. It's a nice smell. Plants and soil and growing things."

"Yes."

"Are we going to walk? Is it far?"

"Not too far."

The man gazed at her intently, a serious expression on his face. "I am very indebted to you, my dear," he said.

Jill nodded.

"I wish to thank you. I must admit I did not expect such a --"

Jill turned abruptly. "What is your name? Your *real* name."

The man's gray eyes flickered. He smiled a little, a kind, gentle smile. "I'm afraid you would not be able to pronounce it. The sounds cannot be formed. . ."

Jill was silent as they walked along, deep in thought. The city lights were coming on all around them. Bright yellow spots in the gloom. "What are you thinking?" the man asked.

"I was thinking perhaps I will still call you Lester," Jill said. "If you don't mind."

"I don't mind," the man said. He put his arm around her, drawing her close to him. He gazed down tenderly as they walked through the thickening darkness, between the yellow candles of light that marked the way. "Anything you wish. Whatever will make you happy."

Foster, You're Dead

School was agony, as always. Only today it was worse. Mike Foster finished weaving his two watertight baskets and sat rigid, while all around him the other children worked. Outside the concrete-and-steel building the late-afternoon sun shone cool. The hills sparkled green and brown in the crisp autumn air. In the overhead sky a few NATS circled lazily above the town.

The vast, ominous shape of Mrs. Cummings, the teacher, silently approached his desk. "Foster, are you finished?"

"Yes, ma'am," he answered eagerly. He pushed the baskets up. "Can I leave now?"

Mrs. Cummings examined his baskets critically. "What about your trap-making?" she demanded.

He fumbled in his desk and brought out his intricate small-animal trap. "All finished, Mrs. Cummings. And my knife, it's done, too." He showed her the razor-edged blade of his knife, glittering metal he had shaped from a discarded gasoline drum. She picked up the knife and ran her expert finger doubtfully along the blade.

"Not strong enough," she stated. "You've oversharpened it. It'll lose its edge the first time you use it. Go down to the main weapons-lab and examine the knives they've got there. Then hone it back some and get a thicker blade."

"Mrs. Cummings," Mike Foster pleaded, "could I fix it *tomorrow?* Could I leave right now, please?"

Everybody in the classroom was watching with interest. Mike Foster flushed; he hated to be singled out and made conspicuous, but he *had* to get away. He couldn't stay in school one minute more.

Inexorable, Mrs. Cummings rumbled, "Tomorrow is digging day. You won't have time to work on your knife."

"I will," he assured her quickly. "After the digging."

"No, you're not too good at digging." The old woman was measuring the boy's spindly arms and legs. "I think you better get your knife finished today. And spend all day tomorrow down at the field."

"What's the use of digging?" Mike Foster demanded, in despair.

"Everybody has to know how to dig," Mrs. Cummings answered patiently. Children were snickering on all sides; she shushed them with a hostile glare. "You all know the importance of digging. When the war begins the whole surface will be littered with debris and rubble. If we hope to survive we'll have to dig down, won't we? Have any of you ever watched a gopher digging around the roots of plants? The gopher knows he'll find something valuable down there under the surface of the ground. We're all going to be little brown gophers. We'll all have to learn to dig down in the rubble and find the good things, because that's where they'll be."

Mike Foster sat miserably plucking his knife, as Mrs. Cummings moved away from his desk and up the aisle. A few children grinned contemptuously at him, but nothing penetrated his haze of wretchedness. Digging wouldn't do him any good. When the bombs came he'd be killed instantly. All the vaccination shots up and down his arms, on his thighs and buttocks, would be of no use. He had wasted his allowance money: Mike Foster wouldn't be alive to catch any of the bacterial plagues. Not unless --

He sprang up and followed Mrs. Cummings to her desk. In an agony of desperation he blurted, "Please, I have to leave. I have to do something."

Mrs. Cumming's tired lips twisted angrily. But the boy's fearful eyes stopped her. "What's wrong?" she demanded. "Don't you feel well?"

The boy stood frozen, unable to answer her. Pleased by the tableau, the class murmured and giggled until Mrs. Cummings rapped angrily on her desk with a writer. "Be quiet," she snapped. Her voice softened a shade. "Michael, if you're not functioning properly, go downstairs to the psyche clinic. There's no point trying to work when your reactions are conflicted. Miss Groves will be glad to optimum you."

"No," Foster said.

"Then what is it?"

The class stirred. Voices answered for Foster; his tongue was stuck with misery and humiliation. "His father's an anti-P," the voices explained. "They don't have a shelter and he isn't registered in Civic Defense. His father hasn't even contributed to the NATS. They haven't done anything."

Mrs. Cummings gazed up in amazement at the mute boy. "You don't have a shelter?"

He shook his head.

A strange feeling filled the woman. "But --" She had started to say, *But you'll die up here.* She changed it to "But where'll you go?"

"Nowhere," the mild voices answered for him. "Everybody else'll be down in their shelters and he'll be up here. He even doesn't have a permit for the school shelter."

Mrs. Cummings was shocked. In her dull, scholastic way she had assumed every child in the school had a permit to the elaborate subsurface chambers under the building. But of course not. Only children whose parents were part of CD, who contributed to arming the community. And if Foster's father was an anti-P. . .

"He's afraid to sit here," the voices chimed in calmly. "He's afraid it'll come while he's sitting here, and everybody else will be safe down in the shelter."

He wandered slowly along, hands deep in his pockets, kicking at dark stones on the sidewalk. The sun was setting. Snub-nosed commute rockets were unloading tired people, glad to be home from the factory strip a hundred miles to the west. On the distant hills something flashed: a radar tower revolving silently in the evening gloom. The circling NATS had increased in number. The twilight hours were the most dangerous; visual observers couldn't spot high-speed missiles coming in close to the ground. Assuming the missiles came.

A mechanical news-machine shouted at him excitedly as he passed. War, death, amazing new weapons developed at home and abroad. He hunched his shoulders and continued on, past the little concrete shells that served as houses, each exactly alike, sturdy reinforced pillboxes. Ahead of him bright neon signs glowed in the settling gloom: the business district, alive with traffic and milling people.

Half a block from the bright cluster of neons he halted. To his right was a public shelter, a dark tunnel-like entrance with a mechanical turnstile glowing dully. Fifty cents admission. If he was here, on the street, and he had fifty cents, he'd be all right. He had pushed down into public shelters many times, during the practice raids. But other times, hideous, nightmare times that never left his mind, he hadn't had the fifty cents. He had stood mute and terrified, while people pushed excitedly past him; and the shrill shrieks of the sirens thundered everywhere.

He continued slowly, until he came to the brightest blotch of light, the great, gleaming showrooms of General Electronics, two blocks long, illuminated on all sides, a vast square of pure color and radiation. He halted and examined for the millionth time the fascinating shapes, the display that always drew him to a hypnotized stop whenever he passed.

In the center of the vast room was a single object. An elaborate pulsing blob of machinery and support struts, beams and walls and sealed locks. All spotlights were turned on it; huge signs announced its hundred and one advantages -- as if there could be any doubt.

THE NEW 1972 BOMBPROOF RADIATION-SEALED
SUBSURFACE SHELTER IS HERE! CHECK THESE
STAR-STUDDED FEATURES:

* automatic descent-lift -- jam-proof, self-powered, e-z locking
* triple-layer hull guaranteed to withstand 5g pressure without buckling
* A-powered heating and refrigeration system -- self-servicing air-purification network
* three decontamination stages for food and water
* four hygienic stages for pre-burn exposure

* complete antibiotic processing
* e-z payment plan

He gazed at the shelter a long time. It was mostly a big tank, with a neck at one end that was the descent tube, and an emergency escape-hatch at the other. It was completely self-contained: a miniature world that supplied its own light, heat, air, water, medicines, and almost inexhaustible food. When fully stocked there were visual and audio tapes, entertainment, beds, chairs, vidscreen, everything that made up the above-surface home. It was, actually, a home below the ground. Nothing was missing that might be needed or enjoyed. A family would be safe, even comfortable, during the most severe H-bomb and bacterial-spray attack.

It cost twenty thousand dollars.

While he was gazing silently at the massive display, one of the salesmen stepped out onto the dark sidewalk, on his way to the cafeteria. "Hi, sonny," he said automatically, as he passed Mike Foster. "Not bad, is it?"

"Can I go inside?" Foster asked quickly. "Can I go down in it?"

The salesman stopped, as he recognized the boy. "You're that kid," he said slowly, "that damn kid who's always pestering us."

"I'd like to go down in it. Just for a couple minutes. I won't bust anything -- I promise. I won't even touch anything."

The salesman was young and blond, a good-looking man in his early twenties. He hesitated, his reactions divided. The kid was a pest. But he had a family, and that meant a reasonable prospect. Business was bad; it was late September and the seasonal slump was still on. There was no profit in telling the boy to go peddle his newstapes; but on the other hand it was bad business encouraging small fry to crawl around the merchandise. They wasted time; they broke things; they pilfered small stuff when nobody was looking.

"No dice," the salesman said. "Look, send your old man down here. Has he seen what we've got?"

"Yes," Mike Foster said tightly.

"What's holding him back?" The salesman waved expansively up at the great gleaming display. "We'll give him a good trade-in on his old one, allowing for depreciation and obsolescence. What model has he got?"

"We don't have any," Mike Foster said.

The salesman blinked. "Come again?" '

"My father says it's a waste of money. He says they're trying to scare people into buying things they don't need. He says --"

"Your father's an anti-P?"

"Yes," Mike Foster answered unhappily.

The salesman let out his breath. "Okay, kid. Sorry we can't do business. It's not your fault." He lingered. "What the hell's wrong with him? Does he put on the NATS?"

"No."

The salesman swore under his breath. A coaster, sliding along, safe because the rest of the community was putting up thirty per cent of its income to keep a constant-defense system going. There were always a few of them, in every town. "How's your mother feel?" the salesman demanded. "She go along with him?"

"She says --" Mike Foster broke off. "Couldn't I go down in it for a little while? I won't bust anything. Just *once.*"

"How'd we ever sell it if we let kids run through it? We're not marking it down as a demonstration model -- we've got roped into that too often." The salesman's curiosity was aroused. "How's a guy get to be anti-P? He always feel this way, or did he get stung with something?"

"He says they sold people as many cars and washing machines and television sets as they could use. He says NATS and bomb shelters aren't good for anything, so people never get all they can use. He says factories can keep turning out guns and gas masks forever, and as long as people are afraid they'll keep paying for them because they think if they don't they might get killed, and maybe a man gets tired of paying for a new car every year and stops, but he's never going to stop buying shelters to protect his children."

"You believe that?" the salesman asked.

"I wish we had that shelter," Mike Foster answered. "If we had a shelter like that I'd go down and sleep in it every night. It'd be there when we needed it."

"Maybe there won't be a war," the salesman said. He sensed the boy's misery and fear, and he grinned good-naturedly down at him. "Don't worry all the time. You probably watch too many vidtapes -- get out and play, for a change."

"Nobody's safe on the surface," Mike Foster said. "We have to be down below. And there's no place I can go."

"Send your old man around," the salesman muttered uneasily. "Maybe we can talk him into it. We've got a lot of time-payment plans. Tell him to ask for Bill O'Neill. Okay?"

Mike Foster wandered away, down the black evening street. He knew he was supposed to be home, but his feet dragged and his body was heavy and dull. His fatigue made him remember what the athletic coach had said the day before, during exercises. They were practicing breath suspension, holding a lungful of air and running. He hadn't done well; the others were still redfaced and racing when he halted, expelled his air, and stood gasping frantically for breath.

"Foster," the coach said angrily, "you're dead. You know that? If this had been a gas attack --" He shook his head wearily. "Go over there and practice by yourself. You've got to do better, if you expect to survive."

But he didn't expect to survive.

When he stepped up onto the porch of his home, he found the living room lights already on. He could hear his father's voice, and more faintly his mother's from the kitchen. He closed the door after him and began unpeeling his coat.

"Is that you?" his father demanded. Bob Foster sat sprawled out in his chair, his lap full of tapes and report sheets from his retail furniture store. "Where have you been? Dinner's been ready half an hour." He had taken off his coat and rolled up his sleeves. His arms were pale and thin, but muscular. He was tired; his eyes were large and dark, his hair thinning. Restlessly, he moved the tapes around, from one stack to another.

"I'm sorry," Mike Foster said.

His father examined his pocket watch; he was surely the only man who still carried a watch. "Go wash your hands. What have you been doing?" He scrutinized his son. "You look odd. Do you feel all right?"

"I was downtown," Mike Foster said.

"What were you doing?"

"Looking at the shelters."

Wordless, his father grabbed up a handful of reports and stuffed them into a folder. His thin lips set; hard lines wrinkled his forehead. He snorted furiously as tapes spilled everywhere; he bent stiffly to pick them up. Mike Foster made no move to help him. He crossed to the closet and gave his coat to the hanger. When he turned away his mother was directing the table of food into the dining room.

They ate without speaking, intent on their food and not looking at each other. Finally his father said, "What'd you see? Same old dogs, I suppose."

"There's the new '72 models," Mike Foster answered.

"They're the same as the '71 models." His father threw down his fork savagely; the table caught and absorbed it. "A few new gadgets, some more chrome. That's all." Suddenly he was facing his son defiantly. "Right?"

Mike Foster toyed wretchedly with his creamed chicken. "The new ones have a jam-proof descent lift. You can't get stuck halfway down. All you have to do is get in it, and it does the rest."

"There'll be one next year that'll pick you up and carry you down. This one'll be obsolete as soon as people buy it. That's what they want -- they want you to keep buying. They keep

424

putting out new ones as fast as they can. This isn't 1972, it's still 1971. What's that thing doing out already? Can't they wait?"

Mike Foster didn't answer. He had heard it all before, many times. There was never anything new, only chrome and gadgets; yet the old ones became obsolete, anyhow. His father's argument was loud, impassioned, almost frenzied, but it made no sense. "Let's get an old one, then," he blurted out. "I don't care, any one'll do. Even a secondhand one."

"No, you want the *new* one. Shiny and glittery to impress the neighbors. Lots of dials and knobs and machinery. How much do they want for it?"

"Twenty thousand dollars."

His father let his breath out. "Just like that."

"They've easy time-payment plans."

"Sure. You pay for it the rest of your life. Interest, carrying charges, and how long is it guaranteed for?"

"Three months."

"What happens when it breaks down? It'll stop purifying and decontaminating. It'll fall apart as soon as the three months are over."

Mike Foster shook his head. "No. It's big and sturdy."

His father flushed. He was a small man, slender and light, brittle-boned. He thought suddenly of his lifetime of lost battles, struggling up the hard way, carefully collecting and holding on to something, a job, money, his retail store, bookkeeper to manager, finally owner. "They're scaring us to keep the wheels going," he yelled desperately at his wife and son. "They don't want another depression."

"Bob," his wife said, slowly and quietly, "you have to stop this. I can't stand any more."

Bob Foster blinked. "What're you talking about?" he muttered. "I'm tired. These goddamn taxes. It isn't possible for a little store to keep open, not with the big chains. There ought to be a law." His voice trailed off. "I guess I'm through eating." He pushed away from the table and got to his feet. "I'm going to lie down on the couch and take a nap."

His wife's thin face blazed. "You have to get one! I can't stand the way they talk about us. All the neighbors and the merchants, everybody who knows. I can't go anywhere or do anything without hearing about it. Ever since that day they put up the flag. *Anti-P.* The last in the whole town. Those things circling around up there, and everybody paying for them but us."

"No," Bob Foster said. "I can't get one."

"Why not?"

"Because," he answered simply, "I can't afford it."

There was silence.

"You've put everything in that store," Ruth said finally. "And it's failing anyhow. You're just like a pack-rat, hoarding everything down at that ratty little hole-in-the-wall. Nobody wants wood furniture anymore. You're a relic -- a curiosity." She slammed at the table and it leaped wildly to gather the empty dishes, like a startled animal. It dashed furiously from the room and back into the kitchen, the dishes churning in its washtank as it raced.

Bob Foster sighed wearily. "Let's not fight. I'll be in the living room. Let me take a nap for an hour or so. Maybe we can talk about it later."

"Always later," Ruth said bitterly.

Her husband disappeared into the living room, a small, hunched-over figure, hair scraggly and gray, shoulder blades like broken wings.

Mike got to his feet. "I'll go study my homework," he said. He followed after his father, a strange look on his face.

The living room was quiet; the vidset was off and the lamp was down low. Ruth was in the kitchen setting the controls on the stove for the next month's meals. Bob Foster lay stretched out on the couch, his shoes off, his head on a pillow. His face was gray with fatigue. Mike hesitated for a moment and then said, "Can I ask you something?"

His father grunted and stirred, opened his eyes. "What?"

Mike sat down facing him. "Tell me again how you gave advice to the President."

His father pulled himself up. "I didn't give any advice to the President. I just talked to him."

"Tell me about it."

"I've told you a million times. Every once in a while, since you were a baby. You were with me." His voice softened, as he remembered. "You were just a toddler -- we had to carry you."

"What did he look like?"

"Well," his father began, slipping into a routine he had worked out and petrified over the years, "he looked about like he does in the vidscreen. Smaller, though."

"Why was he here?" Mike demanded avidly, although he knew every detail. The President was his hero, the man he most admired in all the world. "Why'd he come all the way out here to *our* town?"

"He was on a tour." Bitterness crept into his father's voice. "He happened to be passing through."

"What kind of a tour?"

"Visiting towns all over the country." The harshness increased. "Seeing how we were getting along. Seeing if we had bought enough NATS and bomb shelters and plague shots and gas masks and radar networks to repel attack. The General Electronics Corporation was just beginning to put up its big showrooms and displays -- everything bright and glittering and expensive. The first defense equipment available for home purchase." His lips twisted. "All on easy-payment plans. Ads, posters, searchlights, free gardenias and dishes for the ladies."

Mike Foster's breath panted in his throat. "That was the day we got our Preparedness Flag," he said hungrily. "That was the day he came to give us our flag. And they ran it up on the flagpole in the middle of the town, and everybody was there yelling and cheering."

"You remember that?"

"I -- think so. I remember people and sounds. And it was hot. It was June, wasn't it?"

"June 10,1965. Quite an occasion. Not many towns had the big green flag, then. People were still buying cars and TV sets. They hadn't discovered those days were over. TV sets and cars are good for something -- you can only manufacture and sell so many of them."

"He gave *you* the flag, didn't he?"

"Well, he gave it to all us merchants. The Chamber of Commerce had it arranged. Competition between towns, see who can buy the most the soonest. Improve our town and at the same time stimulate business. Of course, the way they put it, the idea was if we had to *buy* our gas masks and bomb shelters we'd take better care of them. As if we ever damaged telephones and sidewalks. Or highways, because the whole state provided them. Or armies. Haven't there always been armies? Hasn't the government always organized its people for defense? I guess defense costs too much. I guess they save a lot of money, cut down the national debt by this."

"Tell me what he said," Mike Foster whispered.

His father fumbled for his pipe and lit it with trembling hands. "He said, *"Here's your flag, boys. You've done a good job."* Bob Foster choked, as acrid pipe fumes guzzled up. "He was red-faced, sunburned, not embarrassed. Perspiring and grinning. He knew how to handle himself. He knew a lot of first names. Told a funny joke."

The boy's eyes were wide with awe. "He came all the way out here, and you talked to him."

"Yeah," his father said. "I talked to him. They were all yelling and cheering. The flag was going up, the big green Preparedness Flag."

"You said --"

"I said to him, *'Is that all you brought us? A strip of green cloth?'"* Bob Foster dragged tensely on his pipe. "That was when I became an anti-P. Only I didn't know it at the time. All I knew was we were on our own, except for a strip of green cloth. We should have been a country, a whole nation, one hundred and seventy million people working together to defend ourselves. And instead, we're a lot of separate little towns, little walled forts. Sliding and slipping back to the Middle Ages. Raising our separate armies --"

"Will the President ever come back?" Mike asked.

"I doubt it. He was -- just passing through."

"If he comes back," Mike whispered, tense and not daring to hope, "can we go *see* him? Can we *look* at him?"

Bob Foster pulled himself up to a sitting position. His bony arms were bare and white; his lean face was drab with weariness. And resignation. "How much was the damn thing you saw?" he demanded hoarsely. "That bomb shelter?"

Mike's heart stopped beating. "Twenty thousand dollars."

"This is Thursday. I'll go down with you and your mother next Saturday." Bob Foster knocked out his smoldering, half-lit pipe. "I'll get it on the easy-payment plan. The fall buying season is coming up soon. I usually do good -- people buy wood furniture for Christmas gifts." He got up abruptly from the couch. "Is it a deal?"

Mike couldn't answer; he could only nod.

"Fine," his father said, with desperate cheerfulness. "Now you won't have to go down and look at it in the window."

The shelter was installed -- for an additional two hundred dollars -- by a fast-working team of laborers in brown coats with the words GENERAL ELECTRONICS stitched across their backs. The back yard was quickly restored, dirt and shrubs spaded in place, the surface smoothed over, and the bill respectfully slipped under the front door. The lumbering delivery truck, now empty, clattered off down the street and the neighborhood was again silent.

Mike Foster stood with his mother and a small group of admiring neighbors on the back porch of the house. "Well," Mrs. Carlyle said finally, "now you've got a shelter. The best there is."

"That's right," Ruth Foster agreed. She was conscious of the people around her; it had been some time since so many had shown up at once. Grim satisfaction filled her gaunt frame, almost resentment. "It certainly makes a difference," she said harshly.

"Yes," Mr. Douglas from down the street agreed. "Now you have some place to go." He had picked up the thick book of instructions the laborers had left. "It says here you can stock it for a whole year. Live down there twelve months without coming up once." He shook his head admiringly. "Mine's an old '69 model. Good for only six months. I guess maybe --"

"It's still good enough for us," his wife cut in, but there was a longing wistfulness in her voice. "Can we go down and peek at it, Ruth? It's all ready, isn't it?"

Mike made a strangled noise and moved jerkily forward. His mother smiled understandingly. "He has to go down there first. He gets first look at it -- it's really for him, you know."

Their arms folded against the chill September wind, the group of men and women stood waiting and watching, as the boy approached the neck of the shelter and halted a few steps in front of it.

He entered the shelter carefully, almost afraid to touch anything. The neck was big for him; it was built to admit a full grown man. As soon as his weight was on the descent lift it dropped beneath him. With a breathless *whoosh* it plummeted down the pitch-black tube to the body of the shelter. The lift slammed hard against its shock absorbers and the boy stumbled from it. The lift shot back to the surface, simultaneously sealing off the subsurface shelter, an impassable steel-and-plastic cork in the narrow neck.

Lights had come on around him automatically. The shelter was bare and empty; no supplies had yet been carried down. It smelled of varnish and motor grease: below him the generators were throbbing dully. His presence activated the purifying and decontamination systems; on the blank concrete wall meters and dials moved into sudden activity.

He sat down on the floor, knees drawn up, face solemn, eyes wide. There was no sound but that of the generators; the world above was completely cut off. He was in a little self-contained cosmos; everything needed was here -- or would be here, soon: food, water, air, things to do. Nothing else was wanted. He could reach out and touch -- whatever he needed. He could stay here forever, through all time, without stirring. Complete and entire. Not lacking, not fearing, with only the sound of the generators purring below him, and the sheer, ascetic walls around and above him on all sides, faintly warm, completely friendly, like a living container.

Suddenly he shouted, a loud jubilant shout that echoed and bounced from wall to wall. He was deafened by the reverberation. He shut his eyes tight and clenched his fists. Joy filled him. He shouted again -- and let the roar of sound lap over him, his own voice reinforced by the near walls, close and hard and incredibly powerful.

The kids in school knew even before he showed up, the next morning. They greeted him as he approached, all of them grinning and nudging each other. "Is it true your folks got a new General Electronics Model S-72ft?" Earl Peters demanded.

"That's right," Mike answered. His heart swelled with a peaceful confidence he had never known. "Drop around," he said, as casually as he could. "I'll show it to you."

He passed on, conscious of their envious faces.

"Well, Mike," Mrs. Cummings said, as he was leaving the classroom at the end of the day. "How does it feel?"

He halted by her desk, shy and full of quiet pride. "It feels good," he admitted.

"Is your father contributing to the NATS?"

"Yes." ;

"And you've got a permit for our school shelter?"

He happily showed her the small blue seal clamped around his wrist. "He mailed a check to the city for everything. He said, 'As long as I've gone this far I might as well go the rest of the way.' "

"Now you have everything everybody else has." The elderly woman smiled across at him. "I'm glad of that. You're now a pro-P, except there's no such term. You're just -- like everyone else."

The next day the news-machines shrilled out the news. The first revelation of the new Soviet bore-pellets.

Bob Foster stood in the middle of the living room, the newstape in his hands, his thin face flushed with fury and despair. "Goddamn it, it's a plot!" His voice rose in baffled frenzy. "We just bought the thing and now look. *Look!*" He shoved the tape at his wife. "You see? I told you!"

"I've seen it," Ruth said wildly. "I suppose you think the whole world was just waiting with you in mind. They're always improving weapons, Bob. Last week it was those grain-impregnation flakes. This week it's bore-pellets. You don't expect them to stop the wheels of progress because you finally broke down and bought a shelter, do you?"

The man and woman faced each other. "What the hell are we going to do?" Bob Foster asked quietly.

Ruth paced back into the kitchen. "I heard they were going to turn out adaptors."

"Adaptors! What do you mean?"

"So people won't have to buy new shelters. There was a commercial on the vidscreen. They're going to put some kind of metal grill on the market, as soon as the government approves it. They spread it over the ground and it intercepts the bore-pellets. It screens them, makes them explode on the surface, so they can't burrow down to the shelter."

"How much?"

"They didn't say."

Mike Foster sat crouched on the sofa, listening. He had heard the news at school. They were taking their test on berry-identification, examining encased samples of wild berries to distinguish the harmless ones from the toxic, when the bell had announced a general assembly. The principal read them the news about the bore-pellets and then gave a routine lecture on emergency treatment of a new variant of typhus, recently developed.

His parents were still arguing. "We'll have to get one," Ruth Foster said calmly. "Otherwise it won't make any difference whether we've got a shelter or not. The bore-pellets were specifically designed to penetrate the surface and seek out warmth. As soon as the Russians have them in production --"

428

"I'll get one," Bob Foster said. "I'll get an anti-pellet grill and whatever else they have. I'll buy everything they put on the market. I'll never stop buying."

"It's not as bad as that." ¹ ˈ

"You know, this game has one real advantage over selling people cars and TV sets. With something like this we *have* to buy. It isn't a luxury, something big and flashy to impress the neighbors, something we could do without. If we don't buy this we die. They always said the way to sell something was create anxiety in people. Create a sense of insecurity -- tell them they smell bad or look funny. But this makes a joke out of deodorant and hair oil. You can't escape this. If you don't buy, *they'll kill you.* The perfect sales-pitch. Buy or die -- new slogan. Have a shiny new General Electronics H-bomb shelter in your back yard or be slaughtered."

"Stop talking like that!" Ruth snapped.

Bob Foster threw himself down at the kitchen table. "All right. I give up. I'll go along with it."

"You'll get one? I think they'll be on the market by Christmas."

"Oh, yes," Foster said. "They'll be out by Christmas." There was a strange look on his face. "I'll buy one of the damn things for Christmas, and so will everybody else."

The GEC grill-screen adaptors were a sensation.

Mike Foster walked slowly along the crowd-packed December street, through the late-afternoon twilight. Adaptors glittered in every store window. All shapes and sizes, for every kind of shelter. All prices, for every pocket-book. The crowds of people were gay and excited, typical Christmas crowds, shoving good-naturedly, loaded down with packages and heavy overcoats. The air was white with gusts of sweeping snow. Cars nosed cautiously along the jammed streets. Lights and neon displays, immense glowing store windows gleamed on all sides.

His own house was dark and silent. His parents weren't home yet. Both of them were down at the store working; business had been bad and his mother was taking the place of one of the clerks. Mike held his hand up to the code-key, and the front door let him in. The automatic furnace had kept the house warm and pleasant. He removed his coat and put away his schoolbooks.

He didn't stay in the house long. His heart pounding with excitement, he felt his way out the back door and started onto the back porch.

He forced himself to stop, turn around, and reenter the house. It was better if he didn't hurry things. He had worked out every moment of the process, from the first instant he saw the low hinge of the neck reared up hard and firm against the evening sky. He had made a fine art of it; there was no wasted motion. His procedure had been shaped, molded until it was a beautiful thing. The first overwhelming sense of *presence* as the neck of the shelter came around him. Then the blood-freezing rush of air as the descent-lift hurtled down all the way to the bottom.

And the grandeur of the shelter itself.

Every afternoon, as soon as he was home, he made his way down into it, below the surface, concealed and protected in its steel silence, as he had done since the first day. Now the chamber was full, not empty. Filled with endless cans of food, pillows, books, vidtapes, audio-tapes, prints on the walls, bright fabrics, textures and colors, even vases of flowers. The shelter was his place, where he crouched curled up, surrounded by everything he needed.

Delaying things as long as possible, he hurried back through the house and rummaged in the audio-tape file. He'd sit down in the shelter until dinner, listening to *Wind in the Willows.* His parents knew where to find him; he was always down there. Two hours of uninterrupted happiness, alone by himself in the shelter. And then when dinner was over he would hurry back down, to stay until time for bed. Sometimes late at night, when his parents were sound asleep, he got quietly up and made his way outside, to the shelter-neck, and down into its silent depths. To hide until morning.

He found the audio-tape and hurried through the house, out onto the back porch and into the yard. The sky was a bleak gray, shot with streamers of ugly black clouds. The lights of the town were coming on here and there. The yard was cold and hostile. He made his way uncertainly down the steps -- and froze.

A vast yawning cavity loomed. A gaping mouth, vacant and toothless, fixed open to the night sky. There was nothing else. The shelter was gone.

He stood for an endless time, the tape clutched in one hand, the other hand on the porch railing. Night came on; the dead hole dissolved in darkness. The whole world gradually collapsed into silence and abysmal gloom. Weak stars came out; lights in nearby houses came on fitfully, cold and faint. The boy saw nothing. He stood unmoving, his body rigid as stone, still facing the great pit where the shelter had been.

Then his father was standing beside him. "How long have you been here?" his father was saying. "How long, Mike? Answer me!"

With a violent effort Mike managed to drag himself back. "You're home early," he muttered.

"I left the store early on purpose. I wanted to be here when you -- got home."

"It's gone."

"Yes." His father's voice was cold, without emotion. "The shelter's gone. I'm sorry, Mike. I called them and told them to take it back."

"Why?"

"I couldn't pay for it. Not this Christmas, with those grills everyone's getting. I can't compete with them." He broke off and then continued wretchedly, "They were damn decent. They gave me back half the money I put in." His voice twisted ironically. "I knew if I made a deal with them before Christmas I'd come out better. They can resell it to somebody else."

Mike said nothing.

"Try to understand," his father went on harshly. "I had to throw what capital I could scrape together into the store. I have to keep it running. It was either give up the shelter or the store. And if I gave up the store --"

"Then we wouldn't have anything."

His father caught hold of his arm. "Then we'd have to give up the shelter, too." His thin, strong fingers dug in spasmodically. "You're growing up -- you're old enough to understand. We'll get one later, maybe not the biggest, the most expensive, but something. It was a mistake, Mike. I couldn't swing it, not with the goddamn adaptor things to buck. I'm keeping up the NAT payments, though. And your school tab. I'm keeping that going. This isn't a matter of principle," he finished desperately. "I can't help it. Do you understand, Mike? *I had to do it.*"

Mike pulled away.

"Where are you going?" His father hurried after him. "Come back here!" He grabbed for his son frantically, but in the gloom he stumbled and fell. Stars blinded him as his head smashed into the edge of the house; he pulled himself up painfully and groped for some support.

When he could see again, the yard was empty. His son was gone.

"Mike!" he yelled. "Where are you?"

There was no answer. The night wind blew clouds of snow around him, a thin bitter gust of chilled air. Wind and darkness, nothing else.

Bill O'Neill wearily examined the clock on the wall. It was nine thirty: he could finally close the doors and lock up the big dazzling store. Push the milling, murmuring throngs of people outside and on their way home.

"Thank God," he breathed, as he held the door open for the last old lady, loaded down with packages and presents. He threw the code bolt in place and pulled down the shade. "What a mob. I never saw so many people."

"All done," Al Conners said, from the cash register. "I'll count the money -- you go around and check everything. Make sure we got all of them out."

O'Neill pushed his blond hair back and loosened his tie. He lit a cigarette gratefully, then moved around the store, checking light switches, turning off the massive GEC displays and appliances. Finally he approached the huge bomb shelter that took up the center of the floor.

He climbed the ladder to the neck and stepped onto the lift. The lift dropped with a *whoosh* and a second later he stepped out in the cavelike interior of the shelter.

In one corner Mike Foster sat curled up in a tight heap, his knees drawn up against his chin, his skinny arms wrapped around his ankles. His face was pushed down; only his ragged brown hair showed. He didn't move as the salesman approached him, astounded.

"Jesus!" O'Neill exclaimed. "It's that kid."

Mike said nothing. He hugged his legs tighter and buried his head as far down as possible.

"What the hell are you doing down here?" O'Neill demanded, surprised and angry. His outrage increased. "I thought your folks got one of these." Then he remembered. "That's right. We had to repossess it."

Al Conners appeared from the descent-lift. "What's holding you up? Let's get out of here and --" He saw Mike and broke off. "What's he doing down here? Get him out and let's go."

"Come on, kid," O'Neill said gently. "Time to go home."

Mike didn't move.

The two men looked at each other. "I guess we're going to have to drag him out," Conners said grimly. He took off his coat and tossed it over a decontamination fixture. "Come on. Let's get it over with."

It took both of them. The boy fought desperatley, without sound, clawing and struggling and tearing at them with his fingernails, kicking them, slashing at them, biting them when they grabbed him. They half-dragged, half-carried him to the descent-lift and pushed him into it long enough to activate the mechanism. O'Neill rode up with him; Conners came immediately after. Grimly, efficiently, they bundled the boy to the front door, threw him out, and locked the bolts after him.

"Wow," Conners gasped, sinking down against the counter. His sleeve was torn and his cheek was cut and gashed. His glasses hung from one ear; his hair was rumpled and he was exhausted. "Think we ought to call the cops? There's something wrong with that kid."

O'Neill stood by the door, panting for breath and gazing out into the darkness. He could see the boy sitting on the pavement. "He's still out there," he muttered. People pushed by the boy on both sides. Finally one of them stopped and got him up. The boy struggled away, and then disappeared into the darkness. The larger figure picked up its packages, hesitated a moment, and then went on. O'Neill turned away. "What a hell of a thing." He wiped his face with his handkerchief. "He sure put up a fight."

"What was the matter with him? He never said anything, not a goddamn word."

"Christmas is a hell of a time to repossess something," O'Neill said. He reached shakily for his coat. "It's too bad. I wish they could have kept it."

Conners shrugged. "No tickie, no laundry."

"Why the hell can't we give them a deal? Maybe --" O'Neill struggled to get the word out. "Maybe sell the shelter wholesale, to people like that."

Conners glared at him angrily. "*Wholesale?* And then everybody wants it wholesale. It wouldn't be fair -- and how long would we stay in business? How long would GEC last that way?"

"I guess not very long," O'Neill admitted moodily.

"Use your head." Conners laughed sharply. "What you need is a good stiff drink. Come on in the back closet -- I've got a fifty of Haig and Haig in a drawer back there. A little something to warm you up, before you go home. That's what you need."

Mike Foster wandered aimlessly along the dark street, among the crowds of shoppers hurrying home. He saw nothing; people pushed against him but he was unaware of them. Lights, laughing people, the honking of car horns, the clang of signals. He was blank, his mind empty and dead. He walked automatically, without consciousness or feeling.

To his right a garish neon sign winked and glowed in the deepening night shadows. A huge sign, bright and colorful.

PEACE ON EARTH GOOD WILL TO MEN
PUBLIC SHELTER ADMISSION 50¢